THRILLERS

—A Classic Collection—

THRILLERS

-A Classic Collection-

INTRODUCTION BY
ROBERT SHECKLEY

LEOPARD

Thrillers

This edition published in 1996 by Leopard, a division of
Random House UK Ltd, Random House,
20 Vauxhall Bridge Road, London SW1V 2SA.

ISBN 1 85891 316 0

Printed and bound in Guernsey by The Guernsey Press Co. Ltd

INTRODUCTION

There's no question but that the first thing to ask here is why should you, the reader, presently browsing in this my introduction buy this book?

And closely tied to that question, how can I, as an introducer of some reliability, I hope, at least to the extent of never having ended up in the literary equivalent of jail, whatever that might be, or a literal one, either, in case you were wondering, recommend this book for your purchase?

Well, let's have a go at it. There's a short, simple answer. The fact is, it is a generally considered quite a good thing to own at least one collection of curious older stories of the thriller variety, some quite famous, others exceedingly obscure but no less interesting for that. On that basis of idiosyncratic definition, our *Classic Collection* succeeds triumphantly, because that's just what it's about.

Well, you may say, that's all very well, and perhaps I might be tempted toward such a book, but tell me, are the stories the sort of fast, light, rather fluffy reading that I prefer?

At this point we are in trouble, you and me. I hasten to tell you straight out that simplicity is not at all what the anthologists of this collection had in mind. If ease and slangy modern usage are what you're after, I'd like to direct you toward the comic book end of the store, where their own introducers extol their own peculiar virtues in their own introductions. We're in an entirely different line of country at this end of the store. We're selling the well-made tale of strange twists and turns, some of them a little difficult to follow, in which some damned odd thing happens to a chap, usually with dire consequences. We are purveying that prose ode to logic, the short thriller, as performed by, among others, Wilkie Collins, Nathaniel Hawthorne, Sheridan Le Fanu and others less well known to this introducer.

If I have not convinced you yet, let me recommend thinking of this collection as a cross-section of the very notion of 'thriller'. What do we find in this notion? Here is a cask of Poe's Amontillado, and here is a character from an Ambrose Bierce story sitting in a haunted house and reading by the light of a candle. You could conceive of this collection as a giant canvas filled with brilliant individual landscapes, or as a kaleidoscope which constantly changes, presenting each time you look into it another and different picture of what specifically a thriller could be. I'm saying that it's *Multum in Parvo* time. Jorge Luis Borges writes of the Aleph as something that shows the innumerable appearances of everything. The aim of this collection is slightly more modest, but it is still a many-faceted jewel showing the multiplicity inherent in a certain notion, that of the Thriller.

What is a thriller? No use asking the original anonymous anthologizers of the collection. They stand mute, giving no hint as to their principle of selection, leaving all explanation to Mr James Agate, who wrote the original 1934 introduction (not reprinted here) and ingratiated himself with me at once by claiming no knowledge of what a thriller was and no interest in finding out. How simple and honest Mr Agate's words were! Don't know, don't care! We recognize a universal truth in this attitude: Sometimes one simply doesn't want to know what a thriller is, and probably doesn't want to write an introduction about it, either. Sometimes one just wants to sit in a clean well-lighted place staring into the middle distance.

When you ponder the matter for a few seconds, you can see for yourself how difficult it is to say what should be simple and obvious, the criteria for selecting a thriller for anthologization. Should the anthologists choose famous stories? But then you might already have read them. Should they be obscure? Nothing easier, but since when is obscurity a recommendation for publication?

These and other questions occur when one is writing an introduction to an anthology of thrillers, as I believe this book is. The answers, even for one who could expatiate on these matters for as long as required, are not immediately obvious, and this, paradoxically, is one of the ways the book recommends itself for purchase.

One thing I do know: one of the first and very finest things about a collection like this is the instruction it gives in the art of reading. These are stories of a certain age, and, like *grandes dames* of another time, you forgive their insistence on having matters entirely their own way. The modern reader, accustomed to the frequently indented left-hand margin that is a tell-tale sign of our hectic, over-indented age, may shy away at first from the solid blocks of type he (or with a little luck, she) will find in some of these stories. These blocks of type sometimes go as far as to contain unindented dialogue run into the narrative paragraph with no relief for the eye. A strange world, my master.

His eyes exhausted by the endless saccades which they must travel to bring even a modicum of meaning to his brain, the reader may come to resent the sheer difficulty this gives to the reading. Despite this, we can't help but respect the writer's honesty as evinced by contempt for the frilleries of frequent paragraphing. There's something honest and uncompromising about a man who lets his paragraphs run long and shaggy, and you will find excellent examples of what I mean in this book.

It should go without saying that if you've come to *Thrillers – A Classic Collection* looking for one of those fast-paced and barely legible comic-booky sort of things, or one of those scripty sort of things where they rush you along with never a care for your sensibilities, you've come to the wrong place.

This collection, instead of supinely giving in to the reader's desire to read under less than optimum conditions, thus vitiating the plot and the special effects the author has laboured so assiduously to achieve, takes the bold line of prescribing the reader how he should read so and so's story. Thus this collection may claim to be in the category of self-help as well as whatever other rubric it falls under.

One last thing about this collection: it is made up of a number of highly idiosyncratic viewpoints. The characters tell their own stories, as Mr Agate was encouraged to tell his, and as I have been encouraged to tell mine.

Robert Sheckley

CONTENTS

CONTENTS

DONN BYRNE

TALE OF THE PIPER

I FIRST saw him as I rode from the Irish village into the
gates of Destiny—a burly man with a moustache, a cheap
suit of Glasgow reach-me-downs, a cap with a twisted brim,
and the most evilly insolent eyes I have ever seen in a human
face. At the sight of him Pelican, that wisest and steadiest
of horses, reared; and I felt a savage gust of hatred rise in
me.

"Now, who are you?" I asked; "and what are you
doing here?"

"The same question from me to you." And his eyes were
studiedly insulting.

An unaccountable rage made me tremble. I shook out the
thong of the hunting-crop, and edged Pelican towards
him.

"I am the Younger of Destiny," I informed him; "and
when I pass, all folk in Destiny do me the honour of un-
covering."

He fumbled with his cap and took it off. His hair was
shaggy and matted, like a wild man's.

"I am a piper your uncle, Sir Valentine Macfarlane, sent
from the High Country of Scotland home here to await his
coming."

I said no more and rode in. My Aunt Jenepher told me
of my Uncle Valentine's letter which Morag, her Islay maid,
had read to her. My Uncle Valentine had met the man in an
inn in Argyllshire, where he was stalking deer. "None
knows anything about him, and he is most reticent about
himself; but I am persuaded he is the best piper in the
world. Also, he may help revive the lost art of piping in
Ireland."

"Now, if he had only sent me a pair of Ayrshire plough-
men," I grumbled.

At dinner that night the man threw his reeds over his
shoulder and played outside the dining-room window. He
broke into the rollicking country air of the "Palatine's

Daughter." I don't know what he did to it with the knowledge of his art, but out of that tune of frolicsome rural
love-making he produced an atmosphere which made me
uncomfortable, as though some cad were telling foul stories.
He swung from that into " Thorroo a Warralla," the
" Funeral of the Barrel,"—a noted drinking song of how
a barrel of porter went dry after a day's flax-pulling. But
the picture evoked was not that of country men drinking
healthily at a crossroads, but of a thieves' kitchen, where
dreadful blowsy women, as of Hogarth, lay drunk with their
rat-faced cut-purses. . . .

"Stop that man, James Carabine," said my Aunt Jenepher.

He played no more under our window, but in the Irish
village the next day he piped " The Desperate Battle," that
music that only a great piper can touch, and that night the
only faction fight we had had in Destiny for forty years
broke out and raged until the police from the neighbouring
villages were rushed in. He played "" The Belles of Perth "
to the men from the fields, and for days afterwards I saw
maidservants and young girls in the farmhouses around
with red eyelids. And a young under-gardener flung down
his spade and said out of nothing, to nobody: " I'm sick
of the women in this untoward place." And one morning
I heard him play, " Iss fada may an a walla shuh "—" I'm a
long time in this one town "—and my own feet took an
itch for the road.

I said to my Aunt Jenepher at luncheon, " I was thinking
now, with the winter coming, I'll give up hunting for this
one season, and go and see Egypt maybe, or go as far as
India. A young man ought to see the world a bit."

" Shall we talk about it to-night, Kerry? " said my Aunt
Jenepher.

She asked me to go with her into the garden after luncheon,
and sent Carabine for the piper. He arrived with his instrument under his arm.

" You have never played for me yet, piper."

" Your ladyship has never asked me." There was a solid
dignity about him.

" I suppose you have many tunes," said my Aunt Jenepher.

" What I say now would be immodest in another man, but
true in me: no piper has more tunes. I have the lost tunes

of McCrimmon. I have tunes that were lost before Mc-
Crimmon's day—old, dark tunes. Also tunes of my own
making."

" Will you play me the tune of the fishermen, piper, as
they raise the brown sails: ' Christ, Who walked on the sea,
guard us poor fisher folk '! "

" I am sorry, my lady, but I have not that tune."

" Please play me Bruce's Hymn: ' God of Battles '! "

" That also, my lady, is a tune I have not."

" Then a merry song, piper, which you must know: ' The
Marriage Feast which took place in Cana '! "

He was stolid as a rock. " I am afraid I have not that
either."

" One of your favourite tunes is: ' I'm a long while in this
one town '? "

He bowed with a nobleman's courtesy.

" It is a choice tune," he said slowly, " a darling tune."

" Then play it, piper, then play it," said my Aunt Jenepher. " And as you are playing it "—she rose up suddenly
from the seat and looked at him with her blind eyes—
" in God's name, go! "

" I was to wait," said the piper, " until Sir Valentine returned."

Both Carabine and I made a step towards him. My Aunt
Jenepher must have felt us. " Please, Kerry! Please, James
Carabine! "

" Piper, my brother Valentine will not wish you to stay
here an instant longer than I would have you stay, and I
would not have you stay at all."

" Then I had better go," the piper said. And he swung
his reeds to his shoulder; struck the piper's swagger.

" Do you need money for the road? " my Aunt Jenepher
asked.

" I need nothing."

" But you do, piper," said my Aunt Jenepher softly. " I
shall pray for you to-night."

He dropped the pipes from his shoulder and turned
around. " I thank your ladyship," he said simply; " but I
fear it is late for that."

" Nevertheless, I shall," said my Aunt Jenepher.

He turned and went away from us down the garden path,
and what became of him is not known. He did not play

his pipes as he went, but held them crumpled under his arm, and his walk was more like the rapid amble of an animal than the step of a man. I was convinced that were I to look in the gravel I should find not a footprint of a man, but the slot of an animal. But I did not look. I was afraid.

GEORGE ELIOT

THE LIFTED VEIL

I

THE time of my end approaches. I have lately been subject to attacks of *angina pectoris;* and in the ordinary
course of things, my physician tells me, I may fairly hope
that my life will not be protracted many months. Unless,
then, I am cursed with an exceptional physical constitution,
as I am cursed with an exceptional mental character, I shall
not much longer groan under the wearisome burthen of this
earthly existence. If it were to be otherwise—if I were to
live on to the age most men desire and provide for—I should
for once have known whether the miseries of delusive expectation can outweigh the miseries of true prevision. For I
foresee when I shall die, and everything that will happen in
my last moments.

Just a month from this day, on September 20, 1850, I
shall be sitting in this chair, in this study, at ten o'clock at
night, longing to die, weary of incessant insight and foresight,
without delusions and without hope. Just as I am watching
a tongue of blue flame rising in the fire, and my lamp is
burning low, the horrible contraction will begin at my chest.
I shall only have time to reach the bell, and pull it violently,
before the sense of suffocation will come. No one will answer
my bell. I know why. My two servants are lovers, and will
have quarrelled. My housekeeper will have rushed out of the
house in a fury, two hours before, hoping that Perry will
believe she has gone to drown herself. Perry is alarmed at
last, and is gone out after her. The little scullery-maid is
asleep on a bench: she never answers the bell; it does not
wake her. The sense of suffocation increases: my lamp goes
out with a horrible stench: I make a great effort, and snatch
at the bell again. I long for life, and there is no help. I
thirsted for the unknown: the thirst is gone. O God, let me
stay with the known, and be weary of it. I am content.
Agony of pain and suffocation—and all the while the earth,

the fields, the pebbly brook at the bottom of the rookery, the fresh scent after the rain, the light of the morning through my chamber-window, the warmth of the hearth after the frosty air—will darkness close over them for ever?

Darkness—darkness—no pain—nothing but darkness: but I am passing on and on through the darkness: my thought stays in the darkness, but always with a sense of moving onward. . . .

Before that time comes, I wish to use my last hours of ease and strength in telling the strange story of my experience. I have never fully unbosomed myself to any human being; I have never been encouraged to trust much in the sympathy of my fellow-men. But we have all a chance of meeting with some pity, some tenderness, some charity, when we are dead: it is the living only who cannot be forgiven—the living only from whom men's indulgence and reverence are held off, like the rain by the hard east wind. While the heart beats, bruise it—it is your only opportunity; while the eye can still turn towards you with moist, timid entreaty, freeze it with an icy unanswering gaze; while the ear, that delicate messenger to the inmost sanctuary of the soul, can still take in the tones of kindness, put it off with hard civility, or sneering compliment, or envious affectation of indifference; while the creative brain can still throb with the sense of injustice, with the yearning for brotherly recognition—make haste—oppress it with your ill-considered judgments, your trivial comparisons, your careless misrepresentations. The heart will by and by be still—" ubi saeva indignatio ulterius cor lacerare nequit "; the eye will cease to entreat; the ear will be deaf; the brain will have ceased from all wants as well as from all work. Then your charitable speeches may find vent; then you may remember and pity the toil and the struggle and the failure; then you may give due honour to the work achieved; then you may find extenuation for errors, and may consent to bury them.

That is a trivial schoolboy text; why do I dwell on it? It has little reference to me, for I shall leave no works behind me for men to honour. I have no near relatives who will make up, by weeping over my grave, for the wounds they inflicted on me when I was among them. It is only the story of my life that will perhaps win a little more sympathy from strangers when I am dead, than I ever believed it would obtain from my friends while I was living.

My childhood perhaps seems happier to me than it really was, by contrast with all the after-years. For then the curtain of the future was as impenetrable to me as to other children: I had all their delight in the present hour, their sweet indefinite hopes for the morrow; and I had a tender mother: even now, after the dreary lapse of long years, a slight trace of sensation accompanies the remembrance of her caress as she held me on her knee—her arms round my little body, her cheek pressed on mine. I had a complaint of the eyes that made me blind for a little while, and she kept me on her knee from morning till night. That unequalled love soon vanished out of my life, and even to my childish consciousness it was as if that life had become more chill. I rode my little white pony with the groom by my side as before, but there were no loving eyes looking at me as I mounted, no glad arms opened to me when I came back. Perhaps I missed my mother's love more than most children of seven or eight would have done, to whom the other pleasures of life remained as before; for I was certainly a very sensitive child. I remember still the mingled trepidation and delicious excitement with which I was affected by the tramping of the horses on the pavement in the echoing stables, by the loud resonance of the grooms' voices, by the booming bark of the dogs as my father's carriage thundered under the archway of the courtyard, by the din of the gong as it gave notice of luncheon and dinner. The measured tramp of soldiery which I sometimes heard—for my father's house lay near a county town where there were large barracks—made me sob and tremble; and yet when they were gone past, I longed for them to come back again.

I fancy my father thought me an odd child, and had little fondness for me; though he was very careful in fulfilling what he regarded as a parent's duties. But he was already past the middle of life, and I was not his only son. My mother had been his second wife, and he was five-and-forty when he married her. He was a firm, unbending, intensely orderly man, in root and stem a banker, but with a flourishing graft of the active landholder, aspiring to county influence: one of those people who are always like themselves from day to day, who are uninfluenced by the weather, and neither know melancholy nor high spirits. I held him in great awe, and appeared more timid and sensitive in his presence than at other times; a circumstance which, perhaps, helped to confirm him in the intention to educate me on a different plan from the prescriptive one with which he had complied in the case of my elder brother, already a tall youth at Eton. My brother was to be his representative and successor; he must go to Eton and Oxford, for the sake of making connexions, of course: my father was not a man to underrate the bearing of Latin satirists or Greek dramatists on the attainment of an aristocratic position. But, intrinsically, he had slight esteem for " those dead but sceptred spirits "; having qualified himself for forming an independent opinion by reading Potter's *Aeschylus*, and dipping into Francis's *Horace*. To this negative view he added a positive one, derived from a recent connexion with mining speculations; namely, that a scientific education was the really useful training for a younger son. Moreover, it was clear that a shy, sensitive boy like me was not fit to encounter the rough experience of a public school. Mr. Letherall had said so very decidedly. Mr. Letherall was a large man in spectacles, who one day took my small head between his large hands, and pressed it here and there in an exploratory, suspicious manner—then placed each of his great thumbs on my temples, and pushed me a little way from him, and stared at me with glittering spectacles. The contemplation appeared to displease him, for he frowned sternly, and said to my father, drawing his thumbs across my eyebrows—

" The deficiency is there, sir—there; and here," he added, touching the upper sides of my head, " here is the excess. That must be brought out, sir, and this must be laid to sleep."

I was in a state of tremor, partly at the vague idea that I was the object of reprobation, partly in the agitation of my first hatred—hatred of this big, spectacled man, who pulled my head about as if he wanted to buy and cheapen it.

I am not aware how much Mr. Letherall had to do with the system afterwards adopted towards me, but it was presently clear that private tutors, natural history, science, and the modern languages, were the appliances by which the defects of my organization were to be remedied. I was very stupid about machines, so I was to be greatly occupied with them: I had no memory for classification, so it was particularly necessary that I should study systematic zoology and botany; I was hungry for human deeds and humane motions; so I was to be plentifully crammed with the mechanical powers, the elementary bodies, and the phenomena of electricity and magnetism. A better-constituted boy would certainly have profited under my intelligent tutors, with their scientific apparatus; and would, doubtless, have found the phenomena of electricity and magnetism as fascinating as I was, every Thursday, assured they were. As it was, I could have paired off, for ignorance of whatever was taught me, with the worst Latin scholar that was ever turned out of a classical academy. I read Plutarch, and Shakespeare, and Don Quixote by the sly, and supplied myself in that way with wandering thoughts, while my tutor was assuring me that " an improved man, as distinguished from an ignorant one, was a man who knew the reason why water ran downhill." I had no desire to be this improved man; I was glad of the running water; I could watch it and listen to it gurgling among the pebbles and bathing the bright green water-plants, by the hour together. I did not want to know *why* it ran; I had perfect confidence that there were good reasons for what was so very beautiful.

There is no need to dwell on this part of my life. I have said enough to indicate that my nature was of the sensitive, unpractical order, and that it grew up in an uncongenial medium, which could never foster it into happy, healthy development. When I was sixteen I was sent to Geneva to complete my course of education; and the change was a very happy one to me, for the first sight of the Alps, with the setting sun on them, as we descended the Jura, seemed to me like an entrance into heaven; and the three years of my life there were spent in a perpetual sense of exaltation, as if from a draught of delicious wine, at the presence of Nature in all her awful loveliness. You will think, perhaps, that I must have been a poet, from this early sensibility to Nature. But my lot was not so happy as that. A poet pours forth his song and *believes* in the listening ear and answering soul, to which his song will be floated sooner or later. But the poet's sensibility without his voice—the poet's sensibility that finds no vent but in silent tears on the sunny bank, when the noon-day light sparkles on the water, or in an inward shudder at the sound of harsh human tones, the sight of a cold human eye—this dumb passion brings with it a fatal solitude of soul in the society of one's fellow-men. My least solitary moments were those in which I pushed off in my boat, at evening, towards the centre of the lake; it seemed to me that the sky, and the glowing mountain-tops, and the wide blue water, surrounded me with a cherishing love such as no human face had shed on me since my mother's love had vanished out of my life. I used to do as Jean Jacques did—lie down in my boat and let it glide where it would, while I looked up at the departing glow leaving one mountain-top after the other, as if the prophet's chariot of fire were passing over them on its way to the home of light. Then, when the white summits were all sad and corpse-like, I had to push homeward, for I was under careful surveillance, and was allowed no late wanderings. This disposition of mine was not favourable to the formation of intimate friendships among the numerous youths of my own age who are always to be found studying at Geneva. Yet I made *one* such friendship; and, singularly enough, it was with a youth whose intellectual tendencies were the very reverse of my own. I shall call him Charles Meunier; his real surname—an English one, for he was of English extraction—having since become celebrated. He was an orphan, who lived on a miserable pittance while he pursued the medical studies for which he had a special genius. Strange! that with my vague mind, susceptible and unobservant, hating inquiry and given up to contemplation, I should have been drawn towards a youth whose strongest passion was science. But the bond was not an intellectual one; it came from a source that can happily blend the stupid with the brilliant, the dreamy with the practical: it came from community of feeling. Charles was poor and ugly, derided by Genevese *gamins*, and not acceptable in drawingrooms. I saw that he was isolated, as I was, though from a different cause, and stimulated by a sympathetic resentment, I made timid advances towards him. It is enough to say that there sprang up as much comradeship between us as our different habits would allow; and in Charles's rare holidays we went up to the Salève together, or took the boat to Vevay, while I listened dreamily to the monologues in which he unfolded his bold conceptions of future experiment and discovery. I mingled them confusedly in my thought with glimpses of blue water and delicate floating cloud, with the notes of birds and the distant glitter of the glacier. He

knew quite well that my mind was half absent; yet he liked
to talk to me in this way; for don't we talk of our hopes
and our projects even to dogs and birds when they love us?
I have mentioned this one friendship because of its con-
nexion with a strange and terrible scene which I shall have
to narrate in my subsequent life.

This happier life at Geneva was put an end to by a severe
illness, which is partly a blank to me, partly a time of dimly-
remembered suffering, with the presence of my father by
my bed from time to time. Then came the languid monotony of convalescence, the days gradually breaking into
variety and distinctness as my strength enabled me to take
longer and longer drives. On one of these more vividly
remembered days, my father said to me, as he sat beside my
sofa—

" When you are quite well enough to travel, Latimer, I
shall take you home with me. The journey will amuse you
and do you good, for I shall go through the Tyrol and
Austria, and you will see many new places. Our neighbours, the Filmores, are come; Alfred will join us at Basle,
and we shall all go together to Vienna, and back by
Prague " . . .

My father was called away before he had finished his
sentence, and he left my mind resting on the word *Prague*,
with a strange sense that a new and wondrous scene was
breaking upon me: a city under the broad sunshine, that
seemed to me as if it were summer sunshine of a long-past
century arrested in its course—unrefreshed for ages by dews
of night, or the rushing rain-cloud; scorching the dusty,
weary, time-eaten grandeur of a people doomed to live on
in the stale repetition of memories, like deposed and superannuated kings in their regal gold-inwoven tatters. The city
looked so thirsty that the broad river seemed to me a sheet
of metal; and the blackened statues, as I passed under their
blank gaze, along the unending bridge, with their ancient
garments and their saintly crowns, seemed to me the real
inhabitants and owners of this place, while the busy, trivial
men and women, hurrying to and fro, were a swarm of
ephemeral visitants infesting it for a day. It is such grim,
stony beings as these, I thought, who are the fathers of ancient
faded children, in those tanned time-fretted dwellings that
crowd the steep before me; who pay their court in the worn

and crumbling pomp of the palace which stretches its monotonous length on the height; who worship wearily in the stifling air of the churches, urged by no fear or hope, but compelled by their doom to be ever old and undying, to live on in the rigidity of habit, as they live on in perpetual midday, without the repose of night or the new birth of morning.

A stunning clang of metal suddenly thrilled through me, and I became conscious of the objects in my room again: one of the fire-irons had fallen as Pierre opened the door to bring me my draught. My heart was palpitating violently, and I begged Pierre to leave my draught beside me; I would take it presently.

As soon as I was alone again, I began to ask myself whether I had been sleeping. Was this a dream—this wonderfully distinct vision—minute in its distinctness down to a patch of rainbow light on the pavement; transmitted through a coloured lamp in the shape of a star—of a strange city, quite unfamiliar to my imagination! I had seen no picture of Prague: it lay in my mind as a mere name, with vaguely-remembered historical associations—ill-defined memories of imperial grandeur and religious wars.

Nothing of this sort had ever occurred in my dreaming experience before, for I had often been humiliated because my dreams were only saved from being utterly disjointed and commonplace by the frequent terrors of nightmare. But I could not believe that I had been asleep, for I remembered distinctly the gradual breaking-in of the vision upon me, like the new images in a dissolving view, or the growing distinctness of the landscape as the sun lifts up the veil of the morning mist. And while I was conscious of this incipient vision, I was also conscious that Pierre came to tell my father Mr. Filmore was waiting for him, and that my father hurried out of the room. No, it was not a dream; was it—the thought was full of tremulous exultation—was it the poet's nature in me, hitherto only a troubled yearning sensibility, now manifesting itself suddenly as spontaneous creation? Surely it was in this way that Homer saw the plain of Troy, that Dante saw the abodes of the departed, that Milton saw the earthward flight of the Tempter. Was it that my illness had wrought some happy change in my organization—given a firmer tension to my

nerves—carried off some dull obstruction? I had often read
of such effects—in works of fiction at least. Nay; in
genuine biographies I had read of the subtilising or exalting
influence of some diseases on the mental powers. Did not
Novalis feel his inspiration intensified under the progress of
consumption?

When my mind had dwelt for some time on this blissful
idea, it seemed to me that I might perhaps test it by an
exertion of my will. The vision had begun when my father
was speaking of our going to Prague. I did not for a
moment believe it was really a representation of that city;
I believed—I hoped it was a picture that my newly liberated
genius had painted in fiery haste, with the colours snatched
from lazy memory. Suppose I were to fix my mind on some
other place—Venice, for example, which was far more
familiar to my imagination than Prague: perhaps the same
sort of result would follow. I concentrated my thoughts
on Venice; I stimulated my imagination with poetic
memories, and strove to feel myself present in Venice, as I
had felt myself in Prague. But in vain. I was only colouring the Canaletto engravings that hung in my old bedroom
at home; the picture was a shifting one, my mind wandering
uncertainly in search of more vivid images; I could see no
accident of form or shadow without conscious labour after
the necessary conditions. It was all prosaic effort, not rapt
passivity, such as I had experienced half an hour before. I
was discouraged; but I remembered that inspiration was
fitful.

For several days I was in a state of excited expectation,
watching for a recurrence of my new gift. I sent my
thoughts ranging over my world of knowledge, in the hope
that they would find some object which would send a re-
awakening vibration through my slumbering genius. But
no; my world remained as dim as ever, and that flash of
strange light refused to come again, though I watched for
it with palpitating eagerness.

My father accompanied me every day in a drive and a
gradually lengthening walk as my powers of walking increased; and one evening he had agreed to come and fetch
me at twelve the next day, that we might go together to
select a musical box, and other purchases rigorously demanded of a rich Englishman visiting Geneva. He was one

of the most punctual of men and bankers, and I was always nervously anxious to be quite ready for him at the appointed time. But, to my surprise, at a quarter past twelve he had not appeared. I felt all the impatience of a convalescent who has nothing particular to do, and who has just taken a tonic in the prospect of immediate exercise that would carry off the stimulus.

Unable to sit still and reserve my strength, I walked up and down the room, looking out on the current of the Rhone, just where it leaves the dark-blue lake; but thinking all the while of the possible causes that could detain my father.

Suddenly I was conscious that my father was in the room, but not alone: there were two persons with him. Strange! I had heard no footsteps, I had not seen the door open; but I saw my father, and at his right hand our neighbour Mrs. Filmore, whom I remembered very well, though I had not seen her for five years. She was a commonplace middle-aged woman, in silk and cashmere; but the lady on the left of my father was not more than twenty, a tall, slim, willowy figure, with luxuriant blond hair, arranged in cunning braids and folds that looked almost too massive for the slight figure and the small-featured, thin-lipped face they crowned. But the face had not a girlish expression: the features were sharp, the pale grey eyes at once acute, restless, and sarcastic. They were fixed on me in half-smiling curiosity, and I felt a painful sensation as if a sharp wind were cutting me. The pale-green dress, and the green leaves that seemed to form a border about her pale blond hair, made me think of a Water-Nixie—for my mind was full of German lyrics, and this pale, fatal-eyed woman, with the green weeds, looked like a birth from some cold sedgy stream, the daughter of an aged river.

" Well, Latimer, you thought me long," my father said. . . .

But while the last word was in my ears, the whole group vanished, and there was nothing between me and the Chinese painted folding-screen that stood before the door. I was cold and trembling; I could only totter forward and throw myself on the sofa. This strange new power had manifested itself again. . . . But *was* it a power? Might it not rather be a disease—a sort of intermittent delirium, con-

centrating my energy of brain into moments of unhealthy
activity, and leaving my saner hours all the more barren?
I felt a dizzy sense of unreality in what my eye rested on;
I grasped the bell convulsively, like one trying to free himself from nightmare, and rang it twice. Pierre came with
a look of alarm in his face.

"Monsieur ne se trouve pas bien?" he said anxiously.

"I'm tired of waiting, Pierre," I said, as distinctly and
emphatically as I could, like a man determined to be sober
in spite of wine; "I'm afraid something has happened to
my father—he's usually so punctual. Run to the Hôtel
des Bergues and see if he is there."

Pierre left the room at once, with a soothing "Bien,
Monsieur"; and I felt the better for this scene of simple,
waking prose. Seeking to calm myself still further, I went
into my bedroom, adjoining the *salon*, and opened a case of
eau-de-Cologne; took out a bottle; went through the process of taking out the cork very neatly, and then rubbed
the reviving spirit over my hands and forehead, and under
my nostrils, drawing a new delight from the scent because
I had procured it by slow details of labour, and by no
strange sudden madness. Already I had begun to taste
something of the horror that belongs to the lot of a human
being whose nature is not adjusted to simple human conditions.

Still enjoying the scent, I returned to the *salon*, but it
was not unoccupied, as it had been before I left it. In front
of the Chinese folding-screen there was my father, with
Mrs. Filmore on his right hand, and on his left—the slim,
blond-haired girl, with the keen face and the keen eyes fixed
on me in half-smiling curiosity.

"Well, Latimer, you thought me long," my father
said. . . .

I heard no more, felt no more, till I became conscious that
I was lying with my head low on the sofa, Pierre and my
father by my side. As soon as I was thoroughly revived,
my father left the room, and presently returned, saying—

"I've been to tell the ladies how you are, Latimer. They
were waiting in the next room. We shall put off our shop-
ping expedition to-day."

Presently he said, "That young lady is Bertha Grant,
Mrs. Filmore's orphan niece. Filmore has adopted her, and

she lives with them; so you will have her for a neighbour, when we go home—perhaps for a near relation; for there is a tenderness between her and Alfred, I suspect, and I should be gratified by the match, since Filmore means to provide for her in every way as if she were his daughter. It had not occurred to me that you knew nothing about her living with the Filmores."

He made no further allusion to the fact of my having fainted at the moment of seeing her, and I would not for the world have told him the reason: I shrank from the idea of disclosing to any one what might be regarded as a pitiable peculiarity, most of all from betraying it to my father, who would have suspected my sanity ever after.

I do not mean to dwell with particularity on the details of my experience. I have described these two cases at length; because they had definite, clearly traceable results in my after-lot.

Shortly after this last occurrence—I think the very next day—I began to be aware of a phase in my abnormal sensibility, to which, from the languid and slight nature of my intercourse with others since my illness, I had not been alive before. This was the obtrusion on my mind of the mental process going forward in first one person, and then another, with whom I happened to be in contact: the vagrant, frivolous ideas and emotions of some uninteresting acquaintance—Mrs. Filmore, for example—would force themselves on my consciousness like an importunate; ill-played musical instrument, or the loud activity of an imprisoned insect. But this unpleasant sensibility was fitful, and left me moments of rest, when the souls of my companions were once more shut out from me, and I felt a relief such as silence brings to wearied nerves. I might have believed this importunate insight to be merely a diseased activity of the imagination, but that my prevision of incalculable words and actions proved it to have a fixed relation to the mental process in other minds. But this superadded consciousness, wearying and annoying enough when it urged on me the trivial experience of indifferent people, became an intense pain and grief when it seemed to be opening to me the souls of those who were in a close relation to me—when the rational talk, the graceful attentions, the wittily-turned phrases, and the kindly deeds, which used to make the web

of their characters, were seen as if thrust asunder by a micro-
scope vision, that showed all the intermediate frivolities, all
the suppressed egoism, all the struggling chaos of puerilities,
meanness, vague capricious memories, and indolent make-
shift thoughts, from which human words and deeds emerge
like leaflets covering a fermenting heap.

At Basle we were joined by my brother Alfred, now a
handsome, self-confident man of six-and-twenty—a
thorough contrast to my fragile, nervous, ineffectual self.
I believe I was held to have a sort of half-womanish, half-
ghostly beauty; for the portrait-painters, who are thick as
weeds at Geneva, had often asked me to sit to them, and
I had been the model of a dying minstrel in a fancy picture.
But I thoroughly disliked my own physique and nothing
but the belief that it was a condition of poetic genius would
have reconciled me to it. That brief hope was quite fled,
and I saw in my face now nothing but the stamp of a
morbid organization, framed for passive suffering—too
feeble for the sublime resistance of poetic production.
Alfred, from whom I had been almost constantly separated,
and who, in his present stage of character and appearance,
came before me as a perfect stranger, was bent on being
extremely friendly and brother-like to me. He had the
superficial kindness of a good-humoured, self-satisfied
nature, that fears no rivalry, and has encountered no con-
trarieties. I am not sure that my disposition was good
enough for me to have been quite free from envy towards
him, even if our desires had not clashed, and if I had been
in the healthy human condition which admits of generous
confidence and charitable construction. There must always
have been an antipathy between our natures. As it was, he
became in a few weeks an object of intense hatred to me;
and when he entered the room, still more when he spoke, it
was as if a sensation of grating metal had set my teeth on
edge. My diseased consciousness was more intensely and
continually occupied with his thoughts and emotions, than
with those of any other person who came in my way. I
was perpetually exasperated with the petty promptings of
his conceit and his love of patronage, with his self-complacent belief in Bertha Grant's passion for him, with his
half-pitying contempt for me—seen not in the ordinary in-
dications of intonation and phrase and slight action, which

an acute and suspicious mind is on the watch for, but in all their naked skinless complication.

For we were rivals, and our desires clashed, though he was not aware of it. I have said nothing yet of the effect Bertha Grant produced in me on a nearer acquaintance. That effect was chiefly determined by the fact that she made the only exemption, among all the human beings about me, to my unhappy gift of insight. About Bertha I was always in a state of uncertainty: I could watch the expression of her face, and speculate on its meaning; I could ask for her opinion with the real interest of ignorance; I could listen for her words and watch for her smile with hope and fear: she had for me the fascination of an unravelled destiny. I say it was this fact that chiefly determined the strong effect she produced on me: for, in the abstract, no womanly character could seem to have less affinity for that of a shrinking, romantic, passionate youth than Bertha's. She was keen, sarcastic, unimaginative, prematurely cynical, remaining critical and unmoved in the most impressive scenes, inclined to dissect all my favourite poems, and especially contemptuous towards the German lyrics which were my pet literature at that time. To this moment I am unable to define my feeling towards her: it was not ordinary boyish admiration, for she was the very opposite, even to the colour of her hair, of the ideal woman who still remained to me the type of loveliness; and she was without that enthusiasm for the great and good, which, even at the moment of her strongest dominion over me, I should have declared to be the highest element of character. But there is no tyranny more complete than that which a self-centred negative nature exercises over a morbidly sensitive nature perpetually craving sympathy and support. The most independent people feel the effect of a man's silence in heightening their value for his opinion—feel an additional triumph in conquering the reverence of a critic habitually captious and satirical: no wonder, then, that an enthusiastic self-distrusting youth should watch and wait before the closed secret of a sarcastic woman's face, as if it were the shrine of the doubtfully benignant deity who ruled his destiny. For a young enthusiast is unable to imagine the total negation in another mind of the emotions which are stirring his own; they may be feeble, latent, inactive, he thinks, but they are there—

they may be called forth; sometimes, in moments of happy
hallucination, he believes they may be there in all the
greater strength because he sees no outward sign of
them. And this effect, as I have intimated, was heightened
to its utmost intensity in me, because Bertha was the only
being who remained for me in the mysterious seclusion of
soul that renders such youthful delusion possible. Doubtless there was another sort of fascination at work—that
subtle physical attraction which delights in cheating our
psychological predictions, and in compelling the men who
paint sylphs, to fall in love with some *bonne et brave femme,*
heavy-heeled and freckled.

Bertha's behaviour towards me was such as to encourage
all my illusions, to heighten my boyish passion, and make
me more and more dependent on her smiles. Looking back
with my present wretched knowledge, I conclude that her
vanity and love of power were intensely gratified by the
belief that I had fainted on first seeing her purely from the
strong impression her person had produced on me. The
most prosaic woman likes to believe herself the object of a
violent, a poetic passion; and without a grain of romance in
her Bertha had that spirit of intrigue which gave piquancy
to the idea that the brother of the man she meant to marry
was dying with love and jealousy for her sake. That she
meant to marry my brother, was what at that time I did
not believe; for though he was assiduous in his attentions to
her, and I knew well enough that both he and my father had
made up their minds to this result, there was not yet an
understood engagement—there had been no explicit declaration; and Bertha habitually, while she flirted with my
brother, and accepted his homage in a way that implied to
him a thorough recognition of its intention, made me believe, by the subtlest looks and phrases—feminine nothings
which could never be quoted against her—that he was
really the object of her secret ridicule; that she thought him,
as I did, a coxcomb, whom she would have pleasure in dis-
appointing. Me she openly petted in my brother's presence,
as if I were too young and sickly ever to be thought of as
a lover; and that was the view he took of me. But I believe
she must inwardly have delighted in the tremors into which
she threw me by the coaxing way in which she patted my
curls, while she laughed at my quotations. Such caresses

were always given in the presence of our friends; for when we were alone together, she affected a much greater distance towards me, and now and then took the opportunity, by words or slight actions, to stimulate my foolish timid hope that she really preferred me. And why should she not follow her inclination? I was not in so advantageous a position as my brother, but I had fortune, I was not a year younger than she was, and she was an heiress, who would soon be of age to decide for herself.

The fluctuations of hope and fear, confined to this one channel, made each day in her presence a delicious torment. There was one deliberate act of hers which especially helped to intoxicate me. When we were at Vienna her twentieth birthday occurred, and as she was very fond of ornaments, we all took the opportunity of the splendid jewellers' shops in that Teutonic Paris to purchase her a birthday present of jewellery. Mine, naturally, was the least expensive; it was an opal ring—the opal was my favourite stone, because it seems to blush and turn pale as if it had a soul. I told Bertha so when I gave it her, and said that it was an emblem of the poetic nature, changing with the changing light of heaven and of woman's eyes. In the evening she appeared elegantly dressed and wearing conspicuously all the birthday presents except mine. I looked eagerly at her fingers, but saw no opal. I had no opportunity of noticing this to her during the evening; but the next day, when I found her seated near the window alone, after breakfast, I said, " You scorn to wear my poor opal. I should have remembered that you despised poetic natures, and should have given you coral, or turquoise, or some other opaque unresponsive stone." " Do I despise it? " she answered, taking hold of a delicate gold chain which she always wore round her neck and drawing out the end from her bosom with my ring hanging to it; " it hurts me a little, I can tell you," she said, with her usual dubious smile, " to wear it in that secret place; and since your poetical nature is so stupid as to prefer a more public position, I shall not endure the pain any longer."

She took off the ring from the chain and put it on her finger, smiling still, while the blood rushed to my cheeks, and I could not trust myself to say a word of entreaty that she would keep the ring where it was before.

I was completely fooled by this, and for two days shut myself up in my own room whenever Bertha was absent, that I might intoxicate myself afresh with the thought of this scene and all it implied.

I should mention that during these two months—which seemed a long life to me from the novelty and intensity of the pleasures and pains I underwent—my diseased participation in other people's consciousness continued to torment me; now it was my father, and now my brother, now Mrs. Filmore or her husband, and now our German courier, whose stream of thought rushed upon me like a ringing in the ears not to be got rid of, though it allowed my own impulses and ideas to continue their uninterrupted course. It was like a preternaturally heightened sense of hearing, making audible to one a roar of sound where others find perfect stillness. The weariness and disgust of this involuntary intrusion into other souls was counteracted only by my ignorance of Bertha, and my growing passion for her; a passion enormously stimulated, if not produced, by that ignorance. She was my oasis of mystery in the dreary desert of knowledge. I had never allowed my diseased condition to betray itself, or to drive me into any unusual speech or action, except once, when, in a moment of peculiar bitterness against my brother, I had forestalled some words which I knew he was going to utter—a clever observation, which he had prepared beforehand. He had occasionally a slightly-affected hesitation in his speech, and when he paused an instant after the second word, my impatience and jealousy impelled me to continue the speech for him, as if it were something we had both learned by rote. He coloured and looked astonished, as well as annoyed; and the words had no sooner escaped my lips than I felt a shock of alarm lest such an anticipation of words—very far from being words, of course, easy to divine—should have betrayed me as an exceptional being, a sort of quiet energumen, whom every one, Bertha above all, would shudder at and avoid. But I magnified, as usual, the impression any word or deed of mine could produce on others; for no one gave any sign of having noticed my interruption as more than a rudeness, to be forgiven me on the score of my feeble nervous condition.

While this superadded consciousness of the actual was almost constant with me, I had never had a recurrence of

that distinct prevision which I have described in relation to
my first interview with Bertha; and I was waiting with
eager curiosity to know whether or not my vision of Prague
would prove to have been an instance of the same kind.
A few days after the incident of the opal ring, we were
paying one of our frequent visits to the Lichtenberg Palace.
I could never look at many pictures in succession; for pictures, when they are at all powerful, affect me so strongly
that one or two exhaust all my capability of contemplation.
This morning I had been looking at Giorgione's picture of the
cruel-eyed woman, said to be a likeness of Lucrezia Borgia.
I had stood long alone before it, fascinated by the terrible
reality of that cunning, relentless face, till I felt a strange
poisoned sensation, as if I had long been inhaling a fatal
odour, and was just beginning to be conscious of its effects.
Perhaps even then I should not have moved away, if the
rest of the party had not returned to this room, and announced that they were going to the Belvedere Gallery to
settle a bet which had arisen between my brother and Mr.
Filmore about a portrait. I followed them dreamily, and
was hardly alive to what occurred till they had all gone
up to the gallery, leaving me below; for I refused to come
within sight of another picture that day. I made my way
to the Grand Terrace, since it was agreed that we should
saunter in the gardens when the dispute had been decided.
I had been sitting here a short space, vaguely conscious of
trim gardens, with a city and green hills in the distance,
when, wishing to avoid the proximity of the sentinel, I
rose and walked down the broad stone steps, intending to
seat myself farther on in the gardens. Just as I reached the
gravel-walk, I felt an arm slipped within mine, and a light
hand gently pressing my wrist. In the same instant a
strange intoxicating numbness passed over me, like the con-
tinuance or climax of the sensation I was still feeling from
the gaze of Lucrezia Borgia. The gardens, the summer sky,
the consciousness of Bertha's arm being within mine, all
vanished, and I seemed to be suddenly in darkness, out of
which there gradually broke a dim firelight, and I felt myself sitting in my father's leather chair in the library at
home. I knew the fireplace—the dogs for the wood-fire—
the black marble chimney-piece with the white marble
medallion of the dying Cleopatra in the centre. Intense

and hopeless misery was pressing on my soul; the light became stronger, for Bertha was entering with a candle in her hand—Bertha, my wife—with cruel eyes, with green jewels and green leaves on her white ball-dress; every hateful thought within her present to me. . . . " Madman, idiot! why don't you kill yourself, then?" It was a moment of hell. I saw into her pitiless soul—saw its barren worldliness, its scorching hate—and felt it clothe me round like an air I was obliged to breathe. She came with her candle and stood over me with a bitter smile of contempt; I saw the great emerald brooch on her bosom, a studded serpent with diamond eyes. I shuddered—I despised this woman with the barren soul and mean thoughts; but I felt helpless before her, as if she clutched my bleeding heart, and would clutch it till the last drop of life-blood ebbed away. She was my wife, and we hated each other. Gradually the hearth, the dim library, the candle-light disappeared—seemed to melt away into a background of light, the green serpent with the diamond eyes remaining a dark image on the retina. Then I had a sense of my eyelids quivering, and the living daylight broke in upon me; I saw gardens, and heard voices; I was seated on the steps of the Belvedere Terrace, and my friends were round me.

The tumult of mind into which I was thrown by this hideous vision made me ill for several days, and prolonged our stay in Vienna. I shuddered with horror as the scene recurred to me; and it recurred constantly, with all its minutiæ, as if they had been burnt into my memory; and yet, such is the madness of the human heart under the influence of its immediate desires, I felt a wild hell-braving joy that Bertha was to be mine; for the fulfilment of my former prevision concerning her first appearance before me, left me little hope that this last hideous glimpse of the future was the mere diseased play of my own mind, and had no relation to external realities. One thing alone I looked towards as a possible means of casting doubt on my terrible conviction—the discovery that my vision of Prague had been false—and Prague was the next city on our route.

Meanwhile, I was no sooner in Bertha's society again, than I was as completely under her sway as before. What if I saw into the heart of Bertha, the matured woman— Bertha, my wife? Bertha, the *girl*, was a fascinating secret

to me still: I trembled under her touch; I felt the witchery
of her presence; I yearned to be assured of her love. The
fear of poison is feeble against the sense of thirst. Nay, I
was just as jealous of my brother as before—just as much
irritated by his small patronising ways; for my pride, my
diseased sensibility, were there as they had always been, and
winced as inevitably under every offence as my eye winced
from an intruding mote. The future, even when brought
within the compass of feeling by a vision that made me
shudder, had still no more than the force of an idea, compared with the force of present emotion—of my love for
Bertha, of my dislike and jealousy towards my brother.

It is an old story, that men sell themselves to the tempter,
and sign a bond with their blood, because it is only to
take effect at a distant day; then rush on to snatch the cup
their souls thirst after with an impulse not the less savage
because there is a dark shadow beside them for evermore.
There is no short cut, no patent tram-road, to wisdom:
after all the centuries of invention, the soul's path lies
through the thorny wilderness which must be still trodden
in solitude, with bleeding feet, with sobs for help, as it was
trodden by them of old time.

My mind speculated eagerly on the means by which I
should become my brother's successful rival, for I was still
too timid, in my ignorance of Bertha's actual feeling, to
venture on any step that would urge from her an avowal of
it. I thought I should gain confidence even for this, if my
vision of Prague proved to have been veracious; and yet, the
horror of that certitude! Behind the slim girl Bertha, whose
words and looks I watched for, whose touch was bliss, there
stood continually that Bertha with the fuller form, the
harder eyes, the more rigid mouth—with the barren, selfish
soul laid bare; no longer a fascinating secret, but a measured
fact, urging itself perpetually on my unwilling sight. Are
you unable to give me your sympathy—you who read this?
Are you unable to imagine this double consciousness at work
within me, flowing on like two parallel streams which never
mingle their waters and blend into a common hue? Yet you
must have known something of the presentiments that
spring from an insight at war with passion; and my visions
were only like presentiments intensified to horror. You
have known the powerlessness of ideas before the might of

impulse; and my visions, when once they had passed into memory, were mere ideas—pale shadows that beckoned in vain, while my hand was grasped by the living and the loved.

In after-days I thought with bitter regret that if I had foreseen something more or something different—if instead of that hideous vision which poisoned the passion it could not destroy, or if even along with it I could have had a fore-shadowing of that moment when I looked on my brother's face for the last time, some softening influence would have been shed over my feeling towards him: pride and hatred would surely have been subdued into pity, and the record of those hidden sins would have been shortened. But this is one of the vain thoughts with which we men flatter ourselves. We try to believe that the egoism within us would have easily been melted, and that it was only the narrowness of our knowledge which hemmed in our generosity, our awe, our human piety, and hindered them from submerging our hard indifference to the sensations and emotions of our fellows. Our tenderness and self-renunciation seem strong when our egoism has had its day—when, after our mean striving for a triumph that is to be another's loss, the triumph comes suddenly, and we shudder at it, because it is held out by the chill hand of death.

Our arrival in Prague happened at night, and I was glad of this, for it seemed like a deferring of a terribly decisive moment, to be in the city for hours without seeing it. As we were not to remain long in Prague, but to go on speedily to Dresden, it was proposed that we should drive out the next morning and take a general view of the place, as well as visit some of its specially interesting spots, before the heat became oppressive—for we were in August, and the season was hot and dry. But it happened that the ladies were rather late at their morning toilet, and to my father's politely-repressed but perceptible annoyance, we were not in the carriage till the morning was far advanced. I thought with a sense of relief, as we entered the Jews' quarter, where we were to visit the old synagogue, that we should be kept in this flat, shut-up part of the city, until we should all be too tired and too warm to go farther, and so we should return without seeing more than the streets through which we had already passed. That would give me another day's suspense—

suspense, the only form in which a fearful spirit knows the solace of hope. But, as I stood under the blackened, groined arches of that old synagogue, made dimly visible by the seven thin candles in the sacred lamp, while our Jewish cicerone reached down the Book of the Law, and read to us in its ancient tongue—I felt a shuddering impression that this strange building, with its shrunken lights, this surviving withered remnant of mediæval Judaism, was of a piece with my vision. Those darkened dusty Christian saints, with their loftier arches and their larger candles, needed the consolatory scorn with which they might point to a more shrivelled death-in-life than their own.

As I expected, when we left the Jews' quarter the elders of our party wished to return to the hotel. But now, instead of rejoicing in this, as I had done beforehand, I felt a sudden overpowering impulse to go on at once to the bridge, and put an end to the suspense I had been wishing to protract. I declared, with unusual decision, that I would get out of the carriage and walk on alone; they might return without me. My father, thinking this merely a sample of my usual " poetic nonsense," objected that I should only do myself harm by walking in the heat; but when I persisted, he said angrily that I might follow my own absurd devices, but that Schmidt (our courier) must go with me. I assented to this, and set off with Schmidt towards the bridge. I had no sooner passed from under the archway of the grand old gate leading on to the bridge, than a trembling seized me; and I turned cold under the midday sun; yet I went on; I was in search of something—a small detail which I remembered with special intensity as part of my vision. There it was—the patch of rainbow light on the pavement transmitted through a lamp in the shape of a star.

II

BEFORE the autumn was at an end, and while the brown leaves still stood thick on the beeches in our park, my brother and Bertha were engaged to each other, and it was understood that their marriage was to take place early in the next spring. In spite of the certainty I had felt from that moment on the bridge at Prague, that Bertha would one day be my wife, my constitutional timidity and distrust had con-

tinued to benumb me, and the words in which I had sometimes premeditated a confession of my love, had died away
unuttered. The same conflict had gone on within me as
before—the longing for an assurance of love from Bertha's
lips, the dread lest a word of contempt and denial should
fall upon me like a corrosive acid. What was the conviction
of a distant necessity to me? I trembled under a present
glance, I hungered after a present joy, I was clogged and
chilled by a present fear. And so the days passed on: I witnessed Bertha's engagement and heard her marriage discussed
as if I were under a conscious nightmare—knowing it was a
dream that would vanish, but feeling stifled under the grasp
of hard-clutching fingers.

When I was not in Bertha's presence—and I was with her
very often, for she continued to treat me with a playful
patronage that wakened no jealousy in my brother—I spent
my time chiefly in wandering, in strolling, or taking long
rides while the daylight lasted, and then shutting myself up
with my unread books; for books had lost the power of
chaining my attention. My self-consciousness was heightened
to that pitch of intensity in which our own emotions take the
form of a drama which urges itself imperatively on our contemplation, and we begin to weep, less under the sense of
our suffering than at the thought of it. I felt a sort of pity-
ing anguish over the pathos of my own lot: the lot of a being
finely organized for pain, but with hardly any fibres that
responded to pleasure—to whom the idea of future evil
robbed the present of its joy, and for whom the idea of future
good did not still the uneasiness of a present yearning or a
present dread. I went dumbly through that stage of the
poet's suffering, in which he feels the delicious pang of utterance, and makes an image of his sorrows.

I was left entirely without remonstrance concerning this
dreamy wayward life: I knew my father's thought about
me: "That lad will never be good for anything in life: he
may waste his years in an insignificant way on the income
that falls to him: I shall not trouble myself about a career for
him."

One mild morning in the beginning of November, it happened that I was standing outside the portico patting lazy
old Cæsar, a Newfoundland almost blind with age, the only
dog that ever took any notice of me—for the very dogs

shunned me, and fawned on the happier people about me—
when the groom brought up my brother's horse which was
to carry him to the hunt, and my brother himself appeared
at the door, florid, broad-chested, and self-complacent, feeling what a good-natured fellow he was not to behave inso-
lently to us all on the strength of his great advantages.

" Latimer, old boy," he said to me in a tone of compassionate cordiality, " what a pity it is you don't have a run with
the hounds now and then! The finest thing in the world for
low spirits! "

" Low spirits! " I thought bitterly, as he rode away; " that
is the sort of phrase with which coarse, narrow natures like
yours think to describe experience of which you can know
no more than your horse knows. It is to such as you that
the good of this world falls: ready dullness, healthy selfishness, good-tempered conceit—these are the keys to happiness."

The quick thought came, that my selfishness was even
stronger than his—it was only a suffering selfishness instead
of an enjoying one. But then, again, my exasperating insight
into Alfred's self-complacent soul, his freedom from all the
doubts and fears, the unsatisfied yearnings, the exquisite tortures of sensitiveness, that had made the web of my life,
seemed to absolve me from all bonds towards him. This man
needed no pity, no love; those fine influences would have
been as little felt by him as the delicate white mist is felt by
the rock it caresses. There was no evil in store for *him*: if he
was not to marry Bertha, it would be because he had found
a lot pleasanter to himself.

Mr. Filmore's house lay not more than half a mile beyond
our own gates, and whenever I knew my brother was gone in
another direction, I went there for the chance of finding
Bertha at home. Later on in the day I walked thither. By
a rare accident she was alone, and we walked out in the
grounds together, for she seldom went on foot beyond the
trimly-swept gravel-walks. I remember what a beautiful
sylph she looked to me as the low November sun shone on her
blond hair, and she tripped along teasing me with her usual
light banter, to which I listened half-fondly, half-moodily;
it was all the sign Bertha's mysterious inner self ever made to
me. To-day perhaps the moodiness predominated, for I had
not yet shaken off the access of jealous hate which my brother
had raised in me by his parting patronage. Suddenly I inter-

rupted and startled her by saying, almost fiercely, " Bertha, how can you love Alfred? "

She looked at me with surprise for a moment, but soon her light smile came again, and she answered sarcastically, " Why do you suppose I love him? "

" How can you ask that, Bertha? "

" What! your wisdom thinks I must love the man I'm going to marry? The most unpleasant thing in the world. I should quarrel with him; I should be jealous of him; our *ménage* would be conducted in a very ill-bred manner. A little quiet contempt contributes greatly to the elegance of life."

" Bertha, that is not your real feeling. Why do you delight in trying to deceive me by inventing such cynical speeches? "

" I need never take the trouble of invention in order to deceive you, my small Tasso "—(that was the mocking name she usually gave me). " The easiest way to deceive a poet is to tell him the truth."

She was testing the validity of her epigram in a daring way, and for a moment the shadow of my vision—the Bertha whose soul was no secret to me—passed between me and the radiant girl, the playful sylph whose feelings were a fascinating mystery. I suppose I must have shuddered, or betrayed in some other way my momentary chill of horror.

" Tasso! " she said, seizing my wrist, and peeping round into my face, " are you really beginning to discern what a heartless girl I am? Why, you are not half the poet I thought you were; you were actually capable of believing the truth about me."

The shadow passed from between us, and was no longer the object nearest to me. The girl whose light fingers grasped me, whose elfish charming face looked into mine—who, I thought, was betraying an interest in my feelings that she would not have directly avowed—this warm breathing presence again possessed my senses and imagination like a returning siren melody which had been overpowered for an instant by the roar of threatening waves. It was a moment as delicious to me as the waking up to a consciousness of youth after a dream of middle age. I forgot everything but my passion, and said with swimming eyes:

" Bertha, shall you love me when we are first married? I wouldn't mind if you really loved me only for a little while."

Her look of astonishment, as she loosed my hand and started away from me, recalled me to a sense of my strange, my criminal indiscretion.

"Forgive me," I said, hurriedly, as soon as I could speak again; "I did not know what I was saying."

"Ah, Tasso's mad fit has come on, I see," she answered quietly, for she had recovered herself sooner than I had. "Let him go home and keep his head cool. I must go in, for the sun is setting."

I left her—full of indignation against myself. I had let slip words which, if she reflected on them, might rouse in her a suspicion of my abnormal mental condition—a suspicion which of all things I dreaded. And besides that, I was ashamed of the apparent baseness I had committed in uttering them to my brother's betrothed wife. I wandered home slowly, entering our park through a private gate instead of by the lodges. As I approached the house, I saw a man dashing off at full speed from the stable-yard across the park. Had any accident happened at home? No; perhaps it was only one of my father's peremptory business errands that required this headlong haste.

Nevertheless I quickened my pace without any distinct motive, and was soon at the house. I will not dwell on the scene I found there. My brother was dead—had been pitched from his horse, and killed on the spot by a concussion of the brain.

I went up to the room where he lay, and where my father was seated beside him with a look of rigid despair. I had shunned my father more than any one since our return home, for the radical antipathy between our natures made my insight into his inner self a constant affliction to me. But now, as I went up to him, and stood beside him in sad silence, I felt the presence of a new element that blended us as we had never been blent before. My father had been one of the most successful men in the money-getting world: he had had no sentimental sufferings, no illness. The heaviest trouble that had befallen him was the death of his first wife. But he married my mother soon after; and I remember he seemed exactly the same, to my keen childish observation, the week after her death as before. But now, at last, a sorrow had come—the sorrow of old age, which suffers the more from the crushing of its pride and its hopes, in proportion as the

pride and hope are narrow and prosaic. His son was to have
been married soon—would probably have stood for the
borough at the next election. That son's existence was the
best motive that could be alleged for making new purchases
of land every year to round off the estate. It is a dreary thing
to live on doing the same things year after year, without
knowing why we do them. Perhaps the tragedy of disappointed youth and passion is less piteous than the tragedy
of disappointed age and worldliness.

As I saw into the desolation of my father's heart, I felt a
movement of deep pity towards him, which was the beginning of a new affection—an affection that grew and streng-
thened in spite of the strange bitterness with which he
regarded me in the first month or two after my brother's
death. If it had not been for the softening influence of my
compassion for him—the first deep compassion I had ever felt
—I should have been stung by the perception that my father
transferred the inheritance of an eldest son to me with a
mortified sense that fate had compelled him to the unwelcome
course of caring for me as an important being. It was only
in spite of himself that he began to think of me with anxious
regard. There is hardly any neglected child for whom death
has made vacant a more favoured place, who will not understand what I mean.

Gradually, however, my new deference to his wishes, the
effect of that patience which was born of my pity for him,
won upon his affection, and he began to please himself with
the endeavour to make me fill my brother's place as fully as
my feebler personality would admit. I saw that the prospect
which by and by presented itself of my becoming Bertha's
husband was welcome to him, and he even contemplated in
my case what he had not intended in my brother's—that his
son and daughter-in-law should make one household with
him. My softened feeling towards my father made this the
happiest time I had known since childhood;—these last
months in which I retained the delicious illusion of loving
Bertha, of longing and doubting and hoping that she might
love me. She behaved with a certain new consciousness and
distance towards me after my brother's death; and I too was
under a double constraint—that of delicacy towards my
brother's memory, and of anxiety as to the impression my
abrupt words had left on her mind. But the additional screen

this mutual reserve erected between us only brought me more
completely under her power: no matter how empty the
adytum, so that the veil be thick enough. So absolute is our
soul's need of something hidden and uncertain for the maintenance of that doubt and hope and effort which are the
breath of its life, that if the whole future were laid bare to us
beyond to-day, the interest of all mankind would be bent on
the hours that lie between; we should pant after the uncer-
tainties of our one morning and our one afternoon; we
should rush fiercely to the Exchange for our last possibility
of speculation, of success, of disappointment: we should have
a glut of political prophets foretelling a crisis or a no-crisis
within the only twenty-four hours left open to prophecy.
Conceive the condition of the human mind if all propositions
whatsoever were self-evident except one, which was to become self-evident at the close of a summer's day, but in the
meantime might be the subject of question, of hypothesis, of
debate. Art and philosophy, literature and science, would
fasten like bees on that one proposition which had the honey
of probability in it, and be the more eager because their enjoyment would end with sunset. Our impulses, our spiritual
activities, no more adjust themselves to the idea of their
future nullity, than the beating of our heart, or the irritability of our muscles.

Bertha, the slim, fair-haired girl, whose present thoughts
and emotions were an enigma to me amidst the fatiguing ob-
viousness of the other minds around me, was as absorbing to
me as a single unknown to-day—as a single hypothetic proposition to remain problematic till sunset; and all the
cramped, hemmed-in belief and disbelief, trust and distrust,
of my nature, welled out in this one narrow channel.

And she made me believe that she loved me. Without ever
quitting her tone of *badinage* and playful superiority, she
intoxicated me with the sense that I was necessary to her, that
she was never at ease unless I was near her, submitting to her
playful tyranny. It costs a woman so little effort to besot us
in this way! A half-repressed word, a moment's unexpected
silence, even an easy fit of petulance on our account, will
serve us as *hashish* for a long while. Out of the subtlest web
of scarcely perceptible signs, she set me weaving the fancy
that she had always unconsciously loved me better than
Alfred, but that, with the ignorant fluttered sensibility of a

young girl, she had been imposed on by the charm that lay
for her in the distinction of being admired and chosen by a
man who made so brilliant a figure in the world as my
brother. She satirized herself in a very graceful way for her
vanity and ambition. What was it to me that I had the light
of my wretched prevision on the fact that now it was I who
possessed at least all but the personal part of my brother's
advantages? Our sweet illusions are half of them conscious
illusions, like effects of colour that we know to be made up of
tinsel, broken glass, and rags.

We were married eighteen months after Alfred's death, one
cold, clear morning in April, when there came hail and sunshine both together; and Bertha, in her white silk and pale-
green leaves, and the pale hues of her hair and face, looked
like the spirit of the morning. My father was happier than
he had thought of being again: my marriage, he felt sure,
would complete the desirable modification of my character,
and make me practical and wordly enough to take my place
in society among sane men. For he delighted in Bertha's tact
and acuteness, and felt sure she would be mistress of me, and
make me what she chose: I was only twenty-one, and madly
in love with her. Poor father! He kept that hope a little
while after our first year of marriage, and it was not quite
extinct when paralysis came and saved him from utter disappointment.

I shall hurry through the rest of my story, not dwelling so
much as I have hitherto done on my inward experience.
When people are well known to each other, they talk rather
of what befalls them externally, leaving their feelings and
sentiments to be inferred.

We lived in a round of visits for some time after our
return home, giving splendid dinner-parties, and making a
sensation in our neighbourhood by the new lustre of our
equipage, for my father had reserved this display of his increased wealth for the period of his son's marriage; and we
gave our acquaintances liberal opportunity for remarking
that it was a pity I made so poor a figure as an heir and a
bridegroom. The nervous fatigue of this existence, the insin-
cerities and platitudes which I had to live through twice over
—through my inner and outward sense—would have been
maddening to me, if I had not had that sort of intoxicated
callousness which came from the delights of a first passion.

A bride and bridegroom surrounded by all the appliances of wealth, hurried through the day by the whirl of society, filling their solitary moments with hastily-snatched caresses, are prepared for their future life together as the novice is prepared for the cloister—by experiencing its utmost contrast.

Through all these crowded, excited months, Bertha's inward self remained shrouded from me, and I still read her thoughts only through the language of her lips and demeanour: I had still the human interest of wondering whether what I did and said pleased her, of longing to hear a word of affection, of giving a delicious exaggeration of meaning to her smile. But I was conscious of a growing difference in her manner towards me; sometimes strong enough to be called haughty coldness, cutting and chilling me as the hail had done that came across the sunshine on our marriage morning; sometimes only perceptible in the dexterous avoidance of a *tête-à-tête* walk or dinner to which I had been looking forward. I had been deeply pained by this—had even felt a sort of crushing of the heart, from the sense that my brief day of happiness was near its setting; but still I remained dependent on Bertha, eager for the last rays of a bliss that would soon be gone for ever, hoping and watching for some after-glow more beautiful from the impending light.

I remember—how should I not remember?—the time when that dependance and hope utterly left me, when the sadness I had felt in Bertha's growing estrangement became a joy that I looked back upon with longing as a man might look back on the last pains in a paralysed limb. It was just after the close of my father's last illness, which had necessarily withdrawn us from society and thrown us more upon each other. It was the evening of my father's death. On that evening the veil which had shrouded Bertha's soul from me —had made me find in her alone among my fellow-beings the blessed possibility of mystery, and doubt, and expectation —was first withdrawn. Perhaps it was the first day since the beginning of my passion for her, in which that passion was completely neutralized by the presence of an absorbing feeling of another kind. I had been watching by my father's deathbed: I had been witnessing the last fitful yearning glance his soul had cast back on the spent inheritance of life—the last faint consciousness of love he had gathered from the pressure of my hand. What are all our personal loves when we have

been sharing in that supreme agony? In the first moments
when we come away from the presence of death, every other
relation to the living is merged, to our feeling, in the great
relation of a common nature and a common destiny.

In that state of mind I joined Bertha in her private sitting-
room. She was seated in a leaning posture on a settee, with
her back towards the door; the great rich coils of her pale
blond hair surmounting her small neck, visible above the back
of the settee. I remember, as I closed the door behind me, a
cold tremulousness seizing me, and a vague sense of being
hated and lonely—vague and strong, like a presentiment. I
know how I looked at that moment, for I saw myself in
Bertha's thought as she lifted her cutting grey eyes, and
looked at me: a miserable ghost-seer, surrounded by phantoms
in the noonday, trembling under a breeze when the leaves
were still, without appetite for the common objects of human
desires, but pining after the moonbeams. We were front to
front with each other, and judged each other. The terrible
moment of complete illumination had come to me, and I saw
that the darkness had hidden no landscape from me, but only
a blank prosaic wall: from that evening forth, through the
sickening years which followed, I saw all round the narrow
room of this woman's soul—saw petty artifice and mere
negation where I had delighted to believe in coy sensibilities
and in wit at war with latent feeling—saw the light floating
vanities of the girl defining themselves into the systematic
coquetry, the scheming selfishness, of the woman—saw repulsion and antipathy harden into cruel hatred, giving pain only
for the sake of wreaking itself.

For Bertha too, after her kind, felt the bitterness of dis-
illusion. She had believed that my wild poet's passion for
her would make me her slave; and that, being her slave, I
should execute her will in all things. With the essential
shallowness of a negative, unimaginative nature, she was unable to conceive the fact that sensibilities were anything else
than weaknesses. She had thought my weaknesses would put
me in her power, and she found them unmanageable forces.
Our positions were reversed. Before marriage she had completely mastered my imagination, for she was a secret to me;
and I created the unknown thought before which I trembled
as if it were hers. But now that her soul was laid open to
me, now that I was compelled to share the privacy of her

motives, to follow all the petty devices that preceded her words and acts, she found herself powerless with me, except to produce in me the chill shudder of repulsion—powerless, because I could be acted on by no lever within her reach. I was dead to wordly ambitions, to social vanities, to all the incentives within the compass of her narrow imagination, and I lived under influences utterly invisible to her.

She was really pitiable to have such a husband, and so all the world thought. A graceful, brilliant woman, like Bertha, who smiled on morning callers, made a figure in ballrooms, and was capable of that light repartee which, from such a woman, is accepted as wit, was secure of carrying off all sympathy from a husband who was sickly, abstracted, and, as some suspected, crack-brained. Even the servants in our house gave her the balance of their regard and pity. For there were no audible quarrels between us; our alienation, our repulsion from each other, lay within the silence of our own hearts; and if the mistress went out a great deal, and seemed to dislike the master's society, was it not natural, poor thing? The master was odd. I was kind and just to my dependants, but I excited in them a shrinking, half-contemptuous pity; for this class of men and women are but slightly determined in their estimate of others by general considerations, or even experience, of character. They judge of persons as they judge of coins, and value those who pass current at a high rate.

After a time I interfered so little with Bertha's habits that it might seem wonderful how her hatred towards me could grow so intense and active as it did. But she had begun to suspect, by some involuntary betrayal of mine, that there was an abnormal power of penetration in me—that fitfully, at least, I was strangely cognizant of her thoughts and intentions, and she began to be haunted by a terror of me, which alternated every now and then with defiance. She meditated continually how the incubus could be shaken off her life— how she could be freed from this hateful bond to a being whom she at once despised as an imbecile, and dreaded as an inquisitor. For a long while she lived in the hope that my evident wretchedness would drive me to the commission of suicide; but suicide was not in my nature. I was too completely swayed by the sense that I was in the grasp of unknown forces, to believe in my power of self-release.

Towards my own destiny I had become entirely passive; for my one ardent desire had spent itself, and impulse no longer predominated over knowledge. For this reason I never thought of taking any steps towards a complete separation, which would have made our alienation evident to the world. Why should I rush for help to a new course, when I was only suffering from the consequences of a deed which had been the act of my intensest will? That would have been the logic of one who had desires to gratify, and I had no desires. But Bertha and I lived more and more aloof from each other. The rich find it easy to live married and apart.

That course of our life which I have indicated in a few sentences filled the space of years. So much misery—so slow and hideous a growth of hatred and sin, may be compressed into a sentence! And men judge of each other's lives through this summary medium. They epitomize the experience of their fellow-mortal, and pronounce judgment on him in neat syntax, and feel themselves wise and virtuous—conquerors over the temptations they define in well-selected predicates. Seven years of wretchedness glide glibly over the lips of the man who has never counted them out in moments of chill disappointment, of head and heart throbbings, of dread and vain wrestling, of remorse and despair. We learn *words* by rote, but not their meaning; *that* must be paid for with our life-blood, and printed in the subtle fibres of our nerves.

But I will hasten to finish my story. Brevity is justified at once to those who readily understand, and to those who will never understand.

Some years after my father's death, I was sitting by the dim firelight in my library one January evening—sitting in the leather chair that used to be my father's—when Bertha appeared at the door, with a candle in her hand, and advanced towards me. I knew the ball-dress she had on—the white ball-dress, with the green jewels, shone upon by the light of the wax candle which lit up the medallion of the dying Cleopatra on the mantelpiece. Why did she come to me before going out? I had not seen her in the library, which was my habitual place, for months. Why did she stand before me with the candle in her hand, with her cruel contemptuous eyes fixed on me, and the glittering serpent, like a familiar demon, on her breast? For a moment I thought this fulfilment of my vision at Vienna marked some dreadful crisis in my fate, but I saw nothing in Bertha's mind, as she stood before me except scorn for the look of overwhelming misery with which I sat before her. . . . "Fool, idiot, why don't you kill yourself, then?"—that was her thought. But at length her thoughts reverted to her errand, and she spoke aloud. The apparently indifferent nature of the errand seemed to make a ridiculous anticlimax to my prevision and my agitation.

"I have had to hire a new maid. Fletcher is going to be married, and she wants me to ask you to let her husband have the public-house and farm at Molton. I wish him to have it. You must give the promise now, because Fletcher is going to-morrow morning—and quickly, because I'm in a hurry."

"Very well; you may promise her," I said, indifferently, and Bertha swept out of the library again.

I always shrank from the sight of a new person, and all the more when it was a person whose mental life was likely to weary my reluctant insight with wordly ignorant trivialities. But I shrank especially from the sight of this new maid, because her advent had been announced to me at a moment to which I could not cease to attach some fatality: I had a vague dread that I should find her mixed up with the dreary drama of my life—that some new sickening vision would reveal her to me as an evil genius. When at last I did unavoidably meet her, the vague dread was changed into definite disgust. She was a tall, wiry, dark-eyed woman, this Mrs. Archer, with a face handsome enough to give her coarse hard nature the odious finish of bold, self-confident coquetry. That was enough to make me avoid her, quite apart from the contemptuous feeling with which she contemplated me. I seldom saw her; but I perceived that she rapidly became a favourite with her mistress, and, after the lapse of eight or nine months, I began to be aware that there had arisen in Bertha's mind towards this woman a mingled feeling of fear and dependence, and that this feeling was associated with ill-defined images of candle-light scenes in her dressing-room, and the locking-up of something in Bertha's cabinet. My interviews with my wife had become so brief and so rarely solitary, that I had no opportunity of perceiving these images in her mind with more definiteness. The recollections of the past become contracted in the rapidity of thought till they sometimes bear hardly a more distinct resemblance to the external reality than the forms of an oriental alphabet to the objects that suggested them.

Besides, for the last year or more a modification had been going forward in my mental condition, and was growing more and more marked. My insight into the minds of those around me was becoming dimmer and more fitful, and the ideas that crowded my double consciousness became less and less dependent on any personal contact. All that was personal in me seemed to be suffering a gradual death, so that I was losing the organ through which the personal agitations and projects of others could affect me. But along with this relief from wearisome insight, there was a new development of what I concluded—as I have since found rightly—to be a prevision of external scenes. It was as if the relation between me and my fellow-men was more and more deadened, and my relation to what we call the inanimate was quickened into new life. The more I lived apart from society, and in proportion as my wretchedness subsided from the violent throb of agonized passion into the dullness of habitual pain, the more frequent and vivid became such visions as that I had had of Prague—of strange cities, of sandy plains, of gigantic ruins, of midnight skies with strange bright constellations, of mountain-passes, of grassy nooks flecked with the afternoon sunshine through the boughs: I was in the midst of such scenes, and in all of them one presence seemed to weigh on me in all these mighty shapes—the presence of something unknown and pitiless. For continual suffering had annihilated religious faith within me: to the utterly miserable—the unloving and the unloved—there is no religion possible, no worship but a worship of devils. And beyond all these, and continually recurring, was the vision of my death—the pangs, the suffocation, the last struggle, when life would be grasped at in vain.

Things were in this state near the end of the seventh year. I had become entirely free from insight, from my abnormal cognizance of any other consciousness than my own, and instead of intruding involuntarily into the world of other minds, was living continually in my own solitary future. Bertha was aware that I was greatly changed. To my surprise she had of late seemed to seek opportunities of remaining in my society, and had cultivated that kind of distant yet familiar talk which is customary between a husband and wife who live in polite and irrevocable alienation. I bore this with languid submission, and without feeling enough interest in her motives to be roused into keen observation; yet I could not help perceiving something triumphant and excited in her carriage and the expression of her face—something too subtle to express itself in words or tones, but giving one the idea that she lived in a state of expectation or hopeful suspense. My chief feeling was satisfaction that her inner self was once more shut from me; and I almost revelled for the moment in the absent melancholy that made me answer her at cross purposes, and betray utter ignorance of what she had been saying. I remember well the look and the smile with which she one day said, after a mistake of this kind on my part: " I used to think you were a clairvoyant and that was the reason why you were so bitter against other clairvoyants, wanting to keep your monopoly; but I see now you have become rather duller than the rest of the world."

I said nothing in reply. It occurred to me that her recent obtrusion of herself upon me might have been prompted by the wish to test my power of detecting some of her secrets; but I let the thought drop again at once: her motives and her deeds had no interest for me, and whatever pleasures she might be seeking, I had no wish to baulk her. There was still pity in my soul for every living thing, and Bertha was living—was surrounded with possibilities of misery.

Just at this time there occurred an event which roused me somewhat from my inertia, and gave me an interest in the passing moment that I had thought impossible for me. It was a visit from Charles Meunier, who had written me word that he was coming to England for relaxation from too strenuous labour, and would like to see me. Meunier had now a European reputation; but his letter to me expressed that keen remembrance of an early regard, an early debt of sympathy, which is inseparable from nobility of character: and I too felt as if his presence would be to me like a transient resurrection into a happier pre-existence.

He came, and as far as possible, I renewed our old pleasure of making *tête-à-tête* excursions, though, instead of mountains and glaciers and the wide blue lake, we had to content ourselves with mere slopes and ponds and artificial plantations. The years had changed us both, but with what different result! Meunier was now a brilliant figure in society, to whom elegant women pretended to listen, and whose acquaintance was boasted of by noblemen ambitious of brains. He repressed with the utmost delicacy any betrayal of the shock which I am sure he must have received from our meeting, or of a desire to penetrate into my condition and circumstances, and sought by the utmost exertion of his charming social powers to make our reunion agreeable. Bertha was much struck by the unexpected fascinations of a visitor whom she had expected to find presentable only on the score of his celebrity, and put forth all her coquetries and accomplishments. Apparently she succeeded in attracting his admiration, for his manner towards her was attentive and flattering. The effect of his presence on me was so benignant, especially in those renewals of our old *tête-à-tête* wanderings, when he poured forth to me wonderful narratives of his professional experience, that more than once, when his talk turned on the psychological relations of disease, the thought crossed my mind that, if his stay with me were long enough, I might possibly bring myself to tell this man the secrets of my lot. Might there not lie some remedy for *me*, too, in his science? Might there not at least lie some comprehension and sympathy ready for me in his large and susceptible mind? But the thought only flickered feebly now and then, and died out before it could become a wish. The horror I had of again breaking in on the privacy of another soul, made me, by an irrational instinct, draw the shroud of concealment more closely around my own, as we automatically perform the gesture we feel to be wanting in another.

When Meunier's visit was approaching its conclusion, there happened an event which caused some excitement in our household, owing to the surprisingly strong effect it appeared to produce on Bertha—on Bertha, the self-possessed, who usually seemed inaccessible to feminine agitations, and did even her hate in a self-restrained hygienic manner. This event was the sudden severe illness of her maid, Mrs. Archer. I have reserved to this moment the mention of a circumstance which had forced itself on my notice shortly before Meunier's arrival, namely, that there had been some quarrel between Bertha and this maid, apparently during a visit to a distant family, in which she had accompanied her mistress. I had overheard Archer speaking in a tone of bitter insolence, which I should have thought an adequate reason for immediate dismissal. No dismissal followed; on the contrary, Bertha seemed to be silently putting up with personal inconveniences from the exhibitions of this woman's temper. I was the more astonished to observe that her illness seemed a cause of strong solicitude to Bertha; that she was at the bedside night and day, and would allow no one else to officiate as head-nurse. It happened that our family doctor was out on a holiday, an accident which made Meunier's presence in the house doubly welcome, and he apparently entered into the case with an interest which seemed so much stronger than the ordinary professional feeling, that one day when he had fallen into a long fit of silence, after visiting her, I said to him:

"Is this a very peculiar case of disease, Meunier?"

"No," he answered, "it is an attack of peritonitis, which will be fatal, but which does not differ physically from many other cases that have come under my observation. But I'll tell you what I have on my mind. I want to make an experiment on this woman, if you will give me permission. It can do her no harm—will give her no pain—for I shall not make it until life is extinct to all purposes of sensation. I want to try the effect of transfusing blood into her arteries after the heart has ceased to beat for some minutes. I have tried the experiment again and again with animals that have died of this disease, with astounding results, and I want to try it on a human subject. I have the small tubes necessary, in a case I have with me, and the rest of the apparatus could be prepared readily. I should use my own blood—take it from my own arm. This woman won't live through the night, I'm convinced, and I want you to promise me your assistance in making the experiment. I can't do without another hand, but it would perhaps not be well to call in a medical assistant from among your provincial doctors. A disagreeable foolish version of the thing might get abroad."

"Have you spoken to my wife on the subject?" I said, "because she appears to be peculiarly sensitive about this woman: she has been a favourite maid."

"To tell you the truth," said Meunier, "I don't want her to know about it. There are always insuperable difficulties with women in these matters, and the effect on the supposed dead body may be startling. You and I will sit up together, and be in readiness. When certain symptoms appear I shall take you in, and at the right moment we must arrange to get every one else out of the room."

I need not give our further conversation on the subject. He entered very fully into the details, and overcame my repulsion from them, by exciting in me a mingled awe and curiosity concerning the possible results of his experiment.

We prepared everything, and he instructed me in my part as assistant. He had not told Bertha of his absolute conviction that Archer would not survive through the night, and endeavoured to persuade her to leave the patient and take a night's rest. But she was obstinate, suspecting the fact that death was at hand, and supposing that he wished merely to save her nerves. She refused to leave the sickroom. Meunier and I sat up together in the library, he making frequent visits to the sick-room, and returning with the information that the case was taking precisely the course he expected. Once he said to me, "Can you imagine any cause of ill-feeling this woman has against her mistress, who is so devoted to her?"

"I think there was some misunderstanding between them before her illness. Why do you ask?"

"Because I have observed for the last five or six hours—since, I fancy, she has lost all hope of recovery—there seems a strange prompting in her to say something which pain and failing strength forbid her to utter; and there is a look of hideous meaning in her eyes, which she turns continually towards her mistress. In this disease the mind often remains singularly clear to the last."

"I am not surprised at an indication of malevolent feeling in her," I said. "She is a woman who has always inspired me with distrust and dislike, but she managed to insinuate herself into her mistress's favour." He was silent after this, looking at the fire with an air of absorption, till he went upstairs again. He stayed away longer than usual, and on returning, said to me quietly, "Come now."

I followed him to the chamber where death was hovering. The dark hangings of the large bed made a background that gave a strong relief to Bertha's pale face as I entered. She started forward as she saw me enter, and then looked at Meunier with an expression of angry inquiry; but he lifted up his hand as if to impose silence, while he fixed his glance on the dying woman and felt her pulse. The face was pinched and ghastly, a cold perspiration was on the forehead, and the eyelids were lowered so as to conceal the large dark eyes. After a minute or two, Meunier walked round to the other side of the bed where Bertha stood, and with his usual air of gentle politeness towards her begged her to leave the patient under our care—everything should be done for her— she was no longer in a state to be conscious of an affectionate presence. Bertha was hesitating, apparently almost willing to believe his assurance and to comply. She looked round at the ghastly dying face, as if to read the confirmation of that assurance, when for a moment the lowered eyelids were raised again, and it seemed as if the eyes were looking towards Bertha, but blankly. A shudder passed through Bertha's frame, and she returned to her station near the pillow, tacitly implying that she would not leave the room.

The eyelids were lifted no more. Once I looked at Bertha as she watched the face of the dying one. She wore a rich *peignoir*, and her blond hair was half covered by a lace cap: in her attire she was, as always, an elegant woman, fit to figure in a picture of modern aristocratic life: but I asked myself how that face of hers could ever have seemed to me the face of a woman born of woman, with memories of child-hood, capable of pain, needing to be fondled? The features at that moment seemed so preternaturally sharp, the eyes were so hard and eager—she looked like a cruel immortal, finding her spiritual feast in the agonies of a dying race. For across those hard features there came something like a flash when the last hour had been breathed out, and we all felt that the dark veil had completely fallen. What secret was there between Bertha and this woman? I turned my eyes from her with a horrible dread lest my insight should return, and I should be obliged to see what had been breeding about two unloving women's hearts. I felt that Bertha had been watching for the moment of death as the sealing of her secret: I thanked Heaven it could remain sealed for me.

Meunier said quietly, " She is gone." He then gave his arm to Bertha, and she submitted to be led out of the room.

I suppose it was at her order that two female attendants came into the room, and dismissed the younger one who had been present before. When they entered, Meunier had already opened the artery in the long thin neck that lay rigid on the pillow, and I dismissed them, ordering them to remain at a distance till we rang: the doctor, I said, had an operation to perform—he was not sure about the death. For the next twenty minutes I forgot everything but Meunier and the experiment in which he was so absorbed that I think his senses would have been closed against all sounds or sights which had no relation to it. It was my task at first to keep up the artificial respiration in the body after the transfusion had been effected, but presently Meunier relieved me, and I could see the wondrous slow return of life; the breast began to heave, the inspirations became stronger, the eyelids quivered, and the soul seemed to have returned beneath them. The artificial respiration was withdrawn: still the breathing continued, and there was a movement of the lips.

Just then I heard the handle of the door moving: I suppose Bertha had heard from the women that they had been dismissed: probably a vague fear had arisen in her mind, for she entered with a look of alarm. She came to the foot of the bed and gave a stifled cry.

The dead woman's eyes were wide open, and met hers in full recognition of hate. With a sudden strong effort, the hand that Bertha had thought for ever still was pointed towards her, and the haggard face moved. The gasping eager voice said:

" You mean to poison your husband . . . the poison is in the black cabinet . . . I got it for you . . . you laughed at me, and told lies about me behind my back, to make me disgusting . . . because you were jealous . . . are you sorry . . . now? "

The lips continued to murmur, but the sounds were no longer distinct. Soon there was no sound—only a slight movement: the flame had leaped out, and was being extinguished the faster. The wretched woman's heart-strings had been set to hatred and vengeance; the spirit of life had swept the chords for an instant, and was gone again for ever. Great God! Is this what it is to live again . . . to wake up with our unstilled thirst upon us, with our unuttered curses rising to our lips, with our muscles ready to act out their half-committed sins?

Bertha stood pale at the foot of the bed, quivering and helpless, despairing of devices, like a cunning animal whose

hiding-places are surrounded by swift-advancing flame. Even
Meunier looked paralysed; life for that moment ceased to be
a scientific problem to him. As for me, this scene seemed of
one texture with the rest of my existence: horror was my
familiar, and this new revelation was only like an old pain
recurring with new circumstances.

．　　　　．　　　　．　　　　．　　　　．

Since then Bertha and I have lived apart—she in her own
neighbourhood, the mistress of half our wealth, I as a wanderer in foreign countries, until I came to this Devonshire
nest to die. Bertha lives pitied and admired; for what had
I against that charming woman, whom every one but myself could have been happy with? There had been no witness
of the scene in the dying room except Meunier; and while
Meunier lived his lips were sealed by a promise to me.

Once or twice, weary of wandering, I rested in a favourite
spot, and my heart went out towards the men and women
and children whose faces were becoming familiar to me; but
I was driven away again in terror at the approach of my old
insight—driven away to live continually with the one Unknown Presence revealed and yet hidden by the moving
curtain of the earth and sky. Till at last disease took hold
of me and forced me to rest here—forced me to live in dependence on my servants. And then the curse of insight—
of my double consciousness, came again, and has never left
me. I knew all their narrow thoughts, their feeble regard,
their half-wearied pity.

．　　　　．　　　　．　　　　．　　　　．

It is the 20th of September, 1850. I know these figures I
have just written, as if they were a long familiar inscription.
I have seen them on this page in my desk unnumbered times;
when the scene of my dying struggle has opened upon me. . . .

M. R. JAMES

NUMBER 13

AMONG the towns of Jutland, Viborg justly holds a high place. It is the seat of a bishopric; it has a handsome but almost entirely new cathedral, a charming garden, a lake of great beauty, and many storks. Near it is Hald, accounted one of the prettiest things in Denmark; and hard by is Finderup, where Marsk Stig murdered King Erik Glipping on St. Cecilia's Day, in the year 1286. Fifty-six blows of square-headed iron maces were traced on Erik's skull when his tomb was opened in the seventeenth century. But I am not writing a guide-book.

There are good hotels in Viborg—Preisler's and the Phœnix are all that can be desired. But my cousin, whose experiences I have to tell you now, went to the Golden Lion the first time that he visited Viborg. He has not been there since, and the following pages will perhaps explain the reason of his abstention.

The Golden Lion is one of the very few houses in the town that were not destroyed in the great fire of 1726, which practically demolished the cathedral, the Sognekirke, the Raadhuus, and so much else that was old and interesting. It is a great red-brick house—that is, the front is of brick, with corbie steps on the gables and a text over the door; but the courtyard into which the omnibus drives is of black and white " cage-work " in wood and plaster.

The sun was declining in the heavens when my cousin walked up to the door, and the light smote full upon the imposing façade of the house. He was delighted with the old-fashioned aspect of the place, and promised himself a thoroughly satisfactory and amusing stay in an inn so typical of old Jutland.

It was not business in the ordinary sense of the word that had brought Mr. Anderson to Viborg. He was engaged upon some researches into the Church history of Denmark, and it had come to his knowledge that in the Rigsarkiv of Viborg there were papers, saved from the fire, relating to the

last days of Roman Catholicism in the country. He proposed, therefore, to spend a considerable time—perhaps as
much as a fortnight or three weeks—in examining and copying these, and he hoped that the Golden Lion would be able
to give him a room of sufficient size to serve alike as a bedroom
and a study. His wishes were explained to the landlord, and,
after a certain amount of thought, the latter suggested that
perhaps it might be the best way for the gentleman to look at
one or two of the larger rooms and pick one for himself. It
seemed a good idea.

The top floor was soon rejected as entailing too much
getting upstairs after the day's work; the second floor contained no room of exactly the dimensions required; but on
the first floor there was a choice of two or three rooms which
would, so far as size went, suit admirably.

The landlord was strongly in favour of Number 17, but
Mr. Anderson pointed out that its windows commanded only
the blank wall of the next house, and that it would be very
dark in the afternoon. Either Number 12 or Number 14
would be better, for both of them looked on the street, and
the bright evening light and the pretty view would
more than compensate him for the additional amount of
noise.

Eventually Number 12 was selected. Like its neighbours,
it had three windows, all on one side of the room; it was fairly
high and unusually long. There was, of course, no fireplace,
but the stove was handsome and rather old—a cast-iron
erection, on the side of which was a representation of
Abraham sacrificing Isaac, and the inscription, " 1 Bog Mose,
Cap. 22," above. Nothing else in the room was remarkable;
the only interesting picture was an old coloured print of the
town, date about 1820.

Supper-time was approaching, but when Anderson, refreshed by the ordinary ablutions, descended the staircase,
there were still a few minutes before the bell rang. He devoted them to examining the list of his fellow-lodgers. As
is usual in Denmark, their names were displayed on a large
blackboard, divided into columns and lines, the numbers of
the rooms being painted in at the beginning of each line.
The list was not exciting. There was an advocate, or Sagförer, a German, and some bagmen from Copenhagen. The
one and only point which suggested any food for thought

was the absence of any Number 13 from the tale of the
rooms, and even this was a thing which Anderson had already
noticed half a dozen times in his experience of Danish
hotels. He could not help wondering whether the objection
to that particular number, common as it is, was so wide-
spread and so strong as to make it difficult to let a room so
ticketed, and he resolved to ask the landlord if he and his
colleagues in the profession had actually met with many
clients who refused to be accommodated in the thirteenth
room.

He had nothing to tell me (I am giving the story as I heard
it from him) about what passed at supper, and the evening,
which was spent in unpacking and arranging his clothes,
books, and papers, was not more eventful. Towards eleven
o'clock he resolved to go to bed, but with him, as with a
good many other people nowadays, an almost necessary pre-
liminary to bed, if he meant to sleep, was the reading of a
few pages of print, and he now remembered that the particular book which he had been reading in the train, and
which alone would satisfy him at that present moment, was
in the pocket of his greatcoat, then hanging on a peg outside
the dining-room.

To run down and secure it was the work of a moment,
and, as the passages were by no means dark, it was not difficult for him to find his way back to his own door. So, at
least, he thought; but when he arrived there, and turned the
handle, the door entirely refused to open, and he caught the
sound of a hasty movement towards it from within. He had
tried the wrong door, of course. Was his own room to the
right or to the left? He glanced at the number: it was 13.
His room would be on the left; and so it was. And not
before he had been in bed for some minutes, had read his
wonted three or four pages of his book, blown out his light,
and turned over to go to sleep, did it occur to him that,
whereas on the blackboard of the hotel there had been no
Number 13, there was undoubtedly a room numbered 13 in
the hotel. He felt rather sorry he had not chosen it for his
own. Perhaps he might have done the landlord a little service by occupying it, and given him the chance of saying that
a well-born English gentleman had lived in it for three weeks
and liked it very much. But probably it was used as a servant's room or something of the kind. After all, it was most

likely not so large or good a room as his own. And he looked
drowsily about the room, which was fairly perceptible in the
half-light from the street-lamp. It was a curious effect, he
thought. Rooms usually look larger in a dim light than a full
one, but this seemed to have contracted in length and grown
proportionately higher. Well, well! sleep was more important
than these vague ruminations—and to sleep he went.

On the day after his arrival Anderson attacked the
Rigsarkiv of Viborg. He was, as one might expect in Denmark, kindly received, and access to all that he wished to
see was made as easy for him as possible. The documents
laid before him were far more numerous and interesting
than he had at all anticipated. Besides official papers, there
was a large bundle of correspondence relating to Bishop
Jörgen Friis, the last Roman Catholic who held the see, and
in these there cropped up many amusing and what are called
"intimate" details of private life and individual character.
There was much talk of a house owned by the Bishop, but
not inhabited by him, in the town. Its tenant was apparently
somewhat of a scandal and a stumbling-block to the reforming
party. He was a disgrace, they wrote, to the city; he practised secret and wicked arts, and had sold his soul to the
enemy. It was of a piece with the gross corruption and
superstition of the Babylonish Church that such a viper and
blood-sucking *Troldmand* should be patronized and har-
boured by the Bishop. The Bishop met these reproaches
boldly; he protested his own abhorrence of all such things
as secret arts, and required his antagonists to bring the matter
before the proper court—of course, the spiritual court—and
sift it to the bottom. No one could be more ready and
willing than himself to condemn Mag. Nicolas Francken if
the evidence showed him to have been guilty of any of the
crimes informally alleged against him.

Anderson had not time to do more than glance at the next
letter of the Protestant leader, Rasmus Nielsen, before the
record office was closed for the day, but he gathered its general
tenor, which was to the effect that Christian men were now
no longer bound by the decisions of Bishops of Rome, and
that the Bishop's Court was not, and could not be, a fit or
competent tribunal to judge so grave and weighty a cause.

On leaving the office, Mr. Anderson was accompanied by
the old gentleman who presided over it, and, as they walked,

the conversation very naturally turned to the papers of which I have just been speaking.

Herr Scavenius, the Archivist of Viborg, though very well informed as to the general run of the documents under his charge, was not a specialist in those of the Reformation period. He was much interested in what Anderson had to tell him about them. He looked forward with great pleasure, he said, to seeing the publication in which Mr. Anderson spoke of embodying their contents. " This house of the Bishop Friis," he added, " it is a great puzzle to me where it can have stood. I have studied carefully the topography of old Viborg, but it is most unlucky—of the old terrier of the Bishop's property which was made in 1560, and of which we have the greater part in the Arkiv, just the piece which had the list of the town property is missing. Never mind. Perhaps I shall some day succeed to find him."

After taking some exercise—I forget exactly how or where—Anderson went back to the Golden Lion, his supper, his game of patience, and his bed. On the way to his room it occurred to him that he had forgotten to talk to the land-lord about the omission of Number 13 from the hotel, and also that he might as well make sure that Number 13 did actually exist before he made any reference to the matter.

The decision was not difficult to arrive at. There was the door with its number as plain as could be, and work of some kind was evidently going on inside it, for as he neared the door he could hear footsteps and voices, or a voice, within. During the few seconds in which he halted to make sure of the number, the footsteps ceased, seemingly very near the door, and he was a little startled at hearing a quick hissing breathing as of a person in strong excitement. He went on to his own room, and again he was surprised to find how much smaller it seemed now than it had when he selected it. It was a slight disappointment, but only slight. If he found it really not large enough, he could very easily shift to another. In the meantime he wanted something—as far as I remember it was a pocket-handkerchief—out of his portmanteau, which had been placed by the porter on a very inadequate trestle or stool against the wall at the farthest end of the room from his bed. Here was a very curious thing: the portmanteau was not to be seen. It had been moved by officious servants; doubtless the contents had been put in the wardrobe. No, none of them were there. This was vexatious. The idea of a theft he dismissed at once. Such things rarely happen in Denmark, but some piece of stupidity had certainly been performed (which is not so uncommon), and the *stuepige* must be severely spoken to. Whatever it was that he wanted, it was not so necessary to his comfort that he could not wait till the morning for it, and he therefore settled not to ring the bell and disturb the servants. He went to the window— the right-hand window it was—and looked out on the quiet street. There was a tall building opposite, with large spaces of dead wall; no passers-by; a dark night; and very little to be seen of any kind.

The light was behind him, and he could see his own shadow clearly cast on the wall opposite. Also the shadow of the bearded man in Number 11 on the left, who passed to and fro in shirtsleeves once or twice, and was seen first brushing his hair, and later on in a nightgown. Also the shadow of the occupant of Number 13 on the right. This might be more interesting. Number 13 was, like himself, leaning on his elbows on the window-sill looking out into the street. He seemed to be a tall thin man—or was it by any chance a woman?—at least, it was someone who covered his or her head with some kind of drapery before going to bed, and, he thought, must be possessed of a red lamp-shade—and the lamp must be flickering very much. There was a distinct playing up and down of a dull red light on the opposite wall. He craned out a little to see if he could make any more of the figure, but beyond a fold of some light, perhaps white, material on the window-sill he could see nothing.

Now came a distant step in the street, and its approach seemed to recall Number 13 to a sense of his exposed position, for very swiftly and suddenly he swept aside from the window, and his red light went out. Anderson, who had been smoking a cigarette, laid the end of it on the window-sill and went to bed.

Next morning he was woke by the *stuepige* with hot water, etc. He roused himself, and after thinking out the correct Danish words, said as distinctly as he could:

" You must not move my portmanteau. Where is it? "

As is not uncommon, the maid laughed, and went away without making any distinct answer.

Anderson, rather irritated, sat up in bed, intending to call her back, but he remained sitting up, staring straight in front of him. There was his portmanteau on its trestle, exactly where he had seen the porter put it when he first arrived. This was a rude shock for a man who prided himself on his accuracy of observation. How it could possibly have escaped him the night before he did not pretend to understand; at any rate, there it was now.

The daylight showed more than the portmanteau; it let the true proportions of the room with its three windows appear, and satisfied its tenant that his choice after all had not been a bad one. When he was almost dressed he walked to the middle one of the three windows to look out at the weather. Another shock awaited him. Strangely unobservant he must have been last night. He could have sworn ten times over that he had been smoking at the right-hand window the last thing before he went to bed, and here was his cigarette-end on the sill of the middle window.

He started to go down to breakfast. Rather late, but Number 13 was later: here were his boots still outside his door—a gentleman's boots. So then Number 13 was a man, not a woman. Just then he caught sight of the number on the door. It was 14. He thought he must have passed Number 13 without noticing it. Three stupid mistakes in twelve hours were too much for a methodical, accurate-minded man, so he turned back to make sure. The next number to 14 was Number 12, his own room. There was no Number 13 at all.

After some minutes devoted to a careful consideration of everything he had had to eat and drink during the last twenty-four hours, Anderson decided to give the question up. If his sight or his brain were giving way he would have plenty of opportunities for ascertaining that fact; if not, then he was evidently being treated to a very interesting experience. In either case the development of events would certainly be worth watching.

During the day he continued his examination of the episcopal correspondence which I have already summarized. To his disappointment, it was incomplete. Only one other letter could be found which referred to the affair of Mag. Nicolas Francken. It was from the Bishop Jörgen Friis to Rasmus Nielsen. He said:

"Although we are not in the least degree inclined to assent

to your judgment concerning our court, and shall be prepared if need be to withstand you to the uttermost in that behalf, yet forasmuch as our trusty and well-beloved Mag. Nicolas Francken, against whom you have dared to allege certain false and malicious charges, hath been suddenly removed from among us, it is apparent that the question for this time falls. But forasmuch as you further allege that the Apostle and Evangelist St. John in his heavenly Apocalypse describes the Holy Roman Church under the guise and symbol of the Scarlet Woman, be it known to you," etc.

Search as he might, Anderson could find no sequel to this letter nor any clue to the cause or manner of the " removal " of the *casus belli*. He could only suppose that Francken had died suddenly; and as there were only two days between the date of Nielsen's last letter—when Francken was evidently still in being—and that of the Bishop's letter, the death must have been completely unexpected.

In the afternoon he paid a short visit to Hald, and took his tea at Baekkelund; nor could he notice, though he was in a somewhat nervous frame of mind, that there was any indication of such a failure of eye or brain as his experiences of the morning had led him to fear.

At supper he found himself next to the landlord.

" What," he asked him, after some indifferent conversation, " is the reason why in most of the hotels one visits in this country the number thirteen is left out of the list of rooms? I see you have none here."

The landlord seemed amused.

" To think that you should have noticed a thing like that! I've thought about it once or twice myself, to tell the truth. An educated man, I've said, has no business with these superstitious notions. I was brought up myself here in the High School of Viborg, and our old master was always a man to set his face against anything of that kind. He's been dead now this many years—a fine upstanding man he was, and ready with his hands as well as his head. I recollect us boys, one snowy day——"

Here he plunged into reminiscence.

" Then you don't think there is any particular objection to having a Number 13? " said Anderson.

" Ah! to be sure. Well, you understand, I was brought up to the business by my poor old father. He kept an hotel in

Aarhuus first, and then, when we were born, he moved to Viborg here, which was his native place, and had the Phœnix here until he died. That was in 1876. Then I started business in Silkeborg, and only the year before last I moved into this house."

Then followed more details as to the state of the house and business when first taken over.

"And when you came here, was there a Number 13?"

"No, no. I was going to tell you about that. You see, in a place like this, the commercial class—the travellers—are what we have to provide for in general. And put them in Number 13? Why, they'd as soon sleep in the street, or sooner. As far as I'm concerned myself, it wouldn't make a penny difference to me what the number of my room was, and so I've often said to them; but they stick to it that it brings them back luck. Quantities of stories they have among them of men that have slept in a Number 13 and never been the same again, or lost their best customers, or—one thing and another," said the landlord, after searching for a more graphic phrase.

"Then, what do you use your Number 13 for?" said Anderson, conscious as he said the words of a curious anxiety quite disproportionate to the importance of the question.

"My Number 13? Why, don't I tell you that there isn't such a thing in the house? I thought you might have noticed that. If there was it would be next door to your own room."

"Well, yes; only I happened to think—that is, I fancied last night that I had seen a door numbered thirteen in that passage; and, really, I am almost certain I must have been right, for I saw it the night before as well."

Of course, Herr Kristensen laughed this notion to scorn, as Anderson had expected, and emphasized with much iteration the fact that no Number 13 existed or had existed before him in that hotel.

Anderson was in some ways relieved by his certainty but still puzzled, and he began to think that the best way to make sure whether he had indeed been subject to an illusion or not was to invite the landlord to his room to smoke a cigar later on in the evening. Some photographs of English towns which he had with him formed a sufficiently good excuse.

Herr Kristensen was flattered by the invitation, and most willingly accepted it. At about ten o'clock he was to make his appearance, but before that Anderson had some letters to write, and retired for the purpose of writing them. He almost blushed to himself at confessing it, but he could not deny that it was the fact that he was becoming quite nervous about the question of the existence of Number 13; so much so that he approached his room by way of Number 11, in order that he might not be obliged to pass the door, or the place where the door ought to be. He looked quickly and suspiciously about the room when he entered it, but there was nothing, beyond that indefinable air of being smaller than usual, to warrant any misgivings. There was no question of the presence or absence of his portmanteau to-night. He had himself emptied it of its contents and lodged it under his bed. With a certain effort he dismissed the thought of Number 13 from his mind, and sat down to his writing.

His neighbours were quiet enough. Occasionally a door opened in the passage and a pair of boots was thrown out, or a bagman walked past humming to himself, and outside, from time to time a cart thundered over the atrocious cobble-stones, or a quick step hurried along the flags.

Anderson finished his letters, ordered in whisky and soda, and then went to the window and studied the dead wall opposite and the shadows upon it.

As far as he could remember, Number 14 had been occupied by the lawyer, a staid man, who said little at meals, being generally engaged in studying a small bundle of papers beside his plate. Apparently, however, he was in the habit of giving vent to his animal spirits when alone. Why else should he be dancing? The shadow from the next room evidently showed that he was. Again and again his thin form crossed the window, his arms waved, and a gaunt leg was kicked up with surprising agility. He seemed to be bare-footed, and the floor must be well laid, for no sound betrayed his movements. Sagförer Herr Anders Jensen, dancing at ten o'clock at night in a hotel bedroom, seemed a fitting subject for a historical painting in the grand style; and Anderson's thoughts, like those of Emily in the *Mysteries of Udolpho*, began to "arrange themselves in the following lines":

" When I return to my hotel,
  At ten o'clock p.m.,
The waiters think I am unwell;
  I do not care for them.
But when I've locked my chamber door,
  And put my boots outside,
I dance all night upon the floor.
And even if my neighbours swore,
I'd go on dancing all the more,
For I'm acquainted with the law,
And in despite of all their jaw,
Their protests I deride."

Had not the landlord at this moment knocked at the door, it is probable that quite a long poem might have been laid before the reader. To judge from his look of surprise when he found himself in the room, Herr Kristensen was struck, as Anderson had been, by something unusual in its aspect. But he made no remark. Anderson's photographs interested him mightily, and formed the text of many autobiographical discourses. Nor is it quite clear how the conversation could have been diverted into the desired channel of Number 13, had not the lawyer at this moment begun to sing, and to sing in a manner which could leave no doubt in anyone's mind that he was either exceedingly drunk or raving mad. It was a high, thin voice that they heard, and it seemed dry, as if from long disuse. Of words or tune there was no question. It went sailing up to a surprising height, and was carried down with a despairing moan as of a winter wind in a hollow chimney, or an organ whose wind fails suddenly. It was a really horrible sound, and Anderson felt that if he had been alone he must have fled for refuge and society to some neighbour bagman's room.

The landlord sat open-mouthed.

" I don't understand it," he said at last, wiping his forehead. " It is dreadful. I have heard it once before, but I made sure it was a cat."

" Is he mad? " said Anderson.

" He must be; and what a sad thing! Such a good customer, too, and so successful in his business, by what I hear, and a young family to bring up."

Just then came an impatient knock at the door, and the

knocker entered, without waiting to be asked. It was the lawyer, in deshabille and very rough-haired; and very angry he looked.

"I beg pardon, sir," he said, "but I should be much obliged if you would kindly desist——"

Here he stopped, for it was evident that neither of the persons before him was responsible for the disturbance; and after a moment's lull it swelled forth again more wildly than before.

"But what in the name of Heaven does it mean?" broke out the lawyer. "Where is it? Who is it? Am I going out of my mind?"

"Surely, Herr Jensen, it comes from your room next door? Isn't there a cat or something stuck in the chimney?"

This was the best that occurred to Anderson to say, and he realized its futility as he spoke; but anything was better than to stand and listen to that horrible voice, and look at the broad, white face of the landlord, all perspiring and quivering as he clutched the arms of his chair.

"Impossible," said the lawyer, "impossible. There is no chimney. I came here because I was convinced the noise was going on here. It was certainly in the next room to mine."

"Was there no door between yours and mine?" said Anderson eagerly.

"No, sir," said Herr Jensen, rather sharply. "At least, not this morning."

"Ah!" said Anderson. "Nor to-night?"

"I am not sure," said the lawyer with some hesitation.

Suddenly the crying or singing voice in the next room died away, and the singer was heard seemingly to laugh to himself in a crooning manner. The three men actually shivered at the sound. Then there was a silence.

"Come," said the lawyer, "what have you to say, Herr Kristensen? What does this mean?"

"Good Heaven!" said Kristensen. "How should I tell! I know no more than you, gentlemen. I pray I may never hear such a noise again."

"So do I," said Herr Jensen, and he added something under his breath. Anderson thought it sounded like the last words of the Psalter, "*omnis spiritus laudet Dominum,*" but he could not be sure.

" But we must do something," said Anderson—" the three of us. Shall we go and investigate in the next room? "

" But that is Herr Jensen's room," wailed the landlord. " It is no use; he has come from there himself."

" I am not so sure," said Jensen. " I think this gentleman is right: we must go and see."

The only weapons of defence that could be mustered on the spot were a stick and umbrella. The expedition went out into the passage, not without quakings. There was a deadly quiet outside, but a light shone from under the next door. Anderson and Jensen approached it. The latter turned the handle, and gave a sudden vigorous push. No use. The door stood fast.

" Herr Kristensen," said Jensen, " will you go and fetch the strongest servant you have in the place? We must see this through."

The landlord nodded, and hurried off, glad to be away from the scene of action. Jensen and Anderson remained outside looking at the door.

" It *is* Number 13, you see," said the latter.

" Yes; there is your door, and there is mine," said Jensen.

" My room has three windows in the daytime," said Anderson, with difficulty suppressing a nervous laugh.

" By George, so has mine! " said the lawyer, turning and looking at Anderson. His back was now to the door. In that moment the door opened, and an arm came out and clawed at his shoulder. It was clad in ragged, yellowish linen, and the bare skin, where it could be seen, had long grey hair upon it.

Anderson was just in time to pull Jensen out of its reach with a cry of disgust and fright, when the door shut again, and a low laugh was heard.

Jensen had seen nothing, but when Anderson hurriedly told him what a risk he had run, he fell into a great state of agitation, and suggested that they should retire from the enterprise and lock themselves up in one or other of their rooms.

However, while he was developing this plan, the landlord and two able-bodied men arrived on the scene, all looking rather serious and alarmed. Jensen met them with a torrent of description and explanation, which did not at all tend to encourage them for the fray.

The men dropped the crowbars they had brought, and said flatly that they were not going to risk their throats in that devil's den. The landlord was miserably nervous and undecided, conscious that if the danger were not faced his hotel was ruined, and very loth to face it himself. Luckily Anderson hit upon a way of rallying the demoralized force.

"Is this," he said, "the Danish courage I have heard so much of? It isn't a German in there, and if it was, we are five to one."

The two servants and Jensen were stung into action by this, and made a dash at the door.

"Stop!" said Anderson. "Don't lose your heads. You stay out here with the light, landlord, and one of you two men break in the door, and don't go in when it gives way."

The men nodded, and the younger stepped forward, raised his crowbar, and dealt a tremendous blow on the upper panel. The result was not in the least what any of them anticipated. There was no cracking or rending of wood—only a dull sound, as if the solid wall had been struck. The man dropped his tool with a shout, and began rubbing his elbow. His cry drew their eyes upon him for a moment; then Anderson looked at the door again. It was gone; the plaster wall of the passage stared him in the face, with a considerable gash in it where the crowbar had struck it. Number 13 had passed out of existence.

For a brief space they stood perfectly still, gazing at the blank wall. An early cock in the yard beneath was heard to crow; and as Anderson glanced in the direction of the sound, he saw through the window at the end of the long passage that the eastern sky was paling to the dawn.

.   .   .   .   .

"Perhaps," said the landlord, with hesitation, "you gentlemen would like another room for to-night—a double-bedded one?"

Neither Jensen nor Anderson was averse to the suggestion. They felt inclined to hunt in couples after their late experience. It was found convenient, when each of them went to his room to collect the articles he wanted for the night, that the other should go with him and hold the candle. They noticed that both Number 12 and Number 14 had *three* windows.

Next morning the same party reassembled in Number 12. The landlord was naturally anxious to avoid engaging outside help, and yet it was imperative that the mystery attaching to that part of the house should be cleared up. Accordingly the two servants had been induced to take upon them the function of carpenters. The furniture was cleared away, and, at the cost of a good many irretrievably damaged planks, that portion of the floor was taken up which lay nearest to Number 14.

You will naturally suppose that a skeleton—say that of Mag. Nicolas Francken—was discovered. That was not so. What they did find lying between the beams which supported the flooring was a small copper box. In it was a neatly-folded vellum document, with about twenty lines of writing. Both Anderson and Jensen (who proved to be something of a palæographer) were much excited by this discovery, which promised to afford the key to these extraordinary phenomena.

.   .   .   .   .   .

I possess a copy of an astrological work which I have never read. It has, by way of frontispiece, a woodcut by Hans Sebald Beham, representing a number of sages seated round a table. This detail may enable connoisseurs to identify the book. I cannot myself recollect its title, and it is not at this moment within reach; but the fly-leaves of it are covered with writing, and, during the ten years in which I have owned the volume, I have not been able to determine which way up this writing ought to be read, much less in what language it is. Not dissimilar was the position of Anderson and Jensen after the protracted examination to which they submitted the document in the copper box.

After two days' contemplation of it, Jensen, who was the bolder spirit of the two, hazarded the conjecture that the language was either Latin or Old Danish.

Anderson ventured upon no surmises, and was very willing to surrender the box and the parchment to the Historical Society of Viborg to be placed in their museum.

I had the whole story from him a few months later, as we sat in a wood near Upsala, after a visit to the library there, where we—or, rather, I—had laughed over the contract by which Daniel Salthenius (in later life Professor of Hebrew at

Königsberg) sold himself to Satan.   Anderson was not really amused.

" Young idiot! " he said, meaning Salthenius, who was only an undergraduate when he committed that indiscretion, " how did he know what company he was courting? "

And when I suggested the usual considerations he only grunted.   That same afternoon he told me what you have read; but he refused to draw any inferences from it, and to assent to any that I drew for him.

RATS

" And if you was to walk through the bedrooms now, you'd see the ragged, mouldy bedclothes a-heaving and a-heaving like seas." " And a-heaving and a-heaving with what ? " he says. " Why, with the rats under 'em."

BUT was it with the rats? I ask, because in another case it was not. I cannot put a date to the story, but I was young when I heard it, and the teller was old. It is an ill-proportioned tale, but that is my fault, not his.

It happened in Suffolk, near the coast. In a place where the road makes a sudden dip and then a sudden rise; as you go northward, at the top of that rise, stands a house on the left of the road. It is a tall red-brick house, narrow for its height; perhaps it was built about 1770. The top of the front has a low triangular pediment with a round window in the centre. Behind it are stables and offices, and such garden as it has is behind them. Scraggy Scotch firs are near it: an expanse of gorse-covered land stretches away from it. It commands a view of the distant sea from the upper windows of the front. A sign on a post stands before the door; or did so stand, for though it was an inn of repute once, I believe it is so no longer.

To this inn came my acquaintance, Mr. Thomson, when he was a young man, on a fine spring day, coming from the University of Cambridge, and desirous of solitude in tolerable quarters and time for reading. These he found, for the landlord and his wife had been in service and could make a visitor comfortable, and there was no one else staying in the inn. He had a large room on the first floor commanding the road and the view, and if it faced east, why, that could not be helped; the house was well built and warm.

He spent very tranquil and uneventful days: work all the morning, an afternoon perambulation of the country round, a little conversation with country company or the people of the inn in the evening over the then fashionable drink of brandy and water, a little more reading and writing, and bed; and he would have been content that this should continue for the full month he had at disposal, so well was his work progressing, and so fine was the April of that year—which I have reason to believe was that which Orlando Whistlecraft chronicles in his weather record as the " Charming Year."

One of his walks took him along the northern road, which stands high and traverses a wide common, called a heath. On the bright afternoon when he first chose this direction his eye caught a white object some hundreds of yards to the left of the road, and he felt it necessary to make sure what this might be. It was not long before he was standing by it, and found himself looking at a square block of white stone fashioned somewhat like the base of a pillar, with a square hole in the upper surface. Just such another you may see at this day on Thetford Heath. After taking stock of it he contemplated for a few minutes the view, which offered a church tower or two, some red roofs of cottages and windows winking in the sun, and the expanse of sea—also with an occasional wink and gleam upon it—and so pursued his way.

In the desultory evening talk in the bar, he asked why the white stone was there on the common.

" A old-fashioned thing, that is," said the landlord (Mr. Betts), " we was none of us alive when that was put there." " That's right," said another. " It stands pretty high," said Mr. Thomson, " I dare say a sea-mark was on it some time back." " Ah! yes," Mr. Betts agreed, " I 'ave 'eard they could see it from the boats; but whatever there was, it's fell to bits this long time." " Good job too," said a third, " 'twarn't a lucky mark, by what the old men used to say; not lucky for the fishin', I mean to say." " Why ever not? " said Thomson. " Well, I never see it myself," was the answer, " but they 'ad some funny ideas, what I mean, peculiar, them old chaps, and I shouldn't wonder but what they made away with it theirselves."

It was impossible to get anything clearer than this: the company, never very voluble, fell silent, and when next someone spoke it was of village affairs and crops. Mr. Betts was the speaker.

Not every day did Thomson consult his health by taking a country walk. One very fine afternoon found him busily

writing at three o'clock. Then he stretched himself and
rose, and walked out of his room into the passage. Facing
him was another room, then the stair-head, then two more
rooms, one looking out to the back, the other to the south.
At the south end of the passage was a window, to which
he went, considering with himself that it was rather a shame
to waste such a fine afternoon. However, work was paramount just at the moment; he thought he would just take
five minutes off and go back to it; and those five minutes he
would employ—the Bettses could not possibly object—to
looking at the other rooms in the passage, which he had
never seen. Nobody at all, it seemed, was indoors; probably,
as it was market day, they were all gone to the town, except
perhaps a maid in the bar. Very still the house was, and
the sun shone really hot; early flies buzzed in the window-
panes. So he explored. The room facing his own was un-
distinguished except for an old print of Bury St. Edmunds;
the two next him on his side of the passage were gay and
clean, with one window apiece, whereas his had two. Remained the south-west room, opposite to the last which he
had entered. This was locked; but Thomson was in a mood
of quite indefensible curiosity, and feeling confident that
there could be no damaging secrets in a place so easily got at,
he proceeded to fetch the key of his own room, and when that
did not answer, to collect the keys of the other three. One
of them fitted, and he opened the door. The room had two
windows looking south and west, so it was as bright and the
sun as hot upon it as could be. Here there was no carpet,
but bare boards; no pictures, no washing-stand, only a bed,
in the farther corner: an iron bed, with mattress and bolster,
covered with a bluish check counterpane. As featureless a
room as you can well imagine, and yet there was something
that made Thomson close the door very quickly and yet quietly
behind him and lean against the window-sill in the passage,
actually quivering all over. It was this, that under the
counterpane someone lay, and not only lay, but stirred.
That it was some *one* and not some *thing* was certain, because
the shape of a head was unmistakable on the bolster; and
yet it was all covered, and no one lies with covered head but
a dead person; and this was not dead, not truly dead, for it
heaved and shivered. If he had seen these things in dusk
or by the light of a flickering candle, Thomson could have

comforted himself and talked of fancy. On this bright day
that was impossible. What was to be done? First, lock the
door at all costs. Very gingerly he approached it and bending down listened, holding his breath; perhaps there might
be a sound of heavy breathing, and a prosaic explanation.
There was absolute silence. But as, with a rather tremulous
hand, he put the key into its hole and turned it, it rattled,
and on the instant a stumbling padding tread was heard
coming towards the door. Thomson fled like a rabbit to his
room and locked himself in: futile enough, he knew it was;
would doors and locks be any obstacle to what he suspected?
But it was all he could think of at the moment, and in fact
nothing happened; only there was a time of acute suspense—
followed by a misery of doubt as to what to do. The impulse, of course, was to slip away as soon as possible from a
house which contained such an inmate. But only the day
before he had said he should be staying for at least a week
more, and how if he changed plans could he avoid the suspicion of having pried into places where he certainly had no
business? Moreover, either the Bettses knew all about the
inmate, and yet did not leave the house, or knew nothing,
which equally meant that there was nothing to be afraid of,
or knew just enough to make them shut up the room, but
not enough to weigh on their spirits: in any of these cases
it seemed that not much was to be feared, and certainly so far
he had had no sort of ugly experience. On the whole the
line of least resistance was to stay.

Well, he stayed out his week. Nothing took him past that
door, and, often as he would pause in a quiet hour of day
or night in the passage and listen, and listen, no sound whatever issued from that direction. You might have thought
that Thomson would have made some attempt at ferreting
out stories connected with the inn—hardly perhaps from
Betts, but from the parson of the parish, or old people in
the village; but no, the reticence which commonly falls on
people who have had strange experiences, and believe in
them, was upon him. Nevertheless, as the end of his stay
drew near, his yearning after some kind of explanation grew
more and more acute. On his solitary walks he persisted in
planning out some way, the least obtrusive, of getting
another daylight glimpse into that room, and eventually
arrived at this scheme. He would leave by an afternoon

train—about four o'clock. When his fly was waiting, and his luggage on it, he would make one last expedition upstairs to look round his own room and see if anything was left unpacked, and then, with that key, which he had contrived to oil (as if that made any difference!), the door should once more be opened, for a moment, and shut.

So it worked out. The bill was paid, the consequent small talk gone through while the fly was loaded: " pleasant part of the country—been very comfortable, thanks to you and Mrs. Betts—hope to come back some time," on one side: on the other, " very glad you've found satisfaction, sir, done our best—always glad to 'ave your good word—very much favoured we've been with the weather, to be sure." Then, " I'll just take a look upstairs in case I've left a book or something out—no, don't trouble, I'll be back in a minute." And as noiselessly as possible he stole to the door and opened it. The shattering of the illusion! He almost laughed aloud. Propped, or you might say sitting, on the edge of the bed was—nothing in the round world but a scarecrow! A scarecrow out of the garden, of course, dumped into the deserted room. . . . Yes; but here amusement ceased. Have scarecrows bare bony feet? Do their heads loll on to their shoulders? Have they iron collars and links of chain about their necks? Can they get up and move, if never so stiffly, across a floor, with wagging head and arms close at their sides? and shiver?

The slam of the door, the dash to the stair-head, the leap downstairs, were followed by a faint. Awaking, Thomson saw Betts standing over him with the brandy bottle and a very reproachful face. " You shouldn't 'a' done so, sir, really you shouldn't. It ain't a kind way to act by persons as done the best they could for you." Thomson heard words of this kind, but what he said in reply he did not know. Mr. Betts, and perhaps even more Mrs. Betts, found it hard to accept his apologies and his assurances that he would say no word that could damage the good name of the house. However, they *were* accepted. Since the train could not now be caught, it was arranged that Thomson should be driven to the town to sleep there. Before he went the Bettses told him what little they knew. " They says he was landlord 'ere a long time back, and was in with the 'ighwaymen that 'ad their beat about the 'eath. That's how he come by his

end: 'ung in chains, they say, up where you see that stone
what the gallus stood in. Yes, the fishermen made away
with that, I believe, because they see it out at sea and it kep'
the fish off, according to their idea. Yes, we 'ad the account
from the people that 'ad the 'ouse before we come. ' You
keep that room shut up,' they says, ' but don't move the bed
out, and you'll find there won't be no trouble.' And no
more there 'as been; not once he haven't come out into the
'ouse, though what he may do now there ain't no sayin'.
Anyway, you're the first I know on that's seen him since
we've been 'ere: I never set eyes on him myself, nor don't
want. And ever since we've made the servants' rooms in
the stablin', we ain't 'ad no difficulty that way. Only I do
'ope, sir, as you'll keep a close tongue, considerin' 'ow an
'ouse do get talked about ": with more to this effect.

The promise of silence was kept for many years. The
occasion of my hearing the story at last was this: that when
Mr. Thomson came to stay with my father it fell to me to
show him to his room, and instead of letting me open the
door for him, he stepped forward and threw it open himself,
and then for some moments stood in the doorway holding up
his candle and looking narrowly into the interior. Then he
seemed to recollect himself and said: " I beg your pardon.
Very absurd, but I can't help doing that, for a particular
reason." What that reason was I heard some days afterwards, and you have heard now.

COUNT MAGNUS

BY what means the papers out of which I have made a connected story came into my hands is the last point which the reader will learn from these pages. But it is necessary to prefix to my extracts from them a statement of the form in which I possess them.

They consist, then, partly of a series of collections for a book of travels, such a volume as was a common product of the forties and fifties. Horace Marryat's *Journal of a Residence in Jutland and the Danish Isles* is a fair specimen of the class to which I allude. These books usually treated of some unfamiliar district on the Continent. They were illustrated with woodcuts or steel plates. They gave details of hotel accommodation, and of means of communication, such as we now expect to find in any well-regulated guide-book, and they dealt largely in reported conversations with intelligent foreigners, racy innkeepers and garrulous peasants. In a word, they were chatty.

Begun with the idea of furnishing material for such a book, my papers as they progressed assumed the character of a record of one single personal experience, and this record was continued up to the very eve, almost, of its termination.

The writer was a Mr. Wraxall. For my knowledge of him I have to depend entirely on the evidence his writings afford, and from these I deduce that he was a man past middle age, possessed of some private means, and very much alone in the world. He had, it seems, no settled abode in England, but was a denizen of hotels and boarding-houses. It is probable that he entertained the idea of settling down at some future time which never came; and I think it also likely that the Pantechnicon fire in the early seventies must have destroyed a great deal that would have thrown light on his antecedents, for he refers once or twice to property of his that was warehoused at that establishment.

It is further apparent that Mr. Wraxall had published a book, and that it treated of a holiday he had once taken in

Brittany. More than this I cannot say about his work, because a diligent search in bibliographical works has convinced me that it must have appeared either anonymously or under a pseudonym.

As to his character, it is not difficult to form some superficial opinion. He must have been an intelligent and cultivated man. It seems that he was near being a Fellow of his college at Oxford—Brasenose, as I judge from the Calendar. His besetting fault was pretty clearly that of over-inquisitiveness, possibly a good fault in a traveller, certainly a fault for which this traveller paid dearly enough in the end.

On what proved to be his last expedition, he was plotting another book. Scandinavia, a region not widely known to Englishmen forty years ago, had struck him as an interesting field. He must have lighted on some old books of Swedish history or memoirs, and the idea had struck him that there was room for a book descriptive of travel in Sweden, interspersed with episodes from the history of some of the great Swedish families. He procured letters of introduction, therefore, to some persons of quality in Sweden, and set out thither in the early summer of 1863.

Of his travels in the North there is no need to speak, nor of his residence of some weeks in Stockholm. I need only mention that some *savant* resident there put him on the track of an important collection of family papers belonging to the proprietors of an ancient manor-house in Vestergothland, and obtained for him permission to examine them.

The manor-house, or *herrgård*, in question is to be called Råbäck (pronounced something like Roebeck), though that is not its name. It is one of the best buildings of its kind in all the country, and the picture of it in Dahlenberg's *Suecia antiqua et moderna*, engraved in 1694, shows it very much as the tourist may see it to-day. It was built soon after 1600, and is, roughly speaking, very much like an English house of that period in respect of material—red-brick with stone facings—and style. The man who built it was a scion of the great house of De la Gardie, and his descendants possess it still. De la Gardie is the name by which I will designate them when mention of them becomes necessary.

They received Mr. Wraxall with great kindness and courtesy, and pressed him to stay in the house as long as his researches lasted. But, preferring to be independent, and mistrusting his powers of conversing in Swedish, he settled himself at the village inn, which turned out quite sufficiently comfortable, at any rate during the summer months. This arrangement would entail a short walk daily to and from the manor-house of something under a mile. The house itself stood in a park, and was protected—we should say grown up—with large old timber. Near it you found the walled garden, and then entered a close wood fringing one of the small lakes with which the whole country is pitted. Then came the wall of the demesne, and you climbed a steep knoll —a knob of rock lightly covered with soil—and on the top of this stood the church, fenced in with tall dark trees. It was a curious building to English eyes. The nave and aisles were low, and filled with pews and galleries. In the western gallery stood the handsome old organ, gaily painted, and with silver pipes. The ceiling was flat, and had been adorned by a seventeenth-century artist with a strange and hideous " Last Judgment," full of lurid flames, falling cities, burning ships, crying souls, and brown and smiling demons. Handsome brass coronæ hung from the roof; the pulpit was like a doll's-house, covered with little painted wooden cherubs and saints; a stand with three hour-glasses was hinged to the preacher's desk. Such sights as these may be seen in many a church in Sweden now, but what distinguished this one was an addition to the original building. At the eastern end of the north aisle the builder of the manor-house had erected a mausoleum for himself and his family. It was a largish eight-sided building, lighted by a series of oval windows, and it had a domed roof, topped by a kind of pumpkin-shaped object rising into a spire, a form in which Swedish architects greatly delighted. The roof was of copper externally, and was painted black, while the walls, in common with those of the church, were staringly white. To this mausoleum there was no access from the church. It had a portal and steps of its own on the northern side.

Past the churchyard the path to the village goes, and not more than three or four minutes bring you to the inn door.

On the first day of his stay at Råbäck Mr. Wraxall found the church door open, and made those notes of the interior which I have epitomized. Into the mausoleum, however, he could not make his way. He could by looking through the keyhole just descry that there were fine marble effigies and sarcophagi of copper, and a wealth of armorial ornament, which made him very anxious to spend some time in investigation.

The papers he had come to examine at the manor-house proved to be of just the kind he wanted for his book. There were family correspondence, journals, and account-books of the earliest owners of the estate, very carefully kept and clearly written, full of amusing and picturesque detail. The first De la Gardie appeared in them as a strong and capable man. Shortly after the building of the mansion there had been a period of distress in the district, and the peasants had risen and attacked several châteaux and done some damage. The owner of Råbäck took a leading part in suppressing the trouble, and there was reference to executions of ringleaders and severe punishments inflicted with no sparing hand.

The portrait of this Magnus de la Gardie was one of the best in the house, and Mr. Wraxall studied it with no little interest after his day's work. He gives no detailed description of it, but I gather that the face impressed him rather by its power than by its beauty or goodness; in fact, he writes that Count Magnus was an almost phenomenally ugly man.

On this day Mr. Wraxall took his supper with the family, and walked back in the late but still bright evening.

" I must remember," he writes, " to ask the sexton if he can let me into the mausoleum at the church. He evidently has access to it himself, for I saw him to-night standing on the steps, and, as I thought, locking or unlocking the door."

I find that early on the following day Mr. Wraxall had some conversation with his landlord. His setting it down at such length as he does surprised me at first; but I soon realized that the papers I was reading were, at least in their beginning, the materials for the book he was meditating, and that it was to have been one of those quasi-journalistic productions which admit of the introduction of an admixture of conversational matter.

His object, he says, was to find out whether any traditions of Count Magnus de la Gardie lingered on in the scenes of that gentleman's activity, and whether the popular estimate of him were favourable or not. He found that the Count was decidedly not a favourite. If his tenants came late to their work on the days which they owed to him as Lord of the Manor, they were set on the wooden horse, or flogged

and branded in the manor-house yard. One or two cases
there were of men who had occupied lands which encroached
on the lord's domain, and whose houses had been mysteriously
burnt on a winter's night, with the whole family inside. But
what seemed to dwell on the innkeeper's mind most—for he
returned to the subject more than once—was that the Count
had been on the Black Pilgrimage, and had brought something or someone back with him.

You will naturally inquire, as Mr. Wraxall did, what the
Black Pilgrimage may have been. But your curiosity on the
point must remain unsatisfied for the time being, just as his
did. The landlord was evidently unwilling to give a full
answer, or indeed any answer, on the point, and, being called
out for a moment, trotted off with obvious alacrity, only
putting his head in at the door a few minutes afterwards to
say that he was called away to Skara, and should not be back
till evening.

So Mr. Wraxall had to go unsatisfied to his day's work at
the manor-house. The papers on which he was just then
engaged soon put his thoughts into another channel, for he
had to occupy himself with glancing over the correspondence
between Sophia Albertina in Stockholm and her married
cousin Ulrica Leonora at Råbäck in the years 1705–1710.
The letters were of exceptional interest from the light they
threw upon the culture of that period in Sweden, as anyone
can testify who has read the full edition of them in the publi-
cations of the Swedish Historical Manuscripts Commission.

In the afternoon he had done with these, and after returning the boxes in which they were kept to their places on the
shelf, he proceeded, very naturally, to take down some of the
volumes nearest to them, in order to determine which of them
had best be his principal subject of investigation next day.
The shelf he had hit upon was occupied mostly by a collection of account-books in the writing of the first Count
Magnus. But one among them was not an account-book,
but a book of alchemical and other tracts in another sixteenth-
century hand. Not being very familiar with alchemical
literature, Mr. Wraxall spends much space which he might
have spared in setting out the names and beginnings of the
various treatises: The book of the Phœnix, book of the Thirty
Words, book of the Toad, book of Miriam, Turba philoso-
phorum, and so forth; and then he announces with a good

deal of circumstance his delight at finding, on a leaf originally left blank near the middle of the book, some writing of Count Magnus himself headed " Liber nigræ peregrinationis." It is true that only a few lines were written, but there was quite enough to show that the landlord had that morning been referring to a belief at least as old as the time of Count Magnus, and probably shared by him. This is the English of what was written:

" If any man desires to obtain a long life, if he would obtain a faithful messenger and see the blood of his enemies, it is necessary that he should first go into the city of Chorazin, and there salute the prince. . . ." Here there was an erasure of one word, not very thoroughly done, so that Mr. Wraxall felt pretty sure that he was right in reading it as *aëris* (" of the air "). But there was no more of the text copied, only a line in Latin: " Quære reliqua hujus materiei inter secretiora " (See the rest of this matter among the more private things).

It could not be denied that this threw a rather lurid light upon the tastes and beliefs of the Count; but to Mr. Wraxall, separated from him by nearly three centuries, the thought that he might have added to his general forcefulness alchemy, and to alchemy something like magic, only made him a more picturesque figure; and when, after a rather prolonged contemplation of his picture in the hall, Mr. Wraxall set out on his homeward way, his mind was full of the thought of Count Magnus. He had no eyes for his surroundings, no perception of the evening scents of the woods or the evening light on the lake; and when all of a sudden he pulled up short, he was astonished to find himself already at the gate of the churchyard, and within a few minutes of his dinner. His eyes fell on the mausoleum.

" Ah," he said, " Count Magnus, there you are. I should dearly like to see you."

" Like many solitary men," he writes, " I have a habit of talking to myself aloud; and, unlike some of the Greek and Latin particles, I do not expect an answer. Certainly, and perhaps fortunately in this case, there was neither voice nor any that regarded: only the woman who, I suppose, was cleaning up the church dropped some metallic object on the floor, whose clang startled me. Count Magnus, I think, sleeps sound enough."

That same evening the landlord of the inn, who had heard Mr. Wraxall say that he wished to see the clerk or deacon (as he would be called in Sweden) of the parish, introduced him to that official in the inn parlour. A visit to the De la Gardie tomb-house was soon arranged for the next day, and a little general conversation ensued.

Mr. Wraxall, remembering that one function of Scandinavian deacons is to teach candidates for Confirmation, thought he would refresh his own memory on a Biblical point.

" Can you tell me," he said, " anything about Chorazin? "

The deacon seemed startled, but readily reminded him how that village had once been denounced.

" To be sure," said Mr. Wraxall; " it is, I suppose, quite a ruin now? "

" So I expect," replied the deacon. " I have heard some of our old priests say that Antichrist is to be born there; and there are tales——"

" Ah! what tales are those? " Mr. Wraxall put in.

" Tales, I was going to say, which I have forgotten," said the deacon; and soon after that he said good night.

The landlord was now alone, and at Mr. Wraxall's mercy; and that inquirer was not inclined to spare him.

" Herr Nielsen," he said, " I have found out something about the Black Pilgrimage. You may as well tell me what you know. What did the Count bring back with him? "

Swedes are habitually slow, perhaps, in answering, or perhaps the landlord was an exception. I am not sure; but Mr. Wraxall notes that the landlord spent at least one minute in looking at him before he said anything at all. Then he came close up to his guest, and with a good deal of effort he spoke:

" Mr. Wraxall, I can tell you this one little tale, and no more—not any more. You must not ask anything when I have done. In my grandfather's time—that is, ninety-two years ago—there were two men who said: ' The Count is dead; we do not care for him. We will go to-night and have a free hunt in his wood '—the long wood on the hill that you have seen behind Råbäck. Well, those that heard them say this, they said: ' No, do not go; we are sure you will meet with persons walking who should not be walking. They should be resting, not walking.' These men laughed. There were no forest-men to keep the wood, because no one wished to hunt there. The family were not here at the house. These men could do what they wished.

" Very well, they go to the wood that night. My grandfather was sitting here in this room. It was the summer, and a light night. With the window open, he could see out to the wood, and hear.

" So he sat there, and two or three men with him, and they listened. At first they hear nothing at all; then they hear someone—you know how far away it is—they hear someone scream, just as if the most inside part of his soul was twisted out of him. All of them in the room caught hold of each other, and they sat so for three-quarters of an hour. Then they hear someone else, only about three hundred ells off. They hear him laugh out loud: it was not one of those two men that laughed, and, indeed, they have all of them said that it was not any man at all. After that they hear a great door shut.

" Then, when it was just light with the sun, they all went to the priest. They said to him:

" ' Father, put on your gown and your ruff, and come to bury these men, Anders Bjornsen and Hans Thorbjorn."

" You understand that they were sure these men were dead. So they went to the wood—my grandfather never forgot this. He said they were all like so many dead men themselves. The priest, too, he was in a white fear. He said when they came to him:

" ' I heard one cry in the night, and I heard one laugh afterwards. If I cannot forget that, I shall not be able to sleep again.'

" So they went to the wood, and they found these men on the edge of the wood. Hans Thorbjorn was standing with his back against a tree, and all the time he was pushing with his hands—pushing something away from him which was not there. So he was not dead. And they led him away, and took him to the house at Nykjoping, and he died before the winter; but he went on pushing with his hands. Also Anders Bjornsen was there; but he was dead. And I tell you this about Anders Bjornsen, that he was once a beautiful man, but now his face was not there, because the flesh of it was sucked away off the bones. You understand that? My grandfather did not forget that. And they laid him on the bier which they brought, and they put a cloth over his head, and the priest walked before; and they began to sing the psalm for the dead as well as they could. So, as they were singing the end of the first verse, one fell down, who was carrying the head of the bier, and the others looked back, and they saw that the cloth had fallen off, and the eyes of Anders Bjornsen were looking up, because there was nothing to close over them. And this they could not bear. Therefore the priest laid the cloth upon him, and sent for a spade, and they buried him in that place."

The next day Mr. Wraxall records that the deacon called for him soon after his breakfast, and took him to the church and mausoleum. He noticed that the key of the latter was hung on a nail just by the pulpit, and it occurred to him that, as the church door seemed to be left unlocked as a rule, it would not be difficult for him to pay a second and more private visit to the monuments if there proved to be more of interest among them than could be digested at first. The building, when he entered it, he found not unimposing. The monuments, mostly large erections of the seventeenth and eighteenth centuries, were dignified if luxuriant, and the epitaphs and heraldry were copious. The central space of the domed room was occupied by three copper sarcophagi, covered with finely-engraved ornament. Two of them had, as is commonly the case in Denmark and Sweden, a large metal crucifix on the lid. The third, that of Count Magnus, as it appeared, had, instead of that, a full-length effigy engraved upon it, and round the edge were several bands of similar ornament representing various scenes. One was a battle, with cannon belching out smoke, and walled towns, and troops of pikemen. Another showed an execution. In a third, among trees, was a man running at full speed, with flying hair and outstretched hands. After him followed a strange form; it would be hard to say whether the artist had intended it for a man, and was unable to give the requisite similitude, or whether it was intentionally made as monstrous as it looked. In view of the skill with which the rest of the drawing was done, Mr. Wraxall felt inclined to adopt the latter idea. The figure was unduly short, and was for the most part muffled in a hooded garment which swept the ground. The only part of the form which projected from that shelter was not shaped like any hand or arm. Mr. Wraxall compares it to the

tentacle of a devil-fish, and continues: " On seeing this, I said
to myself, ' This, then, which is evidently an allegorical representation of some kind—a fiend pursuing a hunted soul—may
be the origin of the story of Count Magnus and his mysterious
companion.   Let us see how the huntsman is pictured: doubtless it will be a demon blowing his horn.' "   But, as it turned
out, there was no such sensational figure, only the semblance
of a cloaked man on a hillock, who stood leaning on a stick,
and watching the hunt with an interest which the engraver
had tried to express in his attitude.

Mr. Wraxall noted the finely-worked and massive steel
padlocks—three in number—which secured the sarcophagus.
One of them, he saw, was detached, and lay on the pavement.
And then, unwilling to delay the deacon longer or to waste
his own working-time, he made his way onward to the manor-
house.

" It is curious," he notes, " how on retracing a familiar
path one's thoughts engross one to the absolute exclusion of
surrounding objects.   To-night, for the second time, I had
entirely failed to notice where I was going (I had planned a
private visit to the tomb-house to copy the epitaphs), when
I suddenly, as it were, awoke to consciousness, and found
myself (as before) turning in at the churchyard gate, and,
I believe, singing or chanting some such words as, ' Are you
awake, Count Magnus?   Are you asleep, Count Magnus? '
and then something more which I have failed to recollect.
It seemed to me that I must have been behaving in this
nonsensical way for some time."

He found the key of the mausoleum where he had expected to find it, and copied the greater part of what he
wanted; in fact, he stayed until the light began to fail him.

" I must have been wrong," he writes, " in saying that
one of the padlocks of my Count's sarcophagus was un-
fastened; I see to-night that two are loose.   I picked both
up, and laid them carefully on the window-ledge, after trying
unsuccessfully to close them.   The remaining one is still firm,
and, though I take it to be a spring lock, I cannot guess how
it is opened.   Had I succeeded in undoing it, I am almost
afraid I should have taken the liberty of opening the sarcophagus.   It is strange, the interest I feel in the personality of
this, I fear, somewhat ferocious and grim old noble."

The day following was, as it turned out, the last of Mr.

Wraxall's stay at Råbäck. He received letters connected
with certain investments which made it desirable that he
should return to England; his work among the papers was
practically done, and travelling was slow. He decided, therefore, to make his farewells, put some finishing touches to
his notes, and be off.

These finishing touches and farewells, as it turned out,
took more time than he had expected. The hospitable family
insisted on his staying to dine with them—they dined at three
—and it was verging on half-past six before he was outside
the iron gates of Råbäck. He dwelt on every step of his
walk by the lake, determined to saturate himself, now that
he trod it for the last time, in the sentiment of the place and
hour. And when he reached the summit of the churchyard
knoll, he lingered for many minutes, gazing at the limitless
prospect of woods near and distant, all dark beneath a sky
of liquid green. When at last he turned to go, the thought
struck him that surely he must bid farewell to Count
Magnus as well as the rest of the De la Gardies. The church
was but twenty yards away, and he knew where the key
of the mausoleum hung. It was not long before he was
standing over the great copper coffin, and, as usual, talking
to himself aloud. "You may have been a bit of a rascal in
your time, Magnus," he was saying, "but for all that I
should like to see you, or, rather——"

"Just at that instant," he says, "I felt a blow on my
foot. Hastily enough I drew it back, and something fell
on the pavement with a clash. It was the third, the last of
the three padlocks which had fastened the sarcophagus. I
stooped to pick it up, and—Heaven is my witness that I am
writing only the bare truth—before I had raised myself there
was a sound of metal hinges creaking, and I distinctly saw
the lid shifting upwards. I may have behaved like a coward,
but I could not for my life stay for one moment. I was
outside that dreadful building in less time than I can write
—almost as quickly as I could have said—the words; and
what frightens me yet more, I could not turn the key in the
lock. As I sit here in my room noting these facts, I ask
myself (it was not twenty minutes ago) whether that noise
of creaking metal continued, and I cannot tell whether it
did or not. I only know that there was something more
than I have written that alarmed me, but whether it was

sound or sight I am not able to remember. What is this that I have done?"

Poor Mr. Wraxall! He set out on his journey to England on the next day, as he had planned, and he reached England in safety; and yet, as I gather from his changed hand and inconsequent jottings, a broken man. One of several small notebooks that have come to me with his papers gives, not a key to, but a kind of inkling of, his experiences. Much of his journey was made by canal-boat, and I find not less than six painful attempts to enumerate and describe his fellow-passengers. The entries are of this kind:

"24. Pastor of village in Skåne. Usual black coat and soft black hat.
"25. Commercial traveller from Stockholm going to Trollhättan. Black cloak, brown hat.
"26. Man in long black cloak, broad-leafed hat, very old-fashioned."

This entry is lined out, and a note added: "Perhaps identical with No. 13. Have not yet seen his face." On referring to No. 13, I find that he is a Roman priest in a cassock. The net result of the reckoning is always the same. Twenty-eight people appear in the enumeration, one being always a man in a long black cloak and broad hat, and the other a "short figure in dark cloak and hood." On the other hand, it is always noted that only twenty-six passengers appear at meals, and that the man in the cloak is perhaps absent, and the short figure is certainly absent.

On reaching England, it appears that Mr. Wraxall landed at Harwich, and that he resolved at once to put himself out of the reach of some person or persons whom he never specifies, but whom he had evidently come to regard as his pursuers. Accordingly he took a vehicle—it was a closed fly—not trusting the railway, and drove across country to the village of Belchamp St. Paul. It was about nine o'clock on a moonlight August night when he neared the place. He was sitting forward, and looking out of the window at the fields and thickets—there was little else to be seen—racing past him. Suddenly he came to a cross-road. At the corner

two figures were standing motionless; both were in dark
cloaks; the taller one wore a hat, the shorter a hood. He
had no time to see their faces, nor did they make any motion
that he could discern. Yet the horse shied violently and
broke into a gallop, and Mr. Wraxall sank back into his seat
in something like desperation. He had seen them before.

Arrived at Belchamp St. Paul, he was fortunate enough to
find a decent furnished lodging, and for the next twenty-
four hours he lived, comparatively speaking, in peace. His
last notes were written on this day. They are too disjointed
and ejaculatory to be given here in full, but the substance
of them is clear enough. He is expecting a visit from his
pursuers—how or when he knows not—and his constant cry
is " What has he done? " and " Is there no hope? " Doctors,
he knows, would call him mad, policemen would laugh at
him. The parson is away. What can he do but lock his
door and cry to God?

People still remembered last year at Belchamp St. Paul
how a strange gentleman came one evening in August years
back; and how the next morning but one he was found
dead, and there was an inquest; and the jury that viewed the
body fainted, seven of 'em did, and none of 'em wouldn't
speak to what they see, and the verdict was visitation of
God; and how the people as kep' the 'ouse moved out that
same week, and went away from that part. But they do
not, I think, know that any glimmer of light has ever been
thrown, or could be thrown, on the mystery. It so happened that last year the little house came into my hands as
part of a legacy. It had stood empty since 1863, and there
seemed no prospect of letting it; so I had it pulled down,
and the papers of which I have given you an abstract were
found in a forgotten cupboard under the window in the
best bedroom.

G. K. CHESTERTON

THE QUEER FEET

IF you meet a member of that select club, "The Twelve True Fishermen," entering the Vernon Hotel for the annual club dinner, you will observe, as he takes off his overcoat, that his evening coat is green and not black. If (supposing that you have the star-defying audacity to address such a being) you ask him why, he will probably answer that he does it to avoid being mistaken for a waiter. You will then retire crushed. But you will leave behind you a mystery as yet unsolved and a tale worth telling.

If (to pursue the same vein of improbable conjecture) you were to meet a mild, hard-working little priest, named Father Brown, and were to ask him what he thought was the most singular luck of his life, he would probably reply that upon the whole his best stroke was at the Vernon Hotel, where he had averted a crime and, perhaps, saved a soul, merely by listening to a few footsteps in a passage. He is perhaps a little proud of this wild and wonderful guess of his, and it is possible that he might refer to it. But since it is immeasurably unlikely that you will ever rise high enough in the social world to find "The Twelve True Fishermen," or that you will ever sink low enough among slums and criminals to find Father Brown, I fear you will never hear the story at all unless you hear it from me.

The Vernon Hotel at which The Twelve True Fishermen held their annual dinners was an institution such as can only exist in an oligarchical society which has almost gone mad on good manners. It was that topsy-turvy product—an "exclusive" commercial enterprise. That is, it was a thing which paid not by attracting people, but actually by turning people away. In the heart of a plutocracy tradesmen become cunning enough to be more fastidious than their customers. They positively create difficulties so that their wealthy and weary clients may spend money and diplomacy in overcoming them. If there were a fashionable hotel in London which no man could enter who was under six foot, society would meekly

make up parties of six-foot men to dine in it. If there were
an expensive restaurant which by a mere caprice of its proprietor was only open on Thursday afternoon, it would be
crowded on Thursday afternoon. The Vernon Hotel stood,
as if by accident, in the corner of a square in Belgravia. It
was a small hotel; and a very inconvenient one. But its very
inconveniences were considered as walls protecting a particular class. One inconvenience, in particular, was held to
be of vital importance: the fact that practically only twenty-
four people could dine in the place at once. The only big
dinner table was the celebrated terrace table, which stood
open to the air on a sort of veranda overlooking one of the
most exquisite old gardens in London. Thus it happened
that even the twenty-four seats at this table could only be
enjoyed in warm weather; and this making the enjoyment
yet more difficult made it yet more desired. The existing
owner of the hotel was a Jew named Lever; and he made
nearly a million out of it, by making it difficult to get into.
Of course he combined with this limitation in the scope of
his enterprise the most careful polish in its performance. The
wines and cooking were really as good as any in Europe, and
the demeanour of the attendants exactly mirrored the fixed
mood of the English upper class. The proprietor knew all
his waiters like the fingers on his hand; there were only
fifteen of them all told. It was much easier to become a
Member of Parliament than to become a waiter in that hotel.
Each waiter was trained in terrible silence and smoothness,
as if he were a gentleman's servant. And, indeed, there was
generally at least one waiter to every gentleman who dined.

The club of the Twelve True Fishermen would not have
consented to dine anywhere but in such a place, for it insisted on a luxurious privacy; and would have been quite
upset by the mere thought that any other club was even
dining in the same building. On the occasion of their annual
dinner the Fishermen were in the habit of exposing all their
treasures, as if they were in a private house, especially the
celebrated set of fish knives and forks which were, as it were,
the insignia of the society, each being exquisitely wrought
in silver in the form of a fish, and each loaded at the hilt with
one large pearl. These were always laid out for the fish
course, and the fish course was always the most magnificent
in that magnificent repast. The society had a vast number

of ceremonies and observances, but it had no history and no
object; that was where it was so very aristocratic. You did
not have to be anything in order to be one of the Twelve
Fishers; unless you were already a certain sort of person, you
never even heard of them. It had been in existence twelve
years. Its president was Mr. Audley. Its vice-president was
the Duke of Chester.

If I have in any degree conveyed the atmosphere of this
appalling hotel, the reader may feel a natural wonder as to
how I came to know anything about it, and may even speculate as to how so ordinary a person as my friend Father
Brown came to find himself in that golden galley. As far
as that is concerned, my story is simple, or even vulgar.
There is in the world a very aged rioter and demagogue who
breaks into the most refined retreats with the dreadful information that all men are brothers, and wherever this leveller
went on his pale horse it was Father Brown's trade to follow.
One of the waiters, an Italian, had been struck down with a
paralytic stroke that afternoon; and his Jewish employer,
marvelling mildly at such superstitions, had consented to send
for the nearest Popish priest. With what the waiter confessed to Father Brown we are not concerned, for the excellent reason that the cleric kept it to himself; but apparently
it involved him in writing out a note or statement for the
conveying of some message or the righting of some wrong.
Father Brown, therefore, with a meek impudence which he
would have shown equally in Buckingham Palace, asked to be
provided with a room and writing materials. Mr. Lever was
torn in two. He was a kind man, and had also that bad
imitation of kindness, the dislike of any difficulty or scene.
At the same time the presence of one unusual stranger in his
hotel that evening was like a speck of dirt on something just
cleaned. There was never any borderland or ante-room in
the Vernon Hotel, no people waiting in the hall, no customers
coming in on chance. There were fifteen waiters. There
were twelve guests. It would be as startling to find a new
guest in the hotel that night as to find a new brother taking
breakfast or tea in one's own family. Moreover, the priest's
appearance was second-rate and his clothes muddy; a mere
glimpse of him afar off might precipitate a crisis in the club.
Mr. Lever at last hit on a plan to cover, since he might not
obliterate, the disgrace. When you enter (as you never will)

the Vernon Hotel, you pass down a short passage decorated with a few dingy but important pictures, and come to the main vestibule and lounge which opens on your right into passages leading to the public rooms, and on your left to a similar passage pointing to the kitchens and offices of the hotel. Immediately on your left hand is the corner of a glass office, which abuts upon the lounge—a house within a house, so to speak, like the old hotel bar which probably once occupied its place.

In this office sat the representative of the proprietor (nobody in this place ever appeared in person if he could help it), and just beyond the office, on the way to the servants' quarters, was the gentlemen's cloak room, the last boundary of the gentlemen's domain. But between the office and the cloak room was a small private room without other outlet, sometimes used by the proprietor for delicate and important matters, such as lending a duke a thousand pounds or declining to lend him sixpence. It is a mark of the magnificent tolerance of Mr. Lever that he permitted this holy place to be for about half an hour profaned by a mere priest, scribbling away on a piece of paper. The story which Father Brown was writing down was very likely a much better story than this one, only it will never be known. I can merely state that it was very nearly as long, and that the last two or three paragraphs of it were the least exciting and absorbing.

For it was by the time that he had reached these that the priest began a little to allow his thoughts to wander and his animal senses, which were commonly keen, to awaken. The time of darkness and dinner was drawing on; his own forgotten little room was without a light, and perhaps the gathering gloom, as occasionally happens, sharpened the sense of sound. As Father Brown wrote the last and least essential part of his document, he caught himself writing to the rhythm of a recurrent noise outside, just as one sometimes thinks to the tune of a railway train. When he became conscious of the thing he found what it was: only the ordinary patter of feet passing the door, which in an hotel was no very unlikely matter. Nevertheless, he stared at the darkened ceiling, and listened to the sound. After he had listened for a few seconds dreamily, he got to his feet and listened intently, with his head a little on one side. Then he sat down again and buried his brow in his hands, now not merely listening, but listening and thinking also.

The footsteps outside at any given moment were such as one might hear in any hotel; and yet, taken as a whole, there was something very strange about them. There were no other footsteps. It was always a very silent house, for the few familiar guests went at once to their own apartments, and the well-trained waiters were told to be almost invisible until they were wanted. One could not conceive any place where there was less reason to apprehend anything irregular. But these footsteps were so odd that one could not decide to call them regular or irregular. Father Brown followed them with his finger on the edge of the table, like a man trying to learn a tune on the piano.

First, there came a long rush of rapid little steps, such as a light man might make in winning a walking race. At a certain point they stopped and changed to a sort of slow, swinging stamp, numbering not a quarter of the steps, but occupying about the same time. The moment the last echoing stamp had died away would come again the run or ripple of light, hurrying feet, and then again the thud of the heavier walking. It was certainly the same pair of boots, partly because (as has been said) there were no other boots about, and partly because they had a small but unmistakable creak in them. Father Brown had the kind of head that cannot help asking questions; and on this apparently trivial question his head almost split. He had seen men run in order to jump. He had seen men run in order to slide. But why on earth should a man run in order to walk? Or, again, why should he walk in order to run? Yet no other description would cover the antics of this invisible pair of legs. The man was either walking very fast down one-half of the corridor in order to walk very slow down the other half; or he was walking very slow at one end to have the rapture of walking fast at the other. Neither suggestion seemed to make much sense. His brain was growing darker and darker, like his room.

Yet, as he began to think steadily, the very blackness of his cell seemed to make his thoughts more vivid; he began to see as in a kind of vision the fantastic feet capering along the corridor in unnatural or symbolic attitudes. Was it a heathen religious dance? Or some entirely new kind of scientific exercise? Father Brown began to ask himself with

more exactness what the steps suggested. Taking the slow
step first: it certainly was not the step of the proprietor.
Men of his type walk with a rapid waddle, or they sit still.
It could not be any servant or messenger waiting for directions. It did not sound like it. The poorer orders (in an
oligarchy) sometimes lurch about when they are slightly
drunk, but generally, and especially in such gorgeous scenes,
they stand or sit in constrained attitudes. No; that heavy
yet springy step, with a kind of careless emphasis, not specially
noisy, yet not caring what noise it made, belonged to only
one of the animals of this earth. It was a gentleman of
western Europe, and probably one who had never worked for
his living.

Just as he came to this solid certainty, the step changed to
the quicker one, and ran past the door as feverishly as a rat.
The listener remarked that though this step was much swifter
it was also much more noiseless, almost as if the man were
walking on tiptoe. Yet it was not associated in his mind with
secrecy, but with something else—something that he could
not remember. He was maddened by one of those half-
memories that make a man feel half-witted. Surely he had
heard that strange, swift walking somewhere. Suddenly he
sprang to his feet with a new idea in his head, and walked to
the door. His room had no direct outlet on the passage,
but let on one side into the glass office, and on the other into
the cloak room beyond. He tried the door into the office,
and found it locked. Then he looked at the window, now
a square pane full of purple cloud cleft by livid sunset, and
for an instant he smelt evil as a dog smells rats.

The rational part of him (whether the wiser or not) regained its supremacy. He remembered that the proprietor
had told him that he should lock the door, and would come
later to release him. He told himself that twenty things he
had not thought of might explain the eccentric sounds outside; he reminded himself that there was just enough light
left to finish his own proper work. Bringing his paper to
the window so as to catch the last stormy evening light, he
resolutely plunged once more into the almost completed
record. He had written for about twenty minutes, bending
closer and closer to his paper in the lessening light; then suddenly he sat upright. He had heard the strange feet once more.

This time they had a third oddity. Previously the unknown man had walked, with levity indeed and lightning quickness, but he had walked. This time he ran. One could hear the swift, soft, bounding steps coming along the corridor, like the pads of a fleeing and leaping panther. Whoever was coming was a very strong, active man, in still yet tearing excitement. Yet, when the sound had swept up to the office like a sort of whispering whirlwind, it suddenly changed again to the old slow, swaggering stamp.

Father Brown flung down his paper, and, knowing the office door to be locked, went at once into the cloak room on the other side. The attendant of this place was temporarily absent, probably because the only guests were at dinner, and his office was a sinecure. After groping through a grey forest of overcoats, he found that the dim cloak room opened on the lighted corridor in the form of a sort of counter or half-door, like most of the counters across which we have all handed umbrellas and received tickets. There was a light immediately above the semicircular arch of this opening. It threw little illumination on Father Brown himself, who seemed a mere dark outline against the dim sunset window behind him. But it threw an almost theatrical light on the man who stood outside the cloak room in the corridor.

He was an elegant man in very plain evening dress; tall, but with an air of not taking up much room; one felt that he could have slid along like a shadow where many smaller men would have been obvious and obstructive. His face, now flung back in the lamplight, was swarthy and vivacious, the face of a foreigner. His figure was good, his manners good humoured and confident; a critic could only say that his black coat was a shade below his figure and manners, and even bulged and bagged in an odd way. The moment he caught sight of Brown's black silhouette against the sunset, he tossed down a scrap of paper with a number and called out with amiable authority: "I want my hat and coat, please; I find I have to go away at once."

Father Brown took the paper without a word, and obediently went to look for the coat; it was not the first menial work he had done in his life. He brought it and laid it on the counter; meanwhile, the strange gentleman, who had been feeling in his waistcoat pocket, said laughing: "I haven't got any silver; you can keep this." And he threw down half a sovereign, and caught up his coat.

Father Brown's figure remained quite dark and still; but in
that instant he had lost his head. His head was always most
valuable when he had lost it. In such moments he put two
and two together and made four million. Often the Catholic
Church (which is wedded to common sense) did not approve
of it. Often he did not approve of it himself. But it was
real inspiration—important at rare crises—when whosoever
shall lose his head the same shall save it.

" I think, sir," he said civilly, " that you have some silver
in your pocket."

The tall gentleman stared. " Hang it," he cried, " if I give
you gold, why should you complain? "

" Because silver is sometimes more valuable than gold,"
said the priest mildly; " that is, in large quantities."

The stranger looked at him curiously. Then he looked still
more curiously up the passage towards the main entrance.
Then he looked back at Brown again, and then he looked very
carefully at the window beyond Brown's head, still coloured
with the after-glow of the storm. Then he seemed to make
up his mind. He put one hand on the counter, vaulted over
as easily as an acrobat and towered above the priest, putting
one tremendous hand upon his collar.

" Stand still," he said, in a hacking whisper. " I don't
want to threaten you, but——"

" I do want to threaten you," said Father Brown, in a voice
like a rolling drum, " I want to threaten you with the worm
that dieth not, and the fire that is not quenched."

" You're a rum sort of cloak-room clerk," said the other.

" I am a priest, Monsieur Flambeau," said Brown, " and
I am ready to hear your confession."

The other stood gasping for a few moments, and then staggered back into a chair.

The first two courses of the dinner of the Twelve True
Fishermen had proceeded with placid success. I do not
possess a copy of the menu; and if I did it would not convey
anything to anybody. It was written in a sort of super-
French employed by cooks, but quite unintelligible to
Frenchmen. There was a tradition in the club that the *hors
d'œuvre* should be various and manifold to the point of
madness. They were taken seriously because they were
avowedly useless extras, like the whole dinner and the whole

club. There was also a tradition that the soup course should
be light and unpretending—a sort of simple and austere vigil
for the feast of fish that was to come. The talk was that
strange, slight talk which governs the British Empire, which
governs it in secret, and yet would scarcely enlighten an
ordinary Englishman even if he could overhear it. Cabinet
Ministers on both sides were alluded to by their Christian
names with a sort of bored benignity. The Radical Chan-
cellor of the Exchequer, whom the whole Tory party was
supposed to be cursing for his extortions, was praised for
his minor poetry, or his saddle in the hunting field. The
Tory leader, whom all Liberals were supposed to hate as a
tyrant, was discussed and, on the whole, praised—as a Liberal.
It seemed somehow that politicians were very important. And
yet, anything seemed important about them except their
politics. Mr. Audley, the chairman, was an amiable, elderly
man who still wore Gladstone collars; he was a kind of
symbol of all that phantasmal and yet fixed society. He had
never done anything—not even anything wrong. He was
not fast; he was not even particularly rich. He was simply
in the thing; and there was an end of it. No party could
ignore him, and if he had wished to be in the Cabinet he
certainly would have been put there. The Duke of Chester,
the vice-president, was a young and rising politician. That
is to say, he was a pleasant youth, with flat, fair hair and a
freckled face, with moderate intelligence and enormous
estates. In public his appearances were always successful
and his principle was simple enough. When he thought of
a joke he made it, and was called brilliant. When he could
not think of a joke he said that this was no time for trifling,
and was called able. In private, in a club of his own class,
he was simply quite pleasantly frank and silly, like a schoolboy. Mr. Audley, never having been in politics, treated them
a little more seriously. Sometimes he even embarrassed the
company by phrases suggesting that there was some difference
between a Liberal and a Conservative. He himself was a
Conservative, even in private life. He had a roll of grey
hair over the back of his collar, like certain old-fashioned
statesmen, and seen from behind he looked like the man the
empire wants. Seen from the front he looked like a mild,
self-indulgent bachelor, with rooms in the Albany—which
he was.

As has been remarked, there were twenty-four seats at the terrace table, and only twelve members of the club. Thus they could occupy the terrace in the most luxurious style of all, being ranged along the inner side of the table, with no one opposite, commanding an uninterrupted view of the garden, the colours of which were still vivid, though evening was closing in somewhat luridly for the time of year. The chairman sat in the centre of the line, and the vice-president at the right-hand end of it. When the twelve guests first trooped into their seats it was the custom (for some unknown reason) for all the fifteen waiters to stand lining the wall like troops presenting arms to the king, while the fat proprietor stood and bowed to the club with radiant surprise, as if he had never heard of them before. But before the first chink of knife and fork this army of retainers had vanished, only the one or two required to collect and distribute the plates darting about in deathly silence. Mr. Lever, the proprietor, of course had disappeared in convulsions of courtesy long before. It would be exaggerative, indeed irreverent, to say that he ever positively appeared again. But when the important course, the fish course, was being brought on, there was—how shall I put it?—a vivid shadow, a projection of his personality, which told that he was hovering near. The sacred fish course consisted (to the eyes of the vulgar) in a sort of monstrous pudding, about the size and shape of a wedding cake, in which some considerable number of interesting fishes had finally lost the shapes which God had given to them. The Twelve True Fishermen took up their celebrated fish knives and fish forks, and approached it as gravely as if every inch of the pudding cost as much as the silver fork it was eaten with. So it did, for all I know. This course was dealt with in eager and devouring silence; and it was only when his plate was nearly empty that the young duke made the ritual remark: " They can't do this anywhere but here."

" Nowhere," said Mr. Audley, in a deep bass voice, turning to the speaker and nodding his venerable head a number of times. " Nowhere, assuredly, except here. It was represented to me that at the Café Anglais——"

Here he was interrupted and even agitated for a moment by the removal of his plate, but he recaptured the valuable thread of his thoughts. " It was represented to me that the same could be done at the Café Anglais. Nothing like it,

sir," he said, shaking his head ruthlessly, like a hanging judge.
" Nothing like it."

" Overrated place," said a certain Colonel Pound, speaking
(by the look of him) for the first time for some months.

" Oh, I don't know," said the Duke of Chester, who was
an optimist, " it's jolly good for some things. You can't beat
it at———"

A waiter came swiftly along the room, and then stopped
dead. His stoppage was as silent as his tread; but all those
vague and kindly gentlemen were so used to the utter smoothness of the unseen machinery which surrounded and supported their lives, that a waiter doing anything unexpected
was a start and a jar. They felt as you and I would feel if
the inanimate world disobeyed—if a chair ran away from
us.

The waiter stood staring a few seconds, while there
deepened on every face at table a strange shame which is
wholly the product of our time. It is the combination of
modern humanitarianism with the horrible modern abyss
between the souls of the rich and poor. A genuine historic
aristocrat would have thrown things at the waiter, beginning
with empty bottles, and very probably ending with money.
A genuine democrat would have asked him, with a comrade-
like clearness of speech, what the devil he was doing. But
these modern plutocrats could not bear a poor man near to
them, either as a slave or as a friend. That something had
gone wrong with the servants was merely a dull, hot embarrassment. They did not want to be brutal, and they dreaded
the need to be benevolent. They wanted the thing, whatever
it was, to be over. It was over. The waiter, after standing
for some seconds rigid, like a cataleptic, turned round and
ran madly out of the room.

When he reappeared in the room, or rather in the doorway,
it was in company with another waiter, with whom he whispered and gesticulated with southern fierceness. Then the
first waiter went away, leaving the second waiter, and reappeared with a third waiter. By the time a fourth waiter had
joined this hurried synod, Mr. Audley felt it necessary to
break the silence in the interests of Tact. He used a very
loud cough, instead of a presidential hammer, and said:
" Splendid work young Moocher's doing in Burmah. Now,
no other nation in the world could have———"

A fifth waiter had sped towards him like an arrow, and
was whispering in his ear: " So sorry. Important! Might the
proprietor speak to you? "

The chairman turned in disorder, and with a dazed stare
saw Mr. Lever coming towards them with his lumbering
quickness. The gait of the good proprietor was indeed his
usual gait, but his face was by no means usual. Generally it
was a genial copper-brown; now it was a sickly yellow.

" You will pardon me, Mr. Audley," he said, with asth-
matic breathlessness. " I have great apprehensions. Your
fish-plates, they are cleared away with the knife and fork on
them! "

" Well, I hope so," said the chairman, with some warmth.

" You see him? " panted the excited hotel keeper; " you
see the waiter who took them away? You know him? "

" Know the waiter? " answered Mr. Audley indignantly.
" Certainly not! "

Mr. Lever opened his hands with a gesture of agony. " I
never send him," he said. " I know not when or why he
come. I send my waiter to take away the plates, and he find
them already away."

Mr. Audley still looked rather too bewildered to be really
the man the empire wants; none of the company could say
anything except the man of wood—Colonel Pound—who
seemed galvanised into an unnatural life. He rose rigidly
from his chair, leaving all the rest sitting, screwed his eye-
glass into his eye, and spoke in a raucous undertone as if he
had half-forgotten how to speak. " Do you mean," he said,
" that somebody has stolen our silver fish service? "

The proprietor repeated the open-handed gesture with
even greater helplessness; and in a flash all the men at the
table were on their feet.

" Are all your waiters here? " demanded the colonel, in
his low, harsh accent.

" Yes; they're all here. I noticed it myself," cried the
young duke, pushing his boyish face into the inmost ring.
" Always count 'em as I come in; they look so queer standing
up against the wall."

" But surely one cannot exactly remember," began Mr.
Audley, with heavy hesitation.

" I remember exactly, I tell you," cried the duke ex-
citedly. " There never have been more than fifteen waiters

at this place, and there were no more than fifteen to-night, I'll swear; no more and no less."

The proprietor turned upon him, quaking in a kind of palsy of surprise. " You say—you say," he stammered, " that you see all my fifteen waiters? "

" As usual," assented the duke. " What is the matter with that? "

" Nothing," said Lever, with a deepening accent, " only you did not. For one of zem is dead upstairs."

There was a shocking stillness for an instant in that room. It may be (so supernatural is the word death) that each of those idle men looked for a second at his soul, and saw it as a small dried pea. One of them—the duke, I think—even said with the idiotic kindness of wealth: " Is there anything we can do? "

" He has had a priest," said the Jew, not untouched.

Then, as to the clang of doom, they awoke to their own position. For a few weird seconds they had really felt as if the fifteenth waiter might be the ghost of the dead man upstairs. They had been dumb under that oppression, for ghosts were to them an embarrassment, like beggars. But the remembrance of the silver broke the spell of the miraculous; broke it abruptly and with a brutal reaction. The colonel flung over his chair and strode to the door. " If there was a fifteenth man here, friends," he said, " that fifteenth fellow was a thief. Down at once to the front and back doors and secure everything; then we'll talk. The twenty-four pearls are worth recovering."

Mr. Audley seemed at first to hesitate about whether it was gentlemanly to be in such a hurry about anything; but, seeing the duke dash down the stairs with youthful energy, he followed with a more mature motion.

At the same instant a sixth waiter ran into the room, and declared that he had found the pile of fish plates on a sideboard, with no trace of the silver.

The crowd of diners and attendants that tumbled helter-skelter down the passages divided into two groups. Most of the Fishermen followed the proprietor to the front room to demand news of any exit. Colonel Pound, with the chairman, the vice-president, and one or two others darted down the corridor leading to the servants' quarters, as the more likely line of escape. As they did so they passed the dim alcove or cavern of the cloak room, and saw a short, black-coated figure, presumably an attendant, standing a little way back in the shadow of it.

"Hallo, there!" called out the duke. "Have you seen anyone pass?"

The short figure did not answer the question directly, but merely said: "Perhaps I have got what you are looking for, gentlemen."

They paused, wavering and wondering, while he quietly went to the back of the cloak room, and came back with both hands full of shining silver, which he laid out on the counter as calmly as a salesman. It took the form of a dozen quaintly shaped forks and knives.

"You—you——" began the colonel, quite thrown off his balance at last. Then he peered into the dim little room and saw two things: first, that the short, black-clad man was dressed like a clergyman; and, second, that the window of the room behind him was burst, as if someone had passed violently through.

"Valuable things to deposit in a cloak room, aren't they?" remarked the clergyman, with cheerful composure.

"Did—did you steal those things?" stammered Mr. Audley, with staring eyes.

"If I did," said the cleric pleasantly, "at least I am bringing them back again."

"But you didn't," said Colonel Pound, still staring at the broken window.

"To make a clean breast of it, I didn't," said the other, with some humour. And he seated himself quite gravely on a stool.

"But you know who did," said the colonel.

"I don't know his real name," said the priest placidly, "but I know something of his fighting weight, and a great deal about his spiritual difficulties. I formed the physical estimate when he was trying to throttle me, and the moral estimate when he repented."

"Oh, I say—repented!" cried young Chester, with a sort of crow of laughter.

Father Brown got to his feet, putting his hands behind him. "Odd, isn't it," he said, "that a thief and a vagabond should repent, when so many who are rich and secure remain hard and frivolous, and without fruit for God or man? But there, if you will excuse me, you trespass a little upon my province. If you doubt the penitence as a practical fact, there are your knives and forks. You are the Twelve True Fishers, and there are all your silver fish. But He has made me a fisher of men."

" Did you catch this man? " asked the colonel, frowning.

Father Brown looked him full in his frowning face. " Yes," he said, " I caught him, with an unseen hook and an invisible line which is long enough to let him wander to the ends of the world, and still to bring him back with a twitch upon the thread."

There was a long silence. All the other men present drifted away to carry the recovered silver to their comrades, or to consult the proprietor about the queer condition of affairs. But the grim-faced colonel still sat sideways on the counter, swinging his long, lank legs and biting his dark moustache.

At last he said quietly to the priest: " He must have been a clever fellow, but I think I know a cleverer."

" He was a clever fellow," answered the other, " but I am not quite sure of what other you mean."

" I mean you," said the colonel, with a short laugh. " I don't want to get the fellow jailed; make yourself easy about that. But I'd give a good many silver forks to know exactly how you fell into this affair, and how you got the stuff out of him. I reckon you're the most up-to-date devil of the present company."

Father Brown seemed rather to like the saturnine candour of the soldier. " Well," he said, smiling, " I mustn't tell you anything of the man's identity, or his own story, of course; but there's no particular reason why I shouldn't tell you of the mere outside facts which I found out for myself."

He hopped over the barrier with unexpected activity, and sat beside Colonel Pound, kicking his short legs like a little boy on a gate. He began to tell the story as easily as if he were telling it to an old friend by a Christmas fire.

" You see, colonel," he said, " I was shut up in that small room there doing some writing, when I heard a pair of feet in this passage doing a dance that was as queer as the dance of death. First came quick, funny little steps, like a man walking on tiptoe for a wager; then came slow, careless, creaking steps, as of a big man walking about with a cigar. But they were both made by the same feet, I swear, and they came in rotation; first the run and then the walk, and then the run again. I wondered at first idly and then wildly why a man should act these two parts at once. One walk I knew; it was just like yours, colonel. It was the walk of a well-fed gentleman waiting for something, who strolls about rather because he is physically alert than because he is mentally impatient. I knew that I knew the other walk, too, but I could not remember what it was. What wild creature had I met on my travels that tore along on tiptoe in that extra-ordinary style? Then I heard a clink of plates somewhere; and the answer stood up as plain as St. Peter's. It was the walk of a waiter—that walk with the body slanted forward, the eyes looking down, the ball of the toe spurning away the ground, the coat tails and napkin flying. Then I thought for a minute and a half more. And I believe I saw the manner of the crime, as clearly as if I were going to commit it."

Colonel Pound looked at him keenly, but the speaker's mild grey eyes were fixed upon the ceiling with almost empty wistfulness.

" A crime," he said slowly, " is like any other work of art. Don't look surprised; crimes are by no means the only works of art that comes from an infernal workshop. But every work of art, divine or diabolic, has one indispensable mark —I mean, that the centre of it is simple, however much the fulfilment may be complicated. Thus, in *Hamlet*, let us say, the grotesqueness of the grave-digger, the flowers of the mad girl, the fantastic finery of Osric, the pallor of the ghost and the grin of the skull are all oddities in a sort of tangled wreath round one plain tragic figure of a man in black. Well, this also," he said, getting slowly down from his seat with a smile, " this also is the plain tragedy of a man in black. Yes," he went on, seeing the colonel look up in some wonder, " the whole of this tale turns on a black coat. In this, as in *Hamlet*, there are the rococo excrescences—yourselves, let us say. There is the dead waiter, who was there when he could not be there. There is the invisible hand that swept your table clear of silver and melted into air. But every clever crime is founded ultimately on some one quite simple fact— some fact that is not itself mysterious. The mystification comes in covering it up, in leading men's thoughts away from it. This large and subtle and (in the ordinary course) most profitable crime was built on the plain fact that a gentle-

man's evening dress is the same as a waiter's. All the rest was
acting, and thundering good acting, too."

"Still," said the colonel, getting up and frowning at his
boots, "I am not sure that I understand."

"Colonel," said Father Brown, "I tell you that this arch-
angel of impudence who stole your forks walked up and
down this passage twenty times in the blaze of all the lamps,
in the glare of all the eyes. He did not go and hide in dim
corners where suspicion might have searched for him. He
kept constantly on the move in the lighted corridors, and
everywhere that he went he seemed to be there by right.
Don't ask me what he was like; you have seen him yourself
six or seven times to-night. You were waiting with all the
other grand people in the reception-room at the end of the
passage there, with the terrace just beyond. Whenever he
came among you gentlemen, he came in the lightning style of
a waiter, with bent head, flapping napkin and flying feet.
He shot out on to the terrace, did something to the table
cloth, and shot back again towards the office and the waiters'
quarters. By the time he had come under the eye of the
office clerk and the waiters he had become another man in
every inch of his body, in every instinctive gesture. He
strolled among the servants with the absent-minded insolence
which they have all seen in their patrons. It was no new
thing to them that a swell from the dinner party should pace
all parts of the house like an animal at the Zoo; they know
that nothing marks the Smart Set more than a habit of walking where one chooses. When he was magnificently weary
of walking down that particular passage he would wheel
round and pace back past the office; in the shadow of the
arch just beyond he was altered as by a blast of magic, and
went hurrying forward again among the Twelve Fishermen,
an obsequious attendant. Why should the gentlemen look at
a chance waiter? Why should the waiters suspect a first-
rate walking gentleman? Once or twice he played the coolest
tricks. In the proprietor's private quarters he called out
breezily for a syphon of soda water, saying he was thirsty.
He said genially that he would carry it himself, and he
did; he carried it quickly and correctly through the thick of
you, a waiter with an obvious errand. Of course, it could
not have been kept up long, but it only had to be kept up till
the end of the fish course.

"His worst moment was when the waiters stood in a row; but even then he contrived to lean against the wall just round the corner in such a way that for that important instant the waiters thought him a gentleman, while the gentlemen thought him a waiter. The rest went like winking. If any waiter caught him away from the table, that waiter caught a languid aristocrat. He had only to time himself two minutes before the fish was cleared, become a swift servant, and clear it himself. He put the plates down on a sideboard, stuffed the silver in his breast pocket, giving it a bulgy look, and ran like a hare (I heard him coming) till he came to the cloak room. There he had only to be a plutocrat again—a plutocrat called away suddenly on business. He had only to give his ticket to the cloak-room attendant, and go out again elegantly as he had come in. Only—only I happened to be the cloak-room attendant."

"What did you do to him?" cried the colonel, with unusual intensity. "What did he tell you?"

"I beg your pardon," said the priest immovably, "that is where the story ends."

"And the interesting story begins," muttered Pound. "I think I understand his professional trick. But I don't seem to have got hold of yours."

"I must be going," said Father Brown.

They walked together along the passage to the entrance hall, where they saw the fresh, freckled face of the Duke of Chester, who was bounding buoyantly along towards them.

"Come along, Pound," he cried breathlessly. "I've been looking for you everywhere. The dinner's going again in spanking style, and old Audley has got to make a speech in honour of the forks being saved. We want to start some new ceremony, don't you know, to commemorate the occasion. I say, you really got the goods back, what do you suggest?"

"Why," said the colonel, eyeing him with a certain sardonic approval, "I should suggest that henceforward we wear green coats instead of black. One never knows what mistakes may arise when one looks so like a waiter."

"Oh, hang it all!" said the young man, "a gentleman never looks like a waiter."

"Nor a waiter like a gentleman, I suppose," said Colonel Pound, with the same lowering laughter on his face.

"Reverend sir, your friend must have been very smart to act the gentleman."

Father Brown buttoned up his commonplace overcoat to the neck, for the night was stormy, and took his commonplace umbrella from the stand.

"Yes," he said; "it must be very hard work to be a gentleman; but, do you know, I have sometimes thought that it may be almost as laborious to be a waiter."

And saying "Good evening," he pushed open the heavy doors of that palace of pleasures. The golden gates closed behind him, and he went at a brisk walk through the damp, dark streets in search of a penny omnibus.

J. S. FLETCHER

THE IVORY GOD

A T six o'clock Thurston put down his pen, pushed his chair back from the table at which he had been writing, and rose to his feet with a series of gestures indicative of mental and physical fatigue. He glanced at the few sheets of manuscript which represented the result of a long day's labour, and he frowned, as if in anger or distaste.

He had written, or tried to write, from ten o'clock until one, and again from two until six; and his entire product after seven hours' work was comparatively infinitesimal. He had felt no enthusiasm; he had been unable to concentrate his thoughts; the whole thing had been distasteful to him. As he glanced around him he asked himself for the thousandth time whether the game was worth the candle.

More from force of habit than from genuine desire to do it, Thurston proceeded to make some sort of toilet for the evening. He shaved and washed carefully; he put on a clean linen shirt and a dark lounge suit; he was unduly particular about the fold of his tie; in several small ways he showed that he had a gentlemanlike love of cleanliness and orderly habits.

He did everything very slowly. It would have been evident to anyone who might have had an opportunity of watching him that he had no engagement to keep. In point of fact, he had few friends with whom he could have kept any engagement. He was, as he now never cared to remind himself, one of the very loneliest men living. For a while he had reminded himself of this pertinent truth somewhat often; then he wearied of the thought, and put it from him. The fact of the loneliness, however, remained.

Thurston lived in two rooms at the top of a house which stood in a quiet street near the British Museum—a street of an aspect so grey and pathetic that you wondered at first sight of it whether laughter or children's voices were ever heard there. The two rooms opened one into the other by

means of a folding door.   Thurston had furnished them himself when he first came to town.

One room contained a camp bedstead, a chest of drawers,
a dressing-table, a wash-stand, a bath, and a hard-bottomed
chair.   The floor was stained and polished, and destitute of
carpet; but there was a thick bearskin rug at the bedside.
It was absolutely destitute of luxuries or of pictures, but it
possessed a first-rate reading-lamp, attached to the wall at
the head of the bed.

The other room knew the luxury of books; its walls were
covered with them to half their height.   The books related
chiefly to philosophy, theology, history, metaphysics.   There
was little that was light, but a table was strewn with the reviews of several countries, all purchased second-hand and
when a month old.

A desk, littered with papers, stood in the window; an
arm-chair was placed near the hearth; two other chairs of an
easyish sort occurred, sometimes here, sometimes there; a
small table, big enough for one person to eat at, was in the
middle of the room, which, unlike the sleeping-chamber, was
softly carpeted and luxuriant in thick rugs.

It also possessed some luxuries in the way of pictures;
but these, to the English eye of ordinary knowledge, were of
a strange taste, being Japanese.   One skilled in such matters
might have told you that they were all by the most celebrated
Japanese artists.   Even then you would have felt some uneasiness at the prospect of being continually shut up in a
room whose decorations were so purely Eastern.

In these two rooms Thurston had spent five years, every
day corresponding to another day.   He prepared his own
breakfast when he wished for it; he read or wrote when he
desired to do so; he lunched and dined out; he spent his
evenings reading or thinking or dreaming.   It was a strange
life altogether; but it was his.   But, then, the few people
who knew Thurston said he was a strange man, a man who
spoke little, laughed never, smiled seldom, and who was
quite young, in spite of everything.   In point of fact, he was
twenty-seven years old.

At twenty-two he had left Oxford with some reputation
as a scholar and a mystic, and had come to town with the
set purpose of following a literary career.   Whether he had
any ambitions at that time is a debatable question.   It is

quite certain that at twenty-seven none of them had been carried out. He had a little money of his own—sufficient to pay his rent, his housekeeping expenses, his tailor's bills and so on; and there was, therefore, no need to keep his nose to the grindstone.

But he had made no name. He sometimes exhibited a rather heavy, rather pedantic, rather wearisome sort of article to one or other of the leading reviews—the sort of article which is spoken of with great respect by the critics, and read by only a few experts—but to the general public he was as unknown as an unborn babe.

The people who had any dealings with him said that he was unsociable; he had no conversation. If by any chance he was induced to lunch or dine with you, his sole notion seemed to be to get away as quickly as possible. It was evident that he was one of those men who like to be alone.

There were times, however, when Thurston felt his loneliness; and one of them was hanging heavily about him on this particular evening. He had found it difficult to write during the day; and more than once he had caught himself wishing that a friend would come in to break the solitude. But he would have been hard put to it to say where such a friend was to be found.

He never encouraged anyone to visit him at his rooms. One or two men—old college acquaintances—had tracked him down and called upon him, but quickly discovered that they were not wanted. It was not that Thurston wished to be rude; it was simply that a certain shyness and loneliness ran in his blood and his temperament, and made him incapable of entertaining his fellow-creatures. He was essentially an anchorite; and yet there were times when his flesh called for something which it would have found it hard to define in words.

As Thurston drew on his overcoat a light tap came at his door, and he went across and opened it, not without some feeling of surprise that anyone should be there. In the faint light at the top of the landing he saw a man whom he did not recognise—a tall, sloping-shouldered man, whose back was somewhat bowed, whose knees bent in—a man who made a succession of angles in his clothes. Thurston could see that he was shabbily attired, that his hair was long, greasy, and unclean; he had a vague notion that an unwashed atmosphere hung heavily all round and about his visitor. He held the door half open, staring at the man; the man blinked at him.

" Mr. Thurston? " he said inquiringly.

" Well? " replied Thurston.

The man sighed heavily.

" I was sent to you, sir, by Mr. Evanson. I have something to show you which he thought you would like to see. He thought you might not be indisposed to buy it from me. May I come in and show it to you, Mr. Thurston? " said the man, indicating a small parcel which he carried in the crook of one arm.

" I am not disposed to buy anything," answered Thurston, keeping his place.

" But this, sir, is something very uncommon. It is seldom that any collector has such a chance of securing such a valuable curiosity," urged the visitor. " At any rate it will do you no harm to look at it, Mr. Thurston."

" Well," said Thurston, impassively and hesitatingly, " you may bring it in, then, but I really don't want to see it, and I shan't buy it, whatever it may be."

He turned away, and made preparations for lighting a lamp. The man with the parcel lingered at the threshold until the lamp had been placed on the centre table, and the apartment was bathed in a clear, powerful light.

" Now, then," said Thurston, still impassive as ever, " come forward, and let me see what it is! Mr. Evanson has no business to send you to me. I'm merely an acquaintance of his, and I'm certainly not a collector. What is it you have to show me? "

The untidy and unwashed person took small notice of this impatient outburst. He advanced to the table, placed his parcel near the lamp, and proceeded to divest it of its wrappings. He kept himself between Thurston and the parcel while this was going on, and he did not speak until he suddenly turned round, and said, with a note of pride and triumph in his voice:

" There, Mr. Thurston, look at that! "

Thurston, during the unfolding of the parcel, had fallen into a sort of day-dream. He came out of it with a start, and looked at the object which his visitor had placed on the table in the full light of the lamp. A sudden gleam came into his rather dull eyes; a sudden exclamation burst from his lips.

" Ah! " he said.

The man smiled, and rubbed his hands. He chuckled.

" I thought that would move you, Mr. Thurston! " he said. " It's a beauty, isn't it? "

Thurston made no answer to this. He advanced to the table and stood at its edge, contemplating the thing which his visitor had been so anxious to exhibit. He found himself staring at an ivory statue of the god Ganesha, and wondering at the exquisite beauty of the workmanship, the subtle tints of the ivory, the atmosphere of the mystic East, which its mere dumb presence suggested and conveyed.

It was not a thing of any great size—its height was some ten inches, its breadth six; a cigar-box would have held it. And to Thurston, steeped to the lips in the odour and colour of the Orient, it represented a world of art and of dreams. He stared at the god; the god stared at him out of a pair of amethyst eyes, cunningly set into the creamy white of the ivory. A strange intoxication stole into Thurston's soul. He heard himself presently talking in set fashion, calmly, methodically, as though he were in a shop, buying something. He heard his visitor's replies.

" You want to sell this? "

" Yes, sir, I want to sell it. I'll tell you how I came by it, too, Mr. Thurston. All's above-board; and Mr. Evanson, he knows me well, and knew me before I fell on hard times. It was this way, sir: My father was in the army at the time of the Mutiny, and he saw a good deal of fighting out in India —Delhi and Lucknow and elsewhere—and he brought home a good many curiosities, and that image amongst them. It's the image of some Hindu god, so I'm told, and, of course, anybody can see that the workmanship is excellent. My father gave it to me on his deathbed, and charged me never to part with it, because there's some legend about its bringing luck with it. But it's brought no luck to me," continued Thurston's visitor, with a dismal laugh. " I've been down on my luck for some time. However, it will bring luck if you're agreeable to buy it, sir. Perhaps that's where the luck comes in."

" What price do you set upon it? " asked Thurston mechanically.

"Well, sir, I, of course, don't know anything about these matters. I was recommended to take the carving to Mr. Evanson," said the man, "and he advised me to see you. I should be quite satisfied to take what he said he thought it was worth."

"What was that?" said Thurston.

"Twenty pounds, sir."

The man uttered these words with some anxiety, and his eyes fastened themselves on Thurston's face, as if to watch the effect. Thurston, however, was still fascinated by the ivory god, and neither eyes nor lips betrayed anything. He remained silent for some moments. At last he started, as from a reverie.

"I am quite prepared to accept Mr. Evanson's estimate of the carving's value," he said. "I will give you twenty pounds for it."

The man bowed his untidy head, and sighed deeply. It was evident that the prospect of immediate possession of twenty pounds was very grateful to him.

"Thank you, sir," he said.

Thurston went over to his desk, unlocked a drawer, and produced a cashbox, which, on examination, proved to contain twenty-two pound notes and gold. He counted out twenty to his visitor, put two pounds in his own pocket, restored the depleted cashbox to its drawer and locked it up again, and then, asking the vendor his name and address, wrote out a formal receipt. Five minutes later the unkempt person was descending the stairs, happy in the possession of a small fortune, and Thurston was left alone with the ivory god.

The clanging of the street door, far below, plunged the house into a weird silence. In its midst Thurston sighed deeply. There was a strange feeling within him that he had suddenly come into possession of something which he had been wanting all his life. It was akin to the feeling of the lover to whom the much-desired object of affection is at last given.

When the stranger first unwrapped the ivory god and revealed its strange charms to his eyes, Thurston became aware of a sense of satisfaction. This sense was now increasing to a point of something like delight. He drew in his nether lip, and began to utter a soft, sibilant sound, not unlike the purring of a cat. Not for many years had he experienced such a keen feeling of pleasure as that which now filled him.

He began looking about him for a suitable place wherein to enshrine his new acquisition. He glanced at the chimney-piece, already ornamented profusely with carvings from China, Japan, and India, with stones and vases from Peru, and turned away dissatisfied. The ivory god, he said to himself, must have a better setting than the chimney-piece offered. He wanted to have it near him while he wrote. There was something in the lines, in the dull white of the ivory, in the subtle purple tints of the amethyst eyes, which bade fair to soothe and to fascinate. He wished to have the ivory god upon his desk.

Looking about the room, he caught sight of a little triptych which he had bought years ago in Venice, admiring it more for the fineness of the wood and the carving than for the elementary art of the figure of Christ which was placed in the centre niche. Its dark wood, he thought, would make an admirable setting to the pallid tint of the ivory; and without hesitation he took it down from the wall, wrenched away the crucifix from the middle compartment, and installed the figure of the Hindu god in its place. Then he placed the triptych on the ledge above his desk, and stood back from it, admiring the bizarre effect. The amethyst eyes of the ivory god seemed to smile into his own.

Thurston tore himself away from his treasure at last, and went out to dine. He walked through the gloom of the badly-lighted London streets, until he came to the quiet restaurant wherein a certain corner had come to be almost sacred to him. He ate and drank mechanically and sparingly. A small quantity of plainly cooked food satisfied him at all times; he drank no wine or spirits or ale; after dinner he smoked a cigarette to the accompaniment of a cup of coffee, and glanced over his evening newspaper, handed to him by a waiter who knew him for an old and regular customer. Altogether he spent an hour at this restaurant; and on this particular evening there was an itching desire within him all the time to get back to his rooms. He wanted to examine the ivory god again, to look at it, to wonder about it. It was with a feeling of relief and of anticipation of coming pleasure that he finally paid his bill and went quickly away.

Thurston shut himself into his room with a great sense of satisfaction. He was alone in the midst of five millions of people—alone with the only things for which he cared, his books and his curiosities. Other men might dine and wine, go to theatres, balls, social functions. He cared for none of these things. He knew joys which were far deeper, far better worth having, and he could command their presence whenever he pleased to do so. So he fastened his outer door, drew a warm curtain over the inner one, turned up his lamp, and stirred his fire, and looked round about him with a sense of comfort. He saw the ivory god shining in the triptych above his desk, and caught the gleam of its amethyst eyes; and he was once more aware of the feeling that it in some strange way rounded off his life. He was glad to have it and to see it there, sitting above his altar like a presiding deity.

Thurston's next proceedings were significant and explanatory. He divested himself of his overcoat, and of the smartish morning-coat beneath it, and slipped into an old velvet jacket of undoubted antiquity; and, that done, he exchanged his boots for a comfortable and well-worn pair of slippers. And then, having made sure of his preliminaries, he unlocked a cupboard and produced a small decanter of curious shape, half filled with a golden-brown liquid, which seemed to sparkle and coruscate in the lamplight.

He set it on the table in the centre of the room, placed a glass of singular beauty—a deep crystal bowl set in twisted columns—at its side, and proceeded to heat water in a kettle. When the water was heated he made a careful mixture of it and the golden-brown liquid in the glass; and after that he curled himself up in an easy-chair facing the ivory god, with the glass and the decanter at his side.

Thurston had become a slave to the opium habit. Beginning the use of that attractive and insidious drug as a cure for some slight complaint, he had increased his doses, until at twenty-seven he made no excuses to himself for consuming it in large quantities.

During the day he took it in the form of pills, each containing a few grains; at night, following the example of De Quincey, he indulged in laudanum negus, sometimes sitting up until the grey of the morning broke in upon his dreams and fantasies.

He had long since relinquished all thought of giving up the habit. It had destroyed his moral courage once and for all, and had taken complete possession of him, mentally and physically. Under the influence of opium he was indifferent to everything in the world; and it was rarely that its influence was not upon him.

As the subtle charm of the drug stole through his brain, Thurston yielded himself up to the dreams which it induced.

His eyes were fixed on the ivory god. He began to speculate on its history, on the strange things which those amethyst eyes must have seen, on the deeds of blood, the mystic panorama of Eastern life, with its gorgeous colouring, its strange suggestion, which they must have watched unmoved. The phantasmagoria of a hundred worlds began to float, and finally to crystallise, before him.

In his estimation the carving was hundreds upon hundreds of years old. It must certainly have had its orginal abiding place in temple or palace, and of itself formed some part of the gorgeous picture which was rapidly shaping itself in Thurston's imagination.

Thurston's evenings were usually spent in a dream of bliss which was itself a source of deep mental content. He was surprised, on this occasion, to find that contemplation of the ivory god was leading him into a state of unusual unrest.

A strange desire to sit down at his desk—literally at the feet of the god—and write, filled him with strenuous force. It was years since he had ever written anything at night, and the mere thought of doing so now made him almost afraid. But the fear vanished quickly; and he was presently conscious of nothing but that he was shortly going to sit down at his desk. It was as if the ivory god had laid some command upon him. He turned up the flame of his spirit-lamp, heated more water, and mixed himself more of the drug. A little later he found himself laying out paper on his blotting-pad, and examining the nib of a pen. And after a time, as if it had been the most natural thing in the world, he settled himself in his elbow-chair, and after one long, searching look at the ivory god, he dipped his pen in the ink and began to write:

"This is the Story of the Loves and Hates of Men and Women that have long been Dust; the Story of a Day when the Red Earth was Young, and the Gods sat steadfast in their Places; the Story of a Time and Times; and behold it has never been told to Human Ear till Now!"

After that came a long night of work—of work such as Thurston had never before done in his life. It was ten o'clock when he wrote the first words on the top sheet of the pile of manuscript paper which he had laid ready to hand. As each successive hour struck on the silver-voiced clock on the chimney-piece it did but interrupt the gentle scribbling of a rapidly-moving pen.

On Thurston's left hand stood the spirit-lamp, the kettle, the decanter, the glass! now and then he turned to these things and mixed the drug. On his right hand there gradually accumulated a pile of closely-written manuscript. Above him, the amethyst eyes grew purple in the lamplight, the ivory god stared into the gloom beyond the writer's head.

The grey light stole through the cracks and crannies of the shutters, and found Thurston still writing. Much later, the old woman who acted as bedmaker and charwoman knocked loudly at the outer door. Thurston shouted to her to go away and leave him alone; and his pen travelled on and on as if it would never stop.

It was about three days after this that a famous publisher, with whom Thurston was acquainted in slight fashion, was somewhat astonished to find the latter waiting for him in his private room. He stared at Thurston curiously, noting with the keen eye of a practical man of the world that his visitor wore a strange expression, and seemed to be wrapped in an atmosphere of mystery.

He was shaved and washed, and wore his best garments; but there was a strange pallor on his face, a strange light in his eyes, and his voice was as unnaturally steady as the cold, almost lifeless hand which he placed within the publisher's palm.

The publisher, who had never been able to understand Thurston's strangeness of manner, reverted to an earlier suspicion, and wondered if his visitor had been drinking; but he failed to perceive either twitch or tremor in face or hand, and his visitor's voice was even and firm to the verge of monotony.

" Some time ago," said Thurston, " you were good enough to suggest to me that I should write a romance of Eastern life. It seemed to you that I possessed the necessary knowledge of the East to attempt such a book."

" Quite so," said the other. " I don't know any man

better fitted. You've been working in that direction all your life, haven't you? In fact, it's been a wonder to me that you never thought of the thing yourself."

Thurston produced a parcel of manuscript.

"I have here," he said, "a considerable portion of such a work. There is much that I might say to you about it, but at present I prefer not to say anything. Yes, it is not ordinary work, and I should like some assurance from you that it shall be read for you by some one competent to judge of its merits."

"I'll give it to Flintford to read," said the publisher. "How does his name strike you? He's about the best man I can think of."

"I am quite prepared to accept Mr. Flintford's judgment," replied Thurston. "Indeed, I intended suggesting his name to you. Then I will leave this portion of the manuscript with you?"

"Do," answered the publisher. "I'll send it on to Flintford by special messenger at once, and ask him to read it. About the rest of the book, now———"

"The remaining portion," said Thurston, "will be delivered to you when it is written." And with that and a frigid shaking of the publisher's outstretched hand he went away, walking through the outer office, as one of the clerks said, like a ghost.

The next morning Flintford walked into the publisher's office, looking very much excited.

"I say!" he exclaimed. "Where did you get that manuscript which you sent me yesterday? And have you got the rest?"

"Well, what of it?" asked the publisher, ignoring the second part of the question. "Is it good stuff? Will it do? Would it sell?"

"Good! My dear sir, it is the most wonderful piece of imaginative work I ever read in my life. It is amazing, stupendous—quite confusing in its brilliance. I began it last night. I went on reading it until breakfast-time this morning," answered Flintford. "I never read anything quite like it. Indeed, I wouldn't have believed that we had a brain amongst us that could have imagined such a work. Look here! You know I am by no means an enthusiastic person. Well, this book, if it keeps up that level all through, is the biggest find of the last half-century. For sheer imagination the man beats Poe hollow! "

" You think it will make a hit? " inquired the publisher.

" It is the greatest thing I ever had put before me," answered the critic. " I cannot understand the power in it. Who is the man? How does he come to be able to re-create Hindu life as it must have been thousands of years ago? Where did he get such an overwhelming imagination? There's something that's almost unholy, unearthly, about the whole thing. It is a great book—a rare book. I should like to see the author."

" I will try to get him here at three this afternoon," said the publisher. " Come in after lunch. I may tell you that he is a strange person—never done anything but an occasional article in the heavy reviews, but, I fancy, cram full of the East."

" That," said the critic, " is evident. I'll come at three."

At three o'clock Thurston was shown into the publisher's private room, and introduced to the great critic. Thurston, if possible, was more ghostlike than ever; more emotionless; more insensible to any outward influence. He sat with fixed passionless eyes, listening, while the critic praised his work and asked questions. It was not until all this had been said that he spoke.

" I think I may take you both into my confidence," he said. " I conclude, Mr. Mayne, that you will publish this book, and therefore I see no reason why you and Mr. Flintford should be kept in ignorance as to its real history. I may tell you that the story is not mine at all: it is being dictated to me. The circumstances are peculiar; but I feel sure that Mr. Flintford, with his knowledge of the East, will quite understand. I recently came into possession of an image of the god Ganesha, wonderfully wrought in ivory and adorned with amethyst eyes. The story of which you have read some portion is being dictated to me by this image, or, more probably, by this god represented by it. I think you will understand," he said, turning to Flintford with an air which had something appealing in it.

" Yes," said Flintford quietly, " I quite understand."

" I felt the influence of the god," continued Thurston, " as soon as I saw the image. It is a strange, a very fascinating influence. It impelled me to write against my will; and then

I found that I was but a mouthpiece. Everything has been put into my lips—I should say, pen. Clearly, what I have written is the story of the image."

" And when," asked Flintford kindly, " when do you suppose the end of this story will be reached, Mr. Thurston?"

Thurston produced another packet of manuscript. He laid it on the publisher's desk.

" I believe," he said, " I believe the end will come to-night. If "—here he glanced from one face to the other—" if you would like to see the ivory statue, and could call to-morrow morning about noon, I will show it to you. It is certain that it possesses a strange influence."

When Thurston had gone away the two men looked at each other.

" Mad as a hatter! " said the publisher.

The critic shook his head.

" It seems strange," he said; " but, really, I don't think so. Does he drink? "

" I used to think he did," replied the publisher. " He has done work for me now and then, and he sometimes came here with all the symptoms of intoxication upon him, and yet he was always clear-headed and capable, if incoherent of speech. What I don't understand just now is the frightful deliberation with which he speaks, the sort of unearthly coldness and composure of his manner. But—I say!—to tell us that the book is being dictated to him by an ivory statue: surely that is an evidence of insanity! "

" Oh, but then genius and insanity are closely allied," said Flintford. " Well, let us call upon him to-morrow. In the meantime I'll take the manuscript he left with you. I expect it will cost me another sleepless night. You can't get away from it when you once begin—it's a live thing, Mayne."

" Come round about noon to-morrow," said Mayne.

It was half-past twelve next day when they climbed the stairs to Thurston's rooms. They knocked for some time at the outer door and evoked no answer; then Flintford climbed another flight of stairs and discovered the bedmaker woman, who resided nearer the sky, and appeared from a feast wherein onions had played a principal part.

" Mr. Thurston, sir? And indeed I 'aven't set eyes on 'im this morning, sir. Which 'is conduck 'ave of late been most extrornary—me not being able to make no beds, nor

nothink," said she. " A lit'ry gent, sir, which from long
ixperience is very trying to anybody to deal with. You
might knock again, sir; and if so as he doesn't answer, why,
I must open the door with my key, and see if the poor
gentleman isn't well, for never a word did he give me at
ten o'clock."

When the door was opened at last, they found Thurston
quite dead. His arms were crossed over the final page of his
manuscript; his head was bowed upon them, as if, tired out
with his long spell of labour, he had laid it down there and
gone to sleep. Above him, the ivory god looked out of its
amethyst eyes into the shadowy corner of the silent room.

DANIEL DEFOE

THE APPARITION OF MRS. VEAL

THIS thing is so rare in all its circumstances, and on so good authority, that my reading and conversation has not given me anything like it. It is fit to gratify the most ingenious and serious inquirer. Mrs. Bargrave is the person to whom Mrs. Veal appeared after her death; she is my intimate friend, and I can avouch for her reputation for these last fifteen or sixteen years, on my own knowledge; and I can confirm the good character she had from her youth to the time of my acquaintance. Though, since this relation, she is calumniated by some people that are friends to the brother of Mrs. Veal who appeared, who think the relation of this appearance to be a reflection, and endeavour what they can to blast Mrs. Bargrave's reputation and to laugh the story out of countenance. But the circumstances thereof, and the cheerful disposition of Mrs. Bargrave, notwithstanding the unheard-of ill usage of a very wicked husband, there is not the least sign of dejection in her face; nor did I ever hear her let fall a desponding or murmuring expression; nay, not when actually under her husband's barbarity, which I have been witness to, and several other persons of undoubted reputation.

Now you must know that Mrs. Veal was a maiden gentle-woman of about thirty years of age, and for some years last past had been troubled with fits, which were perceived coming on her by her going off from her discourse very abruptly to some impertinence. She was maintained by an only brother, and kept his house in Dover. She was a very pious woman, and her brother a very sober man to all appearance; but now he does all he can to null or quash the story. Mrs. Veal was intimately acquainted with Mrs. Bargrave from her childhood. Mrs. Veal's circumstances were then mean; her father did not take care of his children as he ought, so that they were exposed to hardships. And Mrs. Bargrave in those days had as unkind a father, though she wanted for neither food nor clothing; whilst Mrs. Veal wanted for both.

So that it was in the power of Mrs. Bargrave to be very much her friend in several instances, which mightily endeared Mrs. Veal, insomuch that she would often say, "Mrs. Bargrave, you are not only the best, but the only friend I have in the world; and no circumstances of life shall ever dissolve my friendship." They would often condole each other's adverse fortune and read together *Drelincourt upon Death,* and other good books; and so, like two Christian friends, they comforted each other under their sorrow.

Some time after, Mr. Veal's friends got him a place in the custom-house at Dover, which occasioned Mrs. Veal, by little and little, to fall off from her intimacy with Mrs. Bargrave; though there was never any such thing as a quarrel; but an indifferency came on by degrees, till at last Mrs. Bargrave had not seen her in two years and a half; though above a twelvemonth of the time Mrs. Bargrave had been absent from Dover, and this last half-year has been in Canterbury about two months of the time, dwelling in a house of her own.

In this house, on the eighth of September last, viz. 1705, she was sitting alone in the forenoon, thinking over her unfortunate life, and arguing herself into a due resignation to Providence, though her condition seemed hard: " And," said she, " I have been provided for hitherto, and doubt not but I shall be still, and am well satisfied that my afflictions shall end when it is most fit for me." And then took up her sewing work, which she had no sooner done but she hears a knocking at the door; she went to see who it was there, and this proved to be Mrs. Veal, her old friend, who was in a riding-habit. At that moment of time the clock struck twelve at noon.

" Madam," says Mrs. Bargrave, " I am surprised to see you, you have been so long a stranger "; but told her she was glad to see her, and offered to salute her, which Mrs. Veal complied with, till their lips almost touched, and then Mrs. Veal drew her hand cross her own eyes, and said, " I am not very well," and so waived it. She told Mrs. Bargrave she was going a journey, and had a great mind to see her first. " But," says Mrs. Bargrave, " how came you to take a journey alone? I am amazed at it, because I know you have so fond a brother." " Oh," says Mrs. Veal, " I gave my brother the slip, and came away, because I had so great a mind to see you before I took my journey." So Mrs. Bargrave went in with

her into another room within the first, and Mrs. Veal sat
herself down in an elbow chair, in which Mrs. Bargrave was
sitting when she heard Mrs. Veal knock. Then says Mrs.
Veal, " My dear friend, I am come to renew our old friendship again, and to beg your pardon for my breach of it; and
if you can forgive me, you are one of the best women."
" Oh," says Mrs. Bargrave, " don't mention such a thing; I
have not had an uneasy thought about it. I can easily forgive it." " What did you think of me? " says Mrs. Veal.
Says Mrs. Bargrave, " I thought you were like the rest of
the world, and that prosperity had made you forget yourself
and me." Then Mrs. Veal reminded Mrs. Bargrave of the
many friendly offices she did her in former days, and much
of the conversation they had with each other in the time of
their adversity; what books they read, and what comfort in
particular they received from Drelincourt's *Book of Death*,
which was the best, she said, on that subject was ever wrote.
She also mentioned Doctor Sherlock, and two Dutch books,
which were translated, wrote upon death, and several others.
But Drelincourt, she said, had the clearest notions of death
and of the future state of any who have handled that subject. Then she asked Mrs. Bargrave whether she had Drelincourt. She said, " Yes." Says Mrs. Veal, " Fetch it." And
so Mrs. Bargrave goes upstairs and brings it down. Says
Mrs. Veal, " Dear Mrs. Bargrave, if the eyes of our faith
were as open as the eyes of our body, we should see numbers
of angels about us for our guard. The notions we have of
Heaven now are nothing like what it is, as Drelincourt says;
therefore be comforted under afflictions, and believe that
the Almighty has a particular regard to you, and that your
afflictions are marks of God's favour; and when they have
done the business they were sent for, they shall be removed
from you. And believe me, my dear friend, believe what I
say to you, one minute of future happiness will infinitely
reward you for all your sufferings. For I can never believe "
(and claps her hand upon her knee with a great deal of
earnestness, which, indeed, ran through all her discourse)
" that ever God will suffer you to spend all your days in this
afflicted state. But be assured that your afflictions shall leave
you, or you them, in a short time." She spake in that pathe-
tical and heavenly manner that Mrs. Bargrave wept several
times, she was so deeply affected with it.

Then Mrs. Veal mentioned Doctor Horneck's *Ascetic,* at the end of which he gives an account of the lives of the primitive Christians. Their pattern she recommended to our imitation, and said; " Their conversation was not like this of our age. For now," says she, " there is nothing but frothy vain discourse, which is far different from theirs. Theirs was to edification, and to build one another up in the faith, so that they were not as we are, nor are we as they are. But," said she, " we might do as they did; there was a hearty friendship among them; but where is it now to be found? " Says Mrs. Bargrave, " It is hard indeed to find a true friend in these days." Says Mrs. Veal, " Mr. Norris has a fine copy of verses, called *Friendship in Perfection,* which I wonderfully admire. Have you seen the book? " says Mrs. Veal. " No," says Mrs. Bargrave, " but I have the verses of my own writing out." " Have you? " says Mrs. Veal; " then fetch them "; which she did from above stairs, and offered them to Mrs. Veal to read, who refused, and waived the thing, saying; " holding down her head would make it ache "; and then desired Mrs. Bargrave to read them to her, which she did. As they were admiring *Friendship,* Mrs. Veal said, " Dear Mrs. Bargrave; I shall love you for ever." In the verses there is twice used the word " Elysium." " Ah! " says Mrs. Veal, " these poets have such names for Heaven." She would often draw her hand cross her own eyes, and say, " Mrs. Bargrave, don't you think I am mightily impaired by my fits? " " No," says Mrs. Bargrave; " I think you look as well as ever I knew you."

After all this discourse, which the apparition put in words much finer than Mrs. Bargrave said she could pretend to, and was much more than she can remember—for it cannot be thought that an hour and three quarters' conversation could all be retained, though the main of it she thinks she does —she said to Mrs. Bargrave she would have her write a letter to her brother, and tell him she would have him give rings to such and such; and that there was a purse of gold in her cabinet, and that she would have two broad pieces given to her cousin Watson.

Talking at this rate; Mrs. Bargrave thought that a fit was coming upon her, and so placed herself in a chair just before her knees, to keep her from falling to the ground, if her fits should occasion it; for the elbow-chair, she thought, would

keep her from falling on either side. And to divert Mrs.
Veal, as she thought, she took hold of her gown-sleeve several
times, and commended it. Mrs. Veal told her it was a
scoured silk, and newly made up. But, for all this, Mrs.
Veal persisted in her request, and told Mrs. Bargrave she
must not deny her. And she would have her tell her brother
all their conversation, when she had an opportunity. "Dear
Mrs. Veal," says Mrs. Bargrave, "this seems so impertinent
that I cannot tell how to comply with it; and what a morti-
fying story will our conversation be to a young gentleman."
"Well," says Mrs. Veal, "I must not be denied." "Why,"
says Mrs. Bargrave, "'tis much better, methinks, to do it
yourself." "No," says Mrs. Veal; "though it seems impertinent to you now, you will see more reason for it hereafter." Mrs. Bargrave, then, to satisfy her importunity, was
going to fetch a pen and ink, but Mrs. Veal said, "Let it
alone now, and do it when I am gone; but you must be sure
to do it"; which was one of the last things she enjoined her
at parting, and so she promised her.

Then Mrs. Veal asked for Mrs. Bargrave's daughter. She
said she was not at home. "But if you have a mind to see
her," says Mrs. Bargrave, "I'll send for her." "Do," says
Mrs. Veal; on which she left her, and went to a neighbour's
to send for her; and by the time Mrs. Bargrave was returning, Mrs. Veal was got without the door in the street, in the
face of the beast-market, on a Saturday (which is market-
day), and stood ready to part as soon as Mrs. Bargrave came
to her. She asked her why she was in such haste. She said
she must be going, though perhaps she might not go her
journey till Monday; and told Mrs. Bargrave she hoped she
should see her again at her cousin Watson's before she went
whither she was a-going. Then she said she would not take
her leave of her, and walked from Mrs. Bargrave, in her view,
till a turning interrupted the sight of her, which was three-
quarters after one in the afternoon.

Mrs. Veal died the seventh of September, at twelve o'clock
at noon, of her fits, and had not above four hours' senses
before her death, in which time she received the sacrament.
The next day after Mrs. Veal's appearing, being Sunday,
Mrs. Bargrave was mightily indisposed with a cold and a sore
throat, that she could not go out that day; but on Monday
morning she sends a person to Captain Watson's to know if

Mrs. Veal were there. They wondered at Mrs. Bargrave's inquiry, and sent her word she was not there, nor was expected. At this answer, Mrs. Bargrave told the maid she had certainly mistook the name or made some blunder. And though she was ill, she put on her hood and went herself to Captain Watson's, though she knew none of the family, to see if Mrs. Veal was there or not. They said they wondered at her asking, for that she had not been in town; they were sure, if she had, she would have been there. Says Mrs. Bargrave, "I am sure she was with me on Saturday almost two hours." They said it was impossible, for they must have seen her if she had. In comes Captain Watson, while they were in dispute, and said that Mrs. Veal was certainly dead, and her escutcheons were making. This strangely surprised Mrs. Bargrave, who went to the person immediately who had the care of them, and found it true. Then she related the whole story to Captain Watson's family; and what gown she had on, and how striped; and that Mrs. Veal told her it was scoured. Then Mrs. Watson cried out, "You have seen her indeed, for none knew but Mrs. Veal and myself that the gown was scoured." And Mrs. Watson owned that she described the gown exactly; "for," said she, "I helped her to make it up." This Mrs. Watson blazed all about the town, and avouched the demonstration of the truth of Mrs. Bargrave's seeing Mrs. Veal's apparition. And Captain Watson carried two gentlemen immediately to Mrs. Bargrave's house to hear the relation from her own mouth. And then it spread so fast that gentlemen and persons of quality, the judicious and sceptical part of the world, flocked in upon her, which at last became such a task that she was forced to go out of the way; for they were in general extremely satisfied of the truth of the thing, and plainly saw that Mrs. Bargrave was no hypochondriac, for she always appears with such a cheerful air and pleasing mien that she has gained the favour and esteem of all the gentry; and it is thought a great favour if they can but get the relation from her own mouth. I should have told you before that Mrs. Veal told Mrs. Bargrave that her sister and brother-in-law were just come down from London to see her. Says Mrs. Bargrave, "How came you to order matters so strangely?" "It could not be helped," said Mrs. Veal. And her brother and sister did come to see her, and entered the town of Dover just as

Mrs. Veal was expiring. Mrs. Bargrave asked her whether she would not drink some tea. Says Mrs. Veal, "I do not care if I do; but I'll warrant this mad fellow"—meaning Mrs. Bargrave's husband—"has broke all your trinkets." "But," says Mrs. Bargrave, "I'll get something to drink in for all that"; but Mrs. Veal waived it, and said, "It is no matter; let it alone"; and so it passed.

All the time I sat with Mrs. Bargrave, which was some hours, she recollected fresh sayings of Mrs. Veal. And one material thing more she told Mrs. Bargrave, that old Mr. Breton allowed Mrs. Veal ten pounds a year, which was a secret, and unknown to Mrs. Bargrave till Mrs. Veal told it her.

Mrs. Bargrave never varies in her story, which puzzles those who doubt of the truth, or are unwilling to believe it. A servant in a neighbour's yard adjoining to Mrs. Bargrave's house heard her talking to somebody an hour of the time Mrs. Veal was with her. Mrs. Bargrave went out to her next neighbour's the very moment she parted with Mrs. Veal, and told what ravishing conversation she had with an old friend, and told the whole of it. Drelincourt's *Book of Death* is, since this happened, bought up strangely. And it is to be observed that, notwithstanding all this trouble and fatigue Mrs. Bargrave has undergone upon this account, she never took the value of a farthing, nor suffered her daughter to take anything of anybody, and therefore can have no interest in telling the story.

But Mr. Veal does what he can to stifle the matter, and said he would see Mrs. Bargrave; but yet it is certain matter of fact that he has been at Captain Watson's since the death of his sister, and yet never went near Mrs. Bargrave; and some of his friends report her to be a great liar, and that she knew of Mr. Breton's ten pounds a year. But the person who pretends to say so has the reputation of a notorious liar among persons which I know to be of undoubted repute. Now, Mr. Veal is more a gentleman than to say she lies, but says a bad husband has crazed her; but she needs only present herself and it will effectually confute that pretence. Mr. Veal says he asked his sister on her death-bed whether she had a mind to dispose of anything. And she said no. Now what the things which Mrs. Veal's apparition would have disposed of were so trifling, and nothing of justice aimed at in

their disposal, that the design of it appears to me to be only
in order to make Mrs. Bargrave so to demonstrate the truth
of her appearance as to satisfy the world of the reality thereof
as to what she had seen and heard, and to secure her reputation among the reasonable and understanding part of mankind.   And then, again, Mr. Veal owns that there was a
purse of gold; but it was not found in her cabinet, but in a
comb-box.   This looks improbable; for that Mrs. Watson
owned that Mrs. Veal was so very careful of the key of her
cabinet that she would trust nobody with it; and if so, no
doubt she would not trust her gold out of it.   And Mrs.
Veal's often drawing her hands over her eyes, and asking Mrs.
Bargrave whether her fits had not impaired her, looks to me
as if she did it on purpose to remind Mrs. Bargrave of her
fits, to prepare her not to think it strange that she should
put her upon writing to her brother, to dispose of rings and
gold, which looked so much like a dying person's bequest;
and it took accordingly with Mrs. Bargrave as the effect of
her fits coming upon her, and was one of the many instances
of her wonderful love to her and care of her, that she should
not be affrighted, which, indeed, appears in her whole
management, particularly in her coming to her in the day-
time, waiving the salutation, and when she was alone; and
then the manner of her parting, to prevent a second attempt
to salute her.

Now, why Mr. Veal should think this relation a reflection
—as 'tis plain he does, by his endeavouring to stifle it—I
can't imagine; because the generality believe her to be a good
spirit, her discourse was so heavenly.   Her two great errands
were, to comfort Mrs. Bargrave in her affliction, and to ask
her forgiveness for her breach of friendship, and with a pious
discourse to encourage her.   So that, after all, to suppose that
Mrs. Bargrave could hatch such an invention as this, from
Friday noon to Saturday noon—supposing that she knew of
Mrs. Veal's death the very first moment—without jumbling
circumstances, and without any interest, too, she must be
more witty, fortunate, and wicked too, than any indifferent
person, I dare say, will allow.   I asked Mrs. Bargrave several
times if she was sure she felt the gown.   She answered
modestly, " If my senses be to be relied on, I am sure of it."
I asked her if she heard a sound when she clapped her hand
upon her knee.   She said she did not remember she did, and

she said she appeared to be as much as substance as I did who talked with her. "And I may," said she, "be as soon persuaded that your apparition is talking to me now as that I did not really see her; for I was under no manner of fear, I received her as a friend, and parted with her as such. I would not," says she, "give one farthing to make any one believe it; I have no interest in it; nothing but trouble is entailed upon me for a long time, for aught that I know; and, had it not come to light by accident, it would never have been made public." But now she says she will make her own private use of it, and keep herself out of the way as much as she can; and so she has done since. She says she had a gentleman who came thirty miles to her to hear the relation; and that she had told it to a room full of people at a time. Several particular gentlemen have had the story from Mrs. Bargrave's own mouth.

This thing has very much affected me, and I am as well satisfied, as I am of the best-grounded matter of fact. And why we should dispute matter of fact, because we cannot solve things of which we can have no certain or demonstrative notions, seems strange to me: Mrs. Bargrave's authority and sincerity alone would have been undoubted in any other case.

E. F. BENSON

THE THING IN THE HALL

THE following pages are the account given me by Dr. Assheton of the Thing in the Hall. I took notes, as copious as my quickness of hand allowed me, from his dictation, and subsequently read to him this narrative in its transcribed and connected form. This was on the day before his death, which indeed probably occurred within an hour after I had left him, and, as readers of inquests and such atrocious literature may remember, I had to give evidence before the coroner's jury. Only a week before Dr. Assheton had to give similar evidence, but as a medical expert, with regard to the death of his friend, Louis Fielder, which occurred in a manner identical with his own. As a specialist, he said he believed that his friend had committed suicide while of unsound mind, and the verdict was brought in accordingly. But in the inquest held over Dr. Assheton's body, though the verdict eventually returned was the same, there was more room for doubt.

For I was bound to state that only shortly before his death, I read what follows to him; that he corrected me with extreme precision on a few points of detail, that he seemed perfectly himself, and that at the end he used these words:

"I am quite certain as a brain specialist that I am completely sane, and that these things happened not merely in my imagination, but in the external world. If I had to give evidence again about poor Louis, I should be compelled to take a different line. Please put that down at the end of your account, or at the beginning, if it arranges itself better so."

There will be a few words I must add at the end of this story, and a few words of explanation must precede it. Briefly, they are these.

Francis Assheton and Louis Fielder were up at Cambridge together, and there formed the friendship that lasted nearly till their death. In general attributes no two men could have been less alike, for while Dr. Assheton had become at the age of thirty-five the first and final authority on his subject, which was the functions and diseases of the brain, Louis Fielder at the same age was still on the threshold of achievement. Assheton, apparently without any brilliance at all, had by careful and incessant work arrived at the top of his profession, while Fielder, brilliant at school, brilliant at college, and brilliant ever afterwards, had never done anything. He was too eager, so it seemed to his friends, to set about the dreary work of patient investigation and logical deductions; he was for ever guessing and prying, and striking out luminous ideas, which he left burning, so to speak, to illumine the work of others. But at bottom, the two men had this compelling interest in common, namely, an insatiable curiosity after the unknown, perhaps the most potent bond yet devised between the solitary units that make up the race of man. Both—till the end—were absolutely fearless, and Dr. Assheton would sit by the bedside of a man stricken with bubonic plague to note the gradual surge of the tide of disease with the same absorption as Fielder would study X-rays one week, flying machines the next, and spiritualism the third. The rest of the story, I think, explains itself—or does not quite do so. This, anyhow, is what I read to Dr. Assheton, being the connected narrative of what he had himself told me. It is he, of course, who speaks.

．　　　．　　　．　　　．　　　．

"After I returned from Paris, where I had studied under Charcot, I set up practice at home. The general doctrine of hypnotism, suggestion, and cure by such means had been accepted even in London by this time, and, owing to a few papers I had written on the subject, together with my foreign diplomas, I found that I was a busy man almost as soon as I had arrived in town. Louis Fielder had his ideas about how I should make my début (for he had ideas on every subject, and all of them original), and entreated me to come and live not in the stronghold of doctors, 'Chloroform Square,' as he called it, but down in Chelsea, where there was a house vacant next his own.

"'Who cares where a doctor lives,' he said, 'so long as he cures people? Besides, you don't believe in old methods; why believe in old localities? Oh, there is an atmosphere of painless death in Chloroform Square! Come and make people live instead! And on most evenings I shall have so much to tell you; I can't " drop in " across half London.'

" Now if you have been abroad for five years, it is a great deal to know that you have any intimate friends at all still left in the metropolis, and, as Louis said, to have that intimate friend next door, is an excellent reason for going next door. Above all, I remembered from Cambridge days, what Louis' ' dropping in ' meant. Towards bed-time, when work was over, there would come a rapid step on the landing, and for an hour, or two hours, he would gush with ideas. He simply diffused life, which is ideas, wherever he went. He fed one's brain, which is the one thing which matters. Most people who are ill, are ill because their brain is starving, and the body rebels, and gets lumbago or cancer. That is the chief doctrine of my work such as it has been. All bodily disease springs from the brain. It is merely the brain that has to be fed and rested and exercised properly to make the body absolutely healthy, and immune from all disease. But when the brain is affected, it is as useful to pour medicines down the sink, as make your patient swallow them, unless—and this is a paramount limitation—unless he believes in them.

" I said something of the kind to Louis one night, when, at the end of a busy day, I had dined with him. We were sitting over coffee in the hall, or so it is called, where he takes his meals. Outside, his house is just like mine, and ten thousand other small houses in London, but on entering, instead of finding a narrow passage with a door on one side, leading into the dining-room, which again communicates with a small back room called ' the study,' he has had the sense to eliminate all unnecessary walls, and consequently the whole ground floor of his house is one room, with stairs leading up to the first floor. Study, dining-room, and passage have been knocked into one; you enter a big room from the front door. The only drawback is that the postman makes loud noises close to you, as you dine, and just as I made these commonplace observations to him about the effect of the brain on the body and the senses, there came a loud rap, somewhere close to me, that was startling.

" ' You ought to muffle your knocker,' I said, 'anyhow during the time of meals.'

" Louis leaned back and laughed.

" ' There isn't a knocker,' he said. ' You were startled a
week ago, and said the same thing. So I took the knocker
off. The letters slide in now. But you heard a knock, did
you? '

" ' Didn't you? ' said I.

" ' Why, certainly. But it wasn't the postman. It was
the Thing. I don't know what it is. That makes it so
interesting.'

" Now if there is one thing that the hypnotist, the believer
in unexplained influences, detests and despises, it is the whole
root-notion of spiritualism. Drugs are not more opposed to
his belief than the exploded, discredited idea of the influence
of spirits on our lives. And both are discredited for the
same reason; it is easy to understand how brain can act on
brain, just as it is easy to understand how body can act on
body, so that there is no more difficulty in the reception of
the idea that the strong mind can direct the weak one, than
there is in the fact of a wrestler of greater strength overcoming one of less. But that spirits should rap at furniture and
divert the course of events is as absurd as administering phos-
phorus to strengthen the brain. That was what I thought
then.

" However, I felt sure it was the postman, and instantly
rose and went to the door. There were no letters in the
box, and I opened the door. The postman was just ascend-
ing the steps. He gave the letters into my hand.

" Louis was sipping his coffee when I came back to the
table.

" ' Have you ever tried table-turning? ' he asked. ' It's
rather odd.'

" ' No, and I have not tried violet-leaves as a cure for
cancer,' I said.

" ' Oh, try everything,' he said. ' I know that that is your
plan, just as it is mine. All these years that you have been
away, you have tried all sorts of things, first with no faith,
then with just a little faith, and finally with mountain-
moving faith. Why, you didn't believe in hypnotism at all
when you went to Paris.'

" He rang the bell as he spoke, and his servant came up
and cleared the table. While this was being done we strolled
about the room, looking at prints, with applause for a Barto-
lozzi that Louis had bought in the New Cut, and dead silence

over a ' Perdita ' which he had acquired at considerable cost. Then he sat down again at the table on which we had dined. It was round, and mahogany-heavy, with a central foot divided into claws.

" ' Try its weight,' he said; ' see if you can push it about.'

" So I held the edge of it in my hands, and found that I could just move it. But that was all; it required the exercise of a good deal of strength to stir it.

" ' Now put your hands on the top of it,' he said, ' and see what you can do.'

" I could not do anything, my fingers merely slipped about on it. But I protested at the idea of spending the evening thus.

" ' I would much sooner play chess or noughts and crosses with you,' I said, ' or even talk about politics, than turn tables. You won't mean to push, nor shall I, but we shall push without meaning to.'

" Louis nodded.

" ' Just a minute,' he said, ' let us both put our fingers only on the top of the table and push for all we are worth from right to left.'

" We pushed. At least I pushed, and I observed his finger-nails. From pink they grew to white, because of the pressure he exercised. So I must assume that he pushed too. Once, as we tried this, the table creaked. But it did not move.

" Then there came a quick peremptory rap, not I thought on the front door, but somewhere in the room.

" ' It's the Thing,' said he.

" To-day, as I speak to you, I suppose it was. But on that evening it seemed only like a challenge. I wanted to demonstrate its absurdity.

" ' For five years, on and off, I've been studying rank spiritualism,' he said. ' I haven't told you before, because I wanted to lay before you certain phenomena, which I can't explain, but which now seem to me to be at my command. You shall see and hear, and then decide if you will help me.'

" ' And in order to let me see better, you are proposing to put out the lights,' I said.

" ' Yes; you will see why.'

" ' I am here as a sceptic,' said I.

" ' Scep away,' said he.

"Next moment the room was in darkness, except for a very faint glow of firelight. The window-curtains were thick, and no street-illumination penetrated them, and the familiar cheerful sounds of pedestrians and wheeled traffic came in muffled. I was at the side of the table towards the door; Louis was opposite me, for I could see his figure dimly silhouetted against the glow from the smouldering fire.

"'Put your hands on the table,' he said, 'quite lightly, and—how shall I say it?—expect.'

"Still protesting in spirit, I expected. I could hear his breathing rather quickened, and it seemed to me odd that anybody could find excitement in standing in the dark over a large mahogany table, expecting. Then—through my finger-tips, laid lightly on the table, there began to come a faint vibration, like nothing so much as the vibration through the handle of a kettle when water is beginning to boil inside it. This got gradually more pronounced and violent till it was like the throbbing of a motor-car. It seemed to give off a low humming note. Then quite suddenly the table seemed to slip from under my fingers and began very slowly to revolve.

"'Keep your hands on it and move with it,' said Louis, and as he spoke I saw his silhouette pass away from in front of the fire, moving as the table moved.

"For some moments there was silence, and we continued, rather absurdly, to circle round keeping step, so to speak, with the table. Then Louis spoke again, and his voice was trembling with excitement.

"'Are you there?' he said.

"There was no reply, of course, and he asked it again. This time there came a rap like that which I had thought during dinner to be the postman. But whether it was that the room was dark, or that despite myself I felt rather excited too, it seemed to me now to be far louder than before. Also it appeared to come neither from here nor there, but to be diffused through the room.

"Then the curious revolving of the table ceased, but the intense, violent throbbing continued. My eyes were fixed on it, though owing to the darkness I could see nothing, when quite suddenly a little speck of light moved across it, so that for an instant I saw my own hands. Then came another and another, like the spark of matches struck in the dark, or like fire-flies crossing the dusk in southern gardens. Then came another knock of shattering loudness, and the throbbing of the table ceased, and the lights vanished.

· · · · ·

" Such were the phenomena at the first *séance* at which I was present, but Fielder, it must be remembered, had been studying, ' expecting,' he called it, for some years. To adopt spiritualistic language (which at that time I was very far from doing), he was the medium, I merely the observer, and all the phenomena I had seen that night were habitually produced or witnessed by him. I make this limitation since he told me that certain of them now appeared to be outside his own control altogether. The knockings would come when his mind, as far as he knew, was entirely occupied in other matters, and sometimes he had even been awakened out of sleep by them. The lights were also independent of his volition.

" Now my theory at the time was that all these things were purely subjective in him, and that what he expressed by saying that they were out of his control, meant that they had become fixed and rooted in the unconscious self, of which we know so little, but which, more and more, we see to play so enormous a part in the life of a man. In fact, it is not too much to say that the vast majority of our deeds spring, apparently without volition, from this unconscious self. All hearing is the unconscious exercise of the aural nerve, all seeing of the optic, all walking, all ordinary movement seem to be done without the exercise of will on our part. Nay more, should we take to some new form of progression, skating, for instance, the beginner will learn with falls and difficulty the outside edge, but within a few hours of his having learned his balance on it, he will give no more thought to what he learned so short a time ago as an acrobatic feat, than he gives to the placing of one foot before the other.

" But to the brain specialist all this was intensely interesting, and to the student of hypnotism, as I was, even more so, for (such was the conclusion I came to after this first séance), the fact that I saw and heard just what Louis saw and heard was an exhibition of thought-transference which in all my experience in the Charcot-schools I had never seen surpassed, if indeed rivalled. I knew that I was myself ex-

tremely sensitive to suggestion, and my part in it this evening I believed to be purely that of the receiver of suggestions
so vivid that I visualised and heard these phenomena which
existed only in the brain of my friend.

"We talked over what had occurred upstairs. His view
was that the Thing was trying to communicate with us.
According to him it was the Thing that moved the table and
tapped, and made us see streaks of light.

"'Yes, but the Thing,' I interrupted, 'what do you mean?
Is it a great-uncle—oh, I have seen so many relatives appear
at *séances*, and heard so many of their dreadful platitudes—
or what is it? A spirit? Whose spirit?'

"Louis was sitting opposite to me, and on the little table
before us there was an electric light. Looking at him I saw
the pupil of his eye suddenly dilate. To the medical man—
provided that some violent change in the light is not the
cause of the dilation—that meant only one thing, terror.
But it quickly resumed its normal proportion again.

"Then he got up, and stood in front of the fire.

"'No, I don't think it is great-uncle anybody,' he said.
'I don't know, as I told you, what the Thing is. But if you
ask me what my conjecture is, it is that the Thing is an
Elemental.'

"'And pray explain further. What is an Elemental?'

"Once again his eye dilated.

"'It will take two minutes,' he said. 'But, listen. There
are good things in this world, are there not, and bad things?
Cancer, I take it is bad, and—and fresh air is good; honesty
is good, lying is bad. Impulses of some sort direct both sides,
and some power suggests the impulses. Well, I went into this
spiritualistic business impartially. I learned to "expect," to
throw open the door into the soul, and I said, "Anyone may
come in." And I think Something has applied for admission,
the Thing that tapped and turned the table and struck
matches, as you saw, across it. Now the control of the evil
principle in the world is in the hands of a power which en-
trusts its errands to the things which I call Elementals. Oh,
they have been seen; I doubt not that they will be seen again.
I did not, and do not ask good spirits to come in. I don't
want "The Church's One Foundation" played on a musical
box. Nor do I *want* an Elemental. I only threw open the
door. I believe the Thing has come into my house, and is

"Look, what's that?" he said.   "There on the wall."

establishing communication with me. Oh, I want to go the whole hog. What is it? In the name of Satan, if necessary, what is it? I just want to know.'

.   .   .   .   .

"What followed I thought then might easily be an invention of the imagination, but what I believed to have happened was this. A piano with music on it was standing at the far end of the room by the door, and a sudden draught entered the room, so strong that the leaves turned. Next the draught troubled a vase of daffodils, and the yellow heads nodded. Then it reached the candles that stood close to us, and they fluttered, burning blue and low. Then it reached me, and the draught was cold, and stirred my hair. Then it eddied, so to speak, and went across to Louis, and his hair also moved, as I could see. Then it went downwards towards the fire, and flames suddenly started up in its path, blown upwards. The rug by the fireplace flapped also.

" ' Funny, wasn't it? ' he asked.

" ' And has the Elemental gone up the chimney? ' said I.

" ' Oh, no,' said he, ' the Thing only passed us.'

"Then suddenly he pointed at the wall just behind my chair, and his voice cracked as he spoke.

" ' Look, what's that? ' he said. ' There on the wall.'

"Considerably startled I turned in the direction of his shaking finger. The wall was pale grey in tone, and sharp-cut against it was a shadow that, as I looked, moved. It was like the shadow of some enormous slug, legless and fat, some two feet high by about four feet long. Only at one end of it was a head shaped like the head of a seal, with open mouth and panting tongue.

"Then even as I looked it faded, and from somewhere close at hand there sounded another of those shattering knocks.

"For a moment after there was silence between us, and horror was thick as snow in the air. But, somehow neither Louis nor I was frightened for more than one moment. The whole thing was so absorbingly interesting.

" ' That's what I mean by its being outside my control,' he said. ' I said I was ready for any—any visitor to come in, and by God, we've got a beauty.'

.   .   .   .   .

"Now I was still, even in spite of the appearance of this shadow, quite convinced that I was only taking observations of a most curious case of disordered brain accompanied by the most vivid and remarkable thought-transference. I believed that I had not seen a slug-like shadow at all, but that Louis had visualised this dreadful creature so intensely that I saw what he saw. I found also that his spiritualistic trash-books, which I thought a truer nomenclature than text-books, mentioned this as a common form for Elementals to take. He on the other hand was more firmly convinced than ever that we were dealing not with a subjective but an objective phenomenon.

.   .   .   .   .

"For the next six months or so we sat constantly, but made no further progress, nor did the Thing or its shadow appear again, and I began to feel that we were really wasting time. Then it occurred to me, to get in a so-called medium, induce hypnotic sleep, and see if we could learn anything further. This we did, sitting as before round the dining-room table. The room was not quite dark, and I could see sufficiently clearly what happened.

"The medium, a young man, sat between Louis and myself, and without the slightest difficulty I put him into a light hypnotic sleep. Instantly there came a series of the most terrific raps, and across the table there slid something more palpable than a shadow, with a faint luminance about it, as if the surface of it was smouldering. At the moment the medium's face became contorted to a mask of hellish terror; mouth and eyes were both open, and the eyes were focussed on something close to him. The Thing waving its head came closer and closer to him, and reached out towards his throat. Then with a yell of panic, and warding off this horror with his hands, the medium sprang up, but it had already caught hold, and for the moment he could not get free. Then simultaneously Louis and I went to his aid, and my hands touched something cold and slimy. But pull as we could we could not get it away. There was no firm hand-hold to be taken; it was as if one tried to grasp slimy fur, and the touch of it was horrible, unclean, like a leper. Then, in a sort of despair, though I still could not believe that the horror was real, for it must be a vision of diseased imagination, I remembered that the switch of the four electric lights was close to my hand. I turned them all on. There on the floor lay the medium, Louis was kneeling by him with a face of wet paper, but there was nothing else there. Only the collar of the medium was crumpled and torn, and on his throat were two scratches that bled.

"The medium was still in hypnotic sleep, and I woke him. He felt at his collar, put his hand to his throat and found it bleeding, but, as I expected, knew nothing whatever of what had passed. We told him that there had been an unusual manifestation, and he had, while in sleep, wrestled with something. We had got the result we wished for, and were much obliged to him.

"I never saw him again. A week after that he died of blood-poisoning.

.   .   .   .

"From that evening dates the second stage of this adventure. The Thing had materialised (I use again spiritualistic language which I still did not use at the time). The huge slug, the Elemental, manifested itself no longer by knocks and waltzing tables, nor yet by shadows. It was there in a form that could be seen and felt. But it still—this was my strong point—was only a thing of twilight; the sudden kindling of the electric light had shown us that there was nothing there. In this struggle perhaps the medium had clutched his own throat, perhaps I had grasped Louis' sleeve, he mine. But though I said these things to myself, I am not sure that I believed them in the same way that I believe the sun will rise to-morrow.

"Now as a student of brain-functions and a student in hypnotic affairs, I ought perhaps to have steadily and unremittingly pursued this extraordinary series of phenomena. But I had my practice to attend to, and I found that with the best will in the world, I could think of nothing else except the occurrence in the hall next door. So I refused to take part in any further *séance* with Louis. I had another reason also. For the last four or five months he was becoming depraved. I have been no prude or Puritan in my own life, and I hope I have not turned a Pharisaical shoulder on sinners. But in all branches of life and morals, Louis had become infamous. He was turned out of a club for cheating

at cards, and narrated the event to me with gusto. He had
become cruel; he tortured his cat to death; he had become
bestial. I used to shudder as I passed his house, expecting I
knew not what fiendish thing to be looking at me from the
window.

"Then came a night only a week ago, when I was
awakened by an awful cry, swelling and falling and rising
again. It came from next door. I ran downstairs in my
pyjamas, and out into the street. The policeman on the beat
had heard it too, and it came from the hall of Louis' house,
the window of which was open. Together we burst the door
in. You know what we found. The screaming had ceased
but a moment before, but he was dead already. Both
jugulars were severed, torn open.

.   .   .   .   .

"It was dawn, early and dusky when I got back to my
house next door. Even as I went in something seemed to
push by me, something soft and slimy. It could not be
Louis' imagination this time. Since then I have seen glimpses
of it every evening. I am awakened at night by tappings,
and in the shadows in the corner of my room there sits something more substantial than a shadow."

.   .   .   .   .

Within an hour of my leaving Dr. Assheton, the quiet
street was once more aroused by cries of terror and agony.
He was already dead, and in no other manner than his friend,
when they got into the house.

GUY DE MAUPASSANT

NIGHT

A NIGHTMARE

I LOVE night passionately. I love it as one loves one's country or one's mistress. I love it with all my senses, with my eyes which see it, with my sense of smell which inhales it, with my ears which listen to its silence, with my whole body which is caressed by its shadows. The larks sing in the sunlight, in the blue heavens, in the warm air, in the light air of clear mornings. The owl flies at night, a sombre patch passing through black space, and, rejoicing in the black immensity that intoxicates him, he utters a vibrant and sinister cry.

In the day-time I am tired and bored. The day is brutal and noisy. I rarely get up, I dress myself languidly and I go out regretfully. Every movement, every gesture, every word, every thought, tires me as though I were raising a crushing load.

But when the sun goes down a confused joy invades my whole being. I awaken and become animated. As the shadows lengthen I feel quite different, younger, stronger, more lively, happier. I watch the great soft shadows falling from the sky and growing deeper. They envelop the city like an impenetrable and impalpable wave; they hide, efface and destroy colours and forms; they embrace houses, people and buildings in their imperceptible grasp. Then I would like to cry out with joy like the screech-owls, to run upon the roofs like the cats, and an impetuous, invincible desire to love burns in my veins. I go, I walk, sometimes in the darkened outskirts of Paris, sometimes in the neighbouring woods, where I hear my sisters, the beasts, and my brothers, the poachers, prowling.

One is killed at last by what one loves violently. But how shall I explain what happens to me? How can I ever make people understand that I am able to tell it? I do not know, I cannot tell. I only know that this is—that is all.

Well, yesterday—was it yesterday?—Yes, no doubt, unless
it was earlier, a day, a month, a year earlier . . . I do not
know, but it must have been yesterday, because since then no
day has risen, no sun has dawned. But how long has it been
night? How long? Who can tell? Who will ever know?

Yesterday, then, I went out after dinner, as I do every
evening. It was very fine, very mild, very warm. As I
went down towards the boulevards I looked above my head
at the black streams full of stars, outlined in the sky between
the roofs of the houses, which were turning round and
causing this rolling stream of stars to undulate like a real
river.

Everything was distinct in the clear air, from the planets
to the gas-light. So many lights were burning above, in the
city, that the shadows seemed luminous. Bright nights are
more joyful than days of bright sunshine. The cafés on the
boulevard were flaring; people were laughing, passing up and
down, drinking. I went into a theatre for a few moments.
Into what theatre, I cannot tell. There was so much light in
there that I was depressed, and I came out again with my
heart saddened by the clash of brutal light on the gold of
the balcony, by the factitious glitter of the great crystal
chandelier, by the glaring footlights, by the melancholy of
this artificial and crude light. I arrived at the Champs-
Elysées, where the open-air concerts look like conflagrations
in the branches. The chestnut-trees, touched with yellow
light, look as if they were painted, like phosphorescent trees.
The electric bulbs, like pale dazzling moons, like eggs from
the moon, fallen from heaven, like monstrous, living pearls,
caused the streaks of gas-light, filthy, ugly gas-light and the
garland of coloured, lighted glasses to grow pale beneath their
pearly, mysterious and regal light.

I stopped beneath the Arc de Triomphe to look at the
Avenue, the long and wonderful, starry Avenue, leading to
Paris between two rows of fire and the stars! The stars
above, the unknown stars, thrown haphazard through infinity, where they form those strange shapes which make us
dream and think so much.

I entered the Bois de Boulogne, where I remained for a
long, long time. I was seized by a strange thrill, a powerful
and unforeseen emotion, an exaltation of mind which bordered on frenzy. I walked on and on, and then I returned.

What time was it when I passed again beneath the Arc de
Triomphe? I do not know. The city was sleeping, and
clouds, great black clouds, were slowly spreading over the
sky.

For the first time I felt that something strange was going
to happen, something new.

It seemed to be getting cold, that the air was becoming
thicker, that night, my beloved night, was weighing heavily
upon my heart. The Avenue was deserted now. Two
solitary policemen were walking near the cab-stand, and a
string of vegetable carts was going to the Halles along the
roadway, scarcely lit by the gas-jets, which seemed to be
dying out. They moved along slowly, laden with carrots,
turnips and cabbages. The invisible drivers were asleep, the
horses were walking with an even step, following the carts
in front of them, and making no noise on the wooden pavement. As they passed each lamp on the footpath, the carrots
showed up red in the light, the turnips white, the cabbages
green, and they passed one after another, these carts which
were as red as fire, as white as silver, and as green as emeralds.
I followed them, then I turned into the Rue Royale and
returned to the boulevards. There was nobody to be seen;
none of the cafés was open; only a few belated pedestrians
hurried by. I had never seen Paris so dead and so deserted.
I looked at my watch. It was two o'clock.

Some force was driving me, the desire to walk. So I went
as far as the Bastille. There I became aware that I had never
seen so dark a night, for I could not even see the Colonne de
Juillet, whose Genius in gold was lost in the impenetrable
obscurity. A curtain of clouds as dense as the ether had
buried the stars and seemed to be descending upon the world
to blot it out.

I retraced my steps. There was nobody about me. However, at the Place du Château d'Eau, a drunken man almost
bumped into me, then disappeared. For some time I could
hear his sonorous and uneven steps. I went on. At the top
of the Faubourg Montmartre a cab passed, going in the direction of the Seine. I hailed it but the driver did not reply.
Near the Rue Drouot a woman was loitering: " Listen,
dearie,"—I hastened my steps to avoid her outstretched hand.
Then there was nothing more. In front of the Vaudeville
Theatre a rag-picker was searching in the gutter. His little

lantern was moving just above the ground. I said to him:
" What time is it, my good man? "

" How do I know? " he grumbled. " I have no watch."

Then I suddenly perceived that the lamps had all been
extinguished. I know that at this time of year they are put
out early, before dawn, for the sake of economy. But daylight was still far off, very far off indeed!

" Let us go to the Halles," I said to myself; " there at least
I shall find life."

I set off, but it was too dark even to see the way. I advanced slowly, as one does in a forest, recognising the streets
by counting them. In front of the Crédit Lyonnais a dog
growled. I turned up the Rue de Grammont and lost my
way. I wandered about, and then I recognised the Bourse by
the iron railings around it. The whole of Paris was sleeping,
a deep, terrifying sleep. In the distance a cab rumbled, one
solitary cab, perhaps it was the one which had passed me a
while back. I tried to reach it, going in the direction of the
noise, through streets that were lonely and dark, dark and
sombre as death. Again I lost my way. Where was I?
What nonsense to put out the lights so soon! Not one person
passing by. Not one late reveller, not even
the mewing of an amorous cat? Nothing.

Where on earth were the police? I said to myself: " I
will shout and they will come." I shouted. There was no
answer. I called more loudly. My voice vanished without
an echo, weak, muffled, stifled by the night, the impenetrable
night. I yelled: " Help! Help! Help! " My desperate cry
remained unanswered. What time was it? I pulled out my
watch, but I had no matches. I listened to the gentle tick-
tick of the little mechanism with a strange and unfamiliar
pleasure. It seemed to be a living thing. I felt less lonely.
What a mystery. I resumed my walk like a blind man,
feeling my way along the wall with my stick, and every
moment I raised my eyes to the heavens, hoping that day
would dawn at last. But the sky was dark, all dark, more
profoundly dark than the city.

What could the time be? It seemed to me I had been
walking an infinite length of time, for my legs were giving
way beneath me, my breast was heaving and I was suffering
horribly from hunger. I decided to ring at the first street
door. I pulled the copper bell and it rang sonorously through

the house. It sounded strangely, as if that vibrating noise were alone in the house. I waited. There was no answer. The door did not open. I rang again. I waited again— nothing! I got frightened! I ran to the next house; and, twenty times in succession, I rang the bells in the dark corridors where the concierge was supposed to sleep, but he did not awake. I went on further, pulling the bells and the knockers with all my strength, kicking and knocking with my hand and stick on the doors, which remained obstinately closed.

Suddenly I perceived that I had reached the Halles. The market was deserted, not a sound, not a movement, not a cart, not a man, not a bundle of flowers or vegetables—it was empty, motionless, abandoned, dead. I was seized with a horrible terror. What was happening? Oh, my God, what was happening?

I set off again. But the time? The time? Who would tell me the time? Not a clock struck in the churches or the public buildings. I thought: "I will open the glass of my watch and feel the hands with my fingers." I pulled out my watch. . . . It was not going. . . . It had stopped. Nothing more, nothing more, not a ripple in the city, not a light, not the slightest suspicion of a sound in the air. Nothing! Nothing more! not even the distant rumbling of a cab! Nothing more. I had reached the quays, and a cold chill rose from the river. Was the Seine still flowing? I wanted to know, I found the steps and went down. I could not hear the current rushing under the bridge. . . . A few more steps. . . . Then sand. . . . Mud . . . then water. I dipped my hand into it. It was flowing . . . flowing . . . cold . . . cold . . . cold . . . almost frozen . . . almost dried up . . . almost dead.

I fully realised that I should never have the strength to come up, and that I was going to die there . . . in my turn, of hunger, fatigue and cold.

THE DROWNED MAN

I

EVERY one in Fécamp knew the story of old Mother Patin. She had undoubtedly been unhappy with her man, had old Mother Patin; for her man had beaten her during his lifetime, as a man threshes wheat in his barns.

He was owner of a fishing-smack, and had married her long ago, because she was nice, although she was poor.

Patin, a good seaman, but a brute, frequented old Auban's tavern, where, on ordinary days, he drank four or five brandies, and on days when he had made a good catch, eight or ten, and even more, according how he felt, as he said.

The brandy was served to customers by old Auban's daughter, a pleasant-faced, dark-haired girl, who drew custom to the house merely by her good looks, for no one had ever wagged a tongue against her.

When Patin entered the tavern, he was content to look at her and talk civilly to her, quiet, decent conversation. When he had drunk the first brandy, already he found her nicer; at the second, he was winking at her; at the third, he was saying: "Miss Désirée, if you would only . . ." without ever finishing the sentence; at the fourth, he was trying to hold her by her petticoat to embrace her; and when he had reached the tenth, it was old Auban who served him with the rest.

The old wine-seller, who knew every trick of the trade, used to send Désirée round between the tables to liven up the orders for drinks; and Désirée, who was not old Auban's daughter for nothing, paraded her petticoat among the drinkers and bandied jests, with a smile on her lips, and a twinkle in her eye.

By dint of drinking brandies, Patin grew so familiar with Désirée's face that he thought of it even at sea, when he threw his nets into the water, out on the open sea, on windy

nights and calm nights, on moonlit nights and black nights.
He thought of it as he held the helm in the stern of his boat,
while his four companions slept with their heads on their
arms. He saw her always smiling at him, pouring out the
yellow brandy with a lift of her shoulders, then coming
towards him, saying:
" There! Is this what you want? "
And by dint of treasuring her so in eye and mind, he
reached such a pitch of longing to marry her that, unable to
restrain himself longer, he asked her in marriage.

He was rich, owner of his boat, his nets and a house at the
foot of the cliff, on the Retenue; while old Auban had
nothing. He was, therefore, accepted eagerly, and the wedding took place as quickly as possible, both parties being,
for different reasons, anxious to make it an accomplished
fact.

But three days after the marriage was over, Patin was no
longer able to imagine in the least how he had come to think
Désirée different from other women. He must have been a
rare fool to hamper himself with a penniless girl who had
wheedled him with her cognac, so she had, with the cognac
into which she had put some filthy drug for him.

And he went cursing along the shore, breaking his pipe
between his teeth, swearing at his tackle; and having cursed
heartily, with every term he could think of, everything he
knew, he spat out the anger still left in his stomach on the
fish and crabs that he drew one by one out of his nets, throwing them into the baskets to an accompaniment of oaths and
foul words.

Then, returning to his house, where he had his wife, old
Auban's daughter, within reach of his tongue and his hand,
he soon began to treat her as the lowest of the low. Then,
as she listened resignedly, being used to the paternal violence,
he became exasperated by her calm, and one evening he beat
her. After this, his home became a place of terror.

For ten years, nothing was talked of on the Retenue but
the beatings Patin inflicted on his wife, and his habit of
cursing when he spoke to her, whatever the occasion. He
cursed, in fact, in a unique way, with a wealth of vocabulary
and a forceful vigour of delivery possessed by no other man
in Fécamp. As soon as his boat reached the harbour mouth,
back from fishing, they waited expectantly for the first

broadside he would discharge on the pier, from his deck, the moment he saw the white bonnet of his other half.

Standing in the stern, he tacked, his glance fixed ahead and on the sheets when the sea was running high, and in spite of the close attention required by the narrow, difficult passage, in spite of the great waves running mountain-high in the narrow gully, he endeavoured to pick out—from the midst of the women waiting in the spray of the breakers for the sailors—his woman, old Auban's daughter, the pauper wench.

Then, as soon as he saw her, in spite of the clamour of waves and wind, he poured on her a volley of abuse with such vocal energy that every one laughed at it, although they pitied her deeply. Then, when his boat reached the quay, he had a way of discharging his ballast of civilities, as he said, while he unloaded his fish, which attracted round him all the rascals and idlers of the harbour.

It issued from his mouth, now like cannon-shots, terrible and short, now like thunderclaps that rolled for five minutes, such a tempest of oaths that he seemed to have in his lungs all the storms of the Eternal Father.

Then, when he had left his boat, and met among the curious spectators and fishwives, he fished up again from the bottom of the hold a fresh cargo of insults and hard words, and escorted her in such fashion to their home, she in front, he behind, she weeping, he shouting.

Then, alone with her, doors shut, he beat her on the least pretext. Anything was enough to make him lift his hand, and once he had begun, he never stopped, spitting in her face, all the time, the real causes of his hate. At each blow, at each thump, he yelled: " Oh, you penniless slut, oh, you gutter-snipe, oh, you miserable starveling, I did a fine thing the day I washed my mouth out with the firewater of your scoundrel of a father."

She passed her days now, poor woman, in a state of incessant terror, in a continuous trembling of soul and of body, in stunned expectation of insults and thrashings.

And this lasted for ten years. She was so broken that she turned pale when she talked to anyone, no matter who; and no longer thought of anything but the beatings that threatened her, and she had grown as skinny, yellow and dried up as a smoked fish.

II

ONE night when her man was at sea she was awakened by the noise like the growling of a beast which the wind makes when it gets up, like an unleashed hound. She sat up in bed, uneasy, then, hearing nothing more, lay down again; but almost at once, there was a moaning in the chimney that shook the whole house and ran across the whole sky as if a pack of furious animals had crossed the empty spaces panting and bellowing.

Then she got up and ran to the harbour. Other women were running from all sides with lanterns. Men ran up and every one watched the foam flashing white in the darkness on the crest of the waves out at sea.

The storm lasted fifteen hours. Eleven sailors returned no more, and Patin was among them.

The wreckage of his boat, the *Jeune-Amélie,* was recovered off Dieppe. Near Saint-Valéry, they picked up the bodies of his sailors, but his body was never found. As the hull of the small craft had been cut in two, his wife for a long time expected and dreaded his return; for if there had been a collision, it might have happened that the colliding vessel had taken him on board, and carried him to a distant country.

Then, slowly, she grew used to the thought that she was a widow, even though she trembled every time that a neighbour or a beggar or a tramping pedlar entered her house abruptly.

One afternoon, almost four years after the disappearance of her man, she stopped, on her way along the Rue aux Juifs before the house of an old captain who had died recently, and whose belongings were being sold.

Just at that moment, they were auctioning a parrot, a green parrot with a blue head, which was regarding the crowd with a discontented and uneasy air.

"Three francs," cried the auctioneer, "a bird that talks like a lawyer, three francs."

A friend of Widow Patin jogged her elbow.

"You ought to buy that, you're rich," she said. "It would be company for you; he is worth more than thirty francs, that bird. You can always sell him again for twenty to twenty-five easy."

"Four francs, ladies, four francs," the man repeated.

" He sings vespers and preaches like the priest. He's a phenomenon . . . a miracle! "

Widow Patin raised the bid by fifty centimes; and they handed her the hook-nosed creature in a little cage and she carried him off.

Then she installed him in her house, and as she was opening the iron-wire door to give the creature a drink, she got a bite on the finger that broke the skin and drew blood.

" Oh, the wicked bird," said she.

However, she presented him with hemp-seed and maize, then left him smoothing his feathers while he peered with a malicious air at his new home and his new mistress.

Next morning day was beginning to break, when widow Patin heard, with great distinctness, a loud, resonant, rolling voice, Patin's voice, shouting: " Get up, slut."

Her terror was such that she hid her head under the bed-clothes, for every morning, in the old days, as soon as he had opened his eyes, her dead husband shouted in her ears those three familiar words.

Trembling, huddled into a ball, her back turned to the thrashing that she was momentarily expecting, she murmured, her face hidden in the bed:

" God Almighty, he's here! God Almighty, he's here! He's come back, God Almighty! "

Minutes passed; no other sound broke the silence of her room. Then, shuddering, she lifted her head from the bed, sure that he was there, spying on her, ready to strike.

She saw nothing, nothing but a ray of sun falling across the window-pane, and she thought:

" He's hiding, for sure."

She waited a long time, then, a little reassured, thought:

" I must have been dreaming, seeing he doesn't show himself."

She was shutting her eyes again, a little reassured, when right in her ears the furious voice burst out, the thunderous voice of her drowned man, shouting:

" Damn and blast it, get up, you bitch."

She leaped out of bed, jerked out by her instinctive obedience, the passive obedience of a woman broken in by blows, who still remembers, after four years, and will always remember, and always obey that voice. And she said:

" Here I am, Patin. What do you want? "

But Patin did not answer.

Then, bewildered, she looked round her, and searched everywhere, in the cupboards, in the chimney, under the bed, still finding no one, and at last let herself fall into a chair, distracted with misery, convinced that the spirit of Patin itself was there, near her, come back to torture her.

Suddenly, she remembered the loft, which could be reached from outside by a ladder. He had certainly hidden himself there to take her by surprise. He must have been kept by savages on some shore, unable to escape sooner, and he had come back, more wicked than ever. She could not doubt it; the mere tone of his voice convinced her.

She asked, her head turned towards the ceiling:

" Are you up there, Patin? "

Patin did not answer.

Then she went out, and in an unutterable terror that set her heart beating madly, she climbed the ladder, opened the garret window, looked in, saw nothing, entered, searched, and found nothing.

Seated on a truss of hay, she began to cry; but while she was sobbing, shaken by an acute and supernatural terror, she heard, in the room below her, Patin telling his story. He seemed less angry, calmer, and he was saying:

" Filthy weather . . . high wind . . . filthy weather. I've had no breakfast, damn it."

She called through the ceiling:

" I'm here, Patin; I'll make you some soup. Don't be angry. I'm coming."

She climbed down at a run.

There was no one in her house.

She felt her body giving way as if Death had his hand on her, and she was going to run out to ask help from the neighbours, when just in her ear the voice cried:

" I've had no breakfast, damn it."

The parrot, in his cage, was watching her with his round, malicious, wicked eye.

She stared back at him, in amazement, murmuring:

" Oh, it's you."

He answered, shaking his head:

" Wait, wait, wait, I'll teach you to idle."

What were her thoughts? She felt, she realised that this was none other than the dead man, who had returned and hidden himself in the feathers of this creature, to begin tormenting her again, that he was going to swear, as of old, all day, and find fault with her, and shout insults to attract their neighbours' attention and make them laugh. Then she flung herself across the room, opened the cage, seized the bird, who defended himself and tore her skin with his beak and his claws. But she held him with all her might, in both hands, and throwing herself on the ground, rolled on top of him with mad frenzy, crushed him, made of him a mere rag of flesh, a little, soft, green thing that no longer moved or spoke, and hung limp. Then, wrapping him in a dish-cloth as a shroud, she went out, in her shift, bare-footed, crossed the quay, against which the sea was breaking in small waves, and shaking the cloth, let fall this small, green thing that looked like a handful of grass. Then she returned, threw herself on her knees before the empty cage, and utterly overcome by what she had done, she asked pardon of the good God, sobbing, as if she had just committed a horrible crime.

WHO KNOWS?

I

MY God! My God! So at last I am going to write down what has happened to me. But shall I be able to? Shall I dare?—so fantastic, so inexplicable, so incomprehensible, so crazy is it.

If I were not certain of what I had seen, certain that there has been no faulty link in my reasoning, no error in my investigations, no lacuna in the relentless sequence of my observations, I would have believed myself merely the victim of an hallucination, the sport of a strange vision. After all, who knows?

I am to-day in a private asylum; but I entered it voluntarily, urged thereto by prudence, and fear. Only one living creature knows my story. The doctor here. I am going to write it. I hardly know why. To rid myself of it, for it fills my thoughts like an unendurable nightmare.

Here it is:

I have always been a recluse, a dreamer, a sort of detached philosopher, full of kindly feeling, content with little, with no bitterness against men or resentment against heaven. I lived alone, all my life, because of a sort of uneasiness that the presence of other people induces in me. How can I explain it? I could not explain it. I don't refuse to see people, to talk to them, to dine with friends, but when I have endured their nearness for some time, even those with whom I am most intimate, they weary me, exhaust me, get on my nerves, and I suffer an increasing, exasperating longing to see them go or to go myself, to be alone.

This longing is more than a desire, it is an irresistible necessity. And if I had to endure the continued presence of the people in whose company I was, if I were compelled, not to listen but to go on for any length of time hearing their conversation, some accident would certainly befall me. What? Ah, who knows? Perhaps merely a fainting fit? Yes, probably that!

I have such a passion for solitude that I cannot even endure the nearness of other people sleeping under my roof: I cannot live in Paris because of the indefinable distress I feel there. I endure spiritual death, and I am tortured, too, in my body and my nerves by the vast crowd that swarms and lives round me, even when it sleeps. Ah, the slumber of others is more unendurable to me than their speech! And I can never rest when at the other side of the wall I am aware of lives held in suspense by these regular eclipses of consciousness.

Why am I so made? Who knows? The cause is perhaps quite simple. I am quickly wearied of all that exists outside myself. And there are many like me.

There are two races on earth. Those who need others, who are distracted, occupied and refreshed by others, who are worried, exhausted and unnerved by solitude as by the ascension of a terrible glacier or the crossing of a desert; and those, on the other hand, who are wearied, bored, embarrassed, utterly fatigued by others, while isolation calms them, and the detachment and imaginative activity of their minds bathes them in peace.

In fact, this is a usual psychical phenomenon. Some people are made to live an outward life, others to live within themselves. I myself have a short and quickly exhausted power of attention to the outside world, and as soon as it has reached its limit, I suffer in my whole body and my whole mind an intolerable distress.

The result is that I attach myself, that I attached myself, strongly to inanimate things, that assume for me the importance of living creatures, and that my house has become, had become, a world where I lived a solitary and active life, surrounded by things, furniture, intimate trifles, as sympathetic to my eyes as faces. I had filled it with them little by little. I had decorated it with them, and I felt myself housed, content, satisfied, as happy as in the arms of a loving woman whose familiar caress was become a calm and pleasant need.

I had had this house built in a beautiful garden which shut it off from the roads, and within reach of a town where I could, when occasion arose, find the social resources to which, at odd moments, I felt impelled. All my servants slept in a distant building at the end of the kitchen-garden, which was surrounded by a great wall. The sombre folding down of the nights, in the silence of my habitation, lost, hidden, drowned under the leaves of great trees, was so tranquillising, so pleasant to me, that every evening I delayed going to bed for several hours, to enjoy it the longer.

That particular day, *Sigurd* had been played at the local theatre. It was the first time I had heard this beautiful, fairy-like musical drama, and it had given me the greatest pleasure.

I walked home, at a brisk pace, my head full of sounding rhythms, my eyes filled with visions of loveliness. It was dark, dark, so unfathomably dark that I could hardly make out the high road and several times almost went headlong into the ditch. From the toll-gate to my house is about two-thirds of a mile, perhaps a little more, maybe about twenty minutes' slow walking. It was one o'clock in the morning, one or half-past; the sky grew faintly light in front of me, and a slip of a moon rose, the wan slip of the moon's last quarter. The crescent moon of the first quarter, that rises at four or five o'clock in the evening, is brilliant, gay, gleaming like silver, but the moon that rises after midnight is tawny, sad and sinister: it is a real witches' Sabbath of a moon. Every walker by night must have made this observation. The moon of the first quarter, be it thin as a thread, sends out a small, joyous light that fills the heart with gladness and flings clear shadows over the earth; the moon of the last quarter scarcely spreads a dying light, so wan that it hardly casts any shadow at all.

I saw from some way off the sombre mass of my garden, and, sprung from I know not where, there came to me a certain uneasiness at the idea of entering it. I slackened my step. It was very mild. The heavy clump of trees looked like a tomb in which my house was buried.

I opened my gateway and made my way down the long avenue of sycamores which led to the house, arched and vaulted overhead like a high tunnel, crossing shadowy groves and winding round lawns where under the paling shadows clumps of flowers jewelled the ground with oval stains of indeterminate hues.

As I approached the house, a strange uneasiness took possession of me. I halted. There was no sound. There was not a breath of air in the leaves. " What's the matter with me? " I thought. For ten years I had entered in like manner without feeling the faintest shadow of disquietude. I was not afraid. I have never been afraid at night. The sight of a man, a marauder, a thief, would have filled me with fury, and I would have leaped on him without a moment's hesitation. Besides, I was armed. I had my revolver. But I did not touch it, for I wished to master this sense of terror that was stirring in me.

What was it? A presentiment? The mysterious presentiment that takes possession of one's senses when they are on the verge of seeing the inexplicable? Perhaps? Who knows?

With every step I advanced, I felt my skin creep, and when I was standing under the wall of my vast house, with its closed shutters, I felt the need of waiting a few moments before opening the door and going inside. So I sat down on a bench under the windows of my drawing-room. I remained there, a little shaken, my head leaning against the wall, my eyes open on the shadows of the trees. During these first instants, I noticed nothing unusual round me. I felt a sort of droning sound in my ears, but that often happened to me. It sometimes seems to me that I hear trains passing, that I hear clocks striking, that I hear the footsteps of a crowd.

Then shortly, these droning sounds became more distinct, more differentiated, more recognisable. I had been mistaken. It was not the usual throbbing sound of my pulse that filled my ears with these clamourings, but a very peculiar, though very confused noise that came, no doubt about it, from the interior of my house.

I made it out through the wall, this continuous noise, which was rather a disturbance than a noise, a confused movement of a crowd of things, as if all my furniture was being pushed, moved out of its place and gently dragged about.

For an appreciable time longer I doubted the evidence of my ears. But when I had pressed myself against a shutter the better to make out this strange disturbance of my house, I became convinced, certain, that something abnormal and incomprehensible was taking place in my house. I was not afraid but I was—how shall I say it?—stunned with astonishment. I did not draw my revolver—feeling quite sure that I should not need it. I waited.

I waited a long time, unable to come to any decision, my mind quite lucid, but wildly anxious. I waited, standing there, listening the whole time to the noise, that went on increasing: at times it rose to a violent pitch, and seemed to become a muttering of impatience, of anger, of a mysterious tumult.

Then suddenly, ashamed of my cowardice, I seized my bunch of keys, I chose the one I wanted, I thrust it in the lock, I turned it twice, and pushing the door with all my force, I sent the door clattering against the inner wall.

The crash rang out like a pistol shot, and, amazingly, from top to bottom of my house, a formidable uproar broke out in answer to this explosive sound. It was so sudden, so terrible, so deafening, that I recoiled some steps and although I still felt it to be useless, I drew my revolver from its holster.

I went on waiting, oh, not long. I could distinguish, now, an extraordinary tap-tapping on the steps of my staircase, on the floors, on the carpets, a tap-tapping, not of shoes, of slippers worn by human beings, but of crutches, wooden crutches, and iron crutches that rang out like cymbals. And then all at once I saw, on the threshold of my door, an arm-chair, my big reading-chair, come swaggering out. It set off through the garden. Others followed it, the chairs out of my drawing-room, then the low couches dragging themselves along like crocodiles on their short legs, then all my chairs, leaping like goats, and the little stools trotting along like hares.

Imagine the tumult of my mind! I slipped into a grove of trees, where I stayed, crouched, watching the whole time this march past of my furniture, for they were all taking their departure, one after the other, quickly or slowly, according to their shapes and weight. My piano, my large grand, passed galloping like a runaway horse, with a murmur of music in its depths; the smallest objects glided over the gravel like ants, brushes, glass dishes, goblets, where the moonlight hung glow-worm lamps. The hangings slithered past in whorls, like octopuses. I saw my writing-table appear, a rare piece of the last century, which contained all the letters I have received, the whole story of my heart, an old story which caused me so much suffering. And it held photographs too.

Suddenly, I was no longer afraid, I flung myself on it and seized it as one seizes a thief, as one seizes a flying woman; but it pursued its irresistible course, and in spite of my efforts, in spite of my anger, I could not even retard its progress. As I struggled desperately against this terrible force, I fell on the ground, still wrestling with it. Then it tumbled me over, dragged me over the gravel, and the pieces of furniture that were following it began to walk over me, trampling over my legs and bruising them; then, when I had loosed my hold of it, the others passed over my body like a cavalry charge over a dismounted soldier.

Mad with fear at last, I managed to drag myself out of the main avenue and to hide myself again among the trees, to watch the disappearance of the meanest, smallest, most overlooked by me, most insignificant objects that had belonged to me.

Then far away, in my house, now full of echoing sounds as empty houses are, I heard the dreadful sound of shutting doors. They clashed shut from top to bottom of the building, until the hall door that I myself, in my mad folly, had opened for their flight, had finally shut itself, last of all.

I fled too, running towards the town, and I did not recover my self-control until I was in the streets, and meeting belated wayfarers. I went and rang at the door of a hotel where I was known. I had beaten my clothes with my hands to remove the dust, and I explained that I had lost my bunch of keys which contained also the key of the kitchen-garden, where my servants were sleeping in a house isolated behind the enclosing wall that preserved my fruit and my vegetables from marauding visitors.

I buried myself up to my eyes in the bed they gave me. But I could not sleep, and I waited for daybreak, listening to the beating of my heart. I had given orders that my people were to be warned at dawn, and my man knocked on my door at seven o'clock in the morning.

His face seemed convulsed with emotion.

" A terrible thing happened last night, sir," he said.

" What's that? "

" The whole furniture of the house has been stolen, sir, everything, everything, down to the very smallest articles."

This news pleased me. Why? Who knows? I had myself absolutely in hand, absolutely determined to dissimulate, to say nothing to anyone about what I had seen, to hide it: bury it in my conscience like a frightful secret. I answered:

" They must be the same people who stole my keys. We

must warn the police at once. I will get up and be with you in a few moments."

The investigations lasted five months. They discovered nothing, they did not find the smallest of my possessions, not the faintest trace of the thieves. Lord! if I had told what I knew. If I had told . . . they would have shut me up, me, not the robbers, but the man who had been able to see such a thing.

Oh, I know enough to hold my tongue. But I did not refurnish my house. It was quite useless. The thing would have happened again and gone on happening. I did not want to enter the house again. I did not enter it. I never saw it again.

I went to Paris, to a hotel, and I consulted doctors on my nervous state, which had been giving me much uneasiness since that deplorable night.

They ordered me to travel. I followed their advice.

II

I BEGAN by travelling in Italy. The sun did me good. For six months I wandered from Genoa to Venice, Venice to Florence, Florence to Rome, Rome to Naples. Then I went over Sicily, a country alike notable for its climate and its monuments, relics of the Greek and Norman occupation. I went over to Africa, I peacefully crossed the huge, calm, yellow desert over which camels, gazelles and vagabond Arabs wander, and nothing haunts the light, crystalline air, either by night or day.

I returned to France by Marseilles, and despite the Provençal gaiety, the dimmer light of the sky saddened me. I felt, on returning to the Continent, the strange sensation of a sick man who believed himself cured and is warned by a dull pain that his malady is not yet quite extinct.

Then I came back to Paris. A month later, I was bored with it. It was autumn, and before winter came on, I wanted to make an expedition across Normandy, which I did not know.

I began at Rouen, of course, and for a week I wandered ecstatically, enthusiastically, through this mediæval city, in this amazing mirror of extraordinary Gothic monuments.

One afternoon, about four o'clock, as I was entering an

extraordinary street, in which a stream flows, black as ink, which they call " Robec Water," my attention, which was wholly fixed on the bizarre and antiquated character of the houses, was suddenly distracted by a glimpse of a line of second-hand dealers' shops which succeeded each other from door to door.

How well they had chosen their pitch, these obscene traffickers in rubbish, in this fantastic alley, perched above the evil watercourse, beneath the roofs bristling with tiles and slates on which the weather-cocks of bygone days still creaked!

Higgledy-piggledy in the depths of those dark shops, could be seen carved presses, Rouen, Neders, Moustiers pottery, painted statues, others in oak, Christs, Virgins, saints, church ornaments, chasubles, copes, even chalices, and a painted shrine from which the Almighty had decamped. Curious, are they not? these caverns in these tall houses, in these huge towns, filled from cellar to attic with every kind of article whose existence seemed ended, which outlived their natural owners, their century, their period, their fashion, to be bought by new generations as curiosities.

My weakness for trinkets reawakened in this stronghold of antiquaries. I went from stall to stall, crossing in two strides the bridges made of four rotten planks thrown across the nauseous Robec Water.

Heavens! What a shock! One of my most handsome wardrobes met my eyes at the end of a vault crowded with articles, looking like the entrance to the catacombs of a cemetery for old furniture. I drew nearer, trembling in every limb, trembling so much that I dared not touch it. I put out my hand, I hesitated. It was really it, after all: a unique Louis XIII wardrobe, easily recognisable by anyone who had ever seen it. Suddenly casting my eyes a little further, into the deeper shadows of the gallery, I caught sight of three of my arm-chairs, covered with *petit point* tapestry; then, still further back, my two Henri II tables, so rare that people came from Paris to look at them.

Think! Think of my state of mind!

I went on, aghast, tortured with emotion, still, I went forward, for I am a brave man, as a knight of the Dark Ages thrust his way into a nest of sorcery. Step by step, I found everything which had belonged to me, my chandeliers,

my books, my pictures, my hangings, my armours, everything except the desk full of my letters, which I could see
nowhere.

I went on, climbing down dim galleries, climbing up to
higher floors. I was alone. I shouted; no one answered. I
was alone; there was no one in this vast house, tortuous as a
maze.

Night fell, and I had to sit down in the shadows on one of
my own chairs, for I would not go away. From time to
time I called: "Hallo! Hallo! Is anyone there?"

I must have been there for certainly more than an hour
when I heard steps, light, slow footsteps, I don't know where.
I was on the point of fleeing, but taking heart, I called once
more and saw a light in an adjoining room.

"Who is there?" said a voice.

I replied: "A customer."

The answer came:

"It is very late to come into shops like this."

"I have been waiting for more than an hour," I returned.

"You could come back to-morrow!"

"To-morrow, I shall have left Rouen."

I dared not go forward, and he did not come. All the time,
I was watching the reflection of his light on a tapestry on
which two angels hovered above the bodies on a battle-field.
It, too, belonged to me. I said:

"Well! Are you coming?"

He answered:

"I am waiting for you."

I rose and went towards him.

In the middle of a large room stood a tiny man, tiny and
very fat, fat as a freak, a hideous freak.

He had a thin, straggling beard, thin-grown and yellowish,
and not a hair on his head. Not a hair! As he held his candle
at arm's length to see me the better, his skull looked to me
like a little moon in this vast room cluttered with old furniture. His face was wrinkled and swollen, his eyes scarcely
visible.

I bargained for three chairs, which were mine, and paid a
big price for them on the spot, giving only the number of my
room at the hotel. They were to be delivered before nine
o'clock on the following morning.

Then I went out. He accompanied me politely to the door.

I at once went to the head police station, where I related
the story of the theft of my furniture and of the discovery I
had just made.

He immediately asked for information by telegram from
the Department which had had charge of the burglary, asking me to wait for the reply.   An hour later a quite satisfactory answer arrived.

" I shall have this man arrested and questioned at once,"
the chief told me, " for he may possibly have been suspicious
and made away with your belongings. If you dine and come
back in a couple of hours, I will have him here and make him
undergo a fresh examination in your presence."

" Most certainly, sir.   My warmest thanks. . . ."

I went to my hotel and dined with a better appetite than I
could have believed possible. Still, I was contented enough.
They had him. Two hours later I went back to the chief
inspector, who was waiting for me.

" Well, sir," he said, as soon as he saw me, " they haven't
found your man. My fellows haven't been able to put their
hands on him! "

" Ah! " I felt that I should faint.   " But . . . you have
found his house all right? " I asked.

" Quite. It will be watched and held until he comes back.
But as for himself, vanished! "

" Vanished? "

" Vanished. Usually he spends the evenings with his neighbour, herself a dealer, a queer old witch, Widow Bidoin. She
has not seen him this evening and can give no information
about him. We must wait till to-morrow."

I departed. How sinister, how disturbing, how haunted
the streets of Rouen seemed to me!

I slept badly enough, with nightmares to drag me out of
each bout of sleep. As I did not want to appear either too
worried or in too much haste, I waited on the following day
until ten o'clock before going to the police station.

The dealer had not appeared. His shop was still shut.

The inspector said to me:

" I have taken all the necessary steps. The Department
has charge of the affair; we will go off together to this shop
and have it opened, and you shall point out your belongings
to me."

We were driven there in a carriage. Some policemen with

a locksmith were posted in front of the shop door, which stood open.

When I entered, I found neither my wardrobe, my armchairs, nor my tables, nor anything—nothing of what had furnished my house—absolutely nothing, even though on the previous evening I could not move a step without meeting one of my pieces.

The inspector, surprised, at first looked at me with distrust.

" Good God, sir! " I said, " the disappearance of this furniture coincides amazingly with the disappearance of the dealer."

He smiled:

" True enough. You were wrong to buy and pay for those things of yours yesterday. It put him on his guard! "

I replied:

" What seems incomprehensible to me is that all the places where my furniture stood are now occupied by other pieces! "

" Oh," answered the inspector, " he had the whole night, and accomplices too, no doubt. This house probably communicates with its neighbours. Never mind, sir, I am going to move very quickly in this matter. This rogue won't keep out of our hands very long, now we hold his retreat! "

.   .   .   .   .

Ah, my heart, my poor heart, how it was beating.

.   .   .   .   .

I stayed in Rouen for a fortnight. The man did not return. My God! My God! Is there any man alive who could confound, could overreach him? Then on the morning of the sixteenth day, I received from my gardener, the caretaker of my pillaged and still empty house, the following strange letter:

Sir,—

I beg to inform you that last night there occurred something which no one can fathom, the police no more than ourselves. All the furniture has come back, everything without exception, down to the very smallest objects. The house is now exactly the same as it was on the night of the burglary.

It is enough to drive one off one's head.   It happened during the night of Friday-Saturday.   The drive is cut up as if they had dragged everything from the gate to the door—exactly as it was on the day of the disappearance.

We await you, sir, while remaining,

Your obedient servant,

PHILIPPE RAUDIN.

Ah, no, no, no, no!   I will never go back there!

I took the letter to the police inspector.

" This restitution has been made very skilfully," he said. " Let's pretend to do nothing now.   We'll catch our man one of those days."

. . . . . .

But he is not caught.   No.   They haven't got him, and I am as afraid of him now as if he was a wild beast lurking behind me.

Not to be found!   He is not to be found, this moon-headed monster.   Never will he be caught.   He will never again come back to his house.   What does that matter to him!   I am the only person who could confront him, and I will not.

I will not!   I will not!   I will not!

And If he returns, If he comes back to his shop, who could prove that my furniture was in his place?   Mine is the only evidence against him; and I am well aware that it is regarded with suspicion.

Oh, no, such a life was no longer bearable.   And I could not keep the secret of what I had seen.   I could not go on living like anyone else with the dread that such happenings would begin again.

I went to see the doctor in charge of this private asylum, and told him the whole story.

After questioning me for a long time, he said:

" Would you be willing to remain here for some time? "

" Very willing."

" You have means? "

" Yes."

" You would like separate quarters? "

" Yes."

" Would you care to see friends? "

"No, not a soul. The man from Rouen might dare, for vengeance' sake, to follow me here."

. . . . .

And I have been alone, alone, quite alone, for three months. I am almost at peace. I have only one fear. . . . Suppose the antique-dealer went mad . . . and suppose they brought him to this retreat. . . . The prisons themselves are not safe. . . .

NATHANIEL HAWTHORNE

YOUNG GOODMAN BROWN

YOUNG Goodman Brown came forth at sunset into the street of Salem village; but put his head back, after crossing the threshold, to exchange a parting kiss with his young wife. And Faith, as the wife was aptly named, thrust her own pretty head into the street, letting the wind play with the pink ribbons of her cap while she called to Goodman Brown.

"Dearest heart," whispered she, softly and rather sadly, when her lips were close to his ear, "prithee put off your journey until sunrise and sleep in your own bed to-night. A lone woman is troubled with such dreams and such thoughts that she's afeared of herself sometimes. Pray tarry with me this night, dear husband, of all nights in the year."

"My love and my Faith," replied young Goodman Brown, "of all nights in the year, this one night must I tarry away from thee. My journey, as thou callest it, forth and back again, must needs be done 'twixt now and sunrise. What, my sweet, pretty wife, dost thou doubt me already, and we but three months married?"

"Then God bless you!" said Faith, with the pink ribbons; "and may you find all well when you come back."

"Amen!" cried Goodman Brown. "Say thy prayers, dear Faith, and go to bed at dusk, and no harm will come to thee."

So they parted; and the young man pursued his way until, being about to turn the corner by the meeting-house, he looked back and saw the head of Faith still peeping after him with a melancholy air, in spite of her pink ribbons.

"Poor little Faith!" thought he, for his heart smote him. "What a wretch am I to leave her on such an errand! She talks of dreams, too. Methought as she spoke, there was trouble in her face, as if a dream had warned her what work is to be done to-night. But no, no; 'twould kill her to think it. Well, she's a blessed angel on earth; and after this one night I'll cling to her skirts and follow her to heaven."

With this excellent resolve for the future, Goodman Brown

felt himself justified in making more haste on his present evil purpose. He had taken a dreary road, darkened by all the gloomiest trees of the forest, which barely stood aside to let the narrow path creep through, and closed immediately behind. It was all as lonely as could be; and there is this peculiarity in such a solitude, that the traveller knows not who may be concealed by the innumerable trunks and the thick boughs overhead; so that with lonely footsteps he may yet be passing through an unseen multitude.

" There may be a devilish Indian behind every tree," said Goodman Brown to himself; and he glanced fearfully behind him as he added, " What if the Devil himself should be at my very elbow! "

His head being turned back, he passed a crook of the road, and, looking forward again, beheld the figure of a man, in grave and decent attire, seated at the foot of an old tree. He arose at Goodman Brown's approach and walked onward side by side with him.

" You are late, Goodman Brown," said he. " The clock of the Old South was striking as I came through Boston; and that is full fifteen minutes agone."

" Faith kept me back awhile," replied the young man, with a tremor in his voice, caused by the sudden appearance of his companion, though not wholly unexpected.

It was now deep dusk in the forest, and deepest in that part of it where these two were journeying. As nearly as could be discerned, the second traveller was about fifty years old, apparently in the same rank of life as Goodman Brown, and bearing a considerable resemblance to him, though perhaps more in expression than features. Still they might have been taken for father and son. And yet, though the elder person was as simply clad as the younger and as simple in manner too, he had an indescribable air of one who knew the world, and who would not have felt abashed at the governor's dinner-table or in King William's court, were it possible that his affairs should call him thither. But the only thing about him that could be fixed upon as remarkable was his staff, which bore the likeness of a great black snake, so curiously wrought that it might almost be seen to twist and wriggle itself like a living serpent. This, of course, must have been an ocular deception, assisted by the uncertain light.

"Come, Goodman Brown," cried his fellow-traveller, "this is a dull pace for the beginning of a journey. Take my staff, if you are so soon weary."

"Friend," said the other, exchanging his slow pace for a full stop, "having kept covenant by meeting thee here, it is my purpose now to return whence I came. I have scruples touching the matter thou wot'st of."

"Sayest thou so?" replied he of the serpent, smiling apart. "Let us walk on, nevertheless, reasoning as we go; and if I convince thee not, thou shalt turn back. We are but a little way in the forest yet."

"Too far! too far!" exclaimed the goodman, unconsciously resuming his walk. "My father never went into the woods on such an errand, nor his father before him. We have been a race of honest men and good Christians since the days of the martyrs; and shall I be the first by the name of Brown that ever took this path and kept——"

"Such company, thou wouldst say," observed the elder person, interpreting his pause. "Well said, Goodman Brown! I have been as well acquainted with your family as with ever a one among the Puritans; and that's no trifle to say. I helped your grandfather, the constable, when he lashed the Quaker woman so smartly through the streets of Salem; and it was I that brought your father a pitch-pine knot, kindled at my own hearth, to set fire to an Indian village, in King Philip's war. They were my good friends both; and many a pleasant walk have we had along this path, and returned merrily after midnight. I would fain be friends with you for their sake."

"If it be as thou sayest," replied Goodman Brown, "I marvel they never spoke of these matters; or, verily, I marvel not, seeing that the least rumour of the sort would have driven them from New England. We are a people of prayer, and good works to boot, and abide no such wickedness."

"Wickedness or not," said the traveller with the twisted staff, "I have a very general acquaintance here in New England. The deacons of many a church have drunk the communion wine with me; the select men of divers towns make me their chairman; and a majority of the Great and General Court are firm supporters of my interest. The governor and I, too,—but these are state secrets."

"Can this be so?" cried Goodman Brown, with a stare of

amazement at his undisturbed companion. " Howbeit, I have
nothing to do with the governor and council; they have their
own ways, and are no rule for a simple husbandman like me.
But, were I to go on with thee, how should I meet the eye
of that good old man, our minister, at Salem village? Oh,
his voice would make me tremble both Sabbath day and
lecture day! "

Thus far the elder traveller had listened with due gravity;
but now burst into a fit of irrepressible mirth, shaking himself so violently that his snake-like staff actually seemed to
wriggle in sympathy.

" Ha! ha! ha! " shouted he again and again; then composing himself, " Well, go on, Goodman Brown, go on; but,
prithee, don't kill me with laughing."

" Well, then, to end the matter at once," said Goodman
Brown, considerably nettled, " there is my wife, Faith. It would
break her dear little heart; and I'd rather break my own."

" Nay, if that be the case," answered the other, " e'en go
thy ways, Goodman Brown. I would not for twenty old
women like the one hobbling before us that Faith should
come to any harm."

As he spoke, he pointed his staff at a female figure on the
path, in whom Goodman Brown recognized a very pious and
exemplary dame, who had taught him his catechism in youth,
and was still his moral and spiritual adviser, jointly with the
minister and Deacon Gookin.

" A marvel, truly, that Goody Cloyse should be so far in
the wilderness at nightfall," said he. " But, with your leave,
friend, I shall take a cut through the woods until we have
left this Christian woman behind. Being a stranger to you,
she might ask whom I was consorting with and whither I
was going."

" Be it so," said his fellow-traveller. " Betake you to the
woods, and let me keep the path."

Accordingly the young man turned aside, but took care
to watch his companion, who advanced softly along the road
until he had come within a staff's length of the old dame.
She, meanwhile, was making the best of her way, with
singular speed for so aged a woman, and mumbling some indistinct words—a prayer, doubtless—as she went. The
traveller put forth his staff and touched her withered neck
with what seemed the serpent's tail.

" The Devil! " screamed the pious old lady.

" Then Goody Cloyse knows her old friend? " observed the traveller, confronting her and leaning on his writhing stick.

" Ah, forsooth, and is it your worship indeed? " cried the good old dame.   " Yea, truly is it, and in the very image of my old gossip, Goodman Brown, the grandfather of the silly fellow that now is.   But—would your worship believe it?— my broomstick hath strangely disappeared, stolen as I suspect, by that unhanged witch, Goody Cory, and that, too, when I was all anointed with the juice of smallage, and cinquefoil, and wolf's-bane——"

" Mingled with fine wheat and the fat of a new-born babe," said the shape of old Goodman Brown.

" Ah, your worship knows the recipe," cried the old lady, cackling aloud.   " So, as I was saying, being all ready for the meeting, and no horse to ride on, I made up my mind to foot it; for they tell me there is a nice young man to be taken into communion to-night.   But now your good worship will lend me your arm, and we shall be there in a twinkling."

" That can hardly be," answered her friend.   " I may not spare you my arm, Goody Cloyse; but here is my staff, if you will."

So saying, he threw it down at her feet, where, perhaps, it assumed life, being one of the rods which its owner had formerly lent to the Egyptian magi.   Of this fact, however, Goodman Brown could not take cognizance.   He had cast up his eyes in astonishment, and, looking down again, beheld neither Goody Cloyse nor the serpentine staff, but his fellow-traveller alone, who waited for him as calmly as if nothing had happened.

" That old woman taught me my catechism," said the young man; and there was a world of meaning in this simple comment.

They continued to walk onward, while the elder traveller exhorted his companion to make good speed and persevere in the path, discoursing so aptly that his arguments seemed rather to spring up in the bosom of his auditor than to be suggested by himself.   As they went, he plucked a branch of maple to serve for a walking-stick, and began to strip it of the twigs and little boughs, which were wet with evening dew.   The moment his fingers touched them they became

strangely withered and dried up as with a week's sunshine.
Thus the pair proceeded, at a good free pace, until suddenly,
in a gloomy hollow of the road, Goodman Brown sat himself
down on the stump of a tree and refused to go any farther.

"Friend," said he, stubbornly, "my mind is made up.
Not another step will I budge on this errand. What if a
wretched old woman do choose to go to the Devil when I
thought she was going to heaven: is that any reason why I
should quit my dear Faith and go after her?"

"You will think better of this by and by," said his acquaintance, composedly. "Sit here and rest yourself awhile;
and when you feel like moving again, there's my staff to help
you along."

Without more words, he threw his companion the maple-
stick, and was as speedily out of sight as if he had vanished
into the deepening gloom. The young man sat a few
moments by the roadside, applauding himself greatly, and
thinking with how clear a conscience he should meet the
minister in his morning walk, nor shrink from the eye of
good old Deacon Gookin. And what calm sleep would be
his that very night, which was to have been spent so wickedly,
but so purely and sweetly now, in the arms of Faith! Amidst
these pleasant and praiseworthy meditations, Goodman Brown
heard the tramp of horses along the road, and deemed it
advisable to conceal himself within the verge of the forest,
conscious of the guilty purpose that had brought him thither,
though now so happily turned from it.

On came the hoof-tramps and the voices of the riders, two
grave old voices, conversing soberly as they drew near. These
mingled sounds appeared to pass along the road, within a few
yards of the young man's hiding-place; but, owing doubtless
to the depth of the gloom at that particular spot, neither the
travellers nor their steeds were visible. Though their figures
brushed the small boughs by the wayside, it could not be seen
that they intercepted, even for a moment, the faint gleam
from the strip of bright sky athwart which they must have
passed. Goodman Brown alternately crouched and stood on
tiptoe, pulling aside the branches and thrusting forth his
head as far as he durst, without discerning so much as a
shadow. It vexed him the more, because he could have
sworn, were such a thing possible, that he recognized the
voices of the minister and Deacon Gookin, jogging along

quietly, as they were wont to do, when bound to some ordination or ecclesiastical council. While yet within hearing, one of the riders stopped to pluck a switch.

"Of the two, reverend sir," said the voice like the deacon's, "I had rather miss an ordination dinner than to-night's meeting. They tell me that some of our community are to be here from Falmouth and beyond, and others from Connecticut and Rhode Island, besides several of the Indian powwows, who, after their fashion, know almost as much deviltry as the best of us. Moreover, there is a goodly young woman to be taken into communion."

"Mighty well, Deacon Gookin!" replied the solemn old tones of the minister. "Spur up, or we shall be late. Nothing can be done, you know, until I get on the ground."

The hoofs clattered again; and the voices, talking so strangely in the empty air, passed on through the forest, where no church had ever been gathered or solitary Christian prayed. Whither, then, could these holy men be journeying so deep into the heathen wilderness? Young Goodman Brown caught hold of a tree for support, being ready to sink down on the ground, faint and overburdened with the heavy sickness of his heart. He looked up to the sky, doubting whether there really was a heaven above him. Yet there was the blue arch, and the stars brightening in it.

"With heaven above and Faith below, I will yet stand firm against the Devil!" cried Goodman Brown.

While he still gazed upward into the deep arch of the firmament and had lifted his hands to pray, a cloud, though no wind was stirring, hurried across the zenith and hid the brightening stars. The blue sky was still visible except directly overhead, where this black mass of cloud was sweeping swiftly northward. Aloft in the air, as if from the depths of the cloud, came a confused and doubtful sound of voices. Once the listener fancied that he could distinguish the accents of townspeople of his own, men and women, both pious and ungodly, many of whom he had met at the communion-table, and had seen others rioting at the tavern. The next moment, so indistinct were the sounds, he doubted whether he had heard aught but the murmur of the old forest, whispering without a wind. Then came a stronger swell of those familiar tones, heard daily in the sunshine at Salem village, but never until now from a cloud of night. There

was one voice, of a young woman, uttering lamentations, yet
with an uncertain sorrow, and entreating for some favour,
which, perhaps, it would grieve her to obtain; and all the
unseen multitude, both saints and sinners, seemed to encourage
her onward.

" Faith! " shouted Goodman Brown, in a voice of agony
and desperation; and the echoes of the forest mocked him,
crying, "Faith! Faith!" as if bewildered wretches were
seeking her all through the wilderness.

The cry of grief, rage, and terror was yet piercing the
night, when the unhappy husband held his breath for a
response. There was a scream, drowned immediately in a
louder murmur of voices, fading into far-off laughter, as the
dark cloud swept away, leaving the clear and silent sky above
Goodman Brown. But something fluttered lightly down
through the air and caught on the branch of a tree. The
young man seized it, and beheld a pink ribbon.

"My Faith is gone!" cried he, after one stupefied moment.
"There is no good on earth; and sin is but a name. Come,
Devil; for to thee is this world given."

And, maddened with despair, so that he laughed loud and
long, did Goodman Brown grasp his staff and set forth again,
at such a rate that he seemed to fly along the forest path
rather than to walk or run. The road grew wilder and
drearier and more faintly traced, and vanished at length,
leaving him in the heart of the dark wilderness, still rushing
onward with the instinct that guides mortal man to evil. The
whole forest was peopled with frightful sounds,—the creaking of the trees, the howling of wild beasts, and the yell of
Indians; while sometimes the wind tolled like a distant
church-bell, and sometimes gave a broad roar around the
traveller, as if all Nature were laughing him to scorn. But
he was himself the chief horror of the scene, and shrank not
from its other horrors.

" Ha! ha! ha! " roared Goodman Brown when the wind
laughed at him. "Let us hear which will laugh loudest.
Think not to frighten me with your deviltry. Come witch,
come wizard, come Indian pow-wow, come Devil himself,
and here comes Goodman Brown. You may as well fear him
as he fears you."

In truth, all through the haunted forest there could be
nothing more frightful than the figure of Goodman Brown.

On he flew among the black pines, brandishing his staff with frenzied gestures, now giving vent to an inspiration of horrid blasphemy, and now shouting forth such laughter as set all the echoes of the forest laughing like demons around him. The fiend in his own shape is less hideous than when he rages in the breast of man. Thus sped the demoniac on his course, until, quivering among the trees, he saw a red light before him, as when the felled trunks and branches of a clearing have been set on fire, and throw up their lurid blaze against the sky, at the hour of midnight. He paused, in a lull of the tempest that had driven him onward, and heard the swell of what seemed a hymn rolling solemnly from a distance with the weight of many voices. He knew the tune; it was a familiar one in the choir of the village meeting-house. The verse died heavily away, and was lengthened by a chorus, not of human voices, but of all the sounds of the benighted wilderness pealing in awful harmony together. Goodman Brown cried out; and his cry was lost to his own ear by its unison with the cry of the desert.

In the interval of silence he stole forward until the light glared full upon his eyes. At one extremity of an open space, hemmed in by the dark wall of the forest, arose a rock, bearing some rude, natural resemblance either to an altar or a pulpit and surrounded by four blazing pines, their tops aflame, their stems untouched, like candles at an evening meeting. The mass of foliage that had overgrown the summit of the rock was all on fire, blazing high into the night and fitfully illuminating the whole field. Each pendent twig and leafy festoon was in a blaze. As the red light arose and fell, a numerous congregation alternately shone forth, then disappeared in shadow, and again grew, as it were, out of the darkness, peopling the heart of the solitary woods at once.

"A grave and dark-clad company," quoth Goodman Brown.

In truth they were such. Among them, quivering to and fro between gloom and splendour, appeared faces that would be seen next day at the council board of the province, and others which, Sabbath after Sabbath, looked devoutly heavenward, and benignantly over the crowded pews, from the holiest pulpits in the land. Some affirm that the lady of the governor was there. At least there were high dames well known to her, and wives of honoured husbands, and widows, a great multitude, and ancient maidens, all of excellent repute, and fair young girls, who trembled lest their mothers should espy them. Either the sudden gleams of light flashing over the obscure field bedazzled Goodman Brown, or he recognized a score of the church-members of Salem village famous for their especial sanctity. Good old Deacon Gookin had arrived, and waited at the skirts of that venerable saint, his revered pastor. But, irreverently consorting with these grave, reputable, and pious people, these elders of the church, these chaste dames and dewy virgins, there were men of dissolute lives and women of spotted fame, wretches given over to all mean and filthy vice, and suspected even of horrid crimes. It was strange to see that the good shrank not from the wicked, nor were the sinners abashed by the saints. Scattered also among their pale-faced enemies were the Indian priests, or pow-wows, who had often scared their native forest with more hideous incantations than any known to English witchcraft.

" But where is Faith? " thought Goodman Brown; and, as hope came into his heart, he trembled.

Another verse of the hymn arose, a slow and mournful strain, such as the pious love, but joined to words which expressed all that our nature can conceive of sin, and darkly hinted at far more. Unfathomable to mere mortals is the lore of fiends. Verse after verse was sung; and still the chorus of the desert swelled between like the deepest tone of a mighty organ; and with the final peal of that dreadful anthem there came a sound, as if the roaring wind, the rushing streams, the howling beasts, and every other voice of the unconverted wilderness were mingling and according with the voice of guilty man in homage to the prince of all. The four blazing pines threw up a loftier flame, and obscurely discovered shapes and visages of horror on the smoke-wreaths above the impious assembly. At the same moment the fire on the rock shot redly forth and formed a glowing arch above its base, where now appeared a figure. With reverence be it spoken, the figure bore no slight similitude, both in garb and manner, to some grave divine of the New England churches.

" Bring forth the converts! " cried a voice that echoed through the field and rolled into the forest.

At the word, Goodman Brown stepped forth from the shadow of the trees and approached the congregation, with whom he felt a loathful brotherhood by the sympathy of all that was wicked in his heart. He could have wellnigh sworn that the shape of his own dead father beckoned him to advance, looking downward from a smoke-wreath, while a woman, with dim features of despair, threw out her hand to warn him back. Was it his mother? But he had no power to retreat one step, nor to resist, even in thought, when the minister and good old Deacon Gookin seized his arms and led him to the blazing rock. Thither came also the slender form of a veiled female, led between Goody Cloyse, that pious teacher of the catechism, and Martha Carrier, who had received the Devil's promise to be queen of hell. A rampant hag was she. And there stood the proselytes beneath the canopy of fire.

"Welcome, my children," said the dark figure, " to the communion of your race. Ye have found thus young your nature and your destiny. My children, look behind you! "

They turned; and flashing forth, as it were, in a sheet of flame, the fiend worshippers were seen; the smile of welcome gleamed darkly on every visage.

"There," resumed the sable form, " are all whom ye have reverenced from youth. Ye deemed them holier than yourselves, and shrank from your own sin, contrasting it with their lives of righteousness and prayerful aspirations heavenward. Yet here are they all in my worshipping assembly. This night it shall be granted you to know their secret deeds; how hoary-bearded elders of the church have whispered wanton words to the young maids of their households; how many a woman, eager for widow's weeds, has given her husband a drink at bedtime and let him sleep his last sleep in her bosom; how beardless youths have made haste to inherit their father's wealth; and how fair damsels—blush not, sweet ones—have dug little graves in the garden, and bidden me, the sole guest, to an infant's funeral. By the sympathy of your human hearts for sin ye shall scent out all the places —whether in church, bedchamber, street, field, or forest— where crime has been committed, and shall exult to behold the whole earth one stain of guilt, one mighty blood-spot. Far more than this. It shall be yours to penetrate, in every bosom, the deep mystery of sin, the fountain of all wicked arts, and which inexhaustibly supplies more evil impulses than human power—than my power at its utmost—can make manifest in deeds. And now, my children, look upon each other."

They did so; and, by the blaze of the hell-kindled torches, the wretched man beheld his Faith, and the wife her husband, trembling before that unhallowed altar.

" Lo, there ye stand, my children," said the figure, in a deep and solemn tone, almost sad with its despairing awfulness, as if his once angelic nature could yet mourn for our miserable race. " Depending upon one another's hearts, ye had still hoped that virtue were not all a dream. Now are ye undeceived. Evil is the nature of mankind. Evil must be your only happiness. Welcome again, my children, to the communion of your race."

" Welcome," repeated the fiend worshippers, in one cry of despair and triumph.

And there they stood, the only pair, as it seemed, who were yet hesitating on the verge of wickedness in this dark world. A basin was hollowed, naturally, in the rock. Did it contain water, reddened by the lurid light? or was it blood? or, perchance, a liquid flame? Herein did the shape of evil dip his hand and prepare to lay the mark of baptism upon their foreheads, that they might be partakers of the mystery of sin, more conscious of the secret guilt of others, both in deed and thought, than they could now be of their own. The husband cast one look at his pale wife, and Faith at him. What polluted wretches would the next glance show them to each other, shuddering alike at what they disclosed and what they saw!

" Faith! Faith! " cried the husband, " look up to Heaven, and resist the wicked one."

Whether Faith obeyed, he knew not. Hardly had he spoken, when he found himself amid calm night and solitude, listening to a roar of the wind which died heavily away through the forest. He staggered against the rock, and felt it chill and damp; while a hanging twig, that had been all on fire, besprinkled his cheek with the coldest dew.

The next morning young Goodman Brown came slowly into the street of Salem village, staring around him like a bewildered man. The good old minister was taking a walk along the graveyard to get an appetite for breakfast and meditate his sermon, and bestowed a blessing, as he passed, on Goodman Brown. He shrank from the venerable saint as if to avoid an anathema. Old Deacon Gookin was at domestic worship, and the holy words of his prayer were heard through the open window. " What God doth the wizard pray to? " quoth Goodman Brown. Goody Cloyse, that excellent old Christian, stood in the early sunshine at her own lattice, catechizing a little girl who had brought her a pint of morning's milk. Goodman Brown snatched away the child as from the grasp of the fiend himself. Turning the corner by the meeting-house, he spied the head of Faith, with the pink ribbons, gazing anxiously forth, and bursting into such joy at sight of him that she skipped along the street and almost kissed her husband before the whole village. But Goodman Brown looked sternly and sadly into her face, and passed on without a greeting.

Had Goodman Brown fallen asleep in the forest, and only dreamed a wild dream of a witch-meeting?

Be it so, if you will; but, alas! it was a dream of evil omen for young Goodman Brown. A stern, a sad, a darkly meditative, a distrustful, if not a desperate, man did he become from the night of that fearful dream. On the Sabbath day, when the congregation were singing a holy psalm, he could not listen, because an anthem of sin rushed loudly upon his ear and drowned all the blessed strain. When the minister spoke from the pulpit, with power and fervid eloquence, and with his hand on the open Bible, of the sacred truths of our religion, and of saint-like lives and triumphant deaths, and of future bliss or misery unutterable, then did Goodman Brown turn pale, dreading lest the roof should thunder down upon the grey blasphemer and his hearers. Often, awakening suddenly at midnight, he shrank from the bosom of Faith; and at morning or eventide, when the family knelt down to prayer, he scowled, and muttered to himself, and gazed sternly at his wife, and turned away. And when he had lived long, and was borne to his grave, a hoary corpse, followed by Faith, an aged woman, and children and grandchildren, a goodly procession, besides neighbours not a few, they carved no hopeful verse upon his tombstone; for his dying hour was gloom.

OSCAR WILDE

THE BALLAD OF READING GAOL

I

HE did not wear his scarlet coat,
　For blood and wine are red,
And blood and wine were on his hands
　When they found him with the dead,
The poor dead woman whom he loved,
　And murdered in her bed.

He walked amongst the Trial Men
　In a suit of shabby grey;
A cricket cap was on his head,
　And his step seemed light and gay;
But I never saw a man who looked
　So wistfully at the day.

I never saw a man who looked
　With such a wistful eye
Upon that little tent of blue
　Which prisoners call the sky,
And at every drifting cloud that went
　With sails of silver by.

I walked, with other souls in pain,
　Within another ring,
And was wondering if the man had done
　A great or little thing,
When a voice behind me whispered low,
　" *That fellow's got to swing.*"

Dear Christ! the very prison walls
　Suddenly seemed to reel,
And the sky above my head became
　Like a casque of scorching steel;
And, though I was a soul in pain,
　My pain I could not feel.

I only knew what hunted thought
　　Quickened his step, and why
He looked upon the garish day
　　With such a wistful eye;
The man had killed the thing he loved,
　　And so he had to die.

Yet each man kills the thing he loves,
　　By each let this be heard,
Some do it with a bitter look,
　　Some with a flattering word,
The coward does it with a kiss,
　　The brave man with a sword!

Some kill their love when they are young,
　　And some when they are old;
Some strangle with the hands of Lust,
　　Some with the hands of Gold:
The kindest use a knife, because
　　The dead so soon grow cold.

Some love too little, some too long,
　　Some sell, and others buy;
Some do the deed with many tears,
　　And some without a sigh:
For each man kills the thing he loves,
　　Yet each man does not die.

He does not die a death of shame
　　On a day of dark disgrace,
Nor have a noose about his neck,
　　Nor a cloth upon his face,
Nor drop feet foremost through the floor
　　Into an empty space.

He does not sit with silent men
　　Who watch him night and day;
Who watch him when he tries to weep,
　　And when he tries to pray;
Who watch him lest himself should rob
　　The prison of its prey.

He does not wake at dawn to see
 Dread figures throng his room,
The shivering Chaplain robed in white,
 The Sheriff stern with gloom,
And the Governor all in shiny black,
 With the yellow face of Doom.

He does not rise in piteous haste
 To put on convict clothes,
While some coarse-mouthed Doctor gloats, and notes
 Each new and nerve-twitched pose,
Fingering a watch whose little ticks
 Are like horrible hammer-blows.

He does not know that sickening thirst
 That sands one's throat, before
The hangman with his gardener's gloves
 Slips through the padded door,
And binds one with three leathern thongs,
 That the throat may thirst no more.

He does not bend his head to hear
 The Burial Office read,
Nor, while the terror of his soul
 Tells him he is not dead,
Cross his own coffin, as he moves
 Into the hideous shed.

He does not stare upon the air
 Through a little roof of glass:
He does not pray with lips of clay
 For his agony to pass;
Nor feel upon his shuddering cheek
 The kiss of Caiaphas.

II

SIX weeks our guardsman walked the yard,
 In the suit of shabby grey:
His cricket cap was on his head,
 And his step seemed light and gay,
But I never saw a man who looked
 So wistfully at the day.

I never saw a man who looked
  With such a wistful eye
Upon that little tent of blue
  Which prisoners call the sky,
And at every wandering cloud that trailed
  Its ravelled fleeces by.

He did not wring his hands, as do
  Those witless men who dare
To try to rear the changeling Hope
  In the cave of black Despair:
He only looked upon the sun,
  And drank the morning air.

He did not wring his hands nor weep,
  Nor did he peek or pine,
But he drank the air as though it held
  Some healthful anodyne;
With open mouth he drank the sun
  As though it had been wine!

And I and all the souls in pain,
  Who tramped the other ring,
Forgot if we ourselves had done
  A great or little thing,
And watched with gaze of dull amaze
  The man who had to swing.

And strange it was to see him pass
  With a step so light and gay,
And strange it was to see him look
  So wistfully at the day,
And strange it was to think that he
  Had such a debt to pay.

For oak and elm have pleasant leaves
  That in the spring-time shoot:
But grim to see is the gallows-tree,
  With its adder-bitten root,
And, green or dry, a man must die
  Before it bears its fruit!

The loftiest place is that seat of grace
  For which all worldlings try:
But who would stand in hempen band
  Upon a scaffold high,
And through a murderer's collar take
  His last look at the sky?

It is sweet to dance to violins
  When Love and Life are fair:
To dance to flutes, to dance to lutes
  Is delicate and rare:
But it is not sweet with nimble feet
  To dance upon the air!

So with curious eyes and sick surmise
  We watched him day by day,
And wondered if each one of us
  Would end the self-same way,
For none can tell to what red Hell
  His sightless soul may stray.

At last the dead man walked no more
  Amongst the Trial Men,
And I knew that he was standing up
  In the black dock's dreadful pen,
And that never would I see his face
  In God's sweet world again.

Like two doomed ships that pass in storm
  We had crossed each other's way:
But we made no sign, we said no word,
  We had no word to say;
For we did not meet in the holy night,
  But in the shameful day.

A prison wall was round us both,
  Two outcast men we were:
The world had thrust us from its heart,
  And God from out His care:
And the iron gin that waits for Sin
  Had caught us in its snare.

III

IN Debtors' Yard the stones are hard,
   And the dripping wall is high,
So it was there he took the air
   Beneath the leaden sky,
And by each side a Warder walked,
   For fear the man might die.

Or else he sat with those who watched
   His anguish night and day;
Who watched him when he rose to weep,
   And when he crouched to pray;
Who watched him lest himself should rob
   Their scaffold of its prey.

The Governor was strong upon
   The Regulations Act:
The Doctor said that Death was but
   A scientific fact:
And twice a day the Chaplain called,
   And left a little tract.

And twice a day he smoked his pipe,
   And drank his quart of beer:
His soul was resolute, and held
   No hiding-place for fear;
He often said that he was glad
   The hangman's hands were near.

But why he said so strange a thing
   No Warder dared to ask:
For he to whom a watcher's doom
   Is given as his task
Must set a lock upon his lips,
   And make his face a mask.

Or else he might be moved, and try
   To comfort or console:
And what should Human Pity do
   Pent up in Murderers' Hole?
What word of grace in such a place
   Could help a brother's soul?

With slouch and swing around the ring
  We trod the Fools' Parade!
We did not care: we knew we were
  The Devil's Own Brigade:
And shaven head and feet of lead
  Make a merry masquerade.

We tore the tarry rope to shreds
  With blunt and bleeding nails;
We rubbed the doors, and scrubbed the floors,
  And cleaned the shining rails:
And, rank by rank, we soaked the plank,
  And clattered with the pails.

We sewed the sacks, we broke the stones,
  We turned the dusty drill:
We banged the tins, and bawled the hymns,
  And sweated on the mill:
But in the heart of every man
  Terror was lying still.

So still it lay that every day
  Crawled like a weed-clogged wave:
And we forgot the bitter lot
  That waits for fool and knave,
Till once, as we tramped in from work,
  We passed an open grave.

With yawning mouth the yellow hole
  Gaped for a living thing;
The very mud cried out for blood
  To the thirsty asphalte ring:
And we knew that ere one dawn grew fair
  Some prisoner had to swing.

Right in we went, with soul intent
  On Death and Dread and Doom:
The hangman, with his little bag,
  Went shuffling through the gloom:
And each man trembled as he crept
  Into his numbered tomb.

That night the empty corridors
   Were full of forms of Fear,
And up and down the iron town
   Stole feet we could not hear,
And through the bars that hide the stars
   White faces seemed to peer.

He lay as one who lies and dreams
   In a pleasant meadow-land,
The watchers watched him as he slept,
   And could not understand
How one could sleep so sweet a sleep
   With a hangman close at hand.

But there is no sleep when men must weep
   Who never yet have wept:
So we—the fool, the fraud, the knave—
   That endless vigil kept,
And through each brain on hands of pain
   Another's terror crept.

Alas! it is a fearful thing
   To feel another's guilt!
For, right within, the sword of Sin
   Pierced to its poisoned hilt,
And as molten lead were the tears we shed
   For the blood we had not spilt.

The Warders with their shoes of felt
   Crept by each padlocked door,
And peeped and saw, with eyes of awe,
   Grey figures on the floor,
And wondered why men knelt to pray
   Who never prayed before.

All through the night we knelt and prayed,
   Mad mourners of a corse!
The troubled plumes of midnight were
   The plumes upon a hearse:
And bitter wine upon a sponge
   Was the savour of Remorse.

The grey cock crew, the red cock crew,
　　But never came the day:
And crooked shapes of Terror crouched,
　　In the corners where we lay:
And each evil sprite that walks by night
　　Before us seemed to play.

They glided past, they glided fast,
　　Like travellers through a mist:
They mocked the moon in a rigadoon
　　Of delicate turn and twist,
And with formal pace and loathsome grace
　　The phantoms kept their tryst.

With mop and mow, we saw them go,
　　Slim shadows hand in hand:
About, about, in a ghostly rout
　　They trod a saraband:
And the damned grotesques made arabesques,
　　Like the wind upon the sand!

With the pirouettes of marionettes,
　　They tripped on pointed tread:
But with flutes of Fear they filled the ear,
　　As their grisly masque they led,
And loud they sang, and long they sang,
　　For they sang to wake the dead.

" *Oho!* " they cried, " *The world is wide,*
　　But fettered limbs go lame!
And once, or twice, to throw the dice
　　Is a gentlemanly game,
But he does not win who plays with Sin
　　In the secret House of Shame."

No things of air these antics were,
　　That frolicked with such glee:
To men whose lives were held in gyves,
　　And whose feet might not go free,
Ah! wounds of Christ! they were living things,
　　Most terrible to see.

Around, around, they waltzed and wound;
    Some wheeled in smirking pairs;
With the mincing step of a demirep
    Some sidled up the stairs:
And with subtle sneer, and fawning leer,
    Each helped us at our prayers.

The morning wind began to moan,
    But still the night went on:
Through its giant loom the web of gloom
    Crept till each thread was spun:
And, as we prayed, we grew afraid
    Of the Justice of the Sun.

The moaning wind went wandering round
    The weeping prison-wall:
Till like a wheel of turning steel
    We felt the minutes crawl:
O moaning wind! what had we done
    To have such a seneschal?

At last I saw the shadowed bars,
    Like a lattice wrought in lead,
Move right across the whitewashed wall
    That faced my three-plank bed,
And I knew that somewhere in the world
    God's dreadful dawn was red.

At six o'clock we cleaned our cells,
    At seven all was still,
But the sough and swing of a mighty wing
    The prison seemed to fill,
For the Lord of Death with icy breath
    Had entered in to kill.

He did not pass in purple pomp,
    Nor ride a moon-white steed.
Three yards of cord and a sliding board
    Are all the gallows' need:
So with rope of shame the Herald came
    To do the secret deed.

We were as men who through a fen
    Of filthy darkness grope:
We did not dare to breathe a prayer,
    Or to give our anguish scope:
Something was dead in each of us,
    And what was dead was Hope.

For Man's grim Justice goes its way,
    And will not swerve aside:
It slays the weak, it slays the strong,
    It has a deadly stride:
With iron heel it slays the strong,
    The monstrous parricide!

We waited for the stroke of eight:
    Each tongue was thick with thirst:
For the stroke of eight is the stroke of Fate
    That makes a man accursed,
And Fate will use a running noose
    For the best man and the worst.

We had no other thing to do,
    Save to wait for the sign to come:
So, like things of stone in a valley lone,
    Quiet we sat and dumb:
But each man's heart beat thick and quick,
    Like a madman on a drum!

With sudden shock the prison-clock
    Smote on the shivering air,
And from all the gaol rose up a wail
    Of impotent despair,
Like the sound that frightened marshes hear
    From some leper in his lair.

And as one sees most fearful things
    In the crystal of a dream,
We saw the greasy hempen rope
    Hooked to the blackened beam,
And heard the prayer the hangman's snare
    Strangled into a scream.

And all the woe that moved him so
  That he gave that bitter cry,
And the wild regrets, and the bloody sweats,
  None knew so well as I:
For he who lives more lives than one
  More deaths than one must die.

IV

THERE is no chapel on the day
  On which they hang a man:
The Chaplain's heart is far too sick,
  Or his face is far too wan,
Or there is that written in his eyes
  Which none should look upon.

So they kept us close till nigh on noon,
  And then they rang the bell,
And the Warders with their jingling keys
  Opened each listening cell,
And down the iron stair we tramped,
  Each from his separate Hell.

Out into God's sweet air we went,
  But not in wonted way,
For this man's face was white with fear,
  And that man's face was grey,
And I never saw sad men who looked
  So wistfully at the day.

I never saw sad men who looked
  With such a wistful eye
Upon that little tent of blue
  We prisoners called the sky,
And at every careless cloud that passed
  In happy freedom by.

But there were those amongst us all
  Who walked with downcast head,
And knew that, had each got his due,
  They should have died instead:
He had but killed a thing that lived,
  Whilst they had killed the dead.

For he who sins a second time
   Wakes a dead soul to pain,
And draws it from its spotted shroud,
   And makes it bleed again,
And makes it bleed great gouts of blood,
   And makes it bleed in vain!

Like ape or clown, in monstrous garb
   With crooked arrows starred,
Silently we went round and round
   The slippery asphalte yard;
Silently we went round and round,
   And no man spoke a word.

Silently we went round and round,
   And through each hollow mind
The Memory of dreadful things
   Rushed like a dreadful wind,
And Horror stalked before each man,
   And Terror crept behind.

The Warders strutted up and down,
   And kept their herd of brutes,
Their uniforms were spick and span,
   And they wore their Sunday suits,
But we knew the work they had been at,
   By the quicklime on their boots.

For where a grave had opened wide,
   There was no grave at all:
Only a stretch of mud and sand
   By the hideous prison-wall,
And a little heap of burning lime,
   That the man should have his pall.

For he has a pall, this wretched man,
   Such as few men can claim:
Deep down below a prison-yard,
   Naked for greater shame,
He lies, with fetters on each foot,
   Wrapt in a sheet of flame!

And all the while the burning lime
    Eats flesh and bone away,
It eats the brittle bone by night,
    And the soft flesh by day,
It eats the flesh and bone by turns,
    But it eats the heart alway.

For three long years they will not sow
    Or root or seedling there:
For three long years the unblessed spot
    Will sterile be and bare,
And look upon the wondering sky
    With unreproachful stare.

They think a murderer's heart would taint
    Each simple seed they sow.
It is not true!   God's kindly earth
    Is kindlier than men know,
And the red rose would but blow more red,
    The white rose whiter blow.

Out of his mouth a red, red rose!
    Out of his heart a white!
For who can say by what strange way,
    Christ brings His will to light,
Since the barren staff the pilgrim bore
    Bloomed in the great Pope's sight?

But neither milk-white rose nor red
    May bloom in prison-air;
The shard, the pebble, and the flint,
    Are what they give us there:
For flowers have been known to heal
    A common man's despair.

So never will wine-red rose or white,
    Petal by petal, fall
On that stretch of mud and sand that lies
    By the hideous prison-wall,
To tell the men who tramp the yard
    That God's Son died for all.

Yet though the hideous prison-wall
  Still hems him round and round,
And a spirit may not walk by night
  That is with fetters bound,
And a spirit may but weep that lies
  In such unholy ground,

He is at peace—this wretched man—
  At peace, or will be soon:
There is no thing to make him mad,
  Nor does Terror walk at noon,
For the lampless Earth in which he lies
  Has neither Sun nor Moon.

They hanged him as a beast is hanged:
  They did not even toll
A requiem that might have brought
  Rest to his startled soul,
But hurriedly they took him out,
  And hid him in a hole.

They stripped him of his canvas clothes,
  And gave him to the flies:
They mocked the swollen purple throat,
  And the stark and staring eyes:
And with laughter loud they heaped the shroud
  In which their convict lies.

The Chaplain would not kneel to pray
  By his dishonoured grave:
Nor mark it with that blessed Cross
  That Christ for sinners gave,
Because the man was one of those
  Whom Christ came down to save.

Yet all is well; he has but passed
  To Life's appointed bourne:
And alien tears will fill for him
  Pity's long-broken urn,
For his mourners will be outcast men,
  And outcasts always mourn.

V

I KNOW not whether Laws be right,
   Or whether Laws be wrong;
All that we know who lie in gaol
   Is that the wall is strong;
And that each day is like a year,
   A year whose days are long.

But this I know, that every Law
   That men have made for Man,
Since first Man took his brother's life,
   And the sad world began,
But straws the wheat and saves the chaff
   With a most evil fan.

This too I know—and wise it were
   If each could know the same—
That every prison that men build
   Is built with bricks of shame,
And bound with bars lest Christ should see
   How men their brothers maim.

With bars they blur the gracious moon,
   And blind the goodly sun:
And they do well to hide their Hell,
   For in it things are done
That Son of God nor son of Man
   Ever should look upon!

The vilest deeds like poison weeds,
   Bloom well in prison-air;
It is only what is good in Man
   That wastes and withers there:
Pale Anguish keeps the heavy gate,
   And the Warder is Despair.

For they starve the little frightened child
   Till it weeps both night and day:
And they scourge the weak, and flog the fool,
   And gibe the old and grey,
And some grow mad, and all grow bad,
   And none a word may say.

Each narrow cell in which we dwell
  Is a foul and dark latrine,
And the fetid breath of living Death
  Chokes up each grated screen,
And all, but Lust, is turned to dust
  In Humanity's machine.

The brackish water that we drink
  Creeps with a loathsome slime,
And the bitter bread they weigh in scales
  Is full of chalk and lime,
And Sleep will not lie down, but walks
  Wild-eyed, and cries to Time.

But though lean Hunger and green Thirst
  Like asp with adder fight,
We have little care of prison fare,
  For what chills and kills outright
Is that every stone one lifts by day
  Becomes one's heart by night.

With midnight always in one's heart,
  And twilight in one's cell,
We turn the crank, or tear the rope,
  Each in his separate Hell,
And the silence is more awful far
  Than the sound of a brazen bell.

And never a human voice comes near
  To speak a gentle word:
And the eye that watches through the door
  Is pitiless and hard:
And by all forgot, we rot and rot,
  With soul and body marred.

And thus we rust Life's iron chain
  Degraded and alone:
And some men curse, and some men weep,
  And some men make no moan:
But God's eternal Laws are kind
  And break the heart of stone.

And every human heart that breaks,
　　In prison-cell or yard,
Is as that broken box that gave
　　Its treasure to the Lord,
And filled the unclean leper's house
　　With the scent of costliest nard.

Ah! happy they whose hearts can break
　　And peace of pardon win!
How else may man make straight his plan
　　And cleanse his soul from Sin?
How else but through a broken heart
　　May Lord Christ enter in?

And he of the swollen purple throat,
　　And the stark and staring eyes,
Waits for the holy hands that took
　　The Thief to Paradise;
And a broken and a contrite heart
　　The Lord will not despise.

The man in red who reads the Law
　　Gave him three weeks of life,
Three little weeks in which to heal
　　His soul of his soul's strife,
And cleanse from every blot of blood
　　The hand that held the knife.

And with tears of blood he cleansed the hand,
　　The hand that held the steel:
For only blood can wipe out blood,
　　And only tears can heal:
And the crimson stain that was of Cain
　　Became Christ's snow-white seal.

VI

IN Reading gaol by Reading town
　　There is a pit of shame,
And in it lies a wretched man
　　Eaten by teeth of flame,
In a burning winding-sheet he lies,
　　And his grave has got no name.

And there, till Christ call forth the dead,
   In silence let him lie:
No need to waste the foolish tear,
   Or heave the windy sigh:
The man had killed the thing he loved,
   And so he had to die.

And all men kill the thing they love,
   By all let this be heard,
Some do it with a bitter look,
   Some with a flattering word,
The coward does it with a kiss,
   The brave man with a sword!

EDGAR ALLAN POE

THE TELL-TALE HEART

TRUE!—nervous—very, very dreadfully nervous I had
been and am; but why *will* you say that I am mad?
The disease had sharpened my senses—not destroyed—not
dulled them. Above all was the sense of hearing acute. I
heard all things in the heaven and in the earth. I heard many
things in hell. How, then, am I mad? Hearken! and observe
how healthily—how calmly I can tell you the whole story.

It is impossible to say how first the idea entered my brain;
but once conceived, it haunted me day and night. Object
there was none. Passion there was none. I loved the old man.
He had never wronged me. He had never given me insult.
For his gold I had no desire. I think it was his eye! yes, it
was this! One of his eyes resembled that of a vulture—a pale
blue eye, with a film over it. Whenever it fell upon me, my
blood ran cold; and so by degrees—very gradually—I made
up my mind to take the life of the old man, and thus rid
myself of the eye for ever.

Now this is the point. You fancy me mad. Madmen
know nothing. But you should have seen *me*. You should
have seen how wisely I proceeded—with what caution—with
what foresight—with what dissimulation I went to work!
I was never kinder to the old man than during the whole week
before I killed him. And every night, about midnight, I
turned the latch of his door and opened it—oh, so gently!
And then, when I had made an opening sufficient for my
head, I put in a dark lantern, all closed, closed, so that no
light shone out, and then I thrust in my head. Oh, you
would have laughed to see how cunningly I thrust it in! I
moved it slowly—very, very slowly, so that I might not
disturb the old man's sleep. It took me an hour to place my
whole head within the opening so far that I could see him as
he lay upon his bed. Ha!—would a madman have been so
wise as this? And then, when my head was well in the room,
I undid the lantern, cautiously—oh, so cautiously—cautiously
(for the hinges creaked) I undid it just so much that a single

thin ray fell upon the vulture eye. And this I did for seven
long nights—every night just at midnight—but I found the
eye always closed; and so it was impossible to do the work;
for it was not the old man who vexed me, but his Evil Eye.
And every morning, when the day broke, I went boldly into
the chamber, and spoke courageously to him, calling him by
name in a hearty tone, and inquiring how he had passed the
night. So you see he would have been a very profound old
man, indeed, to suspect that every night, just at twelve, I
looked in upon him while he slept.

Upon the eighth night I was more than usually cautious
in opening the door. A watch's minute hand moves more
quickly than did mine. Never before that night had I *felt*
the extent of my own powers—of my sagacity. I could
scarcely contain my feelings of triumph. To think that there
I was, opening the door, little by little, and he not even to
dream of my secret deeds or thoughts. I fairly chuckled at
the idea; and perhaps he heard me—for he moved on the bed
suddenly, as if startled. Now you may think that I drew
back—but no. His room was as black as pitch with the thick
darkness (for the shutters were close-fastened, through fear
of robbers), and so I knew that he could not see the opening
of the door, and I kept pushing it on steadily, steadily.

I had my head in, and was about to open the lantern, when
my thumb slipped upon the tin fastening, and the old man
sprang up in the bed, crying out, " Who's there? "

I kept quite still and said nothing. For a whole hour I
did not move a muscle, and in the meantime I did not hear
him lie down. He was still sitting up in the bed, listening
—just as I have done, night after night, hearkening to the
death-watches in the wall.

Presently I heard a groan, and I knew it was the groan of
mortal terror. It was not a groan of pain or of grief—oh,
no!—it was the low stifled sound that arises from the bottom
of the soul when overcharged with awe. I knew the sound
well. Many a night, just at midnight, when all the world
slept, it has welled up from my own bosom, deepening, with
its dreadful echo, the terrors that distracted me. I say I knew
it well. I knew what the old man felt, and pitied him,
although I chuckled at heart. I knew that he had been lying
awake ever since the first slight noise, when he had turned
in the bed. His fears had been ever since growing upon him.

He had been trying to fancy them causeless, but could not. He had been saying to himself, " It is nothing but the wind in the chimney—it is only a mouse crossing the floor," or, " It is merely a cricket which has made a single chirp." Yes, he had been trying to comfort himself with these suppositions; but he had found all in vain. *All in vain;* because Death, in approaching him, had stalked with his black shadow before him, and enveloped the victim. And it was the mournful influence of the unperceived shadow that caused him to feel —although he neither saw nor heard—to *feel* the presence of my head within the room.

When I had waited a long time, very patiently, without hearing him lie down, I resolved to open a little—a very, very little crevice in the lantern. So I opened it—you cannot imagine how stealthily, stealthily—until, at length, a single dim ray, like the thread of the spider, shot from out the crevice and fell upon the vulture eye.

It was open—wide, wide open—and I grew furious as I gazed upon it. I saw it with perfect distinctness—all a dull blue, with a hideous veil over it that chilled the very marrow in my bones; but I could see nothing else of the old man's face or person, for I had directed the ray, as if by instinct, precisely upon the damned spot.

And now have I not told you that what you mistake for madness is but over-acuteness of the senses?—now, I say, there came to my ears a low, dull, quick sound, such as a watch makes when enveloped in cotton. I knew *that* sound well, too. It was the beating of the old man's heart. It increased my fury, as the beating of a drum stimulates the soldier into courage.

But even yet I refrained and kept still. I scarcely breathed. I held the lantern motionless. I tried how steadily I could maintain the ray upon the eye. Meantime the hellish tattoo of the heart increased. It grew quicker and quicker, and louder and louder every instant. The old man's terror *must* have been extreme! It grew louder, I say, louder every moment!—do you mark me well? I have told you that I am nervous: so I am. And now, at the dead hour of the night, amid the dreadful silence of that old house, so strange a noise as this excited me to uncontrollable terror. Yet, for some minutes longer, I refrained and stood still. But the beating grew louder, louder! I thought the heart must burst. And now a new anxiety seized me—the sound would be heard by a neighbour! The old man's hour had come! With a loud yell I threw open the lantern and leaped into the room. He shrieked once—once only. In an instant I dragged him to the floor, and pulled the heavy bed over him. I then smiled gaily, to find the deed so far done. But, for many minutes, the heart beat on with a muffled sound. This, however, did not vex me; it would not be heard through the wall. At length it ceased. The old man was dead. I removed the bed and examined the corpse. Yes, he was stone, stone dead. I placed my hand upon the heart and held it there many minutes. There was no pulsation. He was stone dead. His eye would trouble me no more.

If still you think me mad, you will think so no longer when I describe the wise precautions I took for the concealment of the body. The night waned, and I worked hastily, but in silence. First of all I dismembered the corpse. I cut off the head and the arms and the legs.

I then took up three planks from the flooring of the chamber and deposited all between the scantlings. I then replaced the boards so cleverly, so cunningly, that no human eye—not even *his*—could have detected anything wrong. There was nothing to wash out—no stain of any kind—no blood-spot whatever. I had been too wary for that. A tub had caught all—ha! ha!

When I had made an end of these labours, it was four o'clock—still dark as midnight. As the bell sounded the hour, there came a knocking at the street door. I went down to open it with a light heart—for what had I *now* to fear? There entered three men, who introduced themselves, with perfect suavity, as officers of the police. A shriek had been heard by a neighbour during the night; suspicion of foul play had been aroused; information had been lodged at the police office, and they (the officers) had been deputed to search the premises.

I smiled—for *what* had I to fear? I bade the gentlemen welcome. The shriek, I said, was my own in a dream. The old man, I mentioned, was absent in the country. I took my visitors all over the house. I bade them search—search *well*. I led them, at length, to *his* chamber. I showed them his treasures, secure, undisturbed. In the enthusiasm of my confidence, I brought chairs into the room, and desired them *here* to rest from their fatigues, while I myself, in the wild audacity of my perfect triumph, placed my own seat upon the very spot beneath which reposed the corpse of the victim.

The officers were satisfied. My *manner* had convinced them. I was singularly at ease. They sat, and while I answered cheerily, they chatted of familiar things. But, ere long, I felt myself getting pale and wished them gone. My head ached, and I fancied a ringing in my ears; but still they sat and still chatted. The ringing became more distinct—it continued and became more distinct. I talked more freely to get rid of the feeling; but it continued and gained definitiveness—until, at length, I found that the noise was *not* within my ears.

No doubt I now grew *very* pale; but I talked more fluently, and with a heightened voice. Yet the sound increased—and what could I do? It was *a low, dull, quick sound—much such a sound as a watch makes when enveloped in cotton.* I gasped for breath—and yet the officers heard it not. I talked more quickly—more vehemently; but the noise steadily increased. I arose and argued about trifles, in a high key and with violent gesticulations; but the noise steadily increased. Why *would* they not be gone? I paced the floor to and fro with heavy strides, as if excited to fury by the observations of the men—but the noise steadily increased. O God! what *could* I do? I foamed—I raved—I swore! I swung the chair upon which I had been sitting, and grated it upon the boards, but the noise arose over all and continually increased. It grew louder—louder—*louder*! And still the men chatted pleasantly, and smiled. Was it possible they heard not? Almighty God!—no, no! They heard!—they suspected!—they *knew*!—they were making a mockery of my horror!—this I thought, and this I think. But anything was better than this agony! Anything was more tolerable than this derision! I could bear those hypocritical smiles no longer! I felt that I must scream or die!—and now—again!—hark! louder! louder! louder! *louder*!——

"Villains!" I shrieked, "dissemble no more! I admit the deed!—tear up the planks!—here, here!—it is the beating of his hideous heart!"

THE FALL OF THE HOUSE OF USHER

" Son cœur est un luth suspendu;
Sitôt qu'on le touche il résonne."

—De Béranger.

DURING the whole of a dull, dark, and soundless day in the autumn of the year, when the clouds hung oppressively low in the heavens, I had been passing alone, on horseback, through a singularly dreary tract of country; and at length found myself, as the shades of evening drew on, within view of the melancholy House of Usher. I know not how it was—but, with the first glimpse of the building, a sense of insufferable gloom pervaded my spirit. I say insufferable; for the feeling was unrelieved by any of that half-pleasurable, because poetic, sentiment, with which the mind usually receives even the sternest natural images of the desolate or terrible. I looked upon the scene before me—upon the mere house, and the simple landscape features of the domain—upon the bleak walls—upon the vacant eye-like windows—upon a few rank sedges—and upon a few white trunks of decayed trees—with an utter depression of soul which I can compare to no earthly sensation more properly than to the after-dream of the reveller upon opium—the bitter lapse into everyday life—the hideous dropping off of the veil. There was an iciness, a sinking, a sickening of the heart—an unredeemed dreariness of thought which no goading of the imagination could torture into aught of the sublime. What was it—I paused to think—what was it that so unnerved me in the contemplation of the House of Usher? It was a mystery all insoluble; nor could I grapple with the shadowy fancies that crowded upon me as I pondered. I was forced to fall back upon the unsatisfactory conclusion, that while, beyond doubt, there *are* combinations of very simple natural objects which have the power of thus affecting us, still the analysis of this power lies among considerations beyond our depth. It was possible, I reflected, that a mere different arrangement of the particulars of the scene, of the details of the picture, would be sufficient to modify, or perhaps to annihilate its capacity for sorrowful impression; and, acting upon this idea, I reined my horse to the precipitous brink of a black and lurid tarn that lay in unruffled lustre by the dwelling, and gazed down—but with a shudder even more thrilling than before—upon the remodelled and inverted images of the grey sedge, and the ghastly tree-stems, and the vacant and eye-like windows.

Nevertheless, in this mansion of gloom I now proposed to myself a sojourn of some weeks. Its proprietor, Roderick Usher, had been one of my boon companions in boyhood; but many years had elapsed since our last meeting. A letter, however, had lately reached me in a distant part of the country— a letter from him—which, in its wildly importunate nature, had admitted of no other than the personal reply. The MS. gave evidence of nervous agitation. The writer spoke of acute bodily illness—of a mental disorder which oppressed him—and of an earnest desire to see me, as his best, and indeed his only personal friend, with a view of attempting, by the cheerfulness of my society, some alleviation of his malady. It was the manner in which all this, and much more, was said—it was the apparent *heart* that went with his request—which allowed me no room for hesitation; and I accordingly obeyed forthwith what I still considered a very singular summons.

Although, as boys, we had been even intimate associates, yet I really knew little of my friend. His reserve had been always excessive and habitual. I was aware, however, that his very ancient family had been noted, time out of mind, for a peculiar sensibility of temperament, displaying itself through long ages, in many works of exalted art, and manifested, of late, in repeated deeds of munificent yet unobtrusive charity, as well as in a passionate devotion to the intricacies, perhaps even more than to the orthodox and easily recognisable beauties of musical science. I had learned, too, the very remarkable fact, that the stem of the Usher race, all time-honoured as it was, had put forth, at no period, any enduring branch; in other words, that the entire family lay in the direct line of descent, and had always, with very trifling and very temporary variation, so lain. It was this deficiency, I considered, while running over in thought the perfect keeping of the character of the premises with the accredited character of the people, and while speculating upon the possible influence which the one, in the long lapse of centuries, might have exercised upon the other—it was this deficiency, perhaps, of collateral issue, and the consequent undeviating transmission, from sire to son, of the patrimony with the name, which had, at length, so identified the two as to merge the original title of the estate in the quaint and equivocal appellation of the " House of Usher "—an appellation which seemed to include, in the minds of the peasantry who used it, both the family and the family mansion.

I have said that the sole effect of my somewhat childish experiment—that of looking down within the tarn—had been to deepen the first singular impression. There can be no doubt that the consciousness of the rapid increase of my superstition—for why should I not so term it?—served mainly to accelerate the increase itself. Such, I have long known, is the paradoxical law of all sentiments having terror as a basis. And it might have been for this reason only, that, when I again uplifted my eyes to the house itself, from its image in the pool, there grew in my mind a strange fancy— a fancy so ridiculous, indeed, that I but mention it to show the vivid force of the sensations which oppressed me. I had so worked upon my imagination as really to believe that about the whole mansion and domain there hung an atmosphere peculiar to themselves and their immediate vicinity— an atmosphere which had no affinity with the air of heaven, but which had reeked up from the decayed trees, and the grey wall, and the silent tarn—a pestilent and mystic vapour, dull, sluggish, faintly discernible, and leaden-hued.

Shaking off from my spirit what *must* have been a dream, I scanned more narrowly the real aspect of the building. Its principal feature seemed to be that of an excessive antiquity. The discoloration of ages had been great. Minute fungi overspread the whole exterior, hanging in a fine tangled webwork from the eaves. Yet all this was apart from any extraordinary dilapidation. No portion of the masonry had fallen; and there appeared to be a wild inconsistency between its still perfect adaptation of parts, and the crumbling condition of the individual stones. In this there was much that reminded me of the specious totality of old woodwork which has rotted for long years in some neglected vault, with no disturbance

from the breath of the external air. Beyond this indication
of extensive decay, however, the fabric gave little token of
instability. Perhaps the eye of a scrutinising observer might
have discovered a barely perceptible fissure, which, extending
from the roof of the building in front, made its way down
the wall in a zigzag direction, until it became lost in the
sullen waters of the tarn.

Noticing these things, I rode over a short causeway to the
house. A servant in waiting took my horse, and I entered
the Gothic archway of the hall. A valet, of stealthy step,
thence conducted me, in silence, through many dark and
intricate passages in my progress to the studio of his master.
Much that I encountered on the way contributed, I know not
how, to heighten the vague sentiments of which I have already spoken. While the objects around me—while the
carvings of the ceilings, the sombre tapestries of the walls, the
ebon blackness of the floors, and the phantasmagoric armorial
trophies which rattled as I strode, were but matters to which,
or to such as which, I had been accustomed from my infancy
—while I hesitated not to acknowledge how familiar was all
this—I still wondered to find how unfamiliar were the
fancies which ordinary images were stirring up. On one of
the staircases I met the physician of the family. His countenance, I thought, wore a mingled expression of low cunning
and perplexity. He accosted me with trepidation and passed
on. The valet now threw open a door and ushered me into
the presence of his master.

The room in which I found myself was very large and
lofty. The windows were long, narrow, and pointed, and
at so vast a distance from the black oaken floor as to be altogether inaccessible from within. Feeble gleams of encrim-
soned light made their way through the trellised panes, and
served to render sufficiently distinct the more prominent
objects around; the eye, however, struggled in vain to reach
the remoter angles of the chamber, or the recesses of the
vaulted and fretted ceiling. Dark draperies hung upon the
walls. The general furniture was profuse, comfortless,
antique, and tattered. Many books and musical instruments
lay scattered about, but failed to give any vitality to the scene.
I felt that I breathed an atmosphere of sorrow. An air of
stern, deep, and irredeemable gloom hung over and pervaded
all.

Upon my entrance, Usher arose from a sofa on which he had been lying at full length, and greeted me with a vivacious warmth, which had much in it, I at first thought, of an over-done cordiality—of the constrained effort of the *ennuyé* man of the world. A glance, however, at his countenance, con-vinced me of his perfect sincerity. We sat down; and for some moments, while he spoke not, I gazed upon him with a feeling half of pity, half of awe. Surely, man had never before so terribly altered, in so brief a period, as had Roderick Usher! It was with difficulty that I could bring myself to admit the identity of the wan being before me with the com-panion of my early boyhood. Yet the character of his face had been at all times remarkable. A cadaverousness of com-plexion; an eye large, liquid, and luminous beyond compari-son; lips somewhat thin and very pallid, but of a surpassingly beautiful curve; a nose of a delicate Hebrew model, but with a breadth of nostril unusual in similar formations; a finely moulded chin, speaking, in its want of prominence, of a want of moral energy; hair of a more than weblike softness and tenuity; these features, with an inordinate expansion above the regions of the temple, made up altogether a countenance not easily to be forgotten. And now in the mere exaggeration of the prevailing character of these features, and of the ex-pression they were wont to convey, lay so much of change that I doubted to whom I spoke. The now ghastly pallor of the skin, and the now miraculous lustre of the eye, above all things startled and even awed me. The silken hair, too, had been suffered to grow all unheeded, and as, in its wild gos-samer texture, it floated rather than fell about the face, I could not, even with effort, connect its Arabesque expression with any idea of simple humanity.

In the manner of my friend I was at once struck with an incoherence—an inconsistency; and I soon found this to arise from a series of feeble and futile struggles to overcome an habitual trepidancy—an excessive nervous agitation. For something of this nature I had indeed been prepared, no less by his letter, than by reminiscences of certain boyish traits, and by conclusions deduced from his peculiar physical con-formation and temperament. His action was alternately vivacious and sullen. His voice varied rapidly from a tremu-lous indecision (when the animal spirits seemed utterly in abeyance) to that species of energetic concision—that abrupt, weighty, unhurried, and hollow-sounding enunciation—that leaden, self-balanced, and perfectly modulated guttural utterance, which may be observed in the lost drunkard, or the irreclaimable eater of opium, during the periods of his most intense excitement.

It was thus that he spoke of the object of my visit, of his earnest desire to see me, and of the solace he expected me to afford him. He entered, at some length, into what he conceived to be the nature of his malady. It was, he said, a constitutional and a family evil, and one for which he despaired to find a remedy—a mere nervous affection, he immediately added, which would undoubtedly soon pass off. It displayed itself in a host of unnatural sensations. Some of these, as he detailed them, interested and bewildered me; although, perhaps, the terms, and the general manner of the narration had their weight. He suffered much from a morbid acuteness of the senses; the most insipid food was alone endurable; he could wear only garments of certain texture; the odours of all flowers were oppressive; his eyes were tortured by even a faint light; and there were but peculiar sounds, and these from stringed instruments, which did not inspire him with horror.

To an anomalous species of terror I found him a bounden slave. " I shall perish," said he, " I *must* perish in this deplorable folly. Thus, thus, and not otherwise, shall I be lost. I dread the events of the future, not in themselves, but in their results. I shudder at the thought of any, even the most trivial incident, which may operate upon this intolerable agitation of soul. I have, indeed, no abhorrence of danger, except in its absolute effect—in terror. In this unnerved—in this pitiable condition—I feel that the period will sooner or later arrive when I must abandon life and reason together, in some struggle with the grim phantasm, FEAR."

I learned, moreover, at intervals, and through broken and equivocal hints, another singular feature of his mental condition. He was enchained by certain superstitious impressions in regard to the dwelling which he tenanted, and whence, for many years, he had never ventured forth—in regard to an influence whose supposititious force was conveyed in terms too shadowy here to be restated—an influence which some peculiarities in the mere form and substance of his family mansion, had, by dint of long sufferance, he said, obtained over his spirit—an effect which the *physique* of the grey walls and turrets, and of the dim tarn into which they all looked down, had at length brought about upon the *morale* of his existence.

He admitted, however, although with hesitation, that much of the peculiar gloom which thus afflicted him could be traced to a more natural and far more palpable origin— to the severe and long-continued illness—indeed to the evidently approaching dissolution—of a tenderly beloved sister—his sole companion for long years—his last and only relative on earth. " Her decease," he said, with a bitterness which I can never forget, " would leave him (him the hopeless and the frail) the last of the ancient race of the Ushers." While he spoke, the Lady Madeline (for so was she called) passed slowly through a remote portion of the apartment, and, without having noticed my presence, disappeared. I regarded her with an utter astonishment not unmingled with dread—and yet I found it impossible to account for such feelings. A sensation of stupor oppressed me, as my eyes followed her retreating steps. When a door at length closed upon her, my glance sought instinctively and eagerly the countenance of the brother—but he had buried his face in his hands, and I could only perceive that a far more than ordinary wanness had overspread the emaciated fingers, through which trickled many passionate tears.

The disease of the Lady Madeline had long baffled the skill of her physicians. A settled apathy, a gradual wasting away of the person, and frequent although transient affections of a partially cataleptical character, were the unusual diagnosis. Hitherto she had steadily borne up against the pressure of her malady, and had not betaken herself finally to bed; but, on the closing in of the evening of my arrival at the house, she succumbed (as her brother told me at night with inexpressible agitation) to the prostrating power of the Destroyer; and I learned that the glimpse I had obtained of her person would thus probably be the last I should obtain— that the lady, at least while living, would be seen by me no more.

For several days ensuing, her name was unmentioned by either Usher or myself; and during this period I was busied in earnest endeavours to alleviate the melancholy of my friend. We painted and read together; or I listened, as if

in a dream, to the wild improvisations of his speaking guitar.
And thus, as a closer and still closer intimacy admitted me
more unreservedly into the recesses of his spirit, the more
bitterly did I perceive the futility of all attempt at cheering
a mind from which darkness, as if an inherent positive
quality, poured forth upon all objects of the moral and
physical universe, in one unceasing radiation of gloom.

I shall ever bear about me a memory of the many solemn
hours I thus spent alone with the master of the House of
Usher.   Yet I should fail in any attempt to convey an idea
of the exact character of the studies, or of the occupations,
in which he involved me, or led me the way.   An excited and
highly distempered ideality threw a sulphureous lustre over
all.   His long improvised dirges will ring for ever in my
ears.   Among other things, I hold painfully in mind a certain singular perversion and amplification of the wild air of
the last waltz of Von Weber.   From the paintings over
which his elaborate fancy brooded, and which grew, touch
by touch, into vaguenesses at which I shuddered the more
thrillingly, because I shuddered knowing not why—from
these paintings (vivid as their images now are before me) I
would in vain endeavour to educe more than a small portion
which should lie within the compass of merely written words.
By the utter simplicity, by the nakedness of his designs, he
arrested and overawed attention.   If ever mortal painted an
idea, that mortal was Roderick Usher.   For me at least—in
the circumstances then surrounding me—there arose out of
the pure abstractions which the hypochondriac contrived to
throw upon his canvas, an intensity of intolerable awe, no
shadow of which felt I ever yet in the contemplation of the
certainly glowing yet too concrete reveries if Fuseli.

One of the phantasmagoric conceptions of my friend,
partaking not so rigidly of the spirit of abstraction, may
be shadowed forth, although feebly, in words.   A small
picture presented the interior of an immensely long and
rectangular vault or tunnel, with low walls, smooth, white
and without interruption or device.   Certain accessory
points of the design served well to convey the idea that this
excavation lay at an exceeding depth below the surface of
the earth.   No outlet was observed in any portion of its
vast extent, and no torch, or other artificial source of light,
was discernible; yet a flood of intense rays rolled throughout,

and bathed the whole in a ghastly and inappropriate splendour.

I have just spoken of that morbid condition of the auditory nerve which rendered all music intolerable to the sufferer, with the exception of certain effects of stringed instruments. It was, perhaps, the narrow limits to which he thus confined himself upon the guitar, which gave birth, in great measure, to the fantastic character of his performances. But the fervid facility of his impromptus could not be so accounted for. They must have been, and were, in the notes, as well as in the words, of his wild fantasias (for he not unfrequently accompanied himself with rhymed verbal improvisations), the result of that intense mental collectedness and concentration to which I have previously alluded as observable only in particular moments of the highest artificial excitement. The words of one of these rhapsodies I have easily remembered. I was, perhaps, the more forcibly impressed with it, as he gave it, because, in the under or mystic current of its meaning, I fancied that I perceived, and for the first time, a full consciousness on the part of Usher, of the tottering of his lofty reason upon her throne. The verses, which were entitled "The Haunted Palace," ran very nearly, if not accurately, thus:—

I

In the greenest of our valleys,
By good angels tenanted,
Once a fair and stately palace—
Radiant palace—reared its head.
In the monarch Thought's dominion—
It stood there!
Never seraph spread a pinion
Over fabric half so fair.

II

Banners yellow, glorious, golden,
On its roof did float and flow
(This—all this—was in the olden
Time long ago);

And every gentle air that dallied,
  In that sweet day,
Along the ramparts plumed and pallid,
  A winged odour went away.

III

Wanderers in that happy valley
  Through two luminous windows saw
Spirits moving musically
  To a lute's well-tunèd law,
Round about a throne, where sitting
  (Porphyrogene!)
In state his glory well befitting,
  The ruler of the realm was seen.

IV

And all with pearl and ruby glowing
  Was the fair palace door,
Through which came flowing, flowing, flowing
  And sparkling evermore,
A troop of Echoes, whose sweet duty
  Was but to sing,
In voices of surpassing beauty,
  The wit and wisdom of their king.

V

But evil things, in robes of sorrow,
  Assailed the monarch's high estate.
(Ah, let us mourn, for never morrow
  Shall dawn upon him, desolate!)
And, round about his home, the glory
  That blushed and bloomed
Is but a dim-remembered story
  Of the old time entombed.

VI

And travellers now within that valley,
  Through the red-litten windows, see
Vast forms that move fantastically
  To a discordant melody;

While, like a rapid ghastly river,
Through the pale door,
A hideous throng rush out for ever,
And laugh—but smile no more.

I well remember that suggestions arising from this ballad led us into a train of thought wherein there became manifest an opinion of Usher's, which I mention not so much on account of its novelty (for other men have thought thus), as on account of the pertinacity with which he maintained it. This opinion, in its general form, was that of the sentience of all vegetable things. But, in his disordered fancy, the idea had assumed a more daring character, and trespassed, under certain conditions, upon the kingdom of inorganisation. I lack words to express the full extent, or the earnest *abandon* of his persuasion. The belief, however, was connected (as I have previously hinted) with the grey stones of the home of his forefathers. The conditions of the sentience had been here, he imagined, fulfilled in the method of collocation of these stones—in the order of their arrangement, as well as in that of the many fungi which overspread them, and of the decayed trees which stood around—above all, in the long undisturbed endurance of this arrangement, and in its reduplication in the still waters of the tarn. Its evidence—the evidence of the sentience—was to be seen, he said (and I here started as he spoke), in the gradual yet certain condensation of an atmosphere of their own about the waters and the walls. The result was discoverable, he added, in the silent, yet importunate and terrible influence which for centuries had moulded the destinies of his family, and which made *him* what I now saw him—what he was. Such opinions need no comment, and I will make none.

Our books—the books which, for years, had formed no small portion of the mental existence of the invalid—were, as might be supposed, in strict keeping with this character of phantasm. We pored together over such works as the *Ververt et Chartreuse* of Gresset; the *Belphegor* of Machiavelli; the *Heaven and Hell* of Swedenborg; the *Subterranean Voyage of Nicholas Klimn,* by Holberg; the *Chiromancy* of Robert Flud, of Jean D'Indaginé, and of De la Chambre; the *Journey into the Blue Distance* of Tieck; and the *City of the Sun* of Campanella. One favourite volume was a small octavo edition of the *Directorium Inquisitorium*, by the Dominican Eymeric de Gironne; and there were passages in Pomponius Mela, about the old African Satyrs and Œgipans, over which Usher would sit dreaming for hours. His chief delight, however, was found in the perusal of an exceedingly rare and curious book in quarto Gothic—the manual of a forgotten church—the *Vigiliæ Mortuorum secundum Chorum Ecclesiæ Maguntinæ*.

I could not help thinking of the wild ritual of this work, and of its probable influence upon the hypochondriac, when, one evening, having informed me abruptly that the Lady Madeline was no more, he stated his intention of preserving her corpse for a fortnight (previously to its final interment), in one of the numerous vaults within the main walls of the building. The worldly reason, however, assigned for this singular proceeding, was one which I did not feel at liberty to dispute. The brother had been led to his resolution (so he told me) by consideration of the unusual character of the malady of the deceased, of certain obtrusive and eager inquiries on the part of her medical men, and of the remote and exposed situation of the burial-ground of the family. I will not deny that when I called to mind the sinister countenance of the person whom I met upon the staircase, on the day of my arrival at the house, I had no desire to oppose what I regarded as at best but a harmless, and by no means an unnatural, precaution.

At the request of Usher, I personally aided him in the arrangements for the temporary entombment. The body having been encoffined, we two alone bore it to its rest. The vault in which we placed it (and which had been so long unopened that our torches, half smothered in its oppressive atmosphere, gave us little opportunity for investigation) was small, damp, and entirely without means of admission for light; lying, at great depth, immediately beneath that portion of the building in which was my own sleeping apartment. It had been used, apparently, in remote feudal times, for the worst purposes of a donjonkeep, and, in latter days, as a place of deposit for powder, or some other highly combustible substance, as a portion of its floor, and the whole interior of a long archway through which we reached it, were carefully sheathed with copper. The door, of massive iron, had been, also, similarly protected. Its immense weight caused an unusually sharp grating sound, as it moved upon its hinges.

Having deposited our mournful burden upon tressels within this region of horror, we partially turned aside the yet unscrewed lid of the coffin, and looked upon the face of the tenant. A striking similitude between the brother and sister now first arrested my attention; and Usher, divining, perhaps, my thoughts, murmured out some few words from which I learned that the deceased and himself had been twins, and that sympathies of a scarcely intelligible nature had always existed between them. Our glances, however, rested not long upon the dead—for we could not regard her unawed. The disease which had thus entombed the lady in the maturity of youth, had left, as usual in all maladies of a strictly cataleptical character, the mockery of a faint blush upon the bosom and the face, and that suspiciously lingering smile upon the lips which is so terrible in death. We replaced and screwed down the lid, and, having secured the door of iron, made our way, with toil, into the scarcely less gloomy apartments of the upper portion of the house.

And now, some days of bitter grief having elapsed, an observable change came over the features of the mental disorder of my friend. His ordinary manner had vanished. His ordinary occupations were neglected or forgotten. He roamed from chamber to chamber with hurried, unequal, and objectless step. The pallor of his countenance had assumed, if possible, a more ghastly hue—but the luminousness of his eye had utterly gone out. The more occasional huskiness of his tone was heard no more; and a tremulous quaver, as if of extreme terror, habitually characterised his utterance. There were times, indeed, when I thought his unceasingly agitated mind was labouring with some oppressive secret, to divulge which he struggled for the necessary courage. At times, again, I was obliged to resolve all into the mere inexplicable vagaries of madness, for I beheld him gazing upon vacancy for long hours, in an attitude of the profoundest attention, as if listening to some imaginary sound. It was no wonder that his condition terrified—that it infected me. I felt creeping upon me, by slow yet certain degrees, the wild influences of his own fantastic yet impressive superstitions.

It was, especially, upon retiring to bed late in the night of the seventh or eighth day after the placing of the Lady Madeline within the donjon, that I experienced the full power of such feeling. Sleep came not near my couch— while the hours waned and waned away. I struggled to reason off the nervousness which had dominion over me. I endeavoured to believe that much, if not all of what I felt was due to the bewildering influence of the gloomy furniture of the room—of the dark and tattered draperies, which, tortured into motion by the breath of a rising tempest, swayed fitfully to and fro upon the walls, and rustled un-easily about the decorations of the bed. But my efforts were fruitless. An irrepressible tremor gradually pervaded my frame; and, at length, there sat upon my very heart an in-cubus of utterly causeless alarm. Shaking this off with a gasp and a struggle, I uplifted myself upon the pillows, and, peering earnestly within the intense darkness of the chamber, hearkened—I know not why, except that an instinctive spirit prompted me—to certain low and indefinite sounds which came, through the pauses of the storm, at long inter-vals, I knew not whence. Overpowered by an intense senti-ment of horror, unaccountable yet unendurable, I threw on my clothes with haste (for I felt that I should sleep no more during the night), and endeavoured to arouse myself from the pitiable condition into which I had fallen, by pacing rapidly to and fro through the apartment.

I had taken but few turns in this manner, when a light step on an adjoining staircase arrested my attention. I pre-sently recognised it as that of Usher. In an instant after-ward he rapped with a gentle touch, at my door, and entered, bearing a lamp. His countenance was, as usual, cadaverously wan—but, moreover, there was a species of mad hilarity in his eyes—an evidently restrained hysteria in his whole de-meanour. His air appalled me—but anything was prefer-able to the solitude which I had so long endured, and I even welcomed his presence as a relief.

"And you have not seen it?" he said abruptly, after having stared about him for some moments in silence—" you have not then seen it?—but, stay! you shall." Thus speak-ing, and having carefully shaded his lamp, he hurried to one of the casements, and threw it freely open to the storm.

The impetuous fury of the entering gust nearly lifted

us from our feet. It was, indeed, a tempestuous yet sternly beautiful night, and one wildly singular in its terror and its beauty. A whirlwind had apparently collected its force in our vicinity; for there were frequent and violent alterations in the direction of the wind; and the exceeding density of the clouds (which hung so low as to press upon the turrets of the house) did not prevent our perceiving the life-like velocity with which they flew careering from all points against each other, without passing away into the distance. I say that even their exceeding density did not prevent our perceiving this—yet we had no glimpse of the moon or stars —nor was there any flashing forth of the lightning. But the under surfaces of the huge masses of agitated vapour, as well as all terrestrial objects immediately around us, were glowing in the unnatural light of a fæntly luminous and distinctly visible gaseous exhalation which hung about and enshrouded the mansion.

" You must not—you shall not behold this! " said I, shudderingly, to Usher, as I led him, with a gentle violence from the window to a seat. " These appearances, which bewilder you, are merely electrical phenomena not uncommon—or it may be that they have their ghastly origin in the rank miasma of the tarn. Let us close this casement—the air is chilling and dangerous to your frame. Here is one of your favourite romances. I will read, and you shall listen—and so we will pass away this terrible night together."

The antique volume which I had taken up was the *Mad Trist* of Sir Launcelot Canning; but I had called it a favourite of Usher's more in sad jest than in earnest; for, in truth, there is little in its uncouth and unimaginative prolixity which could have had interest for the lofty and spiritual ideality of my friend. It was, however, the only book immediately at hand; and I indulged a vague hope that the excitement which now agitated the hypochondriac, might find relief (for the history of mental disorder is full of similar anomalies) even in the extremeness of the folly which I should read. Could I have judged, indeed, by the wild overstrained air of vivacity with which he hearkened, or apparently hearkened, to the words of the tale, I might well have congratulated myself upon the success of my design.

I had arrived at that well-known portion of the story where Ethelred, the hero of the Trist, having sought in vain for peaceable admission into the dwelling of the hermit, proceeds to make good an entrance by force. Here, it will be remembered, the words of the narrative run thus:—

"And Ethelred, who was by nature of a doughty heart, and who was now mighty withal, on account of the powerfulness of the wine which he had drunken, waited no longer to hold parley with the hermit, who, in sooth, was of an obstinate and maliceful turn, but, feeling the rain upon his shoulders, and fearing the rising of the tempest, uplifted his mace outright, and, with blows, made quickly room in the plankings of the door for his gauntleted hand; and now pulling therewith sturdily, he so cracked, and ripped, and tore all asunder, that the noise of the dry and hollow-sounding wood alarummed and reverberated throughout the forest."

At the termination of this sentence I started, and for a moment paused; for it appeared to me (although I at once concluded that my excited fancy had deceived me)—it appeared to me that, from some very remote portion of the mansion, there came, indistinctly, to my ears, what might have been, in its exact similarity of character, the echo (but a stifled and dull one certainly) of the very cracking and ripping sound which Sir Launcelot had so particularly described. It was, beyond doubt, the coincidence alone which had arrested my attention; for, amid the rattling of the sashes of the casements, and the ordinary commingled noises of the still increasing storm, the sound, in itself, had nothing, surely, which should have interested or disturbed me. I continued the story:—

"But the good champion Ethelred, now entering within the door, was sore enraged and amazed to perceive no signal of the maliceful hermit; but, in the stead thereof, a dragon of a scaly and prodigious demeanour, and of a fiery tongue, which sate in guard before a palace of gold, with a floor of silver; and upon the wall there hung a shield of shining brass with this legend enwritten:—

*'Who entereth herein, a conqueror hath bin;
Who slayeth the dragon, the shield he shall win.'*

And Ethelred uplifted his mace, and struck upon the head of the dragon, which fell before him, and gave up his pesty breath, with a shriek so horrid and harsh, and withal so piercing, that Ethelred had fain to close his ears with his hands against the dreadful noise of it, the like whereof was never before heard."

Here again I paused abruptly, and now with a feeling of wild amazement—for there could be no doubt whatever that, in this instance, I did actually hear (although from what direction it proceeded I found it impossible to say) a low and apparently distant, but harsh, protracted, and most unusual screaming or grating sound—the exact counterpart of what my fancy had already conjured up for the dragon's unnatural shriek as described by the romancer.

Oppressed as I certainly was, upon the occurence of this second and most extraordinary coincidence, by a thousand conflicting sensations, in which wonder and extreme terror were predominant, I still retained sufficient presence of mind to avoid exciting, by any observation, the sensitive nervousness of my companion. I was by no means certain that he had noticed the sound in question; although, assuredly, a strange alteration had, during the last few minutes, taken place in his demeanour. From a position fronting my own, he had gradually brought round his chair, so as to sit with his face to the door of the chamber; and thus I could but partially perceive his features, although I saw that his lips trembled as if he were murmuring inaudibly. His head had dropped upon his breast—yet I knew that he was not asleep, from the wide and rigid opening of the eye as I caught a glance of it in profile. The motion of his body, too, was at variance with this idea—for he rocked from side to side with a gentle yet constant and uniform sway. Having rapidly taken notice of all this, I resumed the narrative of Sir Launcelot, which thus proceeded:—

" And now, the champion, having escaped from the terrible fury of the dragon, bethinking himself of the brazen shield, and of the breaking up of the enchantment which was upon it, removed the carcass from out of the way before him, and approached valorously over the silver pavement of the castle to where the shield was upon the wall; which in sooth tarried not for his full coming, but fell down at his feet upon the silver floor, with a mighty great and terrible ringing sound."

No sooner had these syllables passed my lips, than—as if

a shield of brass had indeed, at the moment, fallen heavily upon a floor of silver—I became aware of a distinct, hollow, metallic, and clangorous, yet apparently muffled reverberation. Completely unnerved, I leaped to my feet; but the measured rocking movement of Usher was undisturbed. I rushed to the chair in which he sat. His eyes were bent fixedly before him, and throughout his whole countenance there reigned a stony rigidity. But, as I placed my hand upon his shoulder, there came a strong shudder over his whole person; a sickly smile quivered on his lips; and I saw that he spoke in a low, hurried, and gibbering murmur, as if unconscious of my presence. Bending closely over him, I at length drank in the hideous import of his words.

"Not hear it?—yes, I hear it, and *have* heard it. Long —long—long—many minutes, many hours, many days, have I heard it—yet I dared not—oh, pity me, miserable wretch that I am!—I dared not—I *dared* not speak! *We have put her living in the tomb!* Said I not that my senses were acute? I *now* tell you that I heard her first feeble movements in the hollow coffin. I heard them—many, many days ago—yet I dared not—*I dared not speak!* And now— to-night—Ethelred—ha! ha!—the breaking of the hermit's door, and the death-cry of the dragon, and the clangour of the shield!—say, rather, the rending of her coffin, and the grating of the iron hinges of her prison, and her struggles within the coppered archway of the vault! Oh, whither shall I fly? Will she not be here anon? Is she not hurrying to upbraid me for my haste? Have I not heard her footstep on the stair? Do I not distinguish that heavy and horrible beating of her heart? Madman! "—here he sprang furiously to his feet, and shrieked out his syllables, as if in the effort he were giving up his soul—"*Madman! I tell you that she now stands without the door!* "

As if in the superhuman energy of his utterance there had been found the potency of a spell—the huge antique panels to which the speaker pointed threw slowly back, upon the instant, their ponderous and ebony jaws. It was the work of the rushing gust—but then without those doors there *did* stand the lofty and enshrouded figure of the Lady Madeline of Usher. There was blood upon her white robes, and the evidence of some bitter struggle upon every portion of her emaciated frame. For a moment she remained trembling and reeling to and fro upon the threshold—then, with a low moaning cry, fell heavily inward upon the person of her brother, and in her violent and now final death-agonies bore him to the floor a corpse, and a victim to the terrors he had anticipated.

From that chamber, and from that mansion, I fled aghast. The storm was still abroad in all its wrath as I found myself crossing the old causeway. Suddenly there shot along the path a wild light, and I turned to see whence a gleam so un-usual could have issued; for the vast house and its shadows were alone behind me. The radiance was that of the full, setting, and blood-red moon, which now shone vividly through that once barely-discernible fissure, of which I have before spoken as extending from the roof of the building, in a zigzag direction, to the base. While I gazed, this fissure rapidly widened—there came a fierce breath of the whirl-wind—the entire orb of the satellite burst at once upon my sight—my brain reeled as I saw the mighty walls rushing asunder—there was a long tumultuous shouting sound like the voice of a thousand waters—and the deep and dark tarn at my feet closed sullenly and silently over the fragments of the " House of Usher."

THE BLACK CAT

FOR the most wild, yet most homely narrative which I am about to pen, I neither expect nor solicit belief. Mad indeed would I be to expect it, in a case where my very senses reject their own evidence. Yet, mad am I not—and very surely do I not dream. But to-morrow I die, and to-day I would unburden my soul. My immediate purpose is to place before the world, plainly, succinctly, and without comment, a series of mere household events. In their consequences, these events have terrified—have tortured—have destroyed me. Yet I will not attempt to expound them. To me, they have presented little but horror—to many they will seem less terrible than *baroques*. Hereafter, perhaps, some intellect may be found which will reduce my phantasm to the commonplace—some intellect more calm, more logical, and far less excitable than my own, which will perceive, in the circumstances I detail with awe, nothing more than an ordinary succession of very natural causes and effects.

From my infancy I was noted for the docility and humanity of my disposition. My tenderness of heart was even so conspicuous as to make me the jest of my companions. I was especially fond of animals, and was indulged by my parents with a great variety of pets. With these I spent most of my time, and never was so happy as when feeding and caressing them. This peculiarity of character grew with my growth, and, in my manhood, I derived from it one of my principal sources of pleasure. To those who have cherished an affection for a faithful and sagacious dog, I need hardly be at the trouble of explaining the nature or the intensity of the gratification thus derivable. There is something in the unselfish and self-sacrificing love of a brute, which goes directly to the heart of him who has had frequent occasion to test the paltry friendship and gossamer fidelity of mere *Man*.

I married early, and was happy to find in my wife a disposition not uncongenial with my own. Observing my partiality for domestic pets, she lost no opportunity of procuring those of the most agreeable kind. We had birds, gold-fish, a fine dog, rabbits, a small monkey, and *a cat*.

This latter was a remarkably large and beautiful animal, entirely black, and sagacious to an astonishing degree. In speaking of his intelligence, my wife, who at heart was not a little tinctured with superstition, made frequent allusion to the ancient popular notion, which regarded all black cats as witches in disguise. Not that she was ever *serious* upon this point—and I mention the matter at all for no better reason than that it happens, just now, to be remembered.

Pluto—this was the cat's name—was my favourite pet and playmate. I alone fed him, and he attended me wherever I went about the house. It was even with difficulty that I could prevent him from following me through the streets.

Our friendship lasted, in this manner, for several years, during which my general temperament and character—through the instrumentality of the fiend Intemperance—had (I blush to confess it) experienced a radical alteration for the worse. I grew, day by day, more moody, more irritable, more regardless of the feelings of others. I suffered myself to use intemperate language to my wife. At length, I even offered her personal violence. My pets, of course, were made to feel the change in my disposition. I not only neglected, but ill-used them. For Pluto, however, I still retained sufficient regard to restrain me from maltreating him, as I made no scruple of maltreating the rabbits, the monkey, or even the dog, when by accident, or through affection, they came in my way. But my disease grew upon me—for what disease is like alcohol?—and at length even Pluto, who was now becoming old, and consequently somewhat peevish—even Pluto began to experience the effects of my ill temper.

One night, returning home, much intoxicated, from one of my haunts about town, I fancied that the cat avoided my presence. I seized him; when, in his fright at my violence, he inflicted a slight wound upon my hand with his teeth. The fury of a demon instantly possessed me. I knew myself no longer. My original soul seemed, at once, to take its flight from my body; and a more than fiendish malevolence, gin-nurtured, thrilled every fibre of my frame. I took from my waistcoat pocket a pen-knife, opened it, grasped the poor beast by the throat, and deliberately cut one of its eyes from the socket! I blush, I burn, I shudder, while I pen the damnable atrocity.

When reason returned with the morning—when I had slept off the fumes of the night's debauch—I experienced a sentiment half of horror, half of remorse, for the crime of which I had been guilty; but it was, at best, a feeble and equivocal feeling, and the soul remained untouched. I again plunged into excess, and soon drowned in wine all memory of the deed.

In the meantime the cat slowly recovered. The socket of the lost eye presented, it is true, a frightful appearance, but he no longer appeared to suffer any pain. He went about the house as usual, but, as might be expected, fled in extreme terror at my approach. I had so much of my old heart left, as to be at first grieved by this evident dislike on the part of a creature which had once so loved me. But this feeling soon gave place to irritation. And then came, as if to my final and irrevocable overthrow, the spirit of PERVERSENESS. Of this spirit philosophy takes no account. Yet I am not more sure that my soul lives, than I am that perverseness is one of the primitive impulses of the human heart—one of the indivisible primary faculties, or sentiments, which give direction to the character of man. Who has not, a hundred times, found himself committing a vile or a silly action, for no other reason than because he knows he should *not*? Have we not a perpetual inclination, in the teeth of our best judgment, to violate that which is *Law*, merely because we understand it to be such? This spirit of perverseness, I say, came to my final overthrow. It was this unfathomable longing of the soul *to vex itself*—to offer violence to its own nature—to do wrong for the wrong's sake only—that urged me to continue and finally to consummate the injury I had inflicted upon the unoffending brute. One morning, in cool blood, I slipped a noose about its neck and hung it to the limb of a tree— hung it with the tears streaming from my eyes, and with the bitterest remorse at my heart—hung it *because* I knew that it had loved me, and *because* I felt it had given me no reason of offence—hung it *because* I knew that in so doing I was committing a sin—a deadly sin that would so jeopardise my immortal soul as to place it—if such a thing were possible— even beyond the reach of the infinite mercy of the Most Merciful and Most Terrible God.

On the night of the day on which this cruel deed was done, I was aroused from sleep by the cry of "Fire!" The curtains of my bed were in flames. The whole house was blazing. It was with great difficulty that my wife, a servant, and myself, made our escape from the conflagration. The destruction was complete. My entire worldly wealth was swallowed up, and I resigned myself thenceforward to despair.

I am above the weakness of seeking to establish a sequence of cause and effect between the disaster and the atrocity. But I am detailing a chain of facts, and wish not to leave even a possible link imperfect. On the day succeeding the fire, I visited the ruins. The walls, with one exception, had fallen in. This exception was found in a compartment wall, not very thick, which stood about the middle of the house, and against which had rested the head of my bed. The plastering had here, in great measure, resisted the action of the fire—a fact which I attributed to its having been recently spread. About this wall a dense crowd were collected, and many persons seemed to be examining a particular portion of it with very minute and eager attention. The words "strange!" "singular!" and other similar expressions, excited my curiosity. I approached and saw, as if graven in bas-relief upon the white surface, the figure of a gigantic *cat*. The impression was given with an accuracy truly marvellous. There was a rope about the animal's neck.

When I first beheld this apparition—for I could scarcely regard it as less—my wonder and my terror were extreme. But at length reflection came to my aid. The cat, I remembered, had been hung in a garden adjacent to the house. Upon the alarm of fire, this garden had been immediately filled by the crowd—by some one of whom the animal must have been cut from the tree and thrown, through an open window, into my chamber. This had probably been done with the view of arousing me from sleep. The falling of other walls had compressed the victim of my cruelty into the substance of the freshly-spread plaster; the lime of which, with the flames and the *ammonia* from the carcass, had then accomplished the portraiture as I saw it.

Although I thus readily accounted to my reason, if not altogether to my conscience, for the startling fact just detailed, it did not the less fail to make a deep impression

I saw the figure of a gigantic cat.

upon my fancy. For months I could not rid myself of the phantasm of the cat; and, during this period, there came back into my spirit a half-sentiment that seemed, but was not, remorse. I went so far as to regret the loss of the animal, and to look about me, among the vile haunts which I now habitually frequented, for another pet of the same species, and of somewhat similar appearance, with which to supply its place.

One night as I sat, half stupefied, in a den of more than infamy, my attention was suddenly drawn to some black object, reposing upon the head of one of the immense hogsheads of gin, or of rum, which constituted the chief furniture of the apartment. I had been looking steadily at the top of this hogshead for some minutes, and what now caused me surprise was the fact that I had not sooner perceived the object thereupon. I approached it, and touched it with my hand. It was a black cat—a very large one—fully as large as Pluto, and closely resembling him in every respect but one. Pluto had not a white hair upon any portion of his body; but this cat had a large, although indefinite, splotch of white, covering nearly the whole region of the breast.

Upon my touching him, he immediately arose, purred loudly, rubbed against my hand, and appeared delighted with my notice. This, then, was the very creature of which I was in search. I at once offered to purchase it of the landlord; but this person made no claim to it—knew nothing of it— had never seen it before.

I continued my caresses, and when I prepared to go home, the animal evinced a disposition to accompany me. I permitted it to do so; occasionally stooping and patting it as I proceeded. When it reached the house it domesticated itself at once, and became immediately a great favourite with my wife.

For my own part, I soon found a dislike to it arising within me. This was just the reverse of what I had anticipated; but —I know not how or why it was—its evident fondness for myself rather disgusted and annoyed me. By slow degrees, these feelings of disgust and annoyance rose into the bitterness of hatred. I avoided the creature; a certain sense of shame, and the remembrance of my former deed of cruelty, preventing me from physically abusing it. I did not, for some weeks, strike, or otherwise violently ill-use it; but gradually—very gradually—I came to look upon it with unutterable loathing, and to flee silently from its odious presence, as from the breath of a pestilence.

What added, no doubt, to my hatred of the beast, was the discovery, on the morning after I brought it home, that, like Pluto, it also had been deprived of one of its eyes. This circumstance, however, only endeared it to my wife, who, as I have already said, possessed, in a high degree, that humanity of feeling which had once been my distinguishing trait, and the source of many of my simplest and purest pleasures.

With my aversion to this cat, however, its partiality for myself seemed to increase. It followed my footsteps with a pertinacity which it would be difficult to make the reader comprehend. Whenever I sat, it would crouch beneath my chair, or spring upon my knees, covering me with its loathsome caresses. If I arose to walk, it would get between my feet, and thus nearly throw me down, or, fastening its long and sharp claws in my dress, clamber, in this manner, to my breast. At such times, although I longed to destroy it with a blow, I was yet withheld from so doing, partly by a memory of my former crime, but chiefly—let me confess it at once—by absolute *dread* of the beast.

This dread was not exactly a dread of physical evil—and yet I should be at a loss how otherwise to define it. I am almost ashamed to own—yes, even in this felon's cell, I am almost ashamed to own—that the terror and horror with which the animal inspired me, had been heightened by one of the merest chimeras it would be possible to conceive. My wife had called my attention, more than once, to the character of the mark of white hair, of which I have spoken, and which constituted the sole visible difference between the strange beast and the one I had destroyed. The reader will remember that this mark, although large, had been originally very indefinite; but, by slow degrees—degrees nearly imperceptible, and which for a long time my reason struggled to reject as fanciful—it had, at length, assumed a rigorous distinctness of outline. It was now the representation of an object that I shudder to name—and for this, above all, I loathed, and dreaded, and would have rid myself of the monster *had I dared*—it was now, I say, the image of a hideous—of a ghastly thing—of the GALLOWS!—oh, mournful and terrible engine of horror and of crime—of agony and of death!

And now was I indeed wretched beyond the wretchedness of mere humanity. And *a brute beast*—whose fellow I had contemptuously destroyed—*a brute beast* to work out for *me* —for me, a man, fashioned in the image of the High God— so much of insufferable woe! Alas! neither by day nor by night knew I the blessing of rest any more! During the former the creature left me no moment alone; and, in the latter, I started, hourly, from dreams of unutterable fear, to find the hot breath of *the thing* upon my face, and its vast weight—an incarnate nightmare that I had no power to shake off—incumbent eternally upon my *heart!*

Beneath the pressure of torments such as these, the feeble remnant of the good within me succumbed. Evil thoughts became my sole intimates—the darkest and most evil of thoughts. The moodiness of my usual temper increased to hatred of all things and of all mankind; while, from the sudden, frequent, and ungovernable outbursts of a fury to which I now blindly abandoned myself, my uncomplaining wife, alas! was the most usual and the most patient of sufferers.

One day she accompanied me, upon some household errand, into the cellar of the old building which our poverty compelled us to inhabit. The cat followed me down the steep stairs, and, nearly throwing me headlong, exasperated me to madness. Uplifting an axe, and forgetting, in my wrath, the childish dread which had hitherto stayed my hand, I aimed a blow at the animal which, of course, would have proved instantly fatal had it descended as I wished. But this blow was arrested by the hand of my wife. Goaded, by the interference, into a rage more than demoniacal, I withdrew my arm from her grasp, and buried the axe in her brain. She fell dead upon the spot, without a groan.

This hideous murder accomplished, I set myself forthwith, and with entire deliberation, to the task of concealing the body. I knew that I could not remove it from the house, either by day or by night, without the risk of being observed by the neighbours. Many projects entered my mind. At one period I thought of cutting the corpse into minute fragments, and destroying them by fire. At another, I resolved to dig a grave for it in the floor of the cellar. Again, I deliberated about casting it into the well in the yard—about packing it in a box, as if merchandise, with the usual arrangements, and so getting a porter to take it from the house. Finally I hit upon what I considered a far better expedient than either of these. I determined to wall it up in the cellar —as the monks of the Middle Ages are recorded to have walled up their victims.

For a purpose such as this the cellar was well adapted. Its walls were loosely constructed, and had lately been plastered throughout with a rough plaster, which the dampness of the atmosphere had prevented from hardening. Moreover, in one of the walls was a projection, caused by a false chimney, or fireplace, that had been filled up, and made to resemble the rest of the cellar. I made no doubt that I could readily displace the bricks at this point, insert the corpse, and wall the whole up as before, so that no eye could detect anything suspicious.

And in this calculation I was not deceived. By means of a crowbar I easily dislodged the bricks, and, having carefully deposited the body against the inner wall, I propped it in that position, while, with little trouble, I relaid the whole structure as it originally stood. Having procured mortar, sand, and hair, with every possible precaution, I prepared a plaster which could not be distinguished from the old, and with this I very carefully went over the new brickwork. When I had finished, I felt satisfied that all was right. The wall did not present the slightest appearance of having been disturbed. The rubbish on the floor was picked up with the minutest care. I looked around triumphantly, and said to myself, "Here at least, then, my labour has not been in vain."

My next step was to look for the beast which had been the cause of so much wretchedness; for I had, at length, firmly resolved to put it to death. Had I been able to meet with it, at the moment, there could have been no doubt of its fate; but it appeared that the crafty animal had been alarmed at the violence of my previous anger, and forbore to present itself in my present mood. It is impossible to describe, or to imagine, the deep, the blissful sense of relief which the absence of the detested creature occasioned in my bosom. It did not make its appearance during the night—and thus for one night at least, since its introduction into the house, I

soundly and tranquilly slept; aye, *slept* even with the burden
of murder upon my soul!

The second and the third day passed, and still my tormentor came not. Once again I breathed as a free man. The
monster, in terror, had fled the premises for ever! I should
behold it no more! My happiness was supreme! The guilt
of my dark deed disturbed me but little. Some few inquiries
had been made, but these had been readily answered. Even
a search had been instituted—but of course nothing was to
be discovered. I looked upon my future felicity as secured.

Upon the fourth day of the assassination, a party of the
police came, very unexpectedly, into the house, and proceeded
again to make rigorous investigation of the premises. Secure,
however, in the inscrutability of my place of concealment, I
felt no embarrassment whatever. The officers bade me
accompany them in their search. They left no nook or
corner unexplored. At length, for the third or fourth time,
they descended into the cellar. I quivered not in a muscle.
My heart beat calmly as that of one who slumbers in innocence. I walked the cellar from end to end. I folded my
arms upon my bosom, and roamed easily to and fro. The
police were thoroughly satisfied, and prepared to depart.
The glee at my heart was too strong to be restrained. I
burned to say if but one word, by way of triumph, and to
render doubly sure their assurance of my guiltlessness.

"Gentlemen," I said at last, as the party ascended the
steps, "I delight to have allayed your suspicions. I wish you
all health, and a little more courtesy. By-the-bye, gentlemen,
this is a very well-constructed house." (In the rabid desire
to say something easily, I scarcely knew what I uttered at
all.) "I may say an *excellently* well-constructed house.
These walls—are you going, gentlemen?—these walls are
solidly put together; " and here, through the mere frenzy of
bravado, I rapped heavily, with a cane which I held in my
hand, upon that very portion of the brickwork behind which
stood the corpse of the wife of my bosom.

But may God shield and deliver me from the fangs of the
Arch-Fiend! No sooner had the reverberation of my blows
sunk into silence, than I was answered by a voice from within the tomb!—by a cry, at first muffled and broken, like the
sobbing of a child, and then quickly swelling into one long,
loud, and continuous scream, utterly anomalous and inhuman

—a howl—a wailing shriek, half of horror and half of triumph, such as might have arisen only out of hell, conjointly from the throats of the damned in their agony and of the demons that exult in the damnation.

Of my own thoughts it is folly to speak. Swooning, I staggered to the opposite wall. For one instant the party upon the stairs remained motionless, through extremity of terror and of awe. In the next, a dozen stout arms were toiling at the wall. It fell bodily. The corpse, already greatly decayed and clotted with gore, stood erect before the eyes of the spectators. Upon its head, with red extended mouth and solitary eye of fire, sat the hideous beast whose craft had seduced me into murder, and whose informing voice had consigned me to the hangman. I had walled the monster up within the tomb!

LIGEIA

"And the will therein lieth, which dieth not. Who knoweth
the mysteries of the will, with its vigour? For God is but a great
will pervading all things by nature of its intentness. Man doth
not yield himself to the angels, nor unto death utterly, save only
through the weakness of his feeble will."—JOSEPH GLANVILL.

I CANNOT, for my soul, remember how, when, or even
precisely where, I first became acquainted with the Lady
Ligeia. Long years have since elapsed, and my memory is
feeble through much suffering. Or, perhaps, I cannot *now*
bring these points to mind, because, in truth, the character
of my beloved, her rare learning, her singular yet placid
cast of beauty, and the thrilling and enthralling eloquence
of her low musical language, made their way into my heart
by paces so steadily and stealthily progressive, that they have
been unnoticed and unknown. Yet I believe that I met her
first and most frequently in some large, old, decaying city
near the Rhine. Of her family—I have surely heard her
speak. That it is of a remotely ancient date cannot be
doubted. Ligeia! Ligeia! Buried in studies of a nature
more than all else adapted to deaden impressions of the outward world, it is by that sweet word alone—by Ligeia—that
I bring before mine eyes in fancy the image of her who is
no more. And now, while I write, a recollection flashes
upon me that I have *never known* the paternal name of her
who was my friend and my betrothed, and who became the
partner of my studies, and finally the wife of my bosom.
Was it a playful charge on the part of my Ligeia? or was it
a test of my strength of affection, that I should institute no
inquiries upon this point? or was it rather a caprice of my
own—a wildly romantic offering on the shrine of the most
passionate devotion? I but indistinctly recall the fact itself
—what wonder that I have utterly forgotten the circumstances which originated or attended it? And, indeed, if
ever that spirit which is entitled *Romance*—if ever she, the

wan and the misty-winged *Ashtophet* of idolatrous Egypt, presided, as they tell, over marriages ill-omened, then most surely she presided over mine.

There is one dear topic, however, on which my memory fails me not. It is the *person* of Ligeia. In stature she was tall, somewhat slender, and, in her latter days, even emaciated. I would in vain attempt to portray the majesty, the quiet ease, of her demeanour, or the incomprehensible lightness and elasticity of her footfall. She came and departed as a shadow. I was never made aware of her entrance into my closed study, save by the dear music of her low sweet voice, as she placed her marble hand upon my shoulder. In beauty of face no maiden ever equalled her. It was the radiance of an opium-dream—an airy and spirit-lifting vision more wildly divine than the fantasies which hovered about the slumbering souls of the daughters of Delos. Yet her features were not of that regular mould which we have been falsely taught to worship in the classical labours of the heathen. "There is no exquisite beauty," says Bacon, Lord Verulam, speaking truly of all the forms and genera of beauty, "without some *strangeness* in the proportion." Yet, although I saw that the features of Ligeia were not of a classic regularity—although I perceived that her loveliness was indeed "exquisite," and felt that there was much of "strangeness" pervading it, yet I have tried in vain to detect the irregularity and to trace home my own perception of "the strange." I examined the contour of the lofty and pale forehead—it was faultless—how cold indeed that word when applied to a majesty so divine!—the skin rivalling the purest ivory, the commanding extent and repose, the gentle prominence of the regions above the temples; and then the raven-black, the glossy, the luxuriant and naturally-curling tresses, setting forth the full force of the Homeric epithet, "hyacinthine!" I looked at the delicate outlines of the nose—and nowhere but in the graceful medallions of the Hebrews had I beheld a similar perfection. There were the same luxurious smoothness of surface, the same scarcely perceptible tendency to the aquiline, the same harmoniously curved nostrils speaking the free spirit. I regarded the sweet mouth. Here was indeed the triumph of all things heavenly —the magnificent turn of the short upper lip—the soft, voluptuous slumber of the under—the dimples which sported,

and the colour which spoke—the teeth glancing back, with a
brilliancy almost startling, every ray of the holy light which
fell upon them in her serene and placid, yet most exultingly
radiant of all smiles. I scrutinised the formation of the chin
—and here, too, I found the gentleness of breadth, the softness and the majesty, the fulness and the spirituality, of the
Greek—the contour which the god Apollo revealed but in a
dream, to Cleomenes, the son of the Athenian. And then I
peered into the large eyes of Ligeia.

For eyes we have no models in the remotely antique. It
might have been, too, that in these eyes of my beloved lay
the secret to which Lord Verulam alludes. They were, I
must believe, far larger than the ordinary eyes of our own
race. They were even fuller than the fullest of the gazelle
eyes of the tribe of the valley of Nourjahad. Yet it was only
at intervals—in moments of intense excitement—that this
peculiarity became more than slightly noticeable in Ligeia.
And at such moments was her beauty—in my heated fancy
thus it appeared, perhaps—the beauty of beings either above
or apart from the earth—the beauty of the fabulous Houri
of the Turk. The hue of the orbs was the most brilliant of
black, and, far over them, hung jetty lashes of great length.
The brows, slightly irregular in outline, had the same tint.
The " strangeness," however, which I found in the eyes, was
of a nature distinct from the formation, or the colour, or the
brilliancy of the features, and must, after all, be referred to
the *expression*. Ah, word of no meaning! behind whose vast
latitude of mere sound we intrench our ignorance of so much
of the spiritual. The expression of the eyes of Ligeia—how
for long hours have I pondered upon it! How have I,
through the whole of a midsummer night, struggled to
fathom it! What was it—that something more profound
than the well of Democritus—which lay far within the pupils
of my beloved? what *was* it? I was possessed with a passion
to discover. Those eyes, those large, those shining, those
divine orbs? they became to me twin stars of Leda, and I to
them devoutest of astrologers.

There is no point, among the many incomprehensible
anomalies of the science of mind, more thrillingly exciting
than the fact—never, I believe, noticed in the schools—that
in our endeavours to recall to memory something long forgotten, we often find ourselves *upon the very verge* of re-

membrance, without being able, in the end, to remember. And thus how frequently, in my intense scrutiny of Ligeia's eyes, have I felt approaching the full knowledge of their expression—felt it approaching—yet not quite be mine— and so at length entirely depart! And (strange—oh, strangest mystery of all!) I found, in the commonest objects of the universe, a circle of analogies to that expression. I mean to say that, subsequently to the period when Ligeia's beauty passed into my spirit, there dwelling as in a shrine, I derived, from many existences in the material world, a sentiment such as I felt always aroused within me by her large and luminous orbs. Yet not the more could I define that sentiment, or analyse, or even steadily view it. I recognised it, let me repeat, sometimes in the survey of a rapidly growing vine—in the contemplation of a moth, a butterfly, a chrysalis, a stream of running water. I have felt it in the ocean; in the falling of a meteor. I have felt it in the glances of unusually aged people. And there are one or two stars in heaven (one especially, a star of the sixth magnitude, double and changeable, to be found near the large star in Lyra), in a telescopic scrutiny of which I have been made aware of the feeling. I have been filled with it by certain sounds from stringed instruments, and not unfrequently by passages from books. Among innumerable other instances, I well remember something in a volume of Joseph Glanvill, which (perhaps merely from its quaintness—who shall say?) never failed to inspire me with the sentiment: "And the will therein lieth, which dieth not. Who knoweth the mysteries of the will, with its vigour? For God is but a great will pervading all things by nature of its intentness. Man doth not yield him to the angels, nor unto death utterly, save only through the weakness of his feeble will."

Length of years and subsequent reflection have enabled me to trace, indeed, some remote connection between this passage in the English moralist and a portion of the character of Ligeia. An *intensity* in thought, action, or speech, was possibly, in her, a result, or at least an index, of that gigantic volition which, during our long intercourse, failed to give other and more immediate evidence of its existence. Of all the women whom I have ever known, she, the outwardly calm, the ever-placid Ligeia, was the most violently a prey to the tumultuous vultures of stern passion. And of such passion I could form no estimate, save by the miraculous expansion of those eyes which at once so delighted and appalled me—by the almost magical melody, modulation, distinctness, and placidity of her very low voice—and by the fierce energy (rendered doubly effective by contrast with her manner of utterance) of the wild words which she habitually uttered.

I have spoken of the learning of Ligeia: it was immense—such as I have never known in woman. In the classical tongues was she deeply proficient, and, as far as my own acquaintance extended in regard to the modern dialects of Europe, I have never known her at fault. Indeed upon any theme of the most admired, because simply the most abstruse of the boasted erudition of the academy, have I *ever* found Ligeia at fault? How singularly—how thrillingly, this one point in the nature of my wife has forced itself, at this late period only, upon my attention! I said her knowledge was such as I have never known in woman—but where breathes the man who has traversed, and successfully, *all* the wide areas of moral, physical, and mathematical science? I saw not then what I now clearly perceive, that the acquisitions of Ligeia were gigantic, were astounding; yet I was sufficiently aware of her infinite supremacy to resign myself, with a childlike confidence, to her guidance through the chaotic world of metaphysical investigation at which I was most busily occupied during the earlier years of our marriage. With how vast a triumph—with how vivid a delight —with how much of all that is ethereal in hope—did I *feel*, as she bent over me in studies but little sought—but less known—that delicious vista by slow degrees expanding before me, down whose long, gorgeous, and all untrodden path, I might at length pass onward to the goal of a wisdom too divinely precious not to be forbidden!

How poignant, then, must have been the grief with which, after some years, I beheld my well-grounded expectations take wings to themselves and fly away! Without Ligeia I was but as a child groping benighted. Her presence, her readings alone, rendered vividly luminous the many mysteries of the transcendentalism in which we were immersed. Wanting the radiant lustre of her eyes, letters, lambent and golden, grew duller than Saturnian lead. And now those eyes shone less and less frequently upon the pages over which I pored.

Ligeia grew ill. The wild eyes blazed with a too—too glorious effulgence; the pale fingers became of the transparent waxen hue of the grave; and the blue veins upon the lofty forehead swelled and sank impetuously with the tides of the most gentle emotion. I saw that she must die—and I struggled desperately in spirit with the grim Azrael. And the struggles of the passionate wife were, to my astonishment, even more energetic than my own. There had been much in her stern nature to impress me with the belief that, to her, death would have come without its terrors; but not so. Words are impotent to convey any just idea of the fierceness of resistance with which she wrestled with the Shadow. I groaned in anguish at the pitiable spectacle. I would have soothed—I would have reasoned; but, in the intensity of her wild desire for life—for life—*but* for life—solace and reason were alike the uttermost of folly. Yet not until the last instance, amid the most convulsive writhings of her fierce spirit, was shaken the external placidity of her demeanour. Her voice grew more gentle—grew more low—yet I would not wish to dwell upon the wild meaning of the quietly uttered words. My brain reeled as I hearkened, entranced, to a melody more than mortal—to assumptions and aspirations which mortality had never before known.

That she loved me I should not have doubted; and I might have been easily aware that, in a bosom such as hers, love would have reigned no ordinary passion. But in death only was I fully impressed with the strength of her affection. For long hours, detaining my hand, would she pour out before me the overflowing of a heart whose more than passionate devotion amounted to idolatry. How had I deserved to be so blessed by such confessions?—how had I deserved to be so cursed with the removal of my beloved in the hour of her making them? But upon this subject I cannot bear to dilate. Let me say only, that in Ligeia's more than womanly abandonment to a love, alas! all unmerited, all unworthily bestowed, I at length recognised the principle of her longing, with so wildly earnest a desire, for the life which was now fleeing so rapidly away. It is this wild longing—it is this eager vehemence of desire for life—*but* for life—that I have no power to portray—no utterance capable of expressing.

At high noon of the day in which she departed, beckoning me, peremptorily, to her side, she bade me repeat certain

verses composed by herself not many days before. I obeyed
her. They were these:—

> Lo! 'tis a gala night
>   Within the lonesome latter years!
> An angel throng, bewinged, bedight
>   In veils, and drowned in tears,
> Sit in a theatre, to see
>   A play of hopes and fears,
> While the orchestra breathes fitfully
>   The music of the spheres.
>
> Mimes, in the form of God on high,
>   Mutter and mumble low,
> And hither and thither fly;
>   Mere puppets they, who come and go
> At bidding of vast formless things
>   That shift the scenery to and fro,
> Flapping from out their condor wings
>   Invisible Woe!
>
> That motley drama!—oh, be sure
>   It shall not be forgot!
> With its Phantom chased for evermore,
>   By a crowd that seize it not,
> Through a circle that ever returneth in
>   To the self-same spot;
> And much of Madness, and more of Sin,
>   And Horror, the soul of the plot!
>
> But see, amid the mimic rout
>   A crawling shape intrude!
> A blood-red thing that writhes from out
>   The scenic solitude!
> It writhes!—it writhes!—with mortal pangs
>   The mimes become its food,
> And the seraphs sob at vermin fangs
>   In human gore imbued.
>
> Out—out are the lights—out all!
>   And over each quivering form,
> The curtain, a funeral pall,
>   Comes down with the rush of a storm—

And the angels, all pallid and wan,
Uprising, unveiling, affirm
That the play is the tragedy, " Man,"
And its hero, the Conqueror Worm.

" O God! " half-shrieked Ligeia, leaping to her feet and extending her arms aloft with a spasmodic movement, as I made an end of these lines—" O God! O Divine Father! —shall these things be undeviatingly so?—shall this conqueror be not once conquered? Are we not part and parcel in Thee? Who—who knoweth the mysteries of the will, with its vigour? Man doth not yield him to the angels, *nor unto death utterly,* save only through the weakness of his feeble will."

And now, as if exhausted with emotion, she suffered her white arms to fall, and returned solemnly to her bed of death. And as she breathed her last sighs, there came mingled with them a low murmur from her lips. I bent to them my ear, and distinguished again the concluding words of the passage in Glanvill: " *Man doth not yield him to the angels, nor unto death utterly, save only through the weakness of his feeble will.*"

She died; and I, crushed into the very dust with sorrow, could no longer endure the lonely desolation of my dwelling in the dim and decaying city by the Rhine. I had no lack of what the world calls wealth. Ligeia had brought me far more, very far more than ordinarily falls to the lot of mortals. After a few months, therefore, of weary and aimless wandering, I purchased, and put in some repair, an abbey, which I shall not name, in one of the wildest and least frequented portions of fair England. The gloomy and dreary grandeur of the building, the almost savage aspect of the domain, the many melancholy and time-honoured memories connected with both, had much in unison with the feelings of utter abandonment which had driven me into that remote and unsocial region of the country. Yet, although the external abbey, with its verdant decay hanging about it, suffered but little alteration, I gave way, with a childlike perversity, and perchance with a faint hope of alleviating my sorrows, to a display of more than regal magnificence within. For such follies, even in childhood, I had imbibed a taste, and now they came back to me as if in the dotage of grief. Alas, I

feel how much even of incipient madness might have been
discovered in the gorgeous and fantastic draperies, in the
solemn carvings of Egypt, in the wild cornices and furniture,
in the Bedlam patterns of the carpets of tufted gold! I had
become a bounden slave in the trammels of opium, and my
labours and my orders had taken a colouring from my
dreams. But these absurdities I must not pause to detail.
Let me speak only of that one chamber, ever accursed,
whither in a moment of mental alienation, I led from the
altar as my bride—as the successor of the unforgotten Ligeia
—the fair-haired and blue-eyed Lady Rowena Trevanion
of Tremaine.

There is no individual portion of the architecture and
decoration of that bridal chamber which is not now visibly
before me. Where were the souls of the haughty family
of the bride, when, through thirst of gold, they permitted
to pass the threshold of an apartment so bedecked, a maiden
and a daughter so beloved? I have said that I minutely
remember the details of the chamber—yet I am sadly for-
getful on topics of deep moment—and here there was no
system, no keeping, in the fantastic display, to take hold
upon the memory. The room lay in a high turret of the
castellated abbey, was pentagonal in shape, and of capacious
size. Occupying the whole southern face of the pentagon
was the sole window—an immense sheet of unbroken glass
from Venice—a single pane, and tinted of a leaden hue, so
that the rays of either the sun or moon passing through it,
fell with a ghastly lustre on the objects within. Over the
upper portion of this huge window extended the trellis-work
of an aged vine, which clambered up the massy walls of the
turret. The ceiling, of gloomy-looking oak, was excessively
lofty, vaulted, and elaborately fretted with the wildest and
most grotesque specimens of a semi-Gothic, semi-Druidical
device. From out the most central recess of this melancholy
vaulting, depended, by a single chain of gold with long links,
a huge censer of the same metal, Saracenic in pattern, and
with many perforations so contrived that there writhed in
and out of them, as if endued with a serpent vitality, a continual succession of parti-coloured fires.

Some few ottomans and golden candelabra, of Eastern
figure, were in various stations about; and there was the
couch, too—the bridal couch—of an Indian model, and low,

and sculptured of solid ebony, with a pall-like canopy above. In each of the angles of the chamber stood on end a gigantic sarcophagus of black granite, from the tombs of the kings over against Luxor, with their aged lids full of immemorial sculpture. But in the draping of the apartment lay, alas! the chief fantasy of all. The lofty walls, gigantic in height —even unproportionably so—were hung from summit to foot, in vast folds, with a heavy and massive-looking tapestry —tapestry of a material which was found alike as a carpet on the floor, as a covering for the ottomans and the ebony bed, as a canopy for the bed, and as the gorgeous volutes of the curtains which partially shaded the window. The material was the richest cloth of gold. It was spotted all over, at irregular intervals, with arabesque figures, about a foot in diameter, and wrought upon the cloth in patterns of the most jetty black. But these figures partook of the true character of the arabesque only when regarded from a single point of view. By a contrivance now common, and indeed traceable to a very remote period of antiquity, they were made changeable in aspect. To one entering the room, they bore the appearance of simple monstrosities; but upon a farther advance, this appearance gradually departed; and, step by step, as the visitor moved his station in the chamber, he saw himself surrounded by an endless succession of the ghastly forms which belong to the superstition of the Norman, or arise in the guilty slumbers of the monk. The Phantasmagoric effect was vastly heightened by the artificial introduction of a strong continual current of wind behind the draperies—giving a hideous and uneasy animation to the whole.

In halls such as these—in a bridal chamber such as this— I passed, with the Lady of Tremaine, the unhallowed hours of the first month of our marriage—passed them with but little disquietude. That my wife dreaded the fierce moodiness of my temper—that she shunned me, and loved me but little—I could not help perceiving; but it gave me rather pleasure than otherwise. I loathed her with a hatred belonging more to demon than to man. My memory flew back (oh, with what intensity of regret!) to Ligeia, the beloved, the august, the beautiful, the entombed. I revelled in recollections of her purity; of her wisdom; of her lofty, her ethereal nature; of her passionate, her idolatrous love.

Now, then, did my spirit fully and freely burn with more than all the fires of her own. In the excitement of my opium dreams (for I was habitually fettered in the shackles of the drug) I would call aloud upon her name, during the silence of the night, or among the sheltered recesses of the glens by day, as if, through the wild eagerness, the solemn passion, the consuming ardour of my longing for the departed, I could restore her to the pathway she had abandoned—ah, *could* it be for ever?—upon the earth.

About the commencement of the second month of the marriage, the Lady Rowena was attacked with sudden illness, from which her recovery was slow. The fever which consumed her rendered her nights uneasy; and in her perturbed state of half-slumber, she spoke of sounds, and of motions, in and about the chamber of the turret, which I concluded had no origin save in the distemper of her fancy, or perhaps in the phantasmagoric influences of the chamber itself. She became at length convalescent—finally, well. Yet but a brief period elapsed ere a second more violent disorder again threw her upon a bed of suffering; and from this attack her frame, at all times feeble, never altogether recovered. Her illnesses were, after this epoch, of alarming character, and of more alarming recurrence, defying alike the knowledge and the great exertions of her physicians. With the increase of the chronic disease, which had thus, apparently, taken too sure hold upon her constitution to be eradicated by human means, I could not fail to observe a similar increase in the nervous irritation of her temperament, and in her excitability by trivial causes of fear. She spoke again, and now more frequently and pertinaciously, of the sounds—of the slight sounds—and of the unusual motions among the tapestries, to which she had formerly alluded.

One night, near the closing in of September, she pressed this distressing subject with more than usual emphasis upon my attention. She had just awakened from an unquiet slumber, and I had been watching, with feelings half of anxiety, half of vague terror, the workings of her emaciated countenance. I sat by the side of her ebony bed, upon one of the ottomans of India. She partly arose, and spoke, in an earnest low whisper, of sounds which she *then* heard, but which I could not hear—of motions which she *then* saw, but which I could not perceive. The wind was rushing hurriedly behind the tapestries, and I wished to show her (what, let me confess it, I could not *all* believe) that those almost inarticulate breathings, and those very gentle variations of the figures upon the wall, were but the natural effects of that customary rushing of the wind.   But a deadly pallor, overspreading her face, had proved to me that my exertions to reassure her would be fruitless.   She appeared to be fainting, and no attendants were within call.   I remembered where was deposited a decanter of light wine which had been ordered by her physicians; and hastened across the chamber to procure it.   But, as I stepped beneath the light of the censer, two circumstances of a startling nature attracted my attention.   I had felt that some palpable although invisible object had passed lightly by my person; and I saw that there lay upon the golden carpet, in the very middle of the rich lustre thrown from the censer, a shadow—a faint, indefinite shadow of angelic aspect—such as might be fancied for the shadow of a shade.   But I was wild with the excitement of an immoderate dose of opium, and heeded these things but little, nor spoke of them to Rowena.   Having found the wine, I recrossed the chamber, and poured out a gobletful, which I held to the lips of the fainting lady.   She had now partially recovered, however, and took the vessel herself, while I sank upon an ottoman near me, with my eyes fastened upon her person.   It was then that I became distinctly aware of a gentle footfall upon the carpet, and near the couch; and in a second therafter, as Rowena was in the act of raising the wine to her lips, I saw, or may have dreamed that I saw, fall within the goblet, as if from some invisible spring in the atmosphere of the room, three or four large drops of a brilliant and ruby-coloured fluid.   If this I saw—not so Rowena.   She swallowed the wine unhesitatingly, and I forbore to speak to her of a circumstance which must, after all, I considered, have been but the suggestion of a vivid imagination, rendered morbidly active by the terror of the lady, by the opium, and by the hour.

Yet I cannot conceal it from my own perception that, immediately subsequent to the fall of the ruby drops, a rapid change for the worse took place in the disorder of my wife; so that, on the third subsequent night, the hands of her menials prepared her for the tomb, and on the fourth, I sat alone, with her shrouded body, in that fantastic chamber which had received her as my bride. Wild visions, opium-engendered, flitted, shadow-like, before me. I gazed with unquiet eye upon the sarcophagi in the angles of the room, upon the varying figures of the drapery, and upon the writh-ing of the parti-coloured fires in the censer overhead. My eyes then fell, as I called to mind the circumstances of a former night, to the spot beneath the glare of the censer where I had seen the faint traces of the shadow. It was there, however, no longer; and breathing with greater freedom, I turned my glances to the pallid and rigid figure upon the bed. Then rushed upon me a thousand memories of Ligeia—and then came back upon my heart, with the turbulent violence of a flood, the whole of that unutterable woe with which I had regarded *her* thus enshrouded. The night waned; and still, with a bosom full of bitter thoughts of the one only and supremely beloved, I remained gazing upon the body of Rowena.

It might have been midnight, or perhaps earlier, or later, for I had taken no note of time, when a sob, low, gentle, but very distinct, startled me from my reverie. I *felt* that it came from the bed of ebony—the bed of death. I listened in an agony of superstitious terror—but there was no repeti-tion of the sound. I strained my vision to detect any motion in the corpse—but there was not the slightest perceptible. Yet I could not have been deceived. I *had* heard the noise, however faint, and my soul was awakened within me. I re-solutely and perseveringly kept my attention riveted upon the body. Many minutes elapsed before any circumstance occurred tending to throw light upon the mystery. At length it became evident that a slight, a very feeble, and barely noticeable tinge of colour had flushed up within the cheeks, and along the sunken small veins of the eyelids. Through a species of unutterable horror and awe, for which the language of mortality has no sufficiently energetic ex-pression, I felt my heart cease to beat, my limbs grow rigid where I sat. Yet a sense of duty finally operated to restore my self-possession. I could no longer doubt that we had been precipitate in our preparations—that Rowena still lived. It was necessary that some immediate exertion be made; yet the turret was altogether apart from the portion of the abbey tenanted by the servants—there were none within call—I had no means of summoning them to my aid without leaving the room for many minutes—and this I could not venture to do. I therefore struggled alone in my endeavours to call back the spirit still hovering. In a short period it was certain, however, that a relapse had taken place; the colour disappeared from both eyelid and cheek, leaving a wanness even more than that of marble; the lips became doubly shrivelled and pinched up in the ghastly expression of death; a repulsive clamminess and coldness overspread rapidly the surface of the body; and all the usual rigorous stiffness immediately supervened. I fell back with a shudder upon the couch from which I had been so startlingly aroused, and again gave myself up to passionate waking visions of Ligeia.

An hour thus elapsed, when (could it be possible?) I was a second time aware of some vague sound issuing from the region of the bed. I listened—in extremity of horror. The sound came again—it was a sigh. Rushing to the corpse, I saw—distinctly saw—a tremor upon the lips. In a minute afterwards they relaxed, disclosing a bright line of the pearly teeth. Amazement now struggled in my bosom with the profound awe which had hitherto reigned there alone. I felt that my vision grew dim, that my reason wandered; and it was only by a violent effort that I at length succeeded in nerving myself to the task which duty thus once more had pointed out. There was now a partial glow upon the forehead and upon the cheek and throat; a perceptible warmth pervaded the whole frame; there was even a slight pulsation at the heart. The lady *lived*; and with redoubled ardour I betook myself to the task of restoration. I chafed and bathed the temples and the hands, and used every exertion which experience, and no little medical reading, could suggest. But in vain. Suddenly, the colour fled, the pulsation ceased, the lips resumed the expression of the dead, and, in an instant afterward, the whole body took upon itself the icy chilliness, the livid hue, the intense rigidity, the sunken outline, and all the loathsome peculiarities of that which has been, for many days, a tenant of the tomb.

And again I sunk into visions of Ligeia—and again (what marvel that I shudder while I write?) *again* there reached my ears a low sob from the region of the ebony bed. But why shall I minutely detail the unspeakable horrors of that night? Why shall I pause to relate how, time after time, until near the period of the grey dawn, this hideous drama of revivifica-

tion was repeated; how each terrific relapse was only into a
sterner and apparently more irredeemable death; how each
agony wore the aspect of a struggle with some invisible foe;
and how each struggle was succeeded by I know not what of
wild change in the personal appearance of the corpse? Let
me hurry to a conclusion.

The greater part of the fearful night had worn away, and
she who had been dead, once again stirred—and now more
vigorously than hitherto, although arousing from a dissolution more appalling in its utter hopelessness than any. I had
long ceased to struggle or to move, and remained sitting
rigidly upon the ottoman, a helpless prey to a whirl of violent
emotions, of which extreme awe was perhaps the least terrible,
the least consuming. The corpse, I repeat, stirred, and now
more vigorously than before. The hues of life flushed up
with unwonted energy into the countenance—the limbs
relaxed—and, save that the eyelids were yet pressed heavily
together and that the bandages and draperies of the grave
still imparted their charnel character to the figure, I might
have dreamed that Rowena had indeed shaken off, utterly, the
fetters of death. But if this idea was not, even then, altogether adopted, I could at least doubt no longer, when arising
from the bed, tottering, with feeble steps, with closed eyes,
and with the manner of one bewildered in a dream, the thing
that was enshrouded advanced boldly and palpably into the
middle of the apartment.

I trembled not—I stirred not—for a crowd of unutterable
fancies connected with the air, the stature, the demeanour of
the figure, rushing hurriedly through my brain, had paralysed—had chilled me into stone. I stirred not—but gazed
upon the apparition. There was a mad disorder in my
thoughts—a tumult unappeasable. Could it, indeed, be the
living Rowena who confronted me? Could it indeed be
Rowena *at all*—the fair-haired, the blue-eyed Lady Rowena
Trevanion of Tremaine? Why, *why* should I doubt it? The
bandage lay heavily about the mouth—but then might it not
be the mouth of the breathing Lady of Tremaine? And the
cheeks—there were the roses as in her noon of life—yes, these
might indeed be the fair cheeks of the living Lady of Tremaine. And the chin, with its dimples, as in health, might
it not be hers?—but *had she then grown taller since her
malady?* What inexpressible madness seized me with that

thought? One bound, and I had reached her feet! Shrinking from my touch, she let fall from her head, unloosened, the ghastly cerements which had confined it, and there streamed forth, into the rushing atmosphere of the chamber, huge masses of long and dishevelled hair; *it was blacker than the raven wings of midnight!* And now slowly opened *the eyes* of the figure which stood before me. " Here then, at least," I shrieked aloud, " can I never—can I never be mistaken— these are the full, and the black, and the wild eyes—of my lost love—of the Lady—of the LADY LIGEIA."

BRAM STOKER

THE SQUAW

NURNBERG at the time was not so much exploited as it has been since then. Irving had not been playing *Faust*, and the very name of the old town was hardly known to the great bulk of the travelling public. My wife and I being in the second week of our honeymoon, naturally wanted someone else to join our party, so that when the cheery stranger, Elias P. Hutcheson, hailing from Isthmain City, Bleeding Gulch, Maple Tree County, Neb., turned up at the station at Frankfort, and casually remarked that he was going on to see the most all-fired old Methuselah of a town in Yurrup, and that he guessed that so much travelling alone was enough to send an intelligent, active citizen into the melancholy ward of a daft house, we took the pretty broad hint and suggested that we should join forces. We found, on comparing notes afterwards, that we had each intended to speak with some diffidence or hesitation so as not to appear too eager, such not being a good compliment to the success of our married life; but the effect was entirely marred by our both beginning to speak at the same instant—stopping simultaneously and then going on together again. Anyhow, no matter how, it was done; and Elias P. Hutcheson became one of our party. Straightway Amelia and I found the pleasant benefit; instead of quarrelling, as we had been doing, we found that the restraining influence of a third party was such that we now took every opportunity of spooning in odd corners. Amelia declares that ever since she has, as the result of that experience, advised all her friends to take a friend on the honeymoon. Well, we "did" Nurnberg together, and much enjoyed the racy remarks of our Transatlantic friend, who, from his quaint speech and his wonderful stock of adventures, might have stepped out of a novel. We kept for the last object of interest in the city to be visited the Burg, and on the day appointed for the visit strolled round the outer wall of the city by the eastern side.

The Burg is seated on a rock dominating the town, and

an immensely deep fosse guards it on the northern side.
Nurnberg has been happy in that it was never sacked; had
it been it would certainly not be so spick-and-span perfect
as it is at present.   The ditch has not been used for centuries,
and now its base is spread with tea-gardens and orchards, of
which some of the trees are of quite respectable growth.   As
we wandered round the wall, dawdling in the hot July sunshine, we often paused to admire the views spread before us,
and in especial the great plain covered with towns and villages
and bounded with a blue line of hills, like a landscape of
Claude Lorraine.   From this we always turned with new
delight to the city itself, with its myriad of quaint old gables
and acre-wide red roofs dotted with dormer windows, tier
upon tier.   A little to our right rose the towers of the Burg,
and nearer still, standing grim, the Torture Tower, which
was, and is, perhaps, the most interesting place in the city.
For centuries the tradition of the Iron Virgin of Nurnberg
has been handed down as an instance of the horrors of cruelty
of which man is capable; we had long looked forward to
seeing it; and here at last was its home.

In one of our pauses we leaned over the wall of the moat
and looked down.   The garden seemed quite fifty or sixty
feet below us, and the sun pouring into it with an intense,
moveless heat like that of an oven.   Beyond rose the grey,
grim wall seemingly of endless height, and losing itself right
and left in the angles of bastion and counterscarp.   Trees and
bushes crowned the wall, and above again towered the lofty
houses on whose massive beauty Time has only set the hand
of approval.   The sun was hot and we were lazy; time was
our own, and we lingered, leaning on the wall.   Just below
us was a pretty sight—a great black cat lying stretched in the
sun, whilst round her gambolled prettily a tiny black kitten.
The mother would wave her tail for the kitten to play with,
or would raise her feet and push away the little one as an
encouragement to further play.   They were just at the foot
of the wall, and Elias P. Hutcheson, in order to help the
play, stooped and took from the walk a moderate-sized
pebble.

" See! " he said, " I will drop it near the kitten, and they
will both wonder where it came from."

" Oh, be careful," said my wife; " you might hit the dear
little thing! "

" Not me, ma'am," said Elias P.   " Why, I'm as tender as
a Maine cherry-tree.   Lor, bless ye, I wouldn't hurt the poor
pooty little critter more'n I'd scalp a baby.   An' you may
bet your variegated socks on that!   See, I'll drop it fur away
on the outside so's not to go near her! "   Thus saying, he
leaned over and held his arm out at full length and dropped
the stone.   It may be that there is some attractive force which
draws lesser matters to greater; or more probably that the
wall was not plumb but sloped to its base—we not noticing
the inclination from above; but the stone fell with a sickening thud that came up to us through the hot air, right on the
kitten's head, and shattered out its little brains then and
there.   The black cat cast a swift upward glance, and we
saw her eyes like green fire fixed an instant on Elias P.
Hutcheson; and then her attention was given to the kitten,
which lay still with just a quiver of her tiny limbs, whilst
a thin red stream trickled from a gaping wound.   With a
muffled cry, such as a human being might give, she bent over
the kitten, licking its wound and moaning.   Suddenly she
seemed to realise that it was dead, and again threw her eyes
up at us.   I shall never forget the sight, for she looked the
perfect incarnation of hate.   Her green eyes blazed with
lurid fire, and the white, sharp teeth seemed to almost shine
through the blood which dabbled her mouth and whiskers.
She gnashed her teeth, and her claws stood out stark and at
full length on every paw.   Then she made a wild rush up the
wall as if to reach us, but when the momentum ended fell
back, and further added to her horrible appearance for she
fell on the kitten, and rose with her back fur smeared with
its brains and blood.   Amelia turned quite faint, and I had
to lift her back from the wall.   There was a seat close by in
shade of a spreading plane-tree, and here I placed her whilst
she composed herself.   Then I went back to Hutcheson, who
stood without moving, looking down on the angry cat below.
    As I joined him, he said:
    " Wall, I guess that air the savagest beast I ever see—'cept
once when an Apache squaw had an edge on a half-breed
what they nicknamed ' Splinters ' 'cos of the way he fixed
up her papoose which he stole on a raid just to show that he
appreciated the way they had given his mother the fire torture.   She got that kinder look so set on her face that it just
seemed to grow there.   She followed Splinters more'n three

year till at last the braves got him and handed him over to her. They did say that no man, white or Injun, had ever been so long a-dying under the tortures of the Apaches. The only time I ever see her smile was when I wiped her out. I kem on the camp just in time to see Splinters pass in his checks, and he wasn't sorry to go either. He was a hard citizen, and though I never could shake with him after that papoose business—for it was bitter bad, and he should have been a white man, for he looked like one—I see he had got paid out in full. Durn me, but I took a piece of his hide from one of his skinnin posts an' had it made into a pocket-book. It's here now! " and he slapped the breast pocket of his coat.

Whilst he was speaking the cat was continuing her frantic efforts to get up the wall. She would take a run back and then charge up, sometimes reaching an incredible height. She did not seem to mind the heavy fall which she got each time but started with renewed vigour; and at every tumble her appearance became more horrible. Hutcheson was a kind-hearted man—my wife and I had both noticed little acts of kindness to animals as well as to persons—and he seemed concerned at the state of fury to which the cat had wrought herself.

" Wall now! " he said, " I du declare that that poor critter seems quite desperate. There! there! poor thing, it was all an accident—though that won't bring back your little one to you. Say! I wouldn't have had such a thing happen for a thousand! Just shows what a clumsy fool of a man can do when he tries to play! Seems I'm too darned slipperhanded to even play with a cat. Say, Colonel! "—it was a pleasant way he had to bestow titles freely—" I hope your wife don't hold no grudge against me on account of this unpleasantness? Why, I wouldn't have had it occur on no account."

He came over to Amelia and apologised profusely, and she with her usual kindness of heart hastened to assure him that she quite understood that it was an accident. Then we all went again to the wall and looked over.

The cat missing Hutcheson's face had drawn back across the moat, and was sitting on her haunches as though ready to spring. Indeed, the very instant she saw him she did spring, and with a blind unreasoning fury, which would have been grotesque, only that it was so frightfully real. She did not try to run up the wall, but simply launched herself at him as though hate and fury could lend her wings to pass straight through the great distance between them. Amelia, womanlike, got quite concerned, and said to Elias P. in a warning voice:

"Oh! you must be very careful. That animal would try to kill you if she were here; her eyes look like positive murder."

He laughed out jovially. "Excuse me, ma'am," he said, "but I can't help laughin'. Fancy a man that has fought grizzlies an' Injuns bein' careful of bein' murdered by a cat!"

When the cat heard him laugh, her whole demeanour seemed to change. She no longer tried to jump or run up the wall, but went quietly over, and sitting again beside the dead kitten began to lick and fondle it as though it were alive.

"See!" said I, "the effect of a really strong man. Even that animal in the midst of her fury recognises the voice of a master, and bows to him!"

"Like a squaw!" was the only comment of Elias P. Hutcheson, as we moved on our way round the city fosse. Every now and then we looked over the wall and each time saw the cat following us. At first she had kept going back to the dead kitten, and then as the distance grew greater took it in her mouth and so followed. After a while, however, she abandoned this, for we saw her following all alone; she had evidently hidden the body somewhere. Amelia's alarm grew at the cat's persistence, and more than once she repeated her warning; but the American always laughed with amusement, till finally, seeing that she was beginning to be worried, he said:

"I say, ma'am, you needn't be skeered over that cat. I go heeled, I du!" Here he slapped his pistol pocket at the back of his lumbar region. "Why, sooner'n have you worried, I'll shoot the critter, right here, an' risk the police interferin' with a citizen of the United States for carryin' arms contrairy to reg'lations!" As he spoke he looked over the wall, but the cat, on seeing him, retreated, with a growl, into a bed of tall flowers, and was hidden. He went on: "Blest if that ar critter ain't got more sense of what's good for her than most Christians. I guess we've seen the last of her! You

bet, she'll go back now to that busted kitten and have a
private funeral of it, all to herself! "

Amelia did not like to say more, lest he might, in mistaken
kindness to her, fulfil his threat of shooting the cat: and so
we went on and crossed the little wooden bridge leading to
the gateway whence ran the steep paved roadway between
the Burg and the pentagonal Torture Tower. As we crossed
the bridge we saw the cat again down below us. When she
saw us her fury seemed to return, and she made frantic efforts
to get up the steep wall. Hutcheson laughed as he looked
down at her, and said:

" Good-bye, old girl. Sorry I in-jured your feelin's, but
you'll get over it in time! So long! " And then we passed
through the long, dim archway and came to the gate of the
Burg.

When we came out again after our survey of this most
beautiful old place which not even the well-intended efforts
of the Gothic restorers of forty years ago have been able to
spoil—though their restoration was then glaring white—we
seemed to have quite forgotten the unpleasant episode of the
morning. The old lime tree with its great trunk gnarled
with the passing of nearly nine centuries, the deep well cut
through the heart of the rock by those captives of old, and
the lovely view from the city wall whence we heard, spread
over almost a full quarter of an hour, the multitudinous
chimes of the city, had all helped to wipe out from our minds
the incident of the slain kitten.

We were the only visitors who had entered the Torture
Tower that morning—so at least said the old custodian—and
as we had the place all to ourselves were able to make a minute
and more satisfactory survey than would have otherwise been
possible. The custodian, looking to us as the sole source of
his gains for the day, was willing to meet our wishes in any
way. The Torture Tower is truly a grim place, even now
when many thousands of visitors have sent a stream of life,
and the joy that follows life, into the place; but at the time
I mention it wore its grimmest and most gruesome aspect.
The dust of ages seemed to have settled on it, and the darkness and the horror of its memories seem to have become
sentient in a way that would have satisfied the Pantheistic
souls of Philo or Spinoza. The lower chamber where we
entered was seemingly, in its normal state, filled with in-

carnate darkness; even the hot sunlight streaming in through
the door seemed to be lost in the vast thickness of the walls,
and only showed the masonry rough as when the builder's
scaffolding had come down, but coated with dust and marked
here and there with patches of dark stain which, if walls
could speak, could have given their own dread memories of
fear and pain. We were glad to pass up the dusty wooden
staircase, the custodian leaving the outer door open to light
us somewhat on our way; for to our eyes the one long-wick'd,
evil-smelling candle stuck in a sconce on the wall gave an
inadequate light. When we came up through the open trap
in the corner of the chamber overhead, Amelia held on to me
so tightly that I could actually feel her heart beat. I must
say for my own part that I was not surprised at her fear,
for this room was even more gruesome than that below.
Here there was certainly more light, but only just sufficient
to realise the horrible surroundings of the place. The builders
of the tower had evidently intended that only they who
should gain the top should have any of the joys of light and
prospect. There, as we had noticed from below, were ranges
of windows, albeit of mediæval smallness, but elsewhere in
the tower were only a very few narrow slits such as were
habitual in places of mediæval defence. A few of these only
lit the chamber, and these so high up in the wall that from no
part could the sky be seen through the thickness of the walls.
In racks, and leaning in disorder against the walls, were a
number of headsmen's swords, great double-handed weapons
with broad blade and keen edge. Hard by were several blocks
whereon the necks of the victims had lain, with here and
there deep notches where the steel had bitten through the
guard of flesh and shored into the wood. Round the
chamber, placed in all sorts of irregular ways, were many
implements of torture which made one's heart ache to see—
chairs full of spikes which gave instant and excruciating
pain; chairs and couches with dull knobs whose torture was
seemingly less, but which, though slower, were equally effi-
cacious; racks, belts, boots, gloves, collars, all made for com-
pressing at will; steel baskets in which the head could be
slowly crushed into a pulp if necessary; watchmen's hooks
with long handle and knife that cut at resistance—this a
specialty of the old Nurnberg police system; and many, many
other devices for man's injury to man. Amelia grew quite

pale with the horror of the things, but fortunately did not faint, for being a little overcome she sat down on a torture chair, but jumped up again with a shriek, all tendency to faint gone. We both pretended that it was the injury done to her dress by the dust of the chair, and the rusty spikes which had upset her, and Mr. Hutcheson acquiesced in accepting the explanation with a kind-hearted laugh.

But the central object in the whole of this chamber of horrors was the engine known as the Iron Virgin, which stood near the centre of the room. It was a rudely-shaped figure of a woman, something of the bell order, or, to make a closer comparison, of the figure of Mrs. Noah in the children's Ark, but without that slimness of waist and perfect *rondeur* of hip which marks the æsthetic type of the Noah family. One would hardly have recognised it as intended for a human figure at all had not the founder shaped on the forehead a rude semblance of a woman's face. This machine was coated with rust without, and covered with dust; a rope was fastened to a ring in the front of the figure, about where the waist should have been, and was drawn through a pulley, fastened on the wooden pillar which sustained the flooring above. The custodian pulling this rope showed that a section of the front was hinged like a door at one side; we then saw that the engine was of considerable thickness, leaving just room enough inside for a man to be placed. The door was of equal thickness and of great weight, for it took the custodian all his strength, aided though he was by the contrivance of the pulley, to open it. This weight was partly due to the fact that the door was of manifest purpose hung so as to throw its weight downwards, so that it might shut of its own accord when the strain was released. The inside was honeycombed with rust—nay more, the rust alone that comes through time would hardly have eaten so deep into the iron walls; the rust of the cruel stains was deep indeed! It was only, however, when we came to look at the inside of the door that the diabolical intention was manifest to the full. Here were several long spikes, square and massive, broad at the base and sharp at the points, placed in such a position that when the door should close the upper ones would pierce the eyes of the victim, and the lower ones his heart and vitals. The sight was too much for poor Amelia, and this time she fainted dead off, and I had to carry her down the stairs, and place

her on a bench outside till she recovered. That she felt it to
the quick was afterwards shown by the fact that my eldest
son bears to this day a rude birthmark on his breast, which
has, by family consent, been accepted as representing the
Nurnberg Virgin.

When we got back to the chamber we found Hutcheson
still opposite the Iron Virgin; he had been evidently philoso-
phising, and now gave us the benefit of his thought in the
shape of a sort of exordium.

" Wall, I guess I've been learnin' somethin' here while
madam has been gettin' over her faint. 'Pears to me that
we're a long way behind the times on our side of the big
drink. We uster think out on the plains that the Injun
could give us points in tryin' to make a man oncomfortable;
but I guess your old mediæval law-and-order party could
raise him every time. Splinters was pretty good in his bluff
on the squaw, but this here young miss held a straight flush
all high on him. The points of them spikes air sharp enough
still, though even the edges air eaten out by what uster be on
them. It'd be a good thing for our Indian section to get
some specimens of this here play-toy to send round to the
Reservations jest to knock the stuffin' out of the bucks, and
the squaws too, by showing them as how old civilisation lays
over them at their best. Guess but I'll get in that box a
minute jest to see how it feels! "

" Oh no! no! " said Amelia. " It is too terrible! "

" Guess, ma'am, nothin's too terrible to the explorin'
mind. I've been in some queer places in my time. Spent
a night inside a dead horse while a prairie fire swept over
me in Montana Territory—an' another time slept inside a
dead buffler when the Comanches was on the war path an'
I didn't keer to leave my kyard on them. I've been two
days in a caved-in tunnel in the Billy Broncho gold mine in
New Mexico, an' was one of the four shut up for three parts
of a day in the caisson what slid over on her side when we
was settin' the foundations of the Buffalo Bridge. I've not
funked an odd experience yet, an' I don't propose to begin
now! "

We saw that he was set on the experiment, so I said:
" Well, hurry up, old man, and get through it quick? "

" All right, General," said he, " but I calculate we ain't
quite ready yet. The gentlemen, my predecessors, what

stood in that thar canister, didn't volunteer for the office—
not much! And I guess there was some ornamental tyin'
up before the big stroke was made. I want to go into this
thing fair and square, so I must get fixed up proper first.
I dare say this old galoot can rise some string and tie me up
accordin' to sample? "

This was said interrogatively to the old custodian, but the
latter, who understood the drift of his speech, though perhaps
not appreciating to the full the niceties of dialect and
imagery, shook his head. His protest was, however, only
formal and made to be overcome. The American thrust a
gold piece into his hand, saying, " Take it, pard! it's your pot;
and don't be skeer'd. This ain't no necktie party that you're
asked to assist in! " He produced some thin frayed rope
and proceeded to bind our companion, with sufficient strict-
ness for the purpose. When the upper part of his body was
bound, Hutcheson said:

" Hold on a moment, Judge. Guess I'm too heavy for you
to tote into the canister. You jest let me walk in, and then
you can wash up regardin' my legs! "

Whilst speaking he had backed himself into the opening
which was just enough to hold him. It was a close fit and no
mistake. Amelia looked on with fear in her eyes, but she
evidently did not like to say anything. Then the custodian
completed his task by tying the American's feet together so
that he was now absolutely helpless and fixed in his voluntary
prison. He seemed to really enjoy it, and the incipient smile
which was habitual to his face blossomed into actuality as
he said:

" Guess this here Eve was made out of the rib of a dwarf!
There ain't much room for a full-grown citizen of the United
States to hustle. We uster make our coffins more roomier in
Idaho territory. Now, Judge, you just begin to let this door
down, slow, on to me. I want to feel the same pleasure
as the other jays had when those spikes began to move towards their eyes! "

" Oh no! no! no! " broke in Amelia hysterically. " It
is too terrible! I can't bear to see it!—I can't! I can't! "

But the American was obdurate. " Say, Colonel," said
he, " Why not take Madame for a little promenade? I
wouldn't hurt her feelin's for the world; but now that I
am here, havin' kem eight thousand miles, wouldn't it be

too hard to give up the very experience I've been pinin' an' pantin' fur? A man can't get to feel like canned goods every time! Me and the Judge here'll fix up this thing in no time, an' then you'll come back, an' we'll all laugh together!"

Once more the resolution that is born of curiosity triumphed, and Amelia stayed holding tight to my arm and shivering whilst the custodian began to slacken slowly inch by inch the rope that held back the iron door. Hutcheson's face was positively radiant as his eyes followed the first movement of the spikes.

"Wall!" he said, "I guess I've not had enjoyment like this since I left Noo York. Bar a scrap with a French sailor at Wapping—an' that warn't much of a picnic neither—I've not had a show fur real pleasure in this dod-rotted Continent, where there ain't no b'ars nor no Injuns, an' wheer nary man goes heeled. Slow there, Judge! Don't you rush this business! I want a show for my money this game—I du!"

The custodian must have had in him some of the blood of his predecessors in that ghastly tower, for he worked the engine with a deliberate and excruciating slowness which after five minutes, in which the outer edge of the door had not moved half as many inches, began to overcome Amelia. I saw her lips whiten, and I felt her hold upon my arm relax. I looked around an instant for a place whereon to lay her, and when I looked at her again found that her eye had become fixed on the side of the Virgin. Following its direction I saw the black cat crouching out of sight. Her green eyes shone like danger lamps in the gloom of the place, and their colour was heightened by the blood which still smeared her coat and reddened her mouth. I cried out:

"The cat! look out for the cat!" for even then she sprang out before the engine. At this moment she looked like a triumphant demon. Her eyes blazed with ferocity, her hair bristled out till she seemed twice her normal size, and her tail lashed about as does a tiger's when the quarry is before it. Elias P. Hutcheson when he saw her was amused, and his eyes positively sparkled with fun as he said:

"Darned if the squaw hain't got on all her war paint! Jest give her a shove off if she comes any of her tricks on me, for I'm so fixed everlastingly by the boss, that durn my skin if I can keep my eyes from her if she wants them!

Easy there, Judge! Don't you slack that ar rope or I'm euchered! "

At this moment Amelia completed her faint, and I had to clutch hold of her round the waist or she would have fallen to the floor. Whilst attending to her I saw the black cat crouching for a spring, and jumped up to turn the creature out.

But at that instant, with a sort of hellish scream, she hurled herself, not as we expected at Hutcheson, but straight at the face of the custodian. Her claws seemed to be tearing wildly as one sees in the Chinese drawings of the dragon rampant, and as I looked I saw one of them light on the poor man's eye, and actually tear through it and down his cheek, leaving a wide band of red where the blood seemed to spurt from every vein.

With a yell of sheer terror which came quicker than even his sense of pain, the man leaped back, dropping as he did so the rope which held back the iron door. I jumped for it, but was too late, for the cord ran like lightning through the pulley-block, and the heavy mass fell forward from its own weight.

As the door closed I caught a glimpse of our poor companion's face. He seemed frozen with terror. His eyes stared with a horrible anguish as if dazed, and no sound came from his lips.

And then the spikes did their work. Happily the end was quick, for when I wrenched open the door they had pierced so deep that they had locked in the bones of the skull through which they had crushed, and actually tore him—it —out of his iron prison till, bound as he was, he fell at full length with a sickly thud upon the floor, the face turning upwards as he fell.

I rushed to my wife, lifted her up and carried her out, for I feared for her very reason if she should wake from her faint to such a scene. I laid her on the bench outside and ran back. Leaning against the wooden column was the custodian moaning in pain whilst he held his reddening hand-kerchief to his eyes. And sitting on the head of the poor American was the cat, purring loudly as she licked the blood which trickled through the gashed sockets of his eyes.

I think no one will call me cruel because I seized one of the old executioner's swords and shore her in two as she sat.

O. HENRY

THE LAST LEAF

IN a little district west of Washington Square the streets have run crazy and broken themselves into small strips called " places." These " places " make strange angles and curves. One street crosses itself a time or two. An artist once discovered a valuable possibility in this street. Suppose a collector with a bill for paints, paper and canvas should, in traversing this route, suddenly meet himself coming back, without a cent having been paid on account!

So, to quaint old Greenwich Village the art people soon came prowling, hunting for north windows and eighteenth-century gables and Dutch attics and low rents. Then they imported some pewter mugs and a chafing dish or two from Sixth Avenue, and became a " colony."

At the top of a squatty, three-storey brick Sue and Johnsy had their studio. " Johnsy " was familiar for Joanna. One was from Maine; the other from California. They had met at the table d'hôte of an Eighth street " Delmonico's," and found their tastes in art, chicory salad and bishop sleeves so congenial that the joint studio resulted.

That was in May. In November a cold, unseen stranger, whom the doctors called Pneumonia, stalked about the colony, touching one here and there with his icy finger. Over on the east side this ravager strode boldly, smiting his victims by scores, but his feet trod slowly through the maze of the narrow and moss-grown " places."

Mr. Pneumonia was not what you would call a chivalric old gentleman. A mite of a little woman with blood thinned by California zephyrs was hardly fair game for the red-fisted, short-breathed old duffer. But Johnsy he smote; and she lay, scarcely moving, on her painted iron bedstead, looking through the small Dutch window-panes at the blank side of the next brick house.

One morning the busy doctor invited Sue into the hall-way with a shaggy, grey eyebrow.

" She has one chance in—let us say, ten," he said, as he

shook down the mercury in his clinical thermometer. " And
that chance is for her to want to live. This way people have
of lining-up on the side of the undertaker makes the entire
pharmacopœia look silly. Your little lady has made up her
mind that she's not going to get well. Has she anything on
her mind? "

" She—she wanted to paint the Bay of Naples some day,"
said Sue.

" Paint?—bosh! Has she anything on her mind worth
thinking about twice—a man, for instance? "

" A man? " said Sue, with a jews'-harp twang in her voice.
" Is a man worth—but, no, doctor; there is nothing of the
kind."

" Well, it is the weakness, then," said the doctor. " I will
do all that science, so far as it may filter through my efforts,
can accomplish. But whenever my patient begins to count
the carriages in her funeral procession I subtract 50 per cent.
from the curative power of medicines. If you will get her
to ask one question about the new winter styles in cloak
sleeves I will promise you a one-in-five chance for her, instead of one in ten."

After the doctor had gone, Sue went into the workroom
and cried a Japanese napkin to a pulp. Then she swaggered
into Johnsy's room with her drawing-board, whistling rag-
time.

Johnsy lay, scarcely making a ripple under the bedclothes,
with her face towards the window. Sue stopped whistling,
thinking she was asleep.

She arranged her board and began a pen-and-ink drawing
to illustrate a magazine story. Young artists must pave
their way to Art by drawing pictures for magazine stories
that young authors write to pave their way to Literature.

As Sue was sketching a pair of elegant horse-show riding
trousers and a monocle on the figure of the hero, an Idaho
cowboy, she heard a low sound, several times repeated. She
went quickly to the bedside.

Johnsy's eyes were open wide. She was looking out the
window and counting—counting backward.

" Twelve," she said, and a little later, " eleven "; and then
" ten," and " nine "; and then " eight " and " seven," almost
together.

Sue looked solicitously out the window. What was there

to count? There was only a bare, dreary yard to be seen, and the blank side of the brick house twenty feet away. An old, old ivy vine, gnarled and decayed at the roots, climbed half-way up the brick wall. The cold breath of autumn had stricken its leaves from the vine until its skeleton branches clung, almost bare, to the crumbling bricks.

" What is it, dear? " asked Sue.

" Six," said Johnsy, in almost a whisper. " They're falling faster now. Three days ago there were almost a hundred. It made my head ache to count them. But now it's easy. There goes another one. There are only five left now."

" Five what, dear? Tell your Sudie."

" Leaves. On the ivy vine. When the last one falls I must go too. I've known that for three days. Didn't the doctor tell you? "

" Oh, I never heard of such nonsense," complained Sue, with magnificent scorn. " What have old ivy leaves to do with your getting well? And you used to love that vine so, you naughty girl. Don't be a goosey. Why, the doctor told me this morning that your chances for getting well real soon were—let's see exactly what he said—he said the chances were ten to one! Why, that's almost as good a chance as we have in New York when we ride on the street cars or walk past a new building. Try to take some broth now, and let Sudie go back to her drawing, so she can sell the editor man with it, and buy port wine for her sick child, and pork chops for her greedy self."

" You needn't get any more wine," said Johnsy, keeping her eyes fixed out the window. " There goes another. No, I don't want any broth. That leaves just four. I want to see the last one fall before it gets dark. Then I'll go too."

" Johnsy, dear," said Sue, bending over her, " will you promise me to keep your eyes closed, and not look out the window until I am done working? I must hand those drawings in by to-morrow. I need the light, or I would draw the shade down."

" Couldn't you draw in the other room? " asked Johnsy, coldly.

" I'd rather be here by you," said Sue. " Besides, I don't want you to keep looking at those silly ivy leaves."

" Tell me as soon as you have finished," said Johnsy, closing her eyes, and lying white and still as a fallen statue, " because I want to see the last one fall. I'm tired of waiting. I'm tired of thinking. I want to turn loose my hold on everything, and go sailing down, down, just like one of those poor, tired leaves."

" Try to sleep," said Sue. " I must call Behrman up to be my model for the old hermit miner. I'll not be gone a minute. Don't try to move till I come back."

Old Behrman was a painter who lived on the ground floor beneath them. He was past sixty and had a Michael Angelo's Moses beard curling down from the head of a satyr along the body of an imp. Behrman was a failure in art. Forty years he had wielded the brush without getting near enough to touch the hem of his Mistress's robe. He had been always about to paint a masterpiece, but had never yet begun it. For several years he had painted nothing except now and then a daub in the line of commerce or advertising. He earned a little by serving as a model to those young artists in the colony who could not pay the price of a professional. He drank gin to excess, and still talked of his coming masterpiece. For the rest he was a fierce little old man, who scoffed terribly at softness in anyone, and who regarded himself as especial mastiff-in-waiting to protect the two young artists in the studio above.

Sue found Behrman smelling strongly of juniper berries in his dimly-lighted den below. In one corner was a blank canvas on an easel that had been waiting there for twenty-five years to receive the first line of the masterpiece. She told him of Johnsy's fancy, and how she feared she would, indeed, light and fragile as a leaf herself, float away when her slight hold upon the world grew weaker.

Old Behrman, with his red eyes plainly streaming, shouted his contempt and derision for such idiotic imaginings.

" Vass! " he cried. " Is dere people in de world mit der foolishness to die because leafs dey drop off from a confounded vine? I haf not heard of such a thing. No, I vill not bose as a model for your fool hermit-dunderhead. Vy do you allow dot silly pusiness to come in der prain of her? Ach, dot poor little Miss Yohnsy."

" She is very ill and weak," said Sue, " and the fever has left her mind morbid and full of strange fancies. Very well, Mr. Behrman, if you do not care to pose for me, you needn't.

But I think you are a horrid old—old flibberti-gibbet."

" You are just like a woman! " yelled Behrman. " Who said I vill not bose? Go on. I come mit you. For half-an-hour I haf peen trying to say dot I am ready to bose. Gott! dis is not any blace in which one so goot as Miss Yohnsy shall lie sick. Some day I vill baint a masterpiece, and ve shall all go avay. Gott! yes."

Johnsy was sleeping when they went upstairs. Sue pulled the shade down to the window-sill and motioned Behrman into the other room. In there they peered out the window fearfully at the ivy vine. Then they looked at each other for a moment without speaking. A persistent, cold rain was falling, mingled with snow. Behrman, in his old blue shirt, took his seat as the hermit-miner on an upturned kettle for a rock.

When Sue awoke from an hour's sleep the next morning she found Johnsy, with dull, wide-open eyes staring at the drawn green shade.

" Pull it up! I want to see," she ordered, in a whisper.

Wearily Sue obeyed.

But, lo! after the beating rain and fierce gusts of wind that had endured through the livelong night, there yet stood out against the brick wall one ivy leaf. It was the last on the vine. Still dark green near its stem, but with its serrated edges tinted with the yellow of dissolution and decay, it hung bravely from a branch some twenty feet above the ground.

" It is the last one," said Johnsy. " I thought it would surely fall during the night. I heard the wind. It will fall to-day, and I shall die at the same time."

" Dear, dear! " said Sue, leaning her worn face down to the pillow; " think of me, if you won't think of yourself. What would I do? "

But Johnsy did not answer. The lonesomest thing in all the world is a soul when it is making ready to go on its mysterious, far journey. The fancy seemed to possess her more strongly as one by one the ties that bound her to friendship and to earth were loosed.

The day wore away, and even through the twilight they could see the lone ivy leaf clinging to its stem against the wall. And then, with the coming of the night the north wind was again loosed, while the rain still beat against the windows and pattered down from the low Dutch eaves.

When it was light enough Johnsy, the merciless, commanded that the shade be raised.

The ivy leaf was still there.

Johnsy lay for a long time looking at it. And then she called to Sue, who was stirring her chicken broth over the gas stove.

" I've been a bad girl, Sudie," said Johnsy. " Something has made that last leaf stay there to show me how wicked I was. It is a sin to want to die. You may bring me a little broth now, and some milk with a little port in it, and—no; bring me a hand-mirror first; and then pack some pillows about me, and I will sit up and watch you cook."

An hour later she said—

" Sudie, some day I hope to paint the Bay of Naples."

The doctor came in the afternoon, and Sue had an excuse to go into the hallway as he left.

" Even chances," said the doctor, taking Sue's thin, shaking hand in his. " With good nursing you'll win. And now I must see another case I have downstairs. Behrman his name is—some kind of an artist, I believe. Pneumonia, too. He is an old, weak man, and the attack is acute. There is no hope for him; but he goes to the hospital to-day to be made more comfortable."

The next day the doctor said to Sue: " She's out of danger. You've won. Nutrition and care now—that's all."

And that afternoon Sue came to the bed where Johnsy lay, contentedly knitting a very blue and very useless woollen shoulder scarf, and put one arm around her, pillows and all.

" I have something to tell you, white mouse," she said. " Mr. Behrman died of pneumonia to-day in hospital. He was ill only two days. The janitor found him on the morning of the first day in his room downstairs helpless with pain. His shoes and clothing were wet through and icy cold. They couldn't imagine where he had been on such a dreadful night. And then they found a lantern, still lighted, and a ladder that had been dragged from its place, and some scattered brushes, and a palette with green and yellow colours mixed on it, and—look out the window, dear, at the last ivy leaf on the wall. Didn't you wonder why it never fluttered or moved when the wind blew? Ah, darling, it's Behrman's masterpiece—he painted it there the night that the last leaf fell."

W. W. JACOBS

THE WELL

I

TWO men were in the billiard-room of an old country house, talking. Play, which had been of a half-hearted nature, was over, and they sat at the open window, looking out over the park stretching away beneath them, conversing idly.

"Your time's nearly up, Jem," said one at length; "this time six weeks you'll be yawning out your honeymoon and cursing the man—woman, I mean—who invented them."

Jem Benson stretched his long limbs in the chair and grunted in dissent.

"I've never understood it," continued Wilfred Carr, yawning. "It's not in my line at all; I never had enough money for my own wants, let alone for two. Perhaps if I were as rich as you, or Crœsus, I might regard it differently."

There was just sufficient meaning in the latter part of the remark for his cousin to forbear replying to it. He continued to gaze out of the window and to smoke slowly.

"Not being as rich as Crœsus—or you," resumed Mr. Carr, regarding him from beneath lowered lids, "I paddle my own canoe down the stream of Time, and tying it to my friends' door-posts, go in to eat their dinners."

"Quite Venetian," said Jem Benson, still looking out of the window. "It's not a bad thing for you, Wilfred, that you have the door-posts and dinners—and friends."

Mr. Carr grunted in his turn. "Seriously though, Jem," he said slowly, "you're a lucky fellow, a very lucky fellow. If there's a better girl above ground than Olive I should like to see her."

"Yes," said the other quietly.

"She's such an exceptional girl," continued Carr, staring out of the window. "She's so good and gentle. She thinks you are a bundle of all the virtues."

He laughed frankly and joyously, but the other man did not join him.

"Strong sense of right and wrong though," continued

Carr, musingly. " Do you know, I believe that if she found out that you were not——"

" Not what? " demanded Benson, turning upon him fiercely. " Not what? " .

" Everything that you are," returned his cousin, with a grin that belied his words. " I believe she'd drop you."

" Talk about something else," said Benson slowly; " your pleasantries are not always in the best taste."

Wilfred Carr rose, and taking a cue from the rack, bent over the board and practised one or two favourite shots. " The only other subject I can talk about just at present is my own financial affairs," he said slowly, as he walked round the table.

" Talk about something else," said Benson again, bluntly.

" And the two things are connected," said Carr, and dropping his cue, he half sat on the table and eyed his cousin.

There was a long silence. Benson pitched the end of his cigar out of the window, and leaning back, closed his eyes.

" Do you follow me? " said Carr at length.

Benson opened his eyes and nodded at the window. " Do you want to follow my cigar? " he demanded.

" I should prefer to depart by the usual way for your sake," returned the other, unabashed. " If I left by the window all sorts of questions would be asked, and you know what a talkative chap I am."

" So long as you don't talk about my affairs," returned the other, restraining himself by an obvious effort, " you can talk yourself hoarse."

" I'm in a mess," said Carr slowly, " a devil of a mess. If I don't raise fifteen hundred pounds by this day fortnight, I may be getting my board and lodging free."

" Would that be any change? " questioned Benson.

" The quality would," retorted the other. " The address also would not be good. Seriously, Jem, will you let me have the fifteen hundred? "

" No," said the other simply.

Carr went white. " It's to save me from ruin," he said thickly.

" I've helped you till I'm tired," said Benson, turning and regarding him, " and it is all to no good. If you've got in a mess, get out of it. You should not be so fond of giving autographs away."

" It's foolish, I admit," said Carr deliberately. " I won't do so any more. By the way, I've got some to sell. You needn't sneer. They're not my own."

" Whose are they? " enquired the other.

" Yours."

Benson got up from his chair and crossed over to him. " What is this? " he asked quietly. " Blackmail? "

" Call it what you like," said Carr. " I've got some letters for sale, price fifteen hundred pounds. And I know a man who wants to buy them at that price for the mere chance of getting Olive from you. I'll give you first offer."

" If you've got any letters bearing my signature, you will be good enough to give them to me," said Benson very slowly.

" They're mine," said Carr lightly; " given to me by the lady you wrote them to. I must say that they are not all in the best possible taste."

His cousin reached forward suddenly, and catching him by the collar of his coat pinned him down on the table.

" Give me those letters," he breathed, sticking his face close to his cousin's.

" They're not here," said Carr, struggling. " I'm not a fool. Let me go, or I'll raise the price."

The other man raised him from the table in his powerful hands, apparently with the intention of dashing his head against it. Then suddenly his hold relaxed as an astonished-looking maid-servant entered the room with letters. Carr sat up hastily.

" That's how it was done," said Benson, for the girl's bene-fit, as he took the letters.

" I don't wonder at the other man making him pay for it then," said Carr blandly.

" You will give me those letters? " said Benson suggestively, as the girl left the room.

" At the price I mentioned, yes," said Carr, " but so sure as I'm a living man, if you lay your clumsy hands on me again, I'll double it. Now, I'll leave you for a time while you think it over."

He took a cigar from the box and lighting it carefully quitted the room. His cousin waited until the door had closed behind him, and then turning to the window sat there in a fit of fury as silent as it was terrible.

The air was fresh and sweet from the park, heavy with the

scent of new-mown grass. The fragrance of a cigar was now added to it, and glancing out he saw his cousin pacing slowly by. He rose and went to the door, and then, apparently altering his mind, returned to the window and watched the figure of his cousin as it moved slowly away into the moonlight. Then he rose again, and for a long time the room was empty.

.   .   .   .   .

It was empty when Mrs. Benson came in some time later to say good night to her son on her way to bed. She walked slowly round the table, and pausing at the window gazed from it in idle thought, until she saw the figure of her son advancing with rapid strides to the house. He looked up at the window.

" Good night," said she.

" Good night," said Benson, in a deep voice.

" Where is Wilfred? "

" Oh, he has gone," said Benson.

" Gone? "

" We had a few words; he was wanting money again, and I gave him a piece of my mind. I don't think we shall see him again."

" Poor Wilfred! " sighed Mrs. Benson. " He is always in trouble of some sort. I hope that you were not too hard upon him."

" No more than he deserved," said her son sternly. " Good night."

II

The well, which had long ago fallen into disuse, was almost hidden by the thick tangle of undergrowth which ran riot at that corner of the old park. It was partly covered by the shrunken half of a lid, above which a rusty windlass creaked in company with the music of the pines when the wind blew strongly. The full light of the sun never reached it, and the ground surrounding it was moist and green when other parts of the park were gaping with the heat.

Two people, walking slowly round the park in the fragrant stillness of a summer evening, strayed in the direction of the well.

"No use going through this wilderness, Olive," said Benson, pausing on the outskirts of the pines and eyeing with some disfavour the gloom beyond.

"Best part of the park," said the girl briskly; "you know it's my favourite spot."

"I know you're very fond of sitting on the coping," said the man slowly, "and I wish you wouldn't. One day you will lean back too far and fall in."

"And make the acquaintance of Truth," said Olive lightly. "Come along."

She ran from him and was lost in the shadow of the pines, the bracken crackling beneath her feet as she ran. Her companion followed slowly, and emerging from the gloom saw her poised daintily on the edge of the well with her feet hidden in the rank grass and nettles which surrounded it. She motioned her companion to take a seat by her side, and smiled softly as she felt a strong arm passed about her waist.

"I like this place," said she, breaking a long silence, "it is so dismal—so uncanny. Do you know I wouldn't dare to sit here alone, Jem. I should imagine that all sorts of dreadful things were hidden behind the bushes and trees, waiting to spring out on me. Ugh!"

"You'd better let me take you in," said her companion tenderly; "the well isn't always wholesome, especially in the hot weather. Let's make a move."

The girl gave an obstinate little shake, and settled herself more securely on her seat.

"Smoke your cigar in peace," she said quietly. "I am settled here for a quiet talk. Has anything been heard of Wilfred yet?"

"Nothing."

"Quite a dramatic disappearance, isn't it?" she continued. "Another scrape, I suppose, and another letter for you in the same old strain: 'Dear Jem, help me out.'"

Jem Benson blew a cloud of fragrant smoke into the air, and holding his cigar between his teeth, brushed away the ash from his coat sleeve.

"I wonder what he would have done without you," said the girl, pressing his arm affectionately. "Gone under long ago, I suppose. When we are married, Jem, I shall presume upon the relationship to lecture him. He is very wild, but he has his good points, poor fellow."

" I never saw them," said Benson, with startling bitterness.
" God knows, I never saw them."

" He is nobody's enemy but his own," said the girl, startled
by this outburst.

" You don't know much about him," said the other shortly.
" He was not above blackmail; not above ruining the life of a
friend to do himself a benefit. A loafer, a cur and a liar! "

The girl looked up at him soberly but timidly, and took his
arm without a word, and they both sat silent while evening
deepened into night and the beams of the moon, filtering
through the branches, surrounded them with a silver network.
Her head sank upon his shoulder, till suddenly, with a sharp
cry, she sprang to her feet.

" What was that? " she cried breathlessly.

" What was what? " demanded Benson, springing up and
clutching her fast by the arm.

She caught her breath and tried to laugh. " You're hurt-
ing me, Jem."

His hold relaxed.

" What is the matter? " he asked gently. " What was it
startled you? "

" I was startled," she said, slowly putting her hands on his
shoulder. " I suppose the words I used just now are ringing
in my ears, but I fancied that somebody behind us whispered,
' Jem, help me out.' "

" Fancy," repeated Benson, and his voice shook; " but these
fancies are not good for you. You—are frightened—at the
dark and the gloom of these trees. Let me take you back to
the house."

" No, I'm not frightened," said the girl, re-seating herself.
" I should never be really frightened of anything when you
were with me, Jem. I'm surprised at myself for being so
silly."

The man made no reply but stood, a strong, dark figure, a
yard or two from the well, as though waiting for her to join
him.

" Come and sit down, sir," cried Olive, patting the brickwork with her small white hand; " one would think that you
did not like your company."

He obeyed slowly and took a seat by her side, drawing so
hard at his cigar that the light of it shone upon his face at
every breath. He passed his arm, firm and rigid as steel,

behind her, with his hand resting on the brickwork beyond.

" Are you warm enough? " he asked tenderly, as she made a little movement.

" Pretty fair," she shivered; " one oughtn't to be cold at this time of the year, but there's a cold damp air comes up from the well."

As she spoke a faint splash sounded from the depths below, and for the second time that evening she sprang from the well with a little cry of dismay.

" What is it now? " he asked in a fearful voice. He stood by her side and gazed at the well, as though half expecting to see the cause of her alarm emerge from it.

" Oh, my bracelet," she cried in distress, " my poor mother's bracelet. I dropped it down the well."

" Your bracelet! " repeated Benson dully. " Your bracelet! The diamond one? "

" The one that was my mother's," said Olive. " Oh, we can get it back, surely. We must have the water drained off."

" Your bracelet! " repeated Benson stupidly.

" Jem," said the girl in terrified tones, " dear Jem, what is the matter? "

For the man she loved was standing regarding her with horror. The moon which touched it was not responsible for all the whiteness of the distorted face, and she shrank back in fear to the edge of the well. He saw her fear, and by a mighty effort regained his composure and took her hand.

" Poor little girl," he murmured, " you frightened me. I was not looking when you cried, and I thought that you were slipping from my arms, down—down——"

His voice broke, and the girl, throwing herself into his arms, clung to him convulsively.

" There, there," said Benson fondly, " don't cry, don't cry."

" To-morrow," said Olive, half laughing, half crying, " we will all come round the well with hook and line and fish for it. It will be quite a new sport."

" No, we must try some other way," said Benson. " You shall have it back."

" How? " asked the girl.

" You shall see," said Benson. " To-morrow morning at

latest you shall have it back. Till then promise me that you
will not mention your loss to anyone. Promise."

"I promise," said Olive wonderingly. "But why not?"

"It is of great value for one thing, and—but there—there
are many reasons. For one thing, it is my duty to get it for
you."

"Wouldn't you like to jump down for it?" she asked mis-
chievously. "Listen."

She stooped for a stone and dropped it down.

"Fancy being where that is now," she said, peering into
the blackness; "fancy going round and round like a mouse
in a pail, clutching at the slimy sides, with the water filling
your mouth, and looking up to the little patch of sky above."

"You had better come in," said Benson very quietly.
"You are developing a taste for the morbid and horrible."

The girl turned, and taking his arm walked slowly in the
direction of the house. Mrs. Benson, who was sitting in the
porch, rose to receive them.

"You shouldn't have kept her out so long," she said chid-
ingly; "where have you been?"

"Sitting on the well," said Olive, smiling, "discussing our
future."

"I don't believe that place is healthy," said Mrs. Benson
emphatically. "I really think it might be filled in, Jem."

"All right," said her son slowly. "Pity it wasn't filled in
long ago."

He took the chair vacated by his mother as she entered the
house with Olive, and with his hands hanging limply over the
sides sat in deep thought. After a time he rose, and going
upstairs to a room which was set apart for sporting requisites
selected a sea fishing line and some hooks and stole softly
downstairs again. He walked swiftly across the park in the
direction of the well, turning before he entered the shadow
of the trees to look back at the lighted windows of the house.
Then, having arranged his line, he sat on the edge of the well
and cautiously lowered it.

He sat with his lips compressed, occasionally looking about
him in a startled fashion, as though he half expected to see
something peering at him from the belt of trees. Time after
time he lowered his line until at length in pulling it up he
heard a little metallic tinkle against the side of the well.

He held his breath then, and forgetting his fears drew the

line in inch by inch, so as not to lose its precious burden. His pulse beat rapidly, and his eyes were bright. As the line came slowly in he saw the catch hanging to the hook, and with a steady hand drew the last few feet in. Then he saw that instead of the bracelet he had hooked a bunch of keys.

With a faint cry he shook them from the hook into the water below, and stood breathing heavily. Not a sound broke the stillness of the night. He walked up and down a bit and stretched his great muscles, then he came back to the well and resumed his task.

For an hour or more the line was lowered without result. In his eagerness he forgot his fear, and with eyes bent down the well fished slowly and carefully. Twice the hook became entangled in something, and was with difficulty released. It caught a third time, and all his efforts failed to free it. Then he dropped the line down the well, and with head bent walked towards the house.

He went first to the stables at the rear, and then retiring to his room for some time paced restlessly up and down. Then without removing his clothes he flung himself upon the bed and fell into a troubled sleep.

III

Long before anybody else was astir he arose and stole softly downstairs. The sunlight was stealing in at every crevice, and flashing in long streaks across the darkened rooms. The dining-room into which he looked struck chill and cheerless in the dark yellow light which came through the lowered blinds. He remembered that it had the same appearance when his father lay dead in the house; now, as then, everything seemed ghastly and unreal; the very chairs, standing as their occupants had left them the night before, seemed to be indulging in some dark communication of ideas.

Slowly and noiselessly he opened the hall door and passed into the fragrant air beyond. The sun was shining on the drenched grass and trees, and a slowly vanishing white mist rolled like smoke about the grounds. For a moment he stood, breathing deeply the sweet air of the morning, and then walked slowly in the direction of the stables.

The rusty creaking of a pump-handle and a spatter of water upon the red-tiled courtyard showed that somebody else was astir, and a few steps farther he beheld a brawny, sandy-haired man gasping wildly under severe self-infliction at the pump.

"Everything ready, George?" he asked quietly.

"Yes, sir," said the man, straightening up suddenly and touching his forehead. "Bob's just finishing the arrangements inside. It's a lovely morning for a dip. The water in that well must be just icy."

"Be as quick as you can," said Benson impatiently.

"Very good, sir," said George, burnishing his face harshly with a very small towel which had been hanging over the top of the pump. "Hurry up, Bob."

In answer to his summons, a man appeared at the door of the stable with a coil of stout rope over his arm and a large metal candlestick in his hand.

"Just to try the air, sir," said George, following his master's glance, "a well gets rather foul sometimes, but if a candle can live down it a man can."

His master nodded, and the man, hastily pulling up the neck of his shirt and thrusting his arms through his waistcoat, followed him as he led the way slowly to the well.

"Beg pardon, sir," said George, drawing up to his side, "but you are not looking over and above well this morning. If you'll let me go down I'd enjoy the bath."

"No, no," said Benson peremptorily.

"You ain't fit to go down, sir," persisted his follower. "I've never seen you look so before. Now, if——"

"Mind your business," said his master curtly.

George became silent, and the three walked with swinging strides through the long, wet grass to the well. Bob flung the rope on the ground, and at a sign from his master handed him the candlestick.

"Here's the line for it, sir," said Bob, fumbling in his pockets.

Benson took it from him and slowly tied it to the candlestick. Then he placed it on the edge of the well and, striking a match, lit the candle and began slowly to lower it.

"Hold hard, sir," said George quickly, laying his hand on his arm; "you must tilt it or the string'll burn through."

Even as he spoke the string parted and the candlestick fell into the water below.

Benson swore quietly.

The face of a dead man came peering over the edge.

"I'll soon get another," said George, starting up.

"Never mind, the well's all right," said Benson.

"It won't take a moment, sir," said the other, over his shoulder.

"Are you master here, or am I?" said Benson hoarsely.

George came back slowly, a glance at his master's face stopped the protest upon his tongue, and he stood by watching him sulkily as he sat on the well and removed his outer garments. Both men watched him curiously, as having completed his preparations he stood grim and silent with his hands by his side.

"I wish you'd let me go sir," said George, plucking up courage to address him. "You ain't fit to go, you've got a chill or something. I shouldn't wonder it's the typhoid. They've got it in the village bad."

For a moment Benson looked at him angrily, then his gaze softened. "Not this time, George," he said quietly. He took the looped end of the rope and placed it under his arms, and sitting down, threw one leg over the side of the well.

"How are you going about it, sir?" queried George, laying hold of the rope and signing to Bob to do the same.

"I'll call out when I reach the water," said Benson; "then pay out three yards more quickly so that I can get to the bottom."

"Very good, sir," answered both.

Their master threw the other leg over the coping and sat motionless. His back was turned towards the men as he sat with head bent, looking down the shaft. He sat for so long that George became uneasy.

"All right, sir?" he enquired.

"Yes," said Benson slowly. "If I tug at the rope, George, pull up at once. Lower away."

The rope passed steadily through their hands until a hollow cry from the darkness below and a faint splashing warned them that he had reached the water. They gave him three yards more, and stood with relaxed grasp and strained ears, waiting.

"He's gone under," said Bob in a low voice.

The other nodded, and moistening his huge palms took a firmer grip of the rope.

Fully a minute passed, and the men began to exchange uneasy glances. Then a sudden tremendous jerk followed by a series of feebler ones nearly tore the rope from their grasp.

" Pull! " shouted George, placing one foot on the side and hauling desperately. " Pull! pull! He's stuck fast; he's not coming; P—U—LL! "

In response to their terrific exertions the rope came slowly in, inch by inch, until at length a violent splashing was heard, and at the same moment a scream of unutterable horror came echoing up the shaft.

" What a weight he is! " panted Bob. " He's stuck fast or something. Keep still, sir; for heaven's sake, keep still."

For the taut rope was being jerked violently by the struggles of the weight at the end of it.

Both men with grunts and sighs hauled it in foot by foot.

" All right, sir," cried George cheerfully.

He had one foot against the well, and was pulling manfully; the burden was nearing the top. A long pull and a strong pull, and the face of a dead man with mud in the eyes and nostrils came peering over the edge. Behind it was the ghastly face of his master; but he saw too late, for with a great cry George let go his hold of the rope and stepped back. The suddenness overthrew his assistant, and the rope tore through his hands. There was a frightful splash.

" You fool! " stammered Bob, and ran to the well helplessly.

" Run! " cried George. " Run for another line."

He bent over the coping and called eagerly down as his assistant sped back to the stables shouting wildly. His voice re-echoed down the shaft, but all else was silence.

CHARLES DICKENS

THE HAUNTED MAN AND THE GHOST'S BARGAIN

I

THE GIFT BESTOWED

EVERYBODY said so.

Far be it from me to assert that what everybody says must be true. Everybody is, often, as likely to be wrong as right. In the general experience, everybody has been wrong so often, and it has taken, in most instances, such a weary while to find out how wrong, that the authority is proved to be fallible. Everybody may sometimes be right; "but *that's* no rule," as the ghost of Giles Scroggins says in the ballad.

The dread word, GHOST, recalls me.

Everybody said he looked like a haunted man. The extent of my present claim for everybody is, that they were so far right. He did.

Who could have seen his hollow cheek; his sunken, brilliant eye; his black-attired figure, indefinably grim, although well-knit and well-proportioned; his grizzled hair hanging, like tangled seaweed, about his face—as if he had been, through his whole life, a lonely mark for the chafing and beating of the great deep of humanity—but might have said he looked like a haunted man?

Who could have observed his manner—taciturn, thoughtful, gloomy, shadowed by habitual reserve, retiring always and jocund never, with a distraught air of reverting to a bygone place and time, or of listening to some old echoes in his mind—but might have said it was the manner of a haunted man?

Who could have heard his voice—slow-speaking, deep, and grave, with a natural fullness and melody in it which he seemed to set himself against and stop—but might have said it was the voice of a haunted man?

Who that had seen him in his inner chamber, part library and part laboratory—for he was, as the world knew, far and wide, a learned man in chemistry, and a teacher on whose lips and hands a crowd of aspiring ears and eyes hung daily —who that had seen him there, upon a winter night, alone, surrounded by his drugs and instruments and books; the shadow of his shaded lamp a monstrous beetle on the wall, motionless among a crowd of spectral shapes raised there by the flickering of the fire upon the quaint objects around him; some of these phantoms (the reflection of glass vessels that held liquids) trembling at heart like things that knew his power to uncombine them, and to give back their component parts to fire and vapour;—who that had seen him then, his work done, and he pondering in his chair before the rusted grate and red flame, moving his thin mouth as if in speech but silent as the dead, would not have said that the man seemed haunted, and the chamber too?

Who might not, by a very easy flight of fancy, have believed that everything about him took this haunted tone, and that he lived on haunted ground?

His dwelling was so solitary and vault-like—an old, retired part of an ancient endowment for students, once a brave edifice, planted in an open place, but now the obsolete whim of forgotten architects, smoke-age-and-weather-darkened, squeezed on every side by the overgrowing of the great city, and choked, like an old well, with stones and bricks; its small quadrangles, lying down in very pits formed by the streets and buildings which, in course of time, had been constructed above its heavy chimney-stacks; its old trees, insulted by the neighbouring smoke, which deigned to droop so low when it was very feeble and the weather very moody; its grass plots, struggling with the mildewed earth to be grass, or to win any show of compromise; its silent pavements, unaccustomed to the tread of feet, and even to the observation of eyes, except when a stray face looked down from the upper world, wondering what nook it was; its sun-dial in a little bricked-up corner, where no sun had straggled for a hundred years, but where, in compensation for the sun's neglect, the snow would lie for weeks when it lay nowhere else, and the black east wind would spin like a huge humming-top, when in all other places it was silent and still.

His dwelling, at its heart and core—within doors—at his

fireside—was so lowering and old, so crazy, yet so strong, with its worm-eaten beams of wood in the ceiling, and its sturdy floor shelving downward to the great oak chimney-piece; so environed and hemmed in by the pressure of the town, yet so remote in fashion, age, and custom; so quiet, yet so thundering with echoes when a distant voice was raised or a door was shut—echoes, not confined to the many low passages and empty rooms, but rumbling and grumbling till they were stifled in the heavy air of the forgotten Crypt where the Norman arches were half-buried in the earth.

You should have seen him in his dwelling about twilight, in the dead winter time.

When the wind was blowing, shrill and shrewd, with the going down of the blurred sun. When it was just so dark as that the forms of things were indistinct and big, but not wholly lost. When sitters by the fire began to see wild faces and figures, mountains and abysses, ambuscades and armies, in the coals. When people in the streets bent down their heads, and ran before the weather. When those who were obliged to meet it were stopped at angry corners, stung by wandering snowflakes alighting on the lashes of their eyes—which fell too sparingly, and were blown away too quickly, to leave a trace upon the frozen ground. When windows of private houses closed up tight and warm. When lighted gas began to burst forth in the busy and the quiet streets, fast blackening otherwise. When stray pedestrians, shivering along the latter, looked down at the glowing fires in kitchens, and sharpened their sharp appetites by sniffing up the fragrance of whole miles of dinners.

When travellers by land were bitter cold, and looked wearily on gloomy landscapes, rustling and shuddering in the blast. When mariners at sea, outlying upon icy yards, were tossed and swung above the howling ocean dreadfully. When lighthouses, on rocks and headlands, showed solitary and watchful, and benighted sea-birds breasted on against their ponderous lanterns, and fell dead. When little readers of story-books, by the firelight, trembled to think of Cassim Baba cut into quarters, hanging in the Robbers' Cave, or had some small misgivings that the fierce little old woman with the crutch, who used to start out of the box in the merchant Abudah's bedroom, might, one of these nights, be found upon the stairs, in the long, cold, dusky journey up to bed.

When, in rustic places, the last glimmering of daylight
died away from the ends of avenues, and the trees, arching
overhead, were sullen and black. When, in parks and woods,
the high wet fern and sodden moss, and beds of fallen leaves
and trunks of trees, were lost to view, in masses of impenetrable shade. When mists arose from dike, and fen, and river.
When lights in old halls and in cottage windows were a
cheerful sight. When the mill stopped, the wheelwright
and the blacksmith shut their workshops, the turnpike gate
closed, the plough and harrow were left lonely in the fields,
the labourer and team went home, and the striking of the
church-clock had a deeper sound than at noon, and the
churchyard wicket would be swung no more that night.

When twilight everywhere released the shadows, prisoned
up all day, that now closed in and gathered like mustering
swarms of ghosts. When they stood lowering, in corners of
rooms, and frowned out from behind half-opened doors.
When they had full possession of unoccupied apartments.
When they danced upon the floors, and walls, and ceilings of
inhabited chambers, while the fire was low, and withdrew
like ebbing waters when it sprung into a blaze. When they
fantastically mocked the shapes of household objects, making
the nurse an ogress, the rocking-horse a monster, the wondering child, half-scared and half-amused, a stranger to itself—
the very tongs upon the hearth a straddling giant with his
arms akimbo, evidently smelling the blood of Englishmen,
and wanting to grind people's bones to make his bread.

When these shadows brought into the minds of older
people other thoughts, and showed them different images.
When they stole from their retreats, in the likenesses of forms
and faces from the past, from the grave, from the deep, deep
gulf where the things that might have been, and never were,
are always wandering.

When he sat, as already mentioned, gazing at the fire.
When, as it rose and fell, the shadows went and came. When
he took no heed of them, with his bodily eyes, but, let them
come or let them go, looked fixedly at the fire. You should
have seen him then.

When the sounds that had arisen with the shadows, and
come out of their lurking-places at the twilight summons,
seemed to make a deeper stillness all about him. When the
wind was rumbling in the chimney, and sometimes crooning,

sometimes howling, in the house. When the old trees outside
were so shaken and beaten, that one querulous old rook,
unable to sleep, protested now and then, in a feeble, dozy
high-up "Caw!" When, at intervals, the window trembled,
the rusty vane upon the turret-top complained, the clock
beneath it recorded that another quarter of an hour was
gone, or the fire collapsed and fell in with a rattle.

When a knock came at his door, in short, as he was sitting
so, and roused him.

"Who's that?" said he. "Come in!"

Surely there had been no figure leaning on the back of his
chair, no face looking over it. It is certain that no gliding
footstep touched the floor, as he lifted up his head, with a
start, and spoke. And yet there was no mirror in the room
on whose surface his own form could have cast its shadow
for a moment; and Something had passed darkly and gone!

"I'm humbly fearful, sir," said a fresh-coloured busy man,
holding the door open with his foot for the admission of
himself and a wooden tray he carried, and letting it go again
by very gentle and careful degrees, when he and the tray had
got in, lest it should close noisily, "that it's a good bit past
the time to-night. But Mrs. William has been taken off her
legs so often——"

"By the wind? Ay! I have heard it rising."

"By the wind, sir—that it's a mercy she got home at all.
Oh dear, yes. Yes. It was by the wind, Mr. Redlaw—by
the wind."

He had by this time put down the tray for dinner, and
was employed in lighting the lamp, and spreading a cloth on
the table. From this employment he desisted in a hurry, to
stir and feed the fire, and then resumed it; the lamp he had
lighted, and the blaze that rose under his hand, so quickly
changing the appearance of the room, that it seemed as if the
mere coming in of his fresh red face and active manner had
made the pleasant alteration.

"Mrs. William is of course subject at any time, sir, to
be taken off her balance by the elements. She is not formed
superior to *that*."

"No," returned Mr. Redlaw good-naturedly, though
abruptly.

"No, sir. Mrs. William may be taken off her balance by
Earth; as, for example, last Sunday week, when sloppy and

greasy, and she going out to tea with her newest sister-in-law,
and having a pride in herself, and wishing to appear perfectly
spotless though pedestrian. Mrs. William may be taken off
her balance by Air; as being once over-persuaded by a
friend to try a swing at Peckham Fair, which acted on her
constitution instantly like a steamboat. Mrs. William may be
taken off her balance by Fire; as on a false alarm of engines
at her mother's, when she went two miles in her nightcap.
Mrs. William may be taken off her balance by Water; as at
Battersea, when rowed into the piers by her young nephew,
Charley Swidger junior, aged twelve, which had no idea of
boats whatever. But these are elements. Mrs. William must
be taken out of elements for the strength of *her* character to
come into play."

As he stopped for a reply, the reply was "Yes," in the
same tone as before.

"Yes, sir. Oh dear, yes!" said Mr. Swidger, still proceeding with his preparations, and checking them off as he
made them. "That's where it is, sir. That's what I always
say myself, sir. Such a many of us Swidgers!—Pepper.
Why, there's my father, sir, superannuated keeper and custodian of this Institution, eigh-ty-seven year old. He's a
Swidger!—Spoon."

"True, William," was the patient and abstracted answer,
when he stopped again.

"Yes, sir," said Mr. Swidger. "That's what I always say,
sir. You may call him the trunk of the tree!—Bread. Then
you come to his successor, my unworthy self—Salt—and Mrs.
William, Swidgers both.—Knife and fork. Then you come
to all my brothers and their families, Swidgers, man and
woman, boy and girl. Why, what with cousins, uncles, aunts,
and relationships of this, that, and t'other degree, and what-
not degree, and marriages, and lyings-in, the Swidgers—
Tumbler—might take hold of hands, and make a ring round
England!"

Receiving no reply at all here from the thoughtful man
whom he addressed, Mr. William approached him nearer,
and made a feint of accidentally knocking the table with a
decanter, to rouse him. The moment he succeeded, he went
on, as if in great alacrity of acquiescence.

"Yes, sir! That's just what I say myself, sir. Mrs.
William and me have often said so. 'There's Swidgers

enough,' we say, ' without *our* voluntary contributions '—
Butter. In fact, sir, my father is a family in himself—
Casters—to take care of; and it happens all for the best that
we have no child of our own, though it's made Mrs. William
rather quiet-like, too.—Quite ready for the fowl and mashed
potatoes, sir? Mrs. William said she'd dish in ten minutes
when I left the Lodge? "

" I am quite ready," said the other, waking as from a
dream, and walking slowly to and fro.

" Mrs. William has been at it again, sir! " said the keeper,
as he stood warming a plate at the fire, and pleasantly shading
his face with it. Mr. Redlaw stopped in his walking, and an
expression of interest appeared in him.

" What I always say myself, sir. She *will* do it! There's
a motherly feeling in Mrs. William's breast that must and
will have went."

" What has she done? "

" Why, sir, not satisfied with being a sort of mother to all
the young gentlemen that come up from a variety of parts,
to attend your courses of lectures at this ancient foundation
—it's surprising how stone-chaney catches the heat, this
frosty weather, to be sure! " Here he turned the plate, and
cooled his fingers.

" Well? " said Mr. Redlaw.

" That's just what I say myself, sir," returned Mr. William,
speaking over his shoulder, as if in ready and delighted
assent. " That's exactly where it is, sir! There ain't one of
our students but appears to regard Mrs. William in that light.
Every day, right through the course, they puts their heads
into the Lodge, one after another, and have all got something
to tell her, or something to ask her. ' Swidge ' is the appellation by which they speak of Mrs. William in general, among
themselves, I'm told; but that's what I say, sir. Better be
called ever so far out of your name, if it's done in real liking,
than have it made ever so much of, and not cared about!
What's a name for? To know a person by. If Mrs. William
is known by something better than her name—I allude to
Mrs. William's qualities and disposition—never mind her
name, though it *is* Swidger by rights. Let 'em call her
Swidge, Widge, Bridge—Lord! London Bridge, Blackfriars',
Chelsea, Putney, Waterloo, or Hammersmith Suspension—if
they like! "

The close of this triumphant oration brought him and the
plate to the table, upon which he half laid and half dropped
it, with a lively sense of its being thoroughly heated, just as
the subject of his praises entered the room, bearing another
tray and a lantern, and followed by a venerable old man with
long grey hair.

Mrs. William, like Mr. William, was a simple, innocent-
looking person, in whose smooth cheeks the cheerful red of
her husband's official waistcoat was very pleasantly repeated.
But whereas Mr. William's light hair stood on end all over
his head, and seemed to draw his eyes up with it in an excess
of bustling readiness for anything, the dark brown hair of
Mrs. William was carefully smoothed down, and waved away
under a trim tidy cap, in the most exact and quiet manner
imaginable. Whereas Mr. William's very trousers hitched
themselves up at the ankles, as if it were not in their iron-grey
nature to rest without looking about them, Mrs. William's
neatly flowered skirts—red and white, like her own pretty
face—were as composed and orderly, as if the very wind
that blew so hard out of doors could not disturb one of their
folds. Whereas his coat had something of a fly-away and
half-off appearance about the collar and breast, her little
bodice was so placid and neat that there should have been
protection for her, in it, had she needed any, with the roughest
people. Who could have had the heart to make so calm
a bosom swell with grief, or throb with fear, or flutter with
a thought of shame? To whom would its repose and peace
have not appealed against disturbance, like the innocent
slumber of a child?

" Punctual, of course, Milly," said her husband, relieving
her of the tray, " or it wouldn't be you. Here's Mrs. William,
sir!—He looks lonelier than ever to-night," whispering to his
wife, as he was taking the tray, " and ghostlier altogether."

Without any show of hurry or noise, or any show of herself
even, she was so calm and quiet, Milly set the dishes she had
brought upon the table—Mr. William, after much clattering
and running about, having only gained possession of a butter-
boat of gravy, which he stood ready to serve.

" What is that the old man has in his arms? " asked Mr.
Redlaw as he sat down to his solitary meal.

" Holly, sir," replied the quiet voice of Milly.

" That's what I say myself, sir," interposed Mr. William,

striking in with the butter-boat. " Berries is so seasonable to the time of year!—Brown gravy! "

" Another Christmas come, another year gone! " murmured the Chemist, with a gloomy sigh. " More figures in the lengthening sum of recollection that we work and work at to our torment, till Death idly jumbles all together, and rubs all out. So, Philip! " breaking off, and raising his voice as he addressed the old man, standing apart, with his glistening burden in his arms, from which the quiet Mrs. William took small branches, which she noiselessly trimmed with her scissors, and decorated the room with, while her aged father-in-law looked on, much interested in the ceremony.

" My duty to you, sir," returned the old man. " Should have spoken before, sir, but know your ways, Mr. Redlaw—proud to say—and wait till spoke to! · Merry Christmas, sir, and happy New Year, and many of 'em. Have had a pretty many of 'em myself—ha, ha!—and may take the liberty of wishing 'em. I'm eighty-seven! "

" Have you had so many that were merry and happy? " asked the other.

" Ay, sir, ever so many," returned the old man.

" Is his memory impaired with age? It is to be expected now," said Mr. Redlaw, turning to the son, and speaking lower.

" Not a morsel of it, sir," replied Mr. William. " That's exactly what I say myself, sir. There never was such a memory as my father's. He's the most wonderful man in the world. He don't know what forgetting means. It's the very observation I'm always making to Mrs. William, sir, if you'll believe me! "

Mr. Swidger, in his polite desire to seem to acquiesce at all events, delivered this as if there were no iota of contradiction in it, and it were all said in unbounded and unqualified assent.

The Chemist pushed his plate away, and, rising from the table, walked across the room to where the old man stood looking at a little sprig of holly in his hand.

" It recalls the time when many of those years were old and new, then? " he said, observing him attentively, and touching him on the shoulder. " Does it? "

" Oh, many, many! " said Philip, half-awaking from his reverie. " I'm eighty-seven! "

" Merry and happy, was it? " asked the Chemist in a low voice. " Merry and happy, old man? "

" Maybe as high as that, no higher," said the old man, holding out his hand a little way above the level of his knee, and looking retrospectively at his questioner, " when I first remember 'em! Cold, sunshiny day it was, out a-walking, when someone—it was my mother as sure as you stand there though I don't know what her blessed face was like, for she took ill and died that Christmas-time—told me they were food for birds. The pretty little fellow thought—that's me, you understand—that birds' eyes were so bright, perhaps, because the berries that they lived on in the winter were so bright. I recollect that. And I'm eighty-seven! "

" Merry and happy! " mused the other, bending his dark eyes upon the stooping figure with a smile of compassion. " Merry and happy—and remember well? "

" Ay, ay, ay! " resumed the old man, catching the last words. " I remember 'em well in my school time, year after year, and all the merrymaking that used to come along with them. I was a strong chap then, Mr. Redlaw; and, if you'll believe me, hadn't my match at football within ten mile. Where's my son William? Hadn't my match at football, William, within ten mile! "

. " That's what I always say, father! " returned the son promptly, and with great respect. " You ARE a Swidger, if ever there was one of the family! "

" Dear! " said the old man, shaking his head as he again looked at the holly. " His mother—my son William's my youngest son—and I have sat among 'em all, boys and girls, little children and babies, many a year, when the berries like these were not shining half so bright all round us as their bright faces. Many of 'em are gone; she's gone; and my son George (our eldest, who was her pride more than all the rest!) is fallen very low. But I can see them, when I look here, alive and healthy, as they used to be in those days and I can see him, thank God, in his innocence. It's a blessed thing to me, at eighty-seven."

The keen look that had been fixed upon him with so much earnestness had gradually sought the ground.

" When my circumstances got to be not so good as formerly, through not being honestly dealt by, and I first come here to be custodian," said the old man—" which was upwards of fifty years ago—where's my son William? More than half a century ago, William!"

"That's what I say, father," replied the son, as promptly and dutifully as before; "that's exactly where it is. Two times ought's an ought, and twice five ten, and there's a hundred of 'em."

"It was quite a pleasure to know that one of our founders —or more correctly speaking," said the old man, with a great glory in his subject and his knowledge of it, "one of the learned gentlemen that helped endow us in Queen Elizabeth's time, for we were founded afore her day—left in his will, among the other bequests he made us, so much to buy holly, for garnishing the walls and windows come Christmas. There was something homely and friendly in it. Being but strange here, then, and coming at Christmas time, we took a liking for his very picter that hangs in what used to be anciently, afore our ten poor gentlemen commuted for an annual stipend in money, our great Dinner Hall.—A sedate gentleman in a peaked beard, with a ruff round his neck, and a scroll below him in old English letters, 'Lord! keep my memory green!' You know all about him, Mr. Redlaw?"

"I know the portrait hangs there, Philip."

"Yes, sure, it's the second on the right, above the panelling. I was going to say—he has helped to keep *my* memory green, I thank him; for going round the building every year, as I'm a-doing now, and freshening up the bare rooms with these branches and berries, freshens up my bare old brain. One year brings back another, and that year another, and those other numbers! At last, it seems to me as if the birth-time of our Lord was the birth-time of all I have ever had affection for, or mourned for, or delighted in—and they're a pretty many, for I'm eighty-seven!"

"Merry and happy," murmured Redlaw to himself.

The room began to darken strangely.

"So you see, sir," pursued old Philip, whose hale wintry cheek had warmed into a ruddier glow, and whose blue eyes had brightened, while he spoke, "I have plenty to keep when I keep this present season. Now, where's my quiet Mouse? Chattering's the sin of my time of life, and there's half the building to do yet, if the cold don't freeze us first, or the wind don't blow us away, or the darkness don't swallow us up."

The quiet Mouse had brought her calm face to his side, and silently taken his arm, before he finished speaking.

"Come away, my dear," said the old man. "Mr. Redlaw won't settle to his dinner, otherwise, till it's cold as the winter. I hope you'll excuse me rambling on, sir, and I wish you good night, and, once again, a merry——"

"Stay!" said Mr. Redlaw, resuming his place at the table, more, it would have seemed from his manner, to reassure the old keeper, than in any remembrance of his own appetite. "Spare me another moment, Philip. William, you were going to tell me something to your excellent wife's honour. It will not be disagreeable to her to hear you praise her. What was it?"

"Why, that's where it is, you see, sir," returned Mr. William Swidger, looking towards his wife in considerable embarrassment. "Mrs. William's got her eye upon me."

"But you're not afraid of Mrs. William's eye?"

"Why, no, sir," returned Mr. Swidger; "that's what I say myself. It wasn't made to be afraid of. It wouldn't have been made so mild, if that was the intention. But I wouldn't like to—Milly!—him, you know. Down in the Buildings."

Mr. William, standing behind the table, and rummaging disconcertedly among the objects upon it, directed persuasive glances at Mrs. William, and secret jerks of his head and thumb at Mr. Redlaw, as alluring her towards him.

"Him, you know, my love," said Mr. William. "Down in the Buildings. Tell, my dear! You're the works of Shakespeare in comparison with myself. Down in the Buildings, you know, my love.—Student."

"Student?" repeated Mr. Redlaw, raising his head.

"That's what I say, sir!" cried Mr. William, in the utmost animation of assent. "If it wasn't the poor student down in the Buildings, why should you wish to hear it from Mrs. William's lips? Mrs. William, my dear—Buildings."

"I didn't know," said Milly, with a quiet frankness, free from any haste, or confusion, "that William had said anything about it, or I wouldn't have come. I asked him not to. It's a sick young gentleman, sir—and very poor, I am afraid—who is too ill to go home this holiday-time, and lives, unknown to any one, in but a common kind of lodging for a gentleman, down in Jerusalem Buildings. That's all, sir."

"Why have I never heard of him?" said the Chemist,

rising hurriedly. "Why has he not made his situation known to me? Sick!—give me my hat and cloak. Poor!—what house?—what number?"

"Oh, you mustn't go there, sir," said Milly, leaving her father-in-law, and calmly confronting him with her collected little face and folded hands.

"Not go there?"

"Oh dear, no!" said Milly, shaking her head as at a most manifest and self-evident impossibility. "It couldn't be thought of!"

"What do you mean? Why not?"

"Why, you see, sir," said Mr. William Swidger, persuasively and confidently, "that's what I say. Depend upon it, the young gentleman would never have made his situation known to one of his own sex. Mrs. William has got into his confidence, but that's quite different. They all confide in Mrs. William; they all trust *her*! A man, sir, couldn't have got a whisper out of him; but woman, sir, and Mrs. William combined——?"

"There is good sense and delicacy in what you say, William," returned Mr. Redlaw, observant of the gentle and composed face at his shoulder. And laying his finger on his lip, he secretly put his purse into her hand.

"Oh dear, no, sir!" cried Milly, giving it back again. "Worse and worse! Couldn't be dreamed of!"

Such a staid, matter-of-fact housewife she was, and so unruffled by the momentary haste of this rejection, that, an instant afterwards, she was tidily picking up a few leaves which had strayed between her scissors and her apron, when she had arranged the holly.

Finding, when she rose from her stooping posture, that Mr. Redlaw was still regarding her with doubt and astonishment, she quietly repeated—looking about, the while, for any other fragments that might have escaped her observation:

"Oh dear, no, sir! He said that of all the world he would not be known to you, or receive help from you—though he is a student in your class. I have made no terms of secrecy with you, but I trust to your honour completely."

"Why did he say so?"

"Indeed I can't tell, sir," said Milly, after thinking a little, "because I am not at all clever, you know; and I wanted to be useful to him in making things neat and comfortable about

him, and employed myself that way. But I know he is poor,
and lonely, and I think he is somehow neglected too.—How
dark it is! "

The room had darkened more and more. There was a
very heavy gloom and shadow gathering behind the Chemist's
chair.

" What more about him? " he asked.

" He is engaged to be married when he can afford it," said
Milly, " and is studying, I think, to qualify himself to earn a
living. I have seen, a long time, that he has studied hard,
and denied himself much.—How very dark it is! "

" It's turned colder, too," said the old man, rubbing his
hands. " There's a chill and dismal feeling in the room.
Where's my son William? William, my boy, turn the lamp,
and rouse the fire? "

Milly's voice resumed, like quiet music very softly played.

" He muttered in his broken sleep yesterday afternoon,
after talking to me " (this was to herself), " about someone
dead, and some great wrong done that could never be forgotten; but whether to him or to another person, I don't
know. Not *by* him, I am sure."

" And, in short, Mrs. William, you see—which she wouldn't
say herself, Mr. Redlaw, if she was to stop here till the new
year after this next one," said Mr. William, coming up to
him to speak in his ear—" has done him worlds of good.
Bless you, worlds of good! All at home just the same as
ever: my father made as snug and comfortable—not a crumb
of litter to be found in the house, if you were to offer fifty
pound ready money for it—Mrs. William apparently never
out of the way—yet Mrs. William backwards and forwards,
backwards and forwards, up and down, up and down, a
mother to him! "

The room turned darker and colder, and the gloom and
shadow gathering behind the chair was heavier.

" Not content with this, sir, Mrs. William goes and finds,
this very night, when she was coming home (why, it's not
above a couple of hours ago), a creature more like a young
wild beast than a young child, shivering upon a doorstep.
What does Mrs. William do but brings it home to dry it, and
feed it, and keep it till our old Bounty of food and flannel
is given away on Christmas morning! If it ever felt a fire
before, it's as much as it ever did; for it's sitting in the old

Lodge chimney, staring at ours as if its ravenous eyes would never shut again. It's sitting there, at least," said Mr. William, correcting himself, on reflection, "unless it's bolted! "

"Heaven keep her happy! " said the Chemist aloud; "and you too, Philip! and you, William! I must consider what to do in this. I may desire to see this student. I'll not detain you longer now. Good night! "

"I thank'ee, sir, I thank'ee! " said the old man, "for Mouse, and for my son William, and for myself. Where's my son William? William, you take the lantern and go on first, through them long dark passages, as you did last year and the year afore. Ha, ha! I remember—though I'm eighty-seven! 'Lord, keep my memory green!' It's a very good prayer, Mr. Redlaw, that of the learned gentleman in the peaked beard, with a ruff round his neck—hangs up, second on the right above the panelling, in what used to be, afore our ten poor gentlemen commuted, our great Dinner Hall. 'Lord, keep my memory green!' It's very good and pious, sir. Amen! Amen! "

As they passed out, and shut the heavy door, which, however carefully withheld, fired a long train of thundering reverberations when it shut at last, the room turned darker.

As he fell a-musing in his chair alone, the healthy holly withered on the wall, and dropped—dead branches.

As the gloom and shadow thickened behind him, in that place where it had been gathering so darkly, it took, by slow degrees—or out of it there came, by some unreal, unsubstantial process, not to be traced by any human sense—an awful likeness of himself!

Ghastly and cold, colourless in its leaden face and hands, but with his features, and his bright eyes, and his grizzled hair, and dressed in the gloomy shadow of his dress, it came into its terrible appearance of existence, motionless, without a sound. As *he* leaned his arm upon the elbow of his chair, ruminating before the fire, *it* leaned back upon the chair-back, close above him, with its appalling copy of his face looking where his face looked, and bearing the expression his face bore.

This, then, was the Something that had passed and gone already. This was the dread companion of the haunted man!

It took, for some moments, no more apparent heed of him

than he of it. The Christmas Waits were playing somewhere in the distance, and, through his thoughtfulness, he seemed to listen to the music. It seemed to listen too.

At length he spoke, without moving or lifting up his face.

" Here again! " he said.

" Here again," replied the Phantom.

" I see you in the fire," said the haunted man; " I hear you in music, in the wind, in the dead stillness of the night."

The Phantom moved its head, assenting.

" Why do you come to haunt me thus? "

" I come as I am called," replied the Ghost.

" No. Unbidden," exclaimed the Chemist.

" Unbidden be it," said the Spectre. " It is enough. I am here."

Hitherto the light of the fire had shone on the two faces—if the dread lineaments behind the chair might be called a face—both addressed towards it, as at first, and neither looking at the other. But now the haunted man turned suddenly and stared upon the Ghost. The Ghost, as sudden in its motion, passed to before the chair, and stared on him.

The living man, and the animated image of himself dead, might so have looked, the one upon the other. An awful survey, in a lonely and remote part of an empty old pile of building, on a winter night, with the loud wind going by upon its journey of mystery—whence, or whither, no man knowing since the world began—and the stars, in unimaginable millions, glittering through it, from eternal space, where the world's bulk is as a grain, and its hoary age is infancy.

" Look upon me! " said the Spectre. " I am he neglected in my youth, and miserably poor, who strove and suffered, and still strove and suffered, until I hewed out knowledge from the mine where it was buried, and made rugged steps thereof, for my worn feet to rest and rise on."

" I *am* that man," returned the Chemist.

" No mother's self-denying love," pursued the Phantom, " no father's counsel, aided *me*. A stranger came into my father's place when I was but a child, and I was easily an alien from my mother's heart. My parents, at the best, were of that sort whose care soon ends, and whose duty is soon done; who cast their offspring loose early, as birds do theirs; and, if they do well, claim the merit, and, if ill, the pity."

It paused, and seemed to tempt and goad him with its look, and with the manner of its speech, and with its smile.

"I am he," pursued the Phantom, "who, in this struggle upward, found a friend. I made him, won him, bound him to me! We worked together, side by side. All the love and confidence that in my earlier youth had had no outlet, and found no expression, I bestowed on him."

"Not all," said Redlaw hoarsely.

"No, not all," returned the Phantom. "I had a sister."

The haunted man, with his head resting on his hands, replied, "I had!"

The Phantom, with an evil smile, drew closer to the chair, and resting its chin upon its folded hands, its folded hands upon the back, and looking down into his face with searching eyes that seemed instinct with fire, went on,—

"Such glimpses of the light of home as I had ever known had streamed from her. How young she was, how fair, how loving! I took her to the first poor roof that I was master of, and made it rich. She came into the darkness of my life, and made it bright.—She is before me!"

"I saw her in the fire but now. I hear her in music, in the wind, in the dead stillness of the night," returned the haunted man.

"*Did* he love her?" said the Phantom, echoing his contemplative tone. "I think he did, once. I am sure he did. Better had she loved him less—less secretly, less dearly, from the shallower depths of a more divided heart!"

"Let me forget it!" said the Chemist, with an angry motion of his hand. "Let me blot it from my memory!"

The Spectre, without stirring, and with its unwinking, cruel eyes still fixed upon his face, went on,—

"A dream like hers stole upon my own life."

"It did," said Redlaw.

"A love, as like hers," pursued the Phantom, "as my inferior nature might cherish, arose in my own heart. I was too poor to bind its object to my fortune then by any thread of promise or entreaty. I loved her far too well to seek to do it. But, more than ever I had striven in my life, I strove to climb! Only an inch gained brought me something nearer to the height. I toiled up! In the late pauses of my labour at that time—my sister (sweet companion!) still sharing with me the expiring embers and the cooling hearth—

when day was breaking, what pictures of the future did I see? "

" I saw them in the fire but now," he murmured. " They come back to me in music, in the wind, in the dead stillness of the night, in the revolving years."

" Pictures of my own domestic life, in after-time, with her who was the inspiration of my toil. Pictures of my sister, made the wife of my dear friend, on equal terms—for he had some inheritance, we none. Pictures of our sobered age and mellowed happiness, and of the golden links, extending back so far, that should bind us and our children in a radiant garland," said the Phantom.

" Pictures," said the haunted man, " that were delusions. Why is it my doom to remember them too well? "

" Delusions! " echoed the Phantom in its changeless voice, and glaring on him with its changeless eyes. " For my friend (in whose breast my confidence was locked as in my own), passing between me and the centre of the system of my hopes and struggles, won her to himself, and shattered my frail universe. My sister, doubly dear, doubly devoted, doubly cheerful in my home, lived on to see me famous, and my old ambition so rewarded when its spring was broken, and then——"

" Then died," he interposed. " Died, gentle as ever, happy, and with no concern but for her brother. Peace! "

The Phantom watched him silently.

" Remembered! " said the haunted man, after a pause. " Yes, so well remembered that even now, when years have passed, and nothing is more idle or more visionary to me than the boyish love so long outlived, I think of it with sympathy, as if it were a younger brother's or a son's. Sometimes I even wonder when her heart first inclined to him, and how it had been affected towards me. Not lightly once, I think.—But that is nothing. Early unhappiness, a wound from a hand I loved and trusted, and a loss that nothing can replace, outlive such fancies."

" Thus," said the Phantom, " I bear within me a Sorrow and a Wrong. Thus I prey upon myself. Thus, memory is my curse; and, if I could forget my sorrow and my wrong, I would! "

" Mocker! " said the Chemist, leaping up, and making, with a wrathful hand, at the throat of his other self. " Why have I always that taunt in my ears? "

"Forbear!" exclaimed the Spectre in an awful voice. "Lay a hand on Me, and die!"

He stopped midway, as if its words had paralysed him, and stood looking on it. It had glided from him; it had its arm raised high in warning; and a smile passed over its unearthly features, as it reared its dark figure in triumph.

"If I could forget my sorrow and wrong, I would," the Ghost repeated. "If I could forget my sorrow and my wrong, I would!"

"Evil spirit of myself," returned the haunted man, in a low, trembling tone, "my life is darkened by that incessant whisper.

"It is an echo," said the Phantom.

"If it be an echo of my thoughts—as now, indeed, I know it is," rejoined the haunted man—"why should I, therefore, be tormented? It is not a selfish thought. I suffer it to range beyond myself. All men and women have their sorrows—most of them their wrongs; ingratitude, and sordid jealousy, and interest besetting all degrees of life. Who would not forget their sorrows and their wrongs?"

"Who would not, truly; and be the happier and better for it?" said the Phantom.

"These revolutions of years, which we commemorate," proceeded Redlaw, "what do *they* recall? Are there any minds in which they do not reawaken some sorrow, or some trouble? What is the remembrance of the old man who was here to-night? A tissue of sorrow and trouble."

"But common natures," said the Phantom, with its evil smile upon its glassy face, "unenlightened minds, and ordinary spirits, do not feel or reason on these things like men of higher cultivation and profounder thought."

"Tempter," answered Redlaw, "whose hollow look and voice I dread more than words can express, and from whom some dim foreshadowing of greater fear is stealing over me while I speak, I hear again an echo of my own mind."

"Receive it as a proof that I am powerful," returned the Ghost. "Hear what I offer! Forget the sorrow, wrong, and trouble you have known!"

"Forget them!" he repeated.

"I have the power to cancel their remembrance—to leave but very faint, confused traces of them, that will die out soon," returned the Spectre. "Say! Is it done?"

" Stay! " cried the haunted man, arresting by a terrified gesture the uplifted hand. " I tremble with distrust and doubt of you, and the dim fear you cast upon me deepens into a nameless horror I can hardly bear. I would not deprive myself of any kindly reflection, or any sympathy that is good for me or others. What shall I lose if I assent to this? What else will pass from my remembrance? "

" No knowledge; no result of study; nothing but the intertwisted chain of feelings and associations, each in its turn dependent on, and nourished by, the banished recollections. Those will go."

" Are they so many? " said the haunted man, reflecting in alarm.

" They have been wont to show themselves in the fire, in music, in the wind, in the dead stillness of the night, in the revolving years," returned the Phantom scornfully.

" In nothing else? "

The Phantom held its peace.

But having stood before him, silent, for a little while, it moved towards the fire; then stopped.

" Decide," it said, " before the opportunity is lost! "

" A moment! I call Heaven to witness," said the agitated man, " that I have never been a hater of my kind; never morose, indifferent, or hard, to anything around me. If, living here alone, I have made too much of all that was and might have been, and too little of what is, the evil, I believe, has fallen on me, and not on others. But if there were poison in my body, should I not, possessed of antidotes and knowledge how to use them, use them? If there be poison in my mind, and through this fearful shadow I can cast it out, shall I not cast it out? "

" Say," said the Spectre, " is it done? "

" A moment longer! " he answered hurriedly. " *I would forget it if I could!* Have *I* thought that alone, or has it been the thought of thousands upon thousands, generation after generation? All human memory is fraught with sorrow and trouble. My memory is as the memory of other men, but other men have not this choice. Yes, I close the bargain. Yes! I WILL forget my sorrow, wrong, and trouble! "

" Say," said the Spectre, " is it done? "

" It is! "

" It is. And take this with you, man whom I here renounce! The gift that I have given, you shall give again, go where you will. Without recovering yourself the power that you have yielded up, you shall henceforth destroy its like in all whom you approach. Your wisdom has discovered that the memory of sorrow, wrong, and trouble is the lot of all mankind; and that mankind would be the happier, in its other memories, without it. Go! Be its benefactor! Freed from such remembrance, from this hour carry involuntarily the blessing of such freedom with you. Its diffusion is inseparable and inalienable from you. Go! Be happy in the good you have won, and in the good you do! "

The Phantom—which had held its bloodless hand above him while it spoke, as if in some unholy invocation, or some ban; and which had gradually advanced its eyes so close to his, that he could see how they did not participate in the terrible smile upon its face, but were a fixed, unalterable, steady horror—melted from before him, and was gone.

As he stood rooted to the spot, possessed by fear and wonder, and imagining he heard repeated in melancholy echoes, dying away fainter and fainter, the words, " Destroy its like in all whom you approach! " a shrill cry reached his ears. It came, not from the passages beyond the door, but from another part of the old building, and sounded like the cry of someone in the dark who had lost the way.

He looked confusedly upon his hands and limbs, as if to be assured of his identity, and then shouted in reply, loudly and wildly; for there was a strangeness and terror upon him, as if he too were lost.

The cry responding, and being nearer, he caught up the lamp, and raised a heavy curtain in the wall, by which he was accustomed to pass into and out of the theatre where he lectured, which adjoined his room. Associated with youth and animation, and a high amphitheatre of faces which his entrance charmed to interest in a moment, it was a ghostly place when all this life was faded out of it, and stared upon him like an emblem of Death.

" Halloa! " he cried. " Halloa! This way! Come to the light! " When, as he held the curtain with one hand, and with the other raised the lamp and tried to pierce the gloom that filled the place, something rushed past him into the room like a wild-cat, and crouched down in a corner.

" What is it? " he said hastily.

He might have asked, "What is it?" even had he seen it well, as presently he did, when he stood looking at it, gathered up in its corner.

A bundle of tatters, held together by a hand, in size and form almost an infant's, but, in its greedy, desperate little clutch, a bad old man's. A face rounded and smoothed by some half-dozen years, but pinched and twisted by the experiences of a life. Bright eyes, but not youthful. Naked feet, beautiful in their childish delicacy—ugly in the blood and dirt that cracked upon them. A baby savage, a young monster, a child who had never been a child, a creature who might live to take the outward form of man, but who, within, would live and perish a mere beast.

Used already to be worried and hunted like a beast, the boy crouched down as he was looked at, and looked back again, and interposed his arm to ward off the expected blow.

"I'll bite," he said, "if you hit me!"

The time had been, and not many minutes since, when such a sight as this would have wrung the Chemist's heart. He looked upon it now coldly; but, with a heavy effort to remember something—he did not know what—he asked the boy what he did there, and whence he came.

"Where's the woman?" he replied. "I want to find the woman."

"Who?"

"The woman. Her that brought me here, and set me by the large fire. She was so long gone that I went to look for her, and lost myself. I don't want you. I want the woman."

He made a spring, so suddenly, to get away, that the dull sound of his naked feet upon the floor was near the curtain, when Redlaw caught him by his rags.

"Come! you let me go!" muttered the boy, struggling, and clenching his teeth. "I've done nothing to you. Let me go, will you, to the woman?"

"That is not the way. There is a nearer one," said Redlaw, detaining him, in the same blank effort to remember some association that ought, of right, to bear upon this monstrous object. "What is your name?"

"Got none."

"Where do you live?"

"Live! What's that?"

The boy shook his hair from his eyes to look at him for a

moment, and then, twisting round his legs and wrestling with him, broke again into his repetition of, " You let me go, will you?   I want to find the woman."

The Chemist led him to the door.   " This way," he said, looking at him still confusedly, but with repugnance and avoidance growing out of his coldness.   " I'll take you to her."

The sharp eyes in the child's head, wandering round the room, lighted on the table where the remnants of the dinner were.

" Give me some of that! " he said covetously.

" Has she not fed you? "

" I shall be hungry again to-morrow, shan't I?   Ain't I hungry every day? "

Finding himself released, he bounded at the table like some small animal of prey, and hugging to his breast bread and meat, and his own rags, all together, said—

" There!   Now take me to the woman! "

As the Chemist, with a new-born dislike to touch him, sternly motioned him to follow, and was going out of the door, he trembled and stopped.

" The gift that I have given, you shall give again, go where you will! "

The Phantom's words were blowing in the wind, and the wind blew chill upon him.

" I'll not go there to-night," he murmured faintly.   " I'll go nowhere to-night.—Boy! straight down this long-arched passage, and past the great dark door into the yard; you will see the fire shining on a window there."

" The woman's fire? " inquired the boy.

He nodded, and the naked feet had sprung away. He came back with his lamp, locked his door hastily, and sat down in his chair, covering his face like one who was frightened at himself.

For now he was, indeed, alone.   Alone, alone!

II

THE GIFT DIFFUSED

A SMALL man sat in a small parlour, partitioned off from a small shop by a small screen pasted all over with small scraps of newspapers. In company with the small man was

almost any amount of small children you may please to name
—at least it seemed so; they made, in that very limited
sphere of action, such an imposing effect, in point of
numbers.

Of these small fry, two had, by some strong machinery,
been got into bed in a corner, where they might have reposed
snugly enough in the sleep of innocence, but for a constitutional propensity to keep awake, and also to scuttle in and
out of bed. The immediate occasion of these predatory
dashes at the waking world was the construction of an oyster-
shell wall in a corner, by two other youths of tender age;
on which fortification the two in bed made harassing descents
(like those accursed Picts and Scots who beleaguer the early
historical studies of most young Britons), and then withdrew
to their own territory.

In addition to the stir attendant on these inroads, and the
retorts of the invaded, who pursued hotly, and made lunges
at the bed-clothes under which the marauders took refuge,
another little boy, in another little bed, contributed his mite
of confusion to the family stock, by casting his boots upon
the waters; in other words, by launching these and several
small objects, inoffensive in themselves, though of a hard
substance considered as missiles, at the disturbers of his repose
—who were not slow to return these compliments.

Besides which, another little boy—the biggest there, but
still little—was tottering to and fro, bent on one side, and
considerably affected in the knees by the weight of a large
baby, which he was supposed, by a fiction that obtains sometimes in sanguine families, to be hushing to sleep. But oh!
the inexhaustible regions of contemplation and watchfulness into which this baby's eyes were then only beginning to
compose themselves to stare, over his unconscious shoulder!

It was a very Moloch of a baby, on whose insatiate altar
the whole existence of this particular young brother was
offered up a daily sacrifice. Its personality may be said to
have consisted in its never being quiet, in any one place, for
five consecutive minutes, and never going to sleep when
required. "Tetterby's baby" was as well known in the
neighbourhood as the postman or the pot-boy. It roved
from doorstep to doorstep, in the arms of little Johnny
Tetterby, and lagged heavily at the rear of troops of juveniles
who followed the Tumblers or the Monkey, and came up,

all on one side, a little too late for everything that was
attractive, from Monday morning until Saturday night.
Wherever childhood congregated to play, there was little
Moloch making Johnny fag and toil. Wherever Johnny desired to stay, little Moloch became fractious, and would not
remain. Whenever Johnny wanted to go out, Moloch was
asleep, and must be watched. Whenever Johnny wanted to
stay at home, Moloch was awake, and must be taken out.
Yet Johnny was verily persuaded that it was a faultless
baby, without its peer in the realm of England, and was
quite content to catch meek glimpses of things in general
from behind its skirts, or over its limp flapping bonnet,
and to go staggering about with it like a very little porter
with a very large parcel, which was not directed to anybody,
and could never be delivered anywhere.

The small man who sat in the small parlour, making fruitless attempts to read his newspaper peaceably in the midst of
this disturbance, was the father of the family, and the chief
of the firm described in the inscription over the little shop
front, by the name and title of A. TETTERBY AND Co., NEWS-
MEN. Indeed, strictly speaking, he was the only personage
answering to that designation, as Co. was a mere poetical
abstraction, altogether baseless and impersonal.

Tetterby's was the corner shop in Jerusalem Buildings.
There was a good show of literature in the window, chiefly
consisting of picture-newspapers out of date, and serial
pirates, and footpads. Walking-sticks, likewise, and marbles
were included in the stock-in-trade. It had once extended
into the light confectionery line; but it would seem that
those elegancies of life were not in demand about Jerusalem
Buildings, for nothing connected with that branch of commerce remained in the window, except a sort of small glass
lantern containing a languishing mass of bull's-eyes, which
had melted in the summer and congealed in the winter, until
all hope of ever getting them out, or of eating them without
eating the lantern too, was gone for ever. Tetterby's had
tried its hand at several things. It had once made a feeble
little dart at the toy business; for, in another lantern, there
was a heap of minute wax dolls, all sticking together upside
down, in the direst confusion, with their feet on one another's
heads, and a precipitate of broken arms and legs at the bottom.
It had made a move in the millinery direction, which a few

dry, wiry bonnet shapes remained in a corner of the window
to attest. It had fancied that a living might be hidden in the
tobacco trade, and had stuck up a representation of a native
of each of the three integral portions of the British empire,
in the act of consuming that fragrant weed, with a poetic
legend attached, importing that united in one cause they sat
and joked, one chewed tobacco, one took snuff, one smoked;
but nothing seemed to have come of it—except flies. Time
had been when it had put a forlorn trust in imitative jewellery, for in one pane of glass there was a card of cheap seals,
and another of pencil cases, and a mysterious black amulet
of inscrutable intention labelled ninepence. But, to that hour,
Jerusalem Buildings had bought none of them. In short,
Tetterby's had tried so hard to get a livelihood out of Jerusalem Buildings in one way or other, and appeared to have
done so indifferently in all, that the best position in the firm
was too evidently Co.'s; Co., as a bodiless creation, being
untroubled with the vulgar inconveniences of hunger and
thirst, being chargeable neither to the poor's-rates nor the
assessed taxes, and having no young family to provide
for.

Tetterby himself, however, in his little parlour, as already
mentioned, having the presence of a young family impressed
upon his mind in a manner too clamorous to be disregarded,
or to comport with the quiet perusal of a newspaper, laid
down his paper; wheeled, in his distraction, a few times
round the parlour, like an undecided carrier-pigeon; made
an ineffectual rush at one or two flying little figures in bed-
gowns that skimmed past him; and then, bearing suddenly
down upon the only unoffending member of the family,
boxed the ears of little Moloch's nurse.

" You bad boy! " said Mr. Tetterby, " haven't you any
feeling for your poor father after the fatigues and anxieties of
a hard winter's day, since five o'clock in the morning, but
must you wither his rest, and corrode his latest intelligence,
with *your* wicious tricks? Isn't it enough, sir, that your
brother 'Dolphus is toiling and moiling in the fog and cold,
and you rolling in the lap of luxury with a—with a baby,
and everythink you can wish for," said Mr. Tetterby, heaping
this up as a great climax of blessings; " but must you make
a wilderness of home, and maniacs of your parents? Must
you, Johnny? Hey? " At each interrogation, Mr. Tetterby

made a feint of boxing his ears again, but thought better of it, and held his hand.

"Oh, father!" whimpered Johnny, "when I wasn't doing anything, I'm sure, but taking such care of Sally, and getting her to sleep. Oh, father!"

"I wish my little woman would come home!" said Mr. Tetterby, relenting and repenting; "I only wish my little woman would come home! I ain't fit to deal with 'em. They make my head go round, and get the better of me. Oh, Johnny! Isn't it enough that your dear mother has provided you with that sweet sister?" indicating Moloch; "isn't it enough that you were seven boys before, without a ray of gal, and that your dear mother went through what she *did* go through, on purpose that you might all of you have a little sister; but must you so behave yourself as to make my head swim?"

Softening more and more, as his own tender feelings and those of his injured son were worked on, Mr. Tetterby concluded by embracing him, and immediately breaking away to catch one of the real delinquents. A reasonably good start occurring, he succeeded, after a short but smart run, and some rather severe cross-country work under and over the bedsteads, and in and out among the intricacies of the chairs, in capturing this infant, whom he condignly punished, and bore to bed. This example had a powerful, and apparently mesmeric, influence on him of the boots, who instantly fell into a deep sleep, though he had been, but a moment before, broad awake, and in the highest possible feather. Nor was it lost upon the two young architects, who retired to bed, in an adjoining closet, with great privacy and speed. The comrade of the Intercepted One also shrinking into his nest with similar discretion, Mr. Tetterby, when he paused for breath, found himself unexpectedly in a scene of peace.

"My little woman herself," said Mr. Tetterby, wiping his flushed face, "could hardly have done it better! I only wish my little woman had had it to do, I do indeed!"

Mr. Tetterby sought upon his screen for a passage appropriate to be impressed upon his children's minds on the occasion, and read the following:

" 'It is an undoubted fact that all remarkable men have had remarkable mothers, and have respected them in after life as their best friends.' Think of your own remarkable mother,

my boys," said Mr. Tetterby, "and know her value while
she is still among you! "

He sat down in his chair by the fire, and composed himself,
cross-legged, over his newspaper.

" Let anybody, I don't care who it is, get out of bed again,"
said Tetterby, as a general proclamation, delivered in a very
soft-hearted manner, " and astonishment will be the portion
of that respected contemporary! "—which expression Mr.
Tetterby selected from his screen. " Johnny, my child, take
care of your only sister, Sally, for she's the brightest gem that
ever sparkled on your early brow."

Johnny sat down on a little stool, and devotedly crushed
himself beneath the weight of Moloch.

" Ah, what a gift that baby is to you, Johnny! " said his
father, " and how thankful you ought to be! ' It is not
generally known,' Johnny "—he was now referring to the
screen again—" ' but it is a fact ascertained, by accurate
calculations, that the following immense percentage of babies
never attain to two years old; that is to say——' "

" Oh, don't, father, please! " cried Johnny. " I can't bear
it, when I think of Sally."

Mr. Tetterby desisting, Johnny, with a profounder sense
of his trust, wiped his eyes, and hushed his sister.

" Your brother 'Dolphus," said his father, poking the fire,
" is late to-night, Johnny, and will come home like a lump of
ice. What's got your precious mother? "

" Here's mother, and 'Dolphus too, father! " exclaimed
Johnny, " I think."

" You're right! " returned his father, listening. " Yes,
that's the footstep of my little woman."

The process of induction, by which Mr. Tetterby had come
to the conclusion that his wife was a little woman, was his
own secret. She would have made two editions of himself
very easily. Considered as an individual, she was rather
remarkable for being robust and portly; but considered with
reference to her husband, her dimensions became magnificent.
Nor did they assume a less imposing proportion, when studied
with reference to the size of her seven sons, who were but
diminutive. In the case of Sally, however, Mrs. Tetterby
had asserted herself at last; as nobody knew better than
the victim Johnny, who weighed and measured that exacting
idol every hour in the day.

Mrs. Tetterby, who had been marketing, and carried a basket, threw back her bonnet and shawl, and sitting down, fatigued, commanded Johnny to bring his sweet charge to her straightway, for a kiss. Johnny having complied, and gone back to his stool, and again crushed himself, Master Adolphus Tetterby, who had by this time unwound his torso out of a prismatic comforter, apparently interminable, requested the same favour. Johnny having again complied, and again gone back to his stool, and again crushed himself, Mr. Tetterby, struck by a sudden thought, preferred the same claim on his own parental part. The satisfaction of this third desire completely exhausted the sacrifice, who had hardly breath enough left to get back to his stool, crushing himself again, and pant at his relations.

" Whatever you do, Johnny," said Mrs. Tetterby, shaking her head, " take care of her, or never look your mother in the face again."

" Nor your brother," said Adolphus.

" Nor your father, Johnny," added Mr. Tetterby.

Johnny, much affected by this conditional renunciation of him, looked down at Moloch's eyes to see that they were all right so far, and skilfully patted her back (which was uppermost), and rocked her with his foot.

" Are you wet, 'Dolphus, my boy? " said his father. " Come and take my chair, and dry yourself."

" No, father, thank'ee," said Adolphus, smoothing himself down with his hands. " I ain't very wet, I don't think. Does my face shine much, father? "

" Well, it *does* look waxy, my boy," returned Mr. Tetterby.

" It's the weather, father," said Adolphus, polishing his cheeks on the worn sleeve of his jacket. " What with rain, and sleet, and wind, and snow, and fog, my face gets quite brought out into a rash sometimes. And shines, it does— oh, don't it, though! "

Master Adolphus was also in the newspaper line of life, being employed, by a more thriving firm than his father and Co., to vend newspapers at a railway station, where his chubby little person, like a shabbily-disguised Cupid, and his shrill little voice (he was not much more than ten years old), were as well known as the hoarse panting of the locomotives, running in and out. His juvenility might have been at some loss for a harmless outlet, in this early application

to traffic, but for a fortunate discovery he made of a means
of entertaining himself, and of dividing the long day into
stages of interest, without neglecting business. This ingenious
invention, remarkable, like many great discoveries, for its
simplicity, consisted in varying the first vowel in the word
" paper," and substituting in its stead, at different periods of
the day, all the other vowels in grammatical succession. Thus,
before daylight in the winter-time, he went to and fro, in his
little oilskin cap and cape, and his big comforter, piercing the
heavy air with his cry of " Morning Pa-per! " which, about
an hour before noon, changed to " Morning Pep-per! "
which, at about two, changed to " Morn-ing Pip-per! "
which, in a couple of hours, changed to " Morn-ing Pop-
per! " and so declined with the sun into " Eve-ning Pup-per! '
to the great relief and comfort of this young gentleman's
spirits.

Mrs. Tetterby, his lady-mother, who had been sitting with
her bonnet and shawl thrown back, as aforesaid, thoughtfully
turning her wedding ring round and round upon her finger,
now rose, and divesting herself of her out-of-door attire,
began to lay the cloth for supper.

" Ah, dear me, dear me, dear me! " said Mrs. Tetterby.
" That's the way the world goes! "

" Which is the way the world goes, my dear? " asked Mr.
Tetterby, looking round.

" Oh, nothing," said Mrs. Tetterby.

Mr. Tetterby elevated his eyebrows, folded his newspaper
afresh, and carried his eyes up it, and down it, and across it,
but was wandering in his attention, and not reading it.

Mrs. Tetterby, at the same time, laid the cloth, but rather
as if she were punishing the table than preparing the family
supper—hitting it unnecessarily hard with the knives and
forks, slapping it with the plates, dinting it with the salt-
cellar, and coming heavily down upon it with the loaf.

" Ah, dear me, dear me, dear me! " said Mrs. Tetterby.
" That's the way the world goes! "

" My duck," returned her husband, looking round again,
" you said that before. Which is the way the world goes? "

" Oh, nothing! " said Mrs. Tetterby.

" Sophia! " remonstrated her husband, " you said *that*
before, too."

" Well, I'll say it again if you like," returned Mrs. Tetterby.

" Oh, nothing—there! And again if you like, Oh, nothing —there! And again if you like, Oh, nothing—now then! "

Mr. Tetterby brought his eye to bear upon the partner of his bosom, and said, in mild astonishment—

" My little woman, what has put you out? "

" I'm sure *I* don't know," she retorted. " Don't ask me. Who said I was put out at all? *I* never did."

Mr. Tetterby gave up the perusal of his newspaper as a bad job, and, taking a slow walk across the room, with his hands behind him and his shoulders raised—his gait according perfectly with the resignation of his manner—addressed himself to his two eldest offspring.

" Your supper will be ready in a minute, 'Dolphus," said Mr. Tetterby. " Your mother has been out in the wet, to the cook's shop, to buy it. It was very good of your mother so to do. *You* shall get some supper, too, very soon, Johnny. Your mother's pleased with you, my man, for being so attentive to your precious sister."

Mrs. Tetterby, without any remark, but with a decided subsidence of her animosity towards the table, finished her preparations, and took from her ample basket a substantial slab of hot pease-pudding wrapped in paper, and a basin covered with a saucer, which, on being uncovered, sent forth an odour so agreeable, that the three pairs of eyes in the two beds opened wide and fixed themselves upon the banquet. Mr. Tetterby, without regarding this tacit invitation to be seated, stood repeating slowly, " Yes, yes, your supper will be ready in a minute, 'Dolphus. Your mother went out in the wet, to the cook's shop, to buy it. It was very good of your mother so to do "—until Mrs. Tetterby, who had been exhibiting sundry tokens of contrition behind him, caught him round the neck, and wept.

" Oh, 'Dolphus! " said Mrs. Tetterby, " how could I go and behave so? "

This reconciliation affected Adolphus the younger and Johnny to that degree, that they both, as with one accord, raised a dismal cry, which had the effect of immediately shutting up the round eyes in the beds, and utterly routing the two remaining little Tetterbys, just then stealing in from the adjoining closet to see what was going on in the eating way.

" I am sure, 'Dolphus," sobbed Mrs. Tetterby, " coming home, I had no more idea than a child unborn——"

Mr. Tetterby seemed to dislike this figure of speech, and observed, " Say than the baby, my dear."

" Had no more idea than the baby," said Mrs. Tetterby.— " Johnny, don't look at me, but look at her, or she'll fall out of your lap and be killed, and then you'll die in agonies of a broken heart, and serve you right.—No more idea I hadn't than that darling, of being cross when I came home; but somehow, 'Dolphus——" Mrs. Tetterby paused, and again turned her wedding ring round and round upon her finger.

" I see! " said Mr. Tetterby. " I understand! My little woman was put out. Hard times, and hard weather, and hard work, make it trying now and then. I see, bless your soul! No wonder! 'Dolf, my man," continued Mr. Tetterby, exploring the basin with a fork, " here's your mother been and bought, at the cook's shop, besides pease-pudding, a whole knuckle of a lovely roast leg of pork, with lots of crackling left upon it, and with seasoning gravy and mustard quite unlimited. Hand in your plate, my boy, and begin while it's simmering."

Master Adolphus, needing no second summons, received his portion with eyes rendered moist by appetite, and withdrawing to his particular stool, fell upon his supper tooth and nail. Johnny was not forgotten, but received his rations on bread, lest he should, in a flush of gravy, trickle any on the baby. He was required, for similar reasons, to keep his pudding, when not on active service, in his pocket.

There might have been more pork on the knuckle-bone —which knuckle-bone the carver at the cook's shop had assuredly not forgotten in carving for previous customers— but there was no stint of seasoning, and that is an accessory dreamily suggesting pork, and pleasantly cheating the sense of taste. The pease-pudding, too, the gravy and mustard, like the Eastern rose in respect of the nightingale, if they were not absolutely pork, had lived near it; so, upon the whole, there was the flavour of a middle-sized pig. It was irresistible to the Tetterbys in bed, who, though professing to slumber peacefully, crawled out when unseen by their parents, and silently appealed to their brothers for any gastronomic token of fraternal affection. They, not hard of heart, presenting scraps in return, it resulted that a party of light skirmishers in night-gowns were careering about the parlour all through supper, which harassed Mr. Tetterby exceedingly, and once or twice imposed upon him the necessity of a charge, before which these guerilla troops retired in all directions and in great confusion.

Mrs. Tetterby did not enjoy her supper. There seemed to be something on Mrs. Tetterby's mind. At one time she laughed without reason, and at another time she cried without reason; and at last she laughed and cried together in a manner so very unreasonable that her husband was confounded.

" My little woman," said Mr. Tetterby, " if the world goes that way, it appears to go the wrong way, and to choke you."

" Give me a drop of water," said Mrs. Tetterby, struggling with herself, " and don't speak to me for the present, or take any notice of me. Don't do it! "

Mr. Tetterby, having administered the water, turned suddenly on the unlucky Johnny (who was full of sympathy), and demanded why he was wallowing there, in gluttony and idleness, instead of coming forward with the baby, that the sight of her might revive his mother. Johnny immediately approached, borne down by its weight; but Mrs. Tetterby holding out her hand to signify that she was not in a condition to bear that trying appeal to her feelings, he was interdicted from advancing another inch, on pain of perpetual hatred from all his dearest connections, and accordingly retired to his stool again, and crushed himself as before.

After a pause, Mrs. Tetterby said she was better now, and began to laugh.

" My little woman," said her husband dubiously, " are you quite sure you're better? Or are you, Sophia, about to break out in a fresh direction? "

" No, 'Dolphus, no," replied his wife. " I'm quite myself." With that, settling her hair and pressing the palms of her hands upon her eyes, she laughed again.

" What a wicked fool I was, to think so for a moment! " said Mrs. Tetterby. " Come nearer, 'Dolphus, and let me ease my mind, and tell you what I mean. Let me tell you all about it."

Mr. Tetterby bringing his chair closer, Mrs. Tetterby laughed again, gave him a hug, and wiped her eyes.

" You know, 'Dolphus, my dear," said Mrs. Tetterby, " that when I was single, I might have given myself away in several directions. At one time, four after me at once; two of them were sons of Mars."

" We're all sons of Ma's, my dear," said Mr. Tetterby,
" jointly with Pa's."

" I don't mean that," replied his wife; " I mean soldiers—
sergeants."

" Oh! " said Mr. Tetterby.

" Well, 'Dolphus, I'm sure I never think of such things
now, to regret them; and I'm sure I've got as good a husband,
and would do as much to prove that I was fond of him,
as——"

" As any little woman in the world," said Mr. Tetterby.
" Very good. *Very* good."

If Mr. Tetterby had been ten feet high, he could not have
expressed a gentler consideration for Mrs. Tetterby's fairy-
like stature; and if Mrs. Tetterby had been two feet high
she could not have felt it more appropriately her due.

" But you see, 'Dolphus," said Mrs. Tetterby, " this being
Christmas-time, when all people who can, make holiday, and
when all people who have got money like to spend some,
I did, somehow, get a little out of sorts when I was in the
streets just now. There were so many things to be sold—
such delicious things to eat, such fine things to look at, such
delightful things to have—and there was so much calculating
and calculating necessary, before I durst lay out a sixpence
for the commonest thing; and the basket was so large, and
wanted so much in it; and my stock of money was so small,
and would go such a little way;—you hate me, don't you,
'Dolphus? "

" Not quite," said Mr. Tetterby, " as yet."

" Well, I'll tell you the whole truth," pursued his wife
penitently, " and then perhaps you will. I felt all this so
much, when I was trudging about in the cold, and when I saw
a lot of other calculating faces and large baskets trudging
about too, that I began to think whether I mightn't have
done better, and been happier, if—I—hadn't——" The
wedding ring went round again, and Mrs. Tetterby shook her
downcast head as she turned it.

" I see," said her husband quietly: " if you hadn't married
at all, or if you had married somebody else? "

" Yes," sobbed Mrs. Tetterby; " that's really what I
thought. Do you hate me now, 'Dolphus? "

" Why, no," said Mr. Tetterby; " I don't find that I do,
as yet."

Mrs. Tetterby gave him a thankful kiss, and went on.

" I begin to hope you won't now, 'Dolphus, though I am afraid I haven't told you the worst. I can't think what came over me. I don't know whether I was ill, or mad, or what I was, but I couldn't call up anything that seemed to bind us to each other, or to reconcile me to my fortune. All the pleasures and enjoyments we had ever had—*they* seemed so poor and insignificant, I hated them. I could have trodden on them. And I could think of nothing else, except our being poor, and the number of mouths there were at home."

" Well, well, my dear," said Mr. Tetterby, shaking her hand encouragingly, " that's truth, after all. We *are* poor, and there *are* a number of mouths at home here."

" Ah! but, Dolf, Dolf! " cried his wife, laying her hands upon his neck, " my good, kind, patient fellow, when I had been at home a very little while—how different! Oh, Dolf dear, how different it was! I felt as if there was a rush of recollection on me, all at once, that softened my hard heart, and filled it up till it was bursting. All our struggles for a livelihood, all our cares and wants since we have been married, all the times of sickness, all the hours of watching, we have ever had by one another, or by the children, seemed to speak to me, and say that they had made us one, and that I never might have been, or could have been, or would have been, any other than the wife and mother I am. Then the cheap enjoyments that I could have trodden on so cruelly, got to be so precious to me—oh, so priceless and dear!—that I couldn't bear to think how much I had wronged them; and I said, and say again a hundred times, how could I ever behave so, 'Dolphus? how could I ever have the heart to do it? "

The good woman, quite carried away by her honest tenderness and remorse, was weeping with all her heart, when she started up with a scream, and ran behind her husband. Her cry was so terrified that the children started from their sleep and from their beds, and clung about her. Nor did her gaze belie her voice, as she pointed to a pale man in a black cloak who had come into the room.

" Look at that man! Look there! What does he want? "

" My dear," returned her husband, " I'll ask him if you'll let me go. What's the matter? How you shake! "

"I saw him in the street, when I was out just now. He looked at me, and stood near me. I am afraid of him."

"Afraid of him! Why?"

"I don't know why—I—— Stop, husband!" for he was going towards the stranger.

She had one hand pressed upon her forehead, and one upon her breast; and there was a peculiar fluttering all over her, and a hurried unsteady motion of her eyes, as if she had lost something.

"Are you ill, my dear?"

"What is it that is going from me again?" she muttered, in a low voice. "What *is* this that is going away?"

Then she abruptly answered, "Ill? No, I am quite well," and stood looking vacantly at the floor.

Her husband, who had not been altogether free from the infection of her fear at first, and whom the present strangeness of her manner did not tend to reassure, addressed himself to the pale visitor in the black cloak, who stood still, and whose eyes were bent upon the ground.

"What may be your pleasure, sir," he asked, "with us?"

"I fear that my coming in unperceived," returned the visitor, "has alarmed you; but you were talking, and did not hear me."

"My little woman says—perhaps you heard her say it," returned Mr. Tetterby—"that it's not the first time you have alarmed her to-night."

"I am sorry for it. I remember to have observed her in the street. I had no intention of frightening her."

As he raised his eyes in speaking, she raised hers. It was extraordinary to see what dread she had of him, and with what dread he observed it—and yet how narrowly and closely.

"My name," he said, "is Redlaw. I come from the old college hard by. A young gentleman who is a student there lodges in your house, does he not?"

"Mr. Denham?" said Tetterby.

"Yes."

It was a natural action, and so slight as to be hardly noticeable, but the little man, before speaking again, passed his hand across his forehead, and looked quickly round the room, as though he were sensible of some change in its atmosphere. The Chemist, instantly transferring to him the look of dread he had directed towards the wife, stepped back, and his face turned paler.

" The gentleman's room," said Tetterby, " is upstairs, sir. There's a more convenient private entrance; but as you have come in here, it will save your going out into the cold, if you'll take this little staircase," showing one communicating directly with the parlour, " and go up to him that way, if you wish to see him."

" Yes, I wish to see him," said the Chemist. " Can you spare a light? "

The watchfulness of his haggard look, and the inexplicable distrust that darkened it, seemed to trouble Mr. Tetterby. He paused, and looking fixedly at him in return, stood for a minute or so, like a man stupefied, or fascinated.

At length he said, " I'll light you, sir, if you'll follow me."

" No," replied the Chemist, " I don't wish to be attended, or announced to him. He does not expect me. I would rather go alone. Please to give me the light, if you can spare it, and I'll find the way."

In the quickness of his expression of this desire, and in taking the candle from the newsman, he touched him on the breast. Withdrawing his hand hastily, almost as though he had wounded him by accident (for he did not know in what part of himself his new power resided, or how it was communicated, or how the manner of its reception varied), he turned and ascended the stair.

But when he reached the top, he stopped and looked down. The wife was standing in the same place, twisting her ring round and round upon her finger. The husband, with his head bent forward on his breast, was musing heavily and sullenly. The children, still clustering about the mother, gazed timidly after the visitor, and nestled together when they saw him looking down.

" Come! " said the father roughly. " There's enough of this. Get to bed here! "

" The place is inconvenient and small enough," the mother added, " without you. Get to bed! "

The whole brood, scared and sad, crept away—little Johnny and the baby lagging last. The mother, glancing contemptuously round the sordid room, and tossing from her the fragments of their meal, stopped on the threshold of her task of clearing the table, and sat down pondering idly and dejectedly. The father betook himself to the chimney-corner, and impatiently raking the small fire together, bent over it as if he would monopolise it all. They did not interchange a word.

The Chemist, paler than before, stole upward like a thief, looking back upon the change below, and dreading equally to go on or return.

" What have I done? " he said confusedly. " What am I going to do? "

" To be the benefactor of mankind," he thought he heard a voice reply.

He looked round, but there was nothing there; and a passage now shutting out the little parlour from his view, he went on, directing his eyes before him at the way he went.

" It is only since last night," he muttered gloomily, " that I have remained shut up, and yet all things are strange to me. I am strange to myself. I am here, as in a dream. What interest have I in this place, or in any place that I can bring to my remembrance? My mind has gone blind! "

There was a door before him, and he knocked at it. Being invited, by a voice within, to enter, he complied.

" Is that my kind nurse? " said the voice. " But I need not ask her. There is no one else to come here."

It spoke cheerfully, though in a languid tone, and attracted his attention to a young man lying on a couch, drawn before the chimney-piece, with the back towards the door. A meagre, scanty stove, pinched and hollowed like a sick man's cheeks, and bricked into the centre of a hearth that it could scarcely warm, contained the fire, to which his face was turned. Being so near the windy house-top, it wasted quickly, and with a busy sound, and the burning ashes dropped down fast.

" They chink when they shoot out here," said the student, smiling, " so, according to the gossips, they are not coffins, but purses. I shall be well and rich yet, some day if it please God, and shall live perhaps to love a daughter, Milly, in remembrance of the kindest nature and the gentlest heart in the world."

He put up his hand as if expecting her to take it, but, being weakened, he lay still, with his face resting on his other hand, and did not turn round.

The Chemist glanced about the room—at the student's books and papers piled upon a table in a corner, where they, and his extinguished reading-lamp, now prohibited and put away, told of the attentive hours that had gone before this illness, and perhaps caused it; at such signs of his old health and freedom, as the out-of-door attire that hung idle on the wall; at those remembrances of other and less solitary scenes, the little miniatures upon the chimney-piece, and the drawing of home; at that token of his emulation, perhaps, in some sort, of his personal attachment too, the framed engraving of himself, the looker-on. The time had been, only yesterday, when not one of these objects, in its remotest association of interest with the living figure before him, would have been lost on Redlaw. Now, they were but objects; or if any gleam of such connection shot upon him, it perplexed, and not enlightened him, as he stood looking round with a dull wonder.

The student, recalling the thin hand which had remained so long untouched, raised himself on the couch, and turned his head.

"Mr. Redlaw!" he exclaimed, and started up.

Redlaw put out his arm.

"Don't come nearer to me. I will sit here. Remain where you are."

He sat down on a chair near the door, and having glanced at the young man standing leaning with his hand upon the couch, spoke with his eyes averted towards the ground.

"I heard, by an accident—by what accident is no matter —that one of my class was ill and solitary. I received no other description of him than that he lived in this street. Beginning my inquiries at the first house in it, I have found him."

"I have been ill, sir," returned the student, not merely with a modest hesitation, but with a kind of awe of him; "but am greatly better. An attack of fever—of the brain, I believe—has weakened me; but I am much better. I cannot say I have been solitary in my illness, or I should forget the ministering hand that has been near me."

"You are speaking of the keeper's wife," said Redlaw.

"Yes." The student bent his head, as if he rendered her some silent homage.

The Chemist, in whom there was a cold, monotonous

apathy, which rendered him more like a marble image on the
tomb of the man who had started from his dinner yesterday
at the first mention of this student's case, than the breathing
man himself, glanced again at the student leaning with his
hand upon the couch, and looked upon the ground, and in
the air, as if for light for his blinded mind.

"I remembered your name," he said, "when it was mentioned to me downstairs just now, and I recollect your face.
We have held but very little personal communication together?"

"Very little."

"You have retired and withdrawn from me more than any
of the rest, I think?"

The student signified assent.

"And why?" said the Chemist, not with the least expression of interest, but with a moody, wayward kind of curiosity.
"Why? How comes it that you have sought to keep especially from me the knowledge of your remaining here, at this
season, when all the rest have dispersed, and of your being ill?
I want to know why this is?"

The young man, who had heard him with increasing agitation, raised his downcast eyes to his face, and clasping his
hands together, cried with sudden earnestness, and with
trembling lips:

"Mr. Redlaw, you have discovered me! You know my
secret!"

"Secret?" said the Chemist harshly. "I know?"

"Yes! Your manner, so different from the interest and
sympathy which endear you to so many hearts, your altered
voice, the constraint there is in everything you say, and in
your looks," replied the student, "warn me that you know
me. That you would conceal it, even now, is but a proof to
me (God knows I need none!) of your natural kindness, and
of the bar there is between us."

A vacant and contemptuous laugh was all his answer.

"But, Mr. Redlaw," said the student, "as a just man, and
a good man, think how innocent I am, except in name and
descent, of participation in any wrong inflicted on you, or in
any sorrow you have borne."

"Sorrow!" said Redlaw, laughing. "Wrong! What are
those to me?"

"For Heaven's sake," entreated the shrinking student,

" do not let the mere interchange of a few words with me change you like this, sir! Let me pass again from your knowledge and notice. Let me occupy my old reserved and distant place among those whom you instruct. Know me only by the name I have assumed, and not by that of Langford——"

" Langford! " exclaimed the other.

He clasped his head with both his hands, and for a moment turned upon the young man his own intelligent and thoughtful face. But the light passed from it, like the sunbeam of an instant, and it clouded as before.

" The name my mother bears, sir," faltered the young man—" the name she took, when she might, perhaps, have taken one more honoured. Mr. Redlaw "—hesitating—" I believe I know that history. Where my information halts, my guesses at what is wanting may supply something not remote from the truth. I am the child of a marriage that has not proved itself a well-assorted or a happy one. From infancy I have heard you spoken of with honour and respect —with something that was almost reverence. I have heard of such devotion, of such fortitude and tenderness, of such rising up against the obstacles which press men down, that my fancy, since I learnt my little lesson from my mother, has shed a lustre on your name. At last, a poor student myself, from whom could I learn but you? "

Redlaw, unmoved, unchanged, and looking at him with a staring frown, answered by no word or sign.

" I cannot say," pursued the other, " I should try in vain to say, how much it has impressed me, and affected me, to find the gracious traces of the past in that certain power of winning gratitude and confidence which is associated among us students (among the humblest of us most) with Mr. Redlaw's generous name. Our ages and positions are so different, sir, and I am so accustomed to regard you from a distance, that I wonder at my own presumption when I touch, however lightly, on that theme. But to one who—I may say, who felt no common interest in my mother once, it may be something to hear, now that is all past, with what indescribable feelings of affection I have, in my obscurity, regarded him; with what pain and reluctance I have kept aloof from his encouragement, when a word of it would have made me rich; yet how I have felt it fit that I should hold my course, content to

know him, and to be unknown. Mr. Redlaw," said the
student faintly, " what I would have said, I have said ill, for
my strength is strange to me as yet; but for anything unworthy in this fraud of mine, forgive me, and for all the
rest forget me."

The staring frown remained on Redlaw's face, and yielded
to no other expression until the student, with these words,
advanced towards him, as if to touch his hand, when he drew
back and cried to him:

" Don't come nearer to me! "

The young man stopped, shocked by the eagerness of his
recoil and by the sternness of his repulsion, and he passed
his hand thoughtfully across his forehead.

" The past is past," said the Chemist. " It dies like the
brutes. Who talks to me of its traces in my life? He raves
or lies! What have I to do with your distempered dreams?
If you want money, here it is. I came to offer it, and that
is all I came for. There can be nothing else that brings me
here," he muttered, holding his head again with both his
hands. " There *can* be nothing else, and yet——"

He had tossed his purse upon the table. As he fell into
this dim cogitation with himself, the student took it up, and
held it out to him.

" Take it back, sir," he said proudly, though not angrily.
" I wish you could take from me, with it, the remembrance
of your words and offer."

" You do? " he retorted, with a wild light in his eyes.
" You do? "

" I do."

The Chemist went close to him, for the first time, and
took the purse, and turned him by the arm, and looked him
in the face.

" There is sorrow and trouble in sickness, is there not? "
he demanded with a laugh.

The wondering student answered, " Yes."

" In its unrest, in its anxiety, in its suspense, in all its train
of physical and mental miseries? " said the Chemist, with a
wild, unearthly exultation. " All best forgotten, are they
not? "

The student did not answer, but again passed his hand
confusedly across his forehead. Redlaw still held him by the
sleeve, when Milly's voice was heard outside.

"I can see very well now," she said; "thank you, Dolf. Don't cry, dear. Father and mother will be comfortable again to-morrow, and home will be comfortable too. A gentleman with him, is there?"

Redlaw released his hold as he listened.

"I have feared, from the first moment," he murmured to himself, "to meet her. There is a steady quality of goodness in her that I dread to influence. I may be the murderer of what is tenderest and best within her bosom."

She was knocking at the door.

"Shall I dismiss it as an idle foreboding, or still avoid her?" he muttered, looking uneasily around.

She was knocking at the door again.

"Of all the visitors who could come here," he said, in a hoarse, alarmed voice, turning to his companion, "this is the one I should desire most to avoid. Hide me!"

The student opened a frail door in the wall, communicating, where the garret roof began to slope towards the floor, with a small inner room. Redlaw passed in hastily, and shut it after him.

The student then resumed his place upon the couch, and called to her to enter.

"Dear Mr. Edmund," said Milly, looking round, "they told me there was a gentleman here."

"There is no one here but I."

"There has been someone?"

"Yes, yes, there has been someone."

She put her little basket on the table, and went up to the back of the couch, as if to take the extended hand; but it was not there. A little surprised, in her quiet way, she leaned over to look at his face, and gently touched him on the brow.

"Are you quite as well to-night? Your head is not so cool as in the afternoon."

"Tut!" said the student petulantly, "very little ails me."

A little more surprise, but no reproach, was expressed in her face, as she withdrew to the other side of the table and took a small packet of needlework from her basket. But she laid it down again, on second thoughts, and going noiselessly about the room, set everything exactly in its place, and in the neatest order, even to the cushions on the couch, which she touched with so light a hand that he hardly seemed to know it, as he lay looking at the fire. When all this was done, and she had swept the hearth, she sat down, in her modest little bonnet, to her work, and was quietly busy on it directly.

" It's the new muslin curtain for the window, Mr. Edmund," said Milly, stitching away as she talked. " It will look very clean and nice, though it costs very little, and will save your eyes, too, from the light. My William says the room should not be too light just now, when you are recovering so well, or the glare might make you giddy."

He said nothing; but there was something so fretful and impatient in his change of position, that her quick fingers stopped, and she looked at him anxiously.

" The pillows are not comfortable," she said, laying down her work and rising. " I will soon put them right."

" They are very well," he answered. " Leave them alone, pray. You make so much of everything."

He raised his head to say this, and looked at her so thanklessly that, after he had thrown himself down again, she stood timidly pausing. However, she resumed her seat, and her needle, without having directed even a murmuring look towards him, and was soon as busy as before.

" I have been thinking, Mr. Edmund, that *you* have been often thinking of late, when I have been sitting by, how true the saying is that adversity is a good teacher. Health will be more precious to you, after this illness, than it has ever been. And years hence, when this time of year comes round, and you remember the days when you lay here sick, alone, that the knowledge of your illness might not afflict those who are dearest to you, your home will be doubly dear and doubly blest. Now, isn't that a good, true thing? "

She was too intent upon her work, and too earnest in what she said, and too composed and quiet altogether, to be on the watch for any look he might direct towards her in reply; so the shaft of his ungrateful glance fell harmless, and did not wound her.

" Ah! " said Milly, with her pretty head inclining thoughtfully on one side, as she looked down, following her busy fingers with her eyes. " Even on me—and I am very different from you, Mr. Edmund, for I have no learning, and don't know how to think properly—this view of such things has made a great impression, since you have been lying ill.

When I have seen you so touched by the kindness and attention of the poor people downstairs, I have felt that you thought even that experience some repayment for the loss of health, and I have read in your face, as plain as if it was a book, that but for some trouble and sorrow we should never know half the good there is about us."

His getting up from the couch interrupted her, or she was going on to say more.

"We needn't magnify the merit, Mrs. William," he rejoined slightingly. "The people downstairs will be paid in good time, I dare say, for any little extra service they may have rendered me; and perhaps they anticipate no less. I am much obliged to you, too."

Her fingers stopped, and she looked at him.

"I can't be made to feel the more obliged by you exaggerating the case," he said. "I am sensible that you have been interested in me, and I say I am much obliged to you. What more would you have?"

Her work fell on her lap, as she still looked at him walking to and fro with an intolerant air, and stopping now and then.

"I say again, I am much obliged to you. Why weaken my sense of what is your due in obligation, by preferring enormous claims upon me? Trouble, sorrow, affliction, adversity! One might suppose I had been dying a score of deaths here!"

"Do you believe, Mr. Edmund," she asked, rising and going nearer to him, "that I spoke of the poor people of the house with any reference to myself? To me?" laying her hand upon her bosom with a simple and innocent smile of astonishment.

"Oh! I think nothing about it, my good creature," he returned. "I have had an indisposition, which your solicitude —observe! I say solicitude—makes a great deal more of than it merits; and it's over, and we can't perpetuate it."

He coldly took a book and sat down at the table.

She watched him for a little while, until her smile was quite gone, and then, returning to where her basket was, said gently:

"Mr. Edmund, would you rather be alone?"

"There is no reason why I should detain you here," he replied.

"Except——" said Milly, hesitating, and showing her work. "Oh! the curtain," he answered, with a supercilious laugh. "That's not worth staying for."

She made up the little packet again, and put it in her basket. Then, standing before him with such an air of patient entreaty that he could not choose but look at her, she said:

"If you should want me, I will come back willingly. When you did want me, I was quite happy to come; there was no merit in it. I think you must be afraid that, now you are getting well, I may be troublesome to you; but I should not have been, indeed. I should have come no longer than your weakness and confinement lasted. You owe me nothing; but it is right that you should deal as justly by me as if I was a lady—even the very lady that you love; and if you suspect me of meanly making much of the little I have tried to do to comfort your sick-room, you do yourself more wrong than ever you can do me. That is why I am sorry; that is why I am very sorry."

If she had been as passionate as she was quiet, as indignant as she was calm, as angry in her look as she was gentle, as loud of tone as she was low and clear, she might have left no sense of her departure in the room, compared with that which fell upon the lonely student when she went away.

He was gazing drearily upon the place where she had been, when Redlaw came out of his concealment, and came to the door.

"When sickness lays its hand on you again," he said, looking fiercely back at him—"may it be soon!—die here! rot here."

"What have you done?" returned the other, catching at his cloak. "What change have you wrought in me? What curse have you brought upon me? Give me back myself!"

"Give me back *myself*!" exclaimed Redlaw, like a madman. "I am infected! I am infectious! I am charged with poison for my own mind, and the minds of all mankind. Where I felt interest, compassion, sympathy, I am turning into stone. Selfishness and ingratitude spring up in my blighting footsteps. I am only so much less base than the wretches whom I make so, that in the moment of their transformation I can hate them."

As he spoke—the young man still holding to his cloak— he cast him off, and struck him; then wildly hurried out into the night air, where the wind was blowing, the snow falling, the cloud-drift sweeping on, the moon dimly shining, and where, blowing in the wind, falling with the snow, drifting with the clouds, shining in the moonlight, and heavily looming in the darkness, were the Phantom's words, " The gift that I have given, you shall give again, go where you will! "

Whither he went he neither knew nor cared, so that he avoided company. The change he felt within him made the busy streets a desert, and himself a desert, and the multitude around him, in their manifold endurances and ways of life, a mighty waste of sand, which the winds tossed into unintelligible heaps, and made a ruinous confusion of. Those traces in his breast which the Phantom had told him would " die out soon," were not, as yet, so far upon their way to death, but that he understood enough of what he was, and what he made of others, to desire to be alone.

This put it in his mind—he suddenly bethought himself, as he was going along, of the boy who had rushed into his room. And then he recollected that, of those with whom he had communicated since the Phantom's disappearance, that boy alone had shown no sign of being changed.

Monstrous and odious as the wild thing was to him, he determined to seek it out, and prove if this were really so; and also to seek it with another intention, which came into his thoughts at the same time.

So, resolving with some difficulty where he was, he directed his steps back to the old college, and to that part of it where the general porch was, and where, alone, the pavement was worn by the tread of the students' feet.

The keeper's house stood just within the iron gates, forming a part of the chief quadrangle. There was a little cloister outside, and from that sheltered place he knew he could look in at the window of their ordinary room, and see who was within. The iron gates were shut; but his hand was familiar with the fastening, and drawing it back by thrusting in his wrist between the bars, he passed through softly, shut it again, and crept up to the window, crumbling the thin crust of snow with his feet.

The fire to which he had directed the boy last night, shining brightly through the glass, made an illuminated place upon the ground. Instinctively avoiding this, and going round it, he looked in at the window. At first, he thought that there was no one there, and that the blaze was reddening only the old beams in the ceiling and the dark walls; but peering in more narrowly, he saw the object of his search coiled asleep before it on the floor. He passed quickly to the door, opened it, and went in.

The creature lay in such a fiery heat that, as the Chemist stooped to rouse him, it scorched his head. So soon as he was touched, the boy, not half awake, clutching his rags together with the instinct of flight upon him, half rolled and half ran into a distant corner of the room, where, heaped upon the ground, he struck his foot out to defend himself.

" Get up! " said the Chemist. " You have not forgotten me? "

" You let me alone! " returned the boy. " This is the woman's house—not yours."

The Chemist's steady eye controlled him somewhat, or inspired him with enough submission to be raised upon his feet, and looked at.

" Who washed them and put those bandages where they were bruised and cracked? " asked the Chemist, pointing to their altered state.

" The woman did."

" And is it she who has made you cleaner in the face, too? "

" Yes. The woman."

Redlaw asked these questions to attract his eyes towards himself, and with the same intent now held him by the chin, and threw his wild hair back, though he loathed to touch him. The boy watched his eyes keenly, as if he thought it needful to his own defence, not knowing what he might do next; and Redlaw could see well that no change came over him.

" Where are they? " he inquired.

" The woman's out."

" I know she is. Where is the old man with the white hair, and his son? "

" The woman's husband, d'ye mean? " inquired the boy.

" Ay. Where are those two? "

" Out. Something's the matter, somewhere. They were fetched out in a hurry, and told me to stop here."

" Come with me," said the Chemist, " and I'll give you money."

" Come where? and how much will you give? "

" I'll give you more shillings than you ever saw, and bring you back soon. Do you know your way to where you came from? "

" You let me go," returned the boy, suddenly twisting out of his grasp. " I'm not a-going to take you there. Let me be, or I'll heave some fire at you! "

He was down before it, and ready, with his savage little hand, to pluck the burning coals out.

What the Chemist had felt, in observing the effect of his charmed influence stealing over those with whom he came in contact, was not nearly equal to the cold vague terror with which he saw the baby-monster put it at defiance. It chilled his blood to look on the immovable, impenetrable thing, in the likeness of a child, with its sharp, malignant face turned up to his, and its almost infant hand ready at the bars.

" Listen, boy! " he said. " You shall take me where you please, so that you take me where the people are very miserable or very wicked. I want to do them good, and not to harm them. You shall have money, as I have told you, and I will bring you back. Get up! Come quickly! " He made a hasty step towards the door, afraid of her returning.

" Will you let me walk by myself, and never hold me, nor yet touch me? " said the boy, slowly withdrawing the hand with which he threatened, and beginning to get up.

" I will! "

" And let me go before, behind, or anyways I like? "

" I will! "

" Give me some money first then, and I'll go."

The Chemist laid a few shillings, one by one, in his extended hand. To count them was beyond the boy's knowledge, but he said " one," every time, and avariciously looked at each as it was given, and at the donor. He had nowhere to put them, out of his hand, but in his mouth, and he put them there. Redlaw then wrote with his pencil, on a leaf of his pocket-book, that the boy was with him; and laying it on the table, signed to him to follow. Keeping his rags together, as usual, the boy complied, and went out with his bare head and his naked feet into the winter night.

Preferring not to depart by the iron gate, by which he had entered, where they were in danger of meeting her whom he so anxiously avoided, the Chemist led the way, through some of those passages among which the boy had lost himself, and by that portion of the building where he lived, to a small door of which he had the key. When they got into the street, he stopped to ask his guide—who instantly retreated from him—if he knew where they were.

The savage thing looked here and there, and at length, nodding his head, pointed in the direction he designed to take. Redlaw going on at once, he followed, something less suspiciously—shifting his money from his mouth into his hand, and back again into his mouth, and stealthily rubbing it bright upon his shreds of dress, as he went along.

Three times, in their progress, they were side by side. Three times they stopped, being side by side. Three times the Chemist glanced down at his face, and shuddered as it forced upon him one reflection.

The first occasion was when they were crossing an old churchyard, and Redlaw stopped among the graves, utterly at a loss how to connect them with any tender, softening, or consolatory thought.

The second was when the breaking forth of the moon induced him to look up at the heavens, where he saw her in her glory, surrounded by a host of stars he still knew by the names and histories which human science has appended to them; but where he saw nothing else he had been wont to see, felt nothing he had been wont to feel, in looking up there, on a bright night.

The third was when he stopped to listen to a plaintive strain of music; but could only hear a tune, made manifest to him by the dry mechanism of the instruments and his own ears, with no address to any mystery within him without a whisper in it of the past, or of the future, powerless upon him as the sound of last year's running water, or the rushing of last year's wind.

At each of these three times, he saw with horror that, in spite of the vast intellectual distance between them, and their being unlike each other in all physical respects, the expression on the boy's face was the expression on his own.

They journeyed on for some time—now through such crowded places, that he often looked over his shoulder thinking he had lost his guide, but generally finding him within his shadow on his other side; now by ways so quiet, that he could have counted his short, quick, naked footsteps coming on behind—until they arrived at a ruinous collection of houses, and the boy touched him and stopped.

"In there!" he said, pointing out one house where there were scattered lights in the windows, and a dim lantern in the doorway, with "Lodgings for Travellers" painted on it.

Redlaw looked about him—from the houses to the waste piece of ground on which the houses stood, or rather did not altogether tumble down, unfenced, undrained, unlighted, and bordered by a sluggish ditch; from that to the sloping line of arches, part of some neighbouring viaduct or bridge with which it was surrounded, and which lessened gradually, towards them, until the last but one was a mere kennel for a dog, the last a plundered little heap of bricks; from that to the child, close to him, cowering and trembling with the cold and limping on one little foot while he coiled the other round his leg to warm it, yet staring at all these things with that frightful likeness of expression so apparent in his face that Redlaw started from him.

"In there!" said the boy, pointing out the house again. "I'll wait."

"Will they let me in?" asked Redlaw.

"Say you're a doctor," he answered, with a nod. "There's plenty ill here."

Looking back on his way to the house-door, Redlaw saw him trail himself upon the dust and crawl within the shelter of the smallest arch, as if he were a rat. He had no pity for the thing, but he was afraid of it, and when it looked out of its den at him he hurried to the house as a retreat.

"Sorrow, wrong, and trouble," said the Chemist, with a painful effort at some more distinct remembrance, "at least haunt this place darkly. He can do no harm who brings forgetfulness of such things here!"

With these words he pushed the yielding door, and went in.

There was a woman sitting on the stairs, either asleep or forlorn, whose head was bent down on her hands and knees. As it was not easy to pass without treading on her, and as she was perfectly regardless of his near approach, he stopped and touched her on the shoulder. Looking up, she showed him quite a young face, but one whose bloom and promise

were all swept away, as if the haggard winter should unnaturally kill the spring.

With little or no show of concern on his account, she moved
nearer to the wall to leave him a wider passage.

" What are you? " said Redlaw pausing, with his hand
upon the broken stair-rail.

" What do you think I am? " she answered, showing him
her face again.

He looked upon the ruined Temple of God, so lately
made, so soon disfigured; and something, which was not compassion—for the springs in which a true compassion for such
miseries has its rise were dried up in his breast—but which
was nearer to it, for the moment, than any feeling that had
lately struggled into the darkening, but not yet wholly
darkened, night of his mind, mingled a touch of softness
with his next words.

" I am come here to give relief, if I can," he said. " Are
you thinking of any wrong? "

She frowned at him, and then laughed; and then her laugh
prolonged itself into a shivering sigh, as she dropped her head
again, and hid her fingers in her hair.

" Are you thinking of a wrong? " he asked once more.

" I am thinking of my life," she said, with a momentary
look at him.

He had a perception that she was one of many, and that he
saw the type of thousands when he saw her drooping at his
feet.

" What are your parents? " he demanded.

" I had a good home once. My father was a gardener,
far away, in the country."

" Is he dead? "

" He's dead to me. All such things are dead to me. You
a gentleman, and not know that! " She raised her eyes again,
and laughed at him.

" Girl! " said Redlaw sternly, " before this death of all
such things was brought about, was there no wrong done to
you? In spite of all that you can do, does no remembrance
of wrong cleave to you? Are there not times upon times
when it is misery to you? "

So little of what was womanly was left in her appearance
that now, when she burst into tears, he stood amazed. But
he was more amazed, and much disquieted, to note that in

her awakened recollection of this wrong, the first trace of her old humanity and frozen tenderness appeared to show itself.

He drew a little off, and in doing so observed that her arms were black, her face cut, and her bosom bruised.

" What brutal hand has hurt you so? " he asked.

" My own. I did it myself! " she answered quickly.

" It is impossible."

" I'll swear I did! He didn't touch me. I did it to myself in a passion, and threw myself down here. He wasn't near me. He never laid a hand upon me! "

In the white determination of her face, confronting him with this untruth, he saw enough of the last perversion and distortion of good surviving in that miserable breast to be stricken with remorse that he had ever come near her.

" Sorrow, wrong, and trouble! " he muttered, turning his fearful gaze away. " All that connects her with the state from which she has fallen has those roots! In the name of God, let me go by! "

Afraid to look at her again, afraid to touch her, afraid to think of having sundered the last thread by which she held upon the mercy of Heaven, he gathered his cloak about him and glided swiftly up the stairs.

Opposite to him, on the landing, was a door, which stood partly open, and which, as he ascended, a man with a candle in his hand came forward from within to shut. But this man, on seeing him, drew back, with much emotion in his manner, and, as if by a sudden impulse, mentioned his name aloud.

In the surprise of such a recognition there, he stopped, endeavouring to recollect the wan and startled face. He had no time to consider it, for, to his yet greater amazement, old Philip came out of the room and took him by the hand.

" Mr. Redlaw," said the old man, " this is like you, this is like you, sir! You have heard of it, and have come after us to render any help you can. Ah, too late, too late! "

Redlaw, with a bewildered look, submitted to be led into the room. A man lay there, on a truckle-bed, and William Swidger stood at the bedside.

" Too late! " murmured the old man, looking wistfully into the Chemist's face, and the tears stole down his cheeks.

" That's what I say, father," interposed his son in a low voice. " That's where it is, exactly. To keep as quiet as

ever we can while he's a-dozing is the only thing to do.
You're right, father! "

Redlaw paused at the bedside, and looked down on the
figure that was stretched upon the mattress. It was that of
a man who should have been in the vigour of his life, but on
whom it was not likely that the sun would ever shine again.
The vices of his forty or fifty years' career had so branded him
that, in comparison with their effects upon his face, the heavy
hand of time upon the old man's face who watched him had
been merciful and beautifying.

" Who is this? " asked the Chemist, looking round.

" My son George, Mr. Redlaw," said the old man, wringing
his hands. " My eldest son, George, who was more his
mother's pride than all the rest! "

Redlaw's eyes wandered from the old man's grey head, as
he laid it down upon the bed, to the person who had recognised
him, and who had kept aloof, in the remotest corner of the
room. He seemed to be about his own age; and although
he knew no such hopelessly decayed and broken man as he
appeared to be, there was something in the turn of his figure,
as he stood with his back towards him, and now went out at
the door, that made him pass his hand uneasily across his brow.

" William," he said, in a gloomy whisper, " who is that
man? "

" Why, you see, sir," returned Mr. William, " that's what I
say, myself. Why should a man ever go and gamble, and the
like of that, and let himself down inch by inch till he can't
let himself down any lower? "

" Has *he* done so? " asked Redlaw, glancing after him
with the same uneasy action as before.

" Just exactly that, sir," returned William Swidger, " as
I'm told. He knows a little about medicine, sir, it seems; and
having been wayfaring towards London with my unhappy
brother that you see here "—Mr. William passed his coat-
sleeve across his eyes— " and being lodging upstairs for the
night—what I say, you see, is that strange companions come
together here sometimes—he looked in to attend upon him,
and came for us at his request. What a mournful spectacle,
sir! But that's where it is. It's enough to kill my father! "

Redlaw looked up at these words, and, recalling where he
was and with whom, and the spell he carried with him—
which his surprise had obscured—retired a little, hurriedly,

debating with himself whether to shun the house that moment or remain.

Yielding to a certain sullen doggedness, which it seemed to be a part of his condition to struggle with, he argued for remaining.

"Was it only yesterday," he said, "when I observed the memory of this old man to be a tissue of sorrow and trouble, and shall I be afraid, to-night, to shake it? Are such remembrances as I can drive away so precious to this dying man that I need fear for *him*? No! I'll stay here."

But he stayed in fear and trembling none the less for these words; and shrouded in his black coat, with his face turned from them, stood away from the bedside, listening to what they said, as if he felt himself a demon in the place.

"Father!" murmured the sick man, rallying a little from his stupor.

"My boy! my son George!" said old Philip.

"You spoke just now of my being mother's favourite long ago. It's a dreadful thing to think now of long ago!"

"No, no, no," returned the old man. "Think of it. Don't say it's dreadful. It's not dreadful to me, my son."

"It cuts you to the heart, father." For the old man's tears were falling on him.

"Yes, yes," said Philip, "so it does; but it does me good. It's heavy sorrow to think of that time; but it does me good, George. Oh, think of it too, think of it too, and your heart will be softened more and more! Where's my son William? William, my boy, your mother loved him dearly to the last, and with her latest breath said, 'Tell him I forgave him, blessed him, and prayed for him.' Those were her words to me. I have never forgotten them, and I am eighty-seven!"

"Father!" said the man upon the bed, "I am dying, I know. I am so far gone that I can hardly speak, even of what my mind most runs on. Is there any hope for me beyond this bed?"

"There is hope," returned the old man, "for all who are softened and penitent. There is hope for all such. Oh!" he exclaimed, clasping his hands and looking up, "I was thankful, only yesterday, that I could remember this unhappy son when he was an innocent child. But what a comfort is it now to think that even God Himself has that remembrance of him!"

Redlaw spread his hands upon his face, and shrunk, like a murderer.

"Ah!" feebly moaned the man upon the bed. "The waste since then, the waste of life since then!"

"But he was a child once," said the old man. "He played with children. Before he lay down on his bed at night, and fell into his guiltless rest, he said his prayers at his poor mother's knee. I have seen him do it, many a time; and seen her lay his head upon her breast and kiss him. Sorrowful as it was to her and me to think of this when he went so wrong, and when our hopes and plans for him were all broken, this gave him still a hold upon us that nothing else could have given. O Father, so much better than the fathers upon earth! O Father, so much more afflicted by the errors of Thy children, take this wanderer back! Not as he is, but as he was then, let him cry to Thee, as he has so often seemed to cry to us!"

As the old man lifted up his trembling hands, the son for whom he made the supplication laid his sinking head against him for support and comfort, as if he were indeed the child of whom he spoke.

When did man ever tremble as Redlaw trembled, in the silence that ensued? He knew it must come upon them, knew that it was coming fast.

"My time is very short, my breath is shorter," said the sick man, supporting himself on one arm, and with the other groping in the air, "and I remember there is something on my mind concerning the man who was here just now. Father and William—wait!—is there really anything in black out there?"

"Yes, yes, it is real," said his aged father.

"Is it a man?"

"What I say myself, George," interposed his brother, bending kindly over him. "It's Mr. Redlaw."

"I thought I had dreamed of him. Ask him to come here."

The Chemist, whiter than the dying man, appeared before him. Obedient to the motion of his hand, he sat upon the bed.

"It has been so ripped up to-night, sir," said the sick man, laying his hand upon his heart, with a look in which the mute, imploring agony of his condition was concentrated, "by the sight of my poor old father, and the thought of all the trouble I have been the cause of, and all the wrong and sorrow lying at my door, that——"

Was it the extremity to which he had come, or was it the dawning of another change, that made him stop?

"——that what I *can* do right, with my mind running on so much, so fast, I'll try to do. There was another man here. Did you see him? "

Redlaw could not reply by any word; for when he saw that fatal sign he knew so well now, of the wandering hand upon the forehead, his voice died at his lips. But he made some indication of assent.

" He is penniless, hungry, and destitute. He is completely beaten down, and has no resource at all. Look after him! Lose no time! I know he has it in his mind to kill himself."

It was working. It was on his face. His face was changing, hardening, deepening in all its shades, and losing all its sorrow.

" Don't you remember? Don't you know him? " he pursued.

He shut his face out for a moment, with the hand that again wandered over his forehead, and then it lowered on Redlaw, reckless, ruffianly, and callous.

" Why, d——n you! " he said, scowling round, " what have you been doing to me here? I have lived bold, and I mean to die bold. To the Devil with you! "

And so lay down upon his bed, and put his arms up, over his head and ears, as resolute from that time to keep out all access, and to die in his indifference.

If Redlaw had been struck by lightning, it could not have struck him from the bedside with a more tremendous shock. But the old man, who had left the bed while his son was speaking to him, now returning, avoided it quickly likewise, and with abhorrence.

" Where's my boy William? " said the old man hurriedly. " William, come away from here. We'll go home."

" Home, father! " returned William. " Are you going to leave your own son? "

" Where's my own son? " replied the old man.

" Where? why, there! "

" That's no son of mine," said Philip, trembling with resentment. " No such wretch as that has any claim on me. My children are pleasant to look at, and they wait upon me, and get my meat and drink ready, and are useful to me. I've a right to it! I'm eighty-seven!"

"You're old enough to be no older," muttered William, looking at him grudgingly, with his hands in his pockets. "I don't know what good you are, myself. We could have a deal more pleasure without you."

"*My* son, Mr. Redlaw!" said the old man. "*My* son, too! The boy talking to me of *my* son! Why, what has he ever done to give me any pleasure, I should like to know?"

"I don't know what you have ever done to give *me* any pleasure," said William sulkily.

"Let me think," said the old man. "For how many Christmas times running have I sat in my warm place, and never had to come out in the cold night air; and have made good cheer, without being disturbed by any such uncomfortable, wretched sight as him there? Is it twenty, William?"

"Nigher forty, it seems," he muttered. "Why, when I look at my father, sir, and come to think of it," addressing Redlaw with an impatience and irritation that were quite new, "I am whipped if I can see anything in him but a calendar of ever so many years of eating, and drinking, and making himself comfortable over and over again.

"I—I'm eighty-seven," said the old man, rambling on, childishly and weakly, "and I don't know as I ever was much put out by anything. I'm not a-going to begin now, because of what he calls my son. He's not my son. I've had a power of pleasant times. I recollect once—no, I don't—no, it's broken off. It was something about a game of cricket and a friend of mine, but it's somehow broken off. I wonder who he was?—I suppose I liked him. And I wonder what became of him?—I suppose he died. But I don't know. And I don't care neither; I don't care a bit."

In his drowsy chuckling, and the shaking of his head, he put his hands into his waistcoat pockets. In one of them he found a bit of holly (left there probably last night), which he now took out and looked at.

"Berries, eh?" said the old man. "Ah! it's a pity they're not good to eat. I recollect, when I was a little chap about as high as that, and out a-walking with—let me see—who was I out a-walking with?—no, I don't remember how that was. I don't remember as I ever walked with anyone particular, or cared for anyone, or anyone for me. Berries, eh? There's good cheer when there's berries. Well, I ought to have my share of it, and to be waited on, and kept warm and comfortable; for I'm eighty-seven, and a poor old man. I'm eigh-ty-seven. Eigh-ty-seven! "

The drivelling, pitiable manner in which, as he repeated this, he nibbled at the leaves, and spat the morsels out; the cold, uninterested eye with which his youngest son (so changed) regarded him; the determined apathy with which his eldest son lay hardened in his sin, impressed themselves no more on Redlaw's observation, for he broke his way from the spot to which his feet seemed to have been fixed, and ran out of the house.

His guide came crawling forth from his place of refuge, and was ready for him before he reached the arches.

" Back to the woman's? " he inquired.

" Back, quickly! " answered Redlaw. " Stop nowhere on the way! "

For a short distance the boy went on before; but their return was more like a flight than a walk, and it was as much as his bare feet could do to keep pace with the Chemist's rapid strides. Shrinking from all who passed, shrouded in his cloak, and keeping it drawn closely about him, as though there were mortal contagion in any fluttering touch of his garments, he made no pause until they reached the door by which they had come out. He unlocked it with his key, went in, accompanied by the boy, and hastened through the dark passages to his own chamber.

The boy watched him as he made the door fast, and withdrew behind the table when he looked round.

" Come! " he said. " Don't you touch me! You've not brought me here to take my money away."

Redlaw threw some more upon the ground. He flung his body on it immediately, as if to hide it from him, lest the sight of it should tempt him to reclaim it; and not until he saw him seated by his lamp, with his face hidden in his hands, began furtively to pick it up. When he had done so, he crept near the fire, and, sitting down in a great chair before it, took from his breast some broken scraps of food, and fell to munching, and to staring at the blaze, and now and then to glancing at his shillings, which he kept clenched up in a bunch, in one hand.

" And this," said Redlaw, gazing on him with increasing repugnance and fear, " is the only one companion I have left on earth! "

How long it was before he was aroused from his contemplation of this creature, whom he dreaded so—whether half an hour, or half the night—he knew not. But the stillness of the room was broken by the boy (whom he had seen listening) starting up, and running towards the door.

" Here's the woman coming! " he exclaimed.

The Chemist stopped him on his way, at the moment when she knocked.

" Let me go to her, will you? " said the boy.

" Not now," returned the Chemist. " Stay here. Nobody must pass in or out of the room now. Who's that? "

" It's I, sir," cried Milly. " Pray, sir, let me in! "

" No! not for the world! " he said.

" Mr. Redlaw, Mr. Redlaw, pray, sir, let me in."

" What is the matter? " he said, holding the boy.

" The miserable man you saw is worse, and nothing I can say will wake him from his terrible infatuation. William's father has turned childish in a moment. William himself is changed. The shock has been too sudden for him; I cannot understand him; he is not like himself. Oh, Mr. Redlaw, pray advise me, help me! "

" No! no! no! " he answered.

" Mr. Redlaw! Dear Sir! George has been muttering, in his doze, about the man you saw there, who, he fears, will kill himself."

" Better he should do it than come near me! "

" He says, in his wandering, that you know him; that he was your friend once, long ago; that he is the ruined father of a student here—my mind misgives me, of the young gentleman who has been ill. What is to be done? How is he to be followed? How is he to be saved? Mr. Redlaw, pray, oh, pray, advise me! Help me! "

All this time he held the boy, who was half-mad to pass him and let her in.

" Phantoms! Punishers of impious thoughts! " cried Redlaw, gazing round in anguish, " look upon me! From the darkness of my mind, let the glimmering of contrition that I know is there shine up, and show my misery! In the material world, as I have long taught, nothing can be spared;

no step or atom in the wondrous structure could be lost, without a blank being made in the great universe. I know now that it is the same with good and evil, happiness and sorrow, in the memories of men. Pity me! Relieve me! "

There was no response but her " Help me, help me, let me in! " and the boy's struggling to get to her.

" Shadow of myself! Spirit of my darker hours! " cried Redlaw, in distraction, " come back, and haunt me day and night, but take this gift away! Or, if it must still rest with me, deprive me of the dreadful power of giving it to others. Undo what I have done. Leave me benighted, but restore the day to those whom I have cursed. As I have spared this woman from the first, and as I never will go forth again, but will die here, with no hand to tend me, save this creature's who is proof against me, hear me! "

The only reply still was, the boy struggling to get to her, while he held him back; and the cry, increasing in its energy, " Help! let me in. He was your friend once—how shall he be followed, how shall he be saved? They are all changed, there is no one else to help me—pray, pray, let me in! "

III

THE GIFT REVERSED

NIGHT was still heavy in the sky. On open plains, from hill-tops, and from the decks of solitary ships at sea, a distant, low-lying line, that promised by and by to change to light, was visible in the dim horizon; but its promise was remote and doubtful, and the moon was striving with the night-clouds busily.

The shadows upon Redlaw's mind succeeded thick and fast to one another, and obscured its light as the night-clouds hovered between the moon and the earth, and kept the latter veiled in darkness. Fitful and uncertain as the shadows which the night-clouds cast were their concealments from him and imperfect revelations to him; and, like the night-clouds still, if the clear light broke forth for a moment, it was only that they might sweep over it, and make the darkness deeper than before.

Without, there was a profound and solemn hush upon the ancient pile of building, and its buttresses and angles made

dark shapes of mystery upon the ground, which now seemed
to retire into the smooth, white snow, and now seemed to
come out of it, as the moon's path was more or less beset.
Within, the Chemist's room was indistinct and murky, by
the light of the expiring lamp; a ghostly silence had succeeded
to the knocking and the voice outside; nothing was audible
but, now and then, a low sound among the whitened ashes of
the fire, as of its yielding up its last breath. Before it, on the
ground, the boy lay fast asleep. In his chair, the Chemist sat,
as he had sat there since the calling at his door had ceased—
like a man turned to stone.

At such a time, the Christmas music he had heard before
began to play. He listened to it at first, as he had listened in
the churchyard; but presently—it playing still, and being
borne towards him on the night air, in a low, sweet, melancholy strain—he rose, and stood stretching his hands about
him, as if there were some friend approaching within his
reach, on whom his desolate touch might rest, yet do no
harm. As he did this, his face became less fixed and wondering, a gentle trembling came upon him; and at last his eyes
filled with tears, and he put his hands before them, and
bowed down his head.

His memory of sorrow, wrong, and trouble had not come
back to him; he knew that it was not restored; he had
no passing belief or hope that it was. But some dumb stir
within him made him capable, again, of being moved by what
was hidden, afar off, in the music. If it were only that it told
him sorrowfully the value of what he had lost, he thanked
Heaven for it with a fervent gratitude.

As the last chord died upon his ear, he raised his head to
listen to its lingering vibration. Beyond the boy, so that his
sleeping figure lay at its feet, the Phantom stood, immovable
and silent, with its eyes upon him.

Ghastly it was, as it had ever been, but not so cruel and
relentless in its aspect—or he thought or hoped so, as he
looked upon it trembling. It was not alone, but in its shadowy
hand it held another hand.

And whose was that? Was the form that stood beside it
indeed Milly's, or but her shade and picture? The quiet
head was bent a little, as her manner was, and her eyes were
looking down, as if in pity, on the sleeping child. A radiant
light fell on her face, but did not touch the Phantom, for,

though close beside her, it was dark and colourless as ever.

" Spectre! " said the Chemist, newly troubled as he looked, " I have not been stubborn or presumptuous in respect of her. Oh, do not bring her here. Spare me that! "

" This is but a shadow," said the Phantom; " when the morning shines, seek out the reality whose image I present before you."

" Is it my inexorable doom to do so? " cried the Chemist.

" It is," replied the Phantom.

" To destroy her peace, her goodness—to make her what I am myself, and what I have made of others! "

" I have said ' seek her out,' " returned the Phantom. " I have said no more."

" Oh, tell me," exclaimed Redlaw, catching at the hope which he fancied might lie hidden in the words. " Can I undo what I have done? "

" No," returned the Phantom.

" I do not ask for restoration to myself," said Redlaw. " What I abandoned, I abandoned of my own will, and have justly lost. But for those to whom I have transferred the fatal gift—who never sought it; who unknowingly received a curse of which they had no warning, and which they had no power to shun—can I do nothing? "

" Nothing," said the Phantom.

" If I cannot, can anyone? "

The Phantom, standing like a statue, kept its gaze upon him for a while; then turned its head suddenly, and looked upon the shadow at its side.

" Ah! can she? " cried Redlaw, still looking upon the shade.

The Phantom released the hand it had retained till now, and softly raised its own with a gesture of dismissal. Upon that, her shadow, still preserving the same attitude, began to move or melt away.

" Stay," cried Redlaw, with an earnestness to which he could not give enough expression. " For a moment! As an act of mercy! I know that some change fell upon me when those sounds were in the air just now. Tell me, have I lost the power of harming her? May I go near her without dread? Oh, let her give me any sign of hope! "

The Phantom looked upon the shade as he did—not at him—and gave no answer.

" At least, say this—has she, henceforth, the consciousness of any power to set right what I have done? "

" She has not," the Phantom answered.

" Has she the power bestowed on her without the consciousness? "

The Phantom answered, " Seek her out." And her shadow slowly vanished.

They were face to face again, and looking on each other, as intently and awfully as at the time of the bestowal of the gift, across the boy who still lay on the ground between them, at the Phantom's feet.

" Terrible instructor," said the Chemist, sinking on his knees before it, in an attitude of supplication, " by whom I was renounced, but by whom I am revisited (in which, and in whose milder aspect, I would fain believe I have a gleam of hope), I will obey without inquiry, praying that the cry I have sent up in the anguish of my soul has been, or will be, heard, in behalf of those whom I have injured beyond human reparation.   But there is one thing——"

" You speak to me of what is lying here," the Phantom interposed, and pointed with its finger to the boy.

" I do," returned the Chemist.   " You know what I would ask. Why has this child alone been proof against my influence, and why, why have I detected in its thoughts a terrible companionship with mine? "

" This," said the Phantom, pointing to the boy, " is the last, completest illustration of a human creature utterly bereft of such remembrances as you have yielded up.   No softening memory of sorrow, wrong, or trouble enters here, because this wretched mortal from his birth has been abandoned to a worse condition than the beasts, and has, within his knowledge, no one contrast, no humanizing touch, to make a grain of such a memory spring up in his hardened breast.   All within this desolate creature is barren wilderness.   All within the man bereft of what you have resigned is the same barren wilderness. Woe to such a man! Woe, tenfold, to the nation that shall count its monsters such as this, lying here, by hundreds and by thousands! "

Redlaw shrunk, appalled, from what he heard.

" There is not," said the Phantom, " one of these—not one—but sows a harvest that mankind MUST reap. From every seed of evil in this boy a field of ruin is grown that shall be gathered in, and garnered up, and sown again in many places in the world, until regions are overspread with wickedness enough to raise the waters of another Deluge. Open and unpunished murder in a city's streets would be less guilty in its daily toleration, than one such spectacle as this."

It seemed to look down upon the boy in his sleep. Redlaw, too, looked down upon him with a new emotion.

"There is not a father," said the Phantom, "by whose side, in his daily or his nightly walk, these creatures pass; there is not a mother among all the ranks of loving mothers in this land; there is no one risen from the state of childhood, but shall be responsible in his or her degree for this enormity. There is not a country throughout the earth on which it would not bring a curse. There is no religion upon earth that it would not deny; there is no people upon earth it would not put to shame."

The Chemist clasped his hands, and looked, with trembling fear and pity, from the sleeping boy to the Phantom, standing above him with its finger pointing down.

"Behold, I say," pursued the Spectre, "the perfect type of what it was your choice to be. Your influence is powerless here, because from this child's bosom you can banish nothing. His thoughts have been in 'terrible companionship' with yours, because you have gone down to his unnatural level. He is the growth of man's indifference; you are the growth of man's presumption. The beneficent design of Heaven is, in each case, overthrown, and from the two poles of the immaterial world you come together."

The Chemist stooped upon the ground beside the boy, and, with the same kind of compassion for him that he now felt for himself, covered him as he slept, and no longer shrunk from him with abhorrence or indifference.

Soon, now, the distant line on the horizon brightened, the darkness faded, the sun rose red and glorious, and the chimney-stacks and gables of the ancient building gleamed in the clear air, which turned the smoke and vapour of the city into a cloud of gold. The very sundial in his shady corner, where the wind was used to spin with such unwindy constancy, shook off the finer particles of snow that had accumulated on his dull old face in the night, and looked out at the little white wreaths eddying round and round him. Doubtless some blind groping of the morning made its way down into the forgotten crypt so cold and earthy, where the Norman arches were half buried in the ground, and stirred the dull sap in the lazy vegetation hanging to the walls, and quickened the slow principle of life within the little world of wonderful and delicate creation which existed there, with some faint knowledge that the sun was up.

The Tetterbys were up and doing. Mr. Tetterby took down the shutters of the shop, and strip by strip, revealed the treasures of the window to the eyes, so proof against their seductions, of Jerusalem Buildings. Adolphus had been out so long already that he was half-way on the Morning Pepper. Five small Tetterbys, whose ten round eyes were much inflamed by soap and friction, were in the tortures of a cool wash in the back kitchen, Mrs. Tetterby presiding. Johnny, who was pushed and hustled through his toilet with great rapidity when Moloch chanced to be in an exacting frame of mind (which was always the case), staggered up and down with his charge before the shop door, under greater difficulties than usual—the weight of Moloch being much increased by a complication of defences against the cold, composed of knitted worsted work, and forming a complete suit of chain armour, with a headpiece and blue gaiters.

It was a peculiarity of this baby to be always cutting teeth. Whether they never came, or whether they came and went away again, is not in evidence; but it had certainly cut enough, on the showing of Mrs. Tetterby, to make a handsome dental provision for the sign of the Bull and Mouth. All sorts of objects were impressed for the rubbing of its gums, notwithstanding that it always carried, dangling at its waist (which was immediately under its chin), a bone ring, large enough to have represented the rosary of a young nun. Knife-handles, umbrella-tops, the heads of walking-sticks selected from the stock, the fingers of the family in general, but especially of Johnny, nutmeg-graters, crusts, the handles of doors, and the cool knobs on the tops of pokers, were among the commonest instruments indiscriminately applied for this baby's relief. The amount of electricity that must have been rubbed out of it in a week is not to be calculated. Still Mrs. Tetterby always said, " it was coming through, and then the child would be herself "; and still it never did come through, and the child continued to be somebody else.

The tempers of the little Tetterbys had sadly changed with

a few hours. Mr. and Mrs. Tetterby themselves were not
more altered than their offspring. Usually they were an
unselfish, good-natured, yielding little race, sharing short
commons when it happened (which was pretty often) contentedly and even generously, and taking a great deal of
enjoyment out of a very little meat. But they were fighting
now, not only for the soap and water, but even for the
breakfast which was yet in perspective. The hand of every
little Tetterby was against the other little Tetterbys; and even
Johnny's hand—the patient, much-enduring, and devoted
Johnny—rose against the baby! Yes. Mrs. Tetterby, going
to the door by a mere accident, saw him viciously pick out
a weak place in the suit of armour where a slap would tell,
and slap that blessed child.

Mrs. Tetterby had him into the parlour, by the collar, in
that same flash of time, and repaid him the assault with usury
thereto.

" You brute, you murdering little boy," said Mrs. Tetterby.
" Had you the heart to do it? "

" Why don't her teeth come through, then," retorted
Johnny, in a loud, rebellious voice, " instead of bothering
me? How would you like it yourself? "

" Like it, sir! " said Mrs. Tetterby, relieving him of his
dishonoured load.

" Yes, like it," said Johnny. " How would you? Not at
all. If you was me, you'd go for a soldier. I will, too.
There ain't no babies in the army."

Mr. Tetterby, who had arrived upon the scene of action,
rubbed his chin thoughtfully, instead of correcting the rebel,
and seemed rather struck by this view of a military life.

" I wish I was in the army myself, if the child's in the
right," said Mrs. Tetterby, looking at her husband, " for I
have no peace of my life here. I'm a slave—a Virginia
slave "; some indistinct association with their weak descent on
the tobacco trade perhaps suggested this aggravated expression
to Mrs. Tetterby. " I never have a holiday, or any pleasures
at all, from year's end to year's end! Why, Lord bless and
save the child! " said Mrs. Tetterby, shaking the baby with an
irritability hardly suited to so pious an aspiration, " what's
the matter with her now? "

Not being able to discover, and not rendering the subject
much clearer by shaking it, Mrs. Tetterby put the baby away

in a cradle, and, folding her arms, sat rocking it angrily with her foot.

" How you stand there, 'Dolphus," said Mrs. Tetterby to her husband.   " Why don't you do something? "

" Because I don't care about doing anything," Mr. Tetterby replied.

" I am sure *I* don't," said Mrs. Tetterby.

" I'll take my oath *I* don't," said Mr. Tetterby.

A diversion arose here among Johnny and his five younger brothers, who, in preparing the family breakfast-table, had fallen to skirmishing for the temporary possession of the loaf, and were buffeting one another with great heartiness, the smallest boy of all, with precocious discretion, hovering outside the knot of combatants and harassing their legs. Into the midst of this fray Mr. and Mrs. Tetterby both precipitated themselves with great ardour, as if such ground were the only ground on which they could now agree; and having, with no visible remains of their late soft-heartedness, laid about them without any lenity, and done much execution, resumed their former relative positions.

" You had better read your paper than do nothing at all, said Mrs. Tetterby.

" What's there to read in a paper? " returned Mr. Tetterby, with excessive discontent.

" What? " said Mrs. Tetterby.   " Police.'

" It's nothing to me," said Tetterby.   " What do I care what people do, or are done to? "

" Suicides," suggested Mrs. Tetterby.

" No business of mine," replied her husband.

" Births, deaths, and marriages, are those nothing to you? ' said Mrs. Tetterby.

" If the births were all over for good and all to-day, and the deaths were all to begin to come off to-morrow, I don't see why it should interest me till I thought it was a-coming to my turn," grumbled Tetterby.   " As to marriages, I've done it myself.   I know quite enough about *them*."

To judge from the dissatisfied expression of her face and manner, Mrs. Tetterby appeared to entertain the same opinions as her husband; but she opposed him, nevertheless, for the gratification of quarrelling with him.

" Oh, you're a consistent man," said Mrs. Tetterby, " ain't you?   You, with the screen of your own making there, made of nothing else but bits of newspapers, which you sit and read to the children by the half-hour together! "

" Say used to, if you please," returned her husband. " You won't find me doing so any more. I'm wiser now."

" Bah! wiser, indeed! " said Mrs. Tetterby. " Are you better? "

The question sounded some discordant note in Mr. Tetterby's breast. He ruminated dejectedly, and passed his hand across and across his forehead.

" Better! " murmured Mr. Tetterby. " I don't know as any of us are better, or happier either. Better, is it? "

He turned to the screen, and traced about it with his finger, until he found a certain paragraph of which he was in quest.

" This used to be one of the family favourites, I recollect," said Tetterby, in a forlorn and stupid way, " and used to draw tears from the children, and make 'em good, if there was any little bickering or discontent among 'em, next to the story of the robin redbreasts in the wood. 'Melancholy case of destitution.—Yesterday a small man, with a baby in his arms, and surrounded by half a dozen ragged little ones, of various ages between ten and two, the whole of whom were evidently in a famishing condition, appeared before the worthy magistrate, and made the following recital '—Ha! I don't understand it, I'm sure," said Tetterby; " I don't see what it has got to do with us."

" How old and shabby he looks," said Mrs. Tetterby, watching him. " I never saw such a change in a man. Ah! dear me, dear me, dear me, it was a sacrifice! "

" What was a sacrifice? " her husband sourly inquired.

Mrs. Tetterby shook her head, and without replying in words, raised a complete sea-storm about the baby, by her violent agitation of the cradle.

" If you mean your marriage was a sacrifice, my good woman——" said her husband.

" I *do* mean it," said his wife.

" Why, then I mean to say," pursued Mr. Tetterby, as sulkily and surlily as she, " that there are two sides to that affair; and that *I* was the sacrifice, and I wish the sacrifice hadn't been accepted."

" I wish it hadn't, Tetterby, with all my heart and soul I do assure you," said his wife. " You can't wish it more than I do, Tetterby."

" I don't know what I saw in her," muttered the newsman,
" I'm sure; certainly, if I saw anything, it's not there now.
I was thinking so last night, after supper, by the fire. She's
fat, she's ageing, she won't bear comparison with most other
women."

" He's common-looking, he has no air with him, he's small,
he's beginning to stoop, and he's getting bald," muttered
Mrs. Tetterby.

" I must have been half out of my mind when I did it,"
muttered Mr. Tetterby.

" My senses must have forsook me. That's the only way
in which I can explain it to myself," said Mrs. Tetterby, with
elaboration.

In this mood they sat down to breakfast. The little
Tetterbys were not habituated to regard that meal in the light
of a sedentary occupation, but discussed it as a dance or trot
—rather resembling a savage ceremony in the occasional
shrill whoops, and brandishings of bread and butter, with
which it was accompanied, as well as in the intricate filings
off into the street and back again, and the hoppings up and
down the doorsteps, which were incidental to the performance. In the present instance, the contentions between these
Tetterby children for the milk-and-water jug, common to all,
which stood upon the table, presented so lamentable an instance of angry passions risen very high indeed, that it was an
outrage on the memory of Doctor Watts. It was not until
Mr. Tetterby had driven the whole herd out at the front door
that a moment's peace was secured; and even that was broken
by the discovery that Johnny had surreptitiously come back,
and was at that instant choking in the jug like a ventriloquist,
in his indecent and rapacious haste.

" These children will be the death of me at last! " said
Mrs. Tetterby, after banishing the culprit. " And the sooner
the better, I think."

" Poor people," said Mr. Tetterby, " ought not to have
children at all. They give *us* no pleasure."

He was at that moment taking up the cup which Mrs.
Tetterby had rudely pushed towards him, and Mrs. Tetterby
was lifting her own cup to her lips, when they both stopped,
as if they were transfixed.

" Here! Mother! Father! " cried Johnny, running into
the room. " Here's Mrs. William coming down the street! "

And if ever, since the world began, a young boy took a baby from a cradle with the care of an old nurse, and hushed and soothed it tenderly, and tottered away with it cheerfully, Johnny was that boy, and Moloch was that baby, as they went out together.

Mr. Tetterby put down his cup; Mrs. Tetterby put down her cup. Mr. Tetterby rubbed his forehead; Mrs. Tetterby rubbed hers. Mr. Tetterby's face began to smooth and brighten; Mrs. Tetterby's began to smooth and brighten.

"Why, Lord forgive me," said Mr. Tetterby to himself, "what evil tempers have I been giving way to? What has been the matter here?"

"How could I ever treat him ill again, after all I said and felt last night?" sobbed Mrs. Tetterby, with her apron to her eyes.

"Am I a brute?" said Mr. Tetterby; "or is there any good in me at all?—Sophia! My little woman!"

"'Dolphus dear," returned his wife.

"I—I've been in a state of mind," said Mr. Tetterby, "that I can't bear to think of, Sophy."

"Oh! It's nothing to what I've been in, Dolf," cried his wife in a great burst of grief.

"My Sophia," said Mr. Tetterby, "don't take on. I never shall forgive myself. I must have nearly broke your heart, I know."

"No, Dolf, no. It was me! Me!" cried Mrs. Tetterby.

"My little woman," said her husband, "don't. You make me reproach myself dreadful, when you show such a noble spirit. Sophia, my dear, you don't know what I thought. I showed it bad enough, no doubt; but what I thought, my little woman——!"

"Oh, dear Dolf, don't! Don't!" cried his wife.

"Sophia," said Mr. Tetterby, "I must reveal it. I couldn't rest in my conscience unless I mentioned it. My little woman——"

"Mrs. William's very nearly here!" screamed Johnny at the door.

"My little woman, I wondered how," gasped Mr. Tetterby, supporting himself by his chair—"I wondered how I had ever admired you. I forgot the previous children you have brought about me, and thought you didn't look as slim as I could wish. I—I never gave a recollection," said Mr. Tetterby, with severe self-accusation, " to the cares you've had as my wife, and along of me and mine, when you might have had hardly any with another man, who got on better and was luckier than me (anybody might have found such a man easily, I am sure) ; and I quarrelled with you for having aged a little in the rough years you've lightened for me. Can you believe it, my little woman? I hardly can myself."

Mrs. Tetterby, in a whirlwind of laughing and crying, caught his face within her hands and held it there.

"Oh, Dolf! " she cried, "I am so happy that you thought so; I am so grateful that you thought so! For I thought that you were common-looking, Dolf; and so you are, my dear, and may you be the commonest of all sights in my eyes, till you close them with your own good hands. I thought that you were small; and so you are, and I'll make much of you because you are, and more of you because I love my husband. I thought that you began to stoop; and so you do, and you shall lean on me, and I'll do all I can to keep you up. I thought there was no air about you; but there is, and it's the air of home, and that's the purest and the best there is, and GOD bless home once more, and all belonging to it, Dolf! "

"Hurrah! Here's Mrs. William! " cried Jŏhnny.

So she was, and all the children with her; and as she came in, they kissed her, and kissed one another, and kissed the baby, and kissed their father and mother, and then ran back and flocked and danced about her, trooping on with her in triumph.

Mr. and Mrs. Tetterby were not a bit behind-hand in the warmth of their reception. They were as much attracted to her as the children were. They ran towards her, kissed her hands, pressed round her, could not receive her ardently or enthusiastically enough. She came among them like the spirit of all goodness, affection, gentle consideration, love, and domesticity.

"What! are *you* all so glad to see me, too, this bright Christmas morning? " said Milly, clapping her hands in a pleasant wonder. "Oh, dear, how delightful this is! "

More shouting from the children, more kissing, more trooping round her, more happiness, more love, more joy, more honour, on all sides, than she could bear.

"Oh, dear! " said Milly, " what delicious tears you make

me shed! How can I ever have deserved this? What have I done to be so loved? "

" Who can help it? " cried Mr. Tetterby.

" Who can help it? " cried Mrs. Tetterby.

" Who can help it? " echoed the children, in a joyful chorus. And they danced and trooped about her again, and clung to her, and laid their rosy faces against her dress, and kissed and fondled it, and could not fondle it or her enough.

" I never was so moved," said Milly, drying her eyes, " as I have been this morning. I must tell you, as soon as I can speak. Mr. Redlaw came to me at sunrise, and with a tenderness in his manner, more as if I had been his darling daughter than myself, implored me to go with him to where William's brother George is lying ill. We went together, and all the way along he was so kind, and so subdued, and seemed to put such trust and hope in me, that I could not help crying with pleasure. When we got to the house, we met a woman at the door (somebody had bruised and hurt her, I am afraid), who caught me by the hand, and blessed me as I passed."

" She was right! " said Mr. Tetterby. Mrs. Tetterby said she was right. All the children cried out she was right.

" Ah, but there's more than that," said Milly. " When we got upstairs into the room, the sick man, who had lain for hours in a state from which no effort could rouse him, rose up in his bed, and bursting into tears, stretched out his arms to me, and said that he had led a misspent life, but that he was truly repentant now, in his sorrow for the past, which was all as plain to him as a great prospect, from which a dense black cloud had cleared away, and that he entreated me to ask his poor father for his pardon and his blessing and to say a prayer beside his bed. And when I did so, Mr. Redlaw joined in it so fervently, and then so thanked and thanked me, and thanked Heaven, that my heart quite overflowed, and I could have done nothing but sob and cry, if the sick man had not begged me to sit down by him, which made me quiet, of course. As I sat there, he held my hand in his until he sunk in a doze; and even then when I withdrew my hand to leave him to come here (which Mr. Redlaw was very earnest indeed in wishing me to do), his hand felt for mine, so that someone else was obliged to take my place and make believe to give him my hand back. Oh, dear, oh, dear! " said Milly, sobbing. " How thankful and how happy I should feel, and do feel, for all this! "

While she was speaking, Redlaw had come in, and, after pausing for a moment to observe the group of which she was the centre, had silently ascended the stairs. Upon those stairs he now appeared again, remaining there, while the young student passed him, and came running down.

" Kind nurse, gentlest, best of creatures," he said, falling on his knee to her, and catching at her hand, " forgive my cruel ingratitude! "

" Oh, dear, oh, dear! " cried Milly innocently, " here's another of them! Oh, dear, here's somebody else who likes me! What shall I ever do? "

The guileless, simple way in which she said it, and in which she put her hands before her eyes and wept for very happiness, was as touching as it was delightful.

" I was not myself," he said. " I don't know what it was —it was some consequence of my disorder perhaps—I was mad. But I am so no longer. Almost as I speak I am restored. I heard the children crying out your name, and the shade passed from me at the very sound of it. Oh, don't weep! Dear Milly, if you could read my heart, and only know with what affection and what grateful homage it is glowing, you would not let me see you weep. It is such deep reproach."

" No, no," said Milly, " it's not that. It's not, indeed. It's joy. It's wonder that you should think it necessary to ask me to forgive so little, and yet it's pleasure that you do."

" And will you come again? and will you finish the little curtain? "

" No," said Milly, drying her eyes, and shaking her head. " You won't care for *my* needlework now."

" Is it forgiving me to say that? "

She beckoned him aside, and whispered in his ear.

" There is news from your home, Mr. Edmund."

" News? How? "

" Either your not writing when you were very ill, or the change in your handwriting when you began to be better, created some suspicion of the truth; however that is—— But you're sure you'll not be the worse for any news, if it's not bad news? "

" Sure."

" Then there's someone come! " said Milly.

" My mother? " asked the student, glancing round involuntarily towards Redlaw, who had come down from the stairs.

" Hush! No," said Milly.

" It can be no one else."

" Indeed? " said Milly. " Are you sure? "

" It is not——" Before he could say more she put her hand upon his mouth.

" Yes, it is! " said Milly. " The young lady (she is very like the miniature, Mr. Edmund, but she is prettier) was too unhappy to rest without satisfying her doubts, and came up, last night, with a little servant-maid. As you always dated your letters from the college, she came there; and before I saw Mr. Redlaw this morning, I saw her. *She* likes me too! " said Milly. " Oh, dear, that's another! "

" This morning! Where is she now? "

" Why, she is now," said Milly, advancing her lips to his ear, " in my little parlour in the Lodge, and waiting to see you."

He pressed her hand, and was darting off, but she detained him.

" Mr. Redlaw is much altered, and has told me this morning that his memory is impaired. Be very considerate to him, Mr. Edmund; he needs that from us all."

The young man assured her, by a look, that her caution was not ill-bestowed; and as he passed the Chemist on his way out, bent respectfully and with an obvious interest before him.

Redlaw returned the salutation courteously and even humbly, and looked after him as he passed on. He drooped his head upon his hand too, as trying to reawaken something he had lost. But it was gone.

The abiding change that had come upon him since the influence of the music, and the Phantom's reappearance, was that now he truly felt how much he had lost, and could compassionate his own condition, and contrast it, clearly, with the natural state of those who were around him. In this, an interest in those who were around him was revived, and a meek, submissive sense of his calamity was bred, resembling that which sometimes obtains in age, when its mental powers are weakened, without insensibility or sullenness being added to the list of its infirmities.

He was conscious that as he redeemed, through Milly, more and more of the evil he had done, and as he was more and more with her, this change ripened itself within him. Therefore, and because of the attachment she inspired him with (but without other hope), he felt that he was quite dependent on her, and that she was his staff in his affliction.

So, when she asked him whether they should go home now, to where the old man and her husband were, and he readily replied " yes "—being anxious in that regard—he put his arm through hers, and walked beside her; not as if he were the wise and learned man to whom the wonders of nature were an open book, and hers were the uninstructed mind, but as if their two positions were reversed, and he knew nothing, and she all.

He saw the children throng about her, and caress her, as he and she went away together thus, out of the house; he heard the ringing of their laughter, and their merry voices; he saw their bright faces, clustering round him like flowers; he witnessed the renewed contentment and affection of their parents; he breathed the simple air of their poor home, restored to its tranquillity; he thought of the unwholesome blight he had shed upon it, and might, but for her, have been diffusing then; and perhaps it is no wonder that he walked submissively beside her, and drew her gentle bosom nearer to his own.

When they arrived at the Lodge, the old man was sitting in his chair in the chimney-corner, with his eyes fixed on the ground, and his son was leaning against the opposite side of the fire-place, looking at him. As she came in at the door, both started, and turned round towards her, and a radiant change came upon their faces.

" Oh, dear, dear, dear, they are pleased to see me like the rest! " cried Milly, clapping her hands in an ecstasy, and stopping short. " Here are two more! "

Pleased to see her! Pleasure was no word for it. She ran into her husband's arms, thrown wide open to receive her; and he would have been glad to have her there, with her head lying on his shoulder, through the short winter's day. But the old man couldn't spare her. He had arms for her too, and he locked her in them.

" Why, where has my quiet Mouse been all this time? "

said the old man. " She has been a long while away. I find that it's impossible for me to get on without Mouse. I—where's my son William?—I fancy I have been dreaming, William."

" That's what I say myself, father," returned his son. " *I* have been in an ugly sort of dream, I think. How are you, father? Are you pretty well? "

" Strong and brave, my boy," returned the old man.

It was quite a sight to see Mr. William shaking hands with his father, and patting him on the back, and rubbing him gently down with his hand, as if he could not possibly do enough to show an interest in him.

" What a wonderful man you are, father! How are you, father? Are you really pretty hearty, though? " said William, shaking hands with him again, and patting him again, and rubbing him gently down again.

" I never was fresher or stouter in my life, my boy."

" What a wonderful man you are, father! But that's exactly where it is," said Mr. William, with enthusiasm. " When I think of all that my father's gone through, and all the chances and changes, and sorrows and troubles, that have happened to him in the course of his long life, and under which his head has grown grey, and years upon years have gathered on it, I feel as if we couldn't do enough to honour the old gentleman, and make his old age easy. How are you, father? Are you really pretty well, though? "

Mr. William might never have left off repeating this inquiry, and shaking hands with him again, and patting him again, and rubbing him down again, if the old man had not espied the Chemist, whom until now he had not seen.

" I ask your pardon, Mr. Redlaw," said Philip, " but didn't know you were here, sir, or should have made less free. It reminds me, Mr. Redlaw, seeing you here on a Christmas morning, of the time when you was a student yourself, and worked so hard that you was backwards and forwards in our Library even at Christmas time. Ha, ha! I'm old enough to remember that; and I remember it right well, I do, though I'm eighty-seven. It was after you left here that my poor wife died. You remember my poor wife, Mr. Redlaw? "

The Chemist answered yes.

" Yes," said the old man. " She was a dear creetur.—I recollect you come here one Christmas morning with a young lady—I ask your pardon, Mr. Redlaw, but I think it was a sister you was very much attached to? "

The Chemist looked at him, and shook his head. "I had a sister," he said vacantly. He knew no more.

"One Christmas morning," pursued the old man, "that you come here with her—and it began to snow, and my wife invited the young lady to walk in, and sit by the fire that is always a-burning on Christmas Day in what used to be, before our ten poor gentlemen commuted, our great Dinner Hall. I was there, and I recollect, as I was stirring up the blaze for the young lady to warm her pretty feet by, she read the scroll out loud that is underneath that picter, 'Lord, keep my memory green!' She and my poor wife fell a-talking about it, and it's a strange thing to think of now, that they both said (both being so unlike to die) that it was a good prayer, and that it was one they would put up very earnestly, if they were called away young, with reference to those who were dearest to them. 'My brother,' says the young lady. 'My husband,' says my poor wife. 'Lord, keep his memory of me green, and do not let me be forgotten!' "

Tears more painful and more bitter than he had ever shed in all his life coursed down Redlaw's face. Philip, fully occupied in recalling his story, had not observed him until now, nor Milly's anxiety that he should not proceed.

"Philip," said Redlaw, laying his hand upon his arm, "I am a stricken man, on whom the hand of Providence has fallen heavily, although deservedly. You speak to me, my friend, of what I cannot follow; my memory is gone."

"Merciful Power!" cried the old man.

"I have lost my memory of sorrow, wrong, and trouble," said the Chemist; "and with that I have lost all man would remember."

To see old Philip's pity for him, to see him wheel his own great chair for him to rest in, and look down upon him with a solemn sense of his bereavement, was to know, in some degree, how precious to old age such recollections are.

The boy came running in, and ran to Milly.

"Here's the man," he said, "in the other room. *I* don't want *him*."

"What man does he mean?" asked Mr. William.

"Hush!" said Milly.

Obedient to a sign from her, he and his old father softly
withdrew. As they went out, unnoticed, Redlaw beckoned
to the boy to come to him.

" I like the woman best," he answered, holding to her
skirts.

" You are right," said Redlaw, with a faint smile. " But
you needn't fear to come to me. I am gentler than I was.
Of all the world, to you, poor child! "

The boy still held back at first; but yielding little by little
to her urging, he consented to approach, and even to sit
down at his feet. As Redlaw laid his hand upon the shoulder
of the child, looking on him with compassion and a fellow-
feeling, he put out his other hand to Milly. She stooped
down on that side of him, so that she could look into his
face, and after silence, said:

" Mr. Redlaw, may I speak to you? "

" Yes," he answered, fixing his eyes upon her. " Your
voice and music are the same to me."

" May I ask you something? "

" What you will."

" Do you remember what I said when I knocked at your
door last night? About one who was your friend once, and
who stood on the verge of destruction? "

" Yes, I remember," he said, with some hesitation.

" Do you understand it? "

He·smoothed the boy's hair, looking at her fixedly the
while, and shook his head.

" This person," said Milly, in her clear, soft voice, which
her mild eyes, looking at him, made clearer and softer, " I
found soon afterwards. I went back to the house, and, with
Heaven's help, traced him. I was not too soon. A very
little, and I should have been too late."

He took his hand from the boy, and laying it on the back
of that hand of hers, whose timid and yet earnest touch
addressed him no less appealingly than her voice and eyes,
looked more intently on her.

" He *is* the father of Mr. Edmund, the young gentleman
we saw just now. His real name is Langford. You recollect
the name? "

" I recollect the name."

" And the man? "

" No, not the man. Did he ever wrong me? "

" Yes! "

" Ah! Then it's hopeless—hopeless."

He shook his head, and softly beat upon the hand he held, as though mutely asking her commiseration.

" I did not go to Mr. Edmund last night," said Milly— " You will listen to me just the same as if you did remember all? "

" To every syllable you say."

"—Both because I did not know then that this really was his father, and because I was fearful of the effect of such intelligence upon him after his illness, if it should be. Since I have known who this person is, I have not gone either; but that is for another reason. He has long been separated from his wife and son—has been a stranger to his home almost from this son's infancy, I learn from him—and has abandoned and deserted what he should have held most dear. In all that time he has been falling from the state of a gentle-man more and more, until——" She rose up hastily, and going out for a moment, returned, accompanied by the wreck that Redlaw had beheld last night.

" Do you know me? " asked the Chemist.

" I should be glad," returned the other—" and that is an unwonted word for me. to use—if I could answer no."

The Chemist looked at the man, standing in self-abasement and degradation before him, and would have looked longer, in an ineffectual struggle for enlightenment, but that Milly resumed her late position by his side, and attracted his atten-tive gaze to her own face.

" See how low he is sunk! how lost he is! " she whispered, stretching out her arm towards him, without looking from the Chemist's face. " If you could remember all that is con-nected with him, do you not think it would move your pity to reflect that one you ever loved (do not let us mind how long ago, or in what belief that he has forfeited) should come to this? "

" I hope it would," he answered. " I believe it would."

His eyes wandered to the figure standing near the door, but came back speedily to her, on whom he gazed intently, as if he strove to learn some lesson from every tone of her voice and every beam of her eyes.

" I have no learning, and you have much," said Milly; " I am not used to think, and you are always thinking. May

I tell you why it seems to me a good thing for us to remember wrong that has been done us? "

" Yes."

" That we may forgive it."

" Pardon me, great Heaven! " said Redlaw, lifting up his eyes, " for having thrown away thine own high attribute! "

" And if," said Milly, " if your memory should one day be restored, as we will hope and pray it may be, would it not be a blessing to you to recall at once a wrong and its forgiveness? "

He looked at the figure by the door, and fastened his attentive eyes on her again: a ray of clearer light appeared to him to shine into his mind from her bright face.

" He cannot go to his abandoned home. He does not seek to go there. He knows that he could only carry shame and trouble to those he has so cruelly neglected; and that the best reparation he can make them now is to avoid them. A very little money, carefully bestowed, would remove him to some distant place, where he might live and do no wrong, and make such atonement as is left within his power for the wrong he has done. To the unfortunate lady who is his wife, and to his son, this would be the best and kindest boon that their best friend could give them—one, too, that they need never know of; and to him, shattered in reputation, mind, and body, it might be salvation."

He took her head between his hands and kissed it, and said, " It shall be done. I trust to you to do it for me, now and secretly; and to tell him that I would forgive him, if I were so happy as to know for what."

As she rose, and turned her beaming face towards the fallen man, implying that her mediation had been successful, he advanced a step, and without raising his eyes, addressed himself to Redlaw.

" You are so generous," he said—" you ever were—that you will try to banish your rising sense of retribution in the spectacle that is before you. I do not try to banish it from myself, Redlaw. If you can, believe me."

The Chemist entreated Milly, by a gesture, to come nearer to him; and, as he listened, looked in her face, as if to find in it the clue to what he heard.

" I am too decayed a wretch to make professions; I recollect my own career too well, to array any such before

you. But from the day on which I made my first step downward, in dealing falsely by you, I have gone down with a
certain, steady, doomed progression. That, I say."

Redlaw, keeping her close at his side, turned his face
towards the speaker, and there was sorrow in it. Something
like mournful recognition too.

" I might have been another man, my life might have been
another life, if I had avoided that first fatal step. I don't
know that it would have been. I claim nothing for the
possibility. Your sister is at rest, and better than she could
have been with me, if I had continued even what you thought
me—even what I once supposed myself to be."

Redlaw made a hasty motion with his hand, as if he would
have put that subject on one side.

" I speak," the other went on, " like a man taken from the
grave. I should have made my own grave, last night, had
it not been for this blessed hand."

" Oh, dear, he likes me too! " sobbed Milly, under her
breath. " That's another! "

" I could not have put myself in your way, last night, even
for bread. But, to-day, my recollection of what has been
between us is so strongly stirred, and is presented to me, I
don't know how, so vividly, that I have dared to come at her
suggestion, and to take your bounty, and to thank you for
it, and to beg you, Redlaw, in your dying hour, to be as
merciful to me in your thoughts as you are in your
deeds."

He turned towards the door, and stopped a moment on his
way forth.

" I hope my son may interest you, for his mother's sake.
I hope he may deserve to do so. Unless my life should be
preserved a long time, and I should know that I have not
misused your aid, I shall never look upon him more."

Going out, he raised his eyes to Redlaw for the first time.
Redlaw, whose steadfast gaze was fixed upon him, dreamily
held out his hand. He returned and touched it—little more
—with both his own; and bending down his head, went
slowly out.

In the few moments that elapsed, while Milly silently took
him to the gate, the Chemist dropped into his chair, and
covered his face with his hands. Seeing him thus, when she
came back, accompanied by her husband and his father (who

were both greatly concerned for him), she avoided disturbing him, or permitting him to be disturbed; and kneeled
down near the chair to put some warm clothing on the
boy.

"That's exactly where it is. That's what I always say,
father!" exclaimed her admiring husband. "There's a
motherly feeling in Mrs. William's breast that must and will
have went!"

"Ay, ay," said the old man, "you're right. My son
William's right!"

"It happens all for the best, Milly dear, no doubt," said
Mr. William tenderly, "that we have no children of our
own; and yet I sometimes wish you had one to love and
cherish. Our little dead child that you built such hopes upon,
and that never breathed the breath of life—it has made you
quiet-like, Milly."

"I am very happy in the recollection of it, William dear,"
she answered. "I think of it every day."

"I was afraid you thought of it a good deal."

"Don't say afraid; it is a comfort to me; it speaks to me
in so many ways. The innocent thing that never lived on
earth, is like an angel to me, William."

"You are like an angel to father and me," said Mr. William
softly. "I know that."

"When I think of all those hopes I built upon it, and the
many times I sat and pictured to myself the little smiling
face upon my bosom that never lay there, and the sweet
eyes turned up to mine that never opened to the light," said
Milly, "I can feel a greater tenderness, I think, for all the
disappointed hopes, in which there is no harm. When I see
a beautiful child in its fond mother's arms, I love it all the
better, thinking that my child might have been like that, and
might have made my heart as proud and happy."

Redlaw raised his head, and looked towards her.

"All through life, it seems by me," she continued, "to tell
me something. For poor neglected children, my little child
pleads as if it were alive, and had a voice I knew with which
to speak to me. When I hear of youth in suffering or shame,
I think that my child might have come to that, perhaps, and
that God took it from me in His mercy. Even in age and
grey hair, such as father's, it is present, saying that it, too,
might have lived to be old, long and long after you and I

were gone, and to have needed the respect and love of younger people."

Her quiet voice was quieter than ever, as she took her husband's arm, and laid her head against it.

"Children love me so, that sometimes I half fancy—it's a silly fancy, William—they have some way I don't know of, of feeling for my little child, and me, and understanding why their love is precious to me. If I have been quiet since, I have been more happy, William, in a hundred ways. Not least happy, dear, in this—that even when my little child was born and dead but a few days, and I was weak and sorrowful, and could not help grieving a little, the thought arose, that if I tried to lead a good life, I should meet in Heaven a bright creature, who would call me Mother!"

Redlaw fell upon his knees with a loud cry.

"O Thou," he said, "who, through the teaching of pure love, hast graciously restored me to the memory which was the memory of Christ upon the Cross, and of all the good who perished in His cause, receive my thanks, and bless her!"

Then he folded her to his heart; and Milly, sobbing more than ever, cried, as she laughed, "He is come back to himself! He likes me very much indeed, too. Oh, dear, dear, dear me, here's another!"

Then the student entered, leading by the hand a lovely girl who was afraid to come. And Redlaw, so changed towards him, seeing in him and in his youthful choice the softened shadow of that chastening passage in his own life, to which, as to a shady tree, the dove so long imprisoned in his solitary ark might fly for rest and company, fell upon his neck, entreating them to be his children.

Then, as Christmas is a time in which, of all times in the year, the memory of every remediable sorrow, wrong, and trouble in the world around us, should be active with us, not less than our own experiences, for all good, he laid his hand upon the boy, and, silently calling Him to witness who laid His hand on children in old time, rebuking, in the majesty of His prophetic knowledge, those who kept them from Him, vowed to protect him, teach him, and reclaim him.

Then he gave his right hand cheerily to Philip, and said that they would that day hold a Christmas dinner in what used to be, before the ten poor gentlemen commuted, their great Dinner Hall; and that they would bid to it as many of that Swidger family (who, his son had told him, were so numerous that they might join hands and make a ring round England) as could be brought together on so short a notice.

And it was that day done. There were so many Swidgers there, grown up and children, that an attempt to state them in round numbers might engender doubts, in the distrustful, of the veracity of this history. Therefore the attempt shall not be made. But there they were, by dozens and scores. And there was good news and good hope there, ready for them, of George, who had been visited again by his father and brother, and by Milly, and again left in a quiet sleep. There, present at the dinner, too, were the Tetterbys, including young Adolphus, who arrived in his prismatic comforter, in good time for the beef. Johnny and the baby were too late, of course, and came in all on one side, the one exhausted, the other in a supposed state of double-tooth; but that was customary, and not alarming.

It was sad to see the child who had no name or lineage watching the other children as they played, not knowing how to talk with them, or sport with them, and more strange to the ways of childhood than a rough dog. It was sad, though in a different way, to see what an instinctive knowledge the youngest children there had of his being different from all the rest, and how they made timid approaches to him with soft words and touches, and with little presents, that he might not be unhappy. But he kept by Milly, and began to love her—that was another, as she said!—and, as they all liked her dearly, they were glad of that, and when they saw him peeping at them from behind her chair, they were pleased that he was so close to it.

All this the Chemist, sitting with the student and his bride that was to be, and Philip, and the rest, saw.

Some people have said since, that he only thought what has been herein set down; others, that he read it in the fire, one winter night about the twilight time; others, that the Ghost was but the representation of his gloomy thoughts, and Milly the embodiment of his better wisdom. *I* say nothing.

—Except this. That as they were assembled in the old Hall, by no other light than that of a great fire (having dined early), the shadows once more stole out of their hiding-places, and danced about the room, showing the children marvellous shapes and faces on the walls, and gradually changing what was real and familiar there to what was wild and magical. But that there was one thing in the Hall, to which the eyes of Redlaw, and of Milly and her husband, and of the old man, and of the student, and his bride that was to be, were often turned, which the shadows did not obscure or change. Deepened in its gravity by the firelight, and gazing from the darkness of the panelled wall like life, the sedate face in the portrait, with the beard and ruff, looked down at them from under its verdant wreath of holly, as they looked up at it; and, clear and plain below, as if a voice had uttered them, were the words:

"Lord, keep my memory green!"

AMBROSE BIERCE

MOXON'S MASTER

"ARE you serious? Do you really believe that a machine thinks? "

I got no immediate reply; Moxon was apparently intent upon the coals in the grate, touching them deftly here and there with the fire-poker till they signified a sense of his attention by a brighter glow. For several weeks I had been observing in him a growing habit of delay in answering even the most trivial of commonplace questions. His air, however, was that of preoccupation rather than deliberation: one might have said that he had " something on his mind."

Presently he said:

"What is a ' machine '? The word has been variously defined. Here is one definition from a popular dictionary: ' Any instrument or organisation by which power is applied and made effective, or a desired effect produced.' Well, then, is not a man a machine? And you will admit that he thinks —or thinks he thinks."

"If you do not wish to answer my question," I said, rather testily, " why not say so? All that you say is mere evasion. You know well enough that when I say ' machine ' I do not mean a man, but something that man has made and controls."

"When it does not control him," he said, rising abruptly and looking out of a window, whence nothing was visible in the blackness of a stormy night. A moment later he turned about and with a smile said: " I beg your pardon; I had no thought of evasion. I considered the dictionary man's unconscious testimony suggestive and worth something in the discussion. I can give your question a direct answer easily enough: I do believe that a machine thinks about the work that it is doing."

That was direct enough, certainly. It was not altogether pleasing, for it tended to confirm a sad suspicion that Moxon's devotion to study and work in his machine-shop had not been good for him. I knew, for one thing, that he suffered from insomnia, and that is no light affliction. Had it affected his

mind? His reply to my question seemed to me then evidence
that it had; perhaps I should think differently about it now.
I was younger then, and among the blessings that are not
denied to youth is ignorance. Incited by that great stimulant
to controversy, I said:

" And what, pray, does it think with—in the absence of
a brain? "

The reply, coming with less than his customary delay, took
his favourite form of counter-interrogation:

" With what does a plant think—in the absence of a
brain? "

" Ah, plants also belong to the philosopher class! I should
be pleased to know some of their conclusions; you may
omit the premises."

" Perhaps," he replied apparently unaffected by my foolish
irony, " you may be able to infer their convictions from
their acts. I will spare you the familiar examples of the
sensitive mimosa, the several insectivorous flowers and those
whose stamens bend down and shake their pollen upon the
entering bee in order that he may fertilise their distant mates.
But observe this. In an open spot in my garden I planted
a climbing vine. When it was barely above the surface I
set a stake into the soil a yard away. The vine at once made
for it, but as it was about to reach it after several days I
removed it a few feet. The vine at once altered its course,
making an acute angle, and again made for the stake. This
manœuvre was repeated several times, but finally, as if discouraged, the vine abandoned the pursuit and ignoring further attempts to divert it, travelled to a small tree, farther
away, which it climbed.

" Roots of the eucalyptus will prolong themselves incredibly
in search of moisture. A well-known horticulturist relates
that one entered an old drain pipe and followed it until it
came to a break, where a section of the pipe had been removed
to make way for a stone wall that had been built across its
course. The root left the drain and followed the wall until it
found an opening where a stone had fallen out. It crept
through, and following the other side of the wall back to the
drain, entered the unexplored part and resumed its journey."

" And all this? "

" Can you miss the significance of it? It shows the consciousness of plants. It proves that they think."

"Even if it did—what then? We were speaking, not of plants, but of machines. They may be composed partly of wood—wood that has no longer vitality—or wholly of metal. Is thought an attribute also of the mineral kingdom?"

"How else do you explain the phenomena, for example, of crystallisation?"

"I do not explain them."

"Because you cannot without affirming what you wish to deny, namely, intelligent co-operation among the constituent elements of the crystals. When soldiers form lines, or hollow squares, you call it reason. When wild geese in flight take the form of a letter V you say instinct. When the homogeneous atoms of a mineral, moving freely in solution, arrange themselves into shapes mathematically perfect, or particles of frozen moisture into the symmetrical and beautiful forms of snowflakes, you have nothing to say. You have not even invented a name to conceal your heroic unreason."

Moxon was speaking with unusual animation and earnestness. As he paused I heard in an adjoining room known to me as his "machine-shop," which no one but himself was permitted to enter, a singular thumping sound, as of someone pounding upon a table with an open hand. Moxon heard it at the same moment and, visibly agitated, rose and hurriedly passed into the room whence it came. I thought it odd that anyone else should be in there, and my interest in my friend —with doubtless a touch of unwarrantable curiosity—led me to listen intently, though, I am happy to say, not at the keyhole. There were confused sounds, as of a struggle or scuffle; the floor shook. I distinctly heard hard breathing and a hoarse whisper which said, "Damn you!" Then all was silent, and presently Moxon reappeared and said, with a rather sorry smile:

"Pardon me for leaving you so abruptly. I have a machine in there that lost its temper and cut up rough."

Fixing my eyes steadily upon his left cheek, which was traversed by four parallel excoriations showing blood, I said:

"How would it do to trim its nails?"

I could have spared myself the jest; he gave it no attention, but seated himself in the chair that he had left and resumed the interrupted monologue as if nothing had occurred:

"Doubtless you do not hold with those (I need not name

them to a man of your reading) who have taught that all matter is sentient, that every atom is a living, feeling, conscious being. *I* do. There is no such thing as dead, inert matter: it is all alive; all instinct with force, actual and potential; all sensitive to the same forces in its environment, and susceptible to the contagion of higher and subtler ones residing in such superior organisms as it may be brought into relation with, as those of man when he is fashioning it into an instrument of his will. It absorbs something of his intelligence and purpose—more of them in proportion to the complexity of the resulting machine and that of its work.

"Do you happen to recall Herbert Spencer's definition of 'Life'? I read it thirty years ago. He may have altered it afterwards, for anything I know, but in all that time I have been unable to think of a single word that could profitably be changed or added or removed. It seems to me not only the best definition, but the only possible one.

"'Life,' he says, 'is a definite combination of heterogeneous changes, both simultaneous and successive, in correspondence with external coexistences and sequences.'"

"That defines the phenomenon," I said, "but gives no hint of its cause."

"That," he replied, "is all that any definition can do. As Mill points out, we know nothing of cause except as an antecedent—nothing of effect except as a consequent. Of certain phenomena one never occurs without another, which is dissimilar: the first in point of time we call cause, the second, effect. One who had many times seen a rabbit pursued by a dog, and had never seen rabbits and dogs otherwise, would think the rabbit the cause of the dog.

"But I fear," he added, laughing naturally enough, "that my rabbit is leading me a long way from the track of my legitimate quarry: I'm indulging in the pleasure of the chase for its own sake. What I want you to observe is that in Herbert Spencer's definition of 'life' the activity of a machine is included—there is nothing in the definition that is not applicable to it. According to this sharpest of observers and deepest of thinkers, if a man during his period of activity is alive, so is a machine when in operation. As an inventor and constructor of machines I know that to be true."

Moxon was silent for a long time, gazing absently into

the fire. It was growing late and I thought it time to be going, but somehow I did not like the notion of leaving him in that isolated house, all alone except for the presence of some person of whose nature my conjectures could go no further than that it was unfriendly, perhaps malign. Leaning towards him and looking earnestly into his eyes while making a motion with my hand through the door of his workshop, I said:

" Moxon, whom have you in there? "

Somewhat to my surprise he laughed lightly and answered without hesitation:

" Nobody; the incident that you have in mind was caused by my folly in leaving a machine in action with nothing to act upon, while I undertook the interminable task of enlightening your understanding. Do you happen to know that Consciousness is the creature of Rhythm? "

" Oh, bother them both! " I replied, rising and laying hold of my overcoat. " I'm going to wish you good night; and I'll add the hope that the machine which you inadvertently left in action will have her gloves on the next time you think it needful to stop her."

Without waiting to observe the effect of my shot I left the house.

Rain was falling, and the darkness was intense. In the sky beyond the crest of a hill towards which I groped my way along precarious plank sidewalks and across miry, unpaved streets I could see the faint glow of the city's lights, but behind me nothing was visible but a single window of Moxon's house. It glowed with what seemed to me a mysterious and fateful meaning. I knew it was an uncurtained aperture in my friend's " machine-shop," and I had little doubt that he had resumed the studies interrupted by his duties as my instructor in mechanical consciousness and the fatherhood of Rhythm. Odd, and in some degree humorous, as his convictions seemed to me at that time, I could not wholly divest myself of the feeling that they had some tragic relation to his life and character—perhaps to his destiny —although I no longer entertained the notion that they were the vagaries of a disordered mind. Whatever might be thought of his views, his exposition of them was too logical for that. Over and over, his last words came back to me: " Consciousness is the creature of Rhythm." Bald and terse

as the statement was, I now found it infinitely alluring.
At each recurrence it broadened in meaning and deepened
in suggestion. Why, here (I thought) is something upon
which to found a philosophy. If Consciousness is the product
of Rhythm all things *are* conscious, for all have motion, and
all motion is rhythmic. I wondered if Moxon knew the
significance and breadth of his thought—the scope of this
momentous generalisation; or had he arrived at his philosophic
faith by the tortuous and uncertain road of observation?

That faith was then new to me, and all Moxon's expound-
ing had failed to make me a convert; but now it seemed as
if a great light shone about me, like that which fell upon
Saul of Tarsus; and out there in the storm and darkness and
solitude I experienced what Lewes calls " the endless variety
and excitement of philosophic thought." I exulted in a new
sense of knowledge, a new pride of reason. My feet seemed
hardly to touch the earth; it was as if I were uplifted and
borne through the air by invisible wings.

Yielding to an impulse to seek further light from him
whom I now recognised as my master and guide, I had unconsciously turned about, and almost before I was aware of
having done so, found myself again at Moxon's door. I was
drenched with rain, but felt no discomfort. Unable in my
excitement to find the door-bell I instinctively tried the knob.
It turned and, entering, I mounted the stairs to the room
that I had so recently left. All was dark and silent; Moxon,
as I had supposed, was in the adjoining room—the " machine-
shop." Groping along the wall until I found the communicating door, I knocked loudly several times, but got no response, which I attributed to the uproar outside, for the
wind was blowing a gale and dashing the rain against the
thin walls in sheets. The drumming upon the shingle roof
spanning the unceilinged room was loud and incessant.

I had never been invited into the machine-shop—had, indeed, been denied admittance, as had all others, with one
exception, a skilled metal worker, of whom no one knew
anything except that his name was Haley and his habit
silence. But in my spiritual exaltation, discretion and civility
were alike forgotten, and I opened the door. What I saw
took all philosophical speculation out of me in short order.

Moxon sat facing me at the farther side of a small table

upon which a single candle made all the light that was in the room. Opposite him, his back towards me, sat another person. On the table between the two was a chess-board; the men were playing. I knew little of chess, but as only a few pieces were on the board it was obvious that the game was near its close. Moxon was intensely interested—not so much, it seemed to me, in the game as in his antagonist, upon whom he had fixed so intent a look that, standing though I did directly in the line of his vision, I was altogether unobserved. His face was ghastly white, and his eyes glittered like diamonds. Of his antagonist I had only a back view, but that was sufficient; I should not have cared to see his face.

He was apparently not more than five feet in height, with proportions suggesting those of a gorilla—a tremendous breadth of shoulders, thick, short neck and broad, squat head, which had a tangled growth of black hair and was topped with a crimson fez. A tunic of the same colour, belted tightly to the waist, reached the seat—apparently a box—upon which he sat; his legs and feet were not seen. His left forearm appeared to rest in his lap; he moved his pieces with his right hand, which seemed disproportionately long.

I had shrunk back and now stood a little to one side of the doorway and in shadow. If Moxon had looked farther than the face of his opponent he could have observed nothing now, except that the door was open. Something forbade me either to enter or to retire, a feeling—I know not how it came—that I was in the presence of an imminent tragedy and might serve my friend by remaining. With a scarcely conscious rebellion against the indelicacy of the act, I remained.

The play was rapid. Moxon hardly glanced at the board before making his moves, and to my unskilled eye seemed to move the piece most convenient to his hand, his motions in doing so being quick, nervous and lacking in precision. The response of his antagonist, while equally prompt in the inception, was made with a slow, uniform, mechanical and, I thought, somewhat theatrical movement of the arm, that was a sore trial to my patience. There was something unearthly about it all, and I caught myself shuddering. But I was wet and cold.

Two or three times after moving a piece the stranger

slightly inclined his head, and each time I observed that
Moxon shifted his king. All at once the thought came to
me that the man was dumb. And then that he was a machine
—an automaton chess-player! Then I remembered that
Moxon had once spoken to me of having invented such a
piece of mechanism, though I did not understand that it
had actually been constructed. Was all this talk about the
consciousness and intelligence of machines merely a prelude
to eventual exhibition of this device—only a trick to in-
tensify the effect of its mechanical action upon me in my
ignorance of its secret?

A fine end this, of all my intellectual transports—my
" endless variety and excitement of philosophic thought "!
I was about to retire in disgust when something occurred to
hold my curiosity. I observed a shrug of the thing's great
shoulders, as if it were irritated: and so natural was this—
so entirely human—that in my new view of the matter it
startled me. Nor was that all, for a moment later it struck
the table sharply with its clenched hand. At that gesture
Moxon seemed even more startled than I: he pushed his chair
a little backward, as in alarm.

Presently Moxon, whose play it was, raised his hand high
above the board, pounced upon one of his pieces like a
sparrow-hawk, and with the exclamation " checkmate! "
rose quickly to his feet and stepped behind his chair. The
automaton sat motionless.

The wind had now gone down, but I heard, at lessening
intervals and progressively louder, the rumble and roll of
thunder. In the pauses between I now became conscious
of a low humming or buzzing which, like the thunder, grew
momentarily louder and more distinct. It seemed to come
from the body of the automaton, and was unmistakably a
whirring of wheels. It gave me the impression of a disordered mechanism which had escaped the repressive and
regulating action of some controlling part—an effect such
as might be expected if a pawl should be jostled from the
teeth of a ratchet-wheel. But before I had time for much
conjecture as to its nature my attention was taken by the
strange motions of the automaton itself. A slight but continuous convulsion appeared to have possession of it. In body
and head, it shook like a man with palsy or an ague chill, and
the motion augmented every moment until the entire figure

was in violent agitation. Suddenly it sprang to its feet and
with a movement almost too quick for the eye to follow
shot forward across table and chair, with both arms thrust
forth to their full length—the posture and lunge of a diver.
Moxon tried to throw himself backward out of reach, but he
was too late: I saw the horrible thing's hands close upon
his throat, his own clutch its wrists. Then the table was
overturned, the candle thrown to the floor and extinguished,
and all was black dark. But the noise of the struggle was
dreadfully distinct, and most terrible of all were the raucous,
squawking sounds made by the strangled man's efforts to
breathe. Guided by the infernal hubbub, I sprang to the
rescue of my friend, but had hardly taken a stride in the
darkness when the whole room blazed with a blinding white
light that burned into my brain and heart and memory a
vivid picture of the combatants on the floor, Moxon underneath, his throat still in the clutch of those iron hands, his
head forced backward, his eyes protruding, his mouth wide
open and his tongue thrust out; and—horrible contrast!—
upon the painted face of his assassin an expression of tranquil
and profound thought, as in the solution of a problem in
chess! This I observed, then all was blackness and silence.

Three days later I recovered consciousness in a hospital.
As the memory of that tragic night slowly evolved in my
ailing brain I recognised in my attendant Moxon's confi-
dential workman, Haley. Responding to a look he approached, smiling.

" Tell me about it," I managed to say, faintly—" all about
it."

" Certainly," he said; " you were carried unconscious from
a burning house—Moxon's. Nobody knows how you came
to be there. You may have to do a little explaining. The
origin of the fire is a bit mysterious, too. My own notion
is that the house was struck by lightning."

" And Moxon? "

" Buried yesterday—what was left of him."

Apparently this reticent person could unfold himself on
occasion. When imparting shocking intelligence to the sick
he was affable enough. After some moments of the keenest
mental suffering I ventured to ask another question:

" Who rescued me? "

" Well, if that interests you—I did."

"Thank you, Mr. Haley, and may God bless you for it. Did you rescue, also, that charming product of your skill, the automaton chess-player that murdered its inventor?"

The man was silent a long time, looking away from me. Presently he turned and gravely said:

"Do you know that?"

"I do," I replied; "I saw it done."

That was many years ago. If asked to-day I should answer less confidently.

THE MIDDLE TOE OF THE RIGHT FOOT

I

IT is well known that the old Manton house is haunted. In all the rural district near about, and even in the town of Marshall, a mile away, not one person of unbiassed mind entertains a doubt of it; incredulity is confined to those opinionated people who will be called " cranks " as soon as the useful word shall have penetrated the intellectual demesne of the Marshall *Advance*. The evidence that the house is haunted is of two kinds: the testimony of disinterested witnesses who have had ocular proof, and that of the house itself. The former may be disregarded and ruled out on any of the various grounds of objection which may be urged against it by the ingenious; but facts within the observation of all are fundamental and controlling.

In the first place, the Manton house has been unoccupied by mortals for more than ten years, and with its outbuildings is slowly falling into decay—a circumstance which in itself the judicious will hardly venture to ignore. It stands a little way off the loneliest reach of the Marshall and Harriston road, in an opening which was once a farm and is still disfigured with strips of rotting fence and half covered with brambles overrunning a stony and sterile soil long unacquainted with the plough. The house itself is in tolerably good condition, though badly weather-stained and in dire need of attention from the glazier, the smaller male population of the region having attested in the manner of its kind its disapproval of dwellings without dwellers. The house is two stories in height, nearly square, its front pierced by a single doorway flanked on each side by a window boarded up to the very top. Corresponding windows above, not protected, serve to admit light and rain to the rooms of the upper floor. Grass and weeds grow pretty rankly all about, and a few shade trees, somewhat the worse for wind and leaning all in one direction, seem to be making a concerted

effort to run away. In short, as the Marshall town humourist
explained in the columns of the *Advance*, " the proposition
that the Manton house is badly haunted is the only logical
conclusion from the premises." The fact that in this dwelling Mr. Manton thought it expedient one night some ten
years ago to rise and cut the throats of his wife and two
small children, removing at once to another part of the
country, has no doubt done its share in directing public
attention to the fitness of the place for supernatural
phenomena.

To this house, one summer evening, came four men in a
waggon. Three of them promptly alighted, and the one who
had been driving hitched the team to the only remaining post
of what had been a fence. The fourth remained seated in
the waggon. " Come," said one of his companions, approaching him, while the others moved away in the direction of the
dwelling—" this is the place."

The man addressed was deathly pale and trembled visibly.
" By God! " he said harshly, " this is a trick, and it looks to
me as if you were in it."

" Perhaps I am," the other said, looking him straight in the
face and speaking in a tone which had something of contempt
in it. " You will remember, however, that the choice of place
was, with your own assent, left to the other side. Of course
if you are afraid of spooks——"

" I am afraid of nothing," the man interrupted with
another oath, and sprang to the ground. The two then
joined the others at the door, which one of them had already
opened with some difficulty, caused by rust of lock and
hinge. All entered. Inside it was dark, but the man who
had unlocked the door produced a candle and matches and
made a light. He then unlocked a door on their right as they
stood in the passage. This gave them entrance to a large,
square room, which the candle but dimly lighted. The floor
had a thick carpeting of dust, which partly muffled their
footfalls. Cobwebs were in the angles of the walls and
depended from the ceiling like strips of rotting lace, making
undulatory movements in the disturbed air. The room had
two windows in adjoining sides, but from neither could anything be seen except the rough inner surfaces of boards a few
inches from the glass. There was no fireplace, no furniture;
there was nothing. Besides the cobwebs and the dust, the

four men were the only objects there which were not a part of the architecture. Strange enough they looked in the yellow light of the candle. The one who had so reluctantly alighted was especially " spectacular "—he might have been called sensational. He was of middle age, heavily built, deep-chested and broad-shouldered. Looking at his figure, one would have said that he had a giant's strength; at his face, that he would use it like a giant. He was clean shaven, his hair rather closely cropped and grey. His low forehead was seamed with wrinkles above the eyes, and over the nose these became vertical. The heavy black brows followed the same law, saved from meeting only by an upward turn at what would otherwise have been the point of contact. Deeply sunken beneath these, glowed in the obscure light a pair of eyes of uncertain colour, but, obviously enough, too small. There was something forbidding in their expression, which was not bettered by the cruel mouth and wide jaw. The nose was well enough, as noses go; one does not expect much of noses. All that was sinister in the man's face seemed accentuated by an unnatural pallor—he appeared altogether blood-less.

The appearance of the other men was sufficiently common-place: they were such persons as one meets and forgets that he met. All were younger than the man described, between whom and the eldest of the others, who stood apart, there was apparently no kindly feeling. They avoided looking at one another.

" Gentlemen," said the man holding the candle and keys, " I believe everything is right. Are you ready, Mr. Rosser? "

The man standing apart from the group bowed and smiled.

" And you, Mr. Grossmith? "

The heavy man bowed and scowled.

" You will please remove your outer clothing."

Their hats, coats, waistcoats, and neckwear were soon removed and thrown outside the door, in the passage. The man with the candle now nodded, and the fourth man—he who had urged Mr. Grossmith to leave the waggon—produced from the pocket of his overcoat two long, murderous-looking bowie knives, which he drew from the scabbards.

" They are exactly alike," he said, presenting one to each

of the two principals—for by this time the dullest observer would have understood the nature of this meeting. It was to be a duel to the death.

Each combatant took a knife, examined it critically near the candle and tested the strength of blade and handle across his lifted knee. Their persons were then searched in turn, each by the second of the other.

"If it is agreeable to you, Mr. Grossmith," said the man holding the light, "you will place yourself in that corner."

He indicated the angle of the room farthest from the door, to which Grossmith retired, his second parting from him with a grasp of the hand which had nothing of cordiality in it. In the angle nearest the door Mr. Rosser stationed himself, and, after a whispered consultation, his second left him, joining the other near the door. At that moment the candle was suddenly extinguished, leaving all in profound darkness. This may have been done by a draught from the open door; whatever the cause, the effect was appalling!

"Gentlemen," said a voice which sounded strangely unfamiliar in the altered condition affecting the relations of the senses, "gentlemen, you will not move until you hear the closing of the outer door."

A sound of trampling ensued, the closing of the inner door; and finally the outer one closed with a concussion which shook the entire building.

A few minutes later a belated farmer's boy met a waggon which was being driven furiously toward the town of Marshall. He declared that behind the two figures on the front seat stood a third with its hands upon the bowed shoulders of the others, who appeared to struggle vainly to free themselves from its grasp. This figure, unlike the others, was clad in white, and had undoubtedly boarded the wagon as it passed the haunted house. As the lad could boast a considerable former experience with the supernatural thereabout, his word had the weight justly due to the testimony of an expert. The story eventually appeared in the *Advance,* with some slight literary embellishments and a concluding intimation that the gentlemen referred to would be allowed the use of the paper's columns for their version of the night's adventure. But the privilege remained without a claimant.

II

THE events which led up to this " duel in the dark " were simple enough. One evening three young men of the town of Marshall were sitting in a quiet corner of the porch of the village hotel, smoking and discussing such matters as three educated young men of a Southern village would naturally find interesting. Their names were King, Sancher, and Rosser. At a little distance, within easy hearing but taking no part in the conversation, sat a fourth. He was a stranger to the others. They merely knew that on his arrival by the stage coach that afternoon he had written in the hotel register the name Robert Grossmith. He had not been observed to speak to anyone except the hotel clerk. He seemed, indeed, singularly fond of his own company—or, as the *personnel* of the *Advance* expressed it, " grossly addicted to evil associations." But then it should be said in justice to the stranger that the *personnel* was himself of a too convivial disposition fairly to judge one differently gifted, and had, moreover, experienced a slight rebuff in an effort at an " interview."

" I hate any kind of deformity in a woman," said King, " whether natural or—or acquired. I have a theory that any physical defect has its correlative mental and moral defect."

" I infer, then," said Rosser, gravely, " that a lady lacking the advantage of a nose would find the struggle to become Mrs. King an arduous enterprise."

" Of course you may put it that way," was the reply; " but, seriously, I once threw over a most charming girl on learning, quite accidentally, that she had suffered amputation of a toe. My conduct was brutal, if you like, but if I had married that girl I should have been miserable and should have made her so."

" Whereas," said Sancher, with a light laugh, " by marrying a gentleman of more liberal views she escaped with a cut throat."

" Ah, you know to whom I refer! Yes, she married Manton, but I don't know about his liberality; I'm not sure but he cut her throat because he discovered that she lacked that excellent thing in woman, the middle toe of the right foot."

" Look at that chap! " said Rosser in a low voice, his eyes fixed upon the stranger.

That person was obviously listening intently to the conversation.

"That's an easy one," Rosser replied, rising. "Sir," he continued, addressing the stranger, "I think it would be better if you would remove your chair to the other end of the verandah. The presence of gentlemen is evidently an unfamiliar situation to you."

The man sprang to his feet and strode forward with clenched hands, his face white with rage. All were now standing. Sancher stepped between the belligerents.

"You are hasty and unjust," he said to Rosser; "this gentleman has done nothing to deserve such language."

But Rosser would not withdraw a word. By the custom of the country and the time, there could be but one outcome to the quarrel.

"I demand the satisfaction due to a gentleman," said the stranger, who had become more calm. "I have not an acquaintance in this region. Perhaps you, sir," bowing to Sancher, "will be kind enough to represent me in this matter."

Sancher accepted the trust—somewhat reluctantly, it must be confessed, for the man's appearance and manner were not at all to his liking. King, who during the colloquy had hardly removed his eyes from the stranger's face, and had not spoken a word, consented with a nod to act for Rosser, and the upshot of it was that, the principals having retired, a meeting was arranged for the next evening. The nature of the arrangements has been already disclosed. The duel with knives in a dark room was once a commoner feature of Southwestern life than it is likely to be again. How thin a veneering of "chivalry" covered the essential brutality of the code under which such encounters were possible, we shall see.

III

IN the blaze of a midsummer noonday, the old Manton house was hardly true to its traditions. It was of the earth, earthy. The sunshine caressed it warmly and affectionately, with evident unconsciousness of its bad reputation. The grass greening all the expanse in its front seemed to grow, not rankly, but with a natural and joyous exuberance, and the weeds blossomed quite like plants. Full of charming lights and shadows, and populous with pleasant-voiced birds, the neglected shade trees no longer struggled to run away, but bent reverently beneath their burdens of sun and song. Even in the glassless upper windows was an expression of peace and contentment, due to the light within. Over the stony fields the visible heat danced with a lively tremor incompatible with the gravity which is an attribute of the supernatural.

Such was the aspect under which the place presented itself to Sheriff Adams and two other men who had come out from Marshall to look at it. One of these men was Mr. King, the sheriff's deputy; the other, whose name was Brewer, was a brother of the late Mrs. Manton. Under a beneficent law of the State relating to property which has been for a certain period abandoned by its owner, whose residence cannot be ascertained, the sheriff was the legal custodian of the Manton farm and the appurtenances thereunto belonging. His present visit was in mere perfunctory compliance with some order of a court in which Mr. Brewer had an action to get possession of the property as heir to his deceased sister. By a mere coincidence the visit was made on the day after the night that Deputy King had unlocked the house for another and very different purpose. His presence now was not of his own choosing: he had been ordered to accompany his superior, and at the moment could think of nothing more prudent than simulated alacrity in obedience. He had intended going anyhow, but in other company.

Carelessly opening the front door, which to his surprise was not locked, the sheriff was amazed to see, lying on the floor of the passage into which it opened, a confused heap of men's apparel. Examination showed it to consist of two hats, and the same number of coats, waistcoats, and scarves, all in a remarkably good state of preservation, albeit somewhat defiled by the dust in which they lay. Mr. Brewer was equally astonished, but Mr. King's emotion is not of record. With a new and lively interest in his own actions, the sheriff now unlatched and pushed open a door on the right, and the three entered. The room was apparently vacant—no; as their eyes became accustomed to the dimmer light, something was visible in the farthest angle of the wall. It was a human figure—that of a man crouching close in the corner. Something in the attitude made the intruders halt when they had barely passed the threshold. The figure more and more clearly defined itself. The man was upon one knee, his back in the angle of the wall, his shoulders elevated to the level of his ears, his hands before his face, palms outward, the fingers spread and crooked like claws; the white face turned upward on the retracted neck had an expression of unutterable fright, the mouth half open, the eyes incredibly expanded. He was stone dead—dead of terror! Yet, with the exception of a knife, which had evidently fallen from his own hand, not another object was in the room.

In the thick dust which covered the floor were some confused footprints near the door and along the wall through which it opened. Along one of the adjoining walls, too, past the boarded-up windows, was the trail made by the man himself in reaching his corner. Instinctively in approaching the body the three men now followed that trail. The sheriff grasped one of the outthrown arms; it was as rigid as iron, and the application of a gentle force rocked the entire body without altering the relation of its parts. Brewer, pale with terror, gazed intently into the distorted face. " God of mercy! " he suddenly cried, " it is Manton! "

" You are right," said King, with an evident attempt at calmness: " I knew Manton. He then wore a full beard and his hair long, but this is he."

He might have added: " I recognised him when he challenged Rosser. I told Rosser and Sancher who he was before we played him this horrible trick. When Rosser left this dark room at our heels, forgetting his clothes in the excitement, and driving away with us in his shirt—all through the discreditable proceedings we knew whom we were dealing with, murderer and coward that he was! "

But nothing of this did Mr. King say. With his better light he was trying to penetrate the mystery of the man's death. That he had not once moved from the corner where he had been stationed, that his posture was that of neither attack nor defence, that he had dropped his weapon, that he had obviously perished of sheer terror of something that he *saw*—these were circumstances which Mr. King's disturbed intelligence could not rightly comprehend.

Groping in intellectual darkness for a clue to his maze of doubt, his gaze directed mechanically downward, as is the way of one who ponders momentous matters, fell upon something which, there, in the light of day, and in the presence of living companions, struck him with an invincible terror. In the dust of years that lay thick upon the floor—leading from the door by which they had entered, straight across the room to within a yard of Manton's crouching corpse—were three parallel lines of footprints—light but definite impressions of bare feet, the outer ones those of small children, the inner a woman's. From the point at which they ended they did not return; they pointed all one way. Brewer, who had observed them at the same moment, was leaning forward in an attitude of rapt attention, horribly pale.

" Look at that! " he cried, pointing with both hands at the nearest print of the woman's right foot, where she had apparently stopped and stood. " The middle toe is missing— it was Gertrude! "

Gertrude was the late Mrs. Manton, sister to Mr. Brewer.

THE DAMNED THING

I

One Does Not Always Eat what is on the Table

BY the light of a tallow candle which had been placed on
one end of a rough table a man was reading something
written in a book. It was an old account book, greatly worn;
and the writing was not, apparently, very legible, for the man
sometimes held the page close to the flame of the candle to
get a stronger light on it. The shadow of the book would
then throw into obscurity a half of the room, darkening a
number of faces and figures; for besides the reader, eight
other men were present. Seven of them sat against the rough
log walls, silent, motionless, and the room being small, not
very far from the table. By extending an arm any one of
them could have touched the eighth man, who lay on the
table, face upward, partly covered by a sheet, his arms at
his sides. He was dead.

The man with the book was not reading aloud, and no one
spoke; all seemed to be waiting for something to occur; the
dead man only was without expectation. From the blank
darkness outside came in, through the aperture that served
for a window, all the ever unfamiliar noises of night in the
wilderness—the long, nameless note of a distant coyote; the
stilly pulsing thrill of tireless insects in trees; strange cries of
night birds, so different from those of the birds of day; the
drone of great blundering beetles, and all that mysterious
chorus of small sounds that seem always to have been but
half heard when they have suddenly ceased, as if conscious of
an indiscretion. But nothing of all this was noted in that
company; its members were not overmuch addicted to idle
interest in matters of no practical importance; that was
obvious in every line of their rugged faces—obvious even in
the dim light of the single candle. They were evidently men
of the vicinity—farmers and woodsmen.

The person reading was a trifle different; one would have said of him that he was of the world, worldly, albeit there was that in his attire which attested a certain fellowship with the organisms of his environment. His coat would hardly have passed muster in San Francisco; his footgear was not of urban origin, and the hat that lay by him on the floor (he was the only one uncovered) was such that if one had considered it as an article of mere personal adornment he would have missed its meaning. In countenance the man was rather prepossessing, with just a hint of sternness; though that he may have assumed or cultivated, as appropriate to one in authority. For he was a coroner. It was by virtue of his office that he had possession of the book in which he was reading; it had been found among the dead man's effects—in his cabin, where the inquest was now taking place.

When the coroner had finished reading he put the book into his breast pocket. At that moment the door was pushed open and a young man entered. He, clearly, was not of mountain birth and breeding: he was clad as those who dwell in cities. His clothing was dusty, however, as from travel. He had, in fact, been riding hard to attend the inquest.

The coroner nodded; no one else greeted him.

"We have waited for you," said the coroner. "It is necessary to have done with this business to-night."

The young man smiled. "I am sorry to have kept you," he said. "I went away, not to evade your summons, but to post to my newspaper an account of what I suppose I am called back to relate."

The coroner smiled.

"The account that you posted to your newspaper," he said, "differs, probably, from that which you will give here under oath."

"That," replied the other, rather hotly and with a visible flush, "is as you please. I used manifold paper and have a copy of what I sent. It was not written as news, for it is incredible, but as fiction. It may go as a part of my testimony under oath."

"But you say it is incredible."

"That is nothing to you, sir, if I also swear that it is true."

The coroner was silent for a time, his eyes upon the floor. The men about the sides of the cabin talked in whispers, but seldom withdrew their gaze from the face of the corpse.

Presently the coroner lifted his eyes and said: "We will resume the inquest."

The men removed their hats. The witness was sworn.

"What is your name?" the coroner asked.

"William Harker."

"Age?"

"Twenty-seven."

"You knew the deceased, Hugh Morgan?"

"Yes."

"You were with him when he died?"

"Near him."

"How did that happen—your presence, I mean?"

"I was visiting him at this place to shoot and fish. A part of my purpose, however, was to study him and his odd, solitary way of life. He seemed a good model for a character in fiction. I sometimes writes stories."

"I sometimes read them."

"Thank you."

"Stories in general—not yours."

Some of the jurors laughed. Against a sombre background humour shows high lights. Soldiers in the intervals of battle laugh easily, and a jest in the death chamber conquers by surprise.

"Relate the circumstances of this man's death," said the coroner. "You may use any notes or memoranda that you please."

The witness understood. Pulling a manuscript from his breast pocket he held it near the candle and, turning the leaves until he found the passage that he wanted, began to read.

II

What may Happen in a Field of Wild Oats

". . . The sun had hardly risen when we left the house. We were looking for quail, each with a shotgun, but we had only one dog. Morgan said that our best ground was beyond a certain ridge that he pointed out, and we crossed it by a trail through the *chaparral*. On the other side was comparatively level ground, thickly covered with wild oats. As we emerged from the *chaparral* Morgan was but a few

yards in advance. Suddenly we heard, at a little distance
to our right and partly in front, a noise as of some animal
thrashing about in the bushes, which we could see were
violently agitated.

" ' We've started a deer,' I said. ' I wish we had brought
a rifle.'

" Morgan, who had stopped and was intently watching
the agitated *chaparral,* said nothing, but had cocked both
barrels of his gun and was holding it in readiness to aim.
I thought him a trifle excited, which surprised me, for he
had a reputation for exceptional coolness, even in moments
of sudden and imminent peril.

" ' Oh, come,' I said. ' You are not going to fill up a
deer with quail-shot, are you? '

" Still he did not reply; but catching a sight of his face
as he turned it slightly towards me I was struck by the
intensity of his look. Then I understood that we had serious
business in hand, and my first conjecture was that we had
' jumped ' a grizzly. I advanced to Morgan's side, cocking
my piece as I moved.

" The bushes were now quiet and the sounds had ceased,
but Morgan was as attentive to the place as before.

" ' What is it? What the devil is it? ' I asked.

" ' The Damned Thing! ' he replied, without turning
his head. His voice was husky and unnatural. He trembled
visibly.

" I was about to speak further, when I observed the wild
oats near the place of the disturbance moving in the most
inexplicable way. I can hardly describe it. It seemed as
if stirred by a streak of wind, which not only bent it, but
pressed it down—crushed it so that it did not rise; and this
movement was slowly prolonging itself directly towards us.

" Nothing that I had ever seen had affected me so strangely
as this unfamiliar and unaccountable phenomenon, yet I am
unable to recall any sense of fear. I remember—and tell it
here because, singularly enough, I recollected it then—that
once in looking carelessly out of an open window I momentarily mistook a small tree close at hand for one of a group
of larger trees at a little distance away. It looked the same
size as the others, but being more distinctly and sharply defined in mass and detail seemed out of harmony with them.
It was a mere falsification of the law of aerial perspective,

but it startled, almost terrified me. We so rely upon the
orderly operation of familiar natural laws that any seeming
suspension of them is noted as a menace to our safety, a
warning of unthinkable calamity. So now the apparently
causeless movement of the herbage and the slow, undeviating
approach of the line of disturbance were distinctly disquiet-
ing. My companion appeared actually frightened, and I
could hardly credit my senses when I saw him suddenly
throw his gun to his shoulder and fire both barrels at the
agitated grain! Before the smoke of the discharge had
cleared away I heard a loud savage cry—a scream like that
of a wild animal—and flinging his gun upon the ground
Morgan sprang away and ran swiftly from the spot. At
the same instant I was thrown violently to the ground by the
impact of something unseen in the smoke—some soft, heavy
substance that seemed thrown against me with great force.

" Before I could get upon my feet and recover my gun,
which seemed to have been struck from my hands, I heard
Morgan crying out as if in mortal agony, and mingling with
his cries were such hoarse, savage sounds as one hears from
fighting dogs. Inexpressibly terrified, I struggled to my feet
and looked in the direction of Morgan's retreat; and may
Heaven in mercy spare me from another sight like that! At
a distance of less than thirty yards was my friend, down
upon one knee, his head thrown back at a frightful angle,
hatless, his long hair in disorder and his whole body in violent
movement from side to side, backward and forward. His
right arm was lifted and seemed to lack the hand—at least,
I could see none. The other arm was invisible. At times,
as my memory now reports this extraordinary scene, I could
discern but a part of his body; it was as if he had been partly
blotted out—I cannot otherwise express it—then a shifting
of his position would bring it all into view again.

" All this must have occurred within a few seconds, yet
in that time Morgan assumed all the postures of a deter-
bined wrestler vanquished by superior weight and strength.
I saw nothing but him, and him not always distinctly. During the entire incident his shouts and curses were heard, as if
through an enveloping uproar of such sounds of rage and
fury as I had never heard from the throat of man or brute!

" For a moment only I stood irresolute, then throwing
down my gun I ran forward to my friend's assistance. I

had a vague belief that he was suffering from a fit, or some form of convulsion. Before I could reach his side he was down and quiet. All sounds had ceased, but with a feeling of such terror as even these awful events had not inspired I now saw again the mysterious movement of the wild oats, prolonging itself from the trampled area about the prostrate man towards the edge of a wood. It was only when it had reached the wood that I was able to withdraw my eyes and look at my companion. He was dead."

III

A Man though Naked may be in Rags

THE coroner rose from his seat and stood beside the dead man. Lifting an edge of the sheet, he pulled it away, exposing the entire body, altogether naked and showing in the candle-light a clay-like yellow. It had, however, broad maculations of bluish black, obviously caused by extravasated blood from contusions. The chest and sides looked as if they had been beaten with a bludgeon. There were dreadful lacerations; the skin was torn in strips and shreds.

The coroner moved round to the end of the table and undid a silk handkerchief which had been passed under the chin and knotted on the top of the head. When the handkerchief was drawn away it exposed what had been the throat. Some of the jurors who had risen to get a better view repented their curiosity and turned away their faces. Witness Harker went to the open window and leaned out across the sill, faint and sick. Dropping the handkerchief upon the dead man's neck, the coroner stepped to an angle of the room and from a pile of clothing produced one garment after another, each of which he held up a moment for inspection. All were torn, and stiff with blood. The jurors did not make a closer inspection. They seemed rather uninterested. They had, in truth, seen all this before; the only thing that was new to them being Harker's testimony.

"Gentlemen," the coroner said, "we have no more evidence, I think. Your duty has been already explained to you; if there is nothing you wish to ask you may go outside and consider your verdict."

The foreman rose—a tall, bearded man of sixty, coarsely clad.

" I should like to ask one question, Mr. Coroner," he said. " What asylum did this yer last witness escape from? "

" Mr. Harker," said the coroner gravely and tranquilly, " from what asylum did you last escape? "

Harker flushed crimson again, but said nothing, and the seven jurors rose and solemnly filed out of the cabin.

" If you have done insulting me, sir," said Harker, as soon as he and the officer were left alone with the dead man, " I suppose I am at liberty to go? "

" Yes."

Harker started to leave, but paused, with his hand on the door latch. The habit of his profession was strong in him—stronger than his sense of personal dignity. He turned about and said:

" The book that you have there—I recognise it as Morgan's diary. You seemed greatly interested in it; you read in it while I was testifying. May I see it? The public would like——"

" The book will cut no figure in this matter," replied the official, slipping it into his coat pocket; " all the entries in it were made before the writer's death."

As Harker passed out of the house the jury re-entered and stood about the table, on which the now covered corpse showed under the sheet with sharp definition. The foreman seated himself near the candle, produced from his breast pocket a pencil and scrap of paper and wrote rather laboriously the following verdict, which with various degrees of effort all signed:

" We, the jury, do find that the remains come to their death at the hands of a mountain lion, but some of us thinks, all the same, they had fits."

IV

An Explanation from the Tomb

IN the diary of the late Hugh Morgan are certain interest-ing entries having, possibly, a scientific value as sugges-tions. At the inquest upon his body the book was not put in evidence; possibly the coroner thought it not worth while to confuse the jury. The date of the first of the entries mentioned cannot be ascertained; the upper part of the leaf is torn away; the part of the entry remaining follows:

". . . would run in a half-circle, keeping his head turned always towards the centre, and again he would stand still, barking furiously. At last he ran away into the brush as fast as he could go. I thought at first that he had gone mad, but on returning to the house found no other alteration in his manner than what was obviously due to fear of punishment.

"Can a dog see with his nose? Do odours impress some cerebral centre with images of the thing that emitted them? . . .

"*Sept.* 2.—Looking at the stars last night as they rose above the crest of the ridge east of the house, I observed them successively disappear—from left to right. Each was eclipsed but an instant, and only a few at the same time, but along the entire length of the ridge all that were within a degree or two of the crest were blotted out. It was as if something had passed along between me and them; but I could not see it, and the stars were not thick enough to define its outline. Ugh! don't like this. . . ."

Several weeks' entries are missing, three leaves being torn from the book.

"*Sept.* 27.—It has been about here again—I find evidences of its presence every day. I watched again all last night in the same cover, gun in hand, double-charged with buckshot. In the morning the fresh footprints were there, as before. Yet I would have sworn that I did not sleep—indeed, I hardly sleep at all. It is terrible, insupportable! If these amazing experiences are real I shall go mad; if they are fanciful I am mad already.

"*Oct.* 3.—I shall not go—it shall not drive me away. No, this is *my* house, *my* land. God hates a coward. . . .

"*Oct.* 5.—I can stand it no longer; I have invited Harker to pass a few weeks with me—he has a level head. I can judge from his manner if he thinks me mad.

"*Oct.* 7.—I have the solution of the mystery; it came to me last night—suddenly, as by revelation. How simple—how terribly simple!

"There are sounds that we cannot hear. At either end

of the scale are notes that stir no chord of that imperfect instrument, the human ear. They are too high or too grave. I have observed a flock of blackbirds occupying an entire tree-top—the tops of several trees—and all in full song. Suddenly—in a moment—at absolutely the same instant— all spring into the air and fly away. How? They could not all see one another—whole tree-tops intervened. At no point could a leader have been visible to all. There must have been a signal of warning or command, high and shrill above the din, but by me unheard. I have observed, too, the same simultaneous flight when all were silent, among not only blackbirds, but other birds—quail, for example, widely separated by bushes—even on opposite sides of a hill.

" It is known to seaman that a school of whales basking or sporting on the surface of the ocean, miles apart, with the convexity of the earth between, will sometimes dive at the same instant—all gone out of sight in a moment. The signal has been sounded—too grave for the ear of the sailor at the masthead and his comrades on the deck—who nevertheless feel its vibrations in the ship as the stones of a cathedral are stirred by the bass of the organ.

" As with sounds, so with colours. At each end of the solar spectrum the chemist can detect the presence of what are known as ' actinic ' rays. They represent colours— integral colours in the composition of light—which we are unable to discern. The human eye is an imperfect instrument; its range is but a few octaves of the real ' chromatic scale.' I am not mad; there are colours that we cannot see.

" And, God help me! the Damned Thing is of such a colour! "

F. MARION CRAWFORD

THE UPPER BERTH

I

SOMEBODY asked for the cigars. We had talked long, and the conversation was beginning to languish; the tobacco smoke had got into the heavy curtains, the wine had got into those brains which were liable to become heavy, and it was already perfectly evident that, unless somebody did something to rouse our oppressed spirits, the meeting would soon come to its natural conclusion, and we, the guests, would speedily go home to bed, and most certainly to sleep. No one had said anything very remarkable; it may be that no one had anything very remarkable to say. Jones had given us every particular of his last hunting adventure in Yorkshire. Mr. Tompkins, of Boston, had explained at elaborate length those working principles, by the due and careful maintenance of which the Atchison, Topeka, and Santa Fé Railroad not only extended its territory, increased its departmental influence, and transported live stock without starving them to death before the day of actual delivery, but, also, had for years succeeded in deceiving those passengers who bought its tickets into the fallacious belief that the corporation aforesaid was really able to transport human life without destroying it. Signor Tombola had endeavoured to persuade us, by arguments which we took no trouble to oppose, that the unity of his country in no way resembled the average modern torpedo, carefully planned, constructed with all the skill of the greatest European arsenals, but, when constructed, destined to be directed by feeble hands into a region where it must undoubtedly explode, unseen, unfeared, and unheard, into the illimitable wastes of political chaos.

It is unnecessary to go into further details. The conversation had assumed proportions which would have bored Prometheus on his rock, which would have driven Tantalus to distraction, and which would have impelled Ixion to seek relaxation in the simple but instructive dialogues of Herr Ollendorff, rather than submit to the greater evil of listening to our talk. We had sat at table for hours; we were bored, we were tired, and nobody showed signs of moving.

Somebody called for cigars. We all instinctively looked towards the speaker. Brisbane was a man of five-and-thirty years of age, and remarkable for those gifts which chiefly attract the attention of men. He was a strong man. The external proportions of his figure presented nothing extraordinary to the common eye, though his size was above the average. He was a little over six feet in height, and moderately broad in the shoulder; he did not appear to be stout, but, on the other hand, he was certainly not thin; his small head was supported by a strong and sinewy neck; his broad, muscular hands appeared to possess a peculiar skill in breaking walnuts without the assistance of the ordinary cracker, and, seeing him in profile, one could not help remarking the extraordinary breadth of his sleeves, and the unusual thickness of his chest. He was one of those men who are commonly spoken of among men as deceptive; that is to say, that though he looked exceedingly strong he was in reality very much stronger than he looked. Of his features I need say little. His head is small, his hair is thin, his eyes are blue, his nose is large, he has a small moustache, and a square jaw. Everybody knows Brisbane, and when he asked for a cigar everybody looked at him.

"It is a very singular thing," said Brisbane. Everybody stopped talking. Brisbane's voice was not loud, but possessed a peculiar quality of penetrating general conversation, and cutting it like a knife. Everybody listened. Brisbane, perceiving that he had attracted their general attention, lit his cigar with great equanimity.

"It is very singular," he continued, "that thing about ghosts. People are always asking whether anybody has seen a ghost. I have."

"Bosh! What, you? You don't mean to say so, Brisbane? Well, for a man of his intelligence!"

A chorus of exclamations greeted Brisbane's remarkable statement. Everybody called for cigars, and Stubbs, the butler, suddenly appeared from the depths of nowhere with a fresh bottle of dry champagne. The situation was saved; Brisbane was going to tell a story.

I am an old sailor, said Brisbane, and as I have to cross

the Atlantic pretty often, I have my favourites. Most men
have their favourites. I have seen a man wait in a Broadway
bar for three-quarters of an hour for a particular car which
he liked. I believe the bar-keeper made at least one-third
of his living by that man's preference. I have a habit of
waiting for certain ships when I am obliged to cross that
duck-pond. It may be a prejudice, but I was never cheated
out of a good passage but once in my life. I remember it
very well; it was a warm morning in June, and the Custom
House officials, who were hanging about waiting for a steamer
already on her way up from the Quarantine, presented a
peculiarly hazy and thoughtful appearance. I had not much
luggage—I never have. I mingled with the crowd of passengers, porters, and officious individuals in blue coats and
brass buttons, who seemed to spring up like mushrooms from
the deck of a moored steamer to obtrude their unnecessary
services upon the independent passenger. I have often noticed
with a certain interest the spontaneous evolution of these
fellows. They are not there when you arrive; five minutes
after the pilot has called " Go ahead! " they, or at least
their blue coats and brass buttons, have disappeared from
deck and gangway as completely as though they had been
consigned to that locker which tradition unanimously ascribes
to Davy Jones. But, at the moment of starting, they are
there, clean shaved, blue coated, and ravenous for fees. I
hastened on board. The *Kamtschatka* was one of my
favourite ships. I say was, because she emphatically no
longer is. I cannot conceive of any inducement which could
entice me to make another voyage in her. Yes, I know what
you are going to say. She is uncommonly clean in the run
aft, she has enough bluffing off in the bows to keep her dry,
and the lower berths are most of them double. She has a lot
of advantages, but I won't cross in her again. Excuse the
digression. I got on board. I hailed a steward, whose red
nose and redder whiskers were equally familiar to me.

"One hundred and five, lower berth," said I, in the
business-like tone peculiar to men who think no more of
crossing the Atlantic than taking a whisky cocktail at down-
town Delmonico's.

The steward took my portmanteau, great-coat, and rug.
I shall never forget the expression of his face. Not that he
turned pale. It is maintained by the most eminent divines

that even miracles cannot change the course of nature. I have no hesitation in saying that he did not turn pale; but, from his expression, I judged that he was either about to shed tears, to sneeze, or to drop my portmanteau. As the latter contained two bottles of particularly fine old sherry presented to me for my voyage by my old friend Snigginson van Pickyns, I felt extremely nervous. But the steward did none of these things.

"Well, I'm d——d!" said he in a low voice, and led the way.

I supposed my Hermes, as he led me to the lower regions, had had a little grog, but I said nothing, and followed him. 105 was on the port side, well aft. There was nothing remarkable about the state-room. The lower berth, like most of those upon the *Kamtschatka*, was double. There was plenty of room; there was the usual washing apparatus calculated to convey an idea of luxury to the mind of a North American Indian; there were the usual inefficient racks of brown wood, in which it is more easy to hang a large-sized umbrella than the common tooth-brush of commerce. Upon the uninviting mattresses were carefully folded together those blankets which a great modern humorist has aptly compared to cold buck-wheat cakes. The question of towels was left entirely to the imagination. The glass decanters were filled with a transparent liquid faintly tinged with brown, but from which an odour less faint, but not more pleasing, ascended to the nostrils like a far-off sea-sick reminiscence of oily machinery. Sad-coloured curtains half closed the upper berth. The hazy June daylight shed a faint illumination upon the desolate little scene. Ugh! how I hate that state-room!

The steward deposited my traps and looked at me, as though he wanted to get away—probably in search of more passengers and more fees. It is always a good plan to start in favour with those functionaries, and I accordingly gave him certain coins there and then.

"I'll try and make yer comfortable all I can," he remarked, as he put the coins in his pocket. Nevertheless, there was a doubtful intonation in his voice which surprised me. Possibly his scale of fees had gone up, and he was not satisfied; but on the whole I was inclined to think that, as he himself would have expressed it, he was "the better for a glass." I was wrong, however, and did the man injustice.

II

NOTHING especially worthy of mention occurred during that day. We left the pier punctually, and it was very pleasant to be fairly under way, for the weather was warm and sultry, and the motion of the steamer produced a refreshing breeze. Everybody knows what the first day at sea is like. People pace the decks and stare at each other, and occasionally meet acquaintances whom they did not know to be on board. There is the usual uncertainty as to whether the food will be good, bad, or indifferent, until the first two meals have put the matter beyond a doubt; there is the usual uncertainty about the weather, until the ship is fairly off Fire Island. The tables are crowded at first, and then suddenly thinned. Pale-faced people spring from their seats and precipitate themselves towards the door, and each old sailor breathes more freely as his sea-sick neighbour rushes from his side, leaving him plenty of elbow-room and an unlimited command over the mustard.

One passage across the Atlantic is very much like another, and we who cross very often do not make the voyage for the sake of novelty. Whales and icebergs are indeed always objects of interest, but, after all, one whale is very much like another whale, and one rarely sees an iceberg at close quarters. To the majority of us the most delightful moment of the day on board an ocean steamer is when we have taken our last turn on deck, have smoked our last cigar, and having succeeded in tiring ourselves, feel at liberty to turn in with a clear conscience. On that first night of the voyage I felt particularly lazy, and went to bed in 105 rather earlier than I usually do. As I turned in, I was amazed to see that I was to have a companion. A portmanteau, very like my own, lay in the opposite corner, and in the upper berth had been deposited a neatly-folded rug, with a stick and umbrella. I had hoped to be alone, and I was disappointed; but I wondered who my room-mate was to be, and I determined to have a look at him.

Before I had been long in bed he entered. He was, as far as I could see, a very tall man, very thin, very pale, with sandy hair and whiskers and colourless grey eyes. He had about him, I thought, an air of rather dubious fashion; the sort of man you might see in Wall Street, without being able precisely to say what he was doing there—the sort of man who frequents the Café Anglais, who always seems to be alone, and who drinks champagne; you might meet him on a race-course, but he would never appear to be doing anything there either. A little over-dressed—a little odd. There are three or four of his kind on every ocean steamer. I made up my mind that I did not care to make his acquaintance, and I went to sleep saying to myself that I would study his habits in order to avoid him. If he rose early, I would rise late; if he went to bed late, I would go to bed early. I did not care to know him. If you once know people of that kind they are always turning up. Poor fellow! I need not have taken the trouble to come to so many decisions about him, for I never saw him again after that first night in 105.

I was sleeping soundly when I was suddenly waked by a loud noise. To judge from the sound, my room-mate must have sprung with a single leap from the upper berth to the floor. I heard him fumbling with the latch and bolt of the door, which opened almost immediately, and then I heard his footsteps as he ran at full speed down the passage, leaving the door open behind him. The ship was rolling a little, and I expected to hear him stumble or fall, but he ran as though he were running for his life. The door swung on its hinges with the motion of the vessel, and the sound annoyed me. I got up and shut it, and groped my way back to my berth in the darkness. I went to sleep again; but I have no idea how long I slept.

When I awoke it was still quite dark, but I felt a disagreeable sensation of cold, and it seemed to me that the air was damp. You know the peculiar smell of a cabin which has been wet with sea-water. I covered myself up as well as I could and dozed off again, framing complaints to be made the next day, and selecting the most powerful epithets in the language. I could hear my room-mate turn over in the upper berth. He had probably returned while I was asleep. Once I thought I heard him groan, and I argued that he was sea-sick. That is particularly unpleasant when one is below. Nevertheless I dozed off and slept till early daylight.

The ship was rolling heavily, much more than on the previous evening, and the grey light which came in through the porthole changed in tint with every movement according as the angle of the vessel's side turned the glass seawards or

skywards. It was very cold—unaccountably so for the
month of June. I turned my head and looked at the porthole, and saw to my surprise that it was wide open and
hooked back. I believe I swore audibly. Then I got up and
shut it. As I turned back I glanced at the upper berth. The
curtains were drawn close together; my companion had
probably felt cold as well as I. It struck me that I had slept
enough. The state-room was uncomfortable, though, strange
to say, I could not smell the dampness which had annoyed
me in the night. My room-mate was still asleep—excellent
opportunity for avoiding him, so I dressed at once and went
on deck. The day was warm and cloudy, with an oily smell
on the water. It was seven o'clock as I came out—much
later than I had imagined. I came across the doctor, who
was taking his first sniff of the morning air. He was a young
man from the West of Ireland—a tremendous fellow, with
black hair and blue eyes, already inclined to be stout; he had
a happy-go-lucky, healthy look about him which was rather
attractive.

"Fine morning," I remarked, by way of introduction.

"Well," said he, eyeing me with an air of ready interest,
"it's a fine morning and it's not a fine morning. I don't
think it's much of a morning."

"Well, no—it is not so very fine," said I.

"It's just what I call fuggly weather," replied the doctor.

"It was very cold last night, I thought," I remarked.
"However, when I looked about, I found that the porthole
was wide open. I had not noticed it when I went to bed.
And the state-room was damp, too."

"Damp!" said he. "Whereabouts are you?"

"One hundred and five——"

To my surprise the doctor started visibly, and stared at
me.

"What is the matter?" I asked.

"Oh—nothing," he answered; "only everybody has complained of that state-room for the last three trips."

"I shall complain too," I said. "It has certainly not been
properly aired. It is a shame!"

"I don't believe it can be helped," answered the doctor.
"I believe there is something—well, it is not my business
to frighten passengers."

"You need not be afraid of frightening me," I replied.

" I can stand any amount of damp. If I should get a bad cold I will come to you."

I offered the doctor a cigar, which he took and examined very critically.

" It is not so much the damp," he remarked. " However, I dare say you will get on very well. Have you a room-mate? "

" Yes; a deuce of a fellow, who bolts out in the middle of the night, and leaves the door open."

Again the doctor glanced curiously at me. Then he lit the cigar and looked grave.

" Did he come back? " he asked presently.

" Yes. I was asleep, but I waked up, and heard him moving. Then I felt cold and went to sleep again. This morning I found the porthole open."

" Look here," said the doctor quietly, " I don't care much for this ship. I don't care a rap for her reputation. I tell you what I will do. I have a good-sized place up here. I will share it with you, though I don't know you from Adam."

I was very much surprised at the proposition. I could not imagine why he should take such a sudden interest in my welfare. However, his manner, as he spoke of the ship, was peculiar.

" You are very good, doctor," I said. " But, really, I be-lieve even now the cabin could be aired, or cleaned out, or something. Why do you not care for the ship? "

" We are not superstitious in our profession, sir," replied the doctor, " but the sea makes people so. I don't want to prejudice you, and I don't want to frighten you, but if you will take my advice you will move in here. I would as soon see you overboard," he added earnestly, " as know that you or any other man was to sleep in 105."

" Good gracious! Why? " I asked.

" Just because on the last three trips the people who have slept there actually have gone overboard," he answered gravely.

The intelligence was startling and exceedingly unpleasant, I confess. I looked hard at the doctor to see whether he was making game of me, but he looked perfectly serious. I thanked him warmly for his offer, but told him I intended to be the exception to the rule by which every one who slept in that particular state-room went overboard. He did not say much, but looked as grave as ever, and hinted that, before we got across, I should probably reconsider his proposal. In the course of time we went to breakfast, at which only an inconsiderable number of passengers assembled. I noticed that one or two of the officers who breakfasted with us looked grave. After breakfast I went into my state-room in order to get a book. The curtains of the upper berth were still closely drawn. Not a word was to be heard. My room-mate was probably still asleep.

As I came out I met the steward whose business it was to look after me. He whispered that the captain wanted to see me, and then scuttled away down the passage as if very anxious to avoid any questions. I went towards the captain's cabin, and found him waiting for me.

" Sir," said he, " I want to ask a favour of you."

I answered that I would do anything to oblige him.

" Your room-mate has disappeared," he said.   " He is known to have turned in early last night. Did you notice anything extraordinary in his manner? "

The question coming, as it did, in exact confirmation of the fears the doctor had expressed half an hour earlier, staggered me.

" You don't mean to say he has gone overboard? " I asked.

" I fear he has," answered the captain.

" This is the most extraordinary thing——" I began.

" Why? " he asked.

" He is the fourth, then? " I explained. In answer to another question from the captain, I explained, without mentioning the doctor, that I had heard the story concerning 105. He seemed very much annoyed at hearing that I knew of it. I told him what had occurred in the night.

" What you say," he replied, " coincides almost exactly with what was told me by the room-mates of two of the other three. They bolt out of bed and run down the passage. Two of them were seen to go overboard by the watch; we stopped and lowered boats, but they were not found. Nobody, however, saw or heard the man who was lost last night—if he is really lost. The steward, who is a superstitious fellow, perhaps, and expected something to go wrong, went to look for him this morning, and found his berth empty, but his clothes lying about, just as he had left them.

The steward was the only man on board who knew him by sight, and he has been searching everywhere for him. He has disappeared! Now, sir, I want to beg you not to mention the circumstance to any of the passengers; I don't want the ship to get a bad name, and nothing hangs about an ocean-goer like stories of suicides. You shall have your choice of any one of the officers' cabins you like, including my own, for the rest of the passage. Is that a fair bargain? "

" Very," said I; " and I am much obliged to you. But since I am alone, and have the state-room to myself, I would rather not move. If the steward will take out that unfortunate man's things, I would as lief stay where I am. I will not say anything about the matter, and I think I can promise you that I will not follow my room-mate."

The captain tried to dissuade me from my intention, but I preferred having a state-room alone to being the chum of any officer on board. I do not know whether I acted foolishly, but if I had taken his advice I should have had nothing more to tell. There would have remained the disagreeable coincidence of several suicides occurring among men who had slept in the same cabin, but that would have been all.

That was not the end of the matter, however, by any means. I obstinately made up my mind that I would not be disturbed by such tales, and I even went so far as to argue the question with the captain. There was something wrong about the state-room, I said. It was rather damp. The port-hole had been left open last night. My room-mate might have been ill when he came on board, and he might have become delirious after he went to bed. He might even now be hiding somewhere on board, and might be found later. The place ought to be aired and the fastening of the port looked to. If the captain would give me leave, I would see what I thought necessary were done immediately.

" Of course you have a right to stay where you are if you please," he replied, rather petulantly; " but I wish you would turn out and let me lock the place up, and be done with it."

I did not see it in the same light, and left the captain, after promising to be silent concerning the disappearance of my companion. The latter had had no acquaintances on board, and was not missed in the course of the day. Towards

evening I met the doctor again, and he asked me whether
I had changed my mind. I told him I had not.

"Then you will before long," he said, very gravely.

III

W E played whist in the evening, and I went to bed late.
I will confess now that I felt a disagreeable sensation
when I entered my state-room. I could not help thinking
of the tall man I had seen on the previous night, who was
now dead, drowned, tossing about in the long swell, two or
three hundred miles astern. His face rose very distinctly
before me as I undressed, and I even went so far as to draw
back the curtains of the upper berth, as though to persuade
myself that he was actually gone. I also bolted the door of
the state-room. Suddenly I became aware that the porthole
was open, and fastened back. This was more than I could
stand. I hastily threw on my dressing-gown and went in
search of Robert, the steward of my passage. I was very
angry, I remember, and when I found him I dragged him
roughly to the door of 105, and pushed him towards the open
porthole.

"What the deuce do you mean, you scoundrel, by leaving
that port open every night? Don't you know it is against
the regulations? Don't you know that if the ship heeled and
the water began to come in, ten men could not shut it?
I will report you to the captain, you blackguard, for endan-
gering the ship!"

I was exceedingly wroth. The man trembled and turned
pale, and then began to shut the round glass plate with the
heavy brass fittings.

"Why don't you answer me?" I said roughly.

"If you please, sir," faltered Robert, "there's nobody
on board as can keep this 'ere port shut at night. You can
try it yourself, sir. I ain't a-going to stop hany longer
on board o' this vessel, sir; I ain't, indeed. But if I was you,
sir, I'd just clear out and go to sleep with the surgeon, or
something, I would. Look 'ere, sir, is that fastened what
you may call securely, or not, sir! Try it, sir, see if it will
move a hinch."

I tried the port, and found it perfectly tight.

"Well, sir," continued Robert triumphantly, "I wager my

reputation as a A1 steward that in 'arf an hour it will be open again; fastened back, too, sir, that's the horful thing— fastened back!"

I examined the great screw and the looped nut that ran on it.

"If I find it open in the night, Robert, I will give you a sovereign. It is not possible. You may go."

"Soverin' did you say, sir? Very good, sir. Thank ye, sir. Good night, sir. Pleasant reepose, sir, and all manner of hinchantin' dreams, sir."

Robert scuttled away, delighted at being released. Of course I thought he was trying to account for his negligence by a silly story, intended to frighten me, and I disbelieved him. The consequence was that he got his sovereign, and I spent a very peculiarly unpleasant night.

I went to bed, and five minutes after I had rolled myself up in my blankets the inexorable Robert extinguished the light that burned steadily behind the ground-glass pane near the door. I lay quite still in the dark trying to go to sleep, but I soon found that impossible. It had been some satisfaction to be angry with the steward, and the diversion had banished that unpleasant sensation I had at first experienced when I thought of the drowned man who had been my chum; but I was no longer sleepy, and I lay awake for some time, occasionally glancing at the porthole, which I could just see from where I lay, and which, in the darkness, looked like a faintly-luminous soup-plate suspended in blackness. I believe I must have lain there for an hour, and, as I remember, I was just dozing into sleep when I was roused by a draught of cold air, and by distinctly feeling the spray of the sea blown upon my face. I started to my feet, and not having allowed in the dark for the motion of the ship, I was instantly thrown violently across the state-room upon the couch which was placed beneath the porthole. I recovered myself immediately, however, and climbed upon my knees. The porthole was again wide open and fastened back!

Now these things are facts. I was wide awake when I got up, and I should certainly have been waked by the fall had I still been dozing. Moreover, I bruised my elbows and knees badly, and the bruises were there on the following morning to testify to the fact, if I myself had doubted it. The porthole was wide open and fastened back—a thing so unaccountable that I remember very well feeling astonishment rather than fear when I discovered it. I at once closed the plate again, and screwed down the loop nut with all my strength. It was very dark in the state-room. I reflected that the port had certainly been opened within an hour after Robert had at first shut it in my presence, and I determined to watch it, and see whether it would open again. Those brass fittings are very heavy and by no means easy to move; I could not believe that the clump had been turned by the shaking of the screw. I stood peering out through the thick glass at the alternate white and grey streaks of the sea that foamed beneath the ship's side. I must have remained there a quarter of an hour.

Suddenly, as I stood, I distinctly heard something moving behind me in one of the berths, and a moment afterwards, just as I turned instinctively to look—though I could, of course, see nothing in the darkness—I heard a very faint groan. I sprang across the state-room, and tore the curtains of the upper berth aside, thrusting in my hands to discover if there were any one there. There was some one.

I remember that the sensation as I put my hands forward was as though I were plunging them into the air of a damp cellar, and from behind the curtains came a gust of wind that smelled horribly of stagnant sea-water. I laid hold of something that had the shape of a man's arm, but was smooth, and wet, and icy cold. But suddenly, as I pulled, the creature sprang violently forward against me, a clammy, oozy mass, as it seemed to me, heavy and wet, yet endowed with a sort of supernatural strength. I reeled across the state-room, and in an instant the door opened and the thing rushed out. I had not had time to be frightened, and quickly recovering myself, I sprang through the door and gave chase at the top of my speed, but I was too late. Ten yards before me I could see—I am sure I saw it—a dark shadow moving in the dimly lighted passage, quickly as the shadow of a fast horse thrown before a dog-cart by the lamp on a dark night. But in a moment it had disappeared, and I found myself holding on to the polished rail that ran along the bulkhead where the passage turned towards the companion. My hair stood on end, and the cold perspiration rolled down my face. I am not ashamed of it in the least: I was very badly frightened.

Still I doubted my senses, and pulled myself together.
It was absurd, I thought. The Welsh rare-bit I had eaten
had disagreed with me. I had been in a nightmare. I made
my way back to my state-room, and entered it with an
effort. The whole place smelled of stagnant sea-water, as it
had when I had waked on the previous evening. It required
my utmost strength to go in, and grope among my things
for a box of wax lights. As I lighted a railway reading-
lantern which I always carry in case I want to read after
the lamps are out, I perceived that the porthole was again
open, and a sort of creeping horror began to take possession
of me which I never felt before, nor wish to feel again.
But I got a light and proceeded to examine the upper berth,
expecting to find it drenched with sea-water.

But I was disappointed. The bed had been slept in, and
the smell of the sea was strong; but the bedding was as dry
as a bone. I fancied that Robert had not had the courage
to make the bed after the accident of the previous night—
it had all been a hideous dream. I drew the curtains back
as far as I could and examined the place very carefully.
It was perfectly dry. But the porthole was open again.
With a sort of dull bewilderment of horror I closed it and
screwed it down, and thrusting my heavy stick through the
brass loop, wrenched it with all my might, till the thick
metal began to bend under the pressure. Then I hooked
my reading-lantern into the red velvet at the head of the
couch, and sat down to recover my senses if I could. I sat
there all night, unable to think of rest—hardly able to think
at all. But the porthole remained closed, and I did not believe it would now open again without the application of a
considerable force.

The morning dawned at last, and I dressed myself slowly,
thinking over all that had happened in the night. It was a
beautiful day and I went on deck, glad to get out into the
early, pure sunshine, and to smell the breeze from the blue
water, so different from the noisome, stagnant odour of my
state-room. Instinctively I turned aft, towards the surgeon's cabin. There he stood, with a pipe in his mouth,
taking his morning airing precisely as on the preceding
day.

"Good morning," said he quietly, but looking at me with
evident curiosity.

"Doctor, you were quite right," said I. "There is something wrong about that place."

"I thought you would change your mind," he answered, rather triumphantly. "You have had a bad night, eh? Shall I make you a pick-me-up? I have a capital recipe."

"No, thanks," I cried. "But I would like to tell you what happened."

I then tried to explain as clearly as possible precisely what had occurred, not omitting to state that I had been scared as I had never been scared in my whole life before. I dwelt particularly on the phenomenon of the porthole, which was a fact to which I could testify, even if the rest had been an illusion. I had closed it twice in the night, and the second time I had actually bent the brass in wrenching it with my stick. I believe I insisted a good deal on this point.

"You seem to think I am likely to doubt the story," said the doctor, smiling at the detailed account of the state of the porthole. "I do not doubt it in the least. I renew my invitation to you. Bring your traps here, and take half my cabin."

"Come and take half of mine for one night," I said. "Help me to get at the bottom of this thing."

"You will get to the bottom of something else if you try," answered the doctor.

"What?" I asked.

"The bottom of the sea. I am going to leave this ship. It is not canny."

"Then you will not help me to find out——"

"Not I," said the doctor quickly. "It is my business to keep my wits about me—not to go fiddling about with ghosts and things."

"Do you really believe it is a ghost?" I enquired, rather contemptuously. But as I spoke I remembered very well the horrible sensation of the supernatural which had got possession of me during the night. The doctor turned sharply on me.

"Have you any reasonable explanation of these things to offer?" he asked. "No; you have not. Well, you say you will find an explanation. I say that you won't, sir, simply because there is not any."

"But, my dear sir," I retorted, "do you, a man of science, mean to tell me that such things cannot be explained?"

"I do," he answered stoutly. "And, if they could, I would not be concerned in the explanation."

I did not care to spend another night alone in the state-room, and yet I was obstinately determined to get at the root of the disturbances. I do not believe there are many men who would have slept there alone, after passing two such nights. But I made up my mind to try it, if I could not get any one to share a watch with me. The doctor was evidently not inclined for such an experiment. He said he was a surgeon, and that in case any accident occurred on board he must be always in readiness. He could not afford to have his nerves unsettled. Perhaps he was quite right, but I am inclined to think that his precaution was prompted by his inclination. On enquiry, he informed me that there was no one on board who would be likely to join me in my investigations, and after a little more conversation I left him. A little later I met the captain, and told him my story. I said that, if no one would spend the night with me, I would ask leave to have the light burning all night, and would try it alone.

"Look here," said he, "I will tell you what I will do. I will share your watch myself, and we will see what happens. It is my belief that we can find out between us. There may be some fellow skulking on board, who steals a passage by frightening the passengers. It is just possible that there may be something queer in the carpentering of that berth."

I suggested taking the ship's carpenter below and examining the place; but I was overjoyed at the captain's offer to spend the night with me. He accordingly sent for the workman and ordered him to do anything I required. We went below at once. I had all the bedding cleared out of the upper berth, and we examined the place thoroughly to see if there was a board loose anywhere, or a panel which could be opened or pushed aside. We tried the planks everywhere, tapped the flooring, unscrewed the fittings of the lower berth and took it to pieces—in short, there was not a square inch of the state-room which was not searched and tested. Everything was in perfect order, and we put everything back in its place. As we were finishing our work, Robert came to the door and looked in.

"Well, sir—find anything, sir?" he asked, with a ghastly grin.

" You were right about the porthole, Robert," I said, and I gave him the promised sovereign. The carpenter did his work silently and skilfully, following my directions. When he had done he spoke.

" I'm a plain man, sir," he said. " But it's my belief you had better just turn out your things, and let me run half a dozen four-inch screws through the door of this cabin. There's no good never came o' this cabin yet, sir, and that's all about it. There's been four lives lost out o' here to my own remembrance, and that in four trips. Better give it up, sir—better give it up! "

" I will try it for one night more," I said.

" Better give it up, sir—better give it up! It's a precious bad job," repeated the workman, putting his tools in his bag and leaving the cabin.

But my spirits had risen considerably at the prospect of having the captain's company, and I made up my mind not to be prevented from going to the end of the strange business. I abstained from Welsh rare-bits and grog that evening, and did not even join in the customary game of whist. I wanted to be quite sure of my nerves, and my vanity made me anxious to make a good figure in the captain's eyes.

IV

THE captain was one of those splendidly tough and cheerful specimens of seafaring humanity whose combined courage, hardihood, and calmness in difficulty leads them naturally into high positions of trust. He was not the man to be led away by an idle tale, and the mere fact that he was willing to join me in the investigation was proof that he thought there was something seriously wrong, which could not be accounted for on ordinary theories, nor laughed down as a common superstition. To some extent, too, his reputation was at stake, as well as the reputation of the ship. It is no light thing to lose passengers overboard, and he knew it.

About ten o'clock that evening, as I was smoking a last cigar, he came up to me, and drew me aside from the beat of the other passengers who were patrolling the deck in the warm darkness.

"This is a serious matter, Mr. Brisbane," he said. "We must make up our minds either way—to be disappointed or to have a pretty rough time of it. You see I cannot afford to laugh at the affair, and I will ask you to sign your name to a statement of whatever occurs. If nothing happens to-night we will try it again to-morrow and next day. Are you ready?"

So we went below, and entered the state-room. As we went in I could see Robert the steward, who stood a little farther down the passage, watching us, with his usual grin, as though certain that something dreadful was about to happen. The captain closed the door behind us and bolted it.

"Supposing we put your portmanteau before the door," he suggested. "One of us can sit on it. Nothing can get out then. Is the port screwed down?"

I found it as I had left it in the morning. Indeed, without using a lever, as I had done, no one could have opened it. I drew back the curtains of the upper berth so that I could see well into it. By the captain's advice I lighted my reading-lantern, and placed it so that it shone upon the white sheets above. He insisted upon sitting on the portmanteau, declaring that he wished to be able to swear that he had sat before the door.

Then he requested me to search the state-room thoroughly, an operation very soon accomplished, as it consisted merely in looking beneath the lower berth and under the couch below the porthole. The spaces were quite empty.

"It is impossible for any human being to get in," I said, "or for any human being to open the port."

"Very good," said the captain calmly. "If we see anything now, it must be either imagination or something supernatural."

I sat down on the edge of the lower berth.

"The first time it happened," said the captain, crossing his legs and leaning back against the door, "was in March. The passenger who slept here, in the upper berth, turned out to have been a lunatic—at all events, he was known to have been a little touched, and he had taken his passage without the knowledge of his friends. He rushed out in the middle of the night, and threw himself overboard, before the officer who had the watch could stop him. We stopped and

lowered a boat; it was a quiet night, just before that heavy
weather came on; but we could not find him. Of course
his suicide was afterwards accounted for on the ground of
his insanity."

"I suppose that often happens?" I remarked, rather absently.

"Not often—no," said the captain; "never before in my
experience, though I have heard of it happening on board of
other ships. Well, as I was saying, that occurred in March.
On the very next trip—— What are you looking at?" he
asked, stopping suddenly in his narration.

I believe I gave no answer. My eyes were riveted upon
the porthole. It seemed to me that the brass loop-nut was
beginning to turn very slowly upon the screw—so slowly,
however, that I was not sure it moved at all. I watched it
intently, fixing its position in my mind, and trying to ascertain whether it changed. Seeing where I was looking, the
captain looked, too.

"It moves!" he exclaimed, in a tone of conviction. "No,
it does not," he added, after a minute.

"If it were the jarring of the screw," said I, "it would
have opened during the day; but I found it this evening
jammed tight as I left it this morning."

I rose and tried the nut. It was certainly loosened, for
by an effort I could move it with my hands.

"The queer thing," said the captain, "is that the second
man who was lost is supposed to have got through that very
port. We had a terrible time over it. It was in the middle
of the night, and the weather was very heavy; there was
an alarm that one of the ports was open and the sea running
in. I came below and found everything flooded, the water
pouring in every time she rolled, and the whole port swinging
from the top bolts—not the porthole in the middle. Well,
we managed to shut it, but the water did some damage. Ever
since that the place smells of sea-water from time to time.
We supposed the passenger had thrown himself out, though
the Lord only knows how he did it. The steward kept telling
me that he cannot keep anything shut here. Upon my word
—I can smell it now, cannot you?" he enquired, sniffing the
air suspiciously.

"Yes—distinctly," I said, and I shuddered as that same
odour of stagnant sea-water grew stronger in the cabin.

"Now, to smell like this, the place must be damp," I continued, "and yet when I examined it with the carpenter this morning everything was perfectly dry. It is most extraordinary—hallo!"

My reading-lantern, which had been placed in the upper berth, was suddenly extinguished. There was still a good deal of light from the pane of ground glass near the door, behind which loomed the regulation lamp. The ship rolled heavily, and the curtain of the upper berth swung far out into the state-room and back again. I rose quickly from my seat on the edge of the bed, and the captain at the same moment started to his feet with a loud cry of surprise. I had turned with the intention of taking down the lantern to examine it, when I heard his exclamation, and immediately afterwards his call for help. I sprang towards him. He was wrestling with all his might with the brass loop of the port. It seemed to turn against his hands in spite of all his efforts. I caught up my cane, a heavy oak stick I always used to carry, and thrust it through the ring and bore on it with all my strength. But the strong wood snapped suddenly and I fell upon the couch. When I rose again the port was wide open, and the captain was standing with his back against the door, pale to the lips.

"There is something in that berth!" he cried, in a strange voice, his eyes almost starting from his head. "Hold the door, while I look—it shall not escape us, whatever it is!"

But instead of taking his place, I sprang upon the lower bed, and seized something which lay in the upper berth.

It was something ghostly, horrible beyond words, and it moved in my grip. It was like the body of a man long drowned, and yet it moved, and had the strength of ten men living; but I gripped it with all my might—the slippery, oozy, horrible thing—the dead white eyes seemed to stare at me out of the dusk; the putrid odour of rank seawater was about it, and its shiny hair hung in foul wet curls over its dead face. I wrestled with the dead thing; it thrust itself upon me and forced me back and nearly broke my arms; it wound its corpse's arms about my neck, the living death, and overpowered me, so that I, at last, cried aloud and fell, and left my hold.

As I fell the thing sprang across me, and seemed to throw itself upon the captain. When I last saw him on his feet his face was white and his lips set. It seemed to me that he struck a violent blow at the dead being, and then he, too, fell forward upon his face, with an inarticulate cry of horror.

The thing paused an instant, seeming to hover over his prostrate body, and I could have screamed again for very fright, but I had no voice left. The thing vanished suddenly, and it seemed to my disturbed senses that it made its exit through the open port, though how that was possible, considering the smallness of the aperture, is more than any one can tell. I lay a long time upon the floor, and the captain lay beside me. At last I partially recovered my senses and moved, and instantly I knew that my arm was broken—the small bone of the left forearm near the wrist.

I got upon my feet somehow, and with my remaining hand I tried to raise the captain. He groaned and moved, and at last came to himself. He was not hurt, but he seemed badly stunned.

Well, do you want to hear any more? There is nothing more. That is the end of my story. The carpenter carried out his scheme of running half a dozen four-inch screws through the door of 105; and if ever you take a passage in the *Kamtschatka*, you may ask for a berth in that stateroom. You will be told that it is engaged—yes—it is engaged by that dead thing.

I finished the trip in the surgeon's cabin. He doctored my broken arm, and advised me not to " fiddle about with ghosts and things " any more. The captain was very silent, and never sailed again in that ship, though it is still running. And I will not sail in her either. It was a very disagreeable experience, and I was very badly frightened, which is a thing I do not like. That is all. That is how I saw a ghost—if it was a ghost. It was dead, anyhow.

MAN OVERBOARD!

YES—I have heard " Man overboard! " a good many times since I was a boy, and once or twice I have seen the man go. There are more men lost in that way than passengers on ocean steamers ever learn of. I have stood looking over the rail on a dark night, when there was a step beside me, and something flew past my head like a big black bat—and then there was a splash! Stokers often go like that. They go mad with the heat, and they slip up on deck and are gone before anybody can stop them, often without being seen or heard. Now and then a passenger will do it, but he generally has what he thinks a pretty good reason. I have seen a man empty his revolver into a crowd of emigrants forward, and then go over like a rocket. Of course, any officer who respects himself will do what he can to pick a man up, if the weather is not so heavy that he would have to risk his ship; but I don't think I remember seeing a man come back when he was once fairly gone more than two or three times in all my life, though we have often picked up the life-buoy, and sometimes the fellow's cap. Stokers and passengers jump over; I never knew a sailor to do that, drunk or sober. Yes, they say it has happened on hard ships, but I never knew a case myself. Once in a long time a man is fished out when it is just too late, and dies in the boat before you can get him aboard, and—well, I don't know that I ever told that story since it happened—I knew a fellow who went over, and came back dead. I didn't see him after he came back; only one of us did, but we all knew he was there.

No, I am not giving you " sharks." There isn't a shark in this story, and I don't know that I would tell it at all if we weren't alone, just you and I. But you and I have seen things in various parts, and maybe you will understand. Anyhow, you know that I am telling what I know about, and nothing else; and it has been on my mind to tell you ever since it happened, only there hasn't been a chance.

It's a long story, and it took some time to happen; and

it began a good many years ago, in October, as well as I can remember. I was mate then; I passed the local Marine Board for master about three years later. She was the *Helen B. Jackson*, of New York, with lumber for the West Indies, four-masted schooner, Captain Hackstaff. She was an old-fashioned one, even then—no steam donkey, and all to do by hand. There were still sailors in the coasting trade in those days, you remember. She wasn't a hard ship, for the Old Man was better than most of them, though he kept to himself and had a face like a monkey-wrench. We were thirteen, all told, in the ship's company; and some of them afterwards thought that might have had something to do with it, but I had all that nonsense knocked out of me when I was a boy. I don't mean to say that I like to go to sea on a Friday, but I *have* gone to sea on a Friday, and nothing has happened; and twice before that we have been thirteen, because one of the hands didn't turn up at the last minute, and nothing ever happened either—nothing worse than the loss of a light spar or two, or a little canvas. Whenever I have been wrecked, we had sailed as cheerily as you please—no thirteens, no Fridays, no dead men in the hold. I believe it generally happens that way.

I daresay you remember those two Benton boys that were so much alike? It's no wonder, for they were twin brothers. They shipped with us as boys on the old *Boston Belle*, when you were mate and I was before the mast. I never was quite sure which was which of those two, even then; and when they both had beards it was harder than ever to tell them apart. One was Jim, and the other was Jack; James Benton and John Benton. The only difference I ever could see was, that one seemed to be rather more cheerful and inclined to talk than the other; but one couldn't even be sure of that. Perhaps they had moods. Anyhow, there was one of them that used to whistle when he was alone. He only knew one tune, and that was " Nancy Lee," and the other didn't know any tune at all; but I may be mistaken about that, too. Perhaps they both knew it.

Well, those two Benton boys turned up on board the *Helen B. Jackson*. They had been on half a dozen ships since the *Boston Belle*, and they had grown up and were good seamen. They had reddish beards and bright blue eyes and freckled faces; and they were quiet fellows, good workmen on rigging, pretty willing, and both good men at the wheel. They managed to be in the same watch—it was the port watch on the *Helen B.*, and that was mine, and I had great confidence in them both. If there was any job aloft that needed two hands, they were always the first to jump into the rigging; but that doesn't often happen on a fore-and-aft schooner. If it breezed up, and the jibtopsail was to be taken in, they never minded a wetting, and they would be out at the bowsprit end before there was a hand at the downhaul. The men liked them for that, and because they didn't blow about what they could do. I remember one day in a reefing job, the downhaul parted and came down on deck from the peak of the spanker. When the weather moderated, and we shook the reefs out, the downhaul was forgotten, until we happened to think we might soon need it again. There was some sea on, and the boom was off and the gaff was slamming. One of those Benton boys was at the wheel, and before I knew what he was doing, the other was out on the gaff with the end of the new downhaul, trying to reeve it through its block. The one who was steering watched him, and got as white as cheese. The other one was swinging about on the gaff end, and every time she rolled to leeward he brought up with a jerk that would have sent anything but a monkey flying into space. But he didn't leave it until he had rove the new rope, and he got back all right. I think it was Jack at the wheel; the one that seemed more cheerful, the one that whistled " Nancy Lee." He had rather have been doing the job himself than watch his brother do it, and he had a scared look; but he kept her as steady as he could in the swell, and he drew a long breath when Jim had worked his way back to the peak-halliard block, and had something to hold on to. I think it was Jim.

They had good togs, too, and they were neat and clean men in the forecastle. I knew they had nobody belonging to them ashore—no mother, no sisters, and no wives; but somehow they both looked as if a woman overhauled them now and then. I remember that they had one ditty bag between them, and they had a woman's thimble in it. One of the men said something about it to them, and they looked at each other; and one smiled, but the other didn't. Most of their clothes were alike, but they had one red guernsey between them. For some time I used to think it was always

the same one that wore it, and I thought that might be a
way to tell them apart.   But then I heard one asking the
other for it, and saying that the other had worn it last.
So that was no sign either.   The cook was a West India man,
called James Lawley; his father had been hanged for putting
lights in coconut trees where they didn't belong.   But he
was a good cook, and knew his business; and it wasn't soup-
and-bully and dog's-body every Sunday.   That's what I
meant to say.   On Sunday the cook called both those boys
Jim, and on week-days he called them Jack.   He used to say
he must be right sometimes if he did that, because even the
hands on a painted clock point right twice a day.

What started me trying for some way of telling the Ben-
tons apart was this.   I heard them talking about a girl.   It
was at night, in our watch, and the wind had headed us off
a little rather suddenly, and when we had flattened in the
jibs, we clewed down the top-sails, while the two Benton
boys got the spanker sheet aft.   One of them was at the
helm.   I coiled down the mizzen-topsail downhaul myself,
and was going aft to see how she headed up, when I stopped
to look at a light, and leaned against the deck-house.   While
I was standing there I heard the two boys talking.   It
sounded as if they had talked of the same thing before, and
as far as I could tell, the voice I heard first belonged to the
one who wasn't quite so cheerful as the other—the one who
was Jim when one knew which he was.

" Does Mamie know? " Jim asked.

" Not yet," Jack answered quietly.   He was at the wheel.
" I mean to tell her next time we get home."

" All right."

That was all I heard, because I didn't care to stand there
listening while they were talking about their own affairs; so
I went aft to look into the binnacle, and I told the one at the
wheel to keep her so as long as she had way on her, for I
thought the wind would back up again before long, and there
was land to leeward.   When he answered, his voice; somehow, didn't sound like the cheerful one.   Perhaps his brother
had relieved the wheel while they had been speaking, but
what I had heard set me wondering which of them it was
that had a girl at home.   There's lots of time for wondering
on a schooner in fair weather.

After that I thought I noticed that the two brothers were

more silent when they were together. Perhaps they guessed that I had overheard something that night, and kept quiet when I was about. Some men would have amused themselves by trying to chaff them separately about the girl at home, and I suppose whichever one it was would have let the cat out of the bag if I had done that. But, somehow, I didn't like to. Yes, I was thinking of getting married myself at that time, so I had a sort of fellow-feeling for whichever one it was, that made me not want to chaff him.

They didn't talk much, it seemed to me; but in fair weather, when there was nothing to do at night, and one was steering, the other was everlastingly hanging round as if he were waiting to relieve the wheel, though he might have been enjoying a quiet nap for all I cared in such weather. Or else, when one was taking his turn at the lookout, the other would be sitting on an anchor beside him. One kept near the other, at night more than in the daytime. I noticed that. They were fond of sitting on that anchor, and they generally tucked away their pipes under it, for the *Helen B.* was a dry boat in most weather, and like most fore-and-afters was better on a wind than going free. With a beam sea we sometimes shipped a little water aft. We were by the stern, anyhow, on that voyage, and that is one reason why we lost the man.

We fell in with a southerly gale, south-east at first; and then the barometer began to fall while you could watch it, and a long swell began to come up from the south'ard. A couple of months earlier we might have been in for a cyclone, but it's "October all over" in those waters, as you know better than I. It was just going to blow, and then it was going to rain, that was all; and we had plenty of time to make everything snug before it breezed up much. It blew harder after sunset, and by the time it was quite dark it was a full gale. We had shortened sail for it, but as we were by the stern we were carrying the spanker close reefed instead of the storm trysail. She steered better so, as long as we didn't have to heave to. I had the first watch with the Benton boys, and we had not been on deck an hour when a child might have seen that the weather meant business.

The Old Man came up on deck and looked round, and in less than a minute he told us to give her the trysail. That meant heaving to, and I was glad of it; for though the *Helen*

B. was a good vessel enough, she wasn't a new ship by a long way, and it did her no good to drive her in that weather. I asked whether I should call all hands, but just then the cook came aft, and the Old Man said he thought we could manage the job without waking the sleepers, and the trysail was handy on deck already, for we hadn't been expecting anything better. We were all in oilskins, of course, and the night was as black as a coal mine, with only a ray of light from the slit in the binnacle shield, and you couldn't tell one man from another except by his voice. The Old Man took the wheel; we got the boom amidships, and he jammed her into the wind until she had hardly any way. It was blowing now, and it was all that I and two others could do to get in the slack of the downhaul, while the others lowered away at the peak and throat, and we had our hands full to get a couple of turns round the wet sail. It's all child's play on a fore-and-after compared with reefing top-sails in anything like weather, but the gear of a schooner sometimes does unhandy things that you don't expect, and those everlasting long halliards get foul of everything if they get adrift. I remember thinking how unhandy that particular job was. Somebody unhooked the throat-halliard block, and thought he had hooked it into the head-cringle of the trysail, and sang out to hoist away, but he had missed it in the dark, and the heavy block went flying into the lee rigging, and nearly killed him when it swung back with the weather roll. Then the Old Man got her up in the wind until the jib was shaking like thunder; then he held her off, and she went off as soon as the head-sails filled, and he couldn't get her back again without the spanker. Then the Helen B. did her favourite trick, and before we had time to say much we had a sea over the quarter and were up to our waists, with the parrels of the trysail only half becketed round the mast, and the deck so full of gear that you couldn't put your foot on a plank, and the spanker beginning to get adrift again, being badly stopped, and the general confusion and hell's delight that you can only have on a fore-and-after when there's nothing really serious the matter. Of course, I don't mean to say that the Old Man couldn't have steered his trick as well as you or I or any other seaman; but I don't believe he had ever been on board the Helen B. before, or had his hand on her wheel till then; and he didn't know her ways.

I don't mean to say that what happened was his fault. I don't know whose fault it was. Perhaps nobody was to blame. But I knew something happened somewhere on board when we shipped that sea, and you'll never get it out of my head. I hadn't any spare time myself, for I was becketing the rest of the trysail to the mast. We were on the starboard tack, and the throat-halliard came down to port as usual, and I suppose there were at least three men at it, hoisting away, while I was at the beckets.

Now I am going to tell you something. You have known me, man and boy, several voyages; and you are older than I am; and you have always been a good friend to me. Now, do you think I am the sort of man to think I hear things where there isn't anything to hear, or to think I see things when there is nothing to see? No, you don't. Thank you. Well now, I had passed the last becket, and I sang out to the men to sway away, and I was standing on the jaws of the spanker-gaff, with my left hand on the bolt-rope of the trysail, so that I could feel when it was board taut, and I wasn't thinking of anything except being glad the job was over, and that we were going to heave her to. It was as black as a coal-pocket, except that you could see the streaks on the seas as they went by, and abaft the deck-house I could see the ray of light from the binnacle on the captain's yellow oilskin as he stood at the wheel—or, rather, I might have seen it if I had looked round at that minute. But I didn't look round. I heard a man whistling. It was "Nancy Lee," and I could have sworn that the man was right over my head in the crosstrees. Only somehow I knew very well that if anybody could have been up there, and could have whistled a tune, there were no living ears sharp enough to hear it on deck then. I heard it distinctly, and at the same time I heard the real whistling of the wind in the weather rigging, sharp and clear as the steam-whistle on a Dago's peanut-cart in New York. That was all right, that was as it should be; but the other wasn't right; and I felt queer and stiff, as if I couldn't move, and my hair was curling against the flannel lining of my sou-wester, and I thought somebody had dropped a lump of ice down my back.

I said that the noise of the wind in the rigging was real, as if the other wasn't, for I felt that it wasn't, though I heard it. But it was, all the same; for the captain heard it too.

When I came to relieve the wheel, while the men were clearing up decks, he was swearing. He was a quiet man, and I hadn't heard him swear before, and I don't think I did again, though several queer things happened after that. Perhaps he said all he had to say then; I don't see how he could have said anything more. I used to think nobody could swear like a Dane, except a Neapolitan or a South American; but when I had heard the Old Man I changed my mind. There's nothing afloat or ashore that can beat one of your quiet American skippers, if he gets off on that tack. I didn't need to ask him what was the matter, for I knew he had heard " Nancy Lee," as I had, only it affected us differently.

He did not give me the wheel, but told me to go forward and get the second bonnet off the staysail, so as to keep her up better. As we tailed on to the sheet when it was done, the man next me knocked his sou'wester off against my shoulder, and his face came so close to me that I could see it in the dark. It must have been very white for me to see it, but I only thought of that afterwards. I don't see how any light could have fallen upon it, but I knew it was one of the Benton boys. I don't know what made me speak to him. " Hullo, Jim! Is that you? " I asked. I don't know why I said Jim, rather than Jack.

" I am Jack," he answered.

We made all fast, and things were much quieter. " The Old Man heard you whistling ' Nancy Lee,' just now," I said, " and he didn't like it."

It was as if there were a white light inside his face, and it was ghastly. I know his teeth chattered. But he didn't say anything, and the next minute he was somewhere in the dark trying to find his sou'wester at the foot of the mast.

When all was quiet, and she was hove to, coming to and falling off her four points as regularly as a pendulum, and the helm lashed a little to the lee, the Old Man turned in again, and I managed to light a pipe in the lee of the deckhouse, for there was nothing more to be done till the gale chose to moderate, and the ship was as easy as a baby in its cradle. Of course the cook had gone below, as he might have done an hour earlier; so there were supposed to be four of us in the watch. There was a man at the lookout, and there was a hand by the wheel, though there was no steering to be done, and I was having my pipe in the lee of the deck-house, and the fourth man was somewhere about decks, probably having a smoke too. I thought some skippers I had sailed with would have called the watch aft, and given them a drink after that job, but it wasn't cold, and I guessed that our Old Man wouldn't be particularly generous in that way. My hands and feet were red-hot, and it would be time enough to get into dry clothes when it was my watch below; so I stayed where I was, and smoked. But by and by, things being so quiet, I began to wonder why nobody moved on deck; just that sort of restless wanting to know where every man is that one sometimes feels in a gale of wind on a dark night. So when I had finished my pipe I began to move about. I went aft, and there was a man leaning over the wheel, with his legs apart and both hands hanging down in the light from the binnacle, and his sou'-wester over his eyes. Then I went forward, and there was a man at the lookout, with his back against the foremast, getting what shelter he could from the staysail. I knew by his small height that he was not one of the Benton boys. Then I went round by the weather side, and poked about in the dark, for I began to wonder where the other man was. But I couldn't find him, though I searched the decks until I got right aft again. It was certainly one of the Benton boys that was missing, but it wasn't like either of them to go below to change his clothes in such warm weather. The man at the wheel was the other, of course. I spoke to him.

" Jim what's become of your brother? "

" I am Jack, sir."

" Well, then, Jack, where's Jim? He's not on deck."

" I don't know, sir."

When I had come up to him he had stood up from force of instinct, and had laid his hands on the spokes as if he were steering, though the wheel was lashed; but he still bent his face down, and it was half hidden by the edge of his sou'wester, while he seemed to be staring at the compass. He spoke in a very low voice, but that was natural, for the captain had left his door open when he turned in, as it was a warm night in spite of the storm, and there was no fear of shipping any more water now.

" What put it into your head to whistle like that, Jack? You've been at sea long enough to know better."

He said something, but I couldn't hear the words; it sounded as if he were denying the charge.

" Somebody whistled," I said.

He didn't answer, and then, I don't know why, perhaps because the Old Man hadn't given us a drink, I cut half an inch off the plug of tobacco I had in my oilskin pocket, and gave it to him. He knew my tobacco was good, and he shoved it into his mouth with a word of thanks. I was on the weather side of the wheel.

" Go forward and see if you can find Jim," I said.

He started a little, and then stepped back and passed behind me, and was going along the weather side. Maybe his silence about the whistling had irritated me, and his taking it for granted that because we were hove to and it was a dark night, he might go forward any way he pleased. Anyhow, I stopped him, though I spoke good-naturedly enough.

" Pass to leeward, Jack," I said.

He didn't answer, but crossed the deck between the binnacle and the deck-house to the lee side. She was only falling off and coming to, and riding the big seas as easily as possible, but the man was not steady on his feet and reeled against the corner of the deck-house and then against the lee rail. I was quite sure he couldn't have had anything to drink, for neither of the brothers were the kind to hide rum from their shipmates, if they had any, and the only spirits that were aboard were locked up in the captain's cabin. I wondered whether he had been hit by the throat-halliard block and was hurt.

I left the wheel and went after him, but when I got to the corner of the deck-house I saw that he was on a full run forward, so I went back. I watched the compass for a while, to see how far she went off, and she must have come to again half a dozen times before I heard voices, more than three or four, forward; and then I heard the little West Indies cook's voice, high and shrill above the rest:

" Man overboard! "

There wasn't anything to be done, with the ship hove to and the wheel lashed. If there was a man overboard, he must be in the water right alongside. I couldn't imagine how it could have happened, but I ran forward instinctively. I came upon the cook first, half dressed in his shirt and trousers, just as he had tumbled out of his bunk. He was jumping into the main rigging, evidently hoping to see the man, as if anyone could have seen anything on such a night, except the foam-streaks on the black water, and now and then the curl of a breaking sea as it went away to leeward. Several of the men were peering over the rail into the dark. I caught the cook by the foot, and asked who was gone. "It's Jim Benton," he shouted down to me. "He's not aboard this ship!"

There was no doubt about that. Jim Benton was gone; and I knew in a flash that he had been taken off by that sea when we were setting the storm trysail. It was nearly half an hour since then; she had run like wild for a few minutes until we got her hove to, and no swimmer that ever swam could have lived as long as that in such a sea. The men knew it as well as I, but still they stared into the foam as if they had any chance of seeing the lost man. I let the cook get into the rigging and joined the men, and asked if they had made a thorough search on board, though I knew they had and that it could not take long, for he wasn't on deck, and there was only the forecastle below.

"That sea took him over, sir, as sure as you're born," said one of the men close beside me.

We had no boat that could have lived in that sea, of course, and we all knew it. I offered to put one over, and let her drift astern two or three cables'-lengths by a line, if the men thought they could haul me aboard again; but none of them would listen to that, and I should probably have been drowned if I had tried it, even with a life-belt; for it was breaking sea. Besides, they all knew as well as I did that the man could not be right in our wake. I don't know why I spoke again.

"Jack Benton, are you there? Will you go if I will?"

"No, sir," answered a voice; and that was all.

By that time the Old Man was on deck, and I felt his hand on my shoulder rather roughly, as if he meant to shake me.

"I'd reckoned you had more sense, Mr. Torkeldsen," he said. "God knows I would risk my ship to look for him, if it were any use; but he must have gone half an hour ago."

He was a quiet man, and the men knew he was right, and that they had seen the last of Jim Benton when they were bending the trysail—if anybody had seen him then. The captain went below again, and for some time the men stood around Jack, quite near him, without saying anything, as sailors do when they are sorry for a man and can't help him; and then the watch below turned in again, and we were three on deck.

Nobody can understand that there can be much consolation in a funeral, unless he has felt that blank feeling there is when a man's gone overboard whom everybody likes. I suppose landsmen think it would be easier if they didn't have to bury their fathers and mothers and friends; but it wouldn't be. Somehow the funeral keeps up the idea of something beyond. You may believe in that something just the same; but a man who has gone in the dark, between two seas, without a cry, seems much more beyond reach than if he were still lying on his bed, and had only just stopped breathing. Perhaps Jim Benton knew that, and wanted to come back to us. I don't know, and I am only telling you what happened, and you may think what you like.

Jack stuck by the wheel that night until the watch was over. I don't know whether he slept afterwards, but when I came on deck four hours later, there he was again, in his oilskins, with his sou'wester over his eyes, staring into the binnacle. We saw that he would rather stand there, and we left him alone. Perhaps it was some consolation to him to get that ray of light when everything was so dark. It began to rain, too, as it can when a southerly gale is going to break up, and we got every bucket and tub on board, and set them under the booms to catch the fresh water for washing our clothes. The rain made it very thick, and I went and stood under the lee of the staysail, looking out. I could tell that day was breaking, because the foam was whiter in the dark where the seas crested, and little by little the black rain grew grey and steamy, and I couldn't see the red glare of the port light on the water when she went off and rolled to leeward. The gale had moderated considerably, and in another hour we should be under way again. I was still standing there when Jack Benton came forward. He stood still a few minutes near me. The rain came down in a solid sheet, and I could see his wet beard and a corner of his cheek, too, grey in the dawn. Then he stooped down and began feeling under the anchor for his pipe. We had hardly shipped any water forward, and I suppose he had some way of tucking the pipe in, so that the rain hadn't floated it off. Presently he got on his legs again, and I saw that he had two pipes in his hand. One of them had belonged to his brother and after looking at them a moment I suppose he recognised his own, for he put it in his mouth, dripping with water. Then he looked at the other fully a minute without moving. When he had made up his mind, I suppose, he quietly chucked it over the lee rail, without even looking round to see whether I was watching him. I thought it was a pity, for it was a good wooden pipe, with a nickel ferrule, and somebody would have been glad to have it. But I didn't like to make any remark, for he had a right to do what he pleased with what had belonged to his dead brother. He blew the water out of his own pipe, and dried it against his jacket; putting his hand inside his oilskin, he filled it, standing under the lee of the foremast, got a light after wasting two or three matches, and turned the pipe upside down in his teeth, to keep the rain out of the bowl. I don't know why I noticed everything he did, and remember it now; but somehow I felt sorry for him, and I kept wondering whether there was anything I could say that would make him feel better. But I didn't think of anything, and as it was broad daylight I went aft again, for I guessed that the Old Man would turn out before long and order the spanker set and the helm up. But he didn't turn out before seven bells, just as the clouds broke and showed blue sky to leeward—" the Frenchman's barometer," you used to call it.

Some people don't seem to be so dead, when they are dead, as others are. Jim Benton was like that. He had been on my watch, and I couldn't get used to the idea that he wasn't about decks with me. I was always expecting to see him, and his brother was so exactly like him that I often felt as if I did see him and forgot he was dead, and made the mistake of calling Jack by his name; though I tried not to, because I knew it must hurt. If ever Jack had been the cheerful one of the two, as I had always supposed he had been, he had changed very much, for he grew to be more silent than Jim had ever been.

One fine afternoon I was sitting on the main-hatch, overhauling the clockwork of the taffrail-log, which hadn't been registering very well of late, and I had got the cook to bring me a coffee-cup to hold the small screws as I took them out, and a saucer for the sperm oil I was going to use. I noticed that he didn't go away, but hung round without exactly watching what I was doing, as if he wanted to say something to me. I thought if it were worth much he would say it anyhow, so I didn't ask him questions; and sure enough he began of his own accord before long. There was nobody on deck but the man at the wheel, and the other man away forward.

" Mr. Torkeldsen," the cook began, and then stopped.

I supposed he was going to ask me to let the watch break out a barrel of flour, or some salt horse.

" Well, doctor? " I asked, as he didn't go on.

" Well, Mr. Torkeldsen," he answered, " I somehow want to ask you whether you think I am giving satisfaction on this ship, or not? "

" So far as I know, you are, doctor. I haven't heard any complaints from the forecastle, and the captain has said nothing, and I think you know your business, and the cabin-boy is bursting out of his clothes. That looks as if you are giving satisfaction. What makes you think you are not? "

I am not good at giving you that West Indies talk, and shan't try; but the doctor beat about the bush awhile, and then he told me he thought the men were beginning to play tricks on him, and he didn't like it, and thought he hadn't deserved it, and would like his discharge at our next port. I told him he was a d——d fool, of course, to begin with; and that men were more apt to try a joke with a chap they liked than with anybody they wanted to get rid of; unless it was a bad joke, like flooding his bunk, or filling his boots with tar. But it wasn't that kind of practical joke. The doctor said that the men were trying to frighten him, and he didn't like it, and that they put things in his way that frightened him. So I told him he was a d——d fool to be frightened, anyway, and I wanted to know what things they put in his way. He gave me a queer answer. He said they were spoons and forks, and odd plates, and a cup now and then, and such things.

I set down the taffrail-log on the bit of canvas I had put under it, and looked at the doctor. He was uneasy, and his eyes had a sort of hunted look, and his yellow face looked grey. He wasn't trying to make trouble. He was in trouble. So I asked him questions.

He said he could count as well as anybody, and do sums

without using his fingers, but that when he couldn't count any other way he did use his fingers, and it always came out the same. He said that when he and the cabin-boy cleared up after the men's meals there were more things to wash than he had given out. There'd be a fork more, or there'd be a spoon more, and sometimes there'd be a spoon and a fork, and there was always a plate more. It wasn't that he complained of that. Before poor Jim Benton was lost they had a man more to feed, and his gear to wash up after meals, and that was in the contract, the doctor said. It would have been if there were twenty in the ship's company; but he didn't think it was right for the men to play tricks like that. He kept his things in good order, and he counted them, and he was responsible for them, and it wasn't right that the men should take more things than they needed when his back was turned, and just soil them and mix them up with their own, so as to make him think——

He stopped there, and looked at me, and I looked at him. I didn't know what he thought, but I began to guess. I wasn't going to humour any such nonsense as that, so I told him to speak to the men himself, and not come bothering me about such things.

"Count the plates and forks and spoons before them when they sit down to table, and tell them that's all they'll get; and when they have finished, count the things again, and if the count isn't right, find out who did it. You know it must be one of them. You're not a green hand; you've been going to sea ten or eleven years, and don't want any lessons about how to behave if the boys play a trick on you."

"If I could catch him," said the cook, "I'd have a knife into him before he could say his prayers."

Those West India men are always talking about knives, especially when they are badly frightened. I knew what he meant, and didn't ask him, but went on cleaning the brass cog-wheels of the patent log and oiling the bearings with a feather. "Wouldn't it be better to wash it out with boiling water, sir?" asked the cook, in an insinuating tone. He knew that he had made a fool of himself, and was anxious to make it right again.

I heard no more about the odd platter and gear for two or three days, though I thought about his story a good deal. The doctor evidently believed that Jim Benton had come

back, though he didn't quite like to say so. His story had
sounded silly enough on a bright afternoon, in fair weather,
when the sun was on the water, and every rag was drawing
in the breeze, and the sea looked as pleasant and harmless as
a cat that has just eaten a canary. But when it was toward
the end of the first watch, and the waning moon had not
risen yet, and the water was like still oil, and the jibs hung
down flat and helpless like the wings of a dead bird—it
wasn't the same then. More than once I have started then,
and looked round when a fish jumped, expecting to see a
face sticking up out of the water with its eyes shut. I think
we all felt something like that at the time.

One afternoon we were putting a fresh service on the jib-
sheet-pennant. It wasn't my watch, but I was standing by
looking on. Just then Jack Benton came up from below,
and went to look for his pipe under the anchor. His face
was hard and drawn, and his eyes were cold like steel balls.
He hardly ever spoke now, but he did his duty as usual, and
nobody had to complain of him, though we were all beginning
to wonder how long his grief for his dead brother was going
to last like that. I watched him as he crouched down, and
ran his hand into the hiding-place for the pipe. When he
stood up he had two pipes in his hand.

Now, I remembered very well seeing him throw one of
those pipes away, early in the morning after the gale; and it
came to me now, and I didn't suppose he kept a stock of
them under the anchor. I caught sight of his face, and it
was greenish white, like the foam on shallow water, and he
stood a long time looking at the two pipes. He wasn't looking to see which was his, for I wasn't five yards from him
as he stood, and one of those pipes had been smoked that
day, and was shiny where his hand had rubbed it, and the
bone mouthpiece was chafed white where his teeth had bitten
it. The other was waterlogged. It was swelled and cracking
with wet, and it looked to me as if there were a little green
weed on it.

Jack Benton turned his head rather stealthily as I looked
away, and then he hid the thing in his trousers pocket, and
went aft on the lee side, out of sight. The men had got the
sheet-pennant on a stretch to serve it, but I ducked under it
and stood where I could see what Jack did, just under the
fore-staysail. He couldn't see me, and he was looking about

for something. His hand shook as he picked up a bit of half-bent iron rod, about a foot long, that had been used for turning an eye-bolt, and had been left on the main-hatch. His hand shook as he got a piece of marline out of his pocket, and made the waterlogged pipe fast to the iron. He didn't mean it to get adrift either, for he took his turns carefully, and hove them taut and then rode them, so that they couldn't slip, and made the end fast with two half-hitches round the iron, and hitched it back on itself. Then he tried it with his hands, and looked up and down the deck furtively, and then quietly dropped the pipe and iron over the rail, so that I didn't even hear the splash. If anybody was playing tricks on board, they weren't meant for the cook.

I asked some questions about Jack Benton, and one of the men told me that he was off his feed, and hardly ate anything, and swallowed all the coffee he could lay his hands on, and had used up all his own tobacco and had begun on what his brother had left.

"The doctor says it ain't so, sir," said the man, looking at me shyly, as if he didn't expect to be believed; "the doctor says there's as much eaten from breakfast to breakfast as there was before Jim fell overboard, though there's a mouth less and another that eats nothing. I says it's the cabin-boy that gets it. He's bu'sting."

I told him that if the cabin-boy ate more than his share, he must work more than his share, so as to balance things. But the man laughed queerly, and looked at me again.

"I only said that, sir, just like that. We all know it ain't so."

"Well, how is it?"

"How is it?" asked the man, half-angry all at once. "I don't know how it is, but there's a hand on board that's getting his whack along with us as regular as the bells."

"Does he use tobacco?" I asked, meaning to laugh it out of him, but as I spoke I remembered the waterlogged pipe.

"I guess he's using his own still," the man answered, in a queer, low voice. "Perhaps he'll take some one else's when his is all gone."

It was about nine o'clock in the morning, I remember, for just then the captain called to me to stand by the chronometer while he took his fore observation. Captain Hackstaff wasn't one of those old skippers who do everything them-

selves with a pocket watch, and keep the key of the chronometer in their waistcoat pocket, and won't tell the mate how
far the dead reckoning is out. He was rather the other way,
and I was glad of it, for he generally let me work the sights
he took, and just ran his eye over my figures afterwards. I
am bound to say his eye was pretty good, for he would pick
out a mistake in a logarithm, or tell me that I had worked the
" Equation of Time " with the wrong sign, before it seemed
to me that he could have got as far as " half the sum, minus
the altitude." He was always right, too, and besides he knew
a lot about iron ships and local deviation, and adjusting the
compass, and all that sort of thing. I don't know how he
came to be in command of a fore-and-aft schooner. He
never talked about himself, and maybe he had just been mate
on one of those big steel square-riggers, and something had
put him back. Perhaps he had been captain, and had got his
ship aground, through no particular fault of his, and had to
begin over again. Sometimes he talked just like you and me,
and sometimes he would speak more like books do, or some
of those Boston people I have heard. I don't know. We
have all been shipmates now and then with men who have
seen better days. Perhaps he had been in the Navy, but what
makes me think he couldn't have been, was that he was a
thorough good seaman, a regular old wind-jammer, and
understood sail, which those Navy chaps rarely do. Why,
you and I have sailed with men before the mast who had
their master's certificates in their pockets—English Board of
Trade certificates, too—who could work a double altitude if
you would lend them a sextant and give them a look at the
chronometer, as well as many a man who commands a big
square-rigger. Navigation ain't everything, nor seamanship
either. You've got to have it in you, if you mean to get there.

I don't know how our captain heard that there was trouble
forward. The cabin-boy may have told him, or the men may
have talked outside his door when they relieved the wheel
at night. Anyhow, he got wind of it, and when he had got
his sight that morning he had all hands aft, and gave them a
lecture. It was just the kind of talk you might have expected
from him. He said he hadn't any complaint to make, and
that so far as he knew everybody on board was doing his
duty, and that he was given to understand that the men
got their whack, and were satisfied. He said his ship was

never a hard ship, and that he liked quiet, and that was the reason he didn't mean to have any nonsense, and the men might just as well understand that too. We'd had a great misfortune, he said, and it was nobody's fault. We had lost a man we all liked and respected, and he felt that everybody in the ship ought to be sorry for the man's brother, who was left behind, and that it was rotten lubberly childishness, and unjust and unmanly and cowardly, to be playing schoolboy tricks with forks and spoons and pipes, and that sort of gear. He said it had got to stop right now, and that was all, and the men might go forward. And so they did.

It got worse after that, and the men watched the cook, and the cook watched the men, as if they were trying to catch each other; but I think everybody felt that there was something else. One evening, at supper-time, I was on deck, and Jack came aft to relieve the wheel while the man who was steering got his supper. He hadn't got past the main-hatch on the lee side, when I heard a man running in slippers that slapped on the deck, and there was a sort of a yell and I saw the coloured cook going for Jack, with a carving-knife in his hand. I jumped to get between them, and Jack turned round short, and put out his hand. I was too far to reach them, and the cook jabbed out with his knife. But the blade didn't get anywhere near Benton. The cook seemed to be jabbing it into the air again and again, at least four feet short of the mark. Then he dropped his right hand, and I saw the whites of his eyes in the dusk, and he reeled up against the pin-rail, and caught hold of a belaying-pin with his left. I had reached him by that time, and grabbed hold of his knife-hand and the other too, for I thought he was going to use the pin, but Jack Benton was standing staring stupidly at him, as if he didn't understand. But instead, the cook was holding on because he couldn't stand, and his teeth were chattering, and he let go of the knife, and the point stuck into the deck.

" He's crazy! " said Jack Benton, and that was all he said; and he went aft.

When he was gone, the cook began to come to, and he spoke quite low, near my ear.

" There were two of them! So help me God, there were two of them! "

I don't know why I didn't take him by the collar, and give him a good shaking; but I didn't. I just picked up the knife

and gave it to him, and told him to go back to his galley, and
not to make a fool of himself. You see, he hadn't struck at
Jack, but at something he thought he saw, and I knew what
it was, and I felt that same thing, like a lump of ice sliding
down my back, that I felt that night when we were bending
the trysail.

When the men had seen him running aft, they jumped up
after him, but they held off when they saw that I had caught
him. By and by, the man who had spoken to me before
told me what had happened. He was a stocky little chap,
with a red head.

"Well," he said, "there isn't much to tell. Jack Benton
had been eating his supper with the rest of us. He always
sits at the after corner of the table, on the port side. His
brother used to sit at the end, next him. The doctor gave
him a thundering big piece of pie to finish up with, and
when he had finished he didn't stop for a smoke, but went
off quick to relieve the wheel. Just as he had gone, the doctor
came in from the galley, and when he saw Jack's empty
plate he stood stock still staring at it; and we all wondered
what was the matter, till we looked at the plate. There were
two forks in it, sir, lying side by side. Then the doctor
grabbed his knife, and flew up through the hatch like a
rocket. The other fork was there all right, Mr. Torkeldsen,
for we all saw it and handled it; and we all had our own.
That's all I know."

I didn't feel that I wanted to laugh when he told me that
story; but I hoped the Old Man wouldn't hear it, for I knew
he wouldn't believe it, and no captain that ever sailed likes
to have stories like that going round about his ship. It gives
her a bad name. But that was all anybody ever saw except
the cook, and he isn't the first man who has thought he saw
things without having any drink in him. I think, if the
doctor had been weak in the head as he was afterwards, he
might have done something foolish again, and there might
have been serious trouble. But he didn't. Only, two or
three times I saw him looking at Jack Benton in a queer,
scared way, and once I heard him talking to himself.

"There's two of them! So help me God, there's two of
them!"

He didn't say anything more about asking for his discharge, but I knew well enough that if he got ashore at the

next port we should never see him again, if he had to leave
his kit behind him, and his money too. He was scared all
through, for good and all; and he wouldn't be right again
till he got another ship. It's no use to talk to a man when he
gets like that, any more than it is to send a boy to the main
truck when he has lost his nerve.

Jack Benton never spoke of what happened that evening.
I don't know whether he knew about the two forks, or not;
or whether he understood what the trouble was. Whatever
he knew from the other men, he was evidently living under
a hard strain. He was quiet enough, and too quiet; but his
face was set, and sometimes it twitched oddly when he was
at the wheel, and he would turn his head round sharp to look
behind him. A man doesn't do that naturally, unless there's
a vessel that he thinks is creeping up on the quarter. When
that happens, if the man at the wheel takes a pride in his
ship, he will almost always keep glancing over his shoulder
to see whether the other fellow is gaining. But Jack Benton
used to look round when there was nothing there; and what
is curious, the other men seemed to catch the trick when they
were steering. One day the Old Man turned out just as the
man at the wheel looked behind him.

"What are you looking at?" asked the captain.

"Nothing, sir," answered the man.

"Then keep your eye on the mizzen-royal," said the Old
Man, as if he were forgetting that we weren't a square-rigger.

"Ay, ay, sir," said the man.

The captain told me to go below and work up the latitude
from the dead-reckoning, and he went forward of the deck-
house and sat down to read, as he often did. When I came
up, the man at the wheel was looking round again, and I
stood beside him and just asked him quietly what everybody
was looking at, for it was getting to be a general habit. He
wouldn't say anything at first, but just answered that it was
nothing. But when he saw that I didn't seem to care, and
just stood there as if there were nothing more to be said,
he naturally began to talk.

He said that it wasn't that he saw anything, because there
wasn't anything to see except the spanker sheet just straining
a little, and working in the sheaves of the blocks as the
schooner rose to the short seas. There wasn't anything to
be seen, but it seemed to him that the sheet made a queer noise

in the blocks. It was a new manilla sheet; and in dry weather it did make a little noise, something between a creak and a wheeze. I looked at it and looked at the man, and said nothing; and presently he went on. He asked me if I didn't notice anything peculiar about the noise. I listened a while, and said I didn't notice anything. Then he looked rather sheepish, but said he didn't think it could be his own ears, because every man who steered his trick heard the same thing now and then—sometimes once in a day, sometimes once in a night, sometimes it would go on a whole hour.

"It sounds like sawing wood," I said, just like that.

"To us it sounds a good deal more like a man whistling 'Nancy Lee.'" He started nervously as he spoke the last words. "There, sir, don't you hear it?" he asked suddenly.

I heard nothing but the creaking of the manilla sheet. It was getting near noon, and fine, clear weather in southern waters—just the sort of day and the time when you would least expect to feel creepy. But I remembered how I had heard that same tune overhead at night in a gale of wind a fortnight earlier, and I am not ashamed to say that the same sensation came over me now, and I wished myself well out of the *Helen B.*, and aboard of any old cargo-dragger, with a windmill on deck, and an eighty-nine forty-eighter for captain, and a fresh leak whenever it breezed up.

Little by little during the next few days life on board that vessel came to be about as unbearable as you can imagine. It wasn't that there was much talk, for I think the men were shy even of speaking to each other freely about what they thought. The whole ship's company grew silent, until one hardly ever heard a voice, except giving an order and the answer. The men didn't sit over their meals when their watch was below, but either turned in at once or sat about on the forecastle smoking their pipes without saying a word. We were all thinking of the same thing. We all felt as if there were a hand on board, sometimes below, sometimes about decks, sometimes aloft, sometimes on the boom end; taking his full share of what the others got, but doing no work for it. We didn't only feel it, we knew it. He took up no room, he cast no shadow, and we never heard his footfall on deck; but he took his whack with the rest as regular as the bells, and—he whistled "Nancy Lee." It was like the worst sort of dream you can imagine; and I daresay a good many of us tried to believe it was nothing else sometimes, when we stood looking over the weather rail in fine weather with the breeze in our faces; but if we happened to turn round and look into each other's eyes, we knew it was something worse than any dream could be; and we would turn away from each other with a queer, sick feeling, wishing that we could just for once see somebody who didn't know what we knew.

There's not much more to tell about the *Helen B. Jackson* so far as I am concerned. We were more like a shipload of lunatics than anything else when we ran in under Morro Castle, and anchored in Havana. The cook had brain fever, and was raving mad in his delirium; and the rest of the men weren't far from the same state. The last three or four days had been awful, and we had been as near to having a mutiny on board as I ever want to be. The men didn't want to hurt anybody: but they wanted to get away out of that ship, if they had to swim for it; to get away from that whistling, from that dead shipmate who had come back, and who filled the ship with his unseen self! I know that if the Old Man and I hadn't kept a sharp lookout the men would have put a boat over quietly on one of those calm nights, and pulled away leaving the captain and me and the mad cook to work the schooner into harbour. We should have done it somehow, of course, for we hadn't far to run if we could get a breeze; and once or twice I found myself wishing that the crew were really gone, for the awful state of fright in which they lived was beginning to work on me too. You see, I partly believed and partly didn't; but, anyhow, I didn't mean to let the thing get the better of me, whatever it was. I turned crusty, too, and kept the men at work on all sorts of jobs, and drove them to it until they wished I was overboard too. It wasn't that the Old Man and I were trying to drive them to desert without their pay, as I am sorry to say a good many skippers and mates do, even now. Captain Hackstaff was as straight as a string, and I didn't mean those poor fellows should be cheated out of a single cent; and I didn't blame them for wanting to leave the ship, but it seemed to me that the only chance to keep everybody sane through those last days was to work the men till they dropped. When they were dead tired they slept a little, and forgot the thing until they had to tumble up on deck and face it again. That

was a good many years ago. Do you believe that I can't hear
"Nancy Lee" now, without feeling cold down my back?
For I heard it too, now and then, after the man had explained
why he was always looking over his shoulder. Perhaps it was
imagination. I don't know. When I look back it seems to
me that I only remember a long fight against something I
couldn't see, against an appalling presence, against something
worse than cholera or Yellow Jack or the plague—and, goodness knows, the mildest of them is bad enough when it
breaks out at sea. The men got as white as chalk, and
wouldn't go about decks alone at night, no matter what I
said to them. With the cook raving in his bunk the forecastle
would have been a perfect hell, and there wasn't a spare
cabin on board. There never is on a fore-and-after. So I
put him into mine, and he was more quiet there, and at last
fell into a sort of stupor as if he were going to die. I don't
know what became of him, for we put him ashore alive and
left him in the hospital.

The men came aft in a body, quiet enough, and asked the
captain if he wouldn't pay them off, and let them go ashore.
Some men wouldn't have done it, for they had shipped for
the voyage, and had signed articles. But the captain knew
that when sailors get an idea into their heads they're no
better than children; and if he forced them to stay aboard
he wouldn't get much work out of them, and couldn't rely
on them in a difficulty. So he paid them off, and let them
go. When they had gone forward to get their kits, he asked
me whether I wanted to go too, and for a minute I had a sort
of weak feeling that I might just as well. But I didn't, and
he was a good friend to me afterwards. Perhaps he was
grateful to me for sticking to him.

When the men went off he didn't come on deck; but it
was my duty to stand by while they left the ship. They
owed me a grudge for making them work during the last
few days, and most of them dropped into the boat without
so much as a word or a look, as sailors will. Jack Benton was
the last to go over the side, and he stood still a minute and
looked at me, and his white face twitched. I thought he
wanted to say something.

"Take care of yourself, Jack," said I. "So long!"

It seemed as if he couldn't speak for two or three seconds;
then his words came thick.

" It wasn't my fault, Mr. Torkeldsen. I swear it wasn't my fault! "

That was all; and he dropped over the side, leaving me to wonder what he meant.

The captain and I stayed on board, and the ship-chandler got a West India boy to cook for us.

That evening, before turning in, we were standing by the rail having a quiet smoke, watching the lights of the city, a quarter of a mile off, reflected in the still water. There was music of some sort ashore, in a sailors' dance-house, I daresay; and I had no doubt that most of the men who had left the ship were there, and already full of jiggy-jiggy. The music played a lot of sailors' tunes that ran into each other, and we could hear the men's voices in the chorus now and then. One followed another, and then it was " Nancy Lee " loud and clear, and the men singing " Yo-ho, heave-ho! "

" I have no ear for music," said Captain Hackstaff, " but it appears to me that's the tune that man was whistling the night we lost the man overboard. I don't know why it has stuck in my head, and of course it's all nonsense: but it seems to me that I have heard it all the rest of the trip."

I didn't say anything to that, but I wondered just how much the Old Man had understood. Then we turned in, and I slept ten hours without opening my eyes.

I stuck to the *Helen B. Jackson* after that as long as I could stand a fore-and-after; but that night when we lay in Havana was the last time I ever heard " Nancy Lee " on board of her. The spare hand had gone ashore with the rest, and he never came back, and he took his tune with him, but all those things are just as clear in my memory as if they had happened yesterday.

After that I was in deep water for a year or more, and after I came home I got my certificate, and what with having friends and having saved a little money, and having had a small legacy from an uncle in Norway, I got the command of a coastwise vessel, with a small share in her. I was at home three weeks before going to sea, and Jack Benton saw my name in the local papers, and wrote to me.

He said that he had left the sea, and was trying farming, and he was going to be married, and he asked if I wouldn't come over for that, for it wasn't more than forty minutes by train; and he and Mamie would be proud to have me

at the wedding.   I remembered how I had heard one brother
ask the other whether Mamie knew. That meant, whether
she knew he wanted to marry her, I suppose. She had taken
her time about it, for it was pretty nearly three years then
since we had lost Jim Benton overboard.

I had nothing particular to do while we were getting ready
for sea; nothing to prevent me from going over for a day, I
mean; and I thought I'd like to see Jack Benton, and have
a look at the girl he was going to marry.   I wondered
whether he had grown cheerful again, and had got rid of
that drawn look he had when he told me it wasn't his fault.
How could it have been his fault, anyhow?   So I wrote to
Jack that I would come down and see him married; and when
the day came I took the train, and got there about ten o'clock
in the morning. I wish I hadn't.   Jack met me at the
station, and he told me that the wedding was to be late in
the afternoon, and that they weren't going off on any silly
wedding trip, he and Mamie, but were just going to walk
home from her mother's house to his cottage. That was
good enough for him, he said.   I looked at him hard for a
minute after we met. When we had parted I had a sort of
idea that he might take to drink, but he hadn't.   He looked
very respectable and well-to-do in his black coat and high
city collar; but he was thinner and bonier than when I had
known him, and there were lines in his face, and I thought
his eyes had a queer look in them, half shifty, half scared.
He needn't have been afraid of me, for I didn't mean to
talk to his bride about the *Helen B. Jackson*.

He took me to his cottage first, and I could see that he
was proud of it.   It wasn't above a cable's-length from high-
water mark, but the tide was running out, and there was
already a broad stretch of hard, wet sand on the other side
of the beach road. Jack's bit of land ran back behind the
cottage about a quarter of a mile, and he said that some of
the trees we saw were his. The fences were neat and well
kept, and there was a fair-sized barn a little way from the
cottage, and I saw some nice-looking cattle in the meadows;
but it didn't look to me to be much of a farm, and I thought
that before long Jack would have to leave his wife to take
care of it, and go to sea again.   But I said it was a nice farm,
so as to seem pleasant, and as I don't know much about these
things I daresay it was, all the same.   I never saw it but that

once.   Jack told me that he and his brother had been born in
the cottage, and that when their father and mother died they
leased the land to Mamie's father, but had kept the cottage
to live in when they came home from sea for a spell.   It
was as neat a little place as you would care to see: the floors
as clean as the decks of a yacht, and the paint as fresh as a
man-o'-war.   Jack always was a good painter.   There was
a nice parlour on the ground floor, and Jack had papered it
and had hung the walls with photographs of ships and foreign
ports, and with things he had brought home from his
voyages: a boomerang, a South Sea club, Japanese straw hats,
and a Gibraltar fan with a bull-fight on it, and all that sort
of gear.   It looked to me as if Miss Mamie had taken a hand
in arranging it.   There was a bran-new polished iron
Franklin stove set into the old fireplace, and a red table-cloth
from Alexandria embroidered with those outlandish Egyptian
letters.   It was all as bright and homelike as possible, and
he showed me everything, and was proud of everything, and
I liked him the better for it.   But I wished that his voice
would sound more cheerful, as it did when we first sailed in
the *Helen B.*, and that the drawn look would go out of his
face for a minute.   Jack showed me everything, and took
me upstairs, and it was all the same: bright and fresh and
ready for the bride.   But on the upper landing there was a
door that Jack didn't open.   When we came out of the
bedroom I noticed that it was ajar, and Jack shut it quickly
and turned the key.

"That lock's no good," he said, half to himself.   "The
door is always open."

I didn't pay much attention to what he said, but as we
went down the short stairs, freshly painted and varnished
so that I was almost afraid to step on them, he spoke again.

"That was his room, sir.   I have made a sort of store-
room of it."

"You may be wanting it in a year or so," I said, wishing
to be pleasant.

"I guess we won't use his room for that," Jack answered
in a low voice.

Then he offered me a cigar from a fresh box in the parlour,
and he took one, and we lit them, and went out; and as we
opened the front door there was Mamie Brewster standing
in the path as if she were waiting for us.   She was a fine-

looking girl, and I didn't wonder that Jack had been willing to wait three years for her. I could see that she hadn't been brought up on steam heat and cold storage, but had grown into a woman by the seashore. She had brown eyes, and fine brown hair, and a good figure.

" This is Captain Torkeldsen," said Jack. " This is Miss Brewster, captain; and she is glad to see you."

" Well, I am," said Miss Mamie, " for Jack has often talked to us about you, captain."

She put out her hand, and took mine and shook it heartily, and I suppose I said something, but I know I didn't say much.

The front door to the cottage looked towards the sea, and there was a straight path leading to the gate on the beach road. There was another path from the steps of the cottage that turned to the right, broad enough for two people to walk easily, and it led straight across the fields through gates to a larger house about a quarter of a mile away. That was where Mamie's mother lived, and the wedding was to be there. Jack asked me whether I would like to look round the farm before dinner, but I told him I didn't know much about farms. Then he said he just wanted to look round himself a bit, as he mightn't have much more chance that day; and he smiled, and Mamie laughed.

" Show the captain the way to the house, Mamie," he said. " I'll be along in a minute."

So Mamie and I began to walk along the path, and Jack went up towards the barn.

" It was sweet of you to come, captain," Miss Mamie began, " for I have always wanted to see you."

" Yes," I said, expecting something more.

" You see, I always knew them both," she went on. " They used to take me out in a dory to catch cod-fish when I was a little girl, and I liked them both," she added thoughtfully. " Jack doesn't care to talk about his brother now. That's natural. But you won't mind telling me how it happened, will you? I should so much like to know."

Well, I told her about the voyage and what happened that night when we fell in with a gale of wind, and that it hadn't been anybody's fault, for I wasn't going to admit that it was my old captain's, if it was. But I didn't tell her anything about what happened afterwards. As she didn't speak, I just went on talking about the two brothers, and how like they had been, and how when poor Jim was drowned and Jack left, I took Jack for him. I told her that none of us had ever been sure which was which.

" I wasn't always sure myself," she said, " unless they were together. Leastways, not for a day or two after they came home from sea. And now it seems to me that Jack is more like poor Jim, as I remembered him, than he ever was, for Jim was always more quiet, as if he were thinking."

I told her I thought so, too. We passed the gate and went into the next field, walking side by side. Then she turned her head to look for Jack, but he wasn't in sight. I shan't forget what she said next.

" Are you sure now? " she asked.

I stood stock still and she went on a step, and then turned and looked at me. We must have looked at each other while you could count five or six.

" I know it's silly," she went on, " it's silly, and it's awful, too, and I have got no right to think it, but sometimes I can't help it. You see it was always Jack I meant to marry."

" Yes," I said stupidly, " I suppose so."

She waited a minute, and began walking on slowly before she went on again.

" I am talking to you as if you were an old friend, captain, and I have only known you five minutes. It was Jack I meant to marry, but now he is so like the other one."

When a woman gets a wrong idea into her head there is only one way to make her tired of it, and that is to agree with her. That's what I did, and she went on talking the same way for a little while, and I kept on agreeing and agreeing until she turned round on me.

" You know you don't believe what you say," she said, and laughed. " You know that Jack is Jack, right enough; and it's Jack I am going to marry."

Of course I said so, for I didn't care whether she thought me a weak creature or not. I wasn't going to say a word that could interfere with her happiness, and I didn't intend to go back on Jack Benton; but I remembered what he had said when he left the ship in Havana: that it wasn't his fault.

" All the same," Miss Mamie went on, as a woman will, without realising what she was saying, " all the same, I wish I had seen it happen. Then I should know."

Next minute she knew that she didn't mean that, and was afraid that I would think her heartless, and began to explain that she would really rather have died herself than have seen poor Jim go overboard. Women haven't got much sense anyhow. All the same, I wondered how she could marry Jack if she had a doubt that he might be Jim after all. I suppose she had really got used to him since he had given up the sea and had stayed ashore, and she cared for him.

Before long we heard Jack coming up behind us, for we had walked very slowly to wait for him.

" Promise not to tell anybody what I said, captain," said Mamie, as girls do as soon as they have told their secrets.

Anyhow, I know I never did tell any one but you. This is the first time I have talked of all that, the first time since I took the train from that place. I am not going to tell you all about the day. Miss Mamie introduced me to her mother, who was a quiet, hard-faced old New England farmer's widow, and to her cousins and relations; and there were plenty of them, too, at dinner, and there was the parson besides. He was what they call a Hard-shell Baptist in those parts, with a long, shaven upper lip and a whacking appetite, and a sort of superior look, as if he didn't expect to see many of us hereafter—the way a New York pilot looks round, and orders things about when he boards an Italian cargo-dragger, as if the ship weren't up to much anyway, though it was his business to see that she didn't get aground. That's the way a good many parsons look, I think. He said grace as if he were ordering the men to sheet home the top gallant sail and get the helm up. After dinner we went out on the piazza, for it was warm autumn weather; and the young folks went off in pairs along the beach road, and the tide had turned and was beginning to come in. The morning had been clear and fine, but by four o'clock it began to look like a fog, and the damp came up out of the sea and settled on everything. Jack said he'd go down to his cottage and have a last look, for the wedding was to be at five o'clock, or soon after, and he wanted to light the lights, so as to have things look cheerful.

" I will just take a last look," he said again, as we reached the house. We went in, and he offered me another cigar, and I lit it and sat down in the parlour. I could hear him moving about, first in the kitchen and then upstairs, and then

I heard him in the kitchen again; and then before I knew anything I heard somebody moving upstairs again. I knew he couldn't have got up those stairs as quick as that. He came into the parlour, and he took a cigar himself, and while he was lighting it I heard those steps again overhead. His hand shook, and he dropped the match.

" Have you got in somebody to help? " I asked.

" No," Jack answered sharply and struck another match.

" There's somebody upstairs, Jack," I said. " Don't you hear footsteps? "

" It's the wind, captain," Jack answered, but I could see he was trembling.

" That isn't any wind, Jack," I said; " it's still and foggy. I'm sure there's somebody upstairs."

" If you are so sure of it, you'd better go and see for yourself, captain," Jack answered, almost angrily.

He was angry because he was frightened. I left him before the fireplace, and went upstairs. There was no power on earth that could make me believe I hadn't heard a man's footsteps overhead. I knew there was somebody there. But there wasn't. I went into the bedroom, and it was all quiet, and the evening light was streaming in, reddish through the foggy air; and I went out on the landing and looked in the little back room that was meant for a servant-girl or a child. And as I came back again I saw that the door of the other room was wide open, though I knew Jack had locked it. He had said the lock was no good. I looked in. It was a room as big as the bedroom, but almost dark, for it had shutters, and they were closed. There was a musty smell, as of old gear, and I could make out that the floor was littered with sea-chests, and that there were oilskins and such stuff piled on the bed. But I still believed that there was somebody upstairs, and I went in and struck a match and looked round. I could see the four walls and the shabby old paper, an iron bed and a cracked looking-glass, and the stuff on the floor. But there was nobody there. So I put out the match, and came out and shut the door and turned the key. Now, what I am telling you is the truth. When I had turned the key, I heard footsteps walking away from the door inside the room. Then I felt queer for a minute, and when I went downstairs I looked behind me, as the men at the wheel used to look behind them on board the *Helen B.*

Jack was already outside on the steps, smoking. I have an idea that he didn't like to stay inside alone.

" Well? " he asked, trying to seem careless.

" I didn't find anybody," I answered, " but I heard somebody moving about."

" I told you it was the wind," said Jack contemptuously. " I ought to know, for I live here, and I hear it often."

There was nothing to be said to that, so we began to walk down towards the beach. Jack said there wasn't any hurry, as it would take Miss Mamie some time to dress for the wedding. So we strolled along, and the sun was setting through the fog, and the tide was coming in. I knew the moon was full, and that when she rose the fog would roll away from the land, as it does sometimes. I felt that Jack didn't like my having heard that noise, so I talked of other things, and asked him about his prospects, and before long we were chatting as pleasantly as possible.

I haven't been at many weddings in my life, and I don't suppose you have, but that one seemed to me to be all right until it was pretty near over; and then, I don't know whether it was part of the ceremony or not, but Jack put out his hand and took Mamie's and held it a minute, and looked at her, while the parson was still speaking.

Mamie turned as white as a sheet and screamed. It wasn't a loud scream, but just a sort of stifled little shriek, as if she were half frightened to death; and the parson stopped, and asked her what was the matter, and the family gathered round.

" Your hand's like ice," said Mamie to Jack, " and it's all wet! "

She kept looking at it, as she got hold of herself again.

" It don't feel cold to me," said Jack, and he held the back of his hand against his cheek. " Try it again."

Mamie held out hers, and touched the back of his hand, timidly at first, and then took hold of it.

" Why, that's funny," she said.

" She's been as nervous as a witch all day," said Mrs. Brewster severely.

" It is natural," said the parson, " that young Mrs. Benton should experience a little agitation at such a moment."

Most of the bride's relations lived at a distance, and were busy people, so it had been arranged that the dinner we'd

had in the middle of the day was to take the place of a
dinner afterwards, and that we should just have a bite after
the wedding was over, and then that everybody should go
home, and the young couple would walk down to the cottage
by themselves. When I looked out I could see the light
burning brightly in Jack's cottage, a quarter of a mile away.
I said I didn't think I could get any train to take me back
before half-past nine, but Mrs. Brewster begged me to stay
until it was time, as she said her daughter would want to
take off her wedding dress before she went home; for she had
put on something white with a wreath, that was very pretty,
and she couldn't walk home like that, could she?

So when we had all had a little supper the party began
to break up, and when they were all gone Mrs. Brewster and
Mamie went upstairs, and Jack and I went on the piazza to
have a smoke, as the old lady didn't like tobacco in the house.

The full moon had risen now, and it was behind me as I
looked down towards Jack's cottage, so that everything was
clear and white, and there was only the light burning in the
window. The fog had rolled down to the water's edge, and
a little beyond, for the tide was high, or nearly, and was
lapping up over the last reach of sand within fifty feet of
the beach road.

Jack didn't say much as we sat smoking, but he thanked
me for coming to his wedding, and I told him I hoped he
would be happy, and so I did. I daresay both of us were
thinking of those footsteps upstairs, just then, and that the
house wouldn't seem so lonely with a woman in it. By and
by we heard Mamie's voice talking to her mother on the
stairs, and in a minute she was ready to go. She had put
on again the dress she had worn in the morning.

Well, they were ready to go now. It was all very quiet
after the day's excitement, and I knew they would like to
walk down that path alone now that they were man and
wife at last. I bade them good-night, although Jack made a
show of pressing me to go with them by the path as far as
the cottage, instead of going to the station by the beach road.
It was all very quiet, and it seemed to me a sensible way of
getting married; and when Mamie kissed her mother good-
night I just looked the other way, and knocked my ashes
over the rail of the piazza. So they started down the straight
path to Jack's cottage, and I waited a minute with Mrs.

Brewster, looking after them, before taking my hat to go. They walked side by side, a little shyly at first, and then I saw Jack put his arm round her waist. As I looked he was on her left and I saw the outline of the two figures very distinctly against the moonlight on the path; and the shadow on Mamie's right was broad and black as ink, and it moved along, lengthening and shortening with the unevenness of the ground beside the path.

I thanked Mrs. Brewster, and bade her good-night; and though she was a hard New England woman her voice trembled a little as she answered, but being a sensible person she went in and shut the door behind her as I stepped out on the path. I looked after the couple in the distance a last time, meaning to go down to the road, so as not to overtake them; but when I had made a few steps I stopped and looked again, for I knew I had seen something queer, though I had only realised it afterwards. I looked again, and it was plain enough now; and I stood stock-still, staring at what I saw. Mamie was walking between two men. The second man was just the same height as Jack, both being about a half a head taller than she; Jack on her left in his black tail-coat and round hat, and the other man on her right—well, he was a sailor-man in wet oilskins. I could see the moonlight shining on the water that ran down him, and on the little puddle that had settled where the flap of his sou'wester was turned up behind: and one of his wet shiny arms was round Mamie's waist, just above Jack's. I was fast to the spot where I stood, and for a minute I thought I was crazy. We'd had nothing but some cider for dinner, and tea in the evening, otherwise I'd have thought something had got into my head, though I was never drunk in my life. It was more like a bad dream after that.

I was glad Mrs. Brewster had gone in. As for me, I couldn't help following the three, in a sort of wonder to see what would happen, to see whether the sailor-man in his wet togs would just melt away into the moonshine. But he didn't.

I moved slowly, and I remembered afterwards that I walked on the grass, instead of on the path, as if I were afraid they might hear me coming. I suppose it all happened in less than five minutes after that, but it seemed as if it must have taken an hour. Neither Jack nor Mamie seemed to notice the sailor. She didn't seem to know that his wet arm was round her, and little by little they got near the cottage, and I wasn't a hundred yards from them when they reached the door. Something made me stand still then. Perhaps it was fright, for I saw everything that happened just as I see you now.

Mamie set her foot on the step to go up, and as she went forward I saw the sailor slowly lock his arm in Jack's, and Jack didn't move to go up. Then Mamie turned round on the step, and they all three stood that way for a second or two. She cried out then—I heard a man cry like that once, when his arm was taken off by a steam-crane—and she fell back in a heap on the little piazza.

I tried to jump forward, but I couldn't move, and I felt my hair rising under my hat. The sailor turned slowly where he stood, and swung Jack round by the arm steadily and easily, and began to walk him down the pathway from the house. He walked him straight down that path, as steadily as Fate; and all the time I saw the moonlight shining on his wet oilskins. He walked him through the gate, and across the beach road, and out upon the wet sand, where the tide was high. Then I got my breath with a gulp, and ran for them across the grass, and vaulted over the fence, and stumbled across the road. But when I felt the sand under my feet, the two were at the water's edge; and when I reached the water they were far out, and up to their waists; and I saw that Jack Benton's head had fallen forward on his breast, and his free arm hung limp beside him, while his dead brother steadily marched him to his death. The moonlight was on the dark water, but the fog-bank was white beyond, and I saw them against it; and they went slowly and steadily down. The water was up to their armpits, and then up to their shoulders, and then I saw it rise up to the black rim of Jack's hat. But they never wavered; and the two heads went straight on, straight on, till they were under, and there was just a ripple in the moonlight where Jack had been.

It has been on my mind to tell you that story, whenever I got a chance. You have known me, man and boy, a good many years; and I thought I would like to hear your opinion. Yes, that's what I always thought. It wasn't Jim that went overboard; it was Jack, and Jim just let him go, when he might have saved him; and then Jim passed himself off for

Jack with us, and with the girl. If that's what happened, he got what he deserved. People said the next day that Mamie found it out as they reached the house, and that her husband just walked out into the sea, and drowned himself; and they would have blamed me for not stopping him if they'd known that I was there. But I never told what I had seen, for they wouldn't have believed me. I just let them think I had come too late.

When I reached the cottage and lifted Mamie up, she was raving mad. She got better afterwards, but she was never right in her head again.

Oh, you want to know if they found Jack's body? I don't know whether it was his, but I read in a paper at a Southern port where I was with my new ship that two dead bodies had come ashore in a gale down East, in pretty bad shape. They were locked together, and one was a skeleton in oilskins.

FREDERICK MARRYAT

THE WEREWOLF

I

BEFORE noon Philip and Krantz had embarked, and made sail in the peroqua.

They had no difficulty in steering their course; the islands by day, and the clear stars by night, were their compass. It is true that they did not follow the more direct track, but they followed the more secure, working up the smooth waters, and gaining to the northward more than to the west. Many times they were chased by the Malay proas, which infested the islands, but the swiftness of their little peroqua was their security; indeed, the chase was, generally speaking, abandoned as soon as the smallness of the vessel was made out by the pirates, who expected that little or no booty was to be gained.

One morning, as they were sailing between the isles, with less wind than usual, Philip observed—

" Krantz, you said that there were events in your own life, or connected with it, which would corroborate the mysterious tale I confided to you. Will you now tell me to what you referred? "

" Certainly," replied Krantz; " I have often thought of doing so, but one circumstance or another has hitherto prevented me; this is, however, a fitting opportunity. Prepare therefore to listen to a strange story, quite as strange, perhaps, as your own.

" I take it for granted that you have heard people speak of the Hartz Mountains," observed Krantz.

" I have never heard people speak of them, that I can recollect," replied Philip; " but I have read of them in some book, and of the strange things which have occurred there."

" It is indeed a wild region," rejoined Krantz, " and many strange tales are told of it; but strange as they are, I have good reason for believing them to be true.

" My father was not born, or originally a resident, in the Hartz Mountains; he was a serf of an Hungarian nobleman,

447

of great possessions, in Transylvania; but although a serf, he was not by any means a poor or illiterate man. In fact, he was rich, and his intelligence and respectability were such, that he had been raised by his lord to the stewardship; but whoever may happen to be born a serf, a serf must he remain, even though he become a wealthy man: such was the condition of my father. My father had been married for about five years; and by his marriage had three children—my eldest brother Cæsar, myself (Hermann), and a sister named Marcella. You know, Philip, that Latin is still the language spoken in that country; and that will account for our high-sounding names. My mother was a very beautiful woman, unfortunately more beautiful than virtuous: she was seen and admired by the lord of the soil; my father was sent away upon some mission; and during his absence, my mother, flattered by the attentions, and won by the assiduities, of this nobleman, yielded to his wishes. It so happened that my father returned very unexpectedly, and discovered the intrigue. The evidence of my mother's shame was positive: he surprised her in the company of her seducer! Carried away by the impetuosity of his feelings, he watched the opportunity of a meeting taking place between them, and murdered both his wife and her seducer. Conscious that, as a serf, not even the provocation which he had received would be allowed as a justification of his conduct, he hastily collected together what money he could lay his hands upon, and, as we were then in the depth of winter, he put his horses to the sleigh, and taking his children with him, he set off in the middle of the night, and was far away before the tragical circumstance had transpired. Aware that he would be pursued, and that he had no chance of escape if he remained in any portion of his native country (in which the authorities could lay hold of him), he continued his flight without intermission until he had buried himself in the intricacies and seclusion of the Hartz Mountains. Of course, all that I have now told you I learned afterwards. My oldest recollections are knit to a rude, yet comfortable cottage, in which I lived with my father, brother, and sister. It was on the confines of one of those vast forests which cover the northern part of Germany; around it were a few acres of ground, which, during the summer months, my father cultivated, and which, though they yielded a doubtful harvest, were sufficient for our support. In the winter we remained much indoors, for, as my father followed the chase, we were left alone, and the wolves during that season incessantly prowled about. My father had purchased the cottage, and land about it, of one of the rude foresters, who gain their livelihood partly by hunting, and partly by burning charcoal, for the purpose of smelting the ore from the neighbouring mines; it was distant about two miles from any other habitation. I can call to mind the whole landscape now; the tall pines which rose up on the mountain above us, and the wide expanse of the forest beneath, on the topmost boughs and heads of whose trees we looked down from our cottage, as the mountain below us rapidly descended into the distant valley. In summer time the prospect was beautiful: but during the severe winter a more desolate scene could not well be imagined.

"I said that, in the winter, my father occupied himself with the chase; every day he left us, and often would he lock the door, that we might not leave the cottage. He had no one to assist him, or to take care of us—indeed, it was not easy to find a female servant who would live in such a solitude; but, could he have found one, my father would not have received her, for he had imbibed a horror of the sex, as the difference of his conduct towards us, his two boys, and my poor little sister Marcella evidently proved. You may suppose we were sadly neglected; indeed, we suffered much, for my father, fearful that we might come to some harm, would not allow us fuel when he left the cottage; and we were obliged, therefore, to creep under the heaps of bears' skins, and there to keep ourselves as warm as we could until he returned in the evening, when a blazing fire was our delight. That my father chose this restless sort of life may appear strange, but the fact was, that he could not remain quiet; whether from the remorse for having committed murder, or from the misery consequent on his change of situation, or from both combined, he was never happy unless he was in a state of activity. Children, however, when left so much to themselves, acquire a thoughtfulness not common to their age. So it was with us; and during the short cold days of winter, we would sit silent, longing for the happy hours when the snow would melt and the leaves burst out, and the birds begin their songs, and when we should again be set at liberty.

"Such was our peculiar and savage sort of life until my

brother Cæsar was nine, myself seven, and my sister five years old, when the circumstances occurred on which is based the extraordinary narrative which I am about to relate.

"One evening my father returned home rather later than usual; he had been unsuccessful, and as the weather was very severe, and many feet of snow were upon the ground, he was not only very cold, but in a very bad humour. He had brought in wood, and we were all three gladly assisting each other in blowing on the embers to create a blaze, when he caught poor little Marcella by the arm and threw her aside; the child fell, struck her mouth, and bled very much. My brother ran to raise her up. Accustomed to ill-usage, and afraid of my father, she did not dare to cry; but looked up in his face very piteously. My father drew his stool nearer to the hearth, muttered something in abuse of women, and busied himself with the fire, which both my brother and I had deserted when our sister was so unkindly treated. A cheerful blaze was soon the result of his exertions; but we did not, as usual, crowd round it. Marcella, still bleeding, retired to a corner, and my brother and I took our seats beside her, while my father hung over the fire gloomily and alone. Such had been our position for about half an hour, when the howl of a wolf, close under the window of the cottage, fell on our ears. My father started up, and seized his gun; the howl was repeated; he examined the priming, and then hastily left the cottage, shutting the door after him. We all waited (anxiously listening), for we thought that if he succeeded in shooting the wolf, he would return in a better humour; and, although he was harsh to all of us, and particularly so to our little sister, still we loved our father, and loved to see him cheerful and happy, for what else had we to look up to? And I may here observe, that perhaps there never were three children who were fonder of each other; we did not, like other children, fight and dispute together; and if, by chance, any disagreement did arise, between my elder brother and me, little Marcella would run to us, and kissing us both, seal, through her entreaties, the peace between us. Marcella was a lovely, amiable child; I can recall her beautiful features even now. Alas! poor little Marcella."

"She is dead, then?" observed Philip.

"Dead! yes, dead! but how did she die?—But I must not anticipate, Philip; let me tell my story.

" We waited for some time, but the report of the gun did not reach us, and my elder brother then said, ' Our father has followed the wolf, and will not be back for some time. Marcella, let us wash the blood from your mouth, and then we will leave this corner and go to the fire to warm ourselves.'

" We did so, and remained there until near midnight, every minute wondering, as it grew later, why our father did not return. We had no idea that he was in any danger, but we thought that he must have chased the wolf for a very long time. ' I will look out and see if father is coming,' said my brother Cæsar, going to the door. ' Take care,' said Marcella; ' the wolves must be about now, and we cannot kill them, brother.' My brother opened the door very cautiously, and but a few inches; he peeped out. ' I see nothing,' said he, after a time, and once more he joined us at the fire. ' We have had no supper,' said I; for my father usually cooked the meat as soon as he came home; and during his absence we had nothing but the fragments of the preceding day.

" ' And if our father comes home, after his hunt, Cæsar,' said Marcella, ' he will be pleased to have some supper; let us cook it for him and for ourselves.' Cæsar climbed upon the stool, and reached down some meat—I forget now whether it was venison or bear's meat, but we cut off the usual quantity, and proceeded to dress it, as we used to do under our father's superintendence. We were all busy putting it into the platters before the fire, to await his coming; when we heard the sound of a horn. We listened—there was a noise outside, and a minute afterwards my father entered, ushered in a young female and a large dark man in a hunter's dress.

" Perhaps I had better now relate what was only known to me many years afterwards. When my father had left the cottage, he perceived a large white wolf about thirty yards from him; as soon as the animal saw my father, it retreated slowly, growling and snarling. My father followed; the animal did not run, but always kept at some distance; and my father did not like to fire until he was pretty certain that his ball would take effect; thus they went on for some time, the wolf now leaving my father far behind, and then stopping and snarling defiance at him; and then, again, on his approach, setting off at speed.

" Anxious to shoot the animal (for the white wolf is very

rare), my father continued the pursuit for several hours, during which he continually ascended the mountain.

"You must know, Philip, that there are peculiar spots on those mountains which are supposed, and, as my story will prove, truly supposed, to be inhabited by the evil influences: they are well known to the huntsmen, who invariably avoid them. Now, one of these spots, an open space in the pine forest above us, had been pointed out to my father as dangerous on that account. But whether he disbelieved these wild stories, or whether, in his eager pursuit of the chase, he disregarded them, I know not; certain, however, it is, that he was decoyed by the white wolf to this open space, when the animal appeared to slacken her speed. My father approached, came close up to her, raised his gun to his shoulder, and was about to fire, when the wolf suddenly disappeared. He thought that the snow on the ground must have dazzled his sight, and he let down his gun to look for the beast—but she was gone; how she could have escaped over the clearance, without his seeing her, was beyond his comprehension. Mortified at the ill-success of his chase, he was about to retrace his steps, when he heard the distant sound of a horn. Astonishment at such a sound—at such an hour—in such a wilderness, made him forget for the moment his disappointment, and he remained riveted to the spot. In a minute the horn was blown a second time, and at no great distance; my father stood still, and listened; a third time it was blown. I forget the term used to express it, but it was the signal which, my father well knew, implied that the party was lost in the woods. In a few minutes more my father beheld a man on horseback, with a female seated on the crupper, enter the cleared space, and ride up to him. At first, my father called to mind the strange stories which he had heard of the supernatural beings who were said to frequent these mountains; but the nearer approach of the parties satisfied him that they were mortals like himself. As soon as they came up to him, the man who guided the horse accosted him. 'Friend hunter, you are out late, the better fortune for us; we have ridden far, and are in fear of our lives, which are eagerly sought after. These mountains have enabled us to elude our pursuers; but if we find not shelter and refreshment, that will avail us little, as we must perish from hunger and the inclemency of the night. My daughter, who rides behind me, is now more dead than alive —say, can you assist us in our difficulty? '

" ' My cottage is some few miles distant,' replied my father, ' but I have little to offer you besides a shelter from the weather; to the little I have you are welcome. May I ask whence you come? '

" ' Yes, friend, it is no secret now; we have escaped from Transylvania, where my daughter's honour and my life were equally in jeopardy! '

" This information was quite enough to raise an interest in my father's heart. He remembered his own escape: he remembered the loss of his wife's honour, and the tragedy by which it was wound up. He immediately, and warmly, offered all the assistance which he could afford them.

" ' There is no time to be lost, then, good sir,' observed the horseman; ' my daughter is chilled with the frost, and cannot hold out much longer against the severity of the weather.'

" ' Follow me,' replied my father, leading the way towards his home.

" ' I was lured away in pursuit of a large white wolf," observed my father; ' it came to the very window of my hut, or I should not have been out at this time of night.'

" ' The creature passed by us just as we came out of the wood,' said the female, in a silvery tone.

" ' I was nearly discharging my piece at it,' observed the hunter; ' but since it did us such good service, I am glad that I allowed it to escape.'

" In about an hour and a half, during which my father walked at a rapid pace, the party arrived at the cottage, and, as I said before, came in.

" ' We are in good time, apparently,' observed the dark hunter, catching the smell of the roasted meat, as he walked to the fire and surveyed my brother and sister and myself. ' You have young cooks here, Meinheer.' ' I am glad that we shall not have to wait,' replied my father. ' Come, mistress, seat yourself by the fire; you require warmth after your cold ride.' ' And where can I put up my horse, Meinheer? ' observed the huntsman. ' I will take care of him,' replied my father, going out of the cottage door.

" The female must, however, be particularly described. She was young, and apparently twenty years of age. She was dressed in a travelling dress, deeply bordered with white fur, and wore a cap of white ermine on her head. Her features were very beautiful, at least I thought so, and so my father has since declared. Her hair was flaxen, glossy, and shining, and bright as a mirror; and her mouth, although somewhat large when it was open, showed the most brilliant teeth I have ever beheld. But there was something about her eyes, bright as they were, which made us children afraid; they were so restless, so furtive; I could not at that time tell why, but I felt as if there was cruelty in her eye; and when she beckoned us to come to her, we approached her with fear and trembling. Still she was beautiful, very beautiful. She spoke kindly to my brother and myself, patted our heads and caressed us; but Marcella would not come near her; on the contrary, she slunk away, and hid herself in the bed, and would not wait for the supper, which half an hour before she had been so anxious for.

"My father, having put the horse into a close shed, soon returned, and supper was placed on the table. When it was over, my father requested the young lady would take possession of the bed, and he would remain at the fire, and sit up with her father. After some hesitation on her part, this arrangement was agreed to, and I and my brother crept into the other bed with Marcella, for we had as yet always slept together.

"But we could not sleep; there was something so unusual, not only in seeing strange people, but in having those people sleep at the cottage, that we were bewildered. As for poor little Marcella, she was quiet, but I perceived that she trembled during the whole night, and sometimes I thought that she was checking a sob. My father had brought out some spirits, which he rarely used, and he and the strange hunter remained drinking and talking before the fire. Our ears were ready to catch the slightest whisper—so much was our curiosity excited.

"'You said you came from Transylvania?' observed my father.

"'Even so, Meinheer,' replied the hunter. 'I was a serf to the noble house of——; my master would insist upon my surrendering up my fair girl to his wishes; it ended in my giving him a few inches of my hunting-knife.'

"'We are countrymen and brothers in misfortune,' replied

my father, taking the huntsman's hand and pressing it warmly.

" ' Indeed!   Are you then from that country? '

" ' Yes; and I too have fled for my life.   But mine is a melancholy tale.'

" ' Your name? ' inquired the hunter.

" ' Krantz.'

" ' What!   Krantz of ——?   I have heard your tale; you need not renew your grief by repeating it now.   Welcome, most welcome, Meinheer, and, I may say, my worthy kinsman.   I am your second cousin, Wilfred of Barnsdorf,' cried the hunter, rising up and embracing my father.

" They filled their horn-mugs to the brim, and drank to one another after the German fashion.   The conversation was then carried on in a low tone; all that we could collect from it was that our new relative and his daughter were to take up their abode in our cottage, at least for the present. In about an hour they both fell back in their chairs and appeared to sleep.

" ' Marcella, dear, did you hear? " said my brother, in a low tone.

" ' Yes,' replied Marcella, in a whisper, ' I heard all.   Oh! brother, I cannot bear to look upon that woman—I feel so frightened.'

" My brother made no reply, and shortly afterwards we were all three fast asleep.

" When we awoke the next morning, we found that the hunter's daughter had risen before us.   I thought she looked more beautiful than ever.   She came up to little Marcella and caressed her; the child burst into tears, and sobbed as if her heart would break.

" But not to detain you with too long a story, the huntsman and his daughter were accommodated in the cottage. My father and he went out hunting daily, leaving Christina with us.   She performed all the household duties; was very kind to us children; and gradually the dislike even of little Marcella wore away.   But a great change took place in my father; he appeared to have conquered his aversion to the sex, and was most attentive to Christina.   Often, after her father and we were in bed, would he sit up with her, conversing in a low tone by the fire.   I ought to have mentioned that my father and the huntsman Wilfred slept in another portion of the cottage, and that the bed which he formerly occupied, and which was in the same room as ours, had been given up to the use of Christina. These visitors had been about three weeks at the cottage, when, one night, after we children had been sent to bed, a consultation was held. My father had asked Christina in marriage, and had obtained both her own consent and that of Wilfred; after this, a conversation took place, which was, as nearly as I can recollect, as follows:—

" ' You may take my child, Meinheer Krantz, and my blessing with her, and I shall then leave you and seek some other habitation—it matters little where.'

" ' Why not remain here, Wilfred? '

" ' No, no, I am called elsewhere; let that suffice, and ask no more questions. You have my child.'

" ' I thank you for her, and will duly value her; but there is one difficulty.'

" ' I know what you would say; there is no priest here in this wild country; true; neither is there any law to bind. Still must some ceremony pass between you, to satisfy a father. Will you consent to marry her after my fashion? if so, I will marry you directly.'

" ' I will,' replied my father.

" ' Then take her by the hand. Now, Meinheer, swear.'

" ' I swear,' repeated my father.

" ' By all the spirits of the Hartz Mountains——'

" ' Nay, why not by Heaven? ' interrupted my father.

" ' Because it is not my humour,' rejoined Wilfred. ' If I prefer that oath, less binding, perhaps, than another, surely you will not thwart me.'

" ' Well, be it so, then; have your humour. Will you make me swear by that in which I do not believe? '

" ' Yet many do so, who in outward appearance are Christians,' rejoined Wilfred; ' say, will you be married, or shall I take my daughter away with me? '

" ' Proceed,' replied my father impatiently.

" ' I swear by all the spirits of the Hartz Mountains, by all their power for good or for evil, that I take Christina for my wedded wife; that I will ever protect her, cherish her, and love her; that my hand shall never be raised against her to harm her.'

" My father repeated the words after Wilfred.

" ' And if I fail in this my vow, may all the vengeance of

the spirits fall upon me and upon my children; may they
perish by the vulture, by the wolf, or other beasts of the
forest; may their flesh be torn from their limbs, and their
bones blanch in the wilderness: all this I swear.'

"My father hesitated, as he repeated the last words; little
Marcella could not restrain herself, and as my father repeated
the last sentence, she burst into tears. This sudden interruption appeared to discompose the party, particularly my
father; he spoke harshly to the child, who controlled her
sobs, burying her face under the bedclothes.

"Such was the second marriage of my father. The next
morning, the hunter Wilfred mounted his horse and rode
away.

"My father resumed his bed, which was in the same room
as ours; and things went on much as before the marriage,
except that our new mother-in-law did not show any kindness towards us; indeed, during my father's absence, she
would often beat us, particularly little Marcella, and her
eyes would flash fire, as she looked eagerly upon the fair and
lovely child.

"One night my sister awoke me and my brother.

"'What is the matter?' said Cæsar.

"'She has gone out,' whispered Marcella.

"'Gone out!'

"'Yes, gone out at the door, in her night-clothes,' replied
the child; 'I saw her get out of bed, look at my father to
see if he slept, and then she went out at the door.'

"What could induce her to leave her bed, and all undressed to go out, in such bitter wintry weather, with the
snow deep on the ground, was to us incomprehensible; we
lay awake, and in about an hour we heard the growl of a
wolf close under the window.

"'There is a wolf,' said Cæsar. 'She will be torn to
pieces.'

"'Oh, no!' cried Marcella.

"In a few minutes afterwards our mother-in-law appeared; she was in her night-dress, as Marcella had stated.
She let down the latch of the door, so as to make no noise,
went to a pail of water and washed her face and hands, and
then slipped into the bed where my father lay.

"We all three trembled—we hardly knew why; but we
resolved to watch the next night. We did so; and not only

on the ensuing night, but on many others, and always at
about the same hour, would our mother-in-law rise from
her bed and leave the cottage; and after she was gone we invariably heard the growl of a wolf under our window, and
always saw her on her return wash herself before she retired
to bed. We observed also that she seldom sat down to meals,
and that when she did she appeared to eat with dislike; but
when the meat was taken down to be prepared for dinner,
she would often furtively put a raw piece into her mouth.

"My brother Cæsar was a courageous boy; he did not like
to speak to my father until he knew more. He resolved
that he would follow her out, and ascertain what she did.
Marcella and I endeavoured to dissuade him from the project; but he would not be controlled; and the very next
night he lay down in his clothes, and as soon as our mother-
in-law had left the cottage he jumped up, took down my
father's gun, and followed her.

"You may imagine in what a state of suspense Marcella
and I remained during his absence. After a few minutes
we heard the report of a gun. It did not awaken my father;
and we lay trembling with anxiety. In a minute afterwards
we saw our mother-in-law enter the cottage—her dress was
bloody. I put my hand to Marcella's mouth to prevent her
crying out, although I was myself in great alarm. Our
mother-in-law approached my father's bed, looked to see if
he was asleep, and then went to the chimney and blew up
the embers into a blaze.

"' Who is there? ' said my father, waking up.

"' Lie still, dearest,' replied my mother-in-law; ' it is only
me; I have lighted the fire to warm some water; I am not
quite well.'

"My father turned round, and was soon asleep; but we
watched our mother-in-law. She changed her linen, and
threw the garments she had worn into the fire; and we then
perceived that her right leg was bleeding profusely, as if
from a gun-shot wound. She bandaged it up, and then
dressing herself, remained before the fire until the break of
day.

"Poor little Marcella, her heart beat quick as she pressed
me to her side—so indeed did mine. Where was our brother
Cæsar? How did my mother-in-law receive the wound unless from his gun? At last my father rose, and then for the

first time I spoke, saying, 'Father, where is my brother Cæsar?'

"'Your brother?' exclaimed he; 'why, where can he be?'

"'Merciful Heaven! I thought as I lay very restless last night,' observed our mother-in-law, 'that I heard somebody open the latch of the door; and, dear me, husband, what has become of your gun?'

"My father cast his eyes up above the chimney, and perceived that his gun was missing. For a moment he looked perplexed; then, seizing a broad axe, he went out of the cottage without saying another word.

"He did not remain away from us long; in a few minutes he returned, bearing in his arms the mangled body of my poor brother; he laid it down, and covered up his face.

"My mother-in-law rose up, and looked at the body, while Marcella and I threw ourselves by its side, wailing and sobbing bitterly.

"'Go to bed again, children,' said she sharply. 'Husband,' continued she, 'your boy must have taken the gun down to shoot a wolf, and the animal has been too powerful for him. Poor boy! he has paid dearly for his rashness.'

"My father made no reply. I wished to speak—to tell all—but Marcella, who perceived my intention, held me by the arm, and looked at me so imploringly, that I desisted.

"My father, therefore, was left in his error; but Marcella and I, although we could not comprehend it, were conscious that our mother-in-law was in some way connected with my brother's death.

"That day my father went out and dug a grave; and when he laid the body in the earth, he piled up stones over it, so that the wolves should not be able to dig it up. The shock of this catastrophe was to my poor father very severe; for several days he never went to the chase, although at times he would utter bitter anathemas and vengeance against the wolves.

"But during this time of mourning on his part, my mother-in-law's nocturnal wanderings continued with the same regularity as before.

"At last my father took down his gun to repair to the forest; but he soon returned, and appeared much annoyed.

"'Would you believe it, Christina, that the wolves—perdition to the whole race!—have actually contrived to dig up

the body of my poor boy, and now there is nothing left of
him but his bones.'

" ' Indeed! ' replied my mother-in-law. Marcella looked at
me, and I saw in her intelligent eye all she would have
uttered.

" ' A wolf growls under our window every night, father,'
said I.

" ' Ay, indeed! Why did you not tell me, boy? Wake
me the next time you hear it.'

" I saw my mother-in-law turn away; her eyes flashed fire,
and she gnashed her teeth.

" My father went out again, and covered up with a
larger pile of stones the little remains of my poor brother
which the wolves had spared. Such was the first act of the
tragedy.

" The spring now came on; the snow disappeared, and we
were permitted to leave the cottage; but never would I quit
for one moment my dear little sister, to whom, since the death
of my brother, I was more ardently attached than ever;
indeed, I was afraid to leave her alone with my mother-in-law,
who appeared to have a particular pleasure in ill-treating the
child. My father was now employed upon his little farm, and
I was able to render him some assistance.

" Marcella used to sit by us while we were at work, leaving
my mother-in-law alone in the cottage. I ought to observe
that, as the spring advanced, so did my mother-in-law de-
crease her nocturnal rambles, and that we never heard the
growl of the wolf under the window after I had spoken of it
to my father.

" One day, when my father and I were in the field, Marcella being with us, my mother-in-law came out, saying that
she was going into the forest to collect some herbs my father
wanted, and that Marcella must go to the cottage and watch
the dinner. Marcella went; and my mother-in-law soon disappeared in the forest, taking a direction quite contrary to
that in which the cottage stood, and leaving my father and
me, as it were, between her and Marcella.

" About an hour afterwards we were startled by shrieks
from the cottage—evidently the shrieks of little Marcella.
' Marcella has burnt herself, father,' said I, throwing down
my spade. My father threw down his, and we both hastened
to the cottage. Before we could gain the door, out darted a

The moon shone full upon her.

large white wolf, which fled with the utmost celerity. My father had no weapon; he rushed into the cottage, and there saw poor little Marcella expiring. Her body was dreadfully mangled and the blood pouring from it had formed a large pool on the cottage floor. My father's first intention had been to seize his gun and pursue; but he was checked by this horrid spectacle; he knelt down by his dying child, and burst into tears. Marcella could just look kindly on us for a few seconds, and then her eyes were closed in death.

" My father and I were still hanging over my poor sister's body, when my mother-in-law came in. At the dreadful sight she expressed much concern; but she did not appear to recoil from the sight of blood, as most women do.

" 'Poor child!' said she, 'it must have been that great white wolf which passed me just now, and frightened me so. She's quite dead, Krantz.'

" 'I know it!—I know it!' cried my father, in agony.

" I thought my father would never recover from the effects of this second tragedy; he mourned bitterly over the body of his sweet child, and for several days would not consign it to its grave, although frequently requested by my mother-in-law to do so. At last he yielded, and dug a grave for her close by that of my poor brother, and took every precaution that the wolves should not violate her remains.

" I was now really miserable as I lay alone in the bed which I had formerly shared with my brother and sister. I could not help thinking that my mother-in-law was implicated in both their deaths, although I could not account for the manner; but I no longer felt afraid of her; my little heart was full of hatred and revenge.

" The night after my sister had been buried, as I lay awake, I perceived my mother-in-law get up and go out of the cottage. I waited some time, then dressed myself, and looked out through the door, which I half opened. The moon shone bright, and I could see the spot where my brother and my sister had been buried; and what was my horror when I perceived my mother-in-law busily removing the stones from Marcella's grave!

" She was in her white night-dress, and the moon shone full upon her. She was digging with her hands, and throwing away the stones behind her with all the ferocity of a wild beast. It was some time before I could collect my senses and decide what I should do. At last I perceived that she had arrived at the body, and raised it up to the side of the grave. I could bear it no longer: I ran to my father and awoke him.

" 'Father, father! ' cried I, 'dress yourself, and get your gun.'

" ' What! ' cried my father, ' the wolves are there, are they? '

" He jumped out of bed, threw on his clothes, and in his anxiety did not appear to perceive the absence of his wife. As soon as he was ready I opened the door, he went out, and I followed him.

" Imagine his horror, when (unprepared as he was for such a sight) he beheld, as he advanced towards the grave, not a wolf, but his wife, in her night-dress, on her hands and knees, crouching by the body of my sister, and tearing off large pieces of the flesh, and devouring them with all the avidity of a wolf. She was too busy to be aware of our approach. My father dropped his gun; his hair stood on end, so did mine; he breathed heavily, and then his breath for a time stopped. I picked up the gun and put it into his hand. Suddenly he appeared as if concentrated rage had restored him to double vigour; he levelled his piece, fired, and with a loud shriek down fell the wretch whom he had fostered in his bosom.

" ' God of heaven! ' cried my father, sinking down upon the earth in a swoon, as soon as he had discharged his gun.

" I remained some time by his side before he recovered. ' Where am I? ' said he, ' what has happened? Oh!—yes, yes! I recollect now. Heaven forgive me! '

" He rose and we walked up to the grave; what again was our astonishment and horror to find that, instead of the dead body of my mother-in-law, as we expected, there was lying over the remains of my poor sister a large white she-wolf.

" ' The white wolf,' exclaimed my father, ' the white wolf which decoyed me into the forest—I see it all now—I have dealt with the spirits of the Hartz Mountains.'

" For some time my father remained in silence and deep thought. He then carefully lifted up the body of my sister, replaced it in the grave, and covered it over as before, having struck the head of the dead animal with the heel of his boot, and raving like a madman. He walked back to the cottage, shut the door, and threw himself on the bed; I did the same, for I was in a stupor of amazement.

"Early in the morning we were both roused by a loud knocking at the door, and in rushed the hunter Wilfred.

"'My daughter—man—my daughter!—where is my daughter?' cried he in a rage.

"'Where the wretch, the fiend should be, I trust,' replied my father, starting up, and displaying equal choler: 'where she should be—in hell! Leave this cottage, or you may fare worse.'

"'Ha!—ha!' replied the hunter, 'would you harm a potent spirit of the Hartz Mountains? Poor mortal, who must needs wed a werewolf.'

"'Out, demon! I defy thee and thy power.'

"'Yet shall you feel it; remember your oath—your solemn oath—never to raise your hand against her to harm her.'

"'I made no compact with evil spirits.'

"'You did, and if you failed in your vow, you were to meet the vengeance of the spirits. Your children were to perish by the vulture, the wolf——'

"'Out, out, demon!'

"'And their bones blanch in the wilderness. Ha!—ha!'

"My father, frantic with rage, seized his axe and raised it over Wilfred's head to strike.

"'All this I swear,' continued the huntsman mockingly.

"The axe descended; but it passed through the form of the hunter, and my father lost his balance, and fell heavily on the floor.

"'Mortal!' said the hunter, striding over my father's body, 'we have power over those only who have committed murder. You have been guilty of a double murder: you shall pay the penalty attached to your marriage vow. Two of your children are gone, the third is yet to follow—and follow them he will, for your oath is registered. Go—it were kindness to kill thee—your punishment is, that you live!'

"With these words the spirit disappeared. My father rose from the floor, embraced me tenderly, and knelt down in prayer.

"The next morning he quitted the cottage for ever. He took me with him, and bent his steps to Holland, where we safely arrived. He had some little money with him; but he had not been many days in Amsterdam before he was seized with a brain fever, and died raving mad. I was put into the asylum, and afterwards was sent to sea before the mast. You now know all my history. The question is, whether I am to pay the penalty of my father's oath? I am myself perfectly convinced that, in some way or another, I shall.

II

ON the twenty-second day the high land of the south of Sumatra was in view: as there were no vessels in sight, they resolved to keep their course through the Straits, and run for Pulo Penang, which they expected, as their vessel lay so close to the wind, to reach in seven or eight days. By constant exposure Philip and Krantz were now so bronzed, that with their long beards and Mussulman dresses, they might easily have passed off for natives. They had steered during the whole of the days exposed to a burning sun; they had lain down and slept in the dew of the night; but their health had not suffered. But for several days, since he had confided the history of his family to Philip, Krantz had become silent and melancholy; his usual flow of spirits had vanished, and Philip had often questioned him as to the cause. As they entered the Straits, Philip talked of what they should do upon their arrival at Goa; when Krantz gravely replied, " For some days, Philip, I have had a presentiment that I shall never see that city."

" You are out of health, Krantz," replied Philip.

" No, I am in sound health, body and mind. I have endeavoured to shake off the presentiment, but in vain; there is a warning voice that continually tells me that I shall not be long with you. Philip, will you oblige me by making me content on one point? I have gold about my person which may be useful to you; oblige me by taking it, and securing it on your own."

" What nonsense, Krantz."

" It is no nonsense, Philip. Have you not had your warnings? Why should I not have mine? You know that I have little fear in my composition, and that I care not about death; but I feel the presentiment which I speak of more strongly every hour. . . ."

" These are the imaginings of a disturbed brain, Krantz; why you, young, in full health and vigour, should not pass your days in peace, and live to a good old age, there is no cause for believing. You will be better to-morrow."

" Perhaps so," replied Krantz; " but still you must yield to my whim, and take the gold. If I am wrong, and we do arrive safe, you know, Philip, you can let me have it back," observed Krantz, with a faint smile—" but you forget, our water is nearly out, and we must look out for a rill on the coast to obtain a fresh supply."

" I was thinking of that when you commenced this unwelcome topic. We had better look out for the water before dark, and as soon as we have replenished our jars, we will make sail again."

At the time that this conversation took place, they were on the eastern side of the Strait, about forty miles to the northward. The interior of the coast was rocky and mountainous, but it slowly descended to low land of alternate forest and jungles, which continued to the beach; the country appeared to be uninhabited. Keeping close in to the shore, they discovered, after two hours' run, a fresh stream which burst in a cascade from the mountains, and swept its devious course through the jungle, until it poured its tribute into the waters of the Strait.

They ran close into the mouth of the stream, lowered the sails, and pulled the peroqua against the current, until they had advanced far enough to assure them that the water was quite fresh. The jars were soon filled, and they were again thinking of pushing off, when, enticed by the beauty of the spot, the coolness of the fresh water, and wearied with their long confinement on board of the peroqua, they proposed to bathe—a luxury hardly to be appreciated by those who have not been in a similar situation. They threw off their Mussulman dresses, and plunged into the stream, where they remained for some time. Krantz was the first to get out; he complained of feeling chilled, and he walked on to the banks where their clothes had been laid. Philip also approached nearer to the beach, intending to follow him.

" And now, Philip," said Krantz, " this will be a good opportunity for me to give you the money. I will open my sash and pour it out, and you can put it into your own before you put it on."

Philip was standing in the water, which was about level with his waist.

"Well, Krantz," said he, "I suppose if it must be so, it must; but it appears to me an idea so ridiculous—however, you shall have your own way."

Philip quitted the run, and sat down by Krantz, who was already busy in shaking the doubloons out of the folds of his sash; at last he said—

"I believe, Philip, you have got them all, now?—I feel satisfied."

"What danger there can be to you, which I am not equally exposed to, I cannot conceive," replied Philip; "however——"

Hardly had he said these words, when there was a tremendous roar—a rush like a mighty wind through the air—a blow which threw him on his back—a loud cry—and a contention. Philip recovered himself, and perceived the naked form of Krantz carried off with the speed of an arrow by an enormous tiger through the jungle. He watched with distended eyeballs; in a few seconds the animal and Krantz had disappeared.

"God of heaven! would that thou hadst spared me this," cried Philip, throwing himself down in agony on his face. "O Krantz! my friend—my brother—too sure was your presentiment. Merciful God! have pity—but Thy will be done;" and Philip burst into a flood of tears.

For more than an hour did he remain fixed upon the spot, careless and indifferent to the danger by which he was surrounded. At last, somewhat recovered, he rose, dressed himself, and then again sat down—his eyes fixed upon the clothes of Krantz, and the gold which still lay on the sand.

"He would give me that gold. He foretold his doom. Yes! yes! it was his destiny, and it has been fulfilled. *His bones will bleach in the wilderness*, and the spirit-hunter and his wolfish daughter are avenged."

J. S. LE FANU

SCHALKEN THE PAINTER

YOU will no doubt be surprised, my dear friend, at the subject of the following narrative. What had I to do with Schalken, or Schalken with me? He had returned to his native land, and was probably dead and buried before I was born; I never visited Holland nor spoke with a native of that country. So much I believe you already know. I must, then, give you my authority, and state to you frankly the ground upon which rests the credibility of the strange story which I am about to lay before you. I was acquainted, in my early days, with a Captain Vandael, whose father had served King William in the Low Countries, and also in my own unhappy land during the Irish campaigns. I know not how it happened that I liked this man's society spite of his politics and religion: but so it was; and it was by means of the free intercourse to which our intimacy gave rise that I became possessed of the curious tale which you are about to hear. I had often been struck, while visiting Vandael, by a remarkable picture, in which, though no *connoisseur* myself, I could not fail to discern some very strong peculiarities, particularly in the distribution of light and shade, as also a certain oddity in the design itself, which interested my curiosity. It represented the interior of what might be a chamber in some antique religious building—the foreground was occupied by a female figure, arrayed in a species of white robe, part of which is arranged so as to form a veil. The dress, however, is not strictly that of any religious order. In its hand the figure bears a lamp, by whose light alone the form and face are illuminated; the features are marked by an arch smile, such as pretty women wear when engaged in successfully practising some roguish trick; in the background, and, excepting where the dim red light of an expiring fire serves to define the form, totally in the shade, stands the figure of a man equipped in the old fashion, with doublet and so forth, in an attitude of alarm, his hand being placed

468

upon the hilt of his sword, which he appears to be in the act of drawing.

"There are some pictures," said I to my friend, " which impress one, I know not how, with a conviction that they represent not the mere ideal shapes and combinations which have floated through the imagination of the artist, but scenes, faces, and situations which have actually existed. When I look upon that picture, something assures me that I behold the representation of a reality."

Vandael smiled, and fixing his eyes upon the painting musingly, he said—

"Your fancy has not deceived you, my good friend, for that picture is the record, and I believe a faithful one, of a remarkable and mysterious occurrence. It was painted by Schalken, and contains, in the face of the female figure, which occupies the most prominent place in the design, an accurate portrait of Rose Velderkaust, the niece of Gerard Douw, the first, and, I believe, the only love of Godfrey Schalken. My father knew the painter well and from Schalken himself he learned the story of the mysterious drama, one scene of which the picture had embodied. This painting, which is accounted a fine specimen of Schalken's style, was bequeathed to my father by the artist's will, and, as you have observed, is a very striking and interesting production."

I had only to request Vandael to tell the story of the painting to be gratified; and thus it is that I am enabled to submit to you a faithful recital of what I heard myself, leaving you to reject or to allow the evidence upon which the truth of the tradition depends, with this one assurance, that Schalken was an honest, blunt Dutchman, and, I believe, wholly incapable of committing a flight of imagination; and further, that Vandael, from whom I heard the story, appeared firmly convinced of its truth.

There are few forms upon which the mantle of mystery and romance could seem to hang more ungracefully than upon that of the uncouth and clownish Schalken—the Dutch boor—the rude and dogged, but most cunning worker of oils, whose pieces delight the initiated of the present day almost as much as his manners disgusted the refined of his own; and yet this man, so rude, so dogged, so slovenly, I had almost said so savage, in mien and manner, during his after successes, had been selected by the capricious goddess, in his early life,

to figure as the hero of a romance by no means devoid of
interest or of mystery. Who can tell how meet he may have
been in his young days to play the part of the lover or of the
hero—who can say that in early life he had been the same
harsh, *unlicked*, and rugged boor which, in his maturer age,
he proved—or how far the neglected rudeness which afterwards marked his air, and garb, and manners, may not have
been the growth of that reckless apathy not unfrequently
produced by bitter misfortunes and disappointments
in early life? These questions can never now be answered.
We must content ourselves, then, with a plain statement
of facts, or what have been received and transmitted as
such, leaving matters of speculation to those who like
them.

When Schalken studied under the immortal Gerard Douw,
he was a young man; and in spite of the phlegmatic constitution and unexcitable manner which he shared (we believe)
with his countrymen, he was not incapable of deep and vivid
impressions, for it is an established fact that the young painter
looked with considerable interest upon the beautiful niece of
his wealthy master. Rose Velderkaust was very young,
having, at the period of which we speak, not yet attained
her seventeenth year, and, if tradition speaks truth, possessed
all the soft dimpling charms of the fair, light-haired Flemish
maidens. Schalken had not studied long in the school of
Gerard Douw, when he felt this interest deepening into something of a keener and intenser feeling than was quite consistent with the tranquillity of his honest Dutch heart; and at
the same time he perceived, or thought he perceived, flattering symptoms of a reciprocity of liking, and this was quite
sufficient to determine whatever indecision he might have
heretofore experienced, and to lead him to devote exclusively
to her every hope and feeling of his heart. In short, he was
as much in love as a Dutchman could be. He was not long
in making his passion known to the pretty maiden herself,
and his declaration was followed by a corresponding confession upon her part. Schalken, however, was a poor man, and
he possessed no counterbalancing advantages of birth or
otherwise to induce the old man to consent to a union which
must involve his niece and ward in the struggles and difficulties of a young and nearly friendless artist. He was, therefore, to wait until time had furnished him with opportunity

and accident with success; and then, if his labours were found
sufficiently lucrative, it was to be hoped that his proposals
might at least be listened to by her jealous guardian. Months
passed away, and, cheered by the smiles of the little Rose,
Schalken's labours were redoubled, and with such effect and
improvement as reasonably to promise the realization of his
hopes, and no contemptible eminence in his art, before many
years should have elapsed.

The even course of this cheering prosperity was, however,
destined to experience a sudden and formidable interruption,
and that, too, in a manner so strange and mysterious as to
baffle all investigation, and throw upon the events themselves
a shadow of almost supernatural horror.

Schalken had one evening remained in the master's studio
considerably longer than his more volatile companions, who
had gladly availed themselves of the excuse which the dusk
of evening afforded, to withdraw from their several tasks,
in order to finish a day of labour in the jollity and conviviality
of the tavern. But Schalken worked for improvement, or
rather for love. Besides, he was now engaged merely in
sketching a design, an operation which, unlike that of colouring, might be continued as long as there was light sufficient
to distinguish between canvas and charcoal. He had not
then, nor, indeed, until long after, discovered the peculiar
powers of his pencil, and he was engaged in composing a
group of extremely roguish-looking and grotesque imps and
demons, who were inflicting various ingenious torments upon
a perspiring and pot-bellied St. Anthony, who reclined in the
midst of them, apparently in the last stage of drunkenness.
The young artist, however, though incapable of executing,
or even of appreciating, anything of true sublimity, had,
nevertheless, discernment enough to prevent his being by
any means satisfied with his work; and many were the patient
erasures and corrections which the limbs and features of saint
and devil underwent, yet all without producing in their new
arrangement anything of improvement or increased effect.
The large, old-fashioned room was silent, and, with the exception of himself, quite deserted by its usual inmates. An hour
had passed—nearly two—without any improved result. Daylight had already declined, and twilight was fast giving way
to the darkness of night. The patience of the young man
was exhausted, and he stood before his unfinished production,

absorbed in no very pleasing ruminations, one hand buried in the folds of his long dark hair, and the other holding the piece of charcoal which had so ill executed its office, and which he now rubbed, without much regard to the sable streaks which it produced, with irritable pressure upon his ample Flemish inexpressibles.—" Pshaw! " said the young man aloud, " would that picture, devils, saint, and all, were where they should be—in hell! " A short, sudden laugh, uttered startlingly close to his ear, instantly responded to the ejaculation. The artist turned sharply round, and now for the first time became aware that his labours had been over-looked by a stranger. Within about a yard and a half, and rather behind him, there stood what was, or appeared to be, the figure of an elderly man: he wore a short cloak, and broad-brimmed hat, with a conical crown, and in his hand, which was protected with a heavy, gauntlet-shaped glove, he carried a long ebony walking-stick, surmounted with what appeared, as it glittered dimly in the twilight, to be a massive head of gold, and upon the breast, through the folds of the cloak, there shone what appeared to be the links of a rich chain of the same metal. The room was so obscure that nothing further of the appearance of the figure could be ascer-tained, and the face was altogether overshadowed by the heavy flap of the beaver which overhung it, so that not a feature could be discerned. A quantity of dark hair escaped from beneath this sombre hat, a circumstance which, con-nected with the firm, upright carriage of the intruder, proved that his years could not yet exceed threescore or thereabouts. There was an air of gravity and importance about the garb of this person, and something indescribably odd, I might say awful, in the perfect stone-like movelessness of the figure, that effectually checked the testy comment which had at once risen to the lips of the irritated artist. He, therefore, as soon as he had sufficiently recovered the surprise, asked the stranger, civilly, to be seated, and desired to know if he had any message to leave for his master.

" Tell Gerard Douw," said the unknown, without altering his attitude in the smallest degree, " that Minheer Vander-hausen, of Rotterdam, desires to speak with him on to-morrow evening at this hour, and, if he please, in this room, upon matters of weight—that is all—good-night."

The stranger, having finished this message, turned

abruptly, and with a quick but silent step quitted the room, before Schalken had time to say a word in reply. The young man felt a curiosity to see in what direction the burgher of Rotterdam would turn on quitting the studio, and for that purpose he went directly to the window which commanded the door. A lobby of considerable extent intervened between the inner door of the painter's room and the street entrance, so that Schalken occupied the post of observation before the old man could possibly have reached the street. He watched in vain, however. There was no other mode of exit. Had the old man vanished, or was he lurking about the recesses of the lobby for some bad purpose? This last suggestion filled the mind of Schalken with a vague horror, which was so unaccountably intense as to make him alike afraid to remain in the room alone and reluctant to pass through the lobby. However, with an effort which appeared very disproportioned to the occasion, he summoned resolution to leave the room, and, having double-locked the door and thrust the key in his pocket, without looking to the right or left, he traversed the passage which had so recently, perhaps still, contained the person of his mysterious visitant, scarcely venturing to breathe till he had arrived in the open street.

"Minheer Vanderhausen," said Gerard Douw within himself, as the appointed hour approached, "Minheer Vanderhausen of Rotterdam! I never heard of the man till yesterday. What can he want of me? A portrait, perhaps, to be painted; or a younger son or a poor relation to be apprenticed; or a collection to be valued; or—pshaw, there's no one in Rotterdam to leave me a legacy. Well, whatever the business may be, we shall soon know it all."

It was now the close of day, and every easel, except that of Schalken, was deserted. Gerard Douw was pacing the apartment with the restless step of impatient expectation, every now and then humming a passage from a piece of music which he was himself composing; for, though no great proficient, he admired the art: sometimes pausing to glance over the work of one of his absent pupils, but more frequently placing himself at the window, from whence he might observe the passengers who threaded the obscure by-street, in which his studio was placed.

"Said you not, Godfrey," exclaimed Douw, after a long and fruitless gaze from his post of observation, and turning to Schalken—" said you not the hour of appointment was at about seven by the clock of the Stadhouse? "

" It had just told seven when I first saw him, sir," answered the student.

" The hour is close at hand, then," said the master, consulting a horologe as large and as round as a full-grown orange. " Minheer Vanderhausen from Rotterdam—is it not so? "

" Such was the name."

" And an elderly man, richly clad? " continued Douw.

" As well as I might see," replied his pupil; " he could not be young, nor yet very old neither, and his dress was rich and grave, as might become a citizen of wealth and consideration."

At this moment the sonorous boom of the Stadhouse clock told, stroke after stroke, the hour of seven; the eyes of both master and student were directed to the door; and it was not until the last peal of the old bell had ceased to vibrate, that Douw exclaimed—

" So, so; we shall have his worship presently—that is, if he means to keep his hour; if not, thou may'st wait for him, Godfrey, if you court the acquaintance of a capricious burgomaster; as for me, I think our old Leyden contains a sufficiency of such commodities, without an importation from Rotterdam."

Schalken laughed, as in duty bound; and after a pause of some minutes, Douw suddenly exclaimed—

" What if it should all prove a jest, a piece of mummery got up by Vankarp, or some such worthy? I wish you had run all risks, and cudgelled the old burgomaster, stadholder, or whatever else he may be, soundly. I would wager a dozen of Rhenish, his worship would have pleaded old acquaintance before the third application."

" Here he comes, sir," said Schalken, in a low admonitory tone; and instantly upon turning towards the door, Gerard Douw observed the same figure which had, on the day before, so unexpectedly greeted the vision of his pupil Schalken.

There was something in the air and mien of the figure which at once satisfied the painter that there was no *mummery* in the case, and that he really stood in the presence of a man of worship; and so, without hesitation, he doffed his cap, and, courteously saluting the stranger, requested him to be seated.

The visitor waved his hand slightly, as if in acknowledgement of the courtesy, but remained standing.

" I have the honour to see Minheer Vanderhausen of Rotterdam? " said Gerard Douw.

" The same," was the laconic reply of his visitant.

" I understand your worship desires to speak with me," continued Douw, " and I am here by appointment to wait your commands."

" Is that a man of trust? " said Vanderhausen, turning towards Schalken, who stood at a little distance behind his master.

" Certainly," replied Gerard.

" Then let him take this box and get the nearest jeweller or goldsmith to value its contents, and let him return hither with a certificate of the valuation."

At the same time, he placed a small case about nine inches square in the hands of Gerard Douw, who was as much amazed at its weight as at the strange abruptness with which it was handed to him. In accordance with the wishes of the stranger, he delivered it into the hands of Schalken, and repeating *his* directions, despatched him upon the mission.

Schalken disposed his precious charge securely beneath the folds of his cloak, and rapidly traversing two or three narrow streets, he stopped at a corner house, the lower part of which was then occupied by the shop of a Jewish goldsmith. Schalken entered the shop, and calling the little Hebrew into the obscurity of its back recesses, he proceeded to lay before him Vanderhausen's packet. On being examined by the light of a lamp, it appeared entirely cased with lead, the outer surface of which was much scraped and soiled, and nearly white with age. This was with difficulty partially removed, and disclosed beneath a box of some dark and singularly hard wood; this too was forced, and after the removal of two or three folds of linen, its contents proved to be a mass of golden ingots, closely packed, and, as the Jew declared, of the most perfect quality. Every ingot underwent the scrutiny of the little Jew, who seemed to feel an epicurean delight in touching and testing these morsels of the glorious metal; and each one of them was replaced in its berth with the exclamation: " Mein Gott, how very perfect! Not one grain of alloy —beautiful, beautiful." The task was at length finished, and the Jew certified under his hand the value of the ingots submitted to his examination, to amount to many thousand rix-dollars. With the desired document in his bosom, and the rich box of gold carefully pressed under his arm, and concealed by his cloak, he retraced his way, and entering the studio, found his master and the stranger in close conference.

Schalken had no sooner left the room, in order to execute the commission he had taken in charge, than Vanderhausen addressed Gerard Douw in the following terms—

" I may not tarry with you to-night more than a few minutes, and so I shall briefly tell you the matter upon which I come. You visited the town of Rotterdam some four months ago, and then I saw in the church of St. Lawrence your niece, Rose Velderkaust. I desire to marry her, and if I satisfy you as to the fact that I am very wealthy, more wealthy than any husband you could dream of for her, I expect that you will forward my views to the utmost of your authority. If you approve my proposals, you must close with it at once, for I cannot command time enough to wait for calculations and delays."

Gerard Douw was, perhaps, as much astonished as any one could be, by the very unexpected nature of Minheer Vanderhausen's communication, but he did not give vent to any unseemly expression of surprise, for besides the motives supplied by prudence and politeness, the painter experienced a kind of chill and oppressive sensation, something like that which is supposed to affect a man who is placed unconsciously in immediate contact with something to which he has a natural antipathy—an undefined horror and dread while standing in the presence of the eccentric stranger, which made him very unwilling to say anything which might reasonably prove offensive.

" I have no doubt," said Gerard, after two or three prefatory hems, " that the connexion which you propose would prove alike advantageous and honourable to my niece; but you must be aware that she has a will of her own, and may not acquiesce in what *we* may design for her advantage."

" Do not seek to deceive me, sir painter," said Vanderhausen; " you are her guardian—she is your ward—she is mine if *you* like to make her so."

The man of Rotterdam moved forward a little as he spoke, and Gerard Douw, he scarce knew why, inwardly prayed for the speedy return of Schalken.

"I desire," said the mysterious gentleman, "to place in your hands at once an evidence of my wealth, and a security for my liberal dealing with your niece. The lad will return in a minute or two with a sum in value five times the fortune which she has a right to expect from a husband. This shall lie in your hands, together with her dowry, and you may apply the united sum as suits her interest best; it shall be all exclusively hers while she lives—is that liberal?"

Douw assented, and inwardly thought that fortune had been extraordinarily kind to his niece; the stranger, he thought, must be both wealthy and generous, and such an offer was not to be despised, though made by a humorist, and one of no very prepossessing presence. Rose had no very high pretensions, for she was almost without dowry; indeed, altogether so, excepting so far as the deficiency had been supplied by the generosity of her uncle; neither had she any right to raise any scruples against the match on the score of birth, for her own origin was by no means elevated, and as to other objections, Gerard resolved, and, indeed, by the usages of the time, was warranted in resolving not to listen to them for a moment.

"Sir," said he, addressing the stranger, "your offer is most liberal, and whatever hesitation I may feel in closing with it immediately, arises solely from my not having the honour of knowing anything of your family or station. Upon these points you can, of course, satisfy me without difficulty?"

"As to my respectability," said the stranger, drily, "you must take that for granted at present; pester me with no inquiries; you can discover nothing more about me than I choose to make known. You shall have sufficient security for my respectability—my word, if you are honourable: if you are sordid, my gold."

"A testy old gentleman," thought Douw, "he must have his own way; but, all things considered, I am justified in giving my niece to him; were she my own daughter, I would do the like by her. I will not pledge myself unnecessarily however."

"You will not pledge yourself unnecessarily," said Vanderhausen, strangely uttering the very words which had just floated through the mind of his companion; "but you will do so if it *is* necessary, I presume; and I will show you that I consider it indispensable. If the gold I mean to leave in your hands satisfy you, and if you desire that my proposal shall not be at once withdrawn, you must, before I leave this room, write your name to this engagement."

Having thus spoken, he placed a paper in the hands of Gerard, the contents of which expressed an engagement entered into by Gerard Douw, to give to Wilken Vanderhausen of Rotterdam, in marriage, Rose Velderkaust, and so forth, within one week of the date thereof. While the painter was employed in reading this covenant, Schalken, as we have stated, entered the studio, and having delivered the box and the valuation of the Jew, into the hands of the stranger, he was about to retire, when Vanderhausen called to him to wait; and, presenting the case and the certificate to Gerald Douw, he waited in silence until he had satisfied himself by an inspection of both as to the value of the pledge left in his hands. At length he said—

" Are you content? "

The painter said he would fain have another day to consider.

" Not an hour," said the suitor coolly.

" Well then," said Douw, " I am content—it is a bargain."

" Then sign at once," said Vanderhausen, " I am weary."

At the same time he produced a small case of writing materials, and Gerard signed the important document.

" Let this youth witness the covenant," said the old man; and Godfrey Schalken unconsciously signed the instrument which bestowed upon another that hand which he had so long regarded as the object and reward of all his labours. The compact being thus completed, the strange visitor folded up the paper, and stowed it safely in an inner pocket.

" I will visit you to-morrow night at nine of the clock, at your house, Gerard Douw, and will see the subject of our contract—farewell "; and so saying, Wilken Vanderhausen moved stiffly but rapidly out of the room.

Schalken, eager to resolve his doubts, had placed himself by the window, in order to watch the street entrance; but the experiment served only to support his suspicions, for the old man did not issue from the door. This was very strange, very odd, very fearful; he and his master returned together, and talked but little on the way, for each had his own subjects of reflection, of anxiety, and of hope. Schalken, however, did not know the ruin which threatened his cherished schemes.

Gerard Douw knew nothing of the attachment which had sprung up between his pupil and his niece; and even if he had, it is doubtful whether he would have regarded its existence as any serious obstruction to the wishes of Minheer Vanderhausen. Marriages were then and there matters of traffic and calculation; and it would have appeared as absurd in the eyes of the guardian to make a mutual attachment an essential element in a contract of marriage, as it would have been to draw up his bonds and receipts in the language of chivalrous romance. The painter, however, did not communicate to his niece the important step which he had taken in her behalf, and his resolution arose not from any anticipation of opposition on her part, but solely from a ludicrous consciousness that if his ward were, as she very naturally might do, to ask him to describe the appearance of the bridegroom whom he destined for her, he would be forced to confess that he had not seen his face, and if called upon, would find it impossible to identify him. Upon the next day, Gerard Douw, having dined, called his niece to him and having scanned her person with an air of satisfaction, he took her hand, and looking upon her pretty, innocent face with a smile of kindness, he said—

" Rose, my girl, that face of yours will make your fortune." Rose blushed and smiled. " Such faces and such tempers seldom go together, and, when they do, the compound is a love potion, which few heads or hearts can resist; trust me, thou wilt soon be a bride, girl; but this is trifling, and I am pressed for time, so make ready the large room by eight o'clock to-night, and give directions for supper at nine. I expect a friend to-night; and observe me, child, do thou trick thyself out handsomely. I would not have him think us poor or sluttish."

With these words he left the chamber, and took his way to the room to which we have already had occasion to introduce our readers—that in which his pupils worked.

When the evening closed in, Gerard called Schalken, who was about to take his departure to his obscure and comfortless lodgings, and asked him to come home and sup with Rose and Vanderhausen. The invitation was, of course, accepted, and Gerard Douw and his pupil soon found themselves in the handsome and somewhat antique-looking room which had been prepared for the reception of the stranger. A

cheerful wood fire blazed in the capacious hearth; a little at
one side an old-fashioned table, with richly carved legs, was
placed—destined, no doubt, to receive the supper, for which
preparations were going forward; and ranged with exact
regularity, stood the tall-backed chairs, whose ungracefulness
was more than counterbalanced by their comfort. The little
party, consisting of Rose, her uncle, and the artist, awaited
the arrival of the expected visitor with considerable impatience. Nine o'clock at length came, and with it a summons
at the street door, which being speedily answered, was followed by a slow and emphatic tread upon the staircase; the
steps moved heavily across the lobby, the door of the room
in which the party which we have described were assembled
slowly opened, and there entered a figure which startled,
almost appalled, the phlegmatic Dutchman, and nearly made
Rose scream with affright; it was the form, and arrayed in
the garb of Minheer Vanderhausen; the air, the gait, the
height were the same, but the features had never been seen
by any of the party before. The stranger stopped at the
door of the room, and displayed his form and face completely.
He wore a dark-coloured cloth cloak, which was short and
full, not falling quite to the knees; his legs were cased in dark
purple silk stockings, and his shoes were adorned with roses
of the same colour. The opening of the cloak in front showed
the under-suit to consist of some very dark, perhaps sable
material, and his hands were enclosed in a pair of heavy
leather gloves, which ran up considerably above the wrist, in
the manner of a gauntlet. In one hand he carried his
walking-stick and his hat, which he had removed, and the
other hung heavily by his side. A quantity of grizzled hair
descended in long tresses from his head, and its folds rested
upon the plaits of a stiff ruff, which effectually concealed
his neck. So far all was well; but the face!—all the flesh of
the face was coloured with the bluish leaden hue, which is
sometimes produced by the operation of metallic medicines,
administered in excessive quantities; the eyes were enormous,
and the white appeared both above and below the iris, which
gave to them an expression of insanity, which was heightened
by their glassy fixedness; the nose was well enough, but the
mouth was writhed considerably to one side, where it opened
in order to give egress to two long, discoloured fangs, which
projected from the upper jaw, far below the lower lip—the

hue of the lips themselves bore the usual relation to that of the face, and was, consequently, nearly black; the character of the face was malignant, even satanic, to the last degree; and, indeed, such a combination of horror could hardly be accounted for, except by supposing the corpse of some atrocious malefactor which had long hung blackening upon the gibbet to have at length become the habitation of a demon— the frightful sport of satanic possession. It was remarkable that the worshipful stranger suffered as little as possible of his flesh to appear, and that during his visit he did not once remove his gloves. Having stood for some moments at the door, Gerard Douw at length found breath and collectedness to bid him welcome, and with a mute inclination of the head, the stranger stepped forward into the room. There was something indescribably odd, even horrible, about all his motions, something undefinable, that was unnatural, un-human—it was as if the limbs were guided and directed by a spirit unused to the management of bodily machinery. The stranger said hardly anything during his visit, which did not exceed half an hour; and the host himself could scarcely muster courage enough to utter the few necessary salutations and courtesies; and, indeed, such was the nervous terror which the presence of Vanderhausen inspired, that very little would have made all his entertainers fly bellowing from the room. They had not so far lost all self-possession, however, as to fail to observe two strange peculiarities of their visitor. During his stay he did not once suffer his eyelids to close, nor even to move in the slightest degree; and farther, there was a death-like stillness in his whole person, owing to the total absence of the heaving motion of the chest, caused by the process of respiration. These two peculiarities, though when told they may appear trifling, produced a very striking and unpleasant effect when seen and observed. Vanderhausen at length relieved the painter of Leyden of his inauspicious presence; and with no small gratification the little party heard the street door close after him.

"Dear uncle," said Rose, "what a frightful man! I would not see him again for the wealth of the States."

"Tush, foolish girl," said Douw, whose sensations were anything but comfortable. "A man may be as ugly as the devil, and yet if his heart and actions are good, he is worth all the pretty-faced, perfumed puppies that walk the Mall.

Rose, my girl, it is very true he has not thy pretty face, but I know him to be wealthy and liberal; and were he ten times more ugly "—(" which is inconceivable," observed Rose)— " these two virtues would be sufficient," continued her uncle, " to counter-balance all his deformity; and if not of power sufficient actually to alter the shape of the features, at least of efficacy enough to prevent one thinking them amiss."

" Do you know, uncle," said Rose, " when I saw him standing at the door, I could not get it out of my head that I saw the old, painted, wooden figure that used to frighten me so much in the church of St. Lawrence of Rotterdam."

Gerard laughed, though he could not help inwardly acknowledging the justness of the comparison. He was resolved, however, as far as he could, to check his niece's inclination to ridicule the ugliness of her intended bridegroom, although he was not a little pleased to observe that she appeared totally exempt from that mysterious dread of the stranger which, he could not disguise it from himself, considerably affected him, as also his pupil Godfrey Schalken.

Early on the next day there arrived from various quarters of the town, rich presents of silks, velvets, jewellery, and so forth, for Rose; and also a packet directed to Gerard Douw, which on being opened, was found to contain a contract of marriage, formally drawn up, between Wilken Vanderhausen of the Boom-quay, in Rotterdam, and Rose Velderkaust of Leyden, niece to Gerard Douw, master in the art of painting, also of the same city; and containing engagements on the part of Vanderhausen to make settlements upon his bride, far more splendid than he had before led her guardian to believe likely, and which were to be secured to her use in the most unexceptionable manner possible—the money being placed in the hands of Gerard Douw himself.

I have no sentimental scenes to describe, no cruelty of guardians, or magnanimity of wards, or agonies of lovers. The record I have to make is one of sordidness, levity, and interest. In less than a week after the first interview which we have just described, the contract of marriage was fulfilled, and Schalken saw the prize which he would have risked anything to secure, carried off triumphantly by his unattractive rival. For two or three days he absented himself from the school; he then returned and worked, if with less cheerfulness, with far more dogged resolution than before—the stimulus

of love had given place to that of ambition. Months passed
away, and, contrary to his expectation, and, indeed, to the
direct promise of the parties, Gerard Douw heard nothing of
his niece or her worshipful spouse. The interest of the money
which was to have been demanded in quarterly sums, lay
unclaimed in his hands. He began to grow extremely uneasy.
Minheer Vanderhausen's direction in Rotterdam he was fully
possessed of; after some irresolution he finally determined to
journey thither—a trifling undertaking, and easily accomplished—and thus to satisfy himself of the safety and comfort
of his ward, for whom he entertained an honest and strong
affection. His search was in vain, however; no one in Rotterdam had ever heard of Minheer Vanderhausen. Gerard Douw
left not a house in the Boom-quay untried; but all in vain—
no one could give him any information whatever touching
the object of his inquiry; and he was obliged to return to
Leyden nothing wiser than when he had left it. On his
arrival he hastened to the establishment from which Vanderhausen had hired the lumbering, though, considering the
times, most luxurious vehicle, which the bridal party had
employed to convey them to Rotterdam. From the driver
of this machine he learned, that having proceeded by slow
stages, they had late in the evening approached Rotterdam;
but that before they entered the city, and while yet nearly
a mile from it, a small party of men, soberly clad, and after
the old fashion, with peaked beards and moustaches, standing
in the centre of the road, obstructed the further progress of
the carriage. The driver reined in his horses, much fearing,
from the obscurity of the hour, and the loneliness of the
road, that some mischief was intended. His fears were, however, somewhat allayed by his observing that these strange
men carried a large litter, of an antique shape, and which
they immediately set down upon the pavement, whereupon
the bridegroom, having opened the coach-door from within,
descended, and having assisted his bride to do likewise, led
her, weeping bitterly and wringing her hands, to the litter,
which they both entered. It was then raised by the men who
surrounded it, and speedily carried towards the city, and
before it had proceeded many yards, the darkness concealed
it from the view of the Dutch charioteer. In the inside of the
vehicle he found a purse, whose contents more than thrice
paid the hire of the carriage and man. He saw and could

tell nothing more of Minheer Vanderhausen and his beautiful
lady. This mystery was a source of deep anxiety and almost
of grief to Gerard Douw. There was evidently fraud in the
dealing of Vanderhausen with him, though for what purpose
committed he could not imagine. He greatly doubted how
far it was possible for a man possessing in his countenance so
strong an evidence of the presence of the most demoniac
feelings, to be in reality anything but a villain, and every day
that passed without his hearing from or of his niece, instead
of inducing him to forget his fears, on the contrary tended
more and more to exasperate them. The loss of his niece's
cheerful society tended also to depress his spirits; and in
order to dispel this despondency, which often crept upon
his mind after his daily employment was over, he was wont
frequently to prevail upon Schalken to accompany him home,
and by his presence to dispel, in some degree, the gloom of
his otherwise solitary supper. One evening, the painter and
his pupil were sitting by the fire, having accomplished a
comfortable supper, and had yielded to that silent pensiveness
sometimes induced by the process of digestion, when their
reflections were disturbed by a loud sound at the street door,
as if occasioned by some person rushing forcibly and
repeatedly against it. A domestic had run without delay to
ascertain the cause of the disturbance, and they heard him
twice or thrice interrogate the applicant for admission, but
without producing an answer or any cessation of the sounds.
They heard him then open the hall door, and immediately
there followed a light and rapid tread upon the staircase.
Schalken laid his hand on his sword, and advanced towards
the door. It opened before he reached it, and Rose rushed
into the room. She looked wild and haggard, and pale with
exhaustion and terror, but her dress surprised them as much
as even her unexpected appearance. It consisted of a kind
of white woollen wrapper, made close about the neck, and
descending to the very ground. It was much deranged and
travel-soiled. The poor creature had hardly entered the
chamber when she fell senseless on the floor. With some
difficulty they succeeded in reviving her, and on recovering
her senses, she instantly exclaimed, in a tone of eager, terrified
impatience—

"Wine, wine, quickly, or I'm lost."

Much alarmed at the strange agitation in which the call

was made, they at once administered to her wishes, and she drank some wine with a haste and eagerness which surprised them. She had hardly swallowed it, when she exclaimed, with the same urgency—

" Food, food, at once, or I perish."

A considerable fragment of a roast joint was upon the table, and Schalken immediately proceeded to cut some, but he was anticipated, for no sooner had she become aware of its presence, than she darted at it with the rapacity of a vulture, and, seizing it in her hands, she tore off the flesh with her teeth, and swallowed it. When the paroxysm of hunger had been a little appeased, she appeared suddenly to become aware how strange her conduct had been, or it may have been that other more agitating thoughts recurred to her mind, for she began to weep bitterly and to wring her hands.

" Oh, send for a minister of God," said she; " I am not safe till he comes; send for him speedily."

Gerard Douw despatched a messenger instantly, and prevailed on his niece to allow him to surrender his bedchamber to her use; he also persuaded her to retire to it at once and to rest; her consent was extorted upon the condition that they would not leave her for a moment.

" Oh that the holy man were here," she said; " he can deliver me—the dead and the living can never be one— God has forbidden it."

With these mysterious words she surrendered herself to their guidance, and they proceeded to the chamber which Gerard Douw had assigned to her use.

" Do not, do not leave me for a moment," said she; " I am lost for ever if you do."

Gerard Douw's chamber was approached through a spacious apartment, which they were now about to enter. Gerard Douw and Schalken each carried a wax candle, so that a sufficient degree of light was cast upon all surrounding objects. They were now entering the large chamber, which, as I have said, communicated with Douw's apartment, when Rose suddenly stopped, and, in a whisper which seemed to thrill with horror, she said—

" Oh, God! he is here, he is here; see, see, there he goes."

She pointed towards the door of the inner room, and Schalken thought he saw a shadowy and ill-defined form

gliding into that apartment. He drew his sword, and, raising
the candle so as to throw its light with increased distinctness
upon the objects in the room, he entered the chamber into
which the shadow had glided. No figure was there—nothing
but the furniture which belonged to the room, and yet he
could not be deceived as to the fact that something had moved
before them into the chamber. A sickening dread came upon
him; and the cold perspiration broke out in heavy drops upon
his forehead; nor was he more composed, when he heard the
increased urgency; the agony of entreaty, with which Rose
implored them not to leave her for a moment.

"I saw him," said she; "he's here. I cannot be deceived—
I know him—he's by me—he is with me—he's in the room;
then, for God's sake, as you would save me, do not stir from
beside me."

They at length prevailed upon her to lie down upon the
bed, where she continued to urge them to stay by her. She
frequently uttered incoherent sentences, repeating, again and
again, "the dead and the living cannot be one—God has
forbidden it;" and then again, "rest to the wakeful—sleep
to the sleep-walkers." These and such mysterious and broken
sentences, she continued to utter until the clergyman arrived.
Gerard Douw began to fear, naturally enough, that the poor
girl, owing to terror or ill-treatment, had become deranged,
and he half-suspected, by the suddenness of her appearance;
and the unseasonableness of the hour, and, above all, from the
wildness and terror of her manner, that she had made her
escape from some place of confinement for lunatics, and was
in immediate fear of pursuit. He resolved to summon
medical advice, as soon as the mind of his niece had been in
some measure set at rest by the offices of the clergyman
whose attendance she had so earnestly desired; and until this
object had been attained, he did not venture to put any
questions to her, which might possibly, by reviving painful
or horrible recollections, increase her agitation. The clergyman soon arrived—a man of ascetic countenance and venerable age—one whom Gerard Douw respected much; forasmuch as he was a veteran polemic, though one, perhaps,
more dreaded as a combatant than beloved as a Christian—
of pure morality, subtle brain, and frozen heart. He entered
the chamber which communicated with that in which Rose
reclined, and immediately on his arrival, she requested him

to pray for her, as for one who lay in the hands of Satan, and who could hope for deliverance—only from heaven.

That our readers may distinctly understand all the circumstances of the event which we are about imperfectly to describe, it is necessary to state the relative positions of the parties who were engaged in it. The old clergyman and Schalken were in the ante-room of which we have already spoken; Rose lay in the inner chamber, the door of which was open; and by the side of the bed, at her urgent desire, stood her guardian; a candle burned in the bedchamber, and three were lighted in the outer apartment. The old man now cleared his voice as if about to commence, but before he had time to begin, a sudden gust of air blew out the candle which served to illuminate the room in which the poor girl lay, and she, with hurried alarm, exclaimed—

" Godfrey, bring in another candle; the darkness is unsafe."

Gerard Douw, forgetting for the moment her repeated injunctions, in the immediate impulse, stepped from the bedchamber into the other, in order to supply what she desired.

" Oh God! do not go, dear uncle," shrieked the unhappy girl—and at the same time she sprang from the bed, and darted after him, in order, by her grasp, to detain him. But the warning came too late, for scarcely had he passed the threshold, and hardly had his niece had time to utter the startling exclamation, when the door which divided the two rooms closed violently after him, as if swung to by a strong blast of wind. Schalken and he both rushed to the door, but their united and desperate efforts could not avail so much as to shake it. Shriek after shriek burst from the inner chamber, with all the piercing loudness of despairing terror. Schalken and Douw applied every energy and strained every nerve to force open the door; but all in vain. There was no sound of struggling from within, but the screams seemed to increase in loudness, and at the same time they heard the bolts of the latticed window withdrawn, and the window itself grated upon the sill as if thrown open. One *last* shriek, so long and piercing and agonized as to be scarcely human, swelled from the room, and suddenly there followed a death-like silence. A light step was heard crossing the floor, as if from the bed to the window; and almost at the same instant the door gave way, and, yielding to the pressure of the external applicants, they were nearly precipitated into the room. It was empty. The window was open, and Schalken sprang to a chair and gazed out upon the street and canal below. He saw no form, but he beheld, or thought he beheld, the waters of the broad canal beneath settling ring after ring in heavy circular ripples, as if a moment before disturbed by the immersion of some large and heavy mass.

No trace of Rose was ever after discovered, nor was anything certain respecting her mysterious wooer detected or even suspected—no clue whereby to trace the intricacies of the labyrinth and to arrive at a distinct conclusion was to be found. But an incident occurred, which, though it will not be received by our rational readers as at all approaching to evidence upon the matter, nevertheless produced a strong and a lasting impression upon the mind of Schalken. Many years after the events which we have detailed, Schalken, then remotely situated, received an intimation of his father's death, and of his intended burial upon a fixed day in the church of Rotterdam. It was necessary that a very considerable journey should be performed by the funeral procession, which, as it will be readily believed, was not very numerously attended. Schalken with difficulty arrived in Rotterdam late in the day upon which the funeral was appointed to take place. It had not then arrived. Evening closed in, and still it did not appear.

Schalken strolled down to the church—he found it open—notice of the arrival of the funeral had been given, and the vault in which the body was to be laid had been opened. The officer, who is analogous to our sexton, on seeing a well-dressed gentleman, whose object was to attend the expected funeral, pacing the aisle of the church, hospitably invited him to share with him the comforts of a blazing wood fire, which, as was his custom in winter time upon such occasions, he had kindled in the hearth of a chamber which communicated, by a flight of steps, with the vault below. In this chamber Schalken and his entertainer seated themselves, and the sexton, after some fruitless attempts to engage his guest in conversation, was obliged to apply himself to his tobacco-pipe and can, to solace his solitude. In spite of his grief and cares, the fatigues of a rapid journey of nearly forty hours gradually overcame the mind and body of Godfrey Schalken, and he sank into a deep sleep, from which he was awakened by some one's shaking him gently by the shoulder.

He first thought that the old sexton had called him, but *he* was no longer in the room. He roused himself, and as soon as he could clearly see what was around him, he perceived a female form, clothed in a kind of light robe of muslin, part of which was so disposed as to act as a veil, and in her hand she carried a lamp. She was moving rather away from him, and towards the flight of steps which conducted towards the vaults. Schalken felt a vague alarm at the sight of this figure, and at the same time an irresistible impulse to follow its guidance. He followed it towards the vaults, but when it reached the head of the stairs, he paused—the figure paused also, and, turning gently round, displayed, by the light of the lamp it carried, the face and features of his first love, Rose Velderkaust. There was nothing horrible, or even sad, in the countenance. On the contrary, it wore the same arch smile which used to enchant the artist long before in his happy days. A feeling of awe and of interest, too intense to be resisted, prompted him to follow the spectre, if spectre it were. She descended the stairs—he followed—and, turning to the left, through a narrow passage, she led him, to his infinite surprise, into what appeared to be an old-fashioned Dutch apartment, such as the pictures of Gerard Douw have served to immortalize. Abundance of costly antique furniture was disposed about the room, and in one corner stood a four-post bed, with heavy black cloth curtains around it; the figure frequently turned towards him with the same arch smile; and when she came to the side of the bed, she drew the curtains, and, by the light of the lamp, which she held towards its contents, she disclosed to the horror-stricken painter, sitting bolt upright in bed, the livid and demoniac form of Vanderhausen. Schalken had hardly seen him, when he fell senseless upon the floor, where he lay until discovered, on the next morning, by persons employed in closing the passages into the vaults. He was lying in a cell of considerable size, which had not been disturbed for a long time, and he had fallen beside a large coffin, which was supported upon small stone pillars, a security against the attacks of vermin.

To his dying day Schalken was satisfied of the reality of the vision which he had witnessed, and he has left behind him a curious evidence of the impression which it wrought upon his fancy, in a painting executed shortly after the event we have narrated, and which is valuable as exhibiting not only the peculiarities which have made Schalken's pictures sought after, but even more so as presenting a portrait as close and faithful as one taken from memory can be, of his early love, Rose Velderkaust, whose mysterious fate must ever remain a matter of speculation. The picture represents a chamber of antique masonry, such as might be found in most old cathedrals, and is lighted faintly by a lamp carried in the hand of a female figure, such as we have above attempted to describe; and in the background, and to the left of him who examines the painting, there stands the form of a man apparently aroused from sleep, and by his attitude, his hand being laid upon his sword, exhibiting considerable alarm; this last figure is illuminated only by the expiring glare of a wood or charcoal fire. The whole production exhibits a beautiful specimen of that artful and singular distribution of light and shade which has rendered the name of Schalken immortal among the artists of his country. This tale is traditionary, and the reader will easily perceive, by our studiously omitting to heighten many points of the narrative, when a little additional colouring might have added effect to the recital, that we have desired to lay before him, not a figment of the brain, but a curious tradition connected with, and belonging to the biography of a famous artist.

CARMILLA

CHAPTER I

AN EARLY FRIGHT

I N Styria, we, though by no means magnificent people, inhabit a castle, or schloss. A small income, in that part of the world, goes a great way. Eight or nine hundred a year does wonders. Scantily enough ours would have answered among wealthy people at home. My father is English, and I bear an English name, although I never saw England. But here, in this lonely and primitive place, where everything is so marvellously cheap, I really don't see how ever so much more money would at all materially add to our comforts, or even luxuries.

My father was in the Austrian service, and retired upon a pension and his patrimony, and purchased this feudal residence, and the small estate on which it stands, a bargain.

Nothing can be more picturesque or solitary. It stands on a slight eminence in a forest. The road, very old and narrow, passes in front of its drawbridge, never raised in my time, and its moat, stocked with perch, and sailed over by many swans, and floating on its surface white fleets of water-lilies.

Over all this the schloss shows its many-windowed front; its towers, and its Gothic chapel.

The forest opens in an irregular and very picturesque glade before its gate, and at the right a steep Gothic bridge carries the road over a stream that winds in deep shadow through the wood.

I have said that this is a very lonely place. Judge whether I say truth. Looking from the hall door towards the road, the forest in which our castle stands extends fifteen miles to the right, and twelve to the left. The nearest inhabited village is about seven of your English miles to the left. The nearest inhabited schloss of any historic associations, is that of old General Spielsdorf, nearly twenty miles away to the right.

I have said " the nearest *inhabited* village," because there is, only three miles westward, that is to say in the direction of General Spielsdorf's schloss, a ruined village, with its quaint little church, now roofless, in the aisle of which are the mouldering tombs of the proud family of Karnstein, now extinct, who once owned the equally-desolate château which, in the thick of the forest, overlooks the silent ruins of the town.

Respecting the cause of the desertion of this striking and melancholy spot, there is a legend which I shall relate to you another time.

I must tell you now, how very small is the party who constitute the inhabitants of our castle. I don't include servants, or those dependants who occupy rooms in the buildings attached to the schloss. Listen, and wonder! My father, who is the kindest man on earth, but growing old; and I, at the date of my story, only nineteen. Eight years have passed since then. I and my father constituted the family at the schloss. My mother, a Styrian lady, died in my infancy, but I had a good-natured governess, who had been with me from, I might almost say, my infancy. I could not remember the time when her fat, benignant face was not a familiar picture in my memory. This was Madame Perrodon, a native of Berne, whose care and good nature in part supplied to me the loss of my mother, whom I do not even remember, so early I lost her. She made a third at our little dinner party. There was a fourth, Mademoiselle de Lafontaine, a lady such as you term, I believe, a " finishing governess." She spoke French and German, Madame Perrodon French and broken English, to which my father and I added English, which, partly to prevent its becoming a lost language among us, and partly from patriotic motives, we spoke every day. The consequence was a Babel, at which strangers used to laugh, and which I shall make no attempt to reproduce in this narrative. And there were two or three young lady friends besides, pretty nearly of my own age, who were occasional visitors, for longer or shorter terms; and these visits I sometimes returned.

These were our regular social resources; but of course there were chance visits from " neighbours " of only five or six leagues' distance. My life was, notwithstanding, rather a solitary one, I can assure you.

My gouvernantes had just so much control over me as you might conjecture such sage persons would have in the case of a rather spoiled girl, whose only parent allowed her pretty nearly her own way in everything.

The first occurrence in my existence, which produced a terrible impression upon my mind, which, in fact, never has been effaced, was one of the very earliest incidents of my life which I can recollect. Some people will think it so trifling that it should not be recorded here. You will see, however, by-and-by, why I mention it. The nursery, as it was called, though I had it all to myself, was a large room in the upper story of the castle, with a steep oak roof. I can't have been more than six years old, when one night I awoke, and looking round the room from my bed, failed to see the nursery-maid. Neither was my nurse there; and I thought myself alone. I was not frightened, for I was one of those happy children who are studiously kept in ignorance of ghost stories, of fairy tales, and of all such lore as makes us cover up our heads when the door creaks suddenly, or the flicker of an expiring candle makes the shadow of a bed-post dance upon the wall, nearer to our faces. I was vexed and insulted at finding myself, as I conceived, neglected, and I began to whimper, preparatory to a hearty bout of roaring; when to my surprise, I saw a solemn, but very pretty face looking at me from the side of the bed. It was that of a young lady who was kneeling, with her hands under the coverlet. I looked at her with a kind of pleased wonder, and ceased whimpering. She caressed me with her hands, and lay down beside me on the bed, and drew me towards her, smiling; I felt immediately delightfully soothed, and fell asleep again. I was wakened by a sensation as if two needles ran into my breast very deep at the same moment, and I cried loudly. The lady started back, with her eyes fixed on me, and then slipped down upon the floor, and, as I thought, hid herself under the bed.

I was now for the first time frightened, and I yelled with all my might and main. Nurse, nursery-maid, housekeeper, all came running in, and hearing my story, they made light of it, soothing me all they could meanwhile. But, child as I was, I could perceive that their faces were pale with an un-

wonted look of anxiety; and I saw them look under the bed,
and about the room, and peep under tables and pluck open
cupboards; and the housekeeper whispered to the nurse: " Lay
your hand along that hollow in the bed; someone *did* lie
there, so sure as you did not; the place is still warm."

I remember the nursery-maid petting me, and all three
examining my chest, where I told them I felt the puncture,
and pronouncing that there was no sign visible that any
such thing had happened to me.

The housekeeper and the two other servants who were
in charge of the nursery, remained sitting up all night; and
from that time a servant always sat up in the nursery until
I was about fourteen.

I was very nervous for a long time after this. A doctor
was called in; he was pallid and elderly. How well I remember his long saturnine face, slightly pitted with small-
pox, and his chestnut wig. For a good while, every second
day, he came and gave me medicine, which of course I hated.

The morning after I saw this apparition I was in a state
of terror, and could not bear to be left alone, daylight though
it was, for a moment.

I remember my father coming up and standing at the bedside, and talking cheerfully, and asking the nurse a number
of questions, and laughing very heartily at one of the answers;
and patting me on the shoulder, and kissing me, and telling
me not to be frightened, that it was nothing but a dream
and could not hurt me.

But I was not comforted, for I knew the visit of the
strange woman was *not* a dream; and I was *awfully* frightened.

I was a little consoled by the nursery-maid's assuring me
that it was she who had come and looked at me, and lain
down beside me in the bed, and that I must have been half-
dreaming not to have known her face. But this, though
supported by the nurse, did not quite satisfy me.

I remember, in the course of that day, a venerable old
man, in a black cassock, coming into the room with the
nurse and housekeeper, and talking a little to them, and
very kindly to me; his face was very sweet and gentle, and
he told me they were going to pray, and joined my hands
together, and desired me to say, softly, while they were
praying, " Lord, hear all good prayers for us, for Jesus'

sake." I think these were the very words, for I often repeated them to myself, and my nurse used for years to make me say them in my prayers.

I remember so well the thoughtful sweet face of that white-haired old man, in his black cassock, as he stood in that rude, lofty, brown room, with the clumsy furniture of a fashion three hundred years old, about him, and the scanty light entering its shadowy atmosphere through the small lattice. He kneeled, and the three women with him, and he prayed aloud with an earnest quavering voice for, what appeared to me, a long time. I forget all my life preceding that event, and for some time after it is all obscure also; but the scenes I have just described stand out vivid as the isolated pictures of the phantasmagoria surrounded by darkness.

CHAPTER II

A GUEST

I AM now going to tell you something so strange that it will require all your faith in my veracity to believe my story. It is not only true, nevertheless, but truth of which I have been an eye-witness.

It was a sweet summer evening, and my father asked me, as he sometimes did, to take a little ramble with him along that beautiful forest vista which I have mentioned as lying in front of the schloss.

"General Spielsdorf cannot come to us so soon as I had hoped," said my father, as we pursued our walk.

He was to have paid us a visit of some weeks, and we had expected his arrival next day. He was to have brought with him a young lady, his niece and ward, Mademoiselle Rheinfeldt, whom I had never seen, but whom I had heard described as a very charming girl, and in whose society I had promised myself many happy days. I was more disappointed than a young lady living in a town, or a bustling neighbourhood, can possibly imagine. This visit, and the new acquaintance it promised, had furnished my day dream for many weeks.

"And how soon does he come?" I asked.

"Not till autumn. Not for two months, I dare say," he

answered. "And I am very glad now, dear, that you never knew Mademoiselle Rheinfeldt."

"And why?" I asked, both mortified and curious.

"Because the poor young lady is dead," he replied. "I quite forgot I had not told you, but you were not in the room when I received the General's letter this evening."

I was very much shocked. General Spielsdorf had mentioned in his first letter, six or seven weeks before, that she was not so well as he would wish her, but there was nothing to suggest the remotest suspicion of danger.

"Here is the General's letter," he said, handing it to me. "I am afraid he is in great affliction; the letter appears to me to have been written very nearly in distraction."

We sat down on a rude bench, under a group of magnificent lime trees. The sun was setting with all its melancholy splendour behind the sylvan horizon, and the stream that flows beside our home, and passes under the steep old bridge I have mentioned, wound through many a group of noble trees, almost at our feet, reflecting in its current the fading crimson of the sky. General Spielsdorf's letter was so extraordinary, so vehement, and in some places so self-contradictory, that I read it twice over—the second time aloud to my father—and was still unable to account for it, except by supposing that grief had unsettled his mind.

It said, "I have lost my darling daughter, for as such I loved her. During the last days of dear Bertha's illness I was not able to write to you. Before then I had no idea of her danger. I have lost her, and now learn *all*, too late. She died in the peace of innocence, and in the glorious hope of a blessed futurity. The fiend who betrayed our infatuated hospitality has done it all. I thought I was receiving into my house innocence, gaiety, a charming companion for my lost Bertha. Heavens! what a fool have I been! I thank God my child died without a suspicion of the cause of her sufferings. She is gone without so much as conjecturing the nature of her illness, and the accursed passion of the agent of all this misery. I devote my remaining days to tracking and extinguishing a monster. I am told I may hope to accomplish my righteous and merciful purpose. At present there is scarcely a gleam of light to guide me. I curse my conceited incredulity, my despicable affection of superiority, my blindness, my obstinacy—all—too late. I

cannot write or talk collectedly now. I am distracted. So
soon as I shall have a little recovered, I mean to devote myself
for a time to enquiry, which may possibly lead me as far as
Vienna. Some time in the autumn, two months hence, or
earlier, if I live, I will see you—that is, if you permit me;
I will then tell you all that I scarce dare put upon paper
now. Farewell. Pray for me, dear friend."

In these terms ended this strange letter. Though I had
never seen Bertha Rheinfeldt, my eyes filled with tears at
the sudden intelligence; I was startled, as well as profoundly
disappointed.

The sun had now set, and it was twilight by the time I
returned the General's letter to my father.

It was a soft clear evening, and we loitered, speculating
upon the possible meanings of the violent and incoherent
sentences which I had just been reading. We had nearly a
mile to walk before reaching the road that passes the schloss
in front, and by that time the moon was shining brilliantly.
At the drawbridge we met Madame Perrodon and Mademoiselle de Lafontaine, who had come out, without their
bonnets, to enjoy the exquisite moonlight.

We heard their voices gabbling in animated dialogue as
we approached. We joined them at the drawbridge, and
turned about to admire with them the beautiful scene.

The glade through which we had just walked lay before
us. At our left the narrow road wound away under clumps
of lordly trees, and was lost to sight amid the thickening
forest. At the right the same road crosses the steep and
picturesque bridge, near which stands a ruined tower, which
once guarded that pass; and beyond the bridge an abrupt
eminence rises, covered with trees, and showing in the
shadow some grey ivy-clustered rocks.

Over the sward and low grounds, a thin film of mist
was stealing, like smoke, marking the distances with a transparent veil; and here and there we could see the river faintly
flashing in the moonlight.

No softer, sweeter scene could be imagined. The news
I had just heard made it melancholy; but nothing could
disturb its character of profound serenity, and the enchanted
glory and vagueness of the prospect.

My father, who enjoyed the picturesque, and I stood looking in silence over the expanse beneath us. The two good

governesses, standing a little way behind us, discoursed upon the scene, and were eloquent upon the moon.

Madame Perrodon was fat, middle-aged, and romantic, and talked and sighed poetically. Mademoiselle de Lafontaine— in right of her father, who was a German, assumed to be psychological, metaphysical, and something of a mystic—now declared that when the moon shone with a light so intense it was well known that it indicated a special spiritual activity. The effect of the full moon, in such a state of brilliancy, was manifold. It acted on dreams, it acted on lunacy, it acted on nervous people; it had marvellous psychical influences connected with life. Mademoiselle related that her cousin, who was mate of a merchant ship, having taken a nap on deck on such a night, lying on his back, with his face full in the light of the moon, had awakened, after a dream of an old woman clawing him by the cheek, with his features horribly drawn to one side; and his countenance had never quite recovered its equilibrium.

" The moon, this night," she said, " is full of idyllic and magnetic influence—and see, when you look behind you at the front of the schloss, how all its windows flash and twinkle with that silvery splendour, as if unseen hands had lighted up the rooms to receive fairy guests."

There are indolent states of the spirits in which, indisposed to talk ourselves, the talk of others is pleasant to our listless ears; and I gazed on, pleased with the tinkle of the ladies' conversation.

" I have got into one of my moping moods to-night," said my father, after a silence, and quoting Shakespeare, whom, by way of keeping up our English, he used to read aloud, he said:

" ' In truth I know not why I am so sad:
  It wearies me; you say it wearies you;
  But how I got it—came by it.'

" I forget the rest. But I feel as if some great misfortune were hanging over us. I suppose the poor General's afflicted letter has had something to do with it."

At this moment the unwonted sound of carriage wheels and many hoofs upon the road, arrested our attention.

They seemed to be approaching from the high ground over-looking the bridge, and very soon the equipage emerged from that point. Two horsemen first crossed the bridge, then came a carriage drawn by four horses, and two men rode behind.

It seemed to be the travelling carriage of a person of rank; and we were all immediately absorbed in watching that very unusual spectacle. It became, in a few moments, greatly more interesting, for just as the carriage had passed the summit of the steep bridge, one of the leaders, taking fright, communicated his panic to the rest, and, after a plunge or two, the whole team broke into a wild gallop together, and dashing between the horsemen who rode in front, came thundering along the road towards us with the speed of a hurricane.

The excitement of the scene was made more painful by the clear, long-drawn screams of a female voice from the carriage window.

We all advanced in curiosity and horror; my father in silence, the rest with various ejaculations of terror.

Our suspense did not last long. Just before you reach the castle drawbridge, on the route they were coming, there stands by the roadside a magnificent lime tree, on the other stands an ancient stone cross, at sight of which the horses, now going at a pace that was perfectly frightful, swerved so as to bring the wheel over the projecting roots of the tree.

I knew what was coming. I covered my eyes, unable to see it out, and turned my head away; at the same moment I heard a cry from my lady friends, who had gone on a little.

Curiosity opened my eyes, and I saw a scene of utter confusion. Two of the horses were on the ground, the carriage lay upon its side, with two wheels in the air; the men were busy removing the traces, and a lady, with a commanding air and figure, had got out, and stood with clasped hands, raising the handkerchief that was in them every now and then to her eyes. Through the carriage door was now lifted a young lady, who appeared to be lifeless. My dear old father was already beside the elder lady, with his hat in his hand, evidently tendering his aid and the resources of his schloss. The lady did not appear to hear him, or to have eyes for anything but the slender girl, who was being placed against the slope of the bank.

I approached; the young lady was apparently stunned, but

she was certainly not dead. My father, who piqued himself on being something of a physician, had just had his fingers to her wrist and assured the lady, who declared herself her mother, that her pulse, though faint and irregular, was undoubtedly still distinguishable. The lady clasped her hands and looked upward, as if in a momentary transport of gratitude; but immediately she broke out again in that theatrical way which is, I believe, natural to some people.

She was what is called a fine-looking woman for her time of life, and must have been handsome; she was tall, but not thin, and dressed in black velvet, and looked rather pale, but with a proud and commanding countenance, though now agitated strangely.

" Was ever being so born to calamity? " I heard her say, with clasped hands, as I came up. " Here am I, on a journey of life and death, in prosecuting which to lose an hour is possibly to lose all. My child will not have recovered sufficiently to resume her route for who can say how long. I must leave her; I cannot, dare not, delay. How far on, sir, can you tell, is the nearest village? I must leave her there; and shall not see my darling, or even hear of her till my return, three months hence."

I plucked my father by the coat, and whispered earnestly in his ear, " Oh! papa, pray ask her to let her stay with us —it would be so delightful. Do, pray."

" If Madame will entrust her child to the care of my daughter, and of her good gouvernante, Madame Perrodon, and permit her to remain as our guest, under my charge, until her return, it will confer a distinction and an obligation upon us, and we shall treat her with all the care and devotion which so sacred a trust deserves."

" I cannot do that, sir, it would be to task your kindness and chivalry too cruelly," said the lady, distractedly.

" It would, on the contrary, be to confer on us a very great kindness at the moment when we most need it. My daughter has just been disappointed by a cruel misfortune, in a visit from which she had long anticipated a great deal of happiness. If you confide this young lady to our care it will be her best consolation. The nearest village on your route is distant, and affords no such inn as you could think of placing your daughter at; you cannot allow her to continue her journey for any considerable distance without danger. If, as you say, you cannot suspend your journey, you must part with her to-night, and nowhere could you do so with more honest assurances of care and tenderness than here."

There was something in this lady's air and appearance so distinguished, and even imposing, and in her manner so engaging, as to impress one, quite apart from the dignity of her equipage, with a conviction that she was a person of consequence.

By this time the carriage was replaced in its upright position, and the horses, quite tractable, in the traces again.

The lady threw on her daughter a glance which I fancied was not quite so affectionate as one might have anticipated from the beginning of the scene; then she beckoned slightly to my father, and withdrew two or three steps with him out of hearing; and talked to him with a fixed and stern countenance, not at all like that with which she had hitherto spoken.

I was filled with wonder that my father did not seem to perceive the change, and also unspeakably curious to learn what it could be that she was speaking, almost in his ear, with so much earnestness and rapidity.

Two or three minutes at most, I think, she remained thus employed, then she turned, and a few steps brought her to where her daughter lay, supported by Madame Perrodon. She kneeled beside her for a moment and whispered, as Madame supposed, a little benediction in her ear; then hastily kissing her, she stepped into her carriage, the door was closed, the footmen in stately liveries jumped up behind, the outriders spurred on, the postilions cracked their whips, the horses plunged and broke suddenly into a furious canter that threatened soon again to become a gallop, and the carriage whirled away, followed at the same rapid pace by the two horsemen in the rear.

CHAPTER III

WE COMPARE NOTES

WE followed the *cortège* with our eyes until it was swiftly lost to sight in the misty wood; and the very sound of the hoofs and wheels died away in the silent night air.

Nothing remained to assure us that the adventure had not

been an illusion of a moment but the young lady, who just at that moment opened her eyes. I could not see, for her face was turned from me, but she raised her head, evidently looking about her, and I heard a very sweet voice ask complainingly, "Where is mamma?"

Our good Madame Perrodon answered tenderly, and added some comfortable assurances.

I then heard her ask:

"Where am I? What is this place?" and after that she said, "I don't see the carriage; and Matska, where is she?"

Madame answered all her questions in so far as she understood them; and gradually the young lady remembered how the misadventure came about, and was glad to hear that no one in, or in attendance on, the carriage was hurt; and on learning that her mamma had left her here, till her return in about three months, she wept.

I was going to add my consolations to those of Madame Perrodon when Mademoiselle de Lafontaine placed her hand upon my arm, saying:

"Don't approach, one at a time is as much as she can at present converse with; a very little excitement would possibly overpower her now."

As soon as she is comfortably in bed, I thought, I will run up to her room and see her.

My father in the meantime had sent a servant on horseback for the physician, who lived about two leagues away; and a bedroom was being prepared for the young lady's reception.

The stranger now rose, and leaning on Madame's arm, walked slowly over the drawbridge and into the castle gate.

In the hall, servants waited to receive her, and she was conducted forthwith to her room.

The room we usually sat in as our drawing-room is long, having four windows, that looked over the moat and drawbridge, upon the forest scene I have just described.

It is furnished in old carved oak, with large carved cabinets, and the chairs are cushioned with crimson Utrecht velvet. The walls are covered with tapestry, and surrounded with great gold frames, the figures being as large as life, in ancient and very curious costume, and the subjects represented are hunting, hawking, and generally festive. It is not too stately to be extremely comfortable; and here we had our tea, for with his usual patriotic leanings my father insisted that the national beverage should make its appearance regularly with our coffee and chocolate.

We sat here this night, and with candles lighted, were talking over the adventure of the evening.

Madame Perrodon and Mademoiselle de Lafontaine were both of our party. The young stranger had hardly lain down in her bed when she sank into a deep sleep; and those ladies had left her in the care of a servant.

" How do you like our guest? " I asked, as soon as Madame entered. " Tell me all about her? "

" I like her extremely," answered Madame; " she is, I almost think, the prettiest creature I ever saw; about your age, and so gentle and nice."

" She is absolutely beautiful," threw in Mademoiselle, who had peeped for a moment into the stranger's room.

" And such a sweet voice! " added Madame Perrodon.

" Did you remark a woman in the carriage, after it was set up again, who did not get out," inquired Mademoiselle, " but only looked from the window? "

No, we had not seen her.

Then she described a hideous black woman, with a sort of coloured turban on her head, who was gazing all the time from the carriage window, nodding and grinning derisively towards the ladies, with gleaming eyes and large white eyeballs, and her teeth set as if in fury.

" Did you remark what an ill-looking pack of men the servants were? " asked Madame.

" Yes," said my father, who had just come in, " ugly, hang-dog looking fellows, as ever I beheld in my life. I hope they mayn't rob the poor lady in the forest. They are clever rogues, however; they got everything to rights in a minute."

" I dare say they are worn out with too long travelling," said Madame. " Besides looking wicked, their faces were so strangely lean, and dark, and sullen. I am very curious, I own; but I dare say the young lady will tell us all about it to-morrow, if she is sufficiently recovered."

" I don't think she will," said my father, with a mysterious smile, and a little nod of his head, as if he knew more about it than he cared to tell us.

This made me all the more inquisitive as to what had passed between him and the lady in the black velvet, in the brief but earnest interview that had immediately preceded her departure.

We were scarcely alone, when I entreated him to tell me. He did not need much pressing.

" There is no particular reason why I should not tell you. She expressed a reluctance to trouble us with the care of her daughter, saying she was in delicate health, and nervous, but not subject to any kind of seizure—she volunteered that—nor to any illusion; being, in fact, perfectly sane."

" How very odd to say all that! " I interpolated. " It was so unnecessary."

" At all events it *was* said," he laughed, " and as you wish to know all that passed, which was indeed very little, I tell you. She then said, ' I am making a long journey of *vital* importance '—she emphasized the word—' rapid and secret; I shall return for my child in three months; in the meantime, she will be silent as to who we are, whence we come, and whither we are travelling.' That is all she said. She spoke very pure French. When she said the word ' secret,' she paused for a few seconds, looking sternly, her eyes fixed on mine. I fancy she makes a great point of that. You saw how quickly she was gone. I hope I have not done a very foolish thing, in taking charge of the young lady."

For my part, I was delighted. I was longing to see and talk to her; and only waiting till the doctor should give me leave. You, who live in towns, can have no idea how great an event the introduction of a new friend is, in such a solitude as surrounded us.

The doctor did not arrive till nearly one o'clock; but I could no more have gone to my bed and slept, than I could have overtaken, on foot, the carriage in which the lady in black velvet had driven away.

When the physician came down to the drawing-room, it was to report very favourably upon his patient. She was now sitting up, her pulse quite regular, apparently perfectly well. She had sustained no injury, and the little shock to her nerves had passed away quite harmlessly. There could be no harm certainly in my seeing her, if we both wished it; and, with this permission, I sent, forthwith, to know whether she would allow me to visit her for a few minutes in her room.

The servant returned immediately to say that she desired nothing more.

You may be sure I was not long in availing myself of this permission.

Our visitor lay in one of the handsomest rooms in the schloss. It was, perhaps, a little stately. There was a sombre piece of tapestry opposite the foot of the bed, representing Cleopatra with the asps to her bosom; and other solemn classic scenes were displayed, a little faded, upon the other walls. But there was gold carving, and rich and varied colour enough in the other decorations of the room, to more than redeem the gloom of the old tapestry.

There were candles at the bedside. She was sitting up; her slender pretty figure enveloped in the soft silk dressing-gown, embroidered with flowers, and lined with thick quilted silk, which her mother had thrown over her feet as she lay upon the ground.

What was it that, as I reached the bedside and had just begun my little greeting, struck me dumb in a moment, and made me recoil a step or two from before her? I will tell you.

I saw the very face which had visited me in my childhood at night, which remained so fixed in my memory, and on which I had for so many years so often ruminated with horror, when no one suspected of what I was thinking.

It was pretty, even beautiful; and when I first beheld it, wore the same melancholy expression.

But this almost instantly lighted into a strange fixed smile of recognition.

There was a silence of fully a minute, and then at length *she* spoke; *I* could not.

" How wonderful! " she exclaimed. " Twelve years ago, I saw your face in a dream, and it has haunted me ever since."

" Wonderful indeed! " I repeated, overcoming with an effort the horror that had for a time suspended my utterances. " Twelve years ago, in vision or reality, *I* certainly saw you. I could not forget your face. It has remained before my eyes ever since."

Her smile had softened. Whatever I had fancied strange in it, was gone, and it and her dimpling cheeks were now delightfully pretty and intelligent.

I felt reassured, and continued more in the vein which hospitality indicated, to bid her welcome, and to tell her how much pleasure her accidental arrival had given us all, and especially what a happiness it was to me.

I took her hand as I spoke. I was a little shy, as lonely people are, but the situation made me eloquent, and even bold. She pressed my hand, she laid hers upon it, and her eyes glowed, as, looking hastily into mine, she smiled again, and blushed.

She answered my welcome very prettily. I sat down beside her, still wondering; and she said:

" I must tell you my vision about you; it is so very strange that you and I should have had, each of the other so vivid a dream, that each should have seen, I you and you me, looking as we do now, when of course we both were mere children. I was a child, about six years old, and I awoke from a confused and troubled dream, and found myself in a room, unlike my nursery, wainscoted clumsily in some dark wood, and with cupboards and bedsteads, and chairs and benches placed about it. The beds were, I thought, all empty, and the room itself without any one but myself in it; and I, after looking about me for some time, and admiring especially an iron candlestick, with two branches, which I should certainly know again, crept under one of the beds to reach the window; but as I got from under the bed, I heard someone crying; and looking up, while I was still upon my knees, I saw *you*—most assuredly you—as I see you now; a beautiful young lady, with golden hair and large blue eyes, and lips—your lips—you, as you are here. Your looks won me; I climbed on the bed and put my arms about you, and I think we both fell asleep. I was aroused by a scream; you were sitting up screaming. I was frightened, and slipped down upon the ground, and, it seemed to me, lost consciousness for a moment; and when I came to myself, I was again in my nursery at home. Your face I have never forgotten since. I could not be misled by mere resemblance. You *are* the lady whom I then saw."

It was now my turn to relate my corresponding vision, which I did, to the undisguised wonder of my new acquaintance.

" I don't know which should be most afraid of the other," she said, again smiling. " If you were less pretty I think I should be very much afraid of you, but being as you are, and you and I both so young, I feel only that I have made

your acquaintance twelve years ago, and have already a right
to your intimacy; at all events, it does seem as if we were
destined, from our earliest childhood, to be friends. I wonder
whether you feel as strangely drawn towards me as I do to
you; I have never had a friend—shall I find one now?"
She sighed, and her fine dark eyes gazed passionately on me.

Now the truth is, I felt rather unaccountably towards the
beautiful stranger. I did feel, as she said, "drawn towards
her," but there was also something of repulsion. In this am-
biguous feeling, however, the sense of attraction immensely
prevailed. She interested and won me; she was so beautiful
and so indescribably engaging.

I perceived now something of languor and exhaustion stealing over her, and hastened to bid her good night.

"The doctor thinks," I added, "that you ought to have a
maid to sit up with you to-night; one of ours is waiting,
and you will find her a very useful and quiet creature."

"How kind of you, but I could not sleep, I never could
with an attendant in the room. I shan't require any assistance
—and, shall I confess my weakness, I am haunted with a
terror of robbers. Our house was robbed once, and two
servants murdered, so I always lock my door. It has become
a habit—and you look so kind I know you will forgive me.
I see there is a key in the lock."

She held me close in her pretty arms for a moment and
whispered in my ear, "Good night, darling, it is very hard
to part with you, but good night; to-morrow, but not early,
I shall see you again."

She sank back on the pillow with a sigh, and her fine eyes
followed me with a fond and melancholy gaze, and she
murmured again "Good night, dear friend."

Young people like, and even love, on impulse. I was flattered by the evident, though as yet undeserved, fondness she
showed me. I liked the confidence with which she at once
received me. She was determined that we should be very
dear friends.

Next day came and we met again. I was delighted with
my companion; that is to say, in many respects.

Her looks lost nothing in daylight—she was certainly the
most beautiful creature I had ever seen, and the unpleasant
remembrance of the face presented in my early dream, had
lost the effect of the first unexpected recognition.

She confessed that she had experienced a similar shock on seeing me, and precisely the same faint antipathy that had mingled with my admiration of her. We now laughed together over our momentary horrors.

CHAPTER IV

HER HABITS——A SAUNTER

I TOLD you that I was charmed with her in most particulars.

There were some that did not please me so well.

She was above the middle height of women. I shall begin by describing her. She was slender, and wonderfully graceful. Except that her movements were languid—*very* languid —indeed, there was nothing in her appearance to indicate an invalid. Her complexion was rich and brilliant; her features were small and beautifully formed; her eyes large, dark, and lustrous; her hair was quite wonderful, I never saw hair so magnificently thick and long when it was down about her shoulders; I have often placed my hands under it, and laughed with wonder at its weight. It was exquisitely fine and soft, and in colour a rich very dark brown, with something of gold. I loved to let it down, tumbling with its own weight, as, in her room, she lay back in her chair talking in her sweet low voice. I used to fold and braid it, and spread it out and play with it. Heavens! If I had but known all!

I said there were particulars which did not please me. I have told you that her confidence won me the first night I saw her; but I found that she exercised with respect to herself, her mother, her history, everything in fact connected with her life, plans, and people, an ever-wakeful reserve. I dare say I was unreasonable, perhaps I was wrong; I dare say I ought to have respected the solemn injunction laid upon my father by the stately lady in black velvet. But curiosity is a restless and unscrupulous passion, and no one girl can endure, with patience, that hers should be baffled by another. What harm could it do anyone to tell me what I so ardently desired to know? Had she no trust in my good sense or honour? Why would she not believe me when I assured her, so solemnly, that I would not divulge one syllable of what she told me to any mortal breathing.

There was a coldness, it seemed to me, beyond her years, in her smiling melancholy persistent refusal to afford me the least ray of light.

I cannot say we quarrelled upon this point, for she would not quarrel upon any. It was, of course, very unfair of me to press her, very ill-bred, but I really could not help it; and I might just as well have let it alone.

What she did tell me amounted, in my unconscionable estimation—to nothing.

It was all summed up in three very vague disclosures:

First.—Her name was Carmilla.

Second.—Her family was very ancient and noble.

Third.—Her home lay in the direction of the west.

She would not tell me the name of her family, nor their armorial bearings, nor the name of their estate, nor even that of the country they lived in.

You are not to suppose that I worried her incessantly on these subjects. I watched opportunity, and rather insinuated than urged my inquiries. Once or twice, indeed, I did attack her more directly. But no matter what my tactics, utter failure was invariably the result. Reproaches and caresses were all lost upon her. But I must add this, that her evasion was conducted with so pretty a melancholy and deprecation, with so many, and even passionate declarations of her liking for me, and trust in my honour, and with so many promises that I should at last know all, that I could not find it in my heart long to be offended with her.

She used to place her pretty arms about my neck, draw me to her, and laying her cheek to mine, murmur with her lips near my ear, " Dearest, your little heart is wounded; think me not cruel because I obey the irresistible law of my strength and weakness; if your dear heart is wounded, my wild heart bleeds with yours. In the rapture of my enormous humiliation I live in your warm life, and you shall die—die, sweetly die—into mine. I cannot help it; as I draw near to you, you, in your turn, will draw near to others, and learn the rapture of that cruelty, which yet is love; so, for a while, seek to know no more of me and mine, but trust me with all your loving spirit."

And when she had spoken such a rhapsody, she would press me more closely in her trembling embrace, and her lips in soft kisses gently glow upon my cheek.

Her agitations and her language were unintelligible to me.

From these foolish embraces, which were not of very frequent occurrence, I must allow, I used to wish to extricate myself; but my energies seemed to fail me. Her murmured words sounded like a lullaby in my ear, and soothed my resistance into a trance, from which I only seemed to recover myself when she withdrew her arms.

In these mysterious moods I did not like her. I experienced a strange tumultuous excitement that was pleasurable, ever and anon, mingled with a vague sense of fear and disgust. I had no distinct thoughts about her while such scenes lasted, but I was conscious of a love growing into adoration, and also of abhorrence. This I know is paradox, but I can make no other attempt to explain the feeling.

I now write, after an interval of more than ten years, with a trembling hand, with a confused and horrible recollection of certain occurrences and situations, in the ordeal through which I was unconsciously passing; though with a vivid and very sharp remembrance of the main current of my story. But, I suspect, in all lives there are certain emotional scenes, those in which our passions have been most wildly and terribly roused, that are of all others the most vaguely and dimly remembered.

Sometimes after an hour of apathy, my strange and beautiful companion would take my hand and hold it with a fond pressure, renewed again and again; blushing softly, gazing in my face with languid and burning eyes, and breathing so fast that her dress rose and fell with the tumultuous respiration. It was like the ardour of a lover; it embarrassed me; it was hateful and yet overpowering; and with gloating eyes she drew me to her, and her hot lips travelled along my cheek in kisses; and she would whisper, almost in sobs, " You are mine, you *shall* be mine, and you and I are one for ever." Then she has thrown herself back in her chair, with her small hands over her eyes, leaving me trembling.

" Are we related," I used to ask; " what can you mean by all this? I remind you perhaps of someone whom you love; but you must not, I hate it; I don't know you—I don't know myself when you look so and talk so."

She used to sigh at my vehemence, then turn away and drop my hand.

Respecting these very extraordinary manifestations I strove

in vain to form any satisfactory theory—I could not refer
them to affectation or trick. It was unmistakably the
momentary breaking out of suppressed instinct and emotion.
Was she, notwithstanding her mother's volunteered denial,
subject to brief visitations of insanity; or was there here a
disguise and a romance? I had read in old story books of
such things. What if a boyish lover had found his way into
the house, and sought to prosecute his suit in masquerade,
with the assistance of a clever old adventuress. But there
were many things against this hypothesis, highly interesting
as it was to my vanity.

I could boast of no little attentions such as masculine gal-
lantry delights to offer. Between these passionate moments
there were long intervals of commonplace; of gaiety, of
brooding melancholy, during which, except that I detected
her eyes so full of melancholy fire, following me, at times I
might have been as nothing to her. Except in these brief
periods of mysterious excitement her ways were girlish; and
there was always a languor about her, quite incompatible with
a masculine system in a state of health.

In some respects her habits were odd. Perhaps not so
singular in the opinion of a town lady like you, as they
appeared to us rustic people. She used to come down very
late, generally not till one o'clock, she would then take a cup
of chocolate, but eat nothing; we then went out for a walk,
which was a mere saunter, and she seemed, almost immediately, exhausted, and either returned to the schloss or
sat on one of the benches that were placed, here and there,
among the trees. This was a bodily languor in which her
mind did not sympathise. She was always an animated talker,
and very intelligent.

She sometimes alluded for a moment to her own home,
or mentioned an adventure or situation, or an early recollection, which indicated a people of strange manners, and
described customs of which we knew nothing. I gathered
from these chance hints that her native country was much
more remote than I had at first fancied.

As we sat thus one afternoon under the trees a funeral
passed us by. It was that of a pretty young girl, whom I had
often seen, the daughter of one of the rangers of the forest.
The poor man was walking behind the coffin of his darling;
she was his only child, and he looked quite heartbroken.

Peasants walking two-and-two came behind, they were singing a funeral hymn.

I rose to mark my respect as they passed, and joined in the
hymn they were very sweetly singing.

My companion shook me a little roughly, and I turned
surprised.

She said brusquely, " Don't you perceive how discordant
that is? "

" I think it very sweet, on the contrary," I answered,
vexed at the interruption, and very uncomfortable, lest the
people who composed the little procession should observe and
resent what was passing.

I resumed, therefore, instantly, and was again interrupted.
" You pierce my ears," said Carmilla, almost angrily, and
stopping her ears with her tiny fingers. " Besides, how can
you tell that your religion and mine are the same; your
forms wound me, and I hate funerals. What a fuss! Why,
you must die—*everyone* must die; and all are happier when
they do. Come home."

" My father has gone on with the clergyman to the churchyard. I thought you knew she was to be buried to-day."

" *She?* I don't trouble my head about peasants. I don't
know who she is," answered Carmilla, with a flash from her
fine eyes.

" She is the poor girl who fancied she saw a ghost a fortnight ago, and has been dying ever since, till yesterday, when
she expired."

" Tell me nothing about ghosts. I shan't sleep to-night if
you do."

" I hope there is no plague or fever coming; all this looks
very like it," I continued. " The swineherd's young wife
died only a week ago, and she thought something seized
her by the throat as she lay in her bed, and nearly strangled
her. Papa says such horrible fancies do accompany some
forms of fever. She was quite well the day before. She sank
afterwards, and died before a week."

" Well, *her* funeral is over, I hope, and *her* hymn sung;
and our ears shan't be tortured with that discord and jargon.
It has made me nervous. Sit down here, beside me; sit close;
hold my hand! press it hard—hard—harder."

We had moved a little back, and had come to another
seat.

She sat down. Her face underwent a change that alarmed and even terrified me for a moment. It darkened, and became horribly livid; her teeth and hands were clenched, and she frowned and compressed her lips, while she stared down upon the ground at her feet, and trembled all over with a continued shudder as irrepressible as ague. All her energies seemed strained to suppress a fit, with which she was then breathlessly tugging; and at length a low convulsive cry of suffering broke from her, and gradually the hysteria subsided. "There! That comes of strangling people with hymns!" she said at last. "Hold me, hold me still. It is passing away."

And so gradually it did; and perhaps to dissipate the sombre impression which the spectacle had left upon me, she became unusually animated and chatty; and so we got home.

This was the first time I had seen her exhibit any definable symptoms of that delicacy of health which her mother had spoken of. It was the first time, also, I had seen her exhibit anything like temper.

Both passed away like a summer cloud; and never but once afterwards did I witness on her part a momentary sign of anger. I will tell you how it happened.

She and I were looking out of one of the long drawing-room windows, when there entered the courtyard, over the drawbridge, a figure of a wanderer whom I knew very well. He used to visit the schloss generally twice a year.

It was the figure of a hunchback, with the sharp lean features that generally accompany deformity. He wore a pointed black beard, and he was smiling from ear to ear, showing his white fangs. He was dressed in buff, black, and scarlet, and crossed with more straps and belts than I could count, from which hung all manner of things. Behind, he carried a magic lantern, and two boxes, which I well knew, in one of which was a salamander, and in the other a mandrake. These monsters used to make my father laugh. They were compounded of parts of monkeys, parrots, squirrels, fish, and hedgehogs, dried and stitched together with great neatness and startling effect. He had a fiddle, a box of conjuring apparatus, a pair of foils and masks attached to his belt, several other mysterious cases dangling about him, and a black staff with copper ferrules in his hand. His companion was a rough spare dog, that followed at his heels, but stopped short, suspiciously, at the drawbridge, and in a little while began to howl dismally.

In the meantime, the mountebank, standing in the midst of the courtyard, raised his grotesque hat, and made us a very ceremonious bow, paying his compliments very volubly in execrable French, and German not much better. Then, disengaging his fiddle, he began to scrape a lively air, to which he sang with a merry discord, dancing with ludicrous airs and activity, that made me laugh, in spite of the dog's howling.

Then he advanced to the window with many smiles and salutations, and his hat in his left hand, his fiddle under his arm, and with a fluency that never took breath, he gabbled a long advertisement of all his accomplishments, and the resources of the various arts which he placed at our service, and the curiosities and entertainments which it was in his power, at our bidding to display.

" Will your ladyships be pleased to buy an amulet against the oupire, which is going like the wolf, I hear, through these woods," he said, dropping his hat on the pavement. " They are dying of it right and left, and here is a charm that never fails; only pinned to the pillow, and you may laugh in his face."

These charms consisted of oblong slips of vellum, with cabalistic ciphers and diagrams upon them.

Carmilla instantly purchased one, and so did I.

He was looking up, and we were smiling down upon him, amused; at least, I can answer for myself. His piercing black eye, as he looked up in our faces, seemed to detect something that fixed for a moment his curiosity.

In an instant he unrolled a leather case, full of all manner of odd little steel instruments.

" See here, my lady," he said, displaying it, and addressing me, " I profess, among other things less useful, the art of dentistry. Plague take the dog! " he interpolated. " Silence, beast! He howls so that your ladyships can scarcely hear a word. Your noble friend, the young lady at your right, has the sharpest tooth—long, thin, pointed, like an awl, like a needle; ha, ha! With my sharp and long sight, as I look up, I have seen it distinctly; now if it happens to hurt the young lady, and I think it must, here am I, here are my file, my punch, my nippers; I will make it round and blunt, if her ladyship pleases; no longer the tooth of a fish, but of a beautiful young lady as she is. Hey? Is the young lady displeased? Have I been too bold? Have I offended her? "

The young lady, indeed, looked very angry as she drew back from the window.

"How dares that mountebank insult us so? Where is your father? I shall demand redress from him. My father would have had the wretch tied up to the pump, and flogged with a cart-whip, and burnt to the bones with the castle brand! "

She retired from the window a step or two, and sat down, and had hardly lost sight of the offender, when her wrath subsided as suddenly as it had risen, and she gradually recovered her usual tone, and seemed to forget the little hunchback and his follies.

My father was out of spirits that evening. On coming in he told us that there had been another case very similar to the two fatal ones which had lately occurred. The sister of a young peasant on his estate, only a mile away, was very ill, had been, as she described it, attacked very nearly in the same way, and was now slowly but steadily sinking.

"All this," said my father, "is strictly referable to natural causes. These poor people infect one another with their superstitions, and so repeat in imagination the images of terror that have infested their neighbours."

"But that very circumstance frightens one horribly," said Carmilla.

"How so? " inquired my father.

"I am so afraid of fancying I see such things; I think it would be as bad as reality."

"We are in God's hands; nothing can happen without His permission, and all will end well for those who love Him. He is our faithful creator; He has made us all, and will take care of us."

"Creator! *Nature!* " said the young lady in answer to my gentle father. "And this disease that invades the country is natural. Nature. All things proceed from Nature—don't they? All things in the heaven, in the earth, and under the earth, act and live as Nature ordains? I think so."

"The doctor said he would come here to-day," said my father, after a silence. "I want to know what he thinks about it, and what he thinks we had better do."

" Doctors never did me any good," said Carmilla.

" Then you have been ill? " I asked.

" More ill than ever you were," she answered.

" Long ago? "

" Yes, a long time. I suffered from this very illness; but I forget all but my pain and weakness, and they were not so bad as are suffered in other diseases."

" You were very young then? "

" I dare say; let us talk no more of it. You would not wound a friend? " She looked languidly in my eyes, and passed her arm round my waist lovingly, and led me out of the room. My father was busy over some papers near the window.

" Why does your papa like to frighten us? " said the pretty girl, with a sigh and a little shudder.

" He doesn't, dear Carmilla, it is the very furthest thing from his mind."

" Are you afraid, dearest? "

" I should be very much if I fancied there was any real danger of my being attacked as those poor people were."

" You are afraid to die? "

" Yes, every one is."

" But to die as lovers may—to die together, so that they may live together. Girls are caterpillars while they live in the world, to be finally butterflies when the summer comes; but in the meantime there are grubs and larvæ, don't you see —each with their peculiar propensities, necessities and structure. So says Monsieur Buffon, in his big book, in the next room."

Later in the day the doctor came, and was closeted with papa for some time. He was a skilful man, of sixty and upwards, he wore powder, and shaved his pale face as smooth as a pumpkin. He and papa emerged from the room together, and I heard papa laugh, and say as they came out:

" Well, I do wonder at a wise man like you. What do you say to hippogriffs and dragons? "

The doctor was smiling, and made answer, shaking his head:

" Nevertheless, life and death are mysterious states, and we know little of the resources of either."

And so they walked on, and I heard no more. I did not then know what the doctor had been broaching, but I think I guess it now.

CHAPTER V

A WONDERFUL LIKENESS

THIS evening there arrived from Gratz the grave, dark-faced son of the picture-cleaner, with a horse and cart laden with two large packing-cases, having many pictures in each. It was a journey of ten leagues, and whenever a messenger arrived at the schloss from our little capital of Gratz, we used to crowd about him in the hall, to hear the news.

This arrival created in our secluded quarters quite a sensation. The cases remained in the hall, and the messenger was taken charge of by the servants till he had eaten his supper. Then with assistants, and armed with hammer, ripping chisel, and turnscrew, he met us in the hall, where we had assembled to witness the unpacking of the cases.

Carmilla sat looking listlessly on, while one after the other the old pictures, nearly all portraits, which had undergone the process of renovation, were brought to light. My mother was of an old Hungarian family, and most of these pictures, which were about to be restored to their places, had come to us through her.

My father had a list in his hand, from which he read, as the artist rummaged out the corresponding numbers. I don't know that the pictures were very good, but they were, undoubtedly very old, and some of them very curious also. They had, for the most part, the merit of being now seen by me, I may say, for the first time; for the smoke and dust of time had all but obliterated them.

" There is a picture that I have not seen yet," said my father. " In one corner, at the top of it, is the name, as well as I could read, ' Marcia Karnstein,' and the date ' 1698 '; and I am curious to see how it has turned out."

I remembered it; it was a small picture, about a foot and a half high, and nearly square, without a frame; but it was so blackened by age that I could not make it out.

The artist now produced it, with evident pride. It was quite beautiful; it was startling; it seemed to live. It was the effigy of Carmilla!

" Carmilla, dear, here is an absolute miracle. Here you are, living, smiling, ready to speak, in this picture. Isn't it beautiful, papa? And see, even the little mole on her throat."

My father laughed, and said " Certainly it is a wonderful likeness," but he looked away, and to my surprise seemed but little struck by it, and went on talking to the picture-cleaner, who was also something of an artist, and discoursed with intelligence about the portraits or other works, which his art had just brought into light and colour, while I was more and more lost in wonder the more I looked at the picture.

" Will you let me hang this picture in my room, papa? " I asked.

" Certainly, dear," said he, smiling, " I'm very glad you think it so like. It must be prettier even than I thought it, if it is."

The young lady did not acknowledge this pretty speech, did not seem to hear it. She was leaning back in her seat, her fine eyes under their long lashes gazing on me in contemplation, and she smiled in a kind of rapture.

" And now you can read quite plainly the name that is written in the corner. It is not Marcia; it looks as if it was done in gold. The name is Mircalla, Countess Karstein, and this is a little coronet over it, and underneath A.D. 1698. I am descended from the Karnsteins; that is, mamma was."

" Ah! " said the lady, languidly, " so am I. I think, a very long descent, very ancient. Are there any Karsteins living now? "

" None who bear the name, I believe. The family were ruined, I believe, in some civil wars, long ago, but the ruins of the castle are only about three miles away."

" How interesting! " she said, languidly. " But see what beautiful moonlight! " She glanced through the hall door, which stood a little open. " Suppose we take a little ramble round the court, and look down at the road and river."

" It is so like the night you came to us," I said.

She sighed, smiling.

She rose, and each with her arm about the other's waist, we walked out upon the pavement.

In silence, slowly we walked down to the drawbridge, where the beautiful landscape opened before us.

" And so you were thinking of the night I came here? " she almost whispered. " Are you glad I came? "

" Delighted, dear Carmilla," I answered.

"And you ask for the picture you think like me, to hang in your room," she murmured with a sigh, as she drew her arm closer about my waist, and let her pretty head sink upon my shoulder.

"How romantic you are, Carmilla," I said. "Whenever you tell me your story, it will be made up chiefly of some one great romance."

She kissed me silently.

"I am sure, Carmilla, you have been in love; that there is, at this moment, an affair of the heart going on."

"I have been in love with no one, and never shall," she whispered, "unless it should be with you."

How beautiful she looked in the moonlight!

Shy and strange was the look with which she quickly hid her face in my neck and hair, with tumultuous sighs, that seemed almost to sob, and pressed in mine a hand that trembled.

Her soft cheek was glowing against mine. "Darling, darling," she murmured, "I live in you; and you would die for me, I love you so."

I started from her.

She was gazing on me with eyes from which all fire, all meaning had flown, and a face colourless and apathetic.

"Is there a chill in the air, dear?" she said drowsily. "I almost shiver; have I been dreaming? Let us come in. Come, come; come in."

"You look ill, Carmilla; a little faint. You certainly must take some wine," I said.

"Yes, I will. I'm better now. I shall be quite well in a few minutes. Yes, do give me a little wine," answered Carmilla, as we approached the door. "Let us look again for a moment; it is the last time, perhaps, I shall see the moonlight with you."

"How do you feel now, dear Carmilla? Are you really better?" I asked.

I was beginning to take alarm, lest she should have been stricken with the strange epidemic that they said had invaded the country about us.

"Papa would be grieved beyond measure," I added, "if he thought you were ever so little ill, without immediately letting us know. We have a very skilful doctor near this, the physician who was with papa to-day."

"I'm sure he is. I know how kind you all are; but, dear child, I am quite well again. There is nothing ever wrong with me, but a little weakness. People say I am languid; I am incapable of exertion; I can scarcely walk as far as a child of three years old; and every now and then the little strength I have falters, and I become as you have just seen me. But after all I am very easily set up again; in a moment ᴛ am perfectly myself. See how I have recovered."

So, indeed, she had; and she and I talked a great deal, and very animated she was; and the remainder of that evening passed without any recurrence of what I called her infatu-ations. I mean her crazy talk and looks, which embarrassed and even frightened me.

But there occurred that night an event which gave my thoughts quite a new turn, and seemed to startle even Car-milla's languid nature into momentary energy.

CHAPTER VI

A VERY STRANGE AGONY

WHEN we got into the drawing-room, and had sat down to our coffee and chocolate, although Carmilla did not take any, she seemed quite herself again, and Madame, and Mademoiselle de Lafontaine, joined us, and made a little card party, in the course of which papa came in for what he called his "dish of tea."

When the game was over he sat down beside Carmilla on the sofa, and asked her, a little anxiously, whether she had heard from her mother since her arrival.

She answered "No."

He then asked her whether she knew where a letter would reach her at present.

"I cannot tell," she answered, ambiguously, "but I have been thinking of leaving you; you have been already too hospitable and too kind to me. I have given you an infinity of trouble, and I should wish to take a carriage to-morrow, and post in pursuit of her; I know where I shall ultimately find her, although I dare not yet tell you."

"But you must not dream of any such thing," exclaimed my father, to my great relief. "We can't afford to lose you so, and I won't consent to your leaving us, except under the

care of your mother, who was so good as to consent to your
remaining with us till she should herself return. I should
be quite happy if I knew that you heard from her; but this
evening the accounts of the progress of the mysterious disease
that has invaded our neighbourhood, grow even more alarming; and my beautiful guest, I do feel the responsibility, un-
aided by advice from your mother, very much. But I shall
do my best; and one thing is certain, that you must not think
of leaving us without her distinct direction to that effect.
We should suffer too much in parting from you to consent to
it easily."

"Thank you, sir, a thousand times for your hospitality,"
she answered, smiling bashfully. "You have all been too
kind to me; I have seldom been so happy in all my life before,
as in your beautiful château, under your care, and in the
society of your dear daughter."

So he gallantly, in his old-fashioned way, kissed her hand,
smiling, and pleased at her little speech.

I accompanied Carmilla as usual to her room, and sat and
chatted with her while she was preparing for bed.

"Do you think," I said, at length, "that you will ever
confide fully in me?"

She turned round smiling, but made no answer, only
continued to smile on me.

"You won't answer that?" I said. "You can't answer
pleasantly; I ought not to have asked you."

"You were quite right to ask me that, or anything. You
do not know how dear you are to me, or you could not think
any confidence too great to look for. But I am under vows,
no nun half so awfully, and I dare not tell my story yet,
even to you. The time is very near when you shall know
everything. You will think me cruel, very selfish, but love
is always selfish; the more ardent the more selfish. How
jealous I am you cannot know. You must come with me,
loving me, to death; or else hate me, and still come with me,
and *hating* me through death and after. There is no such
word as indifference in my apathetic nature."

"Now, Carmilla, you are going to talk your wild nonsense
again," I said hastily.

"Not I, silly little fool as I am, and full of whims and
fancies; for your sake I'll talk like a sage. Were you ever at
a ball?"

"No; how you do run on. What is it like? How charming it must be."

"I almost forget, it is years ago."

I laughed.

"You are not so old. Your first ball can hardly be forgotten yet."

"I remember everything about it—with an effort. I see it all, as divers see what is going on above them, through a medium, dense, rippling, but transparent. There occurred that night what has confused the picture, and made its colours faint. I was all but assassinated in my bed, wounded *here*," she touched her breast, "and never was the same since."

"Were you near dying?"

"Yes, very—a cruel love—strange love, that would have taken my life. Love will have its sacrifices. No sacrifice without blood. Let us go to sleep now; I feel so lazy. How can I get up just now and lock my door?"

She was lying with her tiny hands buried in her rich wavy hair, under her cheek, her little head upon the pillow, and her glittering eyes followed me wherever I moved, with a kind of shy smile that I could not decipher.

I bid her good-night, and crept from the room with an uncomfortable sensation.

I often wondered whether our pretty guest ever said her prayers. *I* certainly had never seen her upon her knees. In the morning she never came down until long after our family prayers were over, and at night she never left the drawing-room to attend our brief evening prayers in the hall.

If it had not been that it had casually come out in one of our careless talks that she had been baptised, I should have doubted her being a Christian. Religion was a subject on which I had never heard her speak a word. If I had known the world better, this particular neglect or antipathy would not have so much surprised me.

The precautions of nervous people are infectious, and persons of a like temperament are pretty sure, after a time, to imitate them. I had adopted Carmilla's habit of locking her bedroom door, having taken into my head all her whimsical alarms about midnight invaders, and prowling assassins. I had also adopted her precaution of making a brief search through the room, to satisfy myself that no lurking assassin or robber was " ensconced."

These wise measures taken, I got into my bed and fell asleep. A light was burning in my room. This was an old habit, of very early date, and which nothing could have tempted me to dispense with.

Thus fortified I might take my rest in peace. But dreams come through stone walls, light up dark rooms, or darken light ones, and their persons make their exits and their entrances as they please, and laugh at locksmiths.

I had a dream that night that was the beginning of a very strange agony.

I cannot call it a nightmare, for I was quite conscious of being asleep. But I was equally conscious of being in my room, and lying in bed, precisely as I actually was. I saw, or fancied I saw, the room and its furniture just as I had seen it last, except that it was very dark, and I saw something moving round the foot of the bed, which at first I could not accurately distinguish. But I soon saw that it was a sooty-black animal that resembled a monstrous cat. It appeared to me about four or five feet long, for it measured fully the length of the hearth-rug as it passed over it; and it continued to-ing and fro-ing with the lithe sinister restlessness of a beast in a cage. I could not cry out although, as you may suppose, I was terrified. Its pace was growing faster, and the room rapidly darker and darker, and at length so dark that I could no longer see anything of it but its eyes. I felt it spring lightly on the bed. The two broad eyes approached my face, and suddenly I felt a stinging pain as if two large needles darted, an inch or two apart, deep into my breast. I waked with a scream. The room was lighted by the candle that burnt there all through the night, and I saw a female figure standing at the foot of the bed, a little at the right side. It was in a dark loose dress, and its hair was down and covered its shoulders. A block of stone could not have been more still. There was not the slightest stir of respiration. As I stared at it, the figure appeared to have changed its place, and was now nearer the door; then, close to it, the door opened, and it passed out.

I was now relieved, and able to breathe and move. My first thought was that Carmilla had been playing me a trick, and that I had forgotten to secure my door. I hastened to it, and found it locked as usual on the inside. I was afraid to open it—I was horrified. I sprang into my bed and covered my head up in the bed-clothes, and lay there more dead than alive till morning.

CHAPTER VII

DESCENDING

IT would be vain my attempting to tell you the horror with which, even now, I recall the occurrence of that night. It was no such transitory terror as a dream leaves behind it. It seemed to deepen by time, and communicated itself to the room and the very furniture that had encompassed the apparition.

I could not bear next day to be alone for a moment. I should have told papa, but for two opposite reasons. At one time I thought he would laugh at my story, and I could not bear its being treated as a jest; and at another, I thought he might fancy that I had been attacked by the mysterious complaint which had invaded our neighbourhood. I had myself no misgivings of the kind, and as he had been rather an invalid for some time, I was afraid of alarming him.

I was comfortable enough with my good-natured companions, Madame Perrodon, and the vivacious Mademoiselle de Lafontaine. They both perceived that I was out of spirits and nervous, and at length I told them what lay so heavy at my heart.

Mademoiselle laughed, but I fancied that Madame Perrodon looked anxious.

" By-the-by," said Mademoiselle, laughing, " the long lime tree walk, behind Carmilla's bedroom window, is haunted! "

" Nonsense! " exclaimed Madame, who probably thought the theme rather inopportune, " and who tells that story, my dear? "

" Martin says that he came up twice, when the old yard-gate was being repaired before sunrise, and twice saw the same female figure walking down the lime tree avenue."

" So he well might, as long as there are cows to milk in the river fields," said Madame.

" I daresay; but Martin chooses to be frightened, and never did I see fool *more* frightened."

" You must not say a word about it to Carmilla, because she can see down that walk from her room window," I interposed, " and she is, if possible, a greater coward than I."

Carmilla came down rather later than usual that day.

" I was so frightened last night," she said, so soon as we were together, " and I am sure I should have seen something dreadful if it had not been for that charm I bought from the poor little hunchback whom I called such hard names. I had a dream of something black coming round my bed, and I awoke in a perfect horror, and I really thought, for some seconds, I saw a dark figure near the chimney piece, but I felt under my pillow for my charm, and the moment my fingers touched it, the figure disappeared, and I felt quite certain, only that I had it by me, that something frightful would have made its appearance, and, perhaps, throttled me, as it did those poor people we heard of."

" Well, listen to me," I began, and recounted my adventure, at the recital of which she appeared horrified.

" And had you the charm near you? " she asked, earnestly.

" No, I had dropped it into a china vase in the drawing-room, but I shall certainly take it with me to-night, as you have so much faith in it."

At this distance of time I cannot tell you, or even understand, how I overcame my horror so effectually as to lie alone in my room that night. I remember distinctly that I pinned the charm to my pillow. I fell asleep almost immediately, and slept even more soundly than usual all night.

Next night I passed as well. My sleep was delightfully deep and dreamless. But I wakened with a sense of lassitude and melancholy, which, however, did not exceed a degree that was almost luxurious.

" Well, I told you so," said Carmilla, when I described my quiet sleep, " I had such delightful sleep myself last night; I pinned the charm to the breast of my nightdress. It was too far away the night before. I am quite sure it was all fancy, except the dreams. I used to think that evil spirits made dreams, but our doctor told me it is no such thing. Only a fever passing by, or some other malady, as they often do, he said, knocks at the door, and not being able to get in, passes on, with that alarm."

" And what do you think the charm is? " said I.

"It has been fumigated or immersed in some drug, and is an antidote against the malaria," she answered.

"Then it acts only on the body?"

"Certainly; you don't suppose that evil spirits are frightened by bits of ribbon, or the perfumes of a druggist's shop? No, these complaints, wandering in the air, begin by trying the nerves, and so infect the brain; but before they can seize upon you, the antidote repels them. That I am sure is what the charm has done for us. It is nothing magical, it is simply natural."

I should have been happier if I could quite have agreed with Carmilla, but I did my best, and the impression was a little losing its force.

For some nights I slept profoundly; but still every morning I felt the same lassitude, and a languor weighed upon me all day. I felt myself a changed girl. A strange melancholy was stealing over me, a melancholy that I would not have interrupted. Dim thoughts of death began to open, and an idea that I was slowly sinking took gentle, and, somehow, not unwelcome possession of me. If it was sad, the tone of mind which this induced was also sweet. Whatever it might be, my soul acquiesced in it.

I would not admit that I was ill, I would not consent to tell my papa, or to have the doctor sent for.

Carmilla became more devoted to me than ever, and her strange paroxysms of languid adoration more frequent. She used to gloat on me with increasing ardour the more my strength and spirits waned. This always shocked me like a momentary glare of insanity.

Without knowing it, I was now in a pretty advanced stage of the strangest illness under which mortal ever suffered. There was an unaccountable fascination in its earlier symptoms that more than reconciled me to the incapacitating effect of that stage of the malady. This fascination increased for a time, until it reached a certain point, when gradually a sense of the horrible mingled itself with it, deepening, as you shall hear, until it discoloured and perverted the whole state of my life.

The first change I experienced was rather agreeable. It was very near the turning point from which began the descent of Avernus.

Certain vague and strange sensations visited me in my

sleep. The prevailing one was of that pleasant, peculiar cold thrill which we feel in bathing, when we move against the current of a river. This was soon accompanied by dreams that seemed interminable, and were so vague that I could never recollect their scenery and persons, or any one connected portion of their action. But they left an awful impression, and a sense of exhaustion, as if I had passed through a long period of great mental exertion and danger. After all these dreams there remained on waking a remembrance of having been in a place very nearly dark, and of having spoken to people whom I could not see; and especially of one clear voice, of a female's, very deep, that spoke as if at a distance, slowly, and producing always the same sensation of indescribable solemnity and fear. Sometimes there came a sensation as if a hand was drawn softly along my cheek and neck. Sometimes it was as if warm lips kissed me, and longer and more lovingly as they reached my throat, but there the caress fixed itself. My heart beat faster, my breathing rose and fell rapidly and full drawn; a sobbing, that rose into a sense of strangulation, supervened, and turned into a dreadful convulsion, in which my senses left me, and I became unconscious.

It was now three weeks since the commencement of this unaccountable state. My sufferings had, during the last week, told upon my appearance. I had grown pale, my eyes were dilated and darkened underneath, and the languor which I had long felt began to display itself in my countenance.

My father asked me often whether I was ill; but, with an obstinacy which now seems to me unaccountable, I persisted in assuring him that I was quite well.

In a sense this was true. I had no pain, I could complain of no bodily derangement. My complaint seemed to be one of the imagination, or the nerves, and, horrible as my sufferings were, I kept them, with a morbid reserve, very nearly to myself.

It could not be that terrible complaint which the peasants call the oupire, for I had now been suffering for three weeks, and they were seldom ill for much more than three days, when death put an end to their miseries.

Carmilla complained of dreams and feverish sensations, but by no means of so alarming a kind as mine. I say that mine were extremely alarming. Had I been capable of comprehending my conditions, I would have invoked aid and advice on my knees. The narcotic of an unsuspected influence was acting upon me, and my perceptions were benumbed.

I am going to tell you now of a dream that led immediately to an odd discovery.

One night, instead of the voice I was accustomed to hear in the dark, I heard one, sweet and tender, and at the same time terrible, which said, " Your mother warns you to beware of the assassin." At the same time a light unexpectedly sprang up, and I saw Carmilla, standing, near the foot of my bed, in her white nightdress, bathed, from her chin to her feet, in one great stain of blood.

I wakened with a shriek, possessed with the one idea that Carmilla was being murdered. I remember springing from my bed, and my next recollection is that of standing on the lobby, crying for help.

Madame and Mademoiselle came scurrying out of their rooms in alarm; a lamp burned always on the lobby, and seeing me, they soon learned the cause of my terror.

I insisted on our knocking at Carmilla's door. Our knocking was unanswered. It soon became a pounding and an uproar. We shrieked her name, but all was vain.

We all grew frightened, for the door was locked. We hurried back, in panic, to my room. There we rang the bell long and furiously. If my father's room had been at that side of the house, we would have called him up at once to our aid. But, alas! he was quite out of hearing, and to reach him involved an excursion for which we none of us had courage.

Servants, however, soon came running up the stairs; I had got on my dressing-gown and slippers meanwhile, and my companions were already similarly furnished. Recognising the voices of the servants on the lobby, we sallied out together; and having renewed, as fruitlessly, our summons at Carmilla's door, I ordered the men to force the lock. They did so, and we stood, holding our lights aloft, in the doorway, and so stared into the room.

We called her by name; but there was still no reply. We looked round the room. Everything was undisturbed. It was exactly in the state in which I left it on bidding her good-night. But Carmilla was gone.

CHAPTER VIII

SEARCH

A T sight of the room, perfectly undisturbed except for our violent entrance, we began to cool a little, and soon recovered our senses sufficiently to dismiss the men. It had struck Mademoiselle that possibly Carmilla had been wakened by the uproar at her door, and in her first panic had jumped from her bed, and hid herself in a press, or behind a curtain, from which she could not, of course, emerge until the major-domo and his myrmidons had withdrawn. We now re-commenced our search, and began to call her by name again.

It was all to no purpose. Our perplexity and agitation in-creased. We examined the windows, but they were secured. I implored of Carmilla, if she had concealed herself, to play this cruel trick no longer—to come out, and to end our anxieties. It was all useless. I was by this time convinced that she was not in the room, nor in the dressing-room, the door of which was still locked on this side. She could not have passed it. I was utterly puzzled. Had Carmilla dis-covered one of those secret passages which the old housekeeper said were known to exist in the schloss, although the tradition of their exact situation had been lost? A little time would, no doubt, explain all—utterly perplexed as, for the present, we were.

It was past four o'clock, and I preferred passing the re-maining hours of darkness in Madame's room. Daylight brought no solution of the difficulty.

The whole household, with my father at its head, was in a state of agitation next morning. Every part of the château was searched. The grounds were explored. Not a trace of the missing lady could be discovered. The stream was about to be dragged; my father was in distraction; what a tale to have to tell the poor girl's mother on her return. I, too, was almost beside myself, though my grief was quite of a different kind.

The morning was passed in alarm and excitement. It was now one o'clock, and still no tidings. I ran up to Carmilla's room, and found her standing at her dressing-table. I was astounded. I could not believe my eyes. She beckoned me to her with her pretty finger, in silence. Her face expressed extreme fear.

I ran to her in an ecstasy of joy; I kissed and embraced her again and again. I ran to the bell and rang it vehemently, to bring others to the spot, who might at once relieve my father's anxiety.

" Dear Carmilla, what has become of you all this time? We have been in agonies of anxiety about you," I exclaimed. " Where have you been? How did you come back? "

" Last night has been a night of wonders," she said.

" For mercy's sake, explain all you can."

" It was past two last night," she said, " when I went to sleep as usual in my bed, with my doors locked, that of the dressing-room, and that opening upon the gallery. My sleep was uninterrupted, and, so far as I know, dreamless; but I awoke just now on the sofa in the dressing-room there, and I found the door between the rooms open, and the other door forced. How could all this have happened without my being wakened? It must have been accompanied with a great deal of noise, and I am particularly easily wakened; and how could I have been carried out of my bed without my sleep having been interrupted, I whom the slightest stir startles? "

By this time, Madame, Mademoiselle, my father, and a number of the servants were in the room. Carmilla was, of course, overwhelmed with inquiries, congratulations, and welcomes. She had but one story to tell, and seemed the least able of all the party to suggest any way of accounting for what had happened.

My father took a turn up and down the room, thinking. I saw Carmilla's eye follow him for a moment with a sly, dark glance.

When my father had sent the servants away, Mademoiselle having gone in search of a little bottle of valerian and salvolatile, and there being no one now in the room with Carmilla except my father, Madame, and myself, he came to her thoughtfully, took her hand very kindly, led her to the sofa, and sat down beside her.

" Will you forgive me, my dear, if I risk a conjecture, and ask a question? "

" Who can have a better right? " she said. " Ask what you please, and I will tell you everything. But my story is simply one of bewilderment and darkness. I know absolutely nothing. Put any question you please. But you know, of course, the limitations mamma has placed me under."

"Perfectly, my dear child. I need not approach the topics on which she desires our silence. Now, the marvel of last night consists in your having been removed from your bed and your room without being wakened, and this removal having occurred apparently while the windows were still secured, and the two doors locked upon the inside. I will tell you my theory, and first ask you a question."

Carmilla was leaning on her hand dejectedly; Madame and I were listening breathlessly.

"Now, my question is this. Have you ever been suspected of walking in your sleep?"

"Never since I was very young indeed."

"But you did walk in your sleep when you were young?"

"Yes; I know I did. I have been told so often by my old nurse."

My father smiled and nodded.

"Well, what has happened is this. You got up in your sleep, unlocked the door, not leaving the key, as usual, in the lock, but taking it out and locking it on the outside; you again took the key out, and carried it away with you to some one of the five-and-twenty rooms on this floor, or perhaps upstairs or downstairs. There are so many rooms and closets, so much heavy furniture, and such accumulations of lumber, that it would require a week to search this old house thoroughly. Do you see, now, what I mean?"

"I do, but not all," she answered.

"And how, papa, do you account for her finding herself on the sofa in the dressing-room, which we had searched so carefully?"

"She came there after you had searched it, still in her sleep, and at last awoke spontaneously, and was as much surprised to find herself where she was as anyone else. I wish all mysteries were as easily and innocently explained as yours, Carmilla," he said, laughing. "And so we may congratulate ourselves on the certainty that the most natural explanation of the occurrence is one that involves no drugging, no tampering with locks, no burglars, or poisoners, or witches—nothing that need alarm Carmilla, or any one else, for our safety."

Carmilla was looking charming. Nothing could be more beautiful than her tints. Her beauty was, I think, enhanced

by that graceful languor that was peculiar to her. I think
my father was silently contrasting her looks with mine, for
he said:

" I wish my poor Laura was looking more like herself ";
and he sighed.

So our alarms were happily ended, and Carmilla restored
to her friends.

CHAPTER IX

THE DOCTOR

AS Carmilla would not hear of an attendant sleeping in
her room, my father arranged that a servant should sleep
outside her door, so that she could not attempt to make
another such excursion without being arrested at her own
door.

That night passed quietly; and next morning early, the
doctor, whom my father had sent for without telling me a
word about it, arrived to see me.

Madame accompanied me to the library; and there the
grave little doctor, with white hair and spectacles, whom I
mentioned before, was waiting to receive me.

I told him my story, and as I proceeded he grew graver
and graver.

We were standing, he and I, in the recess of one of the
windows, facing one another. When my statement was
over, he leaned with his shoulders against the wall, and with
his eyes fixed on me earnestly with an interest in which was
a dash of horror.

After a minute's reflection, he asked Madame if he could
see my father.

He was sent for accordingly, and as he entered, smiling,
he said:

" I dare say, doctor, you are going to tell me that I am
an old fool for having brought you here; I hope I am."

But his smile faded into shadow as the doctor, with a very
grave face, beckoned him to him.

He and the doctor talked for some time in the same recess
where I had just conferred with the physician. It seemed
an earnest and argumentative conversation. The room is very
large, and I and Madame stood together, burning with

curiosity, at the further end. Not a word could we hear, however, for they spoke in a very low tone, and the deep recess of the window quite concealed the doctor from view, and very nearly my father, whose foot, arm, and shoulder only could we see; and the voices were, I suppose, all the less audible for the sort of closet which the thick wall and window formed.

After a time my father's face looked into the room; it was pale, thoughtful, and, I fancied, agitated.

" Laura dear, come here for a moment. Madame, we shan't trouble you, the doctor says, at present."

Accordingly I approached, for the first time a little alarmed; for, although I felt very weak, I did not feel ill; and strength, one always fancies, is a thing that may be picked up when we please.

My father held out his hand to me as I drew near, but he was looking at the doctor, and he said:

" It certainly *is* very odd; I don't understand it quite. Laura, come here, dear; now attend to Doctor Spielsberg, and recollect yourself."

" You mentioned a sensation like that of two needles piercing the skin, somewhere about your neck, on the night when you experienced your first horrible dream. Is there still any soreness?"

" None at all," I answered.

" Can you indicate with your finger about the point at which you think this occurred?"

" Very little below my throat—*here*," I answered.

I wore a morning dress, which covered the place I pointed to.

" Now you can satisfy yourself," said the doctor. " You won't mind your papa's lowering your dress a very little. It is necessary, to detect a symptom of the complaint under which you have been suffering."

I acquiesced. It was only an inch or two below the edge of my collar.

" God bless me!—so it is," exclaimed my father, growing pale.

" You see it now with your own eyes," said the doctor, with a gloomy triumph.

" What is it?" I exclaimed, beginning to be frightened.

" Nothing, my dear young lady, but a small blue spot,

about the size of the tip of your little finger; and now," he continued, turning to papa, " the question is what is best to be done? "

" Is there any danger? " I urged, in great trepidation.

" I trust not, my dear," answered the doctor. " I don't see why you should not recover. I don't see why you should not begin *immediately* to get better. That is the point at which the sense of strangulation begins? "

" Yes," I answered.

" And—recollect as well as you can—the same point was a kind of centre of that thrill which you described just now, like the current of a cold stream running against you? "

" It may have been; I think it was."

" Ay, you see? " he added, turning to my father. " Shall I say a word to Madame? "

" Certainly," said my father.

He called Madame to him, and said:

" I find my young friend here far from well. It won't be of any great consequence, I hope; but it will be necessary that some steps be taken, which I will explain by-and-by; but in the meantime, Madame, you will be so good as not to let Miss Laura be alone for one moment. That is the only direction I need give for the present. It is indispensable."

" We may rely upon your kindness, Madame, I know," added my father.

Madame satisfied him eagerly.

" And you, dear Laura, I know you will observe the doctor's direction."

" I shall have to ask your opinion upon another patient, whose symptoms slightly resemble those of my daughter, that have just been detailed to you—very much milder in degree, but I believe quite of the same sort. She is a young lady—our guest; but as you say you will be passing this way again this evening, you can't do better than take your supper here, and you can then see her. She does not come down till the afternoon."

" I thank you," said the doctor. " I shall be with you, then, at about seven this evening."

And then they repeated their directions to me and to Madame, and with this parting charge my father left us, and walked out with the doctor; and I saw them pacing together up and down between the road and the moat, on the grassy platform in front of the castle, evidently absorbed in earnest conversation.

The doctor, did not return. I saw him mount his horse there, take his leave, and ride away eastward through the forest. Nearly at the same time I saw the man arrive from Dranfeld with the letters, and dismount and hand the bag to my father.

In the meantime, Madame and I were both busy, lost in conjecture as to the reasons of the singular and earnest direction which the doctor and my father had concurred in imposing. Madame, as she afterwards told me, was afraid the doctor apprehended a sudden seizure, and that, without prompt assistance, I might either lose my life in a fit, or at least be seriously hurt.

This interpretation did not strike me; and I fancied, perhaps luckily for my nerves, that the arrangement was prescribed simply to secure a companion, who would prevent my taking too much exercise, or eating unripe fruit, or doing any of the fifty foolish things to which young people are supposed to be prone.

About half an hour after my father came in—he had a letter in his hand—and said:

" This letter has been delayed; it is from General Spielsdorf. He might have been here yesterday, he may not come till to-morrow, or he may be here to-day."

He put the open letter into my hand; but he did not look pleased, as he used to when a guest, especially one so much loved as the General, was coming. On the contrary, he looked as if he wished him at the bottom of the Red Sea. There was plainly something on his mind which he did not choose to divulge.

" Papa, darling, will you tell me this? " said I, suddenly laying my hand on his arm, and looking, I am sure, imploringly in his face.

" Perhaps," he answered, smoothing my hair caressingly over my eyes.

" Does the doctor think me very ill? "

" No, dear; he thinks, if right steps are taken, you will be quite well again, at least on the high road to a complete recovery, in a day or two," he answered, a little dryly. " I wish our good friend, the General, had chosen any other time; that is, I wish you had been perfectly well to receive him."

"But do tell me, papa," I insisted, "*what* does he think is the matter with me?"

"Nothing; you must not plague me with questions," he answered, with more irritation than I ever remember him to have displayed before; and seeing that I looked wounded, I suppose, he kissed me, and added, "You shall know all about it in a day or two; that is, all that *I* know. In the meantime, you are not to trouble your head about it."

He turned and left the room, but came back before I had done wondering and puzzling over the oddity of all this; it was merely to say that he was going to Karnstein, and had ordered the carriage to be ready at twelve, and that I and Madame should accompany him; he was going to see the priest who lived near those picturesque grounds, upon business, and as Carmilla had never seen them, she could follow, when she came down, with Mademoiselle, who would bring materials for what you call a picnic, which might be laid for us in the ruined castle.

At twelve o'clock, accordingly, I was ready, and not long after, my father, Madame and I set out upon our projected drive. Passing the drawbridge we turn to the right, and follow the road over the steep Gothic bridge, westward, to reach the deserted village and ruined castle of Karnstein.

No sylvan drive can be fancied prettier. The ground breaks into gentle hills and hollows, all clothed with beautiful wood, totally destitute of the comparative formality which artificial planting and early culture and pruning impart.

The irregularities of the ground often lead the road out of its course, and cause it to wind beautifully round the sides of broken hollows and the steeper sides of the hills, among varieties of ground almost inexhaustible.

Turning one of these points, we suddenly encountered our old friend, the General, riding towards us, attended by a mounted servant. His portmanteaus were following in a hired waggon, such as we term a cart.

The General dismounted as we pulled up, and, after the usual greetings, was easily persuaded to accept the vacant seat in the carriage, and send his horse on with his servant to the schloss.

CHAPTER X

BEREAVED

IT was about ten months since we had last seen him; but that time had sufficed to make an alteration of years in his appearance. He had grown thinner; something of gloom and anxiety had taken the place of that cordial serenity which used to characterise his features. His dark blue eyes, always penetrating, now gleamed with a sterner light from under his shaggy grey eyebrows. It was not such a change as grief alone usually induces, and angrier passions seemed to have had their share in bringing it about.

We had not long resumed our drive, when the General began to talk, with his usual soldierly directness, of the bereavement, as he termed it, which he had sustained in the death of his beloved niece and ward; and he then broke out in a tone of intense bitterness and fury, inveighing against the "hellish arts" to which she had fallen a victim, and expressing with more exasperation than piety, his wonder that Heaven should tolerate so monstrous an indulgence of the lusts and malignity of hell.

My father, who saw at once that something very extraordinary had befallen, asked him, if not too painful to him, to detail the circumstances which he thought justified the strong terms in which he expressed himself.

"I should tell you all with pleasure," said the General, "but you would not believe me."

"Why should I not?" he asked.

"Because," he answered testily, "you believe in nothing but what consists with your own prejudices and illusions. I remember when I was like you, but I have learned better."

"Try me," said my father; "I am not such a dogmatist as you suppose. Besides which, I very well know that you generally require proof of what you believe, and am, therefore, very strongly predisposed to respect your conclusions."

"You are right in supposing that I have not been led lightly into a belief in the marvellous—for what I have experienced *is* marvellous—and I have been forced by extraordinary evidence to credit that which ran counter, diametrically, to all my theories. I have been made the dupe of a preternatural conspiracy."

Notwithstanding his professions of confidence in the
General's penetration, I saw my father, at this point, glance
at the General, with, as I thought, a marked suspicion of his
sanity.

The General did not see it, luckily. He was looking
gloomily and curiously into the glades and vistas of the woods
that were opening before us.

" You are going to the Ruins of Karnstein? " he said.
" Yes, it is a lucky coincidence; do you know I was going
to ask you to bring me there to inspect them. I have a
special object in exploring. There is a ruined chapel, isn't
there, with a great many tombs of that extinct family? "

" So there are—highly interesting," said my father. " I
hope you are thinking of claiming the title and estates? "

My father said this gaily, but the General did not recollect
the laugh, or even the smile, which courtesy exacts for a
friend's joke; on the contrary, he looked grave and even
fierce, ruminating on a matter that stirred his anger and
horror.

" Something very different," he said, gruffly. " I mean to
unearth some of those fine people. I hope, by God's blessing,
to accomplish a pious sacrilege here, which will relieve our
earth of certain monsters, and enable honest people to sleep
in their beds without being assailed by murderers. I have
strange things to tell you, my dear friend, such as I myself
would have scouted as incredible a few months since."

My father looked at him again, but this time not with a
glance of suspicion—with an eye, rather, of keen intelligence
and alarm.

" The house of Karnstein," he said, " has been long extinct:
a hundred years at least. My dear wife was maternally
descended from the Karnsteins. But the name and title have
long ceased to exist. The castle is a ruin; the very village
is deserted; it is fifty years since the smoke of a chimney
was seen there; not a roof left."

" Quite true. I have heard a great deal about that since
I last saw you; a great deal that will astonish you. But
I had better relate everything in the order in which it occurred," said the General. " You saw my dear ward—my
child, I may call her. No creature could have been more
beautiful, and only three months ago none more blooming."

" Yes, poor thing! when I saw her last she certainly was

quite lovely," said my father. "I was grieved and shocked more than I can tell you, my dear friend; I knew what a blow it was to you."

He took the General's hand, and they exchanged a kind pressure. Tears gathered in the old soldier's eyes. He did not seek to conceal them. He said:

"We have been very old friends; I knew you would feel for me, childless as I am. She had become an object of very dear interest to me, and repaid my care by an affection that cheered my home and made my life happy. That is all gone. The years that remain to me on earth may not be very long; but by God's mercy I hope to accomplish a service to mankind before I die, and to subserve the vengeance of Heaven upon the fiends who have murdered my poor child in the spring of her hopes and beauty!"

"You said, just now, that you intended relating everything as it occurred," said my father. "Pray do; I assure you that it is not mere curiosity that prompts me."

By this time we had reached the point at which the Drunstall road, by which the General had come, diverges from the road which we were travelling to Karnstein.

"How far is it to the ruins?" inquired the General, looking anxiously forward.

"About half a league," answered my father. "Pray let us hear the story you were so good as to promise."

CHAPTER XI

THE STORY

"WITH all my heart," said the General, with an effort; and after a short pause in which to arrange his subject, he commenced one of the strangest narratives I ever heard.

"My dear child was looking forward with great pleasure to the visit you had been so good as to arrange for her to your charming daughter." Here he made me a gallant but melancholy bow. "In the meantime we had an invitation to my old friend the Count Carlsfeld, whose schloss is about six leagues to the other side of Karnstein. It was to attend the series of fêtes which, you remember, were given by him in honour of his illustrious visitor, the Grand Duke Charles."

" Yes; and very splendid, I believe, they were," said my father.

" Princely! But then his hospitalities are quite regal. He has Aladdin's lamp. The night from which my sorrow dates was devoted to a magnificent masquerade. The grounds were thrown open, the trees hung with coloured lamps. There was such a display of fireworks as Paris itself had never witnessed. And such music—music, you know, is my weakness —such ravishing music! The finest instrumental band, perhaps, in the world, and the finest singers who could be collected from all the great operas in Europe. As you wandered through these fantastically illuminated grounds, the moon-lighted château throwing a rosy light from its long rows of windows, you would suddenly hear these ravishing voices stealing from the silence of some grove, or rising from boats upon the lake. I felt myself, as I looked and listened, carried back into the romance and poetry of my early youth.

" When the fireworks were ended, and the ball beginning, we returned to the noble suite of rooms that were thrown open to the dancers. A masked ball, you know, is a beautiful sight; but so brilliant a spectacle of the kind I never saw before.

" It was a very aristocratic assembly. I was myself almost the only ' nobody ' present.

" My dear child was looking quite beautiful. She wore no mask. Her excitement and delight added an unspeakable charm to her features, always lovely. I remarked a young lady, dressed magnificently, but wearing a mask, who appeared to me to be observing my ward with extraordinary interest. I had seen her, earlier in the evening, in the great hall, and again, for a few minutes, walking near us, on the terrace under the castle windows, similarly employed. A lady, also masked, richly and gravely dressed, and with a stately air, like a person of rank, accompanied her as a chaperon. Had the young lady not worn a mask, I could, of course, have been much more certain upon the question whether she was really watching my poor darling. I am now well assured that she was.

" We were now in one of the *salons*. My poor dear child

had been dancing, and was resting a little in one of the chairs near the door; I was standing near. The two ladies I have mentioned had approached, and the younger took the chair next my ward; while her companion stood beside me, and for a little time addressed herself, in a low tone, to her charge.

"Availing herself of the privilege of her mask, she turned to me, and in the tone of an old friend, and calling me by my name, opened a conversation with me, which piqued my curiosity a good deal. She referred to many scenes where she had met me—at Court, and at distinguished houses. She alluded to little incidents which I had long ceased to think of, but which, I found, had only lain in abeyance in my memory, for they instantly started into life at her touch.

"I became more and more curious to ascertain who she was, every moment. She parried my attempts to discover very adroitly and pleasantly. The knowledge she showed of many passages in my life seemed to me all but unaccountable; and she appeared to take a not unnatural pleasure in foiling my curiosity, and in seeing me flounder, in my eager perplexity, from one conjecture to another.

"In the meantime the young lady, whom her mother called by the odd name of Millarca, when she once or twice addressed her, had, with the same ease and grace, got into conversation with my ward.

"She introduced herself by saying that her mother was a very old acquaintance of mine. She spoke of the agreeable audacity which a mask rendered practicable; she talked like a friend; she admired her dress, and insinuated very prettily her admiration of her beauty. She amused her with laughing criticisms upon the people who crowded the ballroom, and laughed at my poor child's fun. She was very witty and lively when she pleased, and after a time they had grown very good friends, and the young stranger lowered her mask, displaying a remarkably beautiful face. I had never seen it before, neither had my dear child. But though it was new to us, the features were so engaging, as well as lovely, that it was impossible not to feel the attraction powerfully. My poor girl did so. I never saw anyone more taken with another at first sight, unless, indeed, it was the stranger herself, who seemed quite to have lost her heart to her.

"In the meantime, availing myself of the licence of a

masquerade, I put not a few questions to the elder lady.

" ' You have puzzled me utterly,' I said, laughing. ' Is that not enough? Won't you, now, consent to stand on equal terms, and do me the kindness to remove your mask? '

" ' Can any request be more unreasonable? ' she replied. ' Ask a lady to yield an advantage! Besides, how do you know you should recognise me? Years make changes.'

" ' As you see,' I said, with a bow, and, I suppose, a rather melancholy little laugh.

" ' As philosophers tell us,' she said; ' and how do you know that a sight of my face would help you? '

" ' I should take chance for that,' I answered. ' It is vain trying to make yourself out an old woman; your figure betrays you.'

" ' Years, nevertheless, have passed since I saw you, rather since you saw me, for that is what I am considering. Millarca, there, is my daughter; I cannot then be young, even in the opinion of people whom time has taught to be indulgent, and I may not like to be compared with what you remember me. You have no mask to remove. You can offer me nothing in exchange.'

" ' My petition is to your pity, to remove it.'

" ' And mine to yours, to let it stay where it is,' she replied.

" ' Well, then, at least you will tell me whether you are French or German; you speak both languages so perfectly.'

" ' I don't think I shall tell you that, General; you intend a surprise, and are meditating the particular point of attack.'

" ' At all events, you won't deny this,' I said, ' that being honoured by your permission to converse, I ought to know how to address you. Shall I say Madame la Comtesse? '

" She laughed, and she would, no doubt, have met me with another evasion—if, indeed, I can treat any occurrence in an interview every circumstance of which was pre-arranged, as I now believe, with the profoundest cunning, as liable to be modified by accident.

" ' As to that,' she began; but she was interrupted, almost as she opened her lips, by a gentleman, dressed in black, who looked particularly elegant and distinguished, with this drawback, that his face was the most deadly pale I ever saw, except in death. He was in no masquerade—in the plain evening dress of a gentleman; and he said, without a smile, but with a courtly and unusually low bow:

"'Will Madame la Comtesse permit me to say a very few words which may interest her?'

"The lady turned quickly to him, and touched her lip in token of silence; she then said to me, 'Keep my place for me, General; I shall return when I have said a few words.'

"And with this injunction, playfully given, she walked a little aside with the gentleman in black, and talked for some minutes, apparently very earnestly. They then walked away slowly together in the crowd, and I lost them for some minutes.

"I spent the interval in cudgelling my brains for conjecture as to the identity of the lady who seemed to remember me so kindly, and I was thinking of turning about and joining in the conversation between my pretty ward and the Countess's daughter, and trying whether, by the time she returned, I might not have a surprise in store for her, by having her name, title, château, and estates at my fingers' ends. But at this moment she returned, accompanied by the pale man in black, who said:

"'I shall return and inform Madame la Comtesse when her carriage is at the door.'

"He withdrew with a bow."

CHAPTER XII

A PETITION

"'THEN we are to lose Madame la Comtesse, but I hope only for a few hours,' I said, with a low bow.

"'It may be that only, or it may be a few weeks. It was very unlucky his speaking to me just now as he did. Do you now know me?'

"I assured her I did not.

"'You shall know me,' she said, 'but not at present. We are older and better friends than, perhaps, you suspect. I cannot yet declare myself. I shall in three weeks pass your beautiful schloss about which I have been making inquiries. I shall then look in upon you for an hour or two, and renew a friendship which I never think of without a thousand pleasant recollections. This moment a piece of news has reached me like a thunderbolt. I must set out now, and travel by a devious route, nearly a hundred miles, with all the dispatch I can possibly make. My perplexities multiply. I am only deterred by the compulsory reserve I practise as to my name from making a very singular request of you. My poor child has not quite recovered her strength. Her horse fell with her, at a hunt which she had ridden out to witness, her nerves have not yet recovered the shock, and our physician says that she must on no account exert herself for some time to come. We came here, in consequence, by very easy stages —hardly six leagues a day. I must now travel day and night, on a mission of life and death—a mission the critical and momentous nature of which I shall be able to explain to you when we meet, as I hope we shall, in a few weeks, without the necessity of any concealment.'

" She went on to make her petition, and it was in the tone of a person from whom such a request amounted to conferring, rather than seeking, a favour. This was only in manner, and, as it seemed, quite unconsciously. Than the terms in which it was expressed, nothing could be more deprecatory. It was simply that I would consent to take charge of her daughter during her absence.

" This was, all things considered, a strange, not to say, an audacious request. She in some sort disarmed me, by stating and admitting everything that could be urged against it, and throwing herself entirely upon my chivalry. At the same moment, by a fatality that seems to have predetermined all that happened, my poor child came to my side, and, in an undertone, besought me to invite her new friend, Millarca, to pay us a visit. She had just been sounding her, and thought, if her mamma would allow her, she would like it extremely.

" At another time I should have told her to wait a little, until, at least, we knew who they were. But I had not a moment to think in. The two ladies assailed me together, and I must confess the refined and beautiful face of the young lady, about which there was something extremely engaging, as well as the elegance and fire of high birth, determined me; and quite overpowered, I submitted, and undertook, too easily, the care of the young lady, whom her mother called Millarca.

" The Countess beckoned to her daughter, who listened

with grave attention, while she told her, in general terms,
how suddenly and peremptorily she had been summoned,
and also of the arrangement she had made for her under my
care, adding that I was one of her earliest and most valued
friends.

"I made, of course, such speeches as the case seemed to
call for, and found myself, on reflection, in a position which
I did not half like.

"The gentleman in black returned, and very ceremoni-
ously conducted the lady from the room.

"The demeanour of this gentleman was such as to impress
me with the conviction that the Countess was a lady of very
much more importance than her modest title alone might
have led me to assume.

"Her last charge to me was that no attempt was to be
made to learn more about her than I might have already
guessed, until her return. Our distinguished host, whose
guest she was, knew her reasons.

"'But here,' she said, 'neither I nor my daughter could
safely remain for more than a day. I removed my mask
imprudently for a moment, about an hour ago, and, too
late, I fancied you saw me. So I resolved to seek an opportunity of talking a little to you. Had I found that you
had seen me, I should have thrown myself on your high sense
of honour to keep my secret for some weeks. As it is, I
am satisfied that you did not see me; but if you now *suspect*,
or, on reflection, *should* suspect, who I am, I commit myself,
in like manner, entirely to your honour. My daughter will
observe the same secrecy, and I well know that you will, from
time to time, remind her, lest she should thoughtlessly disclose
it.'

"She whispered a few words to her daughter, kissed her
hurriedly twice, and went away, accompanied by the pale
gentleman in black, and disappeared in the crowd.

"'In the next room,' said Millarca, 'there is a window that
looks upon the hall door. I should like to see the last of
mamma, and to kiss my hand to her.'

"We assented, of course, and accompanied her to the
window. We looked out, and saw a handsome old-fashioned
carriage, with a troop of couriers and footmen. We saw the
slim figure of the pale gentleman in black, as he held a thick
velvet cloak, and placed it about her shoulders and threw

the hood over her head. She nodded to him, and just touched his hand with hers. He bowed low repeatedly as the door closed, and the carriage began to move.

" ' She is gone,' said Millarca, with a sigh.

" ' She is gone,' I repeated to myself, for the first time—in the hurried moments that had elapsed since my consent—reflecting upon the folly of my act.

" ' She did not look up,' said the young lady, plaintively.

" ' The Countess had taken off her mask, perhaps, and did not care to show her face,' I said; ' and she could not know that you were in the window.'

" She sighed and looked in my face. She was so beautiful that I relented. I was sorry I had for a moment repented of my hospitality, and I determined to make her amends for the unavowed churlishness of my reception.

" The young lady, replacing her mask, joined my ward in persuading me to return to the grounds, where the concert was soon to be renewed. We did so, and walked up and down the terrace that lies under the castle windows. Millarca became very intimate with us, and amused us with lively descriptions and stories of most of the great people whom we saw upon the terrace. I liked her more and more every minute. Her gossip, without being ill-natured, was extremely diverting to me, who had been so long out of the great world. I thought what life she would give to our sometimes lonely evenings at home.

" This ball was not over until the morning sun had almost reached the horizon. It pleased the Grand Duke to dance till then, so loyal people could not go away, or think of bed.

" We had just got through a crowded saloon, when my ward asked me what had become of Millarca. I thought she had been by her side, and she fancied she was by mine. The fact was, we had lost her.

" All my efforts to find her were vain. I feared that she had mistaken, in the confusion of a momentary separation from us, other people for her new friends, and had, possibly, pursued and lost them in the extensive grounds which were thrown open to us.

" Now, in its full force, I recognised a new folly in my having undertaken the charge of a young lady without so much as knowing her name; and fettered as I was by promises, of the reasons for imposing which I knew nothing,

I could not even point my inquiries by saying that the missing young lady was the daughter of the Countess who had taken her departure a few hours before.

"Morning broke. It was clear daylight before I gave up my search. It was not till near two o'clock next day that we heard anything of my missing charge.

"At about that time a servant knocked at my niece's door, to say that he had been earnestly requested by a young lady, who appeared to be in great distress, to make out where she could find the General Baron Spielsdorf and the young lady, his daughter, in whose charge she had been left by her mother.

"There could be no doubt, notwithstanding the slight inaccuracy, that our young friend had turned up; and so she had. Would to Heaven we had lost her!

"She told my poor child a story to account for her having failed to recover us for so long. Very late, she said, she had got into the housekeeper's bedroom in despair of finding us, and had then fallen into a deep sleep which, long as it was, had hardly sufficed to recruit her strength after the fatigues of the ball.

"That day Millarca came home with us. I was only too happy, after all, to have secured so charming a companion for my dear girl."

CHAPTER XIII

THE WOODMAN

"THERE soon, however, appeared some drawbacks. In the first place, Millarca complained of extreme languor —the weakness that remained after her late illness—and she never emerged from her room till the afternoon was pretty far advanced. In the next place, it was accidentally discovered, although she always locked her door on the inside, and never disturbed the key from its place, till she admitted the maid to assist at her toilet, that she was undoubtedly sometimes absent from her room in the very early morning, and at various times later in the day, before she wished it to be understood that she was stirring. She was repeatedly seen from the windows of the schloss, in the first faint grey of the morning, walking through the trees, in an easterly direction, and looking like a person in a trance. This convinced me that she walked in her sleep. But this hypothesis did not solve the puzzle. How did she pass out from her room, leaving the door locked on the inside. How did she escape from the house without unbarring door or window?

" In the midst of my perplexities, an anxiety of a far more urgent kind presented itself.

" My dear child began to lose her looks and health, and that in a manner so mysterious, and even horrible, that I became thoroughly frightened.

" She was at first visited by appalling dreams; then, as she fancied, by a spectre, sometimes resembling Millarca, sometimes in the shape of a beast, indistinctly seen, walking round the foot of her bed, from side to side. Lastly came sensations. One, not unpleasant, but very peculiar, she said, resembled the flow of an icy stream against her breast. At a later time, she felt something like a pair of large needles pierce her, a little below the throat, with a very sharp pain. A few nights after, followed a gradual and convulsive sense of strangulation; then came unconsciousness."

I could hear distinctly every word the kind old General was saying, because by this time we were driving upon the short grass that spreads on either side of the road as you approach the roofless village which had not shown the smoke of a chimney for more than half a century.

You may guess how strangely I felt as I heard my own symptoms so exactly described in those which had been experienced by the poor girl who, but for the catastrophe which followed, would have been at that moment a visitor at my father's château. You may suppose, also, how I felt as I heard him detail habits and mysterious peculiarities which were, in fact, those of our beautiful guest, Carmilla!

A vista opened in the forest; we were on a sudden under the chimneys and gables of the ruined village, and the towers and battlements of the dismantled castle, round which gigantic trees are grouped, overhung us from a slight eminence.

In a frightened dream I got down from the carriage; and in silence, for we had each abundant matter for thinking, we soon mounted the ascent, and were among the spacious chambers, winding stairs, and dark corridors of the castle.

" And this was once the palatial residence of the Karn-

steins! " said the old General at length, as from a great
window he looked out across the village, and saw the wide,
undulating expanse of forest. " It was a bad family, and
here its blood-stained annals were written," he continued.
" It is hard that they should, after death, continue to plague
the human race with their atrocious lusts. That is the chapel
of the Karnsteins, down there."

He pointed down to the grey walls of the Gothic building,
partly visible through the foliage, a little way down the
steep. " And I hear the axe of a woodman," he added,
" busy among the trees that surround it; he possibly may
give us the information of which I am in search, and point
out the grave of Mircalla, Countess of Karnstein. These
rustics preserve the local traditions of great families, whose
stories die out among the rich and titled so soon as the
families themselves become extinct."

" We have a portrait, at home, of Mircalla, the Countess
Karnstein; should you like to see it? " asked my father.

" Time enough, dear friend," replied the General. " I
believe that I have seen the original; and one motive which
has led me to you earlier than I at first intended, was to
explore the chapel which we are now approaching."

" What! see the Countess Mircalla," exclaimed my father;
" why, she has been dead more than a century! "

" Not so dead as you fancy, I am told," answered the
General.

" I confess, General, you puzzle me utterly," replied my
father, looking at him, I fancied, for a moment with a return
of the suspicion I detected before. But although there was
anger and detestation, at times, in the old General's manner,
there was nothing flighty.

" There remains to me," he said, as we passed under the
heavy arch of the Gothic church—for its dimensions would
have justified its being so styled—" but one object which
can interest me during the few years that remain to me on
earth, and that is to wreak on her the vengeance which,
I thank God, may still be accomplished by a mortal
arm."

" What vengeance can you mean? " asked my father, in
increasing amazement.

" I mean, to decapitate the monster," he answered, with
a fierce flush, and a stamp that echoed mournfully through

the hollow ruin, and his clenched hand was at the same moment raised, as if it grasped the handle of an axe, while he shook it ferociously in the air.

" What! " exclaimed my father, more than ever bewildered.

" To strike her head off."

" Cut her head off? "

" Aye, with a hatchet, with a spade, or with anything that can cleave through her murderous throat. You shall hear," he answered, trembling with rage. And hurrying forward, he said:

" That beam will answer for a seat; your dear child is fatigued; let her be seated, and I will, in a few sentences, close my dreadful story."

The squared block of wood, which lay on the grass-grown pavement of the chapel, formed a bench on which I was very glad to seat myself, and in the meantime the General called to the woodman, who had been removing some boughs which leaned upon the old walls; and, axe in hand, the hardy old fellow stood before us.

He could not tell us anything of these monuments; but there was an old man, he said, a ranger of this forest, at present sojourning in the house of the priest, about two miles away, who could point out every monument of the old Karnstein family; and, for a trifle, he undertook to bring him back with him, if we would lend him one of our horses, in little more than half-an-hour.

" Have you been long employed about this forest? " asked my father of the old man.

" I have been a woodman here," he answered in his *patois*, " under the forester, all my days; so has my father before me, and so on, as many generations as I can count up. I could show you the very house in the village here, in which my ancestors lived."

" How came the village to be deserted? " asked the General.

" It was troubled by *revenants*, sir; several were tracked to their graves, there detected by the usual tests, and extinguished in the usual way, by decapitation, by the stake, and by burning; but not until many of the villagers were killed.

" But after all these proceedings according to law," he

continued—" so many graves opened, and so many vampires deprived of their horrible animation—the village was not relieved. But a Moravian nobleman, who happened to be travelling this way, heard how matters were, and being skilled —as many people are in his country—in such affairs, he offered to deliver the village from its tormentor. He did so thus: There being a bright moon that night, he ascended, shortly after sunset, the tower of the chapel here, from whence he could distinctly see the churchyard beneath him; you can see it from that window. From this point he watched until he saw the vampire come out of his grave, and place near it the linen clothes in which he had been folded, and glide away towards the village to plague its inhabitants.

" The stranger, having seen all this, came down from the steeple, took the linen wrappings of the vampire, and carried them up to the top of the tower, which he again mounted. When the vampire returned from his prowlings and missed his clothes, he cried furiously to the Moravian, whom he saw at the summit of the tower, and who, in reply, beckoned him to ascend and take them. Whereupon the vampire, accepting his invitation, began to climb the steeple, and so soon as he had reached the battlements, the Moravian, with a stroke of his sword, clove his skull in twain, hurling him down to the churchyard, whither, descending by the winding stairs, the stranger followed and cut his head off, and next day delivered it and the body to the villagers, who duly impaled and burnt them.

" This Moravian nobleman had authority from the then head of the family to remove the tomb of Mircalla, Countess Karnstein, which he did effectually, so that in a little while its site was quite forgotten."

" Can you point out where it stood? " asked the General eagerly.

The forester shook his head and smiled.

" Not a soul living could tell you that now," he said; " besides, they say her body was removed; but no one is sure of that either."

Having thus spoken, as time pressed, he dropped his axe and departed, leaving us to hear the remainder of the General's strange story.

CHAPTER XIV

THE MEETING

" MY beloved child," he resumed, " was now growing rapidly worse. The physician who attended her had failed to produce the slightest impression upon her disease, for such I then supposed it to be. He saw my alarm, and suggested a consultation. I called in an abler physician, from Gratz. Several days elapsed before he arrived. He was a good and pious, as well as a learned man. Having seen my poor ward together, they withdrew to my library to confer and discuss. I, from the adjoining room, where I awaited their summons, heard these two gentlemen's voices raised in something sharper than a strictly philosophical discussion. I knocked at the door and entered. I found the old physician from Gratz maintaining his theory. His rival was combating it with undisguised ridicule, accompanied with bursts of laughter. This unseemly manifestation subsided and the altercation ended on my entrance.

" ' Sir,' said my first physician, ' my learned brother seems to think that you want a conjuror, and not a doctor.'

" ' Pardon me,' said the old physician from Gratz, looking displeased, ' I shall state my own view of the case in my own way another time. I grieve, Monsieur le Général, that by my skill and science I can be of no use. Before I go I shall do myself the honour to suggest something to you.'

" He seemed thoughtful, and sat down at a table, and began to write. Profoundly disappointed, I made my bow, and as I turned to go, the other doctor pointed over his shoulder to his companion who was writing, and then, with a shrug, significantly touched his forehead.

" This consultation, then, left me precisely where I was. I walked out into the grounds all but distracted. The doctor from Gratz, in ten or fifteen minutes, overtook me. He apologised for having followed me, but said that he could not conscientiously take his leave without a few words more. He told me that he could not be mistaken; no natural disease exhibited the same symptoms; and that death was already very near. There remained, however, a day, or possibly two, of life. If the fatal seizure were at once arrested, with great care and skill her strength might possibly return. But all

hung now upon the confines of the irrevocable. One more
assault might extinguish the last spark of vitality which
is, every moment, ready to die.

"'And what is the nature of the seizure you speak of?'
I entreated.

"'I have stated all fully in this note, which I place in
your hands, upon the distinct condition that you send for
the nearest clergyman, and open my letter in his presence, and
on no account read it till he is with you; you would despise
it else, and it is a matter of life and death. Should the
priest fail you, then, indeed, you may read it.'

"He asked me, before taking his leave finally, whether
I would wish to see a man curiously learned upon the very
subject, which, after I had read his letter, would probably
interest me above all others, and he urged me earnestly to
invite him to visit him there; and so took his leave.

"The ecclesiastic was absent, and I read the letter by myself. At another time, or in another case, it might have
excited my ridicule. But into what quackeries will not
people rush for a last chance, where all accustomed means
have failed, and the life of a beloved object is at stake?

"Nothing, you will say, could be more absurd than the
learned man's letter. It was monstrous enough to have consigned him to a madhouse. He said that the patient was
suffering from the visits of a vampire! The punctures which
she described as having occurred near the throat, were, he
insisted, the insertion of those two long, thin, and sharp
teeth which, it is well known, are peculiar to vampires; and
there could be no doubt, he added, as to the well-defined
presence of the small livid mark which all concurred in
describing as that induced by the demon's lips, and every
symptom described by the sufferer was in exact conformity
with those recorded in every case of a similar visitation.

"Being myself wholly sceptical as to the existence of any
such portent as the vampire, the supernatural theory of the
good doctor furnished, in my opinion, but another instance of
learning and intelligence oddly associated with some one
hallucination. I was so miserable, however, that, rather
than try nothing, I acted upon the instructions of the letter.

"I concealed myself in the dark dressing-room, that opened
upon the poor patient's room, in which a candle was burning,
and watched there till she was fast asleep. I stood at the

door, peeping through the small crevice, my sword laid on
the table beside me, as my directions prescribed, until, a little
after one, I saw a large black object, very ill-defined, crawl,
as it seemed to me, over the foot of the bed, and swiftly
spread itself up to the poor girl's throat, where it swelled, in
a moment, into a great, palpitating mass.

" For a few moments I had stood petrified. I now sprang
forward, with my sword in my hand. The black creature
suddenly contracted towards the foot of the bed, glided over
it, and, standing on the floor about a yard below the foot
of the bed, with a glare of skulking ferocity and horror fixed
on me, I saw Millarca. Speculating I know not what, I
struck at her instantly with my sword; but I saw her standing
near the door, unscathed. Horrified, I pursued and struck
again. She was gone! and my sword flew to shivers against
the door.

" I can't describe to you all that passed on that horrible
night. The whole house was up and stirring. The spectre
Millarca was gone. But her victim was sinking fast, and
before the morning dawned, she died."

The old General was agitated. We did not speak to him.
My father walked to some little distance, and began reading
the inscriptions on the tombstones; and thus occupied, he
strolled into the door of a side chapel to prosecute his re
searches. The General leaned against the wall, dried his eyes,
and sighed heavily. I was relieved on hearing the voices
of Carmilla and Madame, who were at that moment approaching. The voices died away.

In this solitude, having just listened to so strange a story,
connected, as it was, with the great and titled dead, whose
monuments were mouldering among the dust and ivy round
us, and every incident of which bore so awfully upon my
own mysterious case—in this haunted spot, darkened by the
towering foliage that rose on every side, dense and high above
its noiseless walls—a horror began to steal over me, and my
heart sank as I thought that my friends were, after all,
not about to enter and disturb this triste and ominous
scene.

The old General's eyes were fixed on the ground, as he
leaned with his hand upon the basement of a shattered
monument.

Under a narrow, arched doorway, surmounted by one of

those demoniacal grotesques in which the cynical and ghastly
fancy of old Gothic carving delights, I saw very gladly the
beautiful face and figure of Carmilla enter the shadowy
chapel.

I was just about to rise and speak, and nodded smiling,
in answer to her peculiarly engaging smile, when with a cry,
the old man by my side caught up the woodman's hatchet,
and started forward. On seeing him a brutalised change
came over her features. It was an instantaneous and horrible
transformation, as she made a crouching step backwards.
Before I could utter a scream, he struck at her with all his
force, but she dived under his blow, and unscathed, caught
him in her tiny grasp by the wrist. He struggled for a
moment to release his arm, but his hand opened, the axe fell
to the ground, and the girl was gone.

He staggered against the wall. His grey hair stood up on
his head, and a moisture shone over his face, as if he were at
the point of death.

The frightful scene had passed in a moment. The first
thing I recollect after, is Madame standing before me, and
impatiently repeating again and again, the question, " Where
is Mademoiselle Carmilla? "

I answered at length, "I don't know—I can't tell—she
went there," and I pointed to the door through which
Madame had just entered; "only a minute or two
since."

" But I have been standing there, in the passage, ever since
Mademoiselle Carmilla entered; and she did not return."

She then began to call " Carmilla " through every door and
passage and from the windows, but no answer came.

" She called herself Carmilla? " asked the General, still
agitated.

" Carmilla, yes," I answered.

" Aye," he said; " that is Millarca. That is the same person
who long ago was called Mircalla, Countess Karnstein. Depart from this accursed ground, my poor child, as quickly as
you can. Drive to the clergyman's house, and stay there till
we come. Begone! May you never behold Carmilla more;
you will not find her here."

CHAPTER XV

ORDEAL AND EXECUTION

AS he spoke one of the strangest-looking men I ever beheld, entered the chapel at the door through which Carmilla had made her entrance and her exit. He was tall, narrow-chested, stooping, with high shoulders, and dressed in black. His face was brown and dried in with deep furrows; he wore an oddly-shaped hat with a broad leaf. His hair, long and grizzled, hung on his shoulders. He wore a pair of gold spectacles, and walked slowly, with an odd shambling gait, with his face sometimes turned up to the sky, and sometimes bowed down toward the ground, seemed to wear a perpetual smile; his long thin arms were swinging, and his lank hands, in old black gloves ever so much too wide for them, waving and gesticulating in utter abstraction.

" The very man! " exclaimed the General, advancing with manifest delight. " My dear Baron, how happy I am to see you, I had no hope of meeting you so soon." He signed to my father, who had by this time returned, and leading the fantastic old gentleman, whom he called the Baron, to meet him. He introduced him formally, and they at once entered into earnest conversation. The stranger took a roll of paper from his pocket, and spread it on the worn surface of a tomb that stood by. He had a pencil case in his fingers, with which he traced imaginary lines from point to point on the paper, which from their often glancing from it, together, at certain points of the building, I concluded to be a plan of the chapel. He accompanied what I may term his lecture with occasional readings from a dirty little book, whose yellow leaves were closely written over.

They sauntered together down the side aisle, opposite to the spot where I was standing, conversing as they went; then they began measuring distances by paces, and finally they all stood together, facing a piece of the side-wall, which they began to examine with great minuteness; pulling off the ivy that clung over it, and rapping the plaster with the ends of their sticks, scraping here, and knocking there. At length they ascertained the existence of a broad marble tablet, with letters carved in relief upon it.

With the assistance of the woodman, who soon returned,

a monumental inscription, and carved escutcheon, were disclosed. They proved to be those of the long lost monument of Mircalla, Countess Karnstein.

The old General, though not I fear given to the praying mood, raised his hands and eyes to heaven, in mute thanksgiving for some moments.

"To-morrow," I heard him say; "the commissioner will be here, and the Inquisition will be held according to law."

Then turning to the old man with the gold spectacles, whom I have described, he shook him warmly by both hands and said:

"Baron, how can I thank you? How can we all thank you? You will have delivered this region from a plague that has scourged its inhabitants for more than a century. The horrible enemy, thank God, is at last tracked."

My father led the stranger aside, and the General followed. I knew that he had led them out of hearing, that he might relate my case, and I saw them glance often quickly at me, as the discussion proceeded.

My father came to me, kissed me again and again, and leading me from the chapel, said:

"It is time to return, but before we go home, we must add to our party the good priest, who lives but a little way from this, and persuade him to accompany us to the schloss."

In this quest we were successful: and I was glad, being unspeakably fatigued when we reached home. But my satisfaction was changed to dismay, on discovering that there were no tidings of Carmilla. Of the scene that had occurred in the ruined chapel, no explanation was offered to me, and it was clear that it was a secret which my father for the present determined to keep from me.

The sinister absence of Carmilla made the remembrance of the scene more horrible to me. The arrangements for that night were singular. Two servants and Madame were to sit up in my room that night; and the ecclesiastic with my father kept watch in the adjoining dressing-room.

The priest had performed certain solemn rites that night, the purport of which I did not understand any more than I comprehended the reason of this extraordinary precaution taken for my safety during sleep.

I saw all clearly a few days later.

The disappearance of Carmilla was followed by the discontinuance of my nightly sufferings.

You have heard, no doubt, of the appalling superstition that prevails in Upper and Lower Styria, in Moravia, Silesia, in Turkish Servia, in Poland, even in Russia; the superstition, so we must call it, of the vampire.

If human testimony, taken with every care and solemnity, judicially, before commissions innumerable, each consisting of many members, all chosen for integrity and intelligence, and constituting reports more voluminous perhaps than exist upon any one other class of cases, is worth anything, it is difficult to deny, or even to doubt the existence of such a phenomenon as the vampire.

For my part I have heard no theory by which to explain what I myself have witnessed and experienced, other than that supplied by the ancient and well-attested belief of the country.

The next day the formal proceedings took place in the Chapel of Karnstein. The grave of the Countess Mircalla was opened; and the General and my father recognised each his perfidious and beautiful guest, in the face now disclosed to view. The features, though a hundred and fifty years had passed since her funeral, were tinted with the warmth of life. Her eyes were open; no cadaverous smell exhaled from the coffin. The two medical men, one officially present, the other on the part of the promoter of the inquiry, attested the marvellous fact, that there was a faint but appreciable respiration, and a corresponding action of the heart. The limbs were perfectly flexible, the flesh elastic; and the leaden coffin floated with blood, in which to a depth of seven inches, the body lay immersed. Here, then, were all the admitted signs and proofs of vampirism. The body, therefore, in accordance with the ancient practice, was raised, and a sharp stake driven through the heart of the vampire, who uttered a piercing shriek at the moment, in all respects such as might escape from a living person in the last agony. Then the head was struck off, and a torrent of blood flowed from the severed neck. The body and head were next placed on a pile of wood, and reduced to ashes, which were thrown upon the river and borne away, and that territory has never since been plagued by the visits of a vampire.

WILKIE COLLINS

GABRIEL'S MARRIAGE

PEOPLE who go to the Royal Academy Exhibition, and see pictures by famous artists, painted year after year in the same marked style which first made them celebrated, would be amazed indeed if they knew what a Jack-of-all-trades a poor painter must become before he can gain his daily bread. Fresh from painting a bull at a farmhouse, I set forth to copy a Holy Family, by Correggio, at a convent of nuns.

The picture which I was now commissioned to copy had been lent to the nuns by a Catholic gentleman of fortune, who prized it as the gem of his collection, and who had never before trusted it out of his own hands. My copy, when completed, was to be placed over the high altar of the convent chapel; and my work throughout its progress was to be pursued entirely in the parlour of the nunnery, and always in the watchful presence of one or other of the inmates of the house. It was only on such conditions that the owner of the Correggio was willing to trust his treasure out of his own hands, and to suffer it to be copied by a stranger. The restrictions he imposed, which I thought sufficiently absurd, and perhaps offensively suspicious as well, were communicated to me politely enough before I was allowed to undertake the commission. Unless I was inclined to submit to precautionary regulations which would affect any other artist exactly as they affected me, I was told not to think of offering to make the copy; and the nuns would then address themselves to some other person in my profession. After a day's consideration, I submitted to the restrictions, by my wife's advice, and saved the nuns the trouble of making application for a copier of Correggio in any other quarter.

I found the convent was charmingly situated in a quiet little valley in the West of England. The parlour in which I was to paint was a large, well-lighted apartment; and the village inn, about half a mile off, afforded me cheap and excellent quarters for the night. Thus far, therefore, there was nothing to complain of. As for the picture, which was the next object of interest to me, I was surprised to find that the copying of it would be by no means so difficult a task as I had anticipated. I am rather of a revolutionary spirit in matters of art, and am bold enough to think that the old masters have their faults as well as their beauties. I can give my opinion, therefore, on the Correggio at the convent independently at least. Looked at technically, the picture was a fine specimen of colouring and execution; but looked at for the higher merits of delicacy, elevation, and feeling for the subject, it deserved copying as little as the most commonplace work that any unlucky modern artist ever produced. The faces of the Holy Family not only failed to display the right purity and tenderness of expression, but absolutely failed to present any expression at all. It is flat heresy to say so; but the valuable Correggio was nevertheless emphatically, and, in so many words, a very uninteresting picture.

So much for the convent and the work that I was to do in it. My next anxiety was to see how the restrictions imposed on me were to be carried out. The first day, the Mother Superior herself mounted guard in the parlour—a stern, silent, fanatical-looking woman, who seemed determined to awe me and make me uncomfortable, and who succeeded thoroughly in the execution of her purpose. The second day, she was relieved by the officiating priest of the convent: a mild, melancholy, gentlemanlike man, with whom I got on tolerably well. The third day, I had for overlooker the portress of the house—a dirty, dismal, deaf old woman, who did nothing but knit stockings and chew orris-root. The fourth day, a middle-aged nun, whom I heard addressed as Mother Martha, occupied the post of guardian to the precious Correggio; and with her the number of overlookers terminated. She, and the portress, and the priest, and the Mother Superior, relieved each other with military regularity, until I had put the last touch to my copy. I found them ready for me every morning on entering the parlour, and I left them in the chair of observation every evening on quitting it. As for any young and beautiful nuns who might have been in the building, I never so much as set eyes on the ends of their veils. From the door to the parlour, and from the parlour to the door, comprised the whole of my experience of the inside of the convent.

The only one of my superintending companions with whom I established anything like a familiar acquaintance was Mother Martha. She had no outward attractions to recommend her; but she was simple, good-humoured, ready to gossip, and inquisitive to a perfectly incredible degree. Her whole life had been passed in the nunnery; she was thoroughly accustomed to her seclusion; thoroughly content with the monotonous round of her occupations; not at all anxious to see the world for herself; but, on the other hand, insatiably curious to know all about it from others. There was no question connected with myself, my wife, my children, my friends, my profession, my income, my travels, my favourite amusements, and even my favourite sins, which a woman could ask a man, that Mother Martha did not, in the smallest and softest of voices, ask of me. Though an intelligent, well-informed person in all that related to her own special vocation, she was a perfect child in everything else. I constantly caught myself talking to her just as I should have talked at home to one of my own little girls.

I hope no one will think that, in expressing myself thus, I am writing disparagingly of the poor nun. On two accounts, I shall always feel compassionately and gratefully towards Mother Martha. She was the only person in the convent who seemed sincerely anxious to make her presence in the parlour as agreeable to me as possible; and she good-humouredly told me the story which it is my object in these pages to introduce to the reader. In both ways I am deeply indebted to her; and I hope always to remember the obligation.

The circumstances under which the story came to be related to me may be told in very few words.

The interior of a convent parlour being a complete novelty to me, I looked around with some interest on first entering my painting-room at the nunnery. There was but little in it to excite the curiosity of anyone. The floor was covered with common matting, and the ceiling with plain whitewash. The furniture was of the simplest kind: a low chair with a praying-desk fixed to the back, and a finely-carved oak bookcase, studded all over with brass crosses, being the only useful objects that I could discern which had any conventual character about them. As for the ornaments of the room, they were entirely beyond my appreciation. I could feel no interest in the coloured prints of saints, with gold platters at the backs of their heads, that hung on the walls; and I could see nothing particularly impressive in the two plain little alabaster pots for holy water, fastened, one near the door, the other over the chimney-piece. The only object, indeed, in the whole room which in the slightest degree attracted my curiosity, was an old worm-eaten wooden cross, made in the rudest manner, hanging by itself on a slip of wall between two windows. It was so strangely rough and misshapen a thing to exhibit prominently in a neat room, that I suspected some history must be attached to it, and resolved to speak to my friend the nun about it at the earliest opportunity.

"Mother Martha," said I, taking advantage of the first pause in the succession of quaintly innocent questions which she was as usual addressing to me, "I have been looking at that rough old cross hanging between the windows, and fancying that it must surely be some curiosity——"

"Hush! hush!" exclaimed the nun, "you must not speak of that as a ' curiosity ': the Mother Superior calls it a relic."

"I beg your pardon," said I; "I ought to have chosen my expressions more carefully——"

"Not," interposed Mother Martha, nodding to show me that my apology need not be finished,—"not that it is exactly a relic in the strict Catholic sense of the word; but there were circumstances in the life of the person who made it——" Here she stopped, and looked at me doubtfully.

"Circumstances, perhaps, which it is not considered advisable to communicate to strangers," I suggested.

"Oh, no!" answered the nun, "I never heard that they were to be kept a secret. They were not told as a secret to me."

"Then you know all about them?" I asked.

"Certainly. I could tell you the whole history of the wooden cross; but it is all about Catholics, and you are a Protestant."

"That, Mother Martha, does not make it at all less interesting to me."

"Does it not, indeed?" exclaimed the nun, innocently. "What a strange man you are!—And what a remarkable religion yours must be!—What do your priests say about ours?—Are they learned men, your priests?"

I felt that my chance of hearing Mother Martha's story would be a poor one indeed, if I allowed her to begin a fresh string of questions. Accordingly, I dismissed the inquiries about the clergy of the established church with the most irreverent briefness, and recalled her attention forthwith to the subject of the wooden cross.

"Yes, yes," said the good-natured nun; "surely you shall hear all I can tell you about it; but "—she hesitated timidly —"but I must ask the Mother Superior's leave first."

Saying these words, she summoned the portress, to my great amusement, to keep guard over the inestimable Correggio in her absence; and left the room. In less than five minutes she came back, looking quite happy and important in her innocent way.

"The Mother Superior," she said, "has given me leave to tell all I know about the wooden cross. She says it may do you good, and improve your Protestant opinion of us Catholics."

I expressed myself as being both willing and anxious to profit by what I heard; and the nun began her narrative immediately.

She related it in her own simple, earnest, minute way; dwelling as long on small particulars as on important incidents; and making moral reflections for my benefit at every place where it was possible to introduce them. In spite, however, of these drawbacks in the telling of it, the story interested and impressed me in no ordinary degree; and I now purpose putting the events of it together as skilfully and strikingly as I can, in the hope that this written version of the narrative may appeal as strongly to the reader's sympathies as the spoken version did to mine.

I

ONE night, during the period of the first French Revolution, the family of François Sarzeau, a fisherman of Brittany, were all waking and watching at a late hour in their cottage on the peninsula of Quiberon. François had gone out in his boat that evening, as usual, to fish. Shortly after his departure, the wind had risen, the clouds had gathered; and the storm, which had been threatening at intervals throughout the whole day, burst forth furiously about nine o'clock. It was now eleven; and the raging of the wind over the barren, heathy peninsula still seemed to increase with each fresh blast that tore its way out upon the open sea; the crashing of the waves on the beach was awful to hear; the dreary blackness of the sky terrible to behold. The longer they listened to the storm, the oftener they looked out at it, the fainter grew the hopes which the fisherman's family still strove to cherish for the safety of François Sarzeau and of his younger son who had gone with him in the boat.

There was something impressive in the simplicity of the scene that was now passing within the cottage.

On one side of the great rugged black fireplace crouched two little girls; the younger half asleep, with her head in her sister's lap. These were the daughters of the fisherman; and opposite to them sat their eldest brother, Gabriel. His right arm had been badly wounded in a recent encounter at the national game of the *Soule*, a sport resembling our English football; but played on both sides in such savage earnest by the people of Brittany as to end always in bloodshed, often in mutilation, sometimes even in loss of life. On the same bench with Gabriel sat his betrothed wife—a girl of eighteen—clothed in the plain, almost monastic black-and-white costume of her native district. She was the daughter of a small farmer living at some little distance from the coast. Between the groups formed on either side of the fireplace, the vacant space was occupied by the foot of a truckle-bed. In this bed lay a very old man, the father of François Sarzeau. His haggard face was covered with deep wrinkles; his long white hair flowed over the coarse lump of sacking which served him for a pillow, and his light grey eyes wandered incessantly, with a strange expression of terror and suspicion, from person to person, and from object to object, in all parts of the room. Whenever the wind and sea whistled and roared at their loudest, he muttered to himself and tossed his hands fretfully on his wretched coverlid. On these occasions his eyes always fixed themselves intently on a little delf image of the Virgin placed in a niche over the fireplace. Every time they saw him look in this direction Gabriel and the young girls shuddered and crossed themselves; and even the child, who still kept awake, imitated their example. There was one bond of feeling at least between the old man and his grandchildren, which connected his age and their youth unnaturally and closely together. This feeling was reverence for the superstitions which had been handed down to them by their ancestors from centuries and centuries back, as far even as the age of the Druids. The spirit-warnings of disaster and death which the old man heard in the wailing of the wind, in the crashing of the waves, in the dreary monotonous rattling of the casement, the young man and his affianced wife and the little child who cowered by the fireside heard too. All differences in sex, in temperament, in years, superstition was strong enough to strike down to its own dread level, in the fisherman's cottage, on that stormy night.

Besides the benches by the fireside and the bed, the only piece of furniture in the room was a coarse wooden table, with a loaf of black bread, a knife, and a pitcher of cider placed on it. Old nets, coils of rope, tattered sails, hung about the walls and over the wooden partition which separated the room into two compartments. Wisps of straw and ears of barley dropped down through the rotten rafters and gaping boards that made the floor of the granary above.

These different objects, and the persons in the cottage, who composed the only surviving members of the fisherman's family, were strangely and wildly lit up by the blaze of the fire and by the still brighter glare of a resin torch stuck into a block of wood in the chimney-corner. The red and yellow light played full on the weird face of the old man as he lay opposite to it, and glanced fitfully on the figures of the young girl, Gabriel, and the two children; the great gloomy shadows rose and fell, and grew and lessened in bulk about the walls like visions of darkness, animated by a supernatural spectre-life, while the dense obscurity outside spreading before the curtainless window seemed as a wall of solid darkness that had closed in for ever around the fisherman's house. The night-scene within the cottage was almost as wild and as dreary to look upon as the night-scene without.

For a long time the different persons in the room sat together without speaking, even without looking at each other. At last, the girl turned and whispered something into Gabriel's ear.

"Perrine, what were you saying to Gabriel?" asked the child opposite, seizing the first opportunity of breaking the desolate silence—doubly desolate at her age—which was preserved by all around her.

"I was telling him," answered Perrine, simply, "that it

was time to change the bandages on his arm; and I also said to him, what I have often said before, that he must never play at that terrible game of the *Soule* again."

The old man had been looking intently at Perrine and his grandchild as they spoke. His harsh, hollow voice mingled with the last soft tones of the young girl, repeating over and over again the same terrible words: "Drowned! drowned! Son and grandson, both drowned! both drowned!"

"Hush! grandfather," said Gabriel, "we must not lose all hope for them yet. God and the Blessed Virgin protect them!" He looked at the little delf image, and crossed himself; the others imitated him, except the old man. He still tossed his hands over the coverlid, and still repeated, "Drowned! drowned!"

"Oh, that accursed *Soule*!" groaned the young man. "But for this wound I should have been with my father. The poor boy's life might at least have been saved; for we should then have left him here."

"Silence!" exclaimed the harsh voice from the bed. "The wail of dying men rises louder than the loud sea; the devil's psalm-singing roars higher than the roaring wind! Be silent, and listen! François drowned! Pierre drowned! Hark! Hark!"

A terrific blast of wind burst over the house as he spoke, shaking it to its centre, overpowering all other sounds, even to the deafening crash of the waves. The slumbering child awoke, and uttered a scream of fear. Perrine, who had been kneeling before her lover binding the fresh bandages on his wounded arm, paused in her occupation, trembling from head to foot. Gabriel looked towards the window; his experience told him what must be the hurricane fury of that blast of wind out at sea, and he sighed bitterly as he murmured to himself, "God help them both—man's help will be nothing to them now!"

"Gabriel!" cried the voice from the bed in altered tones —very faint and trembling.

He did not hear, or did not attend to the old man. He was trying to soothe and encourage the young girl at his feet.

"Don't be frightened, love," he said, kissing her very gently and tenderly on the forehead. "You are as safe here as anywhere. Was I not right in saying that it would be madness to attempt taking you back to the farmhouse this evening? You can sleep in that room, Perrine, when you are tired—you can sleep with the two girls."

" Gabriel! brother Gabriel! " cried one of the children. " Oh! look at grandfather! "

Gabriel ran to the bedside. The old man had raised himself into a sitting position; his eyes were dilated, his whole face was rigid with terror, his hands were stretched out convulsively towards his grandson. " The White Women! " he screamed. " The White Women! the grave-diggers of the drowned are out on the sea! "

The children, with cries of terror, flung themselves into Perrine's arms; even Gabriel uttered an exclamation of horror, and started back from the bedside.

Still the old man reiterated, " The White Women! The White Women! Open the door, Gabriel! look out westward, where the ebb tide has left the sand dry. You'll see them bright as lightning in the darkness, mighty as the angels in stature, sweeping like the wind over the sea, in their long white garments, with their white hair trailing far behind them! Open the door, Gabriel! You'll see them stop and hover over the place where your father and your brother have been drowned; you'll see them come on till they reach the sand; you'll see them dig in it with their naked feet, and beckon awfully to the raging sea to give up its dead. Open the door, Gabriel!—or, though it should be the death of me, I will get up and open it myself! "

Gabriel's face whitened even to his lips, but he made a sign that he would obey. It required the exertion of his whole strength to keep the door open against the wind while he looked out.

" Do you see them, grandson Gabriel? Speak the truth, and tell me if you see them," cried the old man.

" I see nothing but darkness—pitch darkness," answered Gabriel letting the door close again.

" Ah! woe! woe! " groaned his grandfather, sinking back exhausted on the pillow. " Darkness to *you*; but bright as lightning to the eyes that are allowed to see them. Drowned! drowned! Pray for their souls, Gabriel—*I* see the White Women even where I lie, and dare not pray for them. Son and grandson drowned! both drowned! "

The young man went back to Perrine and the children.

" Grandfather is very ill to-night," he whispered. " You

had better all go into the bedroom, and leave me alone to watch by him."

They rose as he spoke, crossed themselves before the image of the Virgin, kissed him one by one, and, without uttering a word, softly entered the little room on the other side of the partition. Gabriel looked at his grandfather, and saw that he lay quiet now, with his eyes closed as if he were already dropping asleep. The young man then heaped some fresh logs on the fire, and sat down by it to watch till morning.

Very dreary was the moaning of the night-storm; but it was not more dreary than the thoughts which now occupied him in his solitude—thoughts darkened and distorted by the terrible superstitions of his country and his race. Ever since the period of his mother's death he had been oppressed by the conviction that some curse hung over the family. At first they had been prosperous, they had got money, a little legacy had been left them. But this good fortune had availed only for a time; disaster on disaster strangely and suddenly succeeded. Losses, misfortunes, poverty, want itself had overwhelmed them; his father's temper had become so soured, that the oldest friends of François Sarzeau declared he was changed beyond recognition. And now, all this past misfortune—the steady, withering, household blight of many years—had ended in the last, worst misery of all in death. The fate of his father and his brother admitted no longer of a doubt; he knew it, as he listened to the storm, as he reflected on his grandfather's words, as he called to mind his own experience of the perils of the sea. And this double bereavement had fallen on him just as the time was approaching for his marriage with Perrine; just when misfortune was most ominous of evil, just when it was hardest to bear! Forebodings, which he dared not realise, began now to mingle with the bitterness of his grief, whenever his thoughts wandered from the present to the future; and as he sat by the lonely fireside, murmuring from time to time the Church prayer for the repose of the dead, he almost involuntarily mingled with it another prayer, expressed only in his own simple words, for the safety of the living—for the young girl whose love was his sole earthly treasure; for the motherless children who must now look for protection to him alone.

He had sat by the hearth a long, long time, absorbed in his thoughts, not once looking round towards the bed, when he was startled by hearing the sound of his grandfather's voice once more.

"Gabriel," whispered the old man, trembling and shrinking as he spoke, "Gabriel, do you hear a dripping of water —now slow, now quick again—on the floor at the foot of my bed?"

"I hear nothing, grandfather, but the crackling of the fire, and the roaring of the storm outside."

"Drip, drip, drip! Faster and faster; plainer and plainer. Take the torch, Gabriel; look down on the floor—look with all your eyes. Is the place wet there? Is it the rain from heaven that is dropping through the roof?"

Gabriel took the torch with trembling fingers, and knelt down on the floor to examine it closely. He started back from the place, as he saw that it was quite dry—the torch dropped upon the hearth—he fell on his knees before the statue of the Virgin and hid his face.

"Is the floor wet? Answer me, I command you—Is the floor wet?"—asked the old man quickly and breathlessly.

Gabriel rose, went back to the bedside, and whispered to him that no drop of rain had fallen inside the cottage. As he spoke the words, he saw a change pass over his grandfather's face—the sharp features seemed to wither up on a sudden; the eager expression to grow vacant and death-like in an instant. The voice too altered; it was harsh and querulous no more; its tones became strangely soft, slow, and solemn, when the old man spoke again.

"I hear it still," he said, "drip! drip! faster and plainer than ever. That ghostly dropping of water is the last and the surest of the fatal signs which have told of your father's and your brother's deaths to-night, and I know from the place where I hear it—the foot of the bed I lie on—that it is a warning to me of my own approaching end. I am called where my son and my grandson have gone before me: my weary time in this world is over at last. Don't let Perrine and the children come in here, if they should awake—they are too young to look at death."

Gabriel's blood curdled when he heard these words—when he touched his grandfather's hand, and felt the chill that it struck to his own—when he listened to the raging wind, and knew that all help was miles and miles away from the cottage. Still, in spite of the storm, the darkness, and the

distance, he thought not for a moment of neglecting the duty
that had been taught him from his childhood—the duty of
summoning the priest to the bedside of the dying. " I must
call Perrine," he said, " to watch by you while I am away."

" Stop! " cried the old man, " stop, Gabriel; I implore, I
command you not to leave me! "

" The priest, grandfather—your confession——"

" It must be made to you. In this darkness and this hurricane no man can keep the path across the heath. Gabriel! I
am dying—I should be dead before you got back. Gabriel,
for the love of the Blessed Virgin, stop here with me till I
die—my time is short—I have a terrible secret that I must tell
to somebody before I draw my last breath! Your ear to my
mouth—quick! quick! "

As he spoke the last words, a slight noise was audible on
the other side of the partition, the door half opened, and
Perrine appeared at it, looking affrightedly into the room.
The vigilant eyes of the old man—suspicious even in death—
caught sight of her directly.

" Go back! " he exclaimed faintly, before she could utter a
word, " go back—push her back, Gabriel, and nail down
the latch in the door, if she won't shut it of herself! "

" Dear Perrine! go in again," implored Gabriel. " Go in,
and keep the children from disturbing us. You will only
make him worse—you can be of no use here! "

She obeyed without speaking, and shut the door again.

While the old man clutched him by the arm, and repeated,
" Quick! quick!—your ear close to my mouth," Gabriel
heard her say to the children (who were both awake), " Let
us pray for grandfather." And as he knelt down by the
bedside, there stole on his ear the sweet, childish tones of his
little sisters, and the soft, subdued voice of the young girl
who was teaching them the prayer, mingling divinely with
the solemn wailing of wind and sea, rising in a still and awful
purity over the hoarse, gasping whispers of the dying man.

" I took an oath not to tell it, Gabriel—lean down closer!
I'm weak, and they mustn't hear a word in that room—I
took an oath not to tell it; but death is a warrant to all men
for breaking such an oath as that. Listen; don't lose a word
I'm saying! Don't look away into the room: the stain of
blood-guilt has defiled it for ever! Hush! hush! hush! Let
me speak. Now your father's dead, I can't carry the horrid

secret with me into the grave. Just remember, Gabriel—try
if you can't remember the time before I was bedridden—
ten years ago and more—it was about six weeks, you know,
before your mother's death; you can remember it by that.
You and all the children were in that room with your mother;
you were asleep, I think; it was night, not very late—only
nine o'clock. Your father and I were standing at the door,
looking out at the heath in the moonlight. He was so poor
at that time he had been obliged to sell his own boat, and none
of the neighbours would take him out fishing with them—
your father wasn't liked by any of the neighbours. Well;
we saw a stranger coming towards us; a very young man,
with a knapsack on his back. He looked like a gentleman,
though he was but poorly dressed. He came up, and told
us he was dead tired, and didn't think he could reach the
town that night, and asked if we would give him shelter till
morning. And your father said yes, if he would make no
noise, because the wife was ill, and the children were asleep.
So he said all he wanted was to go to sleep himself before the
fire. We had nothing to give him but black bread. He had
better food with him than that, and undid his knapsack to
get at it—and—and—Gabriel! I'm sinking—drink! something to drink—I'm parched with thirst."

Silent and deadly pale, Gabriel poured some of the cider
from the pitcher on the table into a drinking-cup, and gave it
to the old man. Slight as the stimulant was, its effect on him
was almost instantaneous. His dull eyes brightened a little,
and he went on in the same whispering tones as before.

" He pulled the food out of his knapsack rather in a hurry,
so that some of the other small things in it fell on the floor.
Among these was a pocket-book, which your father picked up
and gave him back; and he put it in his coat pocket—there
was a tear in one of the sides of the book, and through the
hole some banknotes bulged out. I saw them, and so did
your father (don't move away, Gabriel; keep close, there's
nothing in me to shrink from). Well, he shared his food,
like an honest fellow, with us; and then put his hand in his
pocket, and gave me four or five livres, and then lay down
before the fire to go to sleep. As he shut his eyes, your
father looked at me in a way I didn't like. He'd been behaving very bitterly and desperately towards us for some
time past; being soured about poverty, and your mother's

illness, and the constant crying out of you children for more
to eat.   So when he told me to go and buy some wood, some
bread, and some wine with the money I had got, I didn't like,
somehow, to leave him alone with the stranger; and so made
excuses, saying (which was true) that it was too late to buy
things in the village that night.   But he told me in a rage
to go and do as he bid me, and knock the people up if the
shop was shut.   So I went out, being dreadfully afraid of
your father—as indeed we all were at that time—but I
couldn't make up my mind to go far from the house: I
was afraid of something happening, though I didn't dare to
think what.   I don't know how it was, but I stole back in
about ten minutes on tiptoe to the cottage; I looked in at
the window, and saw—O God! forgive him!   O God! forgive me!—I saw—I—more to drink, Gabriel!   I can't speak
again—more to drink! "

The voices in the next room had ceased; but in the minute
of silence which now ensued, Gabriel heard his sisters kissing
Perrine, and wishing her good-night.   They were all three
trying to go asleep again.

" Gabriel, pray yourself, and teach your children after you
to pray, that your father may find forgiveness where he is
now gone.   I saw him as plainly as I now see you, kneeling
with his knife in one hand over the sleeping man.   He was
taking the little book with the notes in it out of the stranger's
pocket.   He got the book into his possession, and held it
quite still in his hand for an instant, thinking.   I believe—
oh, no! no!   I'm sure—he was repenting; I'm sure he was
going to put the book back; but just at that moment the
stranger moved, and raised one of his arms, as if he was
waking up.   Then the temptation of the devil grew too
strong for your father—I saw him lift the hand with the
knife in it—but saw nothing more.   I couldn't look in at the
window—I couldn't move away—I couldn't cry out; I stood
with my back turned towards the house, shivering all over,
though it was a warm summer-time, and hearing no cries, no
noises at all, from the room behind me.   I was too frightened
to know how long it was before the opening of the cottage
door made me turn round; but when I did, I saw your father
standing before me in the yellow moonlight, carrying in his
arms the bleeding body of the poor lad who had shared his
food with us and slept on our hearth.   Hush! hush!   Don't

groan and sob in that way! Stifle it with the bed-clothes. Hush! you'll wake them in the next room! "

" Gabriel—Gabriel! " exclaimed a voice from behind the partition. " What has happened? Gabriel! let me come out and be with you! "

" No! no! " cried the old man, collecting the last remains of his strength in the attempt to speak above the wind, which was just then howling at the loudest; " stay where you are —don't speak—don't come out—I command you! Gabriel " (his voice dropped to a faint whisper), " raise me up in bed—you must hear the whole of it, now—raise me; I'm choking so that I can hardly speak. Keep close and listen— I can't say much more. Where was I?—Ah, your father! He threatened to kill me if I didn't swear to keep it secret; and in terror of my life I swore. He made me help him to carry the body—we took it all across the heath—oh! horrible, horrible, under the bright moon—(lift me higher, Gabriel). You know the great stones yonder, set up by the heathens; you know the hollow place under the stones they call ' The Merchant's Table '—we had plenty of room to lay him in that, and hide him so; and then we ran back to the cottage. I never dared to go near the place afterwards; no, nor your father either! (Higher, Gabriel! I'm choking again.) We burnt the pocket-book and the knapsack—never knew his name—we kept the money to spend. (You're not lifting me! you're not listening close enough!) Your father said it was a legacy, when you and your mother asked about the money. (You hurt me, you shake me to pieces, Gabriel, when you sob like that.) It brought a curse on us, the money; the curse has drowned your father and your brother; the curse is killing me; but I've confessed—tell the priest I confessed before I died. Stop her; stop Perrine! I hear her getting up. Take his bones away from The Merchant's Table, and bury them, for the love of God!—and tell the priest—(lift me higher: lift me till I am on my knees)—if your father was alive, he'd murder me—but tell the priest —because of my guilty soul—to pray—and—remember The Merchant's Table—to bury, and to pray—to pray always for——"

As long as Perrine heard faintly the whispering of the old man—though no word that he said reached her ear—she shrank from opening the door in the partition. But, when the whispering sounds—which terrified her she knew not how or why—first faltered, then ceased altogether; when she heard the sobs that followed them; and when her heart told her who was weeping in the next room—then, she began to be influenced by a new feeling which was stronger than the strongest fear, and she opened the door without hesitation —almost without trembling.

The coverlid was drawn up over the old man; Gabriel was kneeling by the bedside with his face hidden. When she spoke to him, he neither answered nor looked at her. After a while, the sobs that shook him ceased; but still he never moved—except once when she touched him, and then he shuddered—shuddered under *her* hand! She called in his little sisters, and they spoke to him, and still he uttered no word in reply. They wept. One by one, often and often, they entreated him with loving words; but the stupor of grief which held him speechless and motionless was beyond the power of human tears, stronger even than the strength of human love.

It was near daybreak, and the storm was lulling—but still no change occurred at the bedside. Once or twice, as Perrine knelt near Gabriel, still vainly endeavouring to arouse him to a sense of her presence, she thought she heard the old man breathing feebly, and stretched out her hand towards the coverlid; but she could not summon courage to touch him or to look at him. This was the first time she had ever been present at a death-bed; the stillness in the room, the stupor of despair that had seized on Gabriel, so horrified her, that she was almost as helpless as the two children by her side. It was not till the dawn looked in at the cottage window—so coldly, so drearily, and yet so reassuringly—that she began to recover her self-possession at all. Then she knew that her best resource would be to summon assistance immediately from the nearest house. While she was trying to persuade the two children to remain alone in the cottage with Gabriel during her temporary absence, she was startled by the sound of footsteps outside the door. It opened; and a man appeared on the threshold, standing still there for a moment in the dim uncertain light.

She looked closer—looked intently at him. It was François Sarzeau himself!

II

THE fisherman was dripping with wet; but his face— always pale and inflexible—seemed to be but little altered in expression by the perils through which he must have passed during the night. Young Pierre lay almost insensible in his arms. In the astonishment and fright of the first moment, Perrine screamed as she recognised him.

"There! there! there!" he said, peevishly, advancing straight to the hearth with his burden; "don't make a noise. You never expected to see us alive again, I dare say. We gave ourselves up as lost, and only escaped after all by a miracle."

He laid the boy down where he could get the full warmth of the fire; and then, turning round, took a wicker-covered bottle from his pocket, and said, "If it hadn't been for the brandy——" He stopped suddenly—started—got down the bottle on the bench near him—and advanced quickly to the bedside.

Perrine looked after him as he went; and saw Gabriel, who had risen when the door was opened, moving back from the bed as François approached. The young man's face seemed to have been suddenly struck to stone—its blank, ghastly whiteness was awful to look at. He moved slowly backward and backward till he came to the cottage wall—then stood quite still, staring on his father with wild vacant eyes, moving his hands to and fro before him, muttering, but never pronouncing one audible word.

François did not appear to notice his son; he had the coverlid of the bed in his hand.

"Anything the matter here?" he asked, as he drew it down.

Still Gabriel could not speak. Perrine saw it, and answered for him.

"Gabriel is afraid that his poor grandfather is dead," she whispered, nervously.

"Dead!" There was no sorrow in the tone as he echoed the word. "Was he very bad in the night before his death happened? Did he wander in his mind? He has been rather light-headed lately."

"He was very restless, and spoke of the ghostly warnings that we all know of: he said he saw and heard many things

which told him from the other world that you and Pierre——
Gabriel! " she screamed, suddenly interrupting herself. " Look
at him!   Look at his face!   Your grandfather is not dead! "

At that moment, François was raising his father's head to
look closely at him.   A faint spasm had indeed passed over
the deathly face; the lips quivered, the jaw dropped.
François shuddered as he looked, and moved away hastily
from the bed.   At the same instant Gabriel started from the
wall: his expression altered, his pale cheeks flushed suddenly,
as he snatched up the wicker-cased bottle, and poured all the
little brandy that was left in it down his grandfather's
throat.

The effect was nearly instantaneous; the sinking vital
forces rallied desperately.   The old man's eyes opened again,
wandered round the room, then fixed themselves intently on
François, as he stood near the fire.   Trying and terrible as his
position was at that moment, Gabriel still retained self-
possession enough to whisper a few words in Perrine's ear.
" Go back again into the bedroom, and take the children with
you," he said.   " We may have something to speak about
which you had better not hear."

" Son Gabriel, your grandfather is trembling all over,"
said François.   " If he is dying at all, he is dying of cold:
help me to lift him, bed and all, to the hearth."

" No, no! don't let him touch me! " gasped the old man.
" Don't let him look at me in that way!   Don't let him
come near me, Gabriel!   Is it his ghost? or is it himself? "

As Gabriel answered, he heard a knocking at the door.   His
father opened it; and disclosed to view some people from the
neighbouring fishing village, who had come—more out of
curiosity than sympathy—to inquire whether François and
the boy Pierre had survived the night.   Without asking anyone to enter, the fisherman surlily and shortly answered the
various questions addressed to him, standing in his own doorway.   While he was thus engaged, Gabriel heard his grandfather muttering vacantly to himself—" Last night—how
about last night, grandson?   What was I talking about last
night?   Did I say your father was drowned?   Very foolish
to say he was drowned, and then see him come back alive
again!   But it wasn't that—I'm so weak in my head, I can't
remember!   What was it, Gabriel?   Something too horrible
to speak of? is that what you're whispering and trembling

about? I said nothing horrible. A crime! Bloodshed! I know nothing of any crime or bloodshed here—I must have been frightened out of my wits to talk in that way! The Merchant's Table? Only a big heap of old stones! What with the storm, and thinking I was going to die, and being afraid about your father, I must have been light-headed. Don't give another thought to that nonsense, Gabriel! I'm better now. We shall all live to laugh at poor grandfather for talking nonsense about crime and bloodshed in his sleep. Ah! poor old man—last night—light-headed—fancies and nonsense of an old man—why don't you laugh at it? I'm laughing—so light-headed—so light!——"

He stopped suddenly. A low cry, partly of terror and partly of pain, escaped him; the look of pining anxiety and imbecile cunning which had distorted his face while he had been speaking faded from it for ever. He shivered a little—breathed heavily once or twice—then became quite still.

Had he died with a falsehood on his lips?

Gabriel looked round and saw that the cottage door was closed, and that his father was standing against it. How long he had occupied that position, how many of the old man's last words he had heard, it was impossible to conjecture, but there was a lowering suspicion in his harsh face as he now looked away from the corpse to his son, which made Gabriel shudder; and the first question that he asked, on once more approaching the bedside, was expressed in tones which, quiet as they were, had a fearful meaning in them.

"What did your grandfather talk about last night?" he asked.

Gabriel did not answer. All that he had heard, all that he had seen, all the misery and horror that might yet be to come, had stunned his mind. The unspeakable dangers of his present position were too tremendous to be realised. He could only feel them vaguely in the weary torpor that oppressed his heart: while in every other direction the use of his faculties, physical and mental, seemed to have suddenly and totally abandoned him.

"Is your tongue wounded, son Gabriel, as well as your arm?" his father went on with a bitter laugh. "I come back to you, saved by a miracle; and you never speak to me. Would you rather I had died than the old man there? He can't hear you now—why shouldn't you tell me what nonsense he was talking last night?—You won't? I say you shall! " (He crossed the room and put his back to the door.) " Before either of us leave this place, you shall confess it! You know that my duty to the Church bids me to go at once and tell the priest of your grandfather's death. If I leave that duty unfulfilled, remember it is through your fault! *You* keep me here—for here I stop till I'm obeyed. Do you hear that, idiot? Speak! Speak instantly, or you shall repent it to the day of your death! I ask again—what did your grandfather say to you when he was wandering in his mind, last night? "

" He spoke of a crime committed by another, and guiltily kept secret by him," answered Gabriel, slowly and sternly. " And this morning he denied his own words with his last living breath. But last night, if he spoke the truth——"

" The truth! " echoed François. " What truth? "

He stopped, his eyes fell, then turned towards the corpse. For a few minutes he stood steadily contemplating it; breathing quickly, and drawing his hand several times across his forehead. Then he faced his son once more. In that short interval he had become in outward appearance a changed man: expression, voice, and manner, all were altered.

" Heaven forgive me! " he went on, " but I could almost laugh at myself, at this solemn moment, for having spoken and acted just now so much like a fool! Denied his words, did he? Poor old man! they say sense often comes back to light-headed people just before death; and he is a proof of it. The fact is, Gabriel, my own wits must have been a little shaken—and no wonder—by what I went through last night, and what I have come home to this morning. As if you, or anybody, could ever really give serious credit to the wandering speeches of a dying old man! (Where is Perrine? Why did you send her away?) I don't wonder at your still looking a little startled, and feeling low in your mind, and all that—for you've had a trying night of it; trying in every way. He must have been a good deal shaken in his wits last night, between fears about himself and fears about me. (To think of my being angry with you, Gabriel, for being a little alarmed—very naturally—by an old man's queer fancies!) Come out, Perrine—come out of the bedroom whenever you are tired of it: you must learn sooner or later to look at death calmly. Shake hands, Gabriel; and let us make it up, and say no more about what has passed. You won't? Still angry with me for what I said to you just now? —Ah! you'll think better about it by the time I return. Come out, Perrine, we've no secrets here."

" Where are you going to? " asked Gabriel, as he saw his father hastily open the door.

" To tell the priest that one of his congregation is dead, and to have the death registered," answered François. " These are *my* duties, and must be performed before I take any rest."

He went out hurriedly as he said these words. Gabriel almost trembled at himself, when he found that he breathed more freely, that he felt less horribly oppressed both in mind and body, the moment his father's back was turned. Fearful as thought was now, it was still a change for the better to be capable of thinking at all. Was the behaviour of his father compatible with innocence? Could the old man's confused denial of his own words in the morning and in the presence of his son, be set for one instant against the circumstantial confession that he had made during the night alone with his grandson? These were the terrible questions which Gabriel now asked himself; and which he shrank involuntarily from answering. And yet that doubt, the solution of which would, one way or the other, irrevocably affect the whole future of his life, must sooner or later be solved at any hazard!

Was there any way of setting it at rest? Yes, one way—to go instantly, while his father was absent, and examine the hollow place under The Merchant's Table. If his grandfather's confession had really been made while he was in possession of his senses, this place (which Gabriel knew to be covered in from wind and weather) had never been visited since the commission of the crime by the perpetrator, or by his unwilling accomplice: though time had destroyed all besides, the hair and the bones of the victim would still be left to bear witness to the truth—if truth had indeed been spoken. As this conviction grew on him, the young man's cheek paled; and he stopped irresolute half-way between the hearth and the door. Then he looked down doubtfully at the corpse on the bed; and then there came upon him suddenly a revulsion of feeling. A wild feverish impatience to know the worst without another instant of delay possessed him. Only telling

Perrine that he should be back soon, and that she must watch by the dead in his absence, he left the cottage at once, without waiting to hear her reply, even without looking back as he closed the door behind him.

There were two tracks to The Merchant's Table. One, the longer of the two, by the coast cliffs; the other across the heath. But this latter path was also, for some little distance, the path which led to the village and the church. He was afraid of attracting his father's attention here, so he took the direction of the coast. At one spot the track trended inland, winding round some of the many Druid monuments scattered over the country. This place was on high ground, and commanded a view, at no great distance, of the path leading to the village, just where it branched off from the heathy ridge which ran in the direction of The Merchant's Table. Here Gabriel descried the figure of a man standing with his back towards the coast.

This figure was too far off to be identified with absolute certainty, but it looked like, and might well be, François Sarzeau. Whoever he was, the man was evidently uncertain which way he should proceed. When he moved forward, it was first to advance several paces towards The Merchant's Table—then he went back again towards the distant cottages and the church. Twice he hesitated thus: the second time pausing long before he appeared finally to take the way that led to the village.

Leaving the post of observation among the stones, at which he had instinctively halted for some minutes past, Gabriel now proceeded on his own path. Could this man really be his father? And if it were so, why did François Sarzeau only determine to go to the village where his business lay, after having twice vainly attempted to persevere in taking the exactly opposite direction of The Merchant's Table? Did he really desire to go there? Had he heard the name mentioned, when the old man referred to it in his dying words? And had he failed to summon courage enough to make all safe by removing——? This last question was too horrible to be pursued: Gabriel stifled it affrightedly in his own heart as he went on.

He reached the great Druid monument without meeting a living soul on his way. The sun was rising, and the mighty storm-clouds of the night were parting asunder wildly over the whole eastward horizon. The waves still leapt and foamed gloriously: but the gale had sunk to a keen, fresh breeze. As Gabriel looked up, and saw how brightly the promise of a lovely day was written in the heavens, he trembled as he thought of the search which he was now about to make. The sight of the fair, fresh sunrise jarred horribly with the suspicions of committed murder that were rankling foully in his heart. But he knew that his errand must be performed, and he nerved himself to go through with it; for he dared not return to the cottage until the mystery had been cleared up at once and for ever.

The Merchant's Table was formed by two huge stones resting horizontally on three others. In the troubled times of more than half a century ago, regular tourists were unknown among the Druid monuments of Brittany; and the entrance to the hollow place under the stones—since often visited by strangers—was at this time nearly choked up by brambles and weeds. Gabriel's first look at this tangled nook of briars convinced him that the place had not been entered —perhaps for years—by any living being. Without allowing himself to hesitate (for he felt that the slightest delay might be fatal to his resolution), he passed as gently as possible through the brambles and knelt down at the low, dusky, irregular entrance of the hollow place under the stones.

His heart throbbed violently, his breath almost failed him; but he forced himself to crawl a few feet into the cavity, and then groped with his hand on the ground about him.

He touched something! Something which it made his flesh creep to handle; something which he would fain have dropped, but which he grasped tight in spite of himself. He drew back into the outer air and sunshine. Was it a human bone? No! he had been the dupe of his own morbid terror —he had only taken up a fragment of dried wood!

Feeling shame at such self-deception as this, he was about to throw the wood from him before he re-entered the place, when another idea occurred to him.

Though it was dimly lighted through one or two chinks in the stones, the far part of the interior of the cavity was still too dusky to admit of perfect examination by the eye, even on a bright sunshiny morning. Observing this, he took out the tinder-box and matches, which, like the other inhabitants of the district, he always carried about with him for the purpose of lighting his pipe, determining to use the piece of wood as a torch which might illuminate the darkest corner of the place when he next entered it. Fortunately the wood had remained so long and had been preserved so dry in its sheltered position, that it caught fire almost as easily as a piece of paper. The moment it was fairly aflame Gabriel went into the cavity, penetrating at once—this time—to its farthest extremity.

He remained among the stones long enough for the wood to burn down nearly to his hand. When he came out, and flung the burning fragment from him, his face was flushed deeply, his eyes sparkled. He leaped carelessly on to the heath, over the bushes through which he had threaded his way so warily but a few minutes before, exclaiming, " I may marry Perrine with a clear conscience now—I am the son of as honest a man as there is in Brittany! "

He had closely examined the cavity in every corner, and not the slightest sign that any dead body had ever been laid there was visible in the hollow place under The Merchant's Table.

III

" I MAY marry Perrine with a clear conscience now! "
There are some parts of the world where it would be drawing no natural picture of human nature to represent a son as believing conscientiously that an offence against life and the laws of hospitality, secretly committed by his father, rendered him, though innocent of all participation in it, unworthy to fulfil his engagement with his affianced wife. Among the simple inhabitants of Gabriel's province, however, such acuteness of conscientious sensibility as this was no extraordinary exception to all general rules. Ignorant and superstitious as they might be, the people of Brittany practised the duties of hospitality as devoutly as they practised the duties of the national religion. The presence of the stranger-guest, rich or poor, was a sacred presence at their hearths. His safety was their especial charge—his property their especial responsibility. They might be half-starved, but they were ready to share the last crust with him, nevertheless, as they would share it with their own children.

Any outrage on the virtue of hospitality, thus born and

bred in the people, was viewed by them with universal disgust, and punished with universal execration. This ignominy was uppermost in Gabriel's thoughts by the side of his grandfather's bed; the dread of his worst dishonour, which there was no wiping out, held him speechless before Perrine, shamed and horrified him so that he felt unworthy to look her in the face; and when the result of his search at The Merchant's Table proved the absence there of all evidence of the crime spoken of by the old man, the blessed relief, the absorbing triumph of that discovery, was expressed entirely in the one thought which had prompted his first joyful words:—He could marry Perrine with a clear conscience, for he was the son of an honest man!

When he returned to the cottage, François had not come back. Perrine was astonished at the change in Gabriel's manner; even Pierre and the children remarked it. Rest and warmth had by this time so far recovered the younger brother, that he was able to give some account of the perilous adventures of the night at sea. They were still listening to the boy's narrative when François at last returned. It was now Gabriel who held out his hand, and made the first advances towards reconciliation.

To his utter amazement, his father recoiled from him. The variable temper of François had evidently changed completely during his absence at the village. A settled scowl of distrust darkened his face as he looked at his son.

"I never shake hands with people who have once doubted me," he exclaimed loudly and irritably; "for I always doubt them for ever after. You are a bad son! You have suspected your father of some infamy that you dare not openly charge him with, on no other testimony than the rambling nonsense of a half-witted, dying old man. Don't speak to me! I won't hear you! An innocent man and a spy are bad company. Go and denounce me, you Judas in disguise! I don't care for your secret or for you. What's that girl Perrine doing here still? Why hasn't she gone home long ago? The priest's coming; we don't want strangers in the house of death. Take her back to the farmhouse, and stop there with her, if you like: nobody wants you here!"

There was something in the manner and look of the speaker as he uttered these words, so strange, so sinister, so indescribably suggestive of his meaning much more than he said, that Gabriel felt his heart sink within him instantly; and almost at the same moment this fearful question forced itself irresistibly on his mind—might not his father have followed him to The Merchant's Table?

Even if he had been desired to speak, he could not have spoken now, while that question and the suspicion that it brought with it were utterly destroying all the reassuring hopes and convictions of the morning. The mental suffering produced by the sudden change from pleasure to pain in all his thoughts, reacted on him physically. He felt as if he were stifling in the air of the cottage, in the presence of his father; and when Perrine hurried on her walking attire, and with a face which alternately flushed and turned pale with every moment, approached the door, he went out with her as hastily as if he had been flying from his home. Never had the fresh air and the free daylight felt like heavenly and guardian influences to him until now!

He could comfort Perrine under his father's harshness, he could assure her of his own affection, which no earthly influence could change, while they walked together towards the farmhouse; but he could do no more. He durst not confide to her the subject that was uppermost in his mind: of all human beings she was the last to whom he could reveal the terrible secret that was festering at his heart. As soon as they got within sight of the farmhouse, Gabriel stopped; and, promising to see her again soon, took leave of Perrine with assumed ease in his manner and with real despair in his heart. Whatever the poor girl might think of it, he felt, at that moment, that he had not courage to face her father, and hear him talk happily and pleasantly, as his custom was, of Perrine's approaching marriage.

Left to himself, Gabriel wandered hither and thither over the open heath, neither knowing nor caring in what direction he turned his steps. The doubts about his father's innocence which had been dissipated by his visit to The Merchant's Table, that father's own language and manner had now revived—had even confirmed, though he dared not yet acknowledge so much to himself. It was terrible enough to be obliged to admit that the result of his morning's search was, after all, not conclusive—that the mystery was in very truth not yet cleared up. The violence of his father's last words of distrust; the extraordinary and indescribable changes in his father's manner while uttering them—what did these things mean? Guilt or innocence? Again, was it any longer reasonable to doubt the death-bed confession made by his grandfather? Was it not, on the contrary, far more probable that the old man's denial in the morning of his own words at night had been made under the influence of a panic terror, when his moral consciousness was bewildered, and his intellectual faculties were sinking? The longer Gabriel thought of these questions, the less competent—possibly also the less willing—he felt to answer them. Should he seek advice from others wiser than he? No: not while the thousandth part of a chance remained that his father was innocent.

This thought was still in his mind, when he found himself once more in sight of his home. He was still hesitating near the door, when he saw it opened cautiously. His brother Pierre looked out, and then came running towards him. "Come in, Gabriel; oh, do come in! " said the boy earnestly. "We are afraid to be alone with father. He's been beating us for talking of you."

Gabriel went in. His father looked up from the hearth where he was sitting, muttered the word "Spy!" and made a gesture of contempt—but did not address a word directly to his son. The hours passed on in silence; afternoon waned into evening, and evening into night; and still he never spoke to any of his children. Soon after it was dark, he went out, and took his net with him—saying that it was better to be alone on the sea than in the house with a spy.

When he returned the next morning there was no change in him. Days passed—weeks, months even elapsed, and still, though his manner insensibly became what it used to be towards his other children, it never altered towards his eldest son. At the rare periods when they now met, except when absolutely obliged to speak, he preserved total silence in his intercourse with Gabriel. He would never take Gabriel out with him in the boat; he would never sit alone with Gabriel in the house; he would never eat a meal with Gabriel; he would never let the other children talk to him about Gabriel; and he would never hear a word in expostulation, a word in reference to anything his dead father had said or done on the night of the storm, from Gabriel himself.

The young man pined and changed, so that even Perrine hardly knew him again, under this cruel system of domestic excommunication; under the wearing influence of the one un-changing doubt which never left him; and, more than all, under the incessant reproaches of his own conscience, aroused by the sense that he was evading a responsibility which it was his solemn, his immediate duty to undertake. But no sting of conscience, no ill-treatment at home, and no self-reproaches for failing in his duty of confession as a good Catholic, were powerful enough in their influence over Gabriel to make him disclose the secret, under the oppression of which his very life was wasting away. He knew that if he once revealed it, whether his father was ultimately proved to be guilty or innocent, there would remain a slur and a suspicion on the family, and on Perrine besides, from her approaching con-nexion with it, which in their time and in their generation could never be removed. The reproach of the world is terrible even in the crowded city, where many of the dwellers in our abiding-place are strangers to us—but it is far more terrible in the country, where none near us are strangers, where all talk of us and know of us, where nothing intervenes between us and the tyranny of the evil tongue. Gabriel had not courage to face this, and dare the fearful chance of life-long ignominy—no, not even to serve the sacred interests of justice, of atonement, and of truth.

IV

WHILE Gabriel still remained prostrated under the afflic-tion that was wasting his energies of body and mind, Brittany was visited by a great public calamity, in which all private misfortunes were overwhelmed for a while.

It was now the time when the ever-gathering storm of the French Revolution had risen to its hurricane climax. Those chiefs of the new republic were in power, whose last, worse madness it was to decree the extinction of religion and the overthrow of everything that outwardly symbolized it throughout the whole of the country that they governed. Already this decree had been executed to the letter in and around Paris; and now the soldiers of the republic were on their way to Brittany, headed by commanders whose com-mission was to root out the Christian religion in the last and the surest of the strongholds still left to it in France.

These men began their work in a spirit worthy of the worst of their superiors who had sent them to do it. They gutted churches, they demolished chapels, they overthrew roadside crosses wherever they found them. The terrible guillotine devoured human lives in the villages of Brittany as it had devoured them in the streets of Paris; the musket and the sword, in highway and by-way, wreaked havoc on the people —even on women and children kneeling in the act of prayer; the priests were tracked night and day from one hiding-place, where they still offered up worship, to another, and were killed as soon as overtaken—every atrocity was committed in every district; but the Christian religion still spread wider than the widest bloodshed; still sprang up with ever-renewed vitality from under the very feet of the men whose vain fury was powerless to trample it down. Everywhere the people remained true to their faith; everywhere the priests stood firm by them in their sorest need. The executioners of the republic had been sent to make Brittany a country of apostates; they did their worst, and left it a country of martyrs.

One evening, while this frightful persecution was still raging, Gabriel happened to be detained unusually late at the cottage of Perrine's father. He had lately spent much of his time at the farmhouse; it was his only refuge now from that place of suffering, of silence, and of secret shame, which he had once called home! Just as he had taken leave of Perrine for the night, and was about to open the farmhouse door, her father stopped him, and pointed to a chair in the chimney-corner. "Leave us alone, my dear," said the old man to his daughter; "I want to speak to Gabriel. You can go to your mother in the next room."

The words which Père Bonan—as he was called by the neighbours—had now to say in private, were destined to lead to very unexpected events. After referring to the alteration which had appeared of late in Gabriel's manner, the old man began by asking him, sorrowfully but not suspiciously, whether he still preserved his old affection for Perrine. On receiving an eager answer in the affirmative, Père Bonan then referred to the persecution still raging through the country, and to the consequent possibility that he, like others of his countrymen, might yet be called to suffer, and perhaps to die, for the cause of his religion. If this last act of self-sacrifice were required of him, Perrine would be left unprotected, unless her affianced husband performed his promise to her, and assumed, without delay, the position of her lawful guardian. "Let me know that you will do this," concluded the old man. "I shall be resigned to all that may be required of me, if I can only know that I shall not die leaving Perrine unprotected." Gabriel gave the promise—gave it with his whole heart. As he took leave of Père Bonan, the old man said to him:

"Come here to-morrow; I shall know more then than I know now—I shall be able to fix with certainty the day for the fulfilment of your engagement with Perrine."

Why did Gabriel hesitate at the farmhouse door, looking back on Père Bonan as though he would fain say something, and yet not speaking a word? Why, after he had gone out and had walked onward several paces, did he suddenly stop, return quickly to the farmhouse, stand irresolute before the gate, and then retrace his steps, sighing heavily as he went, but never pausing again on his homeward way? Because the torment of his horrible secret had grown harder to bear than ever, since he had given the promise that had been required of him. Because, while a strong impulse moved him frankly to lay bare his hidden dread and doubt to the father whose beloved daughter was soon to be his wife, there was a yet stronger passive influence which paralysed on his lips the terrible confession that he knew not whether he was the son of an honest man, or the son of an assassin and a robber. Made desperate by his situation, he determined, while he hastened homeward, to risk the worst, and ask that fatal question of his father in plain words. But this supreme trial for parent and child was not to be. When he entered the cottage François was absent. He had told the younger children that he should not be home again before noon on the next day.

Early in the morning Gabriel repaired to the farmhouse, as he had been bidden. Influenced by his love for Perrine, blindly confiding in the faint hope (which, in despite of heart and conscience, he still forced himself to cherish), that his father might be innocent, he now preserved the appearance at least of perfect calmness. "If I tell my secret to Perrine's father, I risk disturbing in him that confidence in the future safety of his child for which I am his present and only warrant." Something like this thought was in Gabriel's mind as he took the hand of Père Bonan, and waited anxiously to hear what was required of him on that day.

"We have a short respite from danger, Gabriel," said the old man. "News has come to me that the spoilers of our churches and the murderers of our congregations have been stopped on their way hitherwards by tidings which have reached them from another district. This interval of peace and safety will be a short one—we must take advantage of it while it is yet ours. My name is among the names on the list of the denounced. If the soldiers of the republic find me here—but we will say nothing more of this: it is of Perrine and of you that I must now speak. On this very evening your marriage may be solemnized with all the wonted rites of our holy religion, and the blessing may be pronounced over you by the lips of a priest. This evening, therefore, Gabriel, you must become the husband and the protector of Perrine. Listen to me attentively, and I will tell you how."

This was the substance of what Gabriel now heard from Père Bonan:

Not very long before the persecutions broke out in Brittany, a priest, known generally by the name of Father Paul, was appointed to a curacy in one of the northern districts of the province. He fulfilled all the duties of his station in such a manner as to win the confidence and affection of every member of his congregation, and was often spoken of with respect, even in parts of the country distant from the scene of his labours. It was not, however, until the troubles broke out, and the destruction and bloodshed began, that he became renowned far and wide, from one end of Brittany to another. From the date of the very first persecutions the name of Father Paul was a rallying cry of the hunted peasantry; he was their great encouragement under oppression, their example in danger, their last and only consoler in the hour of death. Wherever havoc and ruin raged most fiercely, wherever the pursuit was the hottest and the slaughter most cruel, there the intrepid priest was sure to be seen pursuing his sacred duties in defiance of every peril. His hair-breadth escapes from death; his extraordinary reappearances in parts of the country where no one ever expected to see him again, were regarded by the poorer classes with superstitious awe. Wherever Father Paul appeared, with his black dress, his calm face, and the ivory crucifix which he always carried in his hand, the people reverenced him as more than mortal; and grew at last to believe that, single-handed, he would successfully defend his religion against the armies of the republic. But their simple confidence in his powers of resistance was soon destined to be shaken. Fresh reinforcements arrived in Brittany, and overran the whole province from one end to the other. One morning, after celebrating service in a dismantled church, and after narrowly escaping with his life from those who pursued him, the priest disappeared. Secret inquiries were made after him in all directions; but he was heard of no more.

Many weary days had passed, and the dispirited peasantry had already mourned him as dead, when some fishermen on the northern coast observed a ship of light burden in the offing, making signals to the shore. They put off to her in their boats; and on reaching the deck saw standing before them the well-remembered figure of Father Paul.

The priest had returned to his congregations; and had founded the new altar that they were to worship at on the deck of the ship! Razed from the face of the earth, their church had not been destroyed—for Father Paul and the priests who acted with him had given that church a refuge on the sea. Henceforth, their children could be baptized, their sons and daughters could still be married, the burial of their dead could still be solemnized, under the sanction of the old religion for which, not vainly, they had suffered so patiently and so long.

Throughout the remaining time of trouble, the services were uninterrupted on board the ship. A code of signals was established by which those on shore were always enabled to direct their brethren at sea towards such parts of the coast as happened to be uninfested by the enemies of their worship. On the morning of Gabriel's visit to the farmhouse, these signals had shaped the course of the ship towards the extremity of the peninsula of Quiberon. The people of the district were all prepared to expect the appearance of the vessel some time in the evening, and had their boats ready at a moment's notice to put off and attend the service. At the conclusion of this service Père Bonan had arranged that the marriage of his daughter and Gabriel was to take place.

They waited for evening at the farmhouse. A little before sunset the ship was signalled as in sight; and then Père Bonan and his wife, followed by Gabriel and Perrine, set forth over the heath to the beach. With the solitary exception of François Sarzeau, the whole population of the neighbourhood was already assembled there; Gabriel's brother and sisters being among the number.

It was the calmest evening that had been known for months. There was not a cloud in the lustrous sky—not a ripple on the still surface of the sea. The smallest children were suffered by their mothers to stray down on the beach as they pleased; for the waves of the great ocean slept as tenderly and noiselessly on their sandy bed as if they had been changed into the waters of an inland lake. Slow, almost imperceptible, was the approach of the ship—there was hardly a breath of wind to carry her on—she was just drifting gently with the landward set of the tide at that hour, while her sails hung idly against the masts. Long after the sun had gone down, the congregation still waited and watched on the beach. The moon and stars were arrayed in their glory of the night, before the ship dropped anchor. Then the muffled tolling of a bell came solemnly across the quiet waters; and then, from every creek along the shore, as far as the eye could reach, the black forms of the fishermen's boats shot out swift and stealthy into the shining sea.

By the time the boats had arrived alongside of the ship, the lamp had been kindled before the altar, and its flame was gleaming red and dull in the radiant moonlight. Two of the priests on board were clothed in their robes of office, and were waiting in their appointed places to begin the service. But there was a third, dressed only in the ordinary attire of his calling, who mingled with the congregation, and spoke a few words to each of the persons composing it, as, one by one, they mounted the sides of the ship. Those who had never seen him before knew by the famous ivory crucifix in his hand that the priest who received them was Father Paul. Gabriel looked at this man, whom he now beheld for the first time, with a mixture of astonishment and awe; for he saw that the renowned chief of the Christians of Brittany was, to all appearance, but little older than himself.

The expression on the pale calm face of the priest was so gentle and kind, that children just able to walk tottered up to him, and held familiarly by the skirts of his black gown, whenever his clear blue eyes rested on theirs, while he beckoned them to his side. No one would ever have guessed from the countenance of Father Paul what deadly perils he had confronted, but for the scar of a sabre-wound, as yet hardly healed, which ran across his forehead. That wound had been dealt while he was kneeling before the altar, in the last church in Brittany which had escaped spoliation. He would have died where he knelt, but for the peasants who were praying with him, and who, unarmed as they were, threw themselves like tigers on the soldiery, and at awful sacrifice of their own lives saved the life of their priest. There was not a man now on board the ship who would have hesitated, had the occasion called for it again, to have rescued him in the same way.

The service began. Since the days when the primitive Christians worshipped amid the caverns of the earth, can any service be imagined nobler in itself, or sublimer in the circumstances surrounding it, than that which was now offered up? Here was no artificial pomp, no gaudy profusion of ornament, no attendant grandeur of man's creation. All around this church spread the hushed and awful majesty of the tranquil sea. The roof of this cathedral was the immeasurable heaven, the pure moon its one great light, the countless glories of the stars its only adornment. Here were no hired singers or rich priest-princes; no curious sight-seers, or careless lovers of sweet sounds. This congregation and they who had gathered it together were all poor alike, all persecuted alike, all worshipping alike, to the overthrow of their worldly interests, and at the imminent peril of their lives. How brightly and tenderly the moonlight shone upon the altar and the people before it!—how solemnly and divinely the deep harmonies, as they chanted the penitential Psalms, mingled with the hoarse singing of the freshening night-breeze in the rigging of the ship! how sweetly the still rushing murmur of many voices, as they uttered the responses together, now died away and now rose again softly into the mysterious night!

Of all the members of the congregation—young or old— there was but one over whom that impressive service exercised no influence of consolation or of peace: that one was Gabriel. Often, throughout the day, his reproaching conscience had spoken within him again and again. Often, when he joined the little assembly on the beach, he turned away his face in secret shame and apprehension from Perrine and her father. Vainly, after gaining the deck of the ship, did he try to meet the eye of Father Paul as frankly, as readily, and as affectionately as others met it. The burden of concealment seemed too heavy to be borne in the presence of the priest—and yet, torment as it was, he still bore it! But when he knelt with the rest of the congregation and saw Perrine kneeling by his side—when he felt the calmness of the solemn night and the still sea filling his heart—when the sounds of the first prayers spoke with a dread spiritual language of their own to his soul —then, the remembrance of the confession which he had neglected, and the terror of receiving unprepared the sacrament which he knew would be offered to him—grew too vivid to be endured: the sense that he merited no longer, though once worthy of it, the confidence in his perfect truth and candour placed in him by the woman with whom he was soon to stand before the altar, overwhelmed him with shame: the mere act of kneeling among that congregation, the passive accomplice by his silence and secrecy, for aught he knew to the contrary, of a crime which it was his bounden duty to denounce, appalled him as if he had already committed sacrilege that could never be forgiven. Tears flowed down his cheeks, though he strove to repress them: sobs burst from him, though he tried to stifle them. He knew that others besides Perrine were looking at him in astonishment and alarm; that he could neither control himself, nor move to leave his place, nor raise his eyes even—until suddenly he felt a hand laid on his shoulder. That touch, slight as it was, ran through him instantly. He looked up, and saw Father Paul standing by his side.

Beckoning him to follow, and signing to the congregation not to suspend their devotions, he led Gabriel out of the assembly—then paused for a moment, reflecting—then beckoning him again, took him into the cabin of the ship, and closed the door carefully.

" You have something on your mind," he said, simply and quietly, taking the young man by the hand. " I may be able to relieve you, if you tell me what it is."

As Gabriel heard these gentle words, and saw, by the light of a lamp which burned before a cross fixed against the wall, the sad kindness of expression with which the priest was regarding him, the oppression that had lain so long on his heart seemed to leave it in an instant. The haunting fear of ever divulging his fatal suspicions and his fatal secret had vanished, as it were, at the touch of Father Paul's hand. For the first time he now repeated to another ear—the sounds of prayer and praise rising grandly the while from the congregation above—his grandfather's death-bed confession, word for word almost, as he had heard it in the cottage on the night of the storm.

Once, and once only, did Father Paul interrupt the narrative, which in whispers was addressed to him. Gabriel had hardly repeated the first two or three sentences of his grandfather's confession, when the priest, in quick altered tones, abruptly asked him his name and place of abode.

As the question was answered, Father Paul's calm face became suddenly agitated; but the next moment, resolutely resuming his self-possession, he bowed his head, as a sign that Gabriel was to continue; clasped his trembling hands, and raising them as if in silent prayer, fixed his eyes intently on the cross. He never looked away from it while the terrible narrative proceeded. But when Gabriel described his search at The Merchant's Table; and, referring to his father's behaviour since that time, appealed to the priest to know whether he might, even yet, in defiance of appearances, be still filially justified in doubting whether the crime had been really perpetrated—then Father Paul moved near to him once more, and spoke again.

"Compose yourself, and look at me," he said, with his former sad kindness of voice and manner. "I can end your doubts for ever. Gabriel, your father was guilty in intention and in act; but the victim of his crime still lives. I can prove it."

Gabriel's heart beat wildly; a deadly coldness crept over him as he saw Father Paul loosen the fastening of his cassock round the throat.

At that instant the chanting of the congregation above ceased; and then, the sudden and awful stillness was deepened rather than interrupted by the faint sound of one voice praying. Slowly and with trembling fingers the priest removed the band round his neck—paused a little—sighed heavily—and pointed to a scar which was now plainly visible on one side of his throat. He said something at the same time; but the bell above tolled while he spoke. It was the signal of the elevation of the Host. Gabriel felt an arm passed round him, guiding him to his knees, and sustaining him from sinking to the floor. For one moment longer he was conscious that the bell had stopped, that there was dead silence, that Father Paul was kneeling by him beneath the cross, with bowed head—then all objects around vanished; and he saw and knew nothing more.

When he recovered his senses, he was still in the cabin—the man whose life his father had attempted was bending over him and sprinkling water on his face—and the clear voices of the women and children of the congregation were joining the voices of the men in singing the *Agnus Dei*.

"Look up at me without fear, Gabriel," said the priest. "I desire not to avenge injuries: I visit not the sins of the father on the child. Look up, and listen! I have strange things to speak of: and I have a sacred mission to fulfil before the morning, in which you must be my guide."

Gabriel attempted to kneel and kiss his hand, but Father Paul stopped him, and said, pointing to the cross: "Kneel to that—not to me: not to your fellow-mortal, and your friend—for I will be your friend, Gabriel; believing that God's mercy has ordered it so. And now listen to me," he proceeded, with a brotherly tenderness in his manner which went to Gabriel's heart. "The service is nearly ended. What I have to tell you must be told at once; the errand on which you will guide me must be performed before to-morrow dawns. Sit here near me; and attend to what I now say!"

Gabriel obeyed. Father Paul then proceeded thus:

"I believe the confession made to you by your grandfather to have been true in every particular. On the evening to which he referred you, I approached your cottage, as he said, for the purpose of asking shelter for the night. At that period I had been studying hard to qualify myself for the holy calling which I now pursue; and, on the completion of my studies, had indulged in the recreation of a tour on foot through Brittany, by way of innocently and agreeably occupying the leisure time then at my disposal, before I entered the priesthood. When I accosted your father I had lost my way, had been walking for many hours, and was glad of any rest that I could get for the night. It is unnecessary to pain you now, by reference to the events which followed my

entrance under your father's roof. I remember nothing that
happened from the time when I lay down to sleep before the
fire, until the time when I recovered my senses at the place
which you call The Merchant's Table. My first sensation was
that of being moved into the cold air: when I opened my eyes
I saw the great Druid stones rising close above me, and two
men on either side of me rifling my pockets. They found
nothing valuable there, and were about to leave me where I
lay, when I gathered strength enough to appeal to their
mercy through their cupidity. Money was not scarce with
me then, and I was able to offer them a rich reward (which
they ultimately received as I had promised) if they would
take me to any place where I could get shelter and medical
help. I suppose they inferred by my language and accent—
perhaps also by the linen I wore, which they examined closely
—that I belonged to the higher ranks of the community, in
spite of the plainness of my outer garments; and might therefore be in a position to make good my promise to them. I
heard one say to the other, ' Let us risk it '; and then they
took me in their arms, carried me down to a boat on the
beach, and rowed to a vessel in the offing. The next day they
disembarked me at Paimbœuf, where I got the assistance
which I so much needed. I learnt through the confidence
they were obliged to place in me, in order to give me the
means of sending them their promised reward, that these
men were smugglers, and that they were in the habit of using
the cavity in which I had been laid as a place of concealment
for goods, and for letters of advice to their accomplices. This
accounted for their finding me. As to my wound, I was
informed by the surgeon who attended me, that it had missed
being inflicted in a mortal part by less than a quarter of an
inch, and that, as it was, nothing but the action of the night
air in coagulating the blood over the place had, in the first
instance, saved my life. To be brief, I recovered after a long
illness, returned to Paris, and was called to the priesthood.
The will of my superiors obliged me to perform the first duties
of my vocation in the great city; but my own wish was to be
appointed to a cure of souls in your province, Gabriel. Can
you imagine why? "

The answer to this question was in Gabriel's heart; but he
was still too deeply awed and affected by what he had heard
to give it utterance.

"I must tell you then what my motive was," said Father Paul. "You must know first that I uniformly abstained from disclosing to anyone where and by whom my life had been attempted. I kept this a secret from the men who rescued me—from the surgeon—from my own friends even. My reason for such a proceeding was, I would fain believe, a Christian reason. I hope I had always felt a sincere and humble desire to prove myself, by the help of God, worthy of the sacred vocation to which I was destined. But my miraculous escape from death made an impression on my mind, which gave me another and an infinitely higher view of this vocation—the view which I have since striven, and shall always strive for the future, to maintain. As I lay, during the first days of my recovery, examining my own heart, and considering in what manner it would be my duty to act towards your father when I was restored to health, a thought came into my mind which calmed, comforted, and resolved all my doubts. I said within myself: ' In a few months more I shall be called to be one of the chosen ministers of God. If I am worthy of my vocation, my first desire towards this man who has attempted to take my life, should be, not to know that human justice has overtaken him, but to know that he has truly and religiously repented and made atonement for his guilt. To such repentance and atonement let it be my duty to call him; if he reject that appeal, and be hardened only the more against me because I have forgiven him my injuries, then it will be time enough to denounce him for his crimes to his fellow-men. Surely it must be well for me here and hereafter, if I begin my career in the holy priesthood by helping to save from hell the soul of the man who, of all others, has most cruelly wronged me.' It was for this reason, Gabriel—it was because I desired to go straightway to your father's cottage, and reclaim him after he had believed me to be dead—that I kept the secret and entreated of my superiors that I might be sent to Brittany. But this, as I have said, was not to be at first, and when my desire was granted, my place was assigned me in a far district. The persecution under which we still suffer broke out; the designs of my life were changed; my own will became no longer mine to guide me. But, through sorrow and suffering, and danger and bloodshed, I am now led after many days to the execution of that first purpose which I formed on entering the priesthood.

Gabriel! when the service is over, and the congregation are dispersed, you must guide me to the door of your father's cottage."

He held up his hand, in sign of silence, as Gabriel was about to answer. Just then, the officiating priests above were pronouncing the final benediction. When it was over, Father Paul opened the cabin door. As he ascended the steps, followed by Gabriel, Père Bonan met them. The old man looked doubtfully and searchingly on his future son-in-law, as he respectfully whispered a few words in the ear of the priest. Father Paul listened attentively, answered in a whisper, and then turned to Gabriel, first begging the few people near them to withdraw a little.

"I have been asked whether there is any impediment to your marriage," he said, "and have answered that there is none. What you have said to me has been said in confession, and is a secret between us two. Remember that; and forget not, at the same time, the service which I shall require of you to-night, after the marriage ceremony is over. Where is Perrine Bonan?" he added, aloud, looking round him. Perrine came forward. Father Paul took her hand, and placed it in Gabriel's. "Lead her to the altar steps," he said, "and wait there for me."

It was more than an hour later; the boats had left the ship's side; the congregation had dispersed over the face of the country—but still the vessel remained at anchor. Those who were left in her watched the land more anxiously than usual; for they knew that Father Paul had risked meeting the soldiers of the republic by trusting himself on shore. A boat was awaiting his return on the beach; half of the crew, armed, being posted as scouts in various directions on the high land of the heath. They would have followed and guarded the priest to the place of his destination; but he forbade it; and, leaving them abruptly, walked swiftly onward with one young man only for his companion.

Gabriel had committed his brother and his sisters to the charge of Perrine. They were to go to the farmhouse that night with his newly married wife and her father and mother. Father Paul had desired that this might be done. When Gabriel and he were left alone to follow the path which led to the fisherman's cottage, the priest never spoke while they walked on—never looked aside either to the right or the left

—always held his ivory crucifix clasped to his breast. They
arrived at the door.

"Knock," whispered Father Paul to Gabriel, "and then
wait here with me."

The door was opened. On a lovely moonlight night François Sarzeau had stood on that threshold, years since, with a
bleeding body in his arms. On a lovely moonlight night, he
now stood there again, confronting the very man whose life
he had attempted, and knowing him not.

Father Paul advanced a few paces, so that the moonlight
fell fuller on his features, and removed his hat.

François Sarzeau looked, started, moved one step back,
then stood motionless and perfectly silent, while all traces of
expression of any kind suddenly vanished from his face. Then
the calm, clear tones of the priest stole gently on the dead
silence. "I bring a message of peace and forgiveness from a
guest of former years," he said; and pointed, as he spoke, to
the place where he had been wounded in the neck.

For one moment, Gabriel saw his father trembling violently
from head to foot—then his limbs steadied again—stiffened
suddenly, as if struck by catalepsy. His lips parted, but
without quivering; his eyes glared, but without moving in
their orbits. The lovely moonlight itself looked ghastly and
horrible, shining on the supernatural panic-deformity of that
face! Gabriel turned away his head in terror. He heard the
voice of Father Paul saying to him: "Wait here till I come
back." Then there was an instant of silence again—then a
low groaning sound, that seemed to articulate the name of
God; a sound unlike his father's voice, unlike any human
voice he had ever heard—and then the noise of a closing door.
He looked up, and saw that he was standing alone before the
cottage.

Once, after an interval, he approached the window.

He just saw through it the hand of the priest holding on
high the ivory crucifix; but stopped not to see more, for he
heard such words, such sounds, as drove him back to his
former place. There he stayed, until the noise of something
falling heavily within the cottage struck on his ear. Again
he advanced towards the door; heard Father Paul praying;
listened for several minutes; then heard a moaning voice, now
joining itself to the voice of the priest, now choked in sobs
and bitter wailing. Once more he went back out of hearing,

and stirred not again from his place. He waited a long and a weary time there—so long that one of the scouts on the look-out came towards him, evidently suspicious of the delay in the priest's return. He waved the man back, and then looked again towards the door. At last he saw it open—saw Father Paul approach him, leading François Sarzeau by the hand.

The fisherman never raised his downcast eyes to his son's face; tears trickled silently over his cheeks; he followed the hand that led him, as a little child might have followed it, listening anxiously and humbly at the priest's side to every word that he spoke.

" Gabriel," said Father Paul, in a voice which trembled a little for the first time that night, " Gabriel, it has pleased God to grant the perfect fulfilment of the purpose which brought me to this place; I tell you this, as all that you need —as all, I believe, that you would wish—to know of what has passed while you have been left waiting for me here. Such words as I have now to speak to you, are spoken by your father's earnest desire. It is his own wish that I should communicate to you his confession of having secretly followed you to The Merchant's Table, and of having discovered (as you discovered) that no evidence of his guilt remained there. This admission, he thinks, will be enough to account for his conduct towards yourself from that time to this. I have next to tell you (also at your father's desire) that he has promised in my presence, and now promises again in yours, sincerity of repentance in this manner:—When the persecution of our religion has ceased—as cease it will, and that speedily, be assured of it!—he solemnly pledges himself henceforth to devote his life, his strength, and what worldly possessions he may have, or may acquire, to the task of re-erecting and restoring the roadside crosses which have been sacrilegiously overthrown and destroyed in his native province, and to doing good, good where he may. I have now said all that is required of me, and may bid you farewell— bearing with me the happy remembrance that I have left a father and son reconciled and restored to each other. May God bless and prosper you, and those dear to you, Gabriel! May God accept your father's repentance, and bless him also throughout his future life! "

He took their hands, pressed them long and warmly, then

turned and walked quickly down the path which led to the beach. Gabriel dared not trust himself yet to speak; but he raised his arm, and put it gently round his father's neck. The two stood together so, looking out dimly through the tears that filled their eyes to the sea. They saw the boat put off in the bright track of the moonlight and reach the vessel's side; they watched the spreading of the sails, and followed the slow course of the ship till she disappeared past a distant headland from sight.

After that they went into the cottage together. They knew it not then, but they had seen the last, in this world, of Father Paul.

V

THE events foretold by the good priest happened sooner even than he had anticipated. A new government ruled the destinies of France, and the persecution ceased in Brittany.

Among other propositions which were then submitted to the parliament, was one advocating the restoration of the roadside crosses throughout the province. It was found, however, on inquiry, that these crosses were to be counted by thousands, and that the mere cost of wood required to re-erect them necessitated an expenditure of money which the bankrupt nation could ill afford to spare. While this project was under discussion, and before it was finally rejected, one man had undertaken the task which the government shrank from attempting. When Gabriel left the cottage, taking his brother and sisters to live with his wife and himself at the farmhouse, François Sarzeau left it also, to perform in high-way and by-way his promise to Father Paul. For months and months he laboured without intermission at his task; still, always doing good, and rendering help and kindness and true charity to all whom he could serve. He walked many a weary mile, toiled through many a hard day's work, humbled himself even to beg of others to get wood enough to restore a single cross. No one ever heard him complain, ever saw him impatient, ever detected him in faltering at his task. The shelter in an outhouse, the crust of bread and drink of water, which he could always get from the peasantry, seemed to suffice him. Among the people who watched his perseverance, a belief began to gain ground that his life would be miraculously prolonged until he had completed his under-taking from one end of Brittany to the other. But this was not to be.

He was seen one cold autumn evening, silently and steadily at work as usual, setting up a new cross on the site of one which had been shattered to splinters in the troubled times. In the morning he was found lying dead beneath the sacred symbol which his own hands had completed and erected in its place during the night. They buried him where he lay, and the priest who consecrated the ground allowed Gabriel to engrave his father's epitaph in the wood of the cross. It was simply the initial letters of the dead man's name, followed by this inscription:—" Pray for the repose of his soul: he died penitent, and the doer of good works."

When the nun had concluded her narrative, she pointed to the old wooden cross, and said to me:

" That was one of the many that he made. It was found, a few years since, to have suffered so much from exposure to the weather that it was unfit to remain any longer in its old place. A priest in Brittany gave it to one of the nuns in this convent. Do you wonder now that the Mother Superior always calls it a relic? "

" No," I answered. " And I should have small respect indeed for the religious convictions of anyone who could hear the story of that wooden cross, and not feel that the Mother Superior's name for it is the very best that could have been chosen."

MRS. GASKELL

THE SEXTON'S HERO

THE afternoon sun shed down his glorious rays on the grassy churchyard, making the shadow, cast by the old yew-tree under which we sat, seem deeper and deeper by contrast. The everlasting hum of myriads of summer insects made luxurious lullaby.

Of the view that lay beneath our gaze, I cannot speak adequately. The foreground was the grey-stone wall of the vicarage garden, rich in the colouring made by innumerable lichens, ferns, ivy of most tender green and most delicate tracery, and the vivid scarlet of the crane's-bill, which found a home in every nook and crevice—and at the summit of that old wall flaunted some unpruned tendrils of the vine, and long flower-laden branches of the climbing rose-tree, trained against the inner side. Beyond, lay meadow green and mountain grey, and the blue dazzle of Morecambe Bay, as it sparkled between us and the more distant view.

For a while we were silent, living in sight and murmuring sound. Then Jeremy took up our conversation where, suddenly feeling weariness, as we saw that deep green shadowy resting-place, we had ceased speaking a quarter of an hour before.

It is one of the luxuries of holiday-time that thoughts are not rudely shaken from us by outward violence of hurry and busy impatience, but fall maturely from our lips in the sunny leisure of our days. The stock may be bad, but the fruit is ripe.

" How would you then define a hero? " I asked.

There was a long pause, and I had almost forgotten my question in watching a cloud-shadow floating over the far-away hills, when Jeremy made answer—

" My idea of a hero is one who acts up to the highest idea of duty he has been able to form, no matter at what sacrifice. I think that by this definition, we may include all phases of character, even to the heroes of old, whose sole (and to us, low) idea of duty consisted in personal prowess."

"Then you would even admit the military heroes?" asked I.

"I would; with a certain kind of pity for the circumstances which had given them no higher ideas of duty. Still, if they sacrificed self to do what they sincerely believed to be right, I do not think I could deny them the title of hero."

"A poor, unchristian heroism, whose manifestation consists in injury to others!" I said.

We were both startled by a third voice.

"If I might make so bold, sir"—and then the speaker stopped.

It was the Sexton, whom, when we first arrived, we had noticed, as an accessory to the scene, but whom we had forgotten, as much as though he were as inanimate as one of the moss-covered headstones.

"If I might be so bold," said he again, waiting leave to speak. Jeremy bowed in deference to his white, uncovered head. And, so encouraged, he went on.

"What that gentleman" (alluding to my last speech) "has just now said, brings to my mind one who is dead and gone this many a year ago. I, maybe, have not rightly understood your meaning, gentlemen, but as far as I could gather it, I think you'd both have given in to thinking poor Gilbert Dawson a hero. At any rate," said he, heaving a long, quivering sigh, "I have reason to think him so."

"Will you take a seat, sir, and tell us about him?" said Jeremy, standing up until the old man was seated. I confess I felt impatient at the interruption.

"It will be forty-five year come Martinmass," said the Sexton, sitting down on a grassy mound at our feet, "since I finished my 'prenticeship, and settled down at Lindal. You can see Lindal, sir, at evenings and mornings across the bay; a little to the right of Grange; at least, I used to see it, many a time, and oft, afore my sight grew so dark: and I have spent many a quarter of an hour a-gazing at it far away, and thinking of the days I lived there, till the tears came so thick to my eyes, I could gaze no longer. I shall never look upon it again, either far-off or near; but you may see it, both ways, and a terrible bonny spot it is. In my young days, when I went to settle there, it was full of as wild a set of young fellows as ever were clapped eyes on: all for fighting, poaching, quarrelling, and such-like work.

I were startled myself when I first found what a set I were among, but soon I began to fall into their ways, and I ended by being as rough a chap as any on 'em. I'd been there a matter of two year, and were reckoned by most the cock of the village, when Gilbert Dawson, as I was speaking of, came to Lindal. He were about as strapping a chap as I was (I used to be six feet high, though now I'm so shrunk and doubled up), and, as we were like in the same trade (both used to prepare osiers and wood for the Liverpool coopers, who get a deal of stuff from the copses round the bay, sir), we were thrown together, and took mightily to each other. I put my best leg foremost to be equal with Gilbert, for I'd had some schooling, though since I'd been at Lindal I'd lost a good part of what I'd learnt; and I kept my rough ways out of sight for a time, I felt so ashamed of his getting to know them. But that did not last long. I began to think he fancied a girl I dearly loved, but who had always held off from me. Eh! but she was a pretty one in those days! There's none like her, now. I think I see her going along the road with her dancing tread, and shaking back her long yellow curls, to give me or any other young fellow a saucy word; no wonder Gilbert was taken with her, for all he was grave, and she so merry and light. But I began to think she liked him again; and then my blood was all afire. I got to hate him for everything he did. Aforetime I had stood by, admiring to see him, how he leapt, and what a quoiter and cricketer he was. And now I ground my teeth with hatred whene'er he did a thing which caught Letty's eye. I could read it in her look that she liked him, for all she held herself just as high with him as with all the rest. Lord God forgive me! how I hated that man."

He spoke as if the hatred were a thing of yesterday, so clear within his memory were shown the actions and feelings of his youth. And then he dropped his voice, and said—

"Well! I began to look out to pick a quarrel with him, for my blood was up to fight him. If I beat him (and I were a rare boxer in those days), I thought Letty would cool towards him. So one evening at quoits (I'm sure I don't know how or why, but large doings grow out of small words) I fell out with him, and challenged him to fight. I could see he were very wroth by his colour coming and going—and, as

I said before, he were a fine active young fellow. But all at once he drew in, and said he would not fight. Such a yell as the Lindal lads, who were watching us, set up! I hear it yet. I could na' help but feel sorry for him, to be so scorned, and I thought he'd not rightly taken my meaning, and I'd give him another chance: so I said it again, and dared him, as plain as words could speak, to fight out the quarrel. He told me then, he had no quarrel against me; that he might have said something to put me up; he did not know that he had, but that if he had, he asked pardon; but that he would not fight no-how.

" I was so full of scorn at his cowardliness, that I was vexed I'd given him the second chance, and I joined in the yell that was set up, twice as bad as before. He stood it out, his teeth set, and looking very white, and when we were silent for want of breath, he said out loud, but in a hoarse voice, quite different from his own—

" ' I cannot fight, because I think it is wrong to quarrel, and use violence.'

" Then he turned to go away; I was so beside myself with scorn and hate, that I called out—

" ' Tell truth, lad, at least; if thou dare not fight, dunnot go and tell a lie about it. Mother's moppet is afraid of a black eye, pretty dear. It shannot be hurt, but it munnot tell lies.'

" Well, they laughed, but I could not laugh. It seemed such a thing for a stout young chap to be a coward and afraid!

" Before the sun had set, it was talked of all over Lindal, how I had challenged Gilbert to fight, and how he'd denied me; and the folks stood at their doors, and looked at him going up the hill to his home, as if he'd been a monkey or a foreigner—but no one wished him good e'en. Such a thing as refusing a fight had never been heard of afore at Lindal. Next day, however, they had found voice. The men muttered the word ' coward ' in his hearing, and kept aloof; the women tittered as he passed, and the little impudent lads and lasses shouted out, ' How long is it sin' thou turned Quaker? ' ' Good-bye, Jonathan Broad-brim,' and such-like jests.

" That evening I met him, with Letty by his side, coming up from the shore. She was almost crying as I came upon them at the turn of the lane; and looking up in his face, as

if begging him something. And so she was, she told me it
after. For she did really like him, and could not abide to
hear him scorned by every one for being a coward; and she,
coy as she was, all but told him that very night that she
loved him, and begged him not to disgrace himself, but fight
me as I'd dared him to. When he still stuck to it he could
not, for that it was wrong, she was so vexed and mad-like at
the way she'd spoken, and the feelings she'd let out to coax
him, that she said more stinging things about his being a
coward than all the rest put together (according to what she
told me, sir, afterwards), and ended by saying she'd never
speak to him again, as long as she lived; she did once again,
though—her blessing was the last human speech that reached
his ear in his wild death-struggle.

"But much happened afore that time. From the day I
met them walking, Letty turned towards me; I could see a
part of it was to spite Gilbert, for she'd be twice as kind when
he was near, or likely to hear of it; but by-and-by she got to
like me for my own sake, and it was all settled for our marriage. Gilbert kept aloof from every one, and fell into a sad,
careless way. His very gait was changed; his step used to be
brisk and sounding, and now his foot lingered heavily on the
ground. I used to try and daunt him with my eye, but he
would always meet my look in a steady, quiet way, for all so
much about him was altered; the lads would not play with
him; and, as soon as he found he was to be slighted by them
whenever he came to quoiting or cricket, he just left off
coming.

"The old clerk was the only one he kept company with;
or perhaps, rightly to speak, the only one who would keep
company with him. They got so thick at last, that old Jonas
would say, Gilbert had gospel on his side, and did no more
than gospel told him to do; but we none of us gave much
credit to what he said, more by token our vicar had a brother,
a colonel in the army; and, as we threeped it many a time to
Jonas, would he set himself up to know the gospel better
than the vicar? that would be putting the cart afore the
horse, like the French radicals. And, if the vicar had thought
quarrelling and fighting wicked, and again' the Bible, would
he have made so much work about all the victories, that
were as plenty as blackberries at that time of day, and kept
the little bell of Lindal church for ever ringing; or would he

have thought so much of 'my brother the colonel,' as he was always talking on?

"After I was married to Letty I left off hating Gilbert. I even kind of pitied him—he was so scorned and slighted; and, for all he'd a bold look about him, as if he were not ashamed, he seemed pining and shrunk. It's a wearying thing to be kept at arm's length by one's kind; and so Gilbert found it, poor fellow. The little children took to him, though; they'd be round about him like a swarm of bees—them as was too young to know what a coward was, and only felt that he was ever ready to love and to help them, and was never loud or cross, however naughty they might be. After a while we had our little one, too; such a blessed darling she was, and dearly did we love her; Letty in especial, who seemed to get all the thought I used to think sometimes she wanted, after she had her baby to care for.

"All my kin lived on this side the bay, up above Kellet. Jane (that's her that lies buried near yon white rose-tree) was to be married, and nought would serve her but that Letty and I must come to the wedding; for all my sisters loved Letty, she had such winning ways with her. Letty did not like to leave her baby, nor yet did I want her to take it: so, after a talk, we fixed to leave it with Letty's mother for the afternoon. I could see her heart ached a bit, for she'd never left it till then, and she seemed to fear all manner of evil, even to the French coming and taking it away. Well! we borrowed a shandry, and harnessed my old grey mare, as I used in th' cart, and set off as grand as King George across the sands about three o'clock, for you see it were high-water about twelve, and we'd to go and come back same tide, as Letty could not leave her baby for long. It were a merry afternoon were that; last time I ever saw Letty laugh heartily; and, for that matter, last time I ever laughed downright hearty myself. The latest crossing-time fell about nine o'clock, and we were late at starting. Clocks were wrong; and we'd a piece of work chasing a pig father had given Letty to take home; we bagged him at last, and he screeched and screeched in the back part o' th' shandry, and we laughed and they laughed; and in the midst of all the merriment the sun set, and that sobered us a bit, for then we knew what time it was. I whipped the old mare, but she was a deal beener than she was in the morning, and would neither go

quick up nor down the brows, and they're not a few 'twixt
Kellet and the shore. On the sands it were worse. They
were very heavy, for the fresh had come down after the rains
we'd had. Lord! how I did whip the poor mare, to make
the most of the red light as yet lasted. You, maybe, don't
know the sands, gentlemen. From Bolton side, where we
started from, it is better than six mile to Cart Lane, and two
channels to cross, let alone holes and quicksands. At the
second channel from us the guide waits, all during crossing-
time from sunrise to sunset; but for the three hours on each
side high-water he's not there, in course. He stays after
sunset if he's forespoken, not else. So now you know where
we were that awful night. For we'd crossed the first channel
about two mile, and it were growing darker and darker above
and around us, all but one red line of light above the hills,
when we came to a hollow (for all the sands look so flat,
there's many a hollow in them where you lose all sight of the
shore). We were longer than we should ha' been in crossing
the hollow, the sand was so quick; and when we came up
again, there, again' the blackness, was the white line of the
rushing tide coming up the bay! It looked not a mile from
us; and when the wind blows up the bay it comes swifter
than a galloping horse. 'Lord help us!' said I; and then I
were sorry I'd spoken, to frighten Letty; but the words were
crushed out of my heart by the terror. I felt her shiver up
by my side, and clutch my coat. And as if the pig (as had
screeched himself hoarse some time ago) had found out the
danger we were all in, he took to squealing again, enough
to bewilder any man. I cursed him between my teeth for
his noise; and yet it was God's answer to my prayer, blind
sinner as I was. Ay! you may smile, sir, but God can work
through many a scornful thing, if need be.

" By this time the mare was all in a lather, and trembling
and panting, as if in mortal fright; for, though we were
on the last bank afore the second channel, the water was
gathering up her legs; and she so tired out! When we
came close to the channel she stood still, and not all my
flogging could get her to stir; she fairly groaned aloud, and
shook in a terrible quaking way. Till now Letty had not
spoken: only held my coat tightly. I heard her say something, and bent down my head.

" ' I think, John—I think—I shall never see baby again! '

"And then she sent up such a cry—so loud, and shrill, and pitiful! It fairly maddened me. I pulled out my knife to spur on the old mare, that it might end one way or the other, for the water was stealing sullenly up to the very axle-tree, let alone the white waves that knew no mercy in their steady advance. That one quarter of an hour, sir, seemed as long as all my life since. Thought and fancies, and dreams, and memory ran into each other. The mist, the heavy mist, that was like a ghastly curtain, shutting us in for death, seemed to bring with it the scents of the flowers that grew around our own threshold; it might be, for it was falling on them like blessed dew, though to us it was a shroud. Letty told me 'at after, she heard her baby crying for her, above the gurgling of the rising waters, as plain as ever she heard anything; but the sea-birds were skirling, and the pig shrieking; I never caught it; it was miles away, at any rate.

"Just as I'd gotten my knife out, another sound was close upon us, blending with the gurgle of the near waters, and the roar of the distant (not so distant though); we could hardly see, but we thought we saw something black against the deep lead colour of wave, and mist, and sky. It neared and neared: with slow, steady motion, it came across the channel right to where we were.

"Oh, God! it was Gilbert Dawson on his strong bay horse.

"Few words did we speak, and little time had we to say them in. I had no knowledge at that moment of past or future—only of one present thought—how to save Letty, and, if I could, myself. I only remembered afterwards that Gilbert said he had been guided by an animal's shriek of terror; I only heard when all was over, that he had been uneasy about our return, because of the depth of fresh, and had borrowed a pillion, and saddled his horse early in the evening, and ridden down to Cart Lane to watch for us. If all had gone well, we should ne'er have heard of it. As it was, old Jonas told it, the tears down-dropping from his withered cheeks.

"We fastened his horse to the shandry. We lifted Letty to the pillion. The waters rose every instant with sullen sound. They were all but in the shandry. Letty clung to the pillion handles, but drooped her head as if she had yet no hope of life. Swifter than thought (and yet he might have had time for thought and for temptation, sir—if he had ridden off with Letty, he would have been saved, not me), Gilbert was in the shandry by my side.

"'Quick!' said he, clear and firm. 'You must ride before her, and keep her up. The horse can swim. By God's mercy I will follow. I can cut the traces, and if the mare is not hampered with the shandry, she'll carry me safely through. At any rate, you are a husband and a father. No one cares for me.'

"Do not hate me, gentlemen. I often wish that night was a dream. It has haunted my sleep ever since like a dream, and yet it was no dream. I took his place on the saddle, and put Letty's arms around me, and felt her head rest on my shoulder. I trust in God I spoke some word of thanks; but I can't remember. I only recollect Letty raising her head, and calling out—

"'God bless you, Gilbert Dawson, for saving my baby from being an orphan this night.' And then she fell against me, as if unconscious.

"I bore her through; or, rather, the strong horse swam bravely through the gathering waves. We were dripping wet when we reached the banks in-shore; but we could have but one thought—where was Gilbert? Thick mists and heaving waters compassed us round. Where was he? We shouted. Letty, faint as she was, raised her voice and shouted clear and shrill. No answer came, the sea boomed on with ceaseless sullen beat. I rode to the guide's house. He was a-bed, and would not get up, though I offered him more than I was worth. Perhaps he knew it, the cursed old villain! At any rate, I'd have paid it if I'd toiled my life long. He said I might take his horn and welcome. I did, and blew such a blast through the still, black night; but no human voice or sound was heard—that wild blast could not awaken the dead!

"I took Letty home to her baby, over whom she wept the livelong night. I rode back to the shore about Cart Lane; and to and fro, with weary march, did I pace along the brink of the waters, now and then shouting out into the silence a vain cry for Gilbert. The waters went back and left no trace. Two days afterwards he was washed ashore near Flukeborough. The shandry and poor old mare were found half-buried in a heap of sand by Arnside Knot. As

far as we could guess, he had dropped his knife while trying
to cut the traces, and so had lost all chance of life. Any
rate, the knife was found in a cleft in the shaft.

"His friends came over from Garstang to his funeral. I
wanted to go chief mourner, but it was not my right, and
I might not; though I've never done mourning him to this
day. When his sister packed up his things, I begged hard
for something that had been his. She would give me none
of his clothes (she was a right-down saving woman), as she
had boys of her own, who might grow up into them. But
she threw me his Bible, as she said they'd gotten one already,
and his were but a poor used-up thing. It was his, and so
I cared for it. It were a black leather one, with pockets at
the sides, old-fashioned-wise; and in one were a bunch of
wild flowers, Letty said she could almost be sure were some
she had once given him.

"There were many a text in the Gospel, marked broad
with his carpenter's pencil, which more than bore him out in
his refusal to fight. Of a surety, sir, there's call enough for
bravery in the service of God, and to show love to man,
without quarrelling and fighting.

"Thank you, gentlemen, for listening to me. Your words
called up the thoughts of him, and my heart was full to
speaking. But I must make up; I've to dig a grave for a
little child, who is to be buried to-morrow morning, just
when his playmates are trooping off to school."

"But tell us of Letty; is she yet alive?" asked Jeremy.

The old man shook his head, and struggled against a
choking sigh. After a minute's pause he said—

"She died in less than two year after that night. She
was never like the same again. She would sit thinking—
on Gilbert, I guessed; but I could not blame her. We had
a boy, and we named it Gilbert Dawson Knipe: he that's
stoker on the London railway. Our girl was carried off in
teething; and Letty just quietly drooped, and died in less
than a six week. They were buried here; so I came to be
near them, and away from Lindal, a place I could never
abide after Letty was gone."

He turned to his work; and we, having rested sufficiently,
rose up, and came away.